Worldwide Praise for the Erotica of John Patrick and STARbooks!

"If you're an avid reader of all-male erotica and haven't yet discovered editor John Patrick's series of torrid anthologies, you're in for a treat. ...These books will provide hours of cost-effective entertainment."
- *Lance Sterling, Beau magazine*

"John Patrick is a modern master of the genre! ...This writing is what being brave is all about. It brings up the kinds of things that are usually kept so private that you think you're the only one who experiences them."
– *Gay Times, London*

"'Barely Legal' is a great potpourri... and the coverboy is gorgeous!"
– *Ian Young, Torso magazine*

"A huge collection of highly erotic, short and steamy one-handed tales. Perfect bedtime reading, though you probably won't get much sleep! Prepare to be shocked! Highly recommended!"
– *Vulcan magazine*

"Tantalizing tales of porn stars, hustlers, and other lost boys...John Patrick set the pace with 'Angel'!"
- *The Weekly News, Miami*

"...Some readers may find some of the scenes too explicit; others will enjoy the sudden, graphic sensations each page brings. ...A strange, often poetic vision of sexual obsession. I recommend it to you."
- *Nouveau Midwest*

"'Dreamboys' is so hot I had to put extra baby oil on my fingers, just to turn the pages! ...Those blue eyes on the cover are gonna reach out and touch you..."
- *Bookazine's Hot Flashes*

"Yes, it's another of those bumper collections of steamy tales from STARbooks. The rate at which John Patrick turns out these compilations you'd be forgiven for thinking it's not exactly quality prose. Wrong. These stories are well-crafted, but not over-written, and have a profound effect in the pants department."
– *Vulcan magazine, London*

"For those who share Mr. Patrick's appreciation for cute young men, 'Legends' is a delightfully readable book...I am a fan of John Patrick's...His writing is clear and straight-forward and should be better known in the gay community."
- *Ian Young, Torso Magazine*

"...Touching and gallant in its concern for the sexually addicted, 'Angel' becomes a wonderfully seductive investigation of the mysterious disparity between lust and passion, obsession and desire."
- *Lambda Book Report*

"John Patrick has one of the best jobs a gay male writer could have. In his fiction, he tells tales of rampant sexuality. His non-fiction involves first person explorations of adult male video stars. Talk about choice assignments!"
- *Southern Exposure*

"The title for 'Boys of Spring' is taken from a poem by Dylan Thomas, so you can count on high-caliber imagery throughout."
- *Walter Vatter, Editor, A Different Light Review*

"I just got 'Intimate Strangers' and by the end of the week I had read it all. Great stories! Love it!"
- *L.C., Oregon*

"'Superstars' is a fast read...if you'd like a nice round of fireworks before the Fourth, read this aloud at your next church picnic..."
- *Welcomat, Philadelphia*

Book of the Month Selections in Europe and the U.K.
And Featured By A Different Light, Oscar Wilde Bookshop, Lambda Rising and GR, Australia
And Available at Fine Booksellers Everywhere

These horny lads are so much fun it hurts!

Fresh 'n' Frisky

A New Collection
of Erotic Tales
Edited By
JOHN PATRICK

STARbooks Press
Sarasota, FL

Books by John Patrick

Non-Fiction
A Charmed Life: Vince Cobretti
Lowe Down: Tim Lowe
The Best of the Superstars 1990
The Best of the Superstars 1991
The Best of the Superstars 1992
The Best of the Superstars 1993
The Best of the Superstars 1994
The Best of the Superstars 1995
The Best of the Superstars 1996
The Best of the Superstars 1997
The Best of the Superstars 1998
The Best of the Superstars 1999
The Best of the Superstars 2000
What Went Wrong?
When Boys Are Bad
& Sex Goes Wrong
Legends: The World's Sexiest
Men, Vols. 1 & 2
Legends (Third Edition)
Tarnished Angels (Ed.)

Fiction
Billy & David: A Deadly Minuet
The Bigger They Are...
The Younger They Are...
The Harder They Are...
Angel: The Complete Trilogy
Angel II: Stacy's Story
Angel: The Complete Quintet
A Natural Beauty (Editor)
The Kid (with Joe Leslie)
HUGE (Editor)
Strip: He Danced Alone

Fiction (Continued)
The Boys of Spring
Big Boys/Little Lies (Editor)
Boy Toy
Seduced (Editor)
Insatiable/Unforgettable (Editor)
Heartthrobs
Runaways/Kid Stuff (Editor)
Dangerous Boys/Rent Boys
(Editor)
Barely Legal (Editor)
Country Boys/City Boys (Editor)
My Three Boys (Editor)
Mad About the Boys (Editor)
Lover Boys (Editor)
In the BOY ZONE (Editor)
Boys of the Night (Editor)
Secret Passions (Editor)
Beautiful Boys (Editor)
Juniors (Editor)
Come Again (Editor)
Smooth 'N' Sassy (Editor)
Intimate Strangers (Editor)
Naughty By Nature (Editor)
Dreamboys (Editor)
Raw Recruits (Editor)
Play Hard, Score Big (Editor)
Sweet Temptations (Editor)
Pleasures of the Flesh (Editor)
Juniors 2 (Editor)
Fresh 'N' Frisky (Editor)

Entire Contents Copyrighted © 1999 by John Patrick, Sarasota, FL. All rights reserved. Every effort has been made to credit copyrighted material. The author and the publisher regret any omissions and will correct them in future editions. Note: While the words "boy," "girl," "young man," "youngster," "gal," "kid," "student," "guy," "son," "youth," "fella," and other such terms are occasionally used in text, this work is generally about persons who are at least 18 years of age, unless otherwise noted.

First Edition Published in the U.S. in December, 1999
Library of Congress Card Catalogue No. 99-094435
ISBN No. 1-891855-05-0

Contents

Introduction:
FINDING THE
FRESH 'N' FRISKY
John Patrick...11
IN THE ARMS OF
A STRANGER.
John Patrick..19
FRANKIE &
JOHNNIE
WERE LOVERS
Frank Gardner...28
JACK O'LANTERN
James Lincoln...35
DARK RIDE
James Lincoln...46
SO FRESH, SO
FRISKY
Lance Rush...56
A FEVER IN THE
LOINS
Leo Cardini...64
NIGHT MAZES
Edmund
Miller...86
PLOWBOY'S
PLAYTHING
Thomas C.
Humphrey...97
THE WATCHER
IN THE WOODS
Tony
Anthony...110
OFFSHORE
DRILLER
C. Chezner...119
ROMMATES
Mario Salano...134
A FARMBOY'S
WHIRLWIND
ROMANCE
Mario Salano...137
SEX ON THE RUN
Thom Nickels...141
THE DIVINEST
BOY
John Patrick...157

BOYS LIKE HIM
B. Alexander...165
SEX WEEKEND
R.M. Masters...176
WITHOUT YOU
R.M. Masters...183
GOING WITH
THE FLOW
D. MacMillan...189
DOWN 'N' DIRTY
D. MacMillan...201
COCK-SURE
Peter Gilbert...209
TRUCKSTOP
BOY
Frank Brooks...220
BODY CHECK
Thomas
Wagner...237
BONES
H.A. Bender...244
A RAW FUCKING
John Patrick...251
A PUNK'S
EDUCATION
Frank
Gardner...256
ONE MORE TIME
Jack Ricardo...263
ALL THE MAN I
NEED
John Patrick...270
PAYING
FOR IT
Joe Sexton...279
CAUGHT
IN THE ACT
Ronald James...285
WATCHER IN
THE SKY
Barnabus
Saul...293
NAKED ALTAR
BOY
K. I. Bard...301

A BOY'S BEST
FRIEND
Antler...305
THE MAKING OF
A SOLDIER:
A PRIVATE'S
PART
Rick Jackson...335
A BIRTHDAY AT
THE BATHS
W. Cozad...343
ROCK-SOLID
STUD
W. Cozad...348
TERRY, THE NEW
RECRUIT
Bill Nicholson...354
THE MAKING OF
A SOLDIER
Peter Gilbert...363
SHIPMATES
Tim Scully...383
THE RECRUITING
OFFICER
Peter Gilbert...401
THE CALL OF
THE COCKPIT
T. Wagner...417
INQUISITION
David MacMillan
...422
THE BEST
COCKSUCKER
Thom Nickels...429
CAPTAIN, MY
CAPTAIN
Tony
Anthony....450
SERVICING
SARGE
A. Mitchell...459
Plus
Bonus Book:
FRISKY BOYS
Kevin
Bantan....467

Editor's Note

Most of the stories appearing in this book take place prior to the years of The Plague; the editor and each of the authors represented herein advocate the practice of safe sex at all times.

And, because these stories trespass the boundaries of fiction and non-fiction, to respect the privacy of those involved, we've changed all of the names and other identifying details.

"Alsushi's mind was a place unknown to me, but the rest of his body could keep no secrets, for even his most subtle muscular shifts rippled plainly beneath the skin. I marvel still at the long, protean slenderness of him. His body held everything: a boy's smoothness, a woman's curves, and a man's wiry strength. (But) I saw that 'we' existed only through sex. When I left him, only my hands and mouth mourned his absence...."
—Jaime Cortez, in "Queer PAPI Porn"

John Patrick's favorite frisky boy, porn star/escort Tony Cummings, courtesy Forum Studios. John says, "Finding Tony changed my life. So few porn star/escorts live in Florida and it was simply incredible that I should find Tony here. He was so fresh back then, four years ago, and certainly the friskiest boy I had ever met. Now Tony is indeed the 'pause that refreshes'—better than coke or cola any day."
(Refer to page 16.)

INTRODUCTION: FINDING THE FRESH 'N' FRISKY

John Patrick

Looking for fresh, frisky lovers is taking guys to all corners of the globe. This has meant an economic boom for some venues. For instance, all over Asia and Southeast Asia reporter Edward Chew (for OG magazine) saw many fresh, frisky lads, basically out to make some extra dough for themselves and doing very well at it. "The demand for such services has increased by leaps and bounds, not only from foreign visitors but also from the locals themselves," Chew says. "...Naturally, there is also a thriving nightlife and a rapid rise in its scope and diversity. Besides Bangkok, which more than rivals Tokyo for sheer cultural variety in tourist nightlife, Singapore, Kuala Lumpur and Hong Kong are fast catching up with their own unique nocturnal offerings. ...Kuala Lumpur has Jalan Aior, where the dining is always done under tropical stars and where the men cruising past you are always more beautiful than the women."

While in Singapore, Chew answered an ad: "Thai and Swedish body massage. Give yourself full relaxation and stress relief by young and well-trained male masseur. Call Leslie...". Chew called Leslie and he answered the page within 15 minutes. Leslie was 22, Chinese, a part-time student who had completed his national service. Chew describes him:"Every inch a likeable and stunning young man with black hair, almond-shaped eyes and sensual lips. He is fair-complexioned and in great physical shape. As he stripped down to his 'HOM' briefs, I saw a gym-toned body that awakened all the desires in me and it was with great difficulty that I lay on my stomach stark naked as he rubbed his hands carefully with sweet-smelling aromatherapy oil and began rubbing my back in broad, circular strokes that instantly awoke the tired muscles in my shoulders and lower back areas. I could feel this young adonis's strength and power as he performed a repertoire of muscle-relaxing exercises with his hands, fists and elbows. My back was on fire after fifteen minutes (my frontal area too!) as he continued his invigorating sports rubdown. I found myself drifting off. Leslie then pulled me up with the help of his smooth, naked thighs and knees and it was at this point that all my sense of control broke loose ... I began taking over, and he allowed himself to be submissive. The second part of the massage was 30 minutes of intense love-making between us that I will not soon forget...."

Leslie indicated to Chew that the sexy part of the massage is entirely up to the masseur: "One needs to be imaginative to earn a customer's satisfaction. Usually during the second half of a massage, a customer will be sufficiently aroused and will ask for something 'extra'. I tell them my price. It will cost them $150 to make love to me on top of the massage fee. I do not want to get fucked for all the riches in the world. However, I am prepared to fuck the customer if he so wishes. ...Most of them appreciate a hard rubdown first, then, suddenly, their hands are everywhere! From then on it's the same story.

"I have not yet encountered any requests for kinky sex although, on one occasion a client wanted me to have sex with him while another masseur videotaped us. ...Male prostitution is still a big offence in this country. Only street-wise kids can do this business well. You cannot be a 'greenhorn' in this business. You need to be friendly and you must possess good massage skills for the odd occasion that your customer may only want just that: a sports rubdown and no hanky-panky!

"Guys like Leslie," Chew suggests, "are often between 22 to 30 years of age and not all of them are exclusively gay. Most just work part-time."

In Hong Kong, Chew met Ming, 22, who was tall and boyishly handsome with a nice, sexy body."He resembled one of my favorite OG models, a boy whose pictures I took many years ago in Thailand. Ming worked as a hair stylist and make-up artist and hoped to one day own his own salon back in his hometown, Ipoh.

"Ming gave me a very nice and titillating massage and, of course, all the extras and trimmings as well. He was most enthusiastic about doing a good job on me and I thoroughly enjoyed myself with him. He is one of the handful of male masseurs that I would like to keep in constant contact with. I enjoyed his services and he my company."

Another popular venue for finding fresh, frisky playmates is Amsterdam. Legendary filmmaker William Higgins says that he had lived and worked in Amsterdam for several years before moving to Prague. He says it was nice for about the first year, maybe less: "I am a firm believer in the five-year rule. That is: If you want to have sex with someone the same age or five years younger than yourself, then you don't have to pay. If you want someone younger than that, get out your pocketbook. I like to have paid sex with a lot of, excuse me for being politically incorrect, 'straight boys' (over 18). After four years in Amsterdam, I found that very same group of male hustlers who were working at the various clubs and the Central Station on the very day that I arrived were still plying their trade and little if any new blood had come along.

"Many Americans don't realize this, but because of socialism, everyone who lives in a northern European quasi-socialist country, like Holland, is taken care of quite well from cradle to grave. There are very many reasons not to work there. So, the number of guys who need to exchange money for sex is extremely small in Holland except for those who cannot afford to live on the government dole, which is quite generous. You can pretty much boil it down to junkies and foreigners. Because of the influx after the fall of Communism in 1989, the Dutch government said 'No more foreigners unless they are citizens of the EU.' That dried up the well.

"As far as 'liberal' attitudes towards sex: Anyone who has lived in Holland will tell you that the Dutch are very 'tolerant' people. That does not mean that they like homosexuals or homosexuality. They 'tolerate' us. And the farther that you get from Amsterdam, the less that they 'tolerate' homosexuals. The attitude is far different from that in the Czech Republic. Holland is, believe it or not, a very religious country. The Republic is not. To make a long story short: The Dutch 'tolerate' most sex as long as it does not encroach on their turf, and the Czechs just don't give a shit about sex. Big difference. There is very little religious morality in this countryl that's because Czechs have traditionally not paid much mind to religion. So, sex is no big deal here. The Republic was, after all, pagan for about 900 years after most of the rest of Europe, and it is the

Middle Eastern monotheistic religions that have placed all of these taboos on sex.

"By the way, the Dutch no longer have as liberal attitudes about sex commerce as they once did. Sex businesses are very heavily regulated nowadays, and the Dutch are determined not to let it grow, and would like to shrink it if possible.

"Do I think that America will ever be as mature as Amsterdam or Berlin about sex? Absolutely not. All countries that were heavily colonized by the British have a problem with sex...."

Walter, a semi-official travel correspondent, returned from a visit to Prague, in the Czech Republic, where he said he broke banana" with Higgins. "Actually," he says, "I pilfered a piece from the fruit salad he'd made for himself. "Prague will be recovering from its days as the capital of a Soviet satellite for a few more years; it'll take a while for new construction to replace the drab, dusty, dull buildings that dominate the city. Drake's is one of the few businesses with a sign out front in District 5, the sex section of Prague (spelled 'Praha' in the Czech language). Pay one admission, get access to the free video rooms in the back, the live dancers on-stage, whatever that was down those steep stairs ... Higgins says he's never been down there either, but, from the folks coming up the stairs with a smile on their face, would guess it's a dark room where anything goes. Another customer had brought a copy of a video box to show a lad that his movie was a hit in the U.S. The boys are beautiful! And the prices in Prague, except for hotels, are absurdly low!'

Meanwhile, back in the U.S., just seeing some fresh and frisky boys can be fun, especially when they are celebrities. For instance, as we frequently report in our*Best of the Superstars* annual review, you can spot celebrities (and even interact with them) almost anywhere. In fact, on"Official Celebrity Sightings Correspondents" website one gets to read personal tales from fans. In one case, a fan visited the set of the TV show"Home Improvement." It just happened to be at the time of the taping of the famous "kissing" episode, and the fan noted that Thomas stayed afterward to tape a public service announcement, requesting that people donate used wheelchairs to the needy. The witness commented, "He's sooooo nice!"

E!'s Ted Casablanca spotted our current fave hearthrob Ryan Phillippe and bride Reese Witherspoon (they wed June 5 in Charleston, South Carolina in a small, very private ceremony), dressed down at Pavilions supermarket in West Hollywood:"I suppose sequins aren't really necessary for melon-squeezing. Just shopping, holding hands, bought some flowers, red wine. I could puke it was so adorable." Then, later, the couple was driving a Volvo into the Franklin Canyon recreation area near Beverly Hills: "A Valentine's hike. Love it."

Then Ted attended the "Cruel Intentions" premiere party and reported, "Ryan, unlike his girlfriend, did not stay seated the entire time at a table. He was off—dressed all in black, casual everything—talking to everybody. (I swear he's going to be the next Tom Hanks)." Then, when asked his impression of the depth of their love, Ted replied, "Actually, I found the two adorable but hardly passionate love-a-dub-bub material. Much more like bro and sis, they struck me. But what do I know about people half my age?" Our favroite gossip, Billy Masters, has the great good fortune to live near Ryan and Reese and gives us his assessment: "I see him all the time. We go to the same restaurants, same grocery store, he even says hi to me when he sees me. I'm not a big fan of really young guys (under 30 is pushing it). Yes, I can appreciate young guys but I don't get that crazed over them. Ryan is sweet, but he's nothing special. The face is cute but too pouty for my taste; he is really thin (he works out about six weeks prior to a shoot to get pumped, but isn't that way in real life; it seems like if you blew (air!) he'd blow away! Reese, on the other hand, is a strapping girl who could clearly pin Ryan down; I'm sure she's the top in that relationship!" Billy adds that on one recent occasion, Ryan tipped a waitress ten dollars on a forty-five dollar bill:"What a nice guy!" You can say that again! In fact, even if he weren't nice at all, we'd still love him.

Sighting porn stars is usually a lot easier than sighting movie stars, although you might be disappointed in what you see. For instance, take one fan's sighting of Spike. Spike, as you will recall, is the fresh and frisky porn performer that mannet.com critic Butch Harris described as a real "comer," in more ways than one: "Trust me on this one folks, if you get fucked by Mr. Spike, spiked you have been. Mr. Spike has a really, really big

... really, really hard dick ... devilish good looks and seemingly insatiable appetite for fucking tight asses." But the fan reported Spike looked more like the devil than he could handle:"I saw Spike yesterday at the San Vicente Inn in WeHo, apparently shooting a porn film. I was really disappointed. Nice dick, yes. Very out of shape body though. Plus, I could not believe how queeny he was and you wouldn't believe the nasty shit he was wearing (sleeveless tight black shirt which only emphasized how flabby he was, a tired pair of jeans, white socks and 'bobo' black shoes. Short too. Having fantasized about this guy in the past, I was very disappointed...."

Our favorite frisky porn star/escort Tony Cummings was also in the Stable video shot at the San Vincente Inn and he was one of the lucky cast members to be fucked by Spike. He confirmed that Spike is certainly not much to look at in person, but that the humungous cock stays *very* hard and was a joy to sit on, although he admits he liked Sonny Markham's fucking technique much more in his scene with him five hours after having Spike up his ass! Talk about being frisky, Tony even managed to top Chip Noll during the filming of the video for Stable, and Chip told Peter Scott, his agent, who also represents Tony, that Tony really was a fantastic top: "It felt sooooo good!" (Tony's other appearance as a top on video was in "Something Very Big This Way Cums...." wherein he obviously enjoys topping the now-retired Dean O'Connor. For the record, Tony told me that most of his clients want him to top them! Go figure, I say, since Tony, for my money, is the best bottom in the business.)

Another popular porn star, Chris Steele, who first appeared in the Studio 2000 video "Uncle Jack," is often surprised where he finds his frisky playmates. For example, he told *XXX Showcase*: "...I went to a bisexual orgy when I was sixteen! I was at this party at three o'clock in the morning after the 'Rocky Horror Picture Show' and this guy came up to me and invited me to a party after the party. I said, 'It's three in the morning, what kind of party is it?' And he said, 'Well, it's more like an orgy.' I was so naive. I said, 'What do you do at an orgy?' 'Well, you just find someone you want to be with, and you be with 'em.' That's how he put it to me. I'd never had sex with a guy, but I was very curious and certainly wanted to. I just didn't know what to do. Like when I was a kid—I made all my friends take their clothes off when they spent the night, but then I didn't know what to do from there. Anyway, I went to this party, and the guy started to go down on me and I guess I must have been like turned to stone, because before he put my dick in his mouth he looked up at me and said, 'You've never been with a guy before, have you.' And I go, [hoarse whisper] 'No.'

"I was just terrified. And it was like he put out a bulletin: Sixteen-year-old virgin on the couch! The next thing 1 knew there were five guys all around me wanting to suck my cock. And even then I was still confused—I had to do a girl that night too, just to prove...you know...all that. ...I mean, I always knew I was gay, but this is Texas. Southern Baptists. They lock you in the gym and tell you that homosexuals are going to take over the world and all this evil stuff. So you've got all this guilt. That's why the internet is so popular. All these poor guys who had to go to Southern Baptist Sunday school—they're traumatized from it. So, yeah, I'd had sex with girls a couple times. But boys...that first time it was only oral sex. I didn't do any anal sex. I did watch a muscleboy get fucked. I was very interested in how all that worked. The first time you see two guys fucking it's very bizarre."

IN THE ARMS OF A STRANGER

John Patrick

I am quiet and still on the bed. Naked now, I luxuriate in the smell of my body, in the smell in my skin and my freshly washed hair and the heat that remains from our fucking. I turn my head to the pillow and smell Jeff, his musk cologne, his sweat. I bring the pillow close, hold it as I held him, a few minutes ago, before he said he had to go.

Now I'm alone in our bed and I think that every small sound is his key in the lock, and my body readies itself for him. I roll over and shift my hips slightly. My heart beats faster and faster, and if he were to walk in he'd see my ass in the air, waiting for him again. But he's gone. And I have no idea when he's coming back.

I reach down and find the beer bottle he left. I sip from it, my hand sliding around the cool neck of it, and think how it reminds me of his cock. God, what a cock! I love Jeff's cock. His big, thick, uncut cock. I drop the bottle on the floor and stroke myself remembering how good he felt deep inside me. I fall asleep before I come.

When the night is finally over, I make my way through the empty apartment to make some coffee, then take another shower.

I dress myself carefully, keeping in mind what he would like to see me in if we were to run into each other. Keeping in mind that he likes me in jeans—the tighter the better—and a white long-sleeve shirt. The mirror reveals I've become hollow, gaunt, unsteady. Because of him. Of his promises, all unfulfilled. I know now he will never divorce his wife. Bastard.

I move quickly to the door, before the fear can work on me to hold me home. My keys are in my pocket, my sunglasses shielding me from the light. A few steps to the red convertible, the one he bought me on our first anniversary, and I am safe again, ready to cruise, blocking out his last words. Maybe finding a moment's peace in the arms of a stranger.

I'm late for work, but Stanley doesn't seem to notice; he's

involved with Mrs. Fitch (I call her bitch, and Stanley grimaces). I sit at my desk and begin trying to make sense of the accounts. Stanley has been writing checks again without me, I realize, and the business may well be overdrawn. Bastard will blame me.

Stanley finishes with Mrs. Fitch, promising he'll find her just the right objets d'art for her beach house, and turns his attention to me. "I'm glad to see you finally showed up. I've got a luncheon date." Just like that. That's Stanley. No "Good morning," no nothing. After a quick visit to the john to make sure his toupee is on straight, he's out the door. I take a deep breath and grab the phone. If I can keep a few of those checks from bouncing, I may keep my job.

I take my lunch at my desk. No customers have come in since Mrs. Fitch and I've had a chance to keep the wolf from Stanley's door one more. Then there is a buzz at the door. I consider just letting whomever it is go away, but we need the money so I go to the door. What greets me is the closest thing to Jeff I've seen in months: Tall, dark, handsome, and dressed impeccably. He asks about our recently acquired sculptures by the New York artist Lynda Benglis, who caused a sensation in the early seventies with an advertisement in *ArtForum* magazine depicting herself naked, straddling an enormous dildo. The man, who introduces himself as Spence, says he now finds the sculptures extremely ugly and wonders whatever happened to the dildo. He is obviously a connoisseur, either of art or of dildoes, but it doesn't matter much because I think he's going to leave. But then he decides to look around a bit, and I say, "Take your time," and go back to my desk.

In fifteen minutes he finds me, wonders if I've had lunch. I say I have; he says that's too bad because he'd like to treat me since I have been so very helpful. I chuckle because I haven't done anything but ignore him, but maybe that's what he's into. I look up into his brown eyes. Sometimes you can see it in the eyes of a stranger. You can see a need, a longing. Spence's eyes are sad and lonely. I know that I—only I—could fulfill his wants. But all too often a man will enter the gallery, look around, and leave with his urges unspent, his longings unfulfilled, never knowing that I held the key, that I was the answer to all of his wildest fantasies. I vow not to let that happen this time. I bat my long eyelashes at him and tell him I am free for dinner. He smiles. "Okay. I'm staying at the Radisson. Room 1030. Ring me when you get to the lobby and I'll come down."

I show him to the door. "Till six then?"

"Yes," I say, shaking his hand. I have trouble concentrating on the accounts. Stanley never returns, which I half expected. I lock up and aim my little red car in the direction of the Radisson.

"Oh," Spence says. I have surprised him by coming directly to his room. A mistake, maybe.

But he lets me into the room. Still, he seems flustered. I fear I may have erred, been far too bold for him, but such thoughts are quickly dispelled when he offers me a drink.

We chat about art, the store, Stanley. "You and Stanley ... ?" he asks, pouring himself another drink.

"Oh, no," I answer. "If you could see Stanley...."

He sits on the arm of my chair, offers to freshen my drink. I tell him I'm fine for now and set my drink down on the table next to me and lean back in the chair. "Yes, I'm just fine," I say, wanting him to kiss me, waiting for him to kiss me. Bizarre. Dangerous to have those feelings for a total stranger. But we aren't to remain strangers for long.

"I have the strangest desire," he says, looking me up and down.

"Oh?"

"I think I want to kiss you."

"Then do," I say, reaching up and putting my hands around his neck.

It is a long, passionate kiss. When he finally pulls away, I say, "You're very good." This, of course, leads to his wanting to show me just *how* good he is. As he explores my body I remember how it can be with a stranger: so new, so exciting. Still, the images of the one time Jeff caught me and the price I had to pay fills my mind. I remember I said nothing. Not, "I'm sorry," since he would detect the lie in my voice, and he would be ready with his classic answer: "You're not sorry now. But you will be." Not, "I love you," since he already knew that. And, anyway, Jeff and I don't love each other like that. Not in the classic sense. Yet, his jealousy is more intense than any husband's, so intense I cannot stand it sometimes. That night, after he caught me, I bowed my head, waiting. He pushed me back onto the bed with the simple, brute force of his power. "Little sex machine," he said, a whisper-hiss, prodding me. "Just out for a trick? A good ride? A game?" His words were switchblade sharp and they cut me; he made me tremble."Why do you do it? Why do you cheat on me, my little sex machine? Again and again he screamed at me, so that I could hear the taunting in his voice. He accused me of being a bottomless pit, a fuck-toy for some stranger. He yelled that I had been searching the streets for love, using impersonal sex when I could not find love. I didn't bother telling him that it worked just as well. For a moment or two.

Now, here I am again, with a stranger sucking on my cock. He has made it hard, so hard I fear I will explode before he even gets his clothes off. Two strangers alone in a hotel room with no ties to each other, no weights on each other. Just want. Just need. I watch as he undoes the buttons of his shirt and reveals his hairy chest to me. In a second, he has the fly to his pants unbuttoned, the trousers down and off and kicked into a heap on the floor. All I want in the world is to erase the hurt that lingers in his eyes. Someone else's hurt. Someone else left that look there and it is my job to erase it. His cock is not as big as Jeff's, and cut. It is a nice cock, and he is gentle. The sheets in the hotel are powder blue and they crinkle like tissue paper when he lowers me to the bed. The pillows are thin, so he uses two under my finely boned hips to raise them high enough. I meet his cock as he pushes forward. He plunges it inside me. He begins a heated thrusting that reminds me of Jeff. He loves fucking me; I can taste it in his kisses, can smell it in the perfumed air that surrounds us both. "My sex machine," Jeff always says while he's fucking me, but he's the sex machine, not me. I just lie back and take it. Yes, there's no fuck like the one from a sex machine, and Spence is one too. I must attract them.

Suddenly, Spence pulls his cock out, teases my asslips, and just the feel of it, just gently pressing forward, makes me moan and sigh, my eyelashes fluttering against my flushed cheeks. He works me hard then, suddenly rises up to watch me, needing to see the change in my face as he thrusts inside me, deep inside me. He presses up on his knees, giving me the full length of the cock all at once. Oh, Spence is good. I love the pounding motions, the deeper thrusts. I bring my fingers into the action, and feel his cock sliding back and forth.

Now Spence is up again, banging away. He wants to hear me moan, wants to hear me beg for mercy, but I will not give in. I grip the mattress tighter, drawing the muscles in my back into a taut line, offering myself to him. And he comes. I feel the trembling vibrations work through his body and into mine. He moans, his actions slow, slow, then cease. I move away for only a second, having him roll onto his back and I take my spot above him. As I do, I see the look in his eyes, that haunted look, has changed to one of relief. His lips open and then close, wordlessly, begging me to come. But he is not like Jeff, he does not get hard again, but I move over the cock as I jerk myself until I come, come all over his hairy chest. He watches me come, but he doesn't say anything.

Now, I can't help it, I remember what Jeff said after he found out about the other stranger, the kid I picked up. I could sense the displeasure in his voice as he asked, "Why?" "Please," I begged him. "You need this, don't you?" Jeff asked, though he knew the answer. He knew it all by this time—the tiresome routine, the boring answers. He was just teasing me, testing me, making me wait for my orgasm. "You need me to make you come. That's what I do best, make you come." "Yes, yes," I cried.

And now I realize it is Spence inside me, not Jeff. He is stroking my cock, squeezing out the last drops of cum. "Oh, yes," I cry. It was a great orgasm, leaving me breathless—but still hungry. Jeff would be hard again, fucking me again....

I lie atop Spence. In his eyes there is enough heat to burn me forever. In his heart there is enough darkness to make me afraid of him.

My earlier transgression ended a bit differently. I cruised the kid who I spotted walking along the boulevard.

It didn't take long before we were back at his place. His aprents were out of town. And we quickly went to his room. Oh, how the boy liked to touch my cock, to stroke it, to pull on it while I kissed him.

And then, while I fucked him, how he sighed and moaned

and gave me what I needed from him. He gave me all of the power. Jeff couldn't possibly have any idea how lovingly I kissed that boy I had picked up; how I cradled his sweet face in my hands as I made him come, how I licked and lapped at his mouth until it was bruised from my kisses.

Spence's fuck was hardly loving. The pain was wondrous, all-consuming, much like Jeff's fuck. At this point in my life I have given up denying how much I love it, given up wishing that I did not need it the way I do. Because I do need it. In fact, I think, I deserve it. I deserved this moment with Spence, this moment in the arms of a stranger. Spence has made my fantasies real again in the twisting and turning of a night no longer lonely.

At home, hours later, I listen for the sound of Jeff's key in the lock while I undress. I keep one ear always ready to hear his key in the lock, hoping against hope. There have been no messages and he, obviously, has not been here looking for me.

Naked in bed, I imagine him sliding his cock into me, driving his body hard against mine. A low moan escapes my lips, then a sigh, a silent mouthing of his name with my head thrown back as he comes inside me. I jack off to this memory. My finger explores my ass, and another man's cum covers my fingers....

I fall asleep, my cum coating my fingers. I am disturbed by the ringing of the phone. Jeff's normally lazy drawl has become dangerously menacing. It's got an edge to it that lets me know just how pissed he is. "I'll be over in twenty minutes. You be ready for me, you slut. You be ready. I want you to show me what a good boy you can be."

"Yes...." I start to say more, but he's severed the connection, cut me off. With my hand still holding the phone, I replay the conversation in my mind. A bad boy first, then a good boy. His words echo hollowly as I hang up the receiver. I turn to stare at my reflection in the mirror over the antique hallway table, stare at the image of a unfaithful lover. But we are both sinners. Jeff should be home with his wife, not fucking me, but he can't help it. And I can't help wanting him. Twenty minutes. Twenty minutes to transform myself into a good boy. An impossible goal, so why even try? In the bedroom, I lose myself for a long moment in the late afternoon sunlight that filters through my ricepaper blinds. The light makes shifting designs on the walls, hazy shadows that are somehow comforting. I pull the cord to raise the blinds an inch or two. I squint, staring harder, working to break through the fog that clouds my vision, and trying to picture myself through Jeff s eyes. Yes, it's the confessing of my transgressions to a lover who is my Master, who owns my heart, who holds my soul. Who fills the hole inside me.

I step back and look at myself in the mirror. I keep my hair straight and golden brown, cut short, the way Jeff likes it. My eyes are green-bottle green when I'm serious, darker emerald when I'm afraid. Now they look as dark as I've ever seen them. Am I afraid of Jeff? Yes. He'll want to know where I was last night. Of course he will assume I was unfaithful. He knows everything.

I hear the key in the lock, hear him walking towards the bedroom. No greeting, except, "Little whore." He uses both hands on my shoulders to push me down on my knees in front of him. I look up and gaze into his big brown eyes. I have noticed many times how dark his eyes are when he's angry, but this afternoon they seem darker still, coal-black, hollow or deep, glossy, like marbles. I bow my head to my chest, waiting. He pushes his crotch into my head."Just slumming, was that it?"

"No," I murmur. "I was just flirting."

He takes my head in both hands and pushes my mouth toward the bulge. A shudder, a twinge, then I'm fine again. I peel back his pants to reveal his erection bulging in his briefs. I suck it through the fabric but I need to have more. I need to feel his skin growing flushed beneath the steady strokes, the silky caress, of my hands.

In a rush, it comes, that yearning, that uncontrollable desire to have him in my mouth again. He is digging his hands into my hair, and his cock is soon being excited by the force of my desire.

"Flirting my ass," he says.

"Oh, please. I couldn't help it," I whisper. "Couldn't have stopped if I'd tried."

"Did you fuck him like you did that boy before?"

"No."

He is silent at this. I can almost hear the images being processed. But as I deep throat him, he sighs, "Ohhhhh." Half-moan, half-breath, and I can feel his heart start to race. He lifts me to a standing position and then up and into his arms, then carries me to the bed. "You like to watch," he says, a statement, not a question.

"Oh, yes," I sigh. If I don't watch, then it's not real. I gaze into the mirror and see him preparing my ass. He sticks his fingers in, as if trying to see if the stranger left his calling card. He swallows hard. He's having a difficult time with this. No matter how many times we have been here, it doesn't seem to get any easier for him. But this is especially hard because I have admitted, sort of, that this time I bottomed for the stranger. Another swallow before he is able to speak. "You really need the pain this morning, kid," he says to me, not without compassion.

"I didn't mean for it to happen...."

He's not listening to me, though; he's consumed by the task before him: getting his big cock all the way in me. But I will not be still. I have to tell him. I have to confess my sins. He knows that I will continue tormenting him, torturing him. "I didn't mean for it to happen," I continue. "He was from out of town. He came into the gallery and...." My voice finally becomes a choked sob.

"Did he hurt you?"

"No," I say, swallowing hard. "He was smaller than you. Ordinary. An ordinary stranger."

"It was my fault. I shouldn't have argued with you."

We go back and forth like this, taking the blame, sharing the blame. This isn't a game. This isn't about power or control. This is about giving someone what they need and taking what you need and together, somehow, making it all right. Because somehow it's possible, despite everything that's wrong and dirty, somehow you can make it all tight. And, thinking this, I see my face in the mirror across the room. My eyes are sad, but the need is almost filled.

Breathing heavily now, he turns to look into the mirror himself and sees me watching him fucking me. I begin moving sensually beneath him, now well caught up in my own rising passion. My lithe, supple body squirms excitedly, ass tingling with delight, as I urge him on in husky whispers. I arch up, push my ass up to meet his thrust when he drives into me, seeking even more of the magnificent shaft that fills me so completely. I feel him fucking with renewed fury, sending me over the edge. My orgasm is overwhelming, unstoppable. A spasm of pure pleasure tears through me and, a few seconds later, his own powerful orgasm shakes him in a sudden violent tremor. "Oh shit," he gasps, "I love you so much."

I lie sprawled out in front of him as he slams his erection into me one last time. Then his cock slips from my ass. He goes to the bathroom. Before long, the throbbing in my ass begins to subside. He comes back into the room, toweling off his prick. He pulls me up and rolls me over. Then he kisses me. He is laying claim to me. If it weren't morning, he would have me suck his cock until it hardened again and he would stick it in again. But he must go. I want to keep him here forever, but I cannot. It is enough to know that is what Jeff really wants as well, but it cannot be. I close my eyes and listen to his foolfalls down the hall, out the door. Once more I am reminded, "Things happen for a reason."

FRANKIE AND JOHNNIE WERE LOVERS

Frank Gardner

This happened quite a few years ago, when I was just a kid. I was very slim in those days, and incredibly shy. Music was my thing back then, and I spentmost of my time daydreaming about becoming a world-famous composer. My cousin, Johnnie, was my exact opposite. He was a year older than me and he was big and husky and played on the football team.

We'd both worked on my folks' farm while we were growing up. Dad loved Johnnie 'cause he could lift a bale of hay like it was nothing. But Johnnie never used his size to push me around, like I've seen some guys do to their kin. Johnnie could be surprisingly tender, too. I discovered just how tender he could be one hot summer day .

Like I said, I was shy, and I was especially shy about sex. Of course, on a farm, you have to know something about it—like if a cow was in heat, or "bulling" as we called it, and mounting other cows, you had to get her bred. I remember one time John and I led a young bull up from a neighbor's farm to breed our cow. He was too small to get up on her and really mount her, so we had to get him up on a banking and back her up to him so he could get his long thin, angry red dick into her.

I must have been pretty excited watching the bull ramming into our cow, because I remember Johnnie looking down at my crotch and smiling. My pants were tenting out and I got red in the face. I still found sex pretty embarrassing.

Now, you've probably heard that song about how "Frankie and Johnnie were lovers." Of course, Frankie in the song is supposed to be a girl, but it could have been a guy.

Well, given our names and my obvious shyness—and maybe obvious gayness—I suppose it was inevitable that some wise-guy would try teasing me about how "Frankie and Johnnie were lovers."

It wouldn't have amounted to much, really, if I hadn't been so easy to embarrass. And when some of the guys found out that this song would make me really get red in the face, they would whistle or hum it, just to see the pyrotechnics.

I was walking down the hall one day, and this wise guy said as he went by, "Ohhh! How they did love." As usual I got hot and blushed deeply.

He didn't see Johnnie in back of him. Johnnie didn't say anything, but he gave me a strange thoughtful look as he passed me. I didn't know what it meant then.

I found out that same night, though. That was the night I discovered just how tender my cousin Johnnie could be.

. . .

My bedroom was in the attic of the farmhouse, and often Johnnie would sleep over. One night, he asked me right out of the blue, "Would you like to sleep with me tonight?"

I didn't say anything. I sure thought a lot of him, but even though I liked him, I was still shy about being naked in front of him. I didn't think he would make fun of me, or anything, but I got funny feelings when I saw him undressed, and didn't know what to make of it. Anyway, like I said, I didn't say anything. Maybe my face got a little red.

"Oh, come on," he said, "It's the middle of November and colder than hell. We can keep each other warm." He cuffed me lightly on the shoulder.

I still didn't say anything. I finished undressing, and ended up with just a pair of Jockey shorts. I got into his bed, and he crawled in next to me.

"Golly, it's cold," he said. He shivered and put his arms around me and pulled me close. "Come on, Frankie. Put your arms around me so we can warm each other up."

I finally put my arms around him, and we held each other close for a few minutes, until the blankets had a chance to get warmed up.

Our cheeks were pressed together, and I could feel his chest and belly pressed against mine. Then I felt the beginnings of a warm glow deep down in my crotch. My cock started to stir, and I guess Johnnie could feel it pressing against him.

"Frankie, you know something?" He was nuzzling my cheek.

"What?" I asked.

"I like you."

Since it was dark, and we were alone and safe, I felt free and answered back, "I like you too, Johnnie."

I could feel his breath on my cheek as he laughed. Then he surprised me. He nuzzled my cheek until he found my mouth, and he kissed me right on the lips. I felt my face get really hot, and pulled back a little.

"Didn't you like that?" he asked softly.

"Yeah." I paused. "I sure did, but...it kind of surprised me."

"Kiss me back, Frankie," he asked.

I tried and missed his mouth at first, and kissed his chin. He put his hand up on my cheek and guided me so that I kissed him square on the mouth. It felt good and I liked it. My mouth opened a little as I pressed my lips against his. He pressed back and nibbled a little on mine.

At the same time, I could feel his hand reaching in under my Jockey shorts and feeling my balls. He stroked them softly with the palm of his hand.

"I like that," I said, and he played with them with the tips of his fingers. They're sensitive, but he was so gentle, it was wonderful.

"U-m-m-m, that feels good," I said, and as I did, he pushed his tongue into my mouth and swirled it around.

I didn't know which felt the best, his hand stroking my balls or his tongue slipping in and out of my mouth. Then he pulled his tongue out.

"When I put it in again," he said, "suck on it, I think you'll like it."

"I like your hand on my balls."

"I figured you would." He stripped my balls with his fingers, like you strip a cow's teat at the end of milking.

"Ohhh - that feels good!"

"Like it, huh?" Johnnie kept lightly pulling down on my bag.

"Yeah!"

"I think you'll like this, too." John put his tongue back in my mouth and ran it in and out, and I sucked on it, like I was a kid sucking on his thumb.

His tongue in my mouth felt all warm. A hot glow was beginning in my balls where he was fingering them, and the heat was spreading up into my cock.

My cock got really stiff and pushed through my Jockey shorts against him. As I kept sucking on his tongue, I could feel that his cock was hard too.

He started breathing hard and pulled out his tongue, then kissed my face all over. I kissed him back and felt warm and relaxed.

Johnnie moved his hand up from my balls, feeling his way up the length of my hot prick. "Frankie, do you mind if I pull off your shorts?"

"Please, Johnnie, go ahead. Pull them off. You can do anything you want to me."

He pulled my shorts off and put them up near the pillow, so my cock and balls were right out where he could handle them easily. I wanted to be naked and open to him, so I pulled my legs up and spread them out wide. I really wanted him to handle me.

He caressed my cock up and down its whole length. He was just as easy and gentle and tender with me as could be, and I realized then how much he really thought of me, how he really liked me.

His fingers finally worked up over the end of my cock and he gently stripped it back, then played with the tip with his fingers.

I grunted a little bit and pressed my legs back together, so he knew the head of my cock was pretty sensitive. He put his hand up to his mouth and spit on it, then rubbed the spit on the head of my cock and pulled the foreskin back and forth.

"Yeah!" I moaned.

"I'll remember what you like, then next time I can make it feel even better. Okay?"

"Uh-huh," I grunted. There was going to be a next time! I could feel an excitement building up inside my belly.

"How about spreading your legs apart again?" Johnnie asked.

"All right," I said, and spread my legs out, so he could put his hand between my thighs.

He ran his hand lightly over the inside of my thigh and up beneath my balls.

"That feels good," I said.

"I like it when somebody does it to me too, Frankie," he said. "Now pull your legs way up and keep them spread, so your balls will hang free."

He cupped my balls with his hand, and I pulled my legs up some more and spread them even wider. He pumped my cock up and down with his fingers on the root of it.

"I want to make your balls bounce, Frankie," he said. "I've tried that on myself, and it feels pretty good... Maybe we'd better put a pillow under your ass so they'll really hang free."

He reached up and got the pillow, and as I raised myself he slipped it under my ass. Now I could press my ass back, and my balls could hang free and easy. He caressed my balls and tickled my asshole, and then he kissed me and said,"While I'm doing this, hug me around the neck and kiss me."

He started working the root of my cock up and down, and my balls bounced. I groaned at the feeling, and kissed him and stuck my tongue in his mouth. He really sucked on it, and we were both getting really hot and excited. While he was pumping my cock by the root, my balls were tingling and I was breathing hard.

"Gee, that feels good," I groaned.

"You really like having me jack you off, don't you Frankie?"

"I sure do, Johnnie."

"We should have started doing this a while ago," he said. "I've thought of it lots of times."

"I wish we had," I shoved my cock into his hand every time he pulled down on it. "Rub it all over!"

"Yup."

He rubbed it harder. I could feel the hotness building up in my groin, and I thrashed my ass around and burst out,"I'm going to come!"

"Go ahead, Frankie." He cupped my balls, then slid his hand up my cock, pulling up hard on it."Come right into my hand!"

I let go all over, and panted as my cock jerked and a glowing bubble burst in my balls and shot out into his hand. He kept pulling on my cock and kissing me.

He rubbed me with his other hand around my asshole and played with it. This made it feel all hot. I pumped my seed out into his hand and thrashed my ass around some more until all my cum had spurted out.

Finally I just lay back. All I could say was,"Golly!" I felt warm and relaxed.

He took the cum in his hand and rubbed it into my bellybutton. "This will give you a good grease job," he said.

"Yeah." I was breathing hard.

We lay there for a while; then he pressed his cock against my thigh, and kissed me again.

"I'll bet you want me to do it to you now," I said.

"I sure do. Pull down my shorts."

I pulled them down, and he rolled over on his side, so his ass was right in front of my cock. "While you're pumping my cock," he said, "rub yours in the crack of my ass."

I reached over and grabbed his rod. It was all hot and warm and velvety and hard, and I pumped it.

At the same time, I pressed my prick against his asscrack and rubbed it up and down. His ass was warm and smooth, and this made my hard-on come back.

"Let me spread my asscheeks," he said, "so you can get your cock in between them. It'll feel good."

He reached down and spread his asscheeks, and I pushed my cock deeper in between them. It did feel good. My cock was all warm and hard, and it really felt at home, cuddled there in between his muscled buttocks.

"Pump my cock faster," he said, when I got going again. "I can come better that way."

I went real fast, and he started groaning and shoving his ass back against my cock. I could tell he liked my cock in his asscrack, by the way he kept shoving back against it, and he sure liked my hand working on his hot prick too, because he would really ram into my hand when I pulled his foreskin back.

I kept pushing my cock up and down between his buttocks, and the pressure was building up in my balls. I knew I would come again.

"Make my balls bounce, Frankie," he said, "like I did to yours."

I really wanted to make him feel good, so I started pumping with a long, smooth stroke, all the way up and all the way down. I'd pull down hard so it would stretch the skin tight on the head of his big beautiful cock, then pull it way up so it would pull his bag tight and make his balls bounce.

"Oh boy, that's great," he grunted. "Keep going!" He really

thrashed his ass around, and my cock was so hot that I shot into his asscrack at the same time he spurted into my hand.

"O-h-h-h...a-h-h-h!" He was coming all over my hand as his ass jerked back and forth, squeezing my cock in his asscrack and helping me shoot the rest of my load. I was cupping his cockhead now with my palm, and his cum made my hand all slippery. I squeezed his cock tightly as I continued to slide my cum-covered hand up and down his jerking cock.

"Ahh...uh...ohhh!" Johnnie grunted as he continued to pump his slippery cock in and out of my hand. "Oh boy!" he said as he made a final thrust. "That was great!"

He sure had shot out a big load of cum. His asscrack was all slippery with my cum too, and I kept rubbing my cock up and down.

Finally, we had shot all we had, and just lay there.

"Boy, that was good," Johnnie said, breathing hard. "You're sure a hell of a good cousin, Frankie. Everybody oughta have relatives like you!" Laughing, he rolled over toward me and took me into his arms. "You all warmed up now, boy?"

"Oh, yeah."

"In the morning, would you like to do it again?" he asked, then he kissed me and held me tight.

"Sure would." I kissed him back, hard.

"Okay," he said. "When we wake up, I'll show you another way to do it." He laughed softly, and whispered, melodically, in my ear, "Frankie and Johnnie were lovers, right?"

"Uh-huh," I replied, "Ohhh—how they did love!" I laughed and hugged him tight. Then I burst out with, "You're sure a good lover, Johnnie!"

"I'll get better, Frankie."

"Oh god," I sighed, thinking about all those other ways to do it.

He kissed me again, "Goodnight, Frankie."

"Goodnight, Johnnie."

I cuddled up close to him, and we went off to sleep. It was colder than hell that night, but we were all naked and warm together under the blankets. Two naked and warm farmboy lovers. Yes, "Frankie and Johnnie *were* lovers" all right!

JACK O'LANTERN

James Lincoln

I'm eighteen, Bill would say, giving the word some long, drawn-out gravity. Eighteeeeen. Just barely, his mother would retort dismissively; things don't change overnight. That's my point exactly, he would respond; things didn't change when I turned eighteen. They changed before I turned eighteen. Eighteen finally acknowledged it. But she would hear no more, never letting him do anything, borrow the car, stay out late. Our home, our rules. I could just leave, he'd threaten. Well go on then, she'd counter, knowing he couldn't, not yet anyway. Was there any wonder why he was still a virgin?

Monday began with an attitude, refusing to get light outside; everything was a depressing shade of gray, like mop-water. It was Halloween-time in Epico Hollow, one of the oldest permanent settlements in Westchester County. Cruel October winds shred dead leaves from skeletal trees and they flitted off down the road in little dervishes, threatening to self-organize into some horrifying, familiar shape.

Bill Chambliss woke to the sound of the phone ringing downstairs and he pulled the covers over his head and tried to think of something pleasant . . . like the guy he worked with, Jason Ford. Jason Ford, with his short, dark brown hair and blue-gray eyes and that cynical mouth and....

"Billy?"

Mother, downstairs.

"Yes?" He asked, yelled, raising himself up off the bed.

"That was your boss Mr. Purdy. He wants you to call him when you wake up."

"Aw, come on; I don't have to be in today until later. What does he want?"

"I'm not your answering service," Bill's mother said. He heard the clacking of her footsteps growing softer.

Bill sighed and shook his head. Taking a year off in between high school and college was a mistake. Sure, he needed the money working for Purdy, but this staying at home thing sucked.

Tossing aside the sheets, Bill slipped out of bed, bare feet touching the carpet, and stepped to the bathroom. A fluorescent bulb flickered to life and he winced at it before growing accustomed. He pulled down his shorts to urinate, finished, then pulled them back up while walking past the mirror.

He stopped at his reflection and looked down at his bulge in the white undershorts. He tugged up on the waistband higher, stretching the cotton material over his dick. He could make out its outline. The material felt good pressing against him, and he thought his reflection looked good, too—so long as he imagined his body was Justin Ford's.

He pulled up higher on the waistband of his jockeys, dick straining at the material, growing fatter. Finally he couldn't take it anymore he was so hot and he pulled down the underwear, freeing his massive dick and grabbing it with a fist.

"Uhhn," he moaned. Bill flexed his fist around the base of his cock a few times then stroked up its length. He shuddered.

Bill's eyes fell on the moisturizer now. Squeezing out a good glob of white cream into his hand he coated his dick with the cool stuff, loving the squishy sounds he made. Now his cock was as stiff as he'd ever seen it, bulbous cockhead pulsing. He stared at it in the mirror, pretending it was Justin's, wanting to taste it. He looked up, saw his own face, and the illusion was gone. *That's not Justin—just me, Billy fuckin' Chambliss.* His dick slackened and he went over and started the water to take his shower.

When he got out and toweled off he found himself hard again. Something had to be done. The next thing he knew he was on the floor, kicking his legs up over his head, trying to reach his own dick with his mouth.

"Billy?"

Shit, Mom! Bill could picture her, leaning up the stairway, neck craned, clawed hand on the railing. Her voice was shrewish. "Billy Chambliss, are you up yet?"

There was a moment of indecision, then he said, "Yeah."

He heard one foot placed on the wooden step, the creak of the railing.

He was about to straighten out and get up but his dick beckoned. There was some point he'd passed—an event-horizon—and it was necessary to bring himself off or suffer the consequences. True, his mom was coming up the stairs to check on him, but reason and logic fled from his throbbing sex like frightened forest things.

Billy had begun pumping his cock furiously. It was so close -- his dick was longish, with a sexy curve to it—but his thin lips and fat cockhead were separated by an endless gulf of a few short inches. All he could do was jerk himself off and stare at his pulsating helmet just out of reach of his stretching tongue tip. Close, but no cigar. So to speak.

"Bill Chambliss, why aren't you coming down here?" His mother asked. Another few footfalls on the steps as she got closer upstairs.

He jerked faster. Preseminal fluid was leaking out of his dick in a steady stream and he made sure it got on his tongue. He tasted it. Sweet. This was the first time he had tasted his own jism and it was surprisingly sweet. More leaked onto his lips and face. He pumped faster. He was on the verge, could feel it fomenting in his tightly drawn balls.

Three more hard steps. "Bill!"

"I'm ... coming," he said, feeling it reach critical mass. He tried again to imagine it was Justin's dick in front of him and he opened his eager mouth as he beat faster, loops of clear Preseminal fluid spilling out, and now he felt his juice well up and get ready to explode. He opened his mouth wider still and shot a load of cum into it, a warm, powerful blast.

Another footfall and creak of the railing.

Was his door locked? He thought he locked it when he returned from the bathroom, intent on trying to suck himself, but in his excitement he might not have....

More sperm shot out, splattering his seraphic face and his long blond locks, some more getting into his mouth. He couldn't balance anymore and his legs came down, feet touching the floor hard.

"Billy?"

He groaned, arched his back, and shot off more spumes of sex juice up into the air with a thrust of his ass. It landed hotly on his chest.

"Bill!"

The rest of it dribbled out and he was suddenly enervated. He savored his own taste now, swallowing it all.

Four more hard footfalls then harder clacks as she hit the landing and came up to his door. Bill froze, looking at the handle as it turned.

He was lying spread eagle on the floor, cock in hand, his own come stuck to his face and hair. His heart stopped a moment as the door knob jiggled, then there was a pause, and then a knock.

He sighed. Locked after all. Thank goodness.

"Bill, are you coming downstairs to call Mr. Purdy or not? I told him you wold when you woke up. You aren't going to make me into a liar, now, are you?'

"Okay, Ma," he yelled angrily, licking his lips, swallowing the last of himself. He grabbed the bathtowel, and wiped off his chest and cock. Then he wiped his face while getting up."I'm just getting dressed," he called out, dropping the towel and leaning over to open the bottom dresser drawer. Billy pulled out some briefs and stepped into them, letting the waistband snap against his tight abdomen. Then he put on yesterday's ragged jeans and threw on a big T-shirt. He stayed barefoot, padding over to the door and checking his face and hair with his hands to make sure there were no telltale globs of come on him.

He sighed a moment, wishing he could just lie there and relish his glow. Instead he always found himself jumping up and destroying all the evidence guiltily. For once he'd like to lie naked in his own come, maybe spread it around on his body--

"Billy!" Ma cried.

"Okay!" Now he unlocked the door, tossed his damp blond hair back and looked at the spot where he'd been spread out on the floor, half expecting to see some kind of carpet angel impression that would give him away. Nothing, of course. Indeed, it seemed as if he'd never just jerked off. It seemed, as ridiculous as this was, that some way in his quick cover-up, he had erased the moment completely.

"Well, are you gonna to call Mr. Purdy or not?"

"Okay!" he yelled again, walking downstairs and calling work. Bill got Purdy on the phone and introduced himself.

"Bill, I've got a job for you," he explained. "Store needs a pumpkin. Everyone is really getting into the holiday this year. It's making a revival finally after all those ridiculous razor-blade-in-the-apple scares. So I want you and Justin to go get one and carve it together for the store window."

Bill's eyes opened wide. Did he say Justin?

"Go over to Dell's and pick one out. Tell him it's for me and I'll pay later. You can carve it today and bring it in later. It'll be a slow morning anyway so I won't really need you. Got it?"

"Got it," Bill said, still struck by how fortunate it was that he was being forced into a common activity with Justin Ford. It was almost as if Mr. Purdy read his mind and arranged this whole thing.

The two said their good-byes and Bill hung up, biting his thumbnail. Wow. What luck. He stood there a moment smiling dumbly when the phone rang again. Must be Purdy with something else. Or maybe canceling the whole thing. Bill answered it. "Hello?"

"Chambliss?"

"Yeah?"

"Justin. From the store. Did Purdy call you about—"

"The pumpkin, yeah," Billy said, wondering stupidly if Justin could hear him smile over the phone.

"I guess we gotta do it," Justin griped. "You wanna come pick me up?"

Bill frowned. "I don't think I can get a car for today."

"Well, I can pick you up, then" Justin said and Billy sighed in relief. "I'll be over in a bit."

. . .

Justin Ford liked the Hollow, even if it was a pretentious, stuffy little burg. That was on account of its zeal for conserving a residential, tranquil, and historic character with strict zoning regulations crafted to keep out tower apartments and strip malls and motels and just about anything else that might sully the neighborhood's celebrated old-fashioned charm.

Ford shared a place at the Lexington Apartments with a friend from high school whose job took her all over the country; she was in New Orleans now at some seminar and wouldn't be back for a week.

Justin pulled up in front of the Chambliss house in his beat-up ten-year-old Impala and tapped the horn. He was wearing a banded-collar denim shirt over a NiN concert T-shirt and jeans.

Bill appeared shortly, walking down the steps and around the car. Justin leaned over and pushed open the passenger door for him and Bill scooted his butt inside. "Hey," he said, grinning.

"Chambliss," Justin said. He had decided, for reasons he wasn't quite clear on yet, to act nonchalant and a little annoyed at having to go off and get a pumpkin and carve it with Bill. He reached over and turned up the stereo—Marilyn Manson was playing—and backed out. Shortly they were cruising under that gray sky past the high school and on into the small town on the way to Dell's.

Main Street was decorated for the season. Orange and black things hung. Grinning pumpkins and witches' tell-tale silhouettes and ghost shapes. The storefront windows had been painted this past weekend—an annual event sponsored by the Junior Section of the Woman's Club. Each window was given a number and students grades K through 8 began coming up with their proposed Halloween paintings in mid-September.

"You got any ideas, Chambliss?" Justin asked, turning down the radio.

"I'm sorry?"

"For the pumpkin."

"Oh," Bill said. "Purdy's paying for it, so we should get a giant one. Besides, they're easier to carve."

"I meant, how it's gonna look. Purdy said you're the artistic type...."

"Oh," Bill said again. "No, I just figured a simple generic pumpkin grinning and all. Or maybe looking shocked."

Justin turned off into Dell's dirt lot. It was a fruit-stand with a huge selection of pumpkins out front. The two guys got out and surveyed them, Bill sticking his hands in his back pockets and pacing around, getting good looks. Justin checked out a few promising pumpkins, turning them over, only to find bruises or gashes or other deformities.

"Hey, Chambliss. I'm in love," Ford said suddenly. "Look at

the size of that one...." Indeed, the pumpkin Justin had pointed too was massive and with a shape that resembled a head. The two of them went over and checked it out—just some dirt on the back that needed brushing off. It was perfect.

Justin and Bill looked up at each other and their eyes met and it was clear they had found their pumpkin.

They kept looking at each other.

Their eyes stayed longer than they should have.

A cool October wind blew up around them and ruffled Bill's blond hair.

Finally Justin turned away, breaking the spell which held them. "Well, let's get it," he said awkwardly, reaching down to grab the stem.

"Don't," Bill said. "It'll break off."

"Right. Stupid. I'm not thinking," Justin said, flustered. He picked up the pumpkin and cradled it in his arms. He seemed really distracted, his cool attitude blown by that lingering gaze, his rhythm off.

Shortly they were back on the road and Justin has decided the best place to carve it was his apartment since Judy was gone. They turned onto Sheridan Avenue and drove aways, then slipped onto Carlen Road, which paralleled Black Brook and went under the railroad bridge. The sky was getting darker still, the wind picking up. Mean gales spun dried leaves into whirlwinds across the street as the Impala pulled into the Lexington.

"Well," Justin said and his voice cracked. He coughed into a fist. "Here we are."

. . .

The first thing Justin did was turn on the stereo and put on a Bush CD. Then he slipped out of his denim overshirt while Bill took off his jacket. Justin got all the supplies they'd need for the carving and the drawing of the pumpkin's face and lay down newspapers on the kitchen table. He used a large knife and cut a circle around the stem large enough to reach in and pull out the guts.

"Lift the lid," he said and Billy carefully pulled it up as Justin got under there and severed the stringy membranes. He carefully put the top down and they looked in."Lemme get a scooper and a bowl," Justin said, rummaging around for a soup ladle.

Billy was a little more daring and he reached inside the pumpkin and touched the cool insides, grabbing a fistful of seeds and membrane, pulling it up. By that time Justin had found a large bowl and he dropped the goop in.

"Ew," Justin said. "It's like entrails."

Billy tried a sardonic laugh and held his gooey hand out as if to touch Ford. "Don't!" he said, stumbling backwards against a chair. Billy reached instinctively out to grab him and keep him from falling over, pulling him to his body.

They stayed there like that, Billy holding Justin close.

Then they sort of moved closer still.

Bill felt a flush coming to his smooth cheeks. Justin licked his lips, leaning over slowly until Billy could feel his warm, short breaths on his mouth. They kissed. A gentle press of warm lips against each other. The two held like that a moment.

Bill reached around Justin's waist and pulled him close against his hardening dick.

Justin pulled back, ran his fingers through his tingling scalp. "Um," he said, looking over at the pumpkin. "Maybe we ought to finish this."

Bill felt wounded. He nodded slowly. He understood, he guessed; Justin was confused. It was best not to push things.

"Now, he needs a face ... scary?" Ford was trying to pretend it didn't happen, diving right back into their project. Bill took a moment to compose himself and stepped back to the table. "Um, surprised."

"Okay. Draw it." He handed Bill the magic marker. He took it and drew a wide-eyed face with a cute short line for a nose and a small circle of astonishment for a mouth. He stepped back and looked at it and they laughed.

"Let me cut," Justin said.

"Kay."

Justin tried the mouth first. He poked the knife in. Pulled it out. Did that a few times until he got going, in and out, up and down.

Bill watched him absorbed in what he was doing, kneeling over, intent. His eyes went down to Justin's strong hands, then to the bulge in his pants.

"There," Justin said, pushing the circle into the pumpkin and reaching inside and pulling it out. Mr. Pumpkin had a mouth now.

"Great," Bill said and smiled and their eyes locked once more.

The Bush CD had ended and silence expanded and filled the apartment. Their smiles left and their faces were dead serious.

Justin asked in a quiet, cracking voice, "do you jerk off?"

Billy nodded, thinking about that morning.

"Me too," Justin said. He fidgeted a bit, shifted his weight. Stared at the floor. "I think...." He had trailed off into a mumble, turning his head.

Billy stepped closer. They were almost touching. "You think what?" He whispered.

Justin gulped. "I've been thinking of you when I do recently."

"Oh...?"

Chambliss grew very hard. Then he looked down and saw Justin's stiffness poking out his jeans. Taking the initiative, Bill moved up against him and put his right hand over the hard shape and Justin sucked in hair through his teeth. "My god...."

"Looks like you need to jerk off now," Bill said seductively, surprised at his boldness. "Feels that way, anyhow." He squeezed gently.

"Y-yes," Justin said. "Maybe I should go in the next room?"

"No," Billy said, squeezing harder and moving in for another sweet kiss. "Let's get naked right here."

"Thought you'd never ask," Justin replied. Bill let go of him as he stepped back and pulled his worn Nine-Inch-Nails shirt off and dropped it to the floor. Then he undid the button on his jeans. "Well? You just gonna watch?"

Bill had been transfixed by his bare chest and his tight abs. He was also drawn to the slightly darker material of his jeans at the tip of the huge bulge. Now Ford had undone his fly and was wiggling out of them. He had on paisley boxers which his dick was trying its hardest to poke wetly through.

Bill snapped into action, pulling his own shirt off quickly and undoing his button-fly. His baggy jeans dropped, revealing his own throbbing, curved cock pushing out his briefs.

They kicked off their sneakers and shoes and got out of their pants.

"Socks too?" Justin asked.

"Everything," Bill said, sitting on the floor and pulling his off. Then they were crawling over to each other, hands reaching out, touching, stroking. Justin caressed Billy's silky blond hair and pulled his head to his mouth. They kissed but for a moment, then went off in different directions, exploring each other's bodies with their fingers and tongues.

The two of them stood now, holding each other's cocks, cupping their balls. Then Billy turned Justin around and ran his hands down his back to his smooth ass. Justin gripped the table and leaned over and let Bill kiss him there. Then he felt his dickhead touch something. He looked down.

The pumpkin. With its open mouth.

Justin moaned as he spontaneously slid his throbbing dick into the pumpkin hole. It went into the mushy membranes, the hole gripping his shaft tightly. At the sight of that, Billy's cock grew to a tremendous length. He grabbed Justin's hips and pulled them back so his long dick slid back through the pumpkin mouth with orange membrane on it. Then, just before his cockhead was out in the open, he pushed him forward again, dick sliding in. Justin groaned once more. Bill left Justin going on his own, then moved around the table to look inside the top opening, watching his friend's cock slide in and out.

"Oh fuck, I'm doing a pumpkin," Justin said in stuttering breaths.

Bill reached into the pumpkin and grabbed some more sloppy mess from it and lifted it out. He squeezed the pumpkin gore in his hands, getting them sticky, and leaned over and put them on Justin's shoulders and moved his hands over his arms and chest, coating him with pumpkin guts. Justin continued to fuck the jack-o-lantern, moving faster now, as Bill leaned way over and planted a firm kiss on his lips. Justin's mouth opened and in a moment their tongues intertwined. Bill reached down into the pumpkin and grabbed Justin's sliding cock and made a fist around it. Justin fucked harder. His steady, strong stroke was getting erratic, feral. His breathing was in quick gasps.

"I ... going to come ... in the pumpkin!" Justin said.

"No, don't," Bill said, pushing him back. He moved around the table and genuflected before his friend, sticky hands going up to his cock. He pushed it back and licked up the underside of his balls. The noises Justin made and the tensing of his body told Chambliss he would have to be quick. He licked in an upward motion to the tip of his bulging cock with broad strokes and then slide his moistened tongue lovingly over the head in quick sloppy circles.

"Oh my God," Justin said, tensing even more. There was little time left. Quickly Bill placed Ford's stiff cock inside his mouth and began to suck, his pumpkin-sticky hands going around to Justin's rear, cupping his ass, pulling Justin's dick deep into his mouth so that the tip crammed against the back of his throat as he slid up and down the length with tight, rounded lips. Justin began to thrust his hips faster and faster. Bill let his hand drop to his own curved cock and began to jerk it up and down; he wanted to come when Justin did.

It didn't take long. Justin exploded into Bill's mouth, a warm blast of come squeezed off in quick succession. Justin grabbed Bill's head and tried to force himself all the way down his throat as he shot. The sensation made Bill's cock shoot off almost immediately, squirting white stuff up into the air and against Justin's legs. The two kept on squirting and squirting until they were spent, and then Justin pulled out, dropped to his knees, and hugged his friend.

They kissed again and Justin could taste himself in Bill's mouth. Then the two of them simultaneously looked up to the pumpkin and back at each other and grinned, knowing it would be sitting in the store window for the next two weeks until Halloween.

"I hope he can keep a secret," Justin said and Billy grinned stupidly.

Outside the wind pulled more leaves off the trees and blew them about under a dark, lowering sky.

DARK RIDE

James Lincoln

"Sammy Davis Jr. liked his looks—he knew his face was ugly, but he worked on his body. He had a wonderful V-shaped body, and he loved his little behind. He would make a point of it: 'Isn't that adorable?"
—*Burt Boyar, gossip columnist in the '50s*

I don't know if you know me well enough yet for me to tell you this story. I'll risk it, though, because I think we're like-minded here, you and I. So, you got a moment? I hope you have the time to hear me out and experience what I went through—I mean really experience it fully. So if you need to do a few things first—lock the door, get undressed, pour yourself a drink to have waiting for you on the nightstand after you and are I through here, get a towel or some lubricant—then you tell me and I'll wait for you. I've got time.
You set now?
Okay. It's like this....

"Sorry, dude," Rafe said as I licked my soft ice cream and squinted out the blaring sun. We were sitting on a restful bench overlooking the white sweep of sand lined with tanned bodies lying on colorful beach blankets. The Long Island Sound gleamed beneath a blanched blue sky. An old bi-plane flew with an advertising banner trailing behind, but I couldn't make out what is said because of the glare. You could smell the creosote of the boardwalk, a popcorn smell.

"It's okay," I assured him over the music of the calliope, frowning at a drop of vanilla ice cream that had landed on my blue shirt. I took a finger and tried to scoop it up, but it was too runny. "Please don't apologize."

"I mean, about my sister leaving me with you. You don't have to—"

I put a hand on his bare leg in confidence and looked at the smooth-faced boy with the delicate features. "Stop it right now.

To tell you the truth, I much prefer your company to hers."
A grin broke out on his face.
"But," I added, "that's between you and me, got it?"

It was damn true, that nicety; he was immeasurably better company than his sister, and I was glad she ended up bringing along her little brother to the amusement park ... damn ecstatic when she got that page and had to leave.

Let me see if I can describe him in such a way that gives some idea why he seemed to explode from the surroundings. You see, Rafe was a star, and everyone else was an extra. The world surely revolved around his being as clearly as the hand-carved wooden animals pivoted 'round the center of the carousel behind us.

He was thin and short (not much above "you must be this tall to ride"), but seemed larger than life. He had an amazing, golden tan, dark brown hair with blond streaks, and large, bright blue eyes, with high cheekbones, and a pert nose.

He wore white shorts that stretched across a dead perfect behind. His legs, smooth, carved works of art. An amazing smile with brilliant white teeth.

And he had a wry and cockeyed smile—that strange combination of naivete and wiliness which maddened and excited me.

I looked out now over the various people in tiny bathing suits spread across the beach. Extras, all extras. A crowd of semi-nude bodies serving as scenery. But if Rafe had been out there, with nothing but a tight swimsuit, lycra hugging his teen bulge, curvaceous, so very smooth....

I shifted uncomfortably on the beach, trying not to work myself up. Behind, an old man on a bicycle rolled past, making that distinct rhythmic sound bikes make on old boardwalks. Rafe turned to look at the bike pass and I saw for the first time his tongue had been pierced.

"That hurt?" I asked.
"What?"
"The ... the thing," I explained and pointed to my own tongue. "That."
"A little bit, yeah. Swelled up on me. The worst was I couldn't kiss anybody for a few weeks, though," Rafe said.

The way he tipped his head up at me and squinted out the

blaring sun sent a shiver through me despite the severe heat. I ran my fingers through my perspiration-laden hair and smiled back at him.

I patted his thigh again, then left my hand there. I felt no tension. My hand lingered and he didn't seem to notice or care. I left it there a few moments more.

Nothing.

Rafe began talking, completely at ease with me touching him —in fact, moving his leg slightly in my direction, which had the amazing effect of slipping my hand toward his crotch bulging in those tight white shorts.

I tried to imagine his throbbing teenaged cock in my mouth. Irresistible. Blood gushed to my own member.

"Hey, look," I said. "Go do your thing. I know you like the arcade...."

He thought a moment and looked at me with that cockeyed look, one eye squinted in the brightness. "Okay," he said lightly, "but you come watch." There was sweat on his brow, across his upper lip. I wanted to wipe it off ... with my tongue.

Shrugging nonchalantly I crossed my legs over a pounding erection. "If you want...."

"You like to watch, don't you?" Rafe asked, either oblivious of his intimations or perfectly aware. That uncertainty— seducer or the seduced?—made me harder still.

We walked over to the arcade along the midway. Around us the crowd parted (extras, just extras), carrying mylar balloons and big fluffy mounds of cotton candy on paper tubes. Some had stuffed animals they'd won at the games—giant ones that squatted on their shoulders and you could still see moving in the distance even after the person carrying it had been swallowed by the throng.

"I always wondered," Rafe said, "if they paid people to walk around with those prizes. Like you could really win something that big."

I smiled. "It is hard to win the big prizes," I said, "but you'd be surprised how cheap a giant stuffed animal is. Bigger is not necessarily better."

Rafe looked at me and said flatly, "we'll see."

Around us the sounds of clanging bells and screams of joy

and thumping music and laughter. Occasionally the thunder of the roller coaster as it clambered along the wooden tracks nearby. A clown was juggling three pins, big floppy red shoes and baggy pants with patches. Some big-headed costumed character from the cartoons was shaking hands with kids, their fingers sticky with candy apples and buttered popcorn.

We got to the arcade. Videogames had really changed since the days of Pacman fever. Huge screens, beautiful animation. Rafe was good at everything he tried, and got so preoccupied by them he forgot I was there. One game—I can't remember the name of it -- had him shooting a gun at a host of bad guys. He looked so damn sexy crouching with his gun. I also can't begin to tell you what seeing his hands on a joystick did for me.

When he was through he actually got me to join in at bumper cars (he seemed to revel in behind bashed by my vehicle from behind). We played some games on the midway (I never did win any of those big stuffed animals, only some X-ray glasses which, I'm sorry to say, revealed nothing when I fixed them on Rafe). I was good at skee ball, blowing him away, but Rafe beat me at air hockey -- probably because I kept wanting to be behind him when he leaned across the table to play.

Then I got a beer and he ate some cotton candy that looked like a swaddle of insulation around a paper cone. His tongue turned pink and he stuck it out at me.

"You know that turns me on," I said joking. Or half-joking. You know: one of those "I'm serious if you are, otherwise I'm kidding" kinda things.

He winked at me. "Do me a favor...."

"Yeah?"

"Stop exuding so much sexuality." He winked, then turned and walked off. I stood there for a moment, shook my head at my luck, and then followed him to the ferris wheel.

It was huge, turning at over two revolutions a minute. I hadn't been on one in years, jaded by fast rides, made to forget how breathtaking it was to be hoisted up nine stories high in the open air.

Rafe and I went around several times, looking down at the park. At one point, when the giant wheel was stopped to let people out below, he asked what would happen if we got stuck on the top for hours. My erection returned. I wanted to take him then and there.

"Listen, um," I stammered, "am I still exuding?"

"Huh?" Rafe asked, looking over the edge to peer down at the patrons below. I watch his tight ass rise up out of the seat. "Oh yeah, sexuality. Still exuding. It's overpowering." He turned and smiled at me. The ferris wheel started moving and he lost his balance—or pretended to—and the next thing I knew he was in my lap.

"You okay?" I asked. His ass was on my crotch. I felt his warmth, his life. His sweat smelled great.

"Great now," Rafe said and took my head in his hand. Before I knew it, his tongue was in my mouth. My friend's little brother was actually frenching me!

The wheel dropped downward now as his tongue slid into my throat. My heart beat faster, blood pumped to my cock and threshed in my ears. The combined effect of that—plus the danger of being seen by the line of patrons waiting to go on the ferris wheel— was incredible.

"Uhnnn," I moaned, kissing back. Then I managed to push him away, feeling us sweeping underneath the wheel to its lowest point. We managed to act natural enough as the operator opened our car for us and saw us out. I don't think he noticed my raging hard-on tenting my pants.

Rafe grabbed my hand and pulled me out into the crowd. "Come on," he said. "Let's do the flume ride."

His hand let go of mine and he ran through the crowd. I pushed through it to catch up, following his bouncing hair, his succulent ass.

The flume ride was actually a combination log ride, shoot-the-chute, haunted house attraction called The Spook Mill. Patrons float through a narrow, curving flume in small fiberglass boats which look like logs. The boats are carried by the water which is traveling downward slightly. At the end of the ride, the log travels up a conveyor belt, then drops down into the pool at the end.

We stood in line, waiting. It was a somewhat longer line than other rides -- perhaps due to the excruciating heat and the fact it was an indoor ride.

I watched as one of the boats came out of the tunnel, down a large near-vertical chute, and splashed into the pool of cool blue water with great fanfare. The kids in the log all screamed in excitement.

Rafe turned to me. "That looks like fun."

I nodded and put my arm around Rafe.

Eventually we made it up to the front. It was immediately cooler up under the awning alongside the water. An employee grabbed the next boat for us and helped us down into it, then let it go. We were the only two in it.

Rafe settled back and got comfortable and his hand came down on my thigh. I swallowed, anxious.

The boat moved forward slowly, bobbing up and down. The sun reflected off the water and created undulating heliotropic designs on the roof above. Now we were slipping into the full dark of the ride where it became cooler still.

It felt like time slowed down as we drifted lazily into the cool dark. I felt light-headed. My sweat was chilled.

Rafe whispered. "This is neat."

He scooted closer to me and I put my arm around him again. He snuggled against me and slid his hand up my thigh.

There was a hypnotic lapping sound of the water against the sides. Everything was echoey.

"I like your tongue," I said.

"Thanks."

"Your navel or nipples pierced, too?"

He didn't answer. I knew I was speaking quietly, intimately; maybe he didn't hear? Clearing my throat, I started to ask again when his other hand came over and found mine and held it. I swallowed again. Now he was putting my hand under his shirt and I was touching his flesh.

"No," he whispered.

He guided my hand over his navel. A smooth, flat stomach. An innie. Now he pushed my hand up over his nipples, first his left, then his right. I played with them, drew circles around them.

The boat rocked, slowed down even more. A slight wind blew through the tunnel. It was still pitch black with the exception of an exit sign ahead in an eerie green glow.

"I didn't get my scrotum pierced, either, though I know some people who have," he said.

And then he pushed my hand down over his white shorts. Rafe pressed my hand over his crotch, curling my fingers up under him. I could feel his compact, drawn balls through the material, then the thickening strand of his cock pressed against my palm. We both gasped.

I grasped the hard white outline that was his dick with my fingers. I could feel a small sticky wet spot. The tip of my finger explored this.

Suddenly there was a recorded cackling scream and a light went on to reveal an animatronic skeleton-pirate hoisting his cutlass. I pulled my hand away and tried to compose myself. My own dick was rock-hard, poking painfully against my pants.

The light went out over the diorama and darkness embraced again. I tried to see, straining. My heart was racing.

"Rafe?" I asked.

"Shhh," he said. His hand was back on my thigh. Now it was sliding toward my erection. My dick stiffened more at the prospect of him touching it. "Oh god," I said.

His small fingers brushed over my thickness. Then they found the button of my pants. Now they were pulling the zipper down.

I leaned back and looked up at the dark ceiling. The boat sloshed a little as Rafe worked in between my legs. We were listing to my side. He scooted me over and we evened out, then he pulled my cock out into the coolness and gave it a teasing squeeze with his smooth fingers.

A buzzer went off and a bad Frankenstein's monster raised his hands at us from the side off the boat, illuminated in a greenish light. I jerked uncontrollably, afraid we were being busted, but Rafe just laughed. The green light clicked off and we were in the dark again.

His long, thin, fingers worked on my stiffness now, restoring it completely after my fright. His hand was discovering every inch of my cock. Blood rushed in my ears and I was weak in the knees. My breathing was shallow.

Rafe's fingers wrapped tautly around the base of my cock and stroked upward. The head slid through his fingertips. I quavered. Now he was moving about in the boat. Water sloshed.

"Rafe?"

His fingers, slick with my pre-cum, grabbed my cock again and positioned it, pulling it downward. The next thing I knew it was being licked by the very tip of his warm, wet tongue.

I looked down and tried to see him giving me head but it was too dark. Then another light and buzzer went off somewhere, illuminating Rafe in red just as he opened his mouth into a perfect circle and pushed my massive dick into the yearning hole, past his thin, perfect lips.

I felt his piercing on the tender underside of my dick. He tightening his mouth around me into an asshole and bobbed up and down. Then he pulled away. My prick was leaking hot strands of precum. His fingers spread it around the pulsing knob. My balls drew up tightly and I could feel my sperm readying itself.

"How much time you think we have?"

"Not much," I said. "Please ... finish me off."

"Sure," he said, then took my dick in a tight grip and leaned back over. We passed now through a blacklight section and it was eerie. His shorts glowed brightly. I could see him close his eyes and opened his hot, small mouth. His succulent lips clamped over me tightly. He pumped it's base and sucked quickly with hollowed cheeks. He seemed like such a professional at this, as if he had given blow jobs to everyone, but at the same time his enthusiastic working of my massive dick had the earmark of fresh sexuality, like it was the very first time he'd gotten to taste cock.

I felt his throat relax and my dick slid down it. I gasped.

More displays went off -- screeching bats, hanging spiders -- but I didn't really notice. My blood was thrumming in my ears. Rafe continued to suck and squeeze.

Now the boat listed around a turn and into the flutter of a strobe.

Have you ever watched your dick sucked by someone in a strobe light? The combination of imagery and feeling was indescribable.

Now we were moving ahead into the dark. Rafe continued to fellate me. I leaned back and closed my eyes and hung on every sensation. When I opened them I saw a square of bright light, high up. We were coming to the end.

"Rafe...."

Damned if my dick didn't slacken somewhat at the distraction of the ride ending. But this made Rafe work harder and it bloomed back to full engorged stiffness immediately.

He drew his tongue upward now in sloppy licks. I felt the ball on his tongue slide up smoothly the length of my member. He continued to work on the base with a tight fisted hand.

I put my hands on Rafe's head and guided him up and down my pole, instinctively thrusting myself upward in time with his sucking. The boat sloshed. Then the tempo changed. We were on the conveyor belt now, moving upward at a different, faster speed. I slid backwards, Rafe still clamping his lips to my cock.

"Oh Rafe...."

The sunlight was getting brighter, the opening growing. Rafe was silhouetted now, angelic. I could see him swallowing me whole, encompassing my dick with his lips, drawing back, sliding down. Tension mounted. My sperm massed for a improbable orgasm.

But we were being carried to the opening fast now.

"Hurry...."

He sucked harder.

We were coming out into the sunlight.

"Ra ... Rafe," I said, desperate. "You have to stop."

But he didn't. He kept sucking and jerking me off, trying to get me to explode. My hips thrust upward, burying my hard cock deep in Rafe's throat. I could see him fully now in the bright daylight, crouched in the bottom of the boat, trying to make me come.

I could just see it now—this image of everyone out there turning to see us shoot the chute into the spray, me sitting there with Rafe working my dick.

"Rafe, you gotta...."

I couldn't manage to say anything else, reaching some amazing plateau of delight I haven't reached since ... well, ever. Gripping the sides of the boat strongly and thrusting upward into his mouth that he had made into a tight O, I fucked his face with complete recklessness. We had just passed what I figured must absolutely be the last possible moment where we could stop and compose ourself. But neither of us could stop our sex because we too had passed a point of no return.

I pushed my hips forward in time with Rafe's sucking and held the teen's head. My come built up. I had never felt this pent-up, this much power massed without release.

The boat suddenly hung in the air as he continued to work fast on my ruby head.

We were on the edge. We were coming out of the ride into the open.

There was a strange anti-gravity moment, and then the nose moved downward, fast. My breathing quickened to near-hyperventilation.

As we dropped out, Rafe moved his lips off me and squeezed my cock hard, almost painfully so, and jerked it up and down with a maddening frenzy. The log plummeted down, down, racing down. "Oh, shit!" I screamed, just like everyone else coming out of the ride.

I felt it explode, rushing from my balls through the length of my dick.

The fiberglass boat hit the pool of water just as my cock constricted and then enlarged and discharge a giant hot load of come.

Spu-lash!

Frothy love juice and cool water erupted, spewing everywhere.

Rafe laughed, squeezing me, pumping it all out.

I collapsed, drained, delighted, feeling almost drugged. Rafe slipped me back into my pants and zipped me up surreptitiously, and I swear I don't think anyone noticed at all.

The boat came into a stop and there was that employee.

"How was it?"

"Awesome," I said.

"You wanna go again?" Rafe asked, smiling seductively.

I think you know me well enough now to guess the answer.

SO FRESH, SO FRISKY

Lance Rush

"He grinned with frisky delight. His strength surprised me— so much muscle, so much power in such a little package...."

It wasn't supposed to be this way. You work at something so hard, with such focus, it becomes the nucleus of your existence. Somehow, this charging ambition to succeed so enveloped us, that we'd forgotten we were men—sexual beings. Tikiro Siomaski was a Japanese Olympic hopeful. I was just another hard-nosed freelance journalist, covering the Gymnastic Events for a National magazine. I'd interviewed several team members. My Japanese was rusty. But Tikiro was one of the few athletes who spoke fluent English. He even translated for the shyer guys. I liked him, instantly. His warm, friendly smile made him easy to like. The turning point came during one of their meets. There, I got to see firsthand just what separated the men from the boys in his field.

Once those little warm-up jackets came off, the biceps, the chest, the startling musculature of his flawless torso came into view. But then he quickly took my breath away in a vault through the air, somersaulting, denying every law of gravity. His floor exercises had my mind doing splits. His taut legs sprawled and flexed with quick, balletic grace, I wondered if he used those acrobatic skills in bed. He had speed, agility, strength and form. He was a young Asian Olympic machine. The balance beam portion showed every rippling muscle to startling effect. The guy was a winner. Still, I figured the best I could do was fantasize on slow-hand nights. Who knew if he was gay? Even so, those guys were treated like veal. There were rigid rules, regulations. I assumed I'd never know him intimately. But something was happening between us.

When he spotted me in the hallway, he jogged up and embraced me. I couldn't believe his skin. The smoothness of it, tingled so warm and dewy as he brushed his cheek against my own. A slow, queer smile brightened his aspect. For a moment, his smile did what a flash of sun does to a cloud-shrouded day.

His breaths were strong. It was that strange kind of labored breathing that still stiffens an older stud's cock. It was haunting and exciting all at once.

Later, as I conducted our final interview in his hotel room, I wondered if his trainer would ever leave us alone. After two hours of questions and answers, Tikiro said something in Japanese to his silent mentor. Suddenly their voices raised, and they seemed to be arguing—bitching like lovers.

Finally, the trainer spouted something sharp and clipped, and then he left. Whatever their exchange, whatever was said, it must've hurt Tikiro. He peered with eyes cast down, like a student who'd just been scolded, and yet that face of utter vulnerability never looked hotter.

"Is everything all right, Tikiro?" I asked.

"Fine, fine. Masimo, he is strict, very rigid. But I am not his slave!" he protested.

"But the gold medal is very important to you, isn't it?"

"Gymnastics, it's been my life. All my life. I have no friends. No girls or boys. Nothing but a world of balance beams, and the dreams of others."

I now felt sorry for him; for limitations in his life, all the sacrifices it took in his endless quest for the gold. I wanted to comfort him. He gazed back at me with sad, yet defiant eyes. It was time to leave, but I didn't want to go. He stared directly at my crotch. As I slowly stood, the bulge became even more obvious. He licked his lips.

"Well, it's been a real pleasure meeting you, Tikiro. I wish you the best of luck," I said.

The room was alive with a quiet of things sincerely felt but left unsaid. Tikiro stood and shook my hand. His eyes were two storms of brown light. In a bold move he took my hand and placed it on his ass—round, hard, heroic in its Olympian mold. I clutched it tightly. He ground himself into my burning dick. I just couldn't take all this Asian temptation. Journalistic ethics be damned.

"Since I met you, I've wondered about sex with American men," he said straightforwardly. "I am not so very experience, but...."

Then, he lifted my shirt, and ran the slowest tongue along my hairy chest. I shivered at his touch as he licked each hardening nipple erect, then glided down my belly. Despite his claim of a lack of experience, he seemed to know just what to do. Before he even touched it, my dick was a vicious piece of steel and coursing blood.

"I never been with an American man. But you like me, don't you, Lance?" he sighed, going down slowly on me.

My cock answered "Oh yes!" as he purred like a fine Persian cat at my lap.

Once he unzipped me, and wrestled it free, my cock waved into the air, high and erect, its knob dripping and gooey with pre-cum. His eyes widened, and a slow, excited "Mmmmm...." escaped his lips. He played with it as if it were the latest sex toy, invented just for him. He panted around it, sliding it through both hands. Running his nose along my warm, pulsing shaft, his tongue fluttered through my pubic bush in a tentative fashion.

"Oh, it is so *very* long...." he sighed, like some strange Asian Columbus having just discovered the mythic Penis People. "We'll be safe, yes?" he asked, sliding a rubber on me.

Once he popped its crest through his cherry lips, he looked so right with my dick in his mouth: the perfect blend of butch meeting sensitive. His lips rallied around my wide, heart-shaped crown.

"Ah!" He grunted and eased lower, and lower. I loved the noise he made as he lapped my veiny shaft. His eagerness sent warm gushes of saliva drenching down my swelling scotum.

"Ah!" I began to throb as I surged deeper inside this foreign mouth. He gagged a bit, but soon took it down like a champ. My balls churned beneath his sliding chin. I gazed past his cute sucking face to see his sweats falling. He pushed them past that glorious ass. Two beautifully beefy globes taunted me to distraction. So fresh, so frisky!.

My dick slipped from his mouth. He stood and stripped. His body was trim, hairless, beautifully defined, his chest adorned by rosy brown, dime-sized nipples that seemed perpetually erect. Shoulders broad, waist tiny from years of demanding gymnastics. In clothing, his frame looked delicate; naked was a different story. At five-seven, he was very masculine in a tight, bountiful way. Boyish, yes, but definitely studly. And those eyes. I felt like a prisoner inside them. His cock, a rigid six-inch tube of electric velvet, shot vertically forth. Sizable balls dangled from a pitch black thicket. I was drawn to his erection. I licked and lapped the full column, caressing his large smooth nuts in my fist. My hands encircled him, and massaged his ass. He wiggled it seductively, and I couldn't resist. Jabbing a pinkie up his tender chute, I poked at his gaping pink pucker and slowly whipped his small, fat prick. I pulled away, and suddenly he did a handstand, parting his strong legs. I lashed through his forked thigh and through the crack of his pretty, wincing asshole, hairless, full of musty heat. I lapped it in a rough burrow as his hips swayed and churned to my canine antics.

With his thick thighs trembling to my beat, I found his way with the language enchanting as his voice called out,"I want you to sex me." He tightening his assmuscles, snatching my tongue in its grip.

I brought his feet to the floor, too excited to even take him on his hotel bed. I could barely slide on a rubber with my urgency to fuck his delectable, sweet ass. Tikiro tensed his baby-smooth mounds. His crack revealed the tiniest bud, a lotus blossom, dewy for my juicing prick.

I crouched in a low squat as he parted those beautiful cheeks. In one purposeful lunge, I aimed my cock through his inviting hole. The slick, puckered vice cushioned my pushing dick."A yes!" he cried.

It was part asshole, part clutching inferno, drawing my cock deeper into its blaze. I pulled back and slowly pumped that pretty asshole as its pucker ring flexed and tensed along my dick.

"Am I hurting you, Tikiro?"

"Yes, you hurt me, Lance. But please don't stop!"

In and out, harder, quicker, the machinery of my fuck began. "Oh!" I plodded, then began thrusting into him as hard as I could.

"Love me long time!" He clamped down on me.

Slipping into sexual nirvana, I grabbed his rigid velvet wang and pistoned it quickly in my fist. A charge of cum vibrated through it. I felt that first gust of jism vault from his prick, followed by explosive spurts shooting, shooting in rapid succession. I fisted and tugged his taut, stilted tube, and I suddenly erupted in gobs of white luminosity. His spasm against me sent deep electric shocks as my cock exploded, pelting long slivers of fuck-froth into the rubber.

I kissed him like I had never kissed another man; hard and craven, unable to stop kissing him. He wrapped me tight in strong folds of cashmere skin as I pulsed inside a velvet sweat.

That was three short weeks ago, and now, on his last night here, we must say goodbye.

We arched like divers, he and I, submerging into a rushing tide. Suddenly, washed in an ocean's deafening sound and fury, swirling foam boiled up around us. But then, in an instant, in that one terrible crash, he disappeared, and my heart dropped to the bottom of the ocean's floor. The slow ache of time reminded me just how transitory life was. I knew then, I cared so deeply, too deeply for him, and it scared me. More than simple human concern for another; I suddenly could not imagine life without him. I dove in with desperation swimming through my chest, my limbs.

But then, against a turbulent splashing surf, I see his strong legs kicking, thrusting him forth, his body rising above the tide. When he surfaced again, his wet hair strewn across his face—hair the color of a raven's wing in driving rain—I was more than relieved. Something in his fine Asian features made me want to sweep him up, and drown him in kisses. I looked at his lips, and thought of cherries. His quick, flashing eyes were so dark with the liquid of a small, ancient secret. Strange how everything came together in his startling face, his skin, in a smile that seemed lit from within.

"Why do you panic, Lance?" he cried. "Didn't think I'd make it up?"

I hauled him into my arms. As confusing as the moment was, I hoped my kiss could clarify this blur of me, of my emotions. We kissed until we were both feverish, breathless.

"Come on! Let's go back to shore!" he yelled, swimming hard and anxiously ahead of me.

I watched his taut, naked ass, perhaps for the last time, as he bounded across white sand to the blanket awaiting us. He ran a hand along that ass, gyrating, tempting me with each randy swerve. It was only then that I realized, the whole time, in his own quiet way, he'd been seducing me. He turned on his back. The moon was on his face. His eyes pierced my shivering soul, as if asking: "You fuck me, Lance? You hurt me good?"

I could only smile.

Looking at him, my pounding heart, my throbbing dick answered, "Hell, yes!"

I fell down, tongue first, planting sucking kisses on his neck, shoulders, licking the sparse wires of his pits. He helds my head to his beating chest. I slowly orbited his nipples. He sighed, grabbed my waist and flipped me on my back. He grinned with frisky delight. His strength surprised me! So much muscle, so much power in such a little package.

My salty cock was wet and turgid as he went down the shaft's boiling skin The moisture of his tickling tongue made me throb and shudder. My head sang nasty tunes as he slid a rubber on me. Oh! He opened wide and every inch of my rod was sailing, surfing down to his gullet. My balls pulsed at the ripe cherry of his lips. Already, he'd learned to take it all down. I'd miss those lips—the damp surrender of them sliding across my prick. I'll miss his tongue, tumbling up and down, down as it swabs me in spittle, sending rivers to my balls.

Good-bye sex is the best of all. What was once, a shy, reticent tongue became a quick, warm and desperate one. There was a despondency to his sucking. He lost himself to it. He groped my balls as he kept gurgling along my hardening shaft. OH! An ocean breeze licked our naked skin. But he sucked me, clean out of the atmosphere! With one strong pitch, my slippery dick poked through his jaw, then dislodged, and he laughed. My wet cock slapped his laughing face.

"Am I better, Lance?"

"You're beyond better!" I sighed, collapsing upon him.

I felt his cock pulse and shift, pulse and shift against mine. He stared from dark almond eyes. His beauty was a whole other aesthetic. The yellow toast skin. The small upturned nose. Those tight, moist, puckering lips. I lurched into him. A shock of shiny hair tumbled to his face. But those tight almond eyes never left mine. I wanted to be gentle with him. Maybe it was the way he looked at that moment: part boy, part man. I knew I'd fucked him before—yet, there was a tenderness about him that almost broke my heart.

He tossed me another rubber, winced his little brown ring in and out, calling my dick forth. I entered him in a slow plunge, descending, sinking deep inside a grasping so sweet, I thought I'd cum in a deluge before I could completely savor him. I pulled back, grabbed his tiny waist, drew him in close, and lunged. Ah! The moist cradle of his anus was so intense! Oh! It completely captured my dick in an unyielding constriction of skin and muscle. I swear, it was as if it didn't want to let go of my trembling cock. I squeezed his mounds, eased back and bucked, deep and long within his gripping grotto. But, I couldn't move. My prick latched there, static, soaking in the warm vise of his fuckhole. Ever so slowly, I pull backed and eased through his steaming chute. I heard him groan as my balls rested outside his cheeks.

I pull his legs across my shoulders. His feet entangle my back, slapping together as I thrust. His face grazes mine and he kisses me, hard. My dick's planted deep in the bud of his gripping anus, he grunts. A slow, slow slide of his hips begin to quicken my glide inside him.

"Like it baby?" I ask with a plunge. "Want more?" I taunt, my tongue rattling in his ear.

I could feel him swelling like the push of tide beneath us. Grinding down, I find him violently erect. This excites me. I found a groove, a bouyancy of rhythm, of motion. My pitching dick was soothed in a massage as his asshole gave and clutched. His hips began to dance. Oh! I'm fucking him, loving him, devouring him like a piece of passion fruit.

He's going to kiss me. My lips bare down on his lips. Our tongues touch, as if for the first time, then they lunge. We tunnel and surge, fucked and groaned as the ocean crawls up to our tingling toes.

"Fuck! Yes! Oh! I love it. Give it to me! I want every inch of you inside me," he calls out, kicking his legs behind his head. His erect cock throbs at my neck. I grab the warm surging wang, flogging it rapidly, whipping to my rhythm as it fill my fist with sap. He swoons to my stroke. In this one consuming act, he seems to throw his voice to the exhilarating wind, saying, "'I'm sorry. I'll miss you, forever."

The ocean crashes. Sweat and deep breaths meet in a collision at my heated chest. I fuck, buck him with a deep and sudden abandon. I am making slow, wet, aching love to him, and it feels like the last time. Now, on this secluded beach, I'm alone with him our legs, cocks, balls all pounding. My heat, my rhythm intensifies. The waves drown us wet as I thrust, and pitched in this wordless ceremony. Tides rise and fall, breaking on our trembling skin. I'm a booster rocket about to fire inside him. Our bodies are one continuous spasm. But this jolting makes me sad.

"I am going, going to ... Oh! I don't want to shoot. But I'm, I'm... Oooooooh!" he cried.

Suddenly, his climax catapulted up to my chest, chin, face smearing me warm in sprays of cum. My rhythm slowed to a squirming retreat. I squirmed and retreated till I just couldn't stand the heat anymore. Ocean roared and so did I. I pulled the rubber free. My cum sprayed in white splattering ricochets to his moonlit cheeks.

"Tomorrow, I go, Lance," he panted. "But I write you."

We had learned so much about each other in these past few weeks, even the intricacies of our native languages, but the one word I wished Tikiro had never taught me was the hardest to say: "Sayonara."

A FEVER IN THE LOINS
A BRIEF AUTOBIOGRAPHY

Leo Cardini

PROLOGUE

NEWS ITEM - *Greenwich Village, New York City:* Late last night, a worn out pair of low-rise Jockey briefs came to an unfortunate end during a case of sexual assault. A 25-year-old slaveboy identified as "Teddy" unexpectedly rebelled against his master, a 26-year-old male known as "Mark," and sodomized him. In his haste, he neglected to remove his master's briefs. Instead, he ripped them down the back, and penetrated his victim through the torn cotton.

When interviewed, "Teddy" offered the following comments:

"Yeah, I ripped them. So what? They were just an old pair of jockey shorts. And to tell you the truth, I'm fucking glad I did it. I mean it's a real turn-on to rip apart a guy's briefs when he's still wearing them.

"And I'm not the only guy who gets his rocks off playing rough with men's underwear. I have this one friend; he takes a pair of scissors, cuts a hole in the front of his briefs and pulls his cockhead through it. He likes to show off like that at jackoff clubs. And all night long he keeps ripping the hole wider until finally everything's hanging out.

"And there's this other friend of mine who's into water sports. Well, he takes his briefs off and pisses all over them till they're soaking wet. Then he makes one of his fuck buddies get down on his knees naked and jack off while he wrings out the urine into the guy's mouth.

"And then there's this game I play with another one of my pals. We call it "Good Master, Bad Doggie." I get down on my hands and knees wearing nothing but a dog collar. He stands in front of me dressed only in his briefs, and I have to remove them using just my teeth. And when I finally get them off, he takes them from me, throws them across the room, and makes me run and fetch them, just like a dog. But you know what I always do? When I bring them back to him, I don't let go and he has to yank them out of my mouth. When he finally succeeds, he punishes me for being a bad doggie, which is probably the best part of all.

"I can tell from the expression on your face that you don't like the way I treat Jockey shorts. Well, fuck you, and fuck your straight-laced, narrow-minded morals. I mean, it's not like they're alive or something. They don't think, they don't feel, and they have no appreciation of how it churns up the cum inside me when I play around with them. No, they're just pieces of cotton fabric held together with thread and elastic. So, if I get my rocks off treating them rough, who's to suffer?"

"Besides, if they could express themselves and tell you what they thought about all of this, who's to say they would find it so objectionable?"

ONE

The tight plastic wrapping that securely enclosed me was suddenly and relentlessly stretched beyond resistance. It was helpless against the force of his strong, determined hands as he brutally ripped it apart in a long, jagged gash all the way down the front. He carelessly tossed it aside and it fell to the floor, leaving me wombless and abandoned.

I was overwhelmed by the rapid onslaught of innumerable new sensations, and the jarring realization that the universe was larger and possibly fraught with more danger than I had ever suspected. But before I could even begin to adapt, the thin cardboard insert that held me in position was yanked away and tossed to the floor to join the mutilated plastic wrap. I was left spineless and vulnerable.

In this way, I was unwillingly thrust into the world.

I was a brand new pair of low-rise, thirty-two inch waist Jockey shorts. My white, one-hundred-percent combed cotton fabric had never been sullied, the elastic in my waistband and legholes had never been stretched, and the opening in my pouch had never been pulled open to accommodate the demands of the bladder.

Yes, I was a virgin. And, like all new, unsoiled briefs, I was stuck up; inordinately proud of my pristine condition and born with the firm conviction there was no virtue greater than cleanliness, in both the physical and moral sense.

Within that reservoir of innate knowledge all underwear possess, there was the understanding that my purpose in life was to serve my master and to mold myself to his needs, his comfort, and his desires. I now faced, with a certain amount of apprehension, the question of just what exactly those demands would be.

I was lowered. I felt like I was falling through space at breakneck speed. My pouch had barely touched the carpeted floor when my descent was suddenly halted and I was held suspended in air, wondering what was going to happen next.

One foot forced its way into my left leghole; the other into my right.

And then that dizzying ascent. I brushed haphazardly against his strong, muscular calves. Blond-brown hairs tickled the elastic around my leg openings. His knees bumped against the front of my waistband. My legholes were relentlessly forced to open wider and wider as I was pulled up along his smooth, firm thighs.

What followed next happened so quickly and so thoroughly overwhelmed my senses that I can't quite recall the exact sequence of events.

I felt his balls press against my pouch. Those two large and (I discovered afterwards) sometimes painfully vulnerable egg-shaped spheres jostled around in his loose, pale brown ballsac. The hair that covered it crushed against me, tightly trapped between my pouch and his ballsac. I found myself exquisitely stretched, forced to conform to the comfort of his balls. With time, however, his ballsac and I ultimately negotiated a comfortable truce.

His two firm, asscheeks pressed against my backside. I felt the dimensions of those twin, perfectly sculptured mounds it was my privilege and duty to cover as they molded me into position, stretching me across their terrain.

A deep, dark crevice separated his asscheeks, tantalizing in its inaccessibility. And way down in its center, where it was darkest, there was a pink, puckered entrance. Few hairs surrounded it, making it look strangely forbidding.

I don't know why, but it fascinated me. I felt a strange, compulsive desire to explore it. I plotted that someday when my master wasn't paying any attention to me, I'd edge into that canyon until I'd reach the entrance to that cave, even though this is something a pair of briefs intuitively knows it ought never to do.

Meanwhile, he had adjusted my elastic waistband around his waist exactly where he wanted it. In front, I was stretched across the flat, hard terrain of his lower abdomen. Several inches above me a thin, straight line of hair descended from his navel. It crossed under my waistband, continuing farther down until it reached the lush, ample forest of his pubic hair.

And below, emerging from this forest, his long, pale cockshaft rested heavily in my pouch, its thick, deadweight softness forcing it to lean to one side. I rubbed up against it, intimately exploring every bit of its underside. A network of blue veins meandered along the greater part of it, stopping short of the smoother, pinker stretch of flesh just below his towering, flushed cockhead. His cockslit, taking advantage of my helpless state, pressed against me in a prolonged, wanton kiss.

With his left hand, he grabbed me by my pouch, embracing his soft, ample handful of cock and balls, fondling them with a few appreciative tugs. I found out later that this was a habit of his he was constantly repeating, even when he had pants or Levi's on. And most of the time he wasn't even aware he was doing it.

Then he let his cock and balls settle back into my pouch, commanding the shape I was to take in accommodating their comfort. I was set into position and I assumed my duties, knowing that the sole reason for my existence was to serve and worship this man, holding the most personal parts of his body in my protective and fond embrace.

On this first day of my life I learned many things about my new master.

His name was Mark. He was twenty-five years old and a recent graduate of Princeton. He was now living in Greenwich Village. This had been his dream ever since that night during his freshman year when he had travelled to New York City with two friends to visit the Mineshaft. The doorman there had interrogated him in great detail about the underwear he was wearing, and had seduced him into confessing some of his most intimate sexual secrets. This cross-examination had given him a hard-on, which the doorman had noticed, coaxing him into pulling it out of his Levi's. When he complied and liberated his urgently throbbing cock from the confines of his briefs, the doorman had his assistant suck him off, right then and there in the entrance to the Mineshaft, in full view of anyone who might happen to be entering.

Ever since then, whenever he was horny and the feverish need for sexual satisfaction forced all other preoccupations from his mind, his fantasies were as dark and red-lit as hell. And prominent in them, urgent hard-ons pressed against constraining briefs while confessors and inquisitioners coerced admissions that made his cock ache for orgasmic release.

Anyhow, to get back to that first day, my initiation into the ways of my master was not an easy one. You see, we briefs have a strong sense of morality and abhor the decadent desires that man is usually so helpless in resisting. We may be bound to serve our masters, but we are not obliged to condone their ways. So you can imagine the horror and humiliation I felt when I describe to you my experiences on that first day when I recognized the persuasive ease with which that carnal animal that lurked in his loins was able to take possession of him.

He had scarcely had me on for fifteen minutes and was sitting in his living room browsing through the most recent issue of *Men* when he got a hard-on. I panicked. I had never experienced an erection before, and I didn't know what was going on. His cock just kept growing, pressing mercilessly against me. And the more it pressed against me, the more it seemed encouraged to grow, threatening to stretch me beyond my capabilities. The blue veins along his cockshaft looked like they were going to burst open in response to the internal pressure exerted against their walls as his cock grew and grew and stiffened. His cockhead swelled, its underside becoming so sensitive that the feel of its ascent against my cotton front was driving Mark crazy, and his cockslit oozed a sticky stream of pre-cum against me.

But once he reached full erection and I realized I was safe, I admired his size, awed at the hardness he had attained. I knew it was immoral to feel that way, but I actually enjoyed the sensation of his eight-inch, rock-hard cock pressing against me, and the warm, sticky pre-cum that had so thoroughly soaked me in a rough circle around where his cockslit rested against me.

Then he went into his bedroom, lay down on his bed, and pulled me down to his ankles. He spread his knees apart and clenched his cock with his left hand, running it slowly up and down his steely hard cockshaft. From my closeup position at his ankles, I watched him play with his erection. His cock towered above me in all its unconfined magnificence while his audacious cockslit continued to ooze its steady stream of pre-cum. And as he stroked his thick, totem-pole cock, his two large balls bobbed up and down in response to this self-worship.

Eventually, he tightened his ass muscles and pressed his thighs out, thrusting his ripe, swollen cumswell into clearer view. He accelerated his cockstrokes. His balls were furiously tossing about, as if in agitated rebellion against the constraint of his slightly contracted ballsac.

Finally, I heard him moan as he tossed his head wildly from side to side, flinging away the excess of pleasure that was coursing through his body as spurt after spurt of cum shot out of his cockslit, landing sticky wet all over his chest and face.

Then he relaxed while his cock grew soft again in his hand. He caught his breath as his heartbeat regained its usual, slower-paced tempo.

This was my initiation into masculine sexual behavior. Little did I think then how much more I would come to observe about men and sex. I would not have believed you at the time if you told me that Mark's jackoff behavior was tame—practically juvenile—in comparison with what men are capable of when lust enslaves them.

Horrified, I watched as he removed his hand from his cock, dipped his fingers into the pools of cum on his chest, and brought them to his mouth, licking them clean!

Eventually, he reached under the bed for the towel I came to learn he always kept there, and rubbed the rest of the cum off his face, chest and cock. But, and I was to discover this was always the case, no matter how careful he was in rubbing it off his cock, every time he pulled me up and in place again, his cockslit would discharge a few drops of cum it had mischievously saved just for me.

At first I used to resent this devilish behavior, but to my surprise I found I came to like it. Though it went against the grain of that preoccupation with cleanliness that is characteristic of all underwear, I discovered that every time he jacked off, I actually looked forward to this gift from his cockslit, and the sticky, damp feeling of the mixture of his cum and pre-cum before it dried on me.

Then Mark went into the bathroom and pissed. He pulled his softened cockshaft through the opening in my front pouch, pressing its pliable bulk down against me. With his hand, he coaxed the piss out of him. Each time he pulled on his cock it pressed down on me, stretching the cotton in my front opening and battling against the staying power of my waistband. Finally, a heavy, yellow stream of piss worked its way out of his cockslit, thundering into the toilet bowl. When he was done and had coaxed the last few drops out of his cockslit, he slipped his dick back into my pouch. No sooner had he put himself back in place than his cockslit dribbled a few drops of piss onto me. Oh, how I resented this affront to my self-respect!

At the end of my first day of service, when Mark deposited me into the restful darkness of his laundry bag, I felt taxed, overwhelmed by all I had learned, and humiliated by the mixture of pre-cum, cum, and piss that stained me. And yet, despite all this, I was proud to be serving Mark, privy to the secrets of his crotch, and, I must say, strangely curious about those dark desires that lurked inside him.

As time went on, I became accustomed to my duties, adapting to the smooth, muscled contour of his ass, the narrow passage between his legs, the weight and dimensions of his balls as they rested in his ballsac, and the hair that lightly covered all these territories.

I learned the precise way his cock preferred to rest against me, accommodating Mark's near-obsessive desire to rub it every chance he got. And if not with his hand, then against the corner of a restaurant table when he rose from his chair, or against the well-formed butt of an attractive young man in a crowded subway car. I learned to tolerate these indiscretions, as well as to endure the abuses his cockslit forced on me.

I settled into the cycle of my existence: the demands Mark placed on me throughout a day of wear, the restful recuperation in his laundry bag, the rite of purification in the washer, the exhilarating, invigorating experience of the dryer, and the calm repose of his underwear drawer before I was called upon to serve him again on yet another day.

Now, I mentioned earlier my curiosity with the mystery of his asscrack. Briefs have an instinctual loathing for this area of a man's body. But at the same time, the urge to explore it is irresistible. Sooner or later, every pair of briefs gives in to the temptation and inexcusably crawls into his master's asscrack. Let me tell you, my curiosity was quickly satisfied when I discovered the noxious odors it was capable of emitting, and the filthy excretions it...well, some matters are best left unmentioned. Suffice it to say I learned my lesson.

I got to accompany Mark on his journeys outside the apartment; to the bars, the porn bookstores and cinemas, and the safe sex clubs he frequented. I got used to the chronic hard-ons he got in these locales and the way they'd press against me, agonizing the less accommodating denim in the crotch of his Levis. I grew accustomed to the evaluating grasp of a stranger's hand in Mark's crotch, the pats and light slaps on his ass, and the way some men would hitch their thumbs in his back belt loop and let their fingers fan out over his ass. And I must tell you, I grew to appreciate them. Not in any cheap, carnal way, mind you, but in much the same manner that a connoisseur of fine art wishes to share his appreciation with those around him.

And at the Cell Block's safe sex parties ... well, I know I'm going to sound a little vain, but I felt like a star. As soon as Mark entered, he would go immediately to the coat room and check in everything he was wearing except for me and his boots. All eyes were on us as he walked around allowing everyone to admire that sizeable basket of his that I so provocatively held in place.

And when he brought someone home with him—which was frequently—there were those wonderful moments when they would press their bodies close together, locked in a strong, masculine embrace. I would feel Mark's cock grow hard in no time, his cockhead urgently attempting to crawl up under my waistband. And from outside the stubborn confines of his Levis, I'd feel his partner's cock, as stiff and excited as Mark's, pressing against me while these two dicks made fervent love to each other through the simultaneously tantalizing and frustrating barriers of denim and cotton.

Usually I'd eventually be tossed aside, abandoned on the bedroom floor as Mark and his friend tore the clothes off each other, and continued their impassioned lovemaking as naked and uncontrolled as two wild, rutting animals. If I was lucky, the other man's underwear would be there with me. In that silent communication that goes on between two pairs of briefs when they touch, we would share the secrets of our wearers' loins and the lusty, compelling desires that would emerge from them.

It was as a result of one of these encounters - when I had been in Mark's service for about six months - that I came to alter my unfavorable view of his asshole.

His partner that night was this six-foot-two, brown-haired, broadchested, lumberjack of a man named Colin. Mark had picked him up at the Spike.

After they were a few minutes into their rough love-making, Colin forced Mark in a leaning position against his bureau, the upper part of his chest pressing against it. He folded his arms across the top of the bureau, with his hands clasping his elbows, and rested his head on one side against his right forearm.

With rough, impatient movements, Colin undid Mark's Levis and lowered them and me to his ankles. Mark bent his knees slightly and spread his legs apart, allowing Colin convenient access to his asshole.

Mark's cock hung hard and heavy above me, jerking up and down between his legs every time it twitched. His cumswell was swollen and his ballsac had slightly contracted around his balls. I knew he had lost control of himself.

What followed horrified me. I couldn't understand how he would allow such a thing to happen, even in this state of sexual frenzy.

Colin explored Mark's asshole with his oversized fingers, lubricating it with the KY Mark kept under his bed. And Mark was clearly loving it!

Then Colin paused to lower his own Levis and reach into his right back pocket. He pulled out a small, thin, rectangular package, which he then tore open. He removed the flat, circular rubber object inside and carefully unrolled it over his stiff, nine-inch long log of a cock, all the way down to its base. It fit like the tightest of gloves.

For the first time in my life I experienced jealousy. You see, I had always assumed that no object had more intimate knowledge of a man's cock than his underwear. But to embrace a dick like that, to know even the most minute details of every bit of a man's dick, to map with perfect accuracy the course of every blue-veined canal along a man's cockshaft, to bear witness to the slightest surge of arousal, and to catch and retain in your embrace every iota of precious discharge from the cockslit...well, the thought that came to my mind was that in my next life I wanted to come back as one of those things.

I had second thoughts about this desire, however, when I saw Colin put his hands on Mark's hips and invade his asshole with his sheathed cockshaft. That was not someplace I would ever care to explore. No, not under any conditions. And if the undesirability of such a locale wasn't enough, think of the pain such an intrusion would cause!

And he just kept pushing it into Mark, inch by agonizing inch.

But to my surprise, Mark actually welcomed it into himself! As I watched from below, I heard Mark groan with pleasure as Colin gradually worked his cock all the way into his asshole. Then he slowly and rhythmically moved it in and out. One moment Colin's cock would be all the way in, and his large, hairy balls that hung low and loose in his ballsac would flop below the entrance to Mark's asshole. The next moment, it would be pulled so far out that only his fat cockhead remained inside and the span of his thick cock would loom above me like a tree-trunk bridge between Colin's crotch and Mark's asshole.

Then he started ramming his cock in and out of Mark with greater force and speed. Every time he savagely shoved it all the way in, his belly slapped against Mark's asscheeks. Mark tensed his legs muscles to maintain his position during this assault, and every time crotch and ass made sudden, brutal contact, Mark welcomed it with a low, urgent "Oh!"

And Mark's hard cock, oozing pre-cum, swung up and down between his legs in helpless response to this aggression, so aroused it looked like it was about ready to shoot off with no assistance.

I could feel it in Mark's ankles that the animal in his loins was now fully unleashed and he was in a helpless state of complete ecstasy.

When Colin finally came inside Mark, groaning in a deep bass-baritone voice, he grabbed Mark's cock with his right hand, and jacked him off. Mark came in no time, moaning with pleasure and violently jerking his head back and forth as spurt after spurt of his cum splattered against the bureau.

When Colin's hand had worked the last jet of cum out of Mark's cockslit, Mark's jism began its lazy descent down the front of the bureau. Above, the two of them came to rest, exhausted and breathing heavily after this rough workout that had sent them into such a fierce, uncontrolled ecstasy.

Colin bent over Mark, resting his chest on Mark's back. He wrapped his arms around Mark's torso and remained there while his gradually softening cock slowly and reluctantly exited Mark's asshole. At the same time, Mark's cock also softened. A few last drops of cum dripped out of his cockslit and landed on me.

Later, in the calm repose of Mark's laundry bag, I re-evaluated my opinion of Mark's asshole. As I told you before, briefs have an inbred dislike of a man's rear entryway. But how could something be capable of such loathsome actions as I had experienced that time I sneaked into Mark's asscrack, and yet be equally capable of providing such ecstatic pleasure as I had witnessed that night?

The fever in Mark's loins was eroding my up-to-then unfaltering confidence in my beliefs. Things were not always as they appeared. Goodness and badness were intertwining, somewhat subjective qualities.

For the first time, I questioned the supreme importance of a spotless, bleached-white condition. I had always like the feel of cum, but this evening, as Mark's jism dried crusty-hard on me, I felt absolutely no guilt in my appreciation of it.

I knew my life would never be the same.

TWO

As time went on, Mark changed. I could feel it in the fever that burned in his loins. His cock began taking control of him, whispering its desires so subtly he didn't even realize it was happening. An almost addictive need for rugged contact with other men gradually took over his being. Inside him, a hungry animal stalked through dark corridors in search of appeasement.

I was first aware of these changes the day Mark put me on and I felt something foreign press against me. A silver metal ring encircled his cock and balls. At first I resented this intrusion. I wanted his cock and balls to be mine alone to embrace in the privacy of his Levis. And, to be honest, I envied its ability to keep his cock hard for long periods of time, a constant reminder of its presence.

But as time passed - and this is an example of how my own sense of morality was being sabotaged by the hypnotic power of the beast inside his crotch - I found I came to welcome the company of his cockrings. I grew to admire them all: the metal cockring that would embrace him hard and cold at first, but would then gradually absorb his body heat until it was as warm as his cock; the black rubber cockring that was tight as a noose when Mark got hard; and the two leather snap-on cockrings - one with studs, one without - that he could put on, or remove, even when he already had an erection. I began to see them as companions in the service of my master, and appreciated the way they would keep him pressed hard and large against me.

And then, about two months after the advent of cockrings into my life, I was witness to another change in Mark's crotch. He had shaved his balls! Those blond bristly hairs that I had come to know the ticklish feel of so well were gone. Instead, his balls pressed silky smooth against me. I immediately liked the luxuriant, sensual feel of it.

And as his clean-shaven balls pressed against me, I wondered: what it would be like to experience the adventure of the razor that shaved him? How would it feel to travel slowly and carefully across his furrowed ballsac, careful not to do it any harm while mowing down that precious field of hair?

I guess what followed next was inevitable. Mark began to

seduce men into licking his balls. In bedrooms, or in dark places where he and his partner could carry on unseen, he would entice his partner to get down on his knees and let his tongue explore that same territory the razor had traversed.

Below, I would be at Mark's ankles, shadowed by the man chosen to kneel between Mark's legs. Above, Mark would be watching, grasping his hard cock in his left hand, stroking it while thrusting out his ballsac to provide his partner with easy access to his smooth, clean-shaven nuts.

He loved to give detailed orders to his ball-licking friends, commanding a thorough, worshipful tonguing. And when his partner, cock in hand between his slightly spread-apart legs, would take both of Mark's balls into his mouth and give them a gentle yank, Mark would get this crazed look in his eyes and stroke his cock all the more urgently

Soon, they'd be furiously stroking their desperately hard dicks, ecstatically connected by mouth enclosing ballsac and tongue adoring the nuts contained therein, until the cum erupted out of their cocks, splattering hot, milky-white pools all over. When they were done, and Mark's cum covered his fist, his cockhead and his partner's forehead, and his idolizing friend had shot his load between Mark's legs, an abundant amount of it always landing on me, I'd be pulled up into place again. The wetness of the saliva that coated those precious, smooth-shaven balls would mingle with the cum sticking to my cotton and I'd be glued against Mark's cock in the darkness of his crotch.

When I first served Mark, I felt pride in enclosing him in cleanliness - a clean environment for a clean life. But by now my narrow-minded morality had been upstaged by an ever-increasing hunger to caress him for the sake of the sensation alone, to bear witness to his desires, to feel his smooth-shaven balls, his cockrings, the hard-ons that appeared with increasing frequency, the embrace of his hand against my pouch, and the inquisitive touch of other men's hands as they explored the length and thickness of his cock and the fullness of his ballsac.

I welcomed his increasingly frequent sexual adventures, wallowing in them. But then one evening when Mark's sexual fever had so overwhelmed me that I would have been willing to submit to any demand he placed on me, I was unexpectedly put to the test.

On a Tuesday night shortly after midnight, when Mark really should have been in bed getting enough sleep for another workday, he left the Spike with a man he had met at the Cellblock on several prior occasions.

His name was Teddy. He was about five-foot-ten and packed with the smooth, brawny muscles of a man in his mid-twenties who had spent his youth in a never-ending afternoon of athletic activity and playful roughhousing. He had a handsome, boyish face capped with straight brown hair that inched over his smooth, broad forehead and obscured his ears and the back of his neck.

Everything about him exuded a feeling of wholesomeness and robustness, except for the look in his dark-brown eyes; that same look I'd seen come into Mark's eyes more and more frequently - a burning, lustful, desperate look, seeking out sex infused with danger and violence.

As soon as they entered Mark's bedroom, they embraced. I felt the familiar press of another man against Mark's body. But I had never felt such pressure. Their passion was like a mutual assault, as if each was trying to invade the other's body with all the savagery of a starved animal tearing apart its prey.

Mark's leather-encircled cock hardened instantly and Teddy's equally-hard cock pressed against it. Maybe it was shy of Mark's by a half-inch or so, but its thickness was something impressive. His cockhead crested it like an oversized mushroom. Yes, I'd learned to observe such things in great detail, even through layers of clothing.

But there was also something different about his crotch that I couldn't quite make out - something having to do with texture.

But before I could even begin to figure it out, Mark had placed his hands on Teddy's shoulders and had violently pushed him down to his knees. Then he put his hands behind Teddy's head and forced Teddy's face into his crotch. Teddy let out a muffled exclamation of surprise, but rather than trying to withdraw, he opened his mouth and squirmed his tongue out against the denim in Mark's crotch.

Mark released Teddy's head. With long, slow strokes, Teddy

repeatedly worked his tongue from deep in Mark's crotch crevice all the way up along his dickbulge.

Eventually, Teddy withdrew to undo Mark's Levis and pull them down. He buried his face in Mark's crotch and inhaled. His nose pressed against me to the left of Mark's rockhard cockshaft.

Mark's crotch-smell had the effect of an aphrodisiac on Teddy. When its effect overwhelmed him, he removed his face and resumed his crotch-licking. He started with Mark's ballsac. I felt his wet tongue press against me, jostling Mark's balls in my pouch, leaving me slightly damp with his saliva.

Next, he moved below Mark's ballsac and bit into him. Mark's legs tensed. He moaned with pleasure. With Mark's cumswell clenched between those teeth that threatened to puncture me, he ran his tongue along it, pressing, massaging, churning up Mark's cum.

Then he pulled out from between Mark's legs, manufactured some more saliva in his mouth, moved forward and licked slowly upward along Mark's steely hard cock, all the way up to his cockslit that was just short of pressing against my elastic waistband. When he reached the cockslit and began to delicately tease it through my cotton, Mark's cock surged with one massive twitch.

Teddy prepared a little more saliva in his mouth and repeated his tongue travel along Mark's cockshaft again and again with slow, lavish slurps. His eyes were closed as he was taken over with the overwhelming, intoxicating effect of cockworship.

Soon I was soaked through and through with Teddy's saliva. I clung skintight against Mark's throbbing cock. I could feel the network of blue veins along his cockshaft that protruded like swollen canals, and the promiscuous outpour of pre-cum his cockslit was discharging.

Then, in a frenzy of heated activity, Mark and Teddy tore off their clothes, prior to jumping onto the bed. Mark violently lowered me from his crotch, tearing me unwillingly away from his cockshaft.

I was tossed onto the bedroom floor amidst the chaos of their other tossed-off clothing. I rested against something unfamiliar. It was an odd piece of underwear. Its rough, textured pouch, which had mystified me when I felt it through Teddy's Levis, had elastic running through it. And in the back there was no seat—just two elasticized straps that traversed the ass, meeting the pouch just underneath the balls. In that silent communication that goes on between underwear, I learned that this was a jockstrap, a crude creature whose sole purpose of existence was to protect a man's cock and balls during strenuous exercise. And it performed this function steeped in the crotch-sweat of physical activity. My admiration and envy knew no bounds.

But what fascinated me most at that moment was the realization that here was a piece of underwear which could actually be worn while a man was being fucked. Imagine such proximity during such an act! I wondered what it would be like to hold Mark's cock in my embrace and to experience first hand the effect a cock up his ass would have on it. Since this was something I could never experience myself, I found myself longingly fantasizing over it during the coming weeks.

The bed rocked, the mattress sagged and groaned, and the headboard repeatedly slammed against the wall. Sharp slaps pierced the air. Each one was followed by Teddy's increasingly louder "Aaahs!" as he squirmed to escape Mark's grasp, at the same time thrusting out his ass to receive the next slap.

The two of them tumbled off the bed and into the midst of their disarrayed clothing. They were locked in each other's arms, each struggling for dominance over the other. Mark finally managed to escape Teddy's hold and rose to his feet. Teddy sat up, staring at Mark while trying to catch his breath. His eyes were savage, his face was animal-like, and his chest heaved with inescapable, boundless lust.

Mark reached down, grabbed me and shoved me into Teddy's face, rubbing me all over it. I felt Teddy's heavy breath as he bit into me and tried to pull me out of Mark's grasp. He tossed his head back and forth, trying to wrest me from Mark's grasp, much like a dog trying to yank a favorite toy from his master.

Caught in the midst of their uncontrolled passion, I plunged into the perverse pleasure of being strained and stretched between master and slave, wet with saliva, cruelly manhandled, and in danger of being torn beyond repair.

When Teddy finally let go, Mark grabbed me with both his hands, wrapped me around the back of Teddy's head and forced him forward until his willing mouth took Mark's cock in all the way down to its base. He held him there for what seemed like a blissful eternity. When he released him, holding me by his side with his right hand, Teddy's eager mouth moved up and down on Mark's cock while he worked on his own with his right hand.

When Mark was ready to come, he violently pushed Teddy's mouth off his dick. Teddy nearly fell backwards, breaking his fall with his free hand. Mark took his spit-soaked cock and jacked himself off. With a loud, prolonged "Ahhhh!" he shot his cum all over Teddy's face. Teddy's eyes reflexively shut against the onslaught of the hot, spurting cum that covered his face. His cock erupted with its own outpour of cum, landing in a series of steaming puddles all over the tangle of clothes below him.

When they had milked all the cum out of their cocks and had regained their breath, Mark picked me up and slowly rubbed me all over Teddy's face, massaging his cum into it. Teddy closed his eyes and turned his face upward in passive, blissful acceptance. A low, appreciative "Ummm" gravelled in his throat. I felt Teddy's features; the broad forehead, the soft eyelids, the jut of his nose, the light bristle of beard on his cheeks and chin, and his moist lips. When Mark was finished, I was covered with a coat of sticky cum which mingled with the saliva Teddy had lavished on me a few minutes earlier.

Mark handed me to Teddy and commanded him to put me on. Teddy got up and immediately obeyed.

I had never been worn by another man. I had been molded to Mark's body. Now I covered a new, unfamiliar territory. His brown hair was silkier. His hairy, wrinkled ballsac, tightly wrapped around his nuts, was unshaven. I'd forgotten the feel of ballsac hairs crushing against me, and welcomed that lost sensation. Teddy's ass was more muscled and rounded. And his cock was thicker and stockier, as I had briefly noticed before. His cockslit greeted me with a pearl of Teddy's cum.

I welcomed the feel of Teddy's body against me and hugged every part of his crotch, molding my saliva-and cum-soaked cotton against it, familiarizing myself with every inch of his loins.

At that moment, blissfully abandoning the moral precept that a pair of briefs ought only to be worn by one man, and one man only, I lusted to experience Teddy in the same intimate way I had experienced Mark. And beyond that desire lurked another craving; to experience a multitude of men. I wanted to sample endless variations of cocks and balls and pubic hair and asscheeks. I wanted to know the horny, cock-hardening secrets of a succession of endless men while their crotches rested hidden from the world in the seclusion of my fond embrace.

But when Teddy put his Levis on again and buttoned me into darkness, I momentarily reconsidered. With every step he took—out the apartment door, down the elevator, and through the streets—I was being transported farther and farther from Mark. And Mark, who should had protected me, had allowed it!

I was being separated from all I knew. I felt torn between the pain of separation and the exhilaration of adventure.

When we reached Teddy's grubby Chelsea apartment, he went directly to his bedroom and stripped. He held me to his nose and inhaled, smelling the mix of sweat, saliva and cum that pervaded my cotton. He jacked off right then and there, still standing, and used me to catch his cum and to wipe off his cock when he was done.

Then he tossed me to the floor and jumped into his unmade bed. I found myself amidst the rank-smelling jungle of all his other worn clothing that had been deposited there.

How different men can be. Mark had a laundry bag; Teddy had a floor.

The rest of the room was equally messy. A disorganized assortment of gay male magazines rested under his bed, along with a dirty towel steeped in dry cum, a huge, lifelike, rubber phallus, and three containers of lubricants, two of them empty. His night table and bureau were similarly covered with clutter; several small brown bottles, half-used packages of E-Z Wider, condoms, cockrings, tit clamps, a dog-eared copy of *Mineshaft Nights*, and other signs of a hedonistic lifestyle.

As soon as I got over my initial reaction of disgust, I found an odd sense of liberation in such carelessness.

That night, while Teddy slept, I evaluated my situation. I

was held captive and helpless in an unfamiliar environment, one of moral and physical laxity. The rules here were different. They were more casual. All signs, in fact, pointed to a downright depraved existence. And, although I missed Mark and the comparably calm order of his apartment, I was loving it.

As the days went by, that stabbing feeling of loss that I would experience now and then gradually lessened. I felt myself settling into this new life, basking in the devil-may-care disorder of Teddy's bedroom floor. Piss-stained briefs, sweaty jockstraps, T-shirts reeking of sweat in their armpits, and white gym socks rich with the pungent odor of feet all mingled in masculine camaraderie.

Not a day went by without Teddy noticing me. He'd pick me up, press me against his face, and inhale. Sometimes he'd wear me around his apartment, usually with his dick hanging out my front opening. He'd tug at his cock and I'd feel his balls reposition inside me. And sometimes when he lay on his bed and jacked off, he would put me in his mouth. And whenever he came, he'd use me to wipe the cum off his cock and chest.

When his cum initially accumulated on me, I felt humiliated, debased. But after three or four deposits, I felt strangely liberated and I found myself lusting for it. His cum was like an aphrodisiac that suffused me with a dense, lazy eroticism.

But still, however slight and dwindling, there was always that aching feeling whenever I thought of Mark.

Then one night, Teddy put me on, and for the first time since he brought me to his apartment, he placed a pair of Levis over me. Then I felt the tucked-in bottom of a T-shirt.

We were going out.

But where? Out his apartment building. Walking. Walking. Seemingly endless steps down seemingly endless streets. Finally he entered another building and went up an elevator.

When he unbuttoned his Levis again we were back in Mark's bedroom.

Teddy stripped off all his other clothes, but he kept me on. He kneeled in front of Mark with his hands clasped behind his back. Mark towered above him with his arms crossed across his chest and his legs slightly spread apart. He was shirtless, dressed in boots and Levis. He had never appeared so stern and threatening.

When he saw the condition I was in, he chastised Teddy for his slovenly lack of self-respect. Maybe Mark was right. But I wasn't so sure.

He took his left hand and slapped Teddy across the face with the back of it. Teddy's head jerked to the right in response. He closed his eyes and lowered his head to his chest. Shame and humiliation flushed through his body, heating up his loins and sending an arousing surge through his cock.

Mark told Teddy he'd have to be punished. He commanded him to remove me. Teddy complied with his wishes, tossing me onto the floor beside Mark's bed.

I landed next to Teddy's abandoned jockstrap, that article of clothing that had held such fascination for me just a few weeks before. He smelled of Mark's crotchsweat. A few drops of dried, crusty cum stuck to its pouch at cockslit level. I knew instantly that everything I had experienced at Teddy's apartment had been paralleled here between Mark and Teddy's jockstrap, though, I was certain, in a less extreme manner.

At Mark's command, Teddy picked up his jockstrap and put it on, but not without surreptitiously sniffing its pouch first.

That evening, Mark put Teddy through a workout I would never have thought him capable of before. He spanked Teddy until his asscheeks were red. He tormented his nipples with his thumbs, forefingers and teeth, until I thought Teddy wouldn't be able to stand it any longer. He relentlessly raped Teddy's mouth, and every time Teddy tried to cry out, he muffled his cry with another deep thrust of cock down his throat.

Yet all this time, Teddy's cock pressed hard against his jockstrap.

Finally, he ordered Teddy to lie on his back and hold his legs up and apart in ass-vulnerable position. After he had lubricated Teddy's asshole and unrolled a condom over his own dick, he placed his hands behind Teddy's knees, pushed until they were on either side of Teddy's head, and fucked him.

How I envied that jockstrap. That fantasy I knew could never come true for me, that fantasy that had haunted me since I first saw Teddy's jockstrap, was now a reality for that fortunate, strap-stretched, backless jockstrap. How I longed to feel the force of Mark's hips against Teddy's asscheeks as cock plunged into asshole, and to feel the frenzy of orgasm as cum shot deep inside Teddy while he handshot his own cum all over his chest.

When Teddy left that evening, he was still wearing his jockstrap. I was left behind, confused with the conflicting emotions of happiness and regret.

Before Mark went to sleep that night, he tossed me into the bedroom closet next to his laundry bag. I was too filthy to mingle with his other dirty clothes.

The next day he washed me separately in the bathroom sink, using extra bleach. But after all I had been through with Teddy, I could never be restored to my former whiteness. And I didn't even care!

Other changes followed. The elastic in my waistband was giving out. It could no longer hold me in place around Mark's waist. When his cock and balls pressed down on my now-sagging pouch, my waistband would give way and follow the trail of Mark's below-the-navel hairs as they approached his pubic forest.

Similarly, the elastic in my legholes was also losing its resiliency. Mark's left ball would constantly slip out of my pouch, quickly followed by his cockhead, as if it was curious about the world outside.

Initially, this loss of vigor upset me. I was afraid I'd be abandoned, and the adventures I had been through with Mark and with Teddy (who still came around regularly) would become nothing more than fond, fading memories.

Instead, I found I'd acquired a new position in Mark's life. Around this time he bought a VCR. He would put me on and wear me around the apartment, reaching underneath my now-more-accommodating waistband to play with himself, or tugging at his balls through my left leghole. When he was sufficiently aroused, he'd put a porn tape on the VCR, recline on his sofa, and jack off to the encounters that greeted delivery men, window washers, gym instructors, and the like, as they went about their duties.

You never know what life is going to bring you. I began my existence aspiring to a pure, unsullied, bleach-white career of service to my master. Little did I think I would come to discover other values, other desires. And little did I think I would be deeply content to end my days in service to a man who lived in willing servitude to the cock-hardening desires that dwelt within his loins.

EPILOGUE

NEWS ITEM - *Greenwich Village, New York City:* Late last night, a worn pair of low-rise Jockey briefs came to an unfortunate end during a case of sexual assault. A twenty-five year old slaveboy identified as "Teddy" unexpectedly rebelled against his master, a twenty-six year old male known as "Mark," and sodomized him. In his haste, he neglected to remove his master's briefs. Instead, he ripped them down the back, and penetrated his victim through the torn cotton.

NIGHT MAZES

Edmund Miller

I remember quite clearly the first time I saw him. I was on my way home alone one night after leaving Splash. As I turned a corner, a number of hawkers in the bright Chelsea night handed me fagtags and other discount flyers. That night one of these was for the j.o. party "He's Gotta Have It," an event publicized with the blurb "Our last party brought in over 200 HOT MEN!" "What the hell," I thought, "all the muscle clones at Splash are so into playing games, maybe a jack-off party is a way to cut to the chase." According to the flyer, He's Gotta Have It only just opens at midnight, so I was still in time. And it was only a few blocks away.

I walked the short distance to the address on Fourteenth Street and headed upstairs at the location. At the top of the slightly tilted staircase (this is New York), I found a makeshift ticket table and paid the modest fee. I was also handed the following also modest and somehow not entirely reassuring notice:

He's Gotta Have It! is a safer sex j.o. party for men of all colors, sizes and ages. We choose not to discriminate at the door because our community is already oppressed enough from the outside.

The space was a thousand-square-foot work loft with an unfinished look. And despite the somewhat contradictory poses about the hot quotient of the participants as indicated by the flyer and the announcement given me at the door, the place did seem to be full of swirling bodies.

"Do you want to check anything?" This was the guy at the makeshift coatcheck/refreshment stand. I decided to keep everything for the time being. I walked across a floor covered in sheets of plastic down an entry corridor framed with hanging bedsheets. At the end of the corridor of bedsheets, there was a little TV lounge with windows overlooking Fourteenth Street. A few people were hanging around here, but the action seemed to be in the middle part of the loft, an area enclosed by walls of bedsheets. I ventured into this tent-like enclosure to find a large crowd inside. Most of the guys were circling an interior partition that divided the space into dark and darker.

There were perhaps even more men present than the two hundred promised, all of them horny if not necessarily hot. And there was enough of a range of types and ages to justify the politically correct pose of the on-the-spot advertising (or disclaimer), including more Asians (maybe twenty percent of the total) than I can recall seeing in other dark rooms. Another ten or fifteen percent of the patrons were Hispanic. There were also a few blacks, but just a few. Only a small percent of the men there were in their early twenties or more than sixty, though there were a few in each age group. Almost everybody was presentable for his type rather than either drop-dead irresistible on the one hand or beyond the pale on the other.

I got caught up in a counterclockwise movement through the curtained cruising space and began to feel like a mouse in a multicultural maze. At first I found myself somewhat disconcerted attempting to cruise in a place without furniture or even walls to lean against and with a dense crowd always shifting and moving around me, particularly in the darker dark room. After a few more circuits, I began to encounter spots of traffic congestion in the inner, darker space. And as my eyes adjusted to the dim, I saw there was a certain logic to our movement. A few guys were stopped here and there along the route, and occasionally someone would break free and stand a little too close to one of these. Action tended to pocket around the younger and better looking and to spread among those pressed in close to watch.

Then I saw him for the first time. A Hollywood blond stationed in the middle of one side of the space was getting hit on a lot. But he just waved everyone along, or if someone seemed particularly distasteful, he turned his head to the side and folded his arms across his chest. But he was hot stuff; I had to grant him that. He had a swimmer's build, lean and sleek. His hair had a supernatural golden glow to it and unnatural curliness. And his face was male-model pretty with big pouty lips.

As I slowed down to check him out, some congestion

suddenly snarled the movement of traffic and blocked my view. I soon made out that someone had made contact—but not with the Hollywood blond. I could still glimpse his shape in the distance. The circling crowd was rubbernecking the successful couple. Two guys were apparently groping one another and kissing, and others had begun to press in close against them. One of the two guys at the center of activity swatted away a stray hand and then another. But soon these hands were busy groping others in the crowd that had gathered behind, and eventually there was a mass of fifteen or twenty guys groping in various directions. I saw a bit of cock here and there and a flash of hip. And hands were everywhere.

But I moved on. The Hollywood blond was getting less attention now, so I saw my chance with him. Slowing down a bit as I passed him the next time around, I ran my eyes and fingers across his chest. I snagged a nipple but moved on. The next time I went by I reached out for his chest again only to have him grab me by the wrist rather more firmly than necessary and pull me toward him. With his face practically in mine, he whispered (there is no talking in a dark room, of course), "Don't do that. I'm ticklish." I was leaning up against him and could feel the fullness of his cock against my leg. With my free hand I cupped his ass through the thin fabric of his slacks and felt his passion rising. I pressed forward to touch his lips with mine, but he turned his head away. He did let me kiss his cheek and neck, and he let go of my right hand. I kneaded the round globes of his ass, and he clenched his glutes in response, making them as hard as marble. I reached down to rub his swelling erection with one hand as I slipped the other inside the waistband of his slacks and briefs in back to slide the hand down his warm, damp curves.

I had almost forgotten the other men in the room until someone pressed rudely up against me from behind. Glancing over my shoulder, I was not pleased with what I saw. I pushed the fellow back a bit, and he stopped thrusting. But he could not have gone away if he had wanted to, I realized, because my Hollywood blond and I were at the center of a dense mass of bodies. "What the hell," I thought, warming my right hand in the depth of his cleft as my Hollywood blond alternately squeezed it tight and than relaxed and as I slowly lowered the zipper on his fly. I reached inside and released his cock from the waistband of his briefs. The briefs slid down the long shaft in front, and I yanked them down behind. He was not helping me at all or touching me in any way. But he was occasionally swatting away a hand in the crowd and pushing back some of the bolder assaults—both on him and on me.

I started jerking his fully erect cock with one hand while reaching under from behind with the other to play with his balls and press him from underneath. The wide, flat shaft of his cock reached up past his waistline. As I kneaded the cock with my fingers and ran a nail up and down the shaft and around the rim of the head, I was rewarded by a series of contented moans. As I pressed upward from underneath with my right hand, I raised him up on tiptoe, and he began to drip precum. I rubbed this along the shaft of his cock and found my hand sliding up and down easily and propelled to move more and more rapidly. I started to squeeze harder as I jerked him off and was rewarded by louder moans at first and then by heavy breathing. He started to spew and I deftly slid my body around behind him, pressing my cock against his cleft through my slacks from behind. I moved quickly because I sensed he was ready to shoot. I cannot say that others in the crowd had the same forewarning. "Yuck," said a guy whose shoes were suddenly dripping with come. Another guy pulled out some Kleenex to wipe up his trousers. But the brunt of the explosion splashed across the bare chest of my Hollywood blond himself, and he just smiled serenely and started rubbing his fingers in the mess.

After a few lazy minutes, he shoved his cock back inside his briefs, pulled up his pants, and zipped up. Then he dipped his head a bit to duck through the crowd and, slapping my hand behind with the same movement, disappeared into the crowd and was gone. "Well, that was interesting," I thought, as I struggled to make it through the crowd myself, swatting away the various hands that groped for the erection still visibly outlined through my pants. I started looking for the bathroom.

At the first one I came to, there was something of a commotion in progress. A plaintive voice inside was whining, "Let me out! Let me out!" The doorknob had fallen off, and with the outer part lying on the floor, someone was trying to manipulate the opening like a sensitive asshole unwilling to release its firm grip. "There's another one by the entrance to the left," the guy working on the sensitive hole informed me. I walked over to the entrance and waited my turn in the short line. When I got my chance, I was glad to find the place a clean and tidy no-frills affair.

It was after 2:00 a.m. by my watch when I came out of the bathroom. I looked around for the Hollywood blond. But I figured he must have left. I asked at the front desk about the Big Dick Contest promised in the advertising flyer only to be told that this was not to take place until 2:00. When I pointed out that it was already after 2:00, all the doorman could say was, "Oh, yeah, it is." I milled around for a little while longer, but nothing in the crowd struck my fancy. Certainly nothing came close to my Hollywood blond.

Then promptly at 2:30 (or nearly so) seventy-five men converged on the lounge area for the promised Big Dick Contest. According to the flyer, the winner would be taking home a $50 first prize. This was not quite enough of an incentive to get me involved as more than a voyeur—even if I had been blessed with a really competitive edge in this department. My reluctance seemed to be shared by many of the others who had converged on the scene, for it took quite a while to get anyone at all to put his cards on the table. At last a few did thrust themselves forward at the urging of an overweight black person of indeterminate sex who pointed out that the money would be lost by default. Our indeterminate master of ceremonies then calculated the pecking order with a standard wooden ruler. Peeking over the head of those around me, it appeared that not a few contestants were wilted on the vine in face of this clinical procedure. But it was pretty much impossible to get a sustained look at anything—even on the simulcast video monitor above the heads of the crowd since the cameraman was standing on a chair right in front of the screen. I did hear the master of ceremonies asking for a volunteer hand to help one of the wilting contestants face the ruler. With the contest a bust, I was ready to call it a night and left before a winner measured up.

That night's experience whetted my appetite for sex clubs. And I wanted to find my Hollywood blond again. So the following week I decided to check out Hands On, a $10 Friday night jack-off party at the Maze. I arrived at the somewhat seedy address in the meatpacking district to find the asking price was, not $10 as advertised, but $35. No big deal, of course. Having paid, I took the staircase down below street level to enter a freakish world where a lot of men and a few man-woman couples were gawking at such live acts as two chubby Lesbians engaged in S/M play, a transvestite self-dildoing, and a black man jacking off in a cage with obtuse political incorrectness. After checking out this house of ill fame for a half an hour or so, I engaged the doorman (who was cuter than anyone else on the premises) in banter, observing that the place was not at all my idea of a gay jack-off party. He pointed out that I had inadvertently wandered into the Vault and told me that the place I wanted was upstairs. I did not get my money back, but the doorman did get me into the Maze upstairs without any additional payment. A real cutie.

"This is more like it," I thought as I checked out the surroundings upstairs. In this upstairs space, the simple 1890s diversions of the straights down below gave way to 1970s raunch. The place was large and not particularly crowded. It seemed to be reasonably clean, considering. And the music got my special praise for not being blastingly loud. There were some pockets of action in progress, most of it concentrated in one dark nook. The crowd was mostly thirtyish or older, running to beefy, hairy types but with a mix of this and that. One guy in underwear was standing facing the wall and holding a paddle in his hand. I took it from him and gave him a few whacks, but when I started to feel him up through his white briefs, he swatted my hand away and asked for more of the paddle. While O.K. as foreplay, spanking is something I cannot get into for its own sake, so I gave him one last whack for disappointing me and moved on.

And then I saw him again, the golden boy, my Hollywood blond. He was, already and understandably, the focus of considerable, well-deserved attention. He was actually out in the middle of a room nearly naked, his legs intertwined with an ugly but muscular, somewhat older guy. They were facing each other but leaning back, working each other's cock and preventing them from falling over by this conduit of cock. A lot of other guys were gathered around although not touching. But the gym-built chest (of the Mr. Teen U.S.A. variety) and the already-familiar male-model face were too much for me. I rubbed my hand along the chest a bit and then moved right to the bare ass: his pants and briefs were down around his ankles. I reached into my pocket for a rubber glove and without ceremony or lube touched his inviting pucker. I slid right in. I found his sensitive spot and began working it over. I was rewarded by seeing his cock jump in the hand of his jack-off companion. The three of us developed a rhythm of thrust and pull, and I think maybe his cock grew a little bit more as a result of my hard work, especially after I slipped in a second finger. We kept it up—in more ways than one—for fully half an hour and attracted an even bigger crowd than had already been there. My Hollywood blond did pull my hand back a little after a while, leaving me to tickle the rim. Finally one soul bolder than the rest came over and plucked my hand away entirely. My gloved finger was replaced by the newcomer's probing tongue. The rimming enthusiast for whom I made way was proceeding, rather unwisely I thought, without a dental dam.

I circulated in the shadows for a while after that. I observed a good deal of fellatio, most of this also apparently unprotected. The few couples I observed fucking did seem to be using protection, however. In one of the dark corners, I tripped over a hefty black man down on his knees giving head. As my eyes adjusted to double darkness, I saw that he had lowered his trousers, exposing his full, round rump. As I felt the smooth surface, he turned his head part way toward me—as well as he could with his mouth full—and nodded. I slipped on another pair of gloves and got back to work. His hole opened easily to my touch, and I was soon spreading him wide with my thumbs. But that is another story.

The next time I saw my Hollywood blond was a few months later and again at the Maze. This time it was at the monthly Forever Fisting party. There is a mandatory clothing check of all one is wearing above the waist, below the waist down to the feet, or both. This checkroom policy cuts down on mere gawkers and gives an immediate visual take on the top and bottom status of everyone on the premises. I kept my pants on.

The place was festooned with slings for the occasion. And

Crisco, rubber gloves (although I always travel with my own), and paper towels were set out at various locations. The lighting was dim but not so dark as on the regular nights. There was a strong enough aroma of poppers in the air so that I was starting to get off on it. And the volume of the music was again tolerable.

As I made a circuit of the rooms, I noted a plethora of gut-heavy daddy types with plenty of body hair—not my scene. There were also a good number of very skinny guys. I crossed these off my dance card as well. But there were some more conventionally handsome types as well and some guys with good muscle tone—something more important than youth to me.

As I moved around I saw a lot of guys chatting and socializing, more so than in other kinds of dark rooms. Fisting is an in-group, clubby sort of thing, and after all—despite the dress-coded appearance of everyone—there are some technical details to be worked out that require conversation. I saw two lean, muscular guys undressed for versatility comparing hand sizes. I marked them down for future notice, particularly the brunet with dimples in his glutes. The crew-cut blond had smaller hands, so as I passed by I heard them agree that the brunet was going to bottom. The pairing-up process is a lot like the traditional bar pick-up dance in the old days before AIDS and before loud music. Guys need to get to know one another a bit before plunging in. Fisting is an exercise in trust.

And plunging there was. In the course of the evening, three or four scenes were always in progress, usually in the slings but sometimes on the floor or leaning over furniture. As I entered one small room, a daddy type with a gut hanging out over the waistband of his leather pants was just finishing up and pulling out of a skinny guy in a sling. I heard a distinct plop as he pulled out. "Help me out, will ya?" the guy in the sling said.

"No. You got in there yourself. You can get out," this very unpaternal Daddy snapped back as he walked away. "Well," I thought, "that's not according to the house rules," as I offered my hand to the fellow in the sling—offered my hand to help him down, that is. Skinny guys do nothing for me.

In the main room shortly afterwards, I found a muscular

Chinese guy taking on all comers. As one guy pounded his arm to the point of exhaustion, another stepped up to replace him. A bookish type with glasses was just taking over as I wandered into the scene. I slapped the bottom boy a couple of times here and there to test his muscle tone. He passed. I put the gloves on and began feeling up his ass from both sides and then underneath, spreading his hole with my thumbs to give the bookish top man deeper access. I started feeling up the sensitive ass lips with my thumbs, noting with approval that they were distended and loose. As the top pulled back (he was stroking slowly), I let my thumbs sink in around the edges, and when he pushed back in I let him carry my thumbs in along with him. Our bottom went into convulsions, so we just vibrated in place for a while getting off on what was happening. When the bookworm screwed his way out, pulling my thumbs along with him, I got into position with two fingers of one hand so that they would be sucked in on the next go round. But then I glanced across the room and saw my Hollywood blond just entering. I pulled my fingers back from the abyss, not without some difficulty and also not without some regret. I tossed away the gloves I had been using and went off in pursuit.

A crowd was starting to form around him, but I caught his eye, and he reached his hand between two guys loitering in the vicinity and pulled me into the inner circle. Naked except for boots and a dog collar, he took my hand in his and placed it palm to palm, then smiled when he saw my delicate fingers dwarfed by his thick ones. He pulled me along to a vacant sling. It was in the corner of the main room. He let me help hoist him up, and I got a chance to run my hands over the lean muscularity of his hairless swimmer's build. I carefully placed his feet in the ankle loops and dropped my head down to give his cock a few licks for good luck. It sprang to attention and soon outgrew my capacity to take it all in. I let it fall back against his belly, throbbing, and put my gloves back on.

Dipping out a large scoop of Crisco, I started playing with his asshole, tickling it rapidly and watching it open to my touch, its redness reaching out to me and expanding against the cool gold of his skin. Then all of a sudden I stuck four fingers in together, two from each hand, and was rewarded by a grunt of pleasure from my Hollywood blond and a few additional gasps from the good-sized crowd that had begun to accumulate around us, watching. I spread him wide with the fingers and blew softly into the dark interior. He squeezed himself closed around my fingers and tightened up so that Crisco started to ooze out between fingers and climb up my palm. I sucked out the fingers of my left hand and slapped him on the ass. I left a greasy smear in the deep, hard indentation of his glute. He loosened up to the touch of my other hand, and I slipped three fingers in easily and then the fourth. Stopping to apply some lube with my other hand, I lined up the four fingers that were deep inside and started to rock my open hand side to side. As I shoved in up to the thumb, he gave a little gasp, and someone in the crowd let out a much bigger one. I started to turn my hand by degrees. I heard him purring as he opened up to me. I could see a space opening around my hand, so pretty soon there was a circular opening as wide as the widest part of my hand. I brought my thumb over and let it dance in the open space, touching the rim with it and then pulling it back to touch my palm.

Finally I slipped inside. There was no resistance. I sank in almost twelve inches right with the first thrust. His ass lips closed gently to kiss my wrist, and with my left hand I tugged at the edges of the rubber glove just barely visible on the brink and pulled it up as best I could. Inside I slowly curled my fingers around to form a fist, which I turned gently in the heat of the interior. A smile crossed his face, and his eyes glazed over. Then I pulled back, or tried to. The suction held me back, and for every inch of retreat I had to plunge forward again and try two or three times. Finally the widest part of my fist was back at his ass lips, and I slipped out the rest of the way in a moment.

His ass lips were pulsating, imploring me to go back in. I scooped up some more lube and slathered it all over his ass. Then I began playing with those pulsating ass lips, tickling them with all my fingers at once. I slipped my right hand back inside and then pulled it out again teasingly before he could close around it. Then I put my left in and pulled it out. I started alternating hands, pressing back on the edge on each side in turn as I pulled out. When he was loose enough, I pushed in four fingers of each hand, clasping my palms together. I began rocking my clasped hands and wriggling them down till my thumbs hit his ass. Then I started turning half circles faster and faster and pulling in and out, back to the edge and all the way in again, faster and faster. Then I started pulling my hands apart a bit as best I could and clapping them together again. When he was loosened up some more, I tucked my thumbs in against my palms and pushed downward. At first he resisted. But I pulled out and slathered up with some more Crisco, then tried again. This time I slid in easily. I pushed my right hand ahead of my left and then snaked my hands across one another. And then he shot off all over himself. The come pooled in his belly and then started dripping down his sides. When it started dripping toward his ass, I figured I had to pull out. But, after all, my work was done.

As he lay there panting in large heaves and dripping come, I noticed a drip of blood too. I disposed of the gloves and wiped up the more conspicuous elements of the mess. And I tidied up the playspace. By this time, he was coming around to more normal consciousness. I helped him down and called his attention to the minor bleeding. We stuffed him with paper, and that seemed to do the trick. Mentioning the possible contamination of the open Crisco, I brought that off to the doorman, while my Hollywood blond went back to the checkroom to get dressed.

When I joined him at the checkroom, I told him my name and offered to give him my number.

"No, sorry. I don't see men socially, just for fucking," he said.

"But we hit it off so well!"

"Yes, I know, and if you see me around again I want you to do me. You were great. But I'm straight. I just like to get fucked."

"Straight? But you like it so much," I said, in a good deal of confusion.

"Yes, I know," my Hollywood blond replied calmly, "but that's the way it is. And I don't want to talk about it anymore. See ya!" And with that he disappeared into the crowd.

THE PLOWBOY'S PLAYTHING

Thomas C. Humphrey

What I learned from Buford Railsback that summer wasn't taught in school. But Buford was an inspired teacher, and once his lessons caught hold of me, I quickly became an enthusiastic student. I wanted to learn everything. And I learned fast.

I wound up with Buford after some of my buddies and I had gone wild our senior year of prep school, and, just before graduation, Ed Tollison had finally smashed up his car driving us home from a night of boozing and pill-popping in Atlanta.

After I stubbornly refused to see a counselor about what my dad considered my "problem," I was banished to Grandma and Grandpa's farm for a summer of hard labor. My punishment was tempered, though, by Dad's last-minute promise of a new Mustang if I laid off the drugs and made it through the summer without getting fucked up. Man, neither one of us had any idea how thoroughly fucked I was going to get!

Buford and I knew each other from childhood, when I would visit the farm for a week or so during the summer. His parents had owned a neighboring farm and had been close friends of Grandma and Grandpa's. When he didn't have chores, Buford and I would romp through the woods playing war games, or strip off our clothes and dam up the branch dividing the two farms to make a pool for skinny-dipping.

Then, for several years, our paths did not cross on my rare, hurried weekend trips, and for the past couple of years, I had managed to beg off from visiting altogether. I had heard, though, that both of Buford's parents were killed in a car wreck when he was sixteen, and that Grandpa had leased the Railsback property, put the money in trust, and moved Buford in with them until he was old enough to make a decision about the family farm.

I wasn't quite prepared for the eighteen-year-old Buford who presented himself after coming in from a date late that first Sunday afternoon. I remembered him as a painfully shy, pale, skinny reed of a boy with a mop of flaming red hair and freckles. In the intervening years, he had grown so tall he towered over me, and his chest and shoulders were as thickly muscled as a college running back's. His hair had darkened to the hue of brick dust, and his rare redhead's even tan framed his blue eyes, as pale as a wisp of smoke across a valley. He approached me with a wide, disarming smile and extended his callused, big-knuckled paw, which engulfed my hand in a vise-grip as he slapped me on the back in welcome. As we shook hands, I experienced an unfamiliar tightness in my chest, and my legs went suddenly weak. Nobody had ever affected me quite that way before.

Becoming reacquainted with him at least cooled some of the seething anger that had been building in me for weeks. It was bad enough to be stuck in a hick south Georgia town for months, without a car, instead of hacking around with my hell-raising friends in Atlanta. But to make matters worse, when I got to the farm, I found out that Aunt Catherine and her gaggle of daughters had come for an extended visit, and that I would have to share a room—and bed—with Buford. By the time he showed up, I was about ready to tell everybody to take a flying fuck and strike off on my own. But that was before I saw him.

After his initial exuberant welcome, though, he gave most of his attention to my Cousin Cindy, who was about sixteen and apparently deeply infatuated with him. I sat fidgeting, feeling what I suspected were pangs of jealousy and fretting over my unfamiliar reaction.

During dinner, I mostly stared at my plate, speaking only when one of the adults asked me a question. Meanwhile, Buford and Cindy sat side by side and giggled and teased throughout the meal.

Finally, Buford pushed back from the table and stood up. "Come on, Ryan, go with me to feed the livestock," he said, snapping me out of the blue funk I had slipped into.

He kept up a line of chatter while we poured grain and forked out hay for the horses and cows. Then he leaned against a support post and wiped at his forehead.

"Cindy's a real babe, don't you think?" he asked.

"I donno," I shrugged. "I never thought about it. She's just one of my cousins. I suppose she looks all right."

"Well, she's not my cousin, so I can think she's pretty hot."

"I thought you had a steady girlfriend."

"I do, but that don't stop me from looking. How 'bout you? You got a steady back in Atlanta?"

Although I had managed to bed a couple of girls, I had found the experience sorely disappointing and, each time, had rationalized that I was so wasted I could barely get it up. Somehow, Buford's question reminded me of my less-than-ecstatic experiences and, embarrassed, I felt my face heat up. "Naw, nothing steady," I mumbled.

"I hear you're down here because of some trouble you got into up there. That right?" When I didn't answer, he repeated his question. "Say, Big City, is that why you're spending the summer down here?"

My temper exploded before I could get it in check. "The name's Ryan, not Big City, okay? What's the matter? You resent that I don't live on a farm, or are you envious because you do? Maybe I'll just call you Plowboy. And as for your question, it's none of your damned business, and you're not going to make it your business."

Buford quickly backpedaled. "I'm sorry," he said, flashing another disarming smile. "You're right; it's not any of my business. I guess I'm just curious about your life in Atlanta. About all I know is this little town, but I don't plan to spend my life here. I guess maybe I do envy you for living in a big city. But I'm sorry I pissed you off. I promise not to nose around in your business again. Friends? he said, extending his big hand.

"Friends," I said, reaching for him. Again, as we touched, I felt a peculiar knotting in my stomach, and my knees trembled.

"I guess you get the inside of the bed," Buford said as we started to undress.

He had his back to me as he slipped his clothes off and folded them over a chair while I stripped to my underwear. He turned to face me, and I noticed his large, dark nipples and broad muscular chest, dusted with a faint copper down that thickened into a fish-bone trail across his tight, rippled abdomen before it disappeared into his briefs. I had to pry my eyes away from the bulging mound in his crotch. I had checked out guys in the shower before, had even felt a pang of desire for a couple of them, but the strength of my reaction to Buford was a totally new experience.

"Do you sleep in your underwear or bare?" he asked.

"Sometimes one, sometimes the other," I said.

"I usually sleep bare."

"That's okay with me," I answered. "Bare it is." I slipped off my underwear and hurried into bed.

Buford turned out the light, and in the pale moonlight glimmering through the sheer curtains, I caught a glimpse of his pale, untanned buttocks. Then he turned to face me and stood, weight on one leg, as if he were posing. I stared at his Greek-statue physique, and my breath became shallow and ragged. If I had noticed when we were kids, I had long ago forgotten that he was uncut. Now, I was fascinated by the way the foreskin shrouded the broad crown of his cock, completely obscuring it. I had seen better-hung guys among my soccer teammates, but Buford's thick shaft curved straight down lazily over massive balls, which made his rod protrude almost as if he had an erection. In the blue-tinged moonlight, it glowed temptingly, almost daring me to reach out and touch it. My own cock sprang to life and pressed painfully tight against my belly as I experienced a visceral surge of lust for the vision before me.

Buford broke his pose and crawled into bed beside me. He lay on his back, hands behind his head, and talked about his just-completed school year and playing football while I propped on an elbow and watched him, unsuccessfully trying to will my erection away. After a while, the talk stopped and, within a few seconds, Buford was breathing deeply, sound asleep. I turned my back to him and hugged the wall, desperately trying to get my emotions under control, emotions that were unfamiliar and disturbing, but also exciting and filled with vague hopes for the future.

I slept restlessly, falling into deep sleep only just before dawn. The rain was beating a steady tattoo against the tin roof when Grandpa woke us up just after daylight. Buford rolled out of the sagging double bed, turned on the lamp, and stood twisting his shoulders, stretching his back, oblivious to the hard-on climbing his belly. After risking a few glances, I stifled a yawn and turned against the wall, unaccustomed to getting up in the middle of the night.

"Get a move on, Big City," Buford said, reaching for his jeans. "Your Grandma gets upset when folks are late to the table."

I chose to ignore the "Big City" remark. It wasn't worth a fight. "In a minute," I said, curling up and closing my eyes. I was so sleepy I didn't particularly care who got upset.

"Come on, up and at 'em!" Buford snatched the sheet off, leaving me exposed, erection and all. I tried to curl up again to hide my nakedness, but he grabbed my feet and tugged me to the edge of the bed. "Well, at least part of you is awake," he said, staring at my hard-on, a big grin spreading across his face.

"All right! All right! I'm up," I said swinging my feet off the side of the bed.

At the table, I dawdled over the huge breakfast Grandma set in front of me and dreamed of going back to sleep, since surely we couldn't work with it pouring rain.

Buford soon dashed those hopes. "I thought Ryan and I would get the barn cleaned and straightened up, unless you've got something else for us to do," he said to Grandpa as we finished up breakfast.

"No, that'll be fine," Grandpa said. "I've got paperwork to get done myself."

Cleaning the barn wasn't even close to what Buford had in mind that dreary morning. He immediately led me up the ladder into the hayloft and stretched out on a pile of loose hay. I flopped down beside him.

"Man, I don't feel like working today," he said.

"Me neither," I agreed. "I just feel like sleeping."

"I can think of things I'd rather do," he said, lightly fondling himself. "You ever slam the ham?"

"Huh?" I said, not understanding.

"You know," he said, making an up-and-down gesture with his hand. "Choke the old chicken, whack off."

"Oh," I said, catching on. "Yeah, sometimes."

"Me, too," he said. "When I'm real horny. And this morning, I'm so hard up I'd fuck mud."

I snickered at the note of desperation in his voice. "Well, you're in luck; there's plenty of mud outside, the way it's raining."

"Smart ass," he said, tossing a handful of hay at me.

He moved against me and tickled my ribs. Laughing, I crammed a handful of hay down his jeans and rolled away from him. As I stood up, he tackled me and sat on my chest.

"Now I'll be all itchy," he said, pulling hay out of his waistband. "Just for that, I'm going to take your pants off and make you run around bare-assed."

As I halfheartedly struggled to escape him, both of us laughing all the time, he twisted around and sat with his back toward my head, his legs clamping my arms against my sides. He quickly unsnapped my jeans and tugged them down over my hips, exposing my hard cock. As if on a signal, our laughter suddenly stopped. His hand slid downward through my pubic hair, and he fondled my bulging dick. I lay still, my breath quick and sharp, as he gently slid his fingers up and down my shaft, which throbbed in his hand.

"Man, that's a pretty good dick for a little guy!" he said.

He turned my rod loose and rolled onto his side, tight up against me. He pushed my hand into his crotch. "See how much I've got," he said, squeezing my hand around his thumping shaft. I kneaded his dick through his jeans and it blossomed in my hand. He unfastened his jeans, raised his hips, and shoved jeans and briefs down to his knees. His dick was throbbing against his belly, straight, milk-white, and perfectly formed. Touching somebody else for the first time in my life, I wrapped my hand around it and slowly moved up and down, retracting the foreskin all the way from the broad knob of his cock and then pushing it back up until the head was completely covered. The movement of the crown beneath his foreskin fascinated me. Buford turned onto his back, still tight against me, and I felt the tremors running through his body as he sighed with pleasure.

"Put your mouth on it," he whispered huskily, trying to push my head into his crotch.

"Uh-uh, I can't do that," I said, wrenching away from his grasp on my neck. I still held onto his cock.

"Come on, Ryan, just try it," he persuaded. "I need something besides jacking off real bad. Come on!"

He again tugged my head downward, and this time I did not

offer much resistance. Overcoming all the macho aversion that had been built into my thinking for most of my life, I opened my mouth and let him shove his dick in. I ran my tongue over the broad crown, which I felt creeping out of its hood. At the same time, I fondled his big balls and rolled them around in my palm.

His cock was velvety soft against the lining of my mouth, and he barely moved it in and out as he wound his fingers in my hair and guided my head up and down on his rod. As I swirled my tongue around the rim of his cockhead, I kept thinking: *I'm sucking a guy's cock, and I'm loving it!*

As I brought him closer and closer to the finish, Buford got more and more active. The muscles in his buttocks clenched until they were as hard as steel, and he lifted himself off the hay to drive into my mouth. "Yeah! Oh, yeah! That's it! Yeah!" he kept whispering.

Just when I knew he was close to exploding and was about to jerk my mouth off his rod to avoid his cum, he sagged back into the hay and pulled my head up. "Just a minute," he said, standing up.

As I watched in puzzlement, he pulled his jeans up and walked over to the ladder and climbed down. I lay fingering my stiff cock and wondering why he had stopped just as he was ready to shoot. Before I knew it, he was back up the ladder, his hard-on sticking through his open fly. He had a can of something in his hand.

He pulled me to my feet and stripped my jeans down around my ankles. "Here, lean over this bale," he instructed.

Wondering at my ready compliance, I dropped to my knees and draped myself across the bale. "What're you going to do?" I asked.

"I want to butt-fuck you," he replied, his voice hoarse and throaty.

"Uh-uh, that'll hurt," I objected. "I couldn't take it."

"Yeah, you can," he insisted. "I'll go slow and gentle, I promise. Besides, I got some good grease here that'll make it go in real easy."

He slid his jeans down and kneeled between my legs. He took a big glob of grease out of the can and dabbed it around my ass. His finger slid in and moved around, then a second one joined it. There was only a little pain. As he pulled his fingers apart, stretching my opening, he reached under with his other hand and started jacking my dick. His fingers plopped out, and, looking back, I watched him coat his rod with grease. It looked a whole lot bigger now that I knew where it was about to go. I was a little scared, but I never considered stopping him. Although I had never even thought about getting fucked before, I knew I wanted it now.

As he stroked his cock a few times, it leaked big raindrops of pre-cum onto my buttocks. Then he jabbed it home, and I let out a loud yell. "Stop! Take it out! It feels like I'm on fire!" I whimpered.

"It's in now. I'll go easy; just relax!" he whispered soothingly, holding my hips in a tight grasp to keep me from escaping him.

He reached for my dick again and began sliding his hand back and forth. My rod bulged in his palm and the pleasure took my mind off the burning pain in my ass. Without my really knowing it, he gently worked his cock all the way in me. He lay down heavily on my back, manipulated my thumping shaft with one hand, squeezed my balls with the other, and started thrusting lightly, rotating his pelvis as he eased all the way back in time after time. As he got more and more excited, the speed and force of his thrusts increased. I felt his pistoning tube swell inside me, felt my own nuts churning, and, just as I blasted my load against the bale of hay, he sighed a long, "Aaaah!" and melted onto my back as I felt his hot cum spurting as deep inside me as he could go.

"That was good, damned good!" he said, adjusting his clothes. "Thanks, Ryan. You're a real buddy!"

We did get the barn straightened up and cleaned, at least enough so Grandpa could see we had worked. But we spent most of the day teasing and punching each other and wrestling in the hay. I couldn't remember having a better time, and Buford's whole attitude told me he was having a great time, too.

We had hardly settled in bed that night before Buford's hand was between my legs, playing with my cock, which was instantly ready for action. I reached for him and discovered that he was fully aroused and throbbing in my hand.

"Let me fuck you again," he whispered.

"I donno," I said, knowing that I wanted him to.

"Come on, let me do it," he urged. I turned onto my stomach. "Uh-uh, turn back over," he said.

I lay on my back, and he kneeled between my legs and lifted them onto his shoulders. The thought of this new position fired me up, and my cock thumped against my stomach. He dug at my ass cheeks with his thumbs, spreading them open.

"Get it good and wet," I whispered.

He spat on his dick a couple of times and then spat in his hand and rubbed it in my crack. He probed around with his dick and then pushed his broad head in.

"Go slow," I said. "It hurts if you go too fast."

He patiently worked his cock all the way inside me. Then he pushed forward on my legs, almost bending me double, and lifted my ass completely off the bed. He reached under my armpits and grabbed my shoulders from underneath. He started thrusting like a rabbit, popping all the way out a couple of times and then driving all the way back in with one hard shove. It hurt like hell, but deep inside some form of pleasure overrode the pain, and I started moving my ass in rhythm with his thrusts.

The springs of the old bed began sounding off, "squee-squonk, squee-squonk," with every lunge. He was pounding into me so hard and tugging at my shoulders and pushing so frantically to drive himself even deeper into me that my head rammed against the loose headboard, which banged into the wall, "thump-thonk, thump-thonk," faster and faster, louder and louder.

"You boys cut out whatever you're doing in there and go to sleep," Grandpa shouted from the room next to ours.

Buford went rigid for a few seconds and then started fucking me more gently. He was so hot, though, that in a little bit, it was the same old, "squee-squonk, thump-thonk," as he rammed it to me.

"Cut it out, damn it!" Grandpa growled, but Buford was too close to pay him any mind. He kept hunching away, unconcerned about the noise we were making. He buried his head against my neck, kissing and sucking until I was afraid I'd have a hickey, and fired jet after jet of hot cum into me.

When he rolled off me, I was hoping he'd give me a hand job, but he got up and went down the hall to the bathroom without touching me. He came back in smelling of soap and crawled into bed without a word. He turned his back to me, and, within moments, I heard his deep, steady breathing. I lay fingering my aching dick, accepting that I was nothing but a plaything to satisfy his needs. After a while, I went to the bathroom and jacked off, thinking about his dick moving inside me.

Just after sunrise next morning, I woke to the pressure of his stiff cock pushing against my buttocks as he lay tight against me, one arm across my chest.

"I want to fuck you again," he whispered when he knew I was awake.

"Uh-uh, I'm sore from yesterday," I said. I really was more concerned that Grandpa, who surely was up, might come in the room to check out the noise if it started again.

He rolled away from me. "I need to cum again," he said. "Why don't you suck it some?"

He tugged me over against him and pressed my head down until my lips were just inches away from his throbbing dick. Without hesitating, I slid on down and ran my tongue over the magenta crown, which was already inching out of his foreskin. I licked all the way down his big-veined shaft, returning now and then to tease his cockhead, or taking first one and then the other ball in my mouth. He lay sighing and trembling, clenching his thigh muscles and twining his fingers through my hair.

As he got closer and closer, he cradled my head in a tight grip and really pounded into my mouth, brushing against my tonsils and trying to push on past them into my throat. I struggled to back off to keep from gagging.

"I'm about to let you have it," he rasped out. "Don't pull your mouth off. Take my load! Take all of it!"

The tube on the underside of his shaft swelled as big as my thumb, and the first hard blast of his cum splatted against the roof of my mouth, followed by four or five other rapid bursts. His dick danced around in my mouth from the force of his load. He completely flooded me, and little driblets of his cum seeped out of my lips and dropped into his pubic hair.

When he began to soften, he sagged back onto the mattress and took his dick out of my mouth with his hand. He milked it a couple of times, gently pulling the foreskin up over his reddened, ultra-sensitive crown. "That was great!" he whispered, grinning at me.

As I pondered what to do with a mouthful of cum, he spat in his hand and reached for my rock-hard dick. As he started moving up and down on it, I thought, "What the hell," and swallowed his load. I didn't mind the taste of him, after all.

"You boys gonna sleep all day?" Grandpa called from the hallway just as I spurted my load all over my chest. "Get moving. We got things to do, and breakfast is getting cold."

I wiped myself off with a dirty tee shirt, jumped into my jeans, and shifted my still-hard cock straight up my belly so it wouldn't be too obvious. I was so excited that it didn't go down until sometime in the middle of breakfast.

It was too wet to work the fields, so Grandpa, Buford, and I spent the morning replacing rotted fence posts and stringing new barbed wire around the perimeter of the farm. After we went in for a good hot meal, Grandpa had to go into town to meet with his accountant, so Buford and I returned to setting posts. The afternoon temperature hovered in the mid-nineties, and by two o'clock, we were dirty and soaked with sweat. My muscles were tight from the unfamiliar exertion.

"Let's walk down to the branch and cool off for a while," Buford suggested.

We cut through a stand of oak trees until we were completely out of sight of the fields. We kept going until we reached a clearing where the slow-moving stream gurgled over big rocks, the same spot where we had played when we were kids.

"Let's go skinny-dipping," Buford said with the same enthusiasm he had shown as a child.

We quickly shucked our clothes on the bank and waded into the shallow, cool stream. Buford began splashing handfuls of water onto my bare chest. I fought back, skipping my hand across the surface, sending big sheets of water onto him each time. Giggling, he wrestled me down into the branch. Then he raised up and looked at me.

"Your dick's already hard and standing up," he said.

"It's been hard since we got out of bed this morning," I said.

"What you need is my dick up your ass to cool you off," he said. He tugged me to my feet and half-dragged me over to a fallen tree and draped me across it, my ass sticking up inviting him. He shoved my legs wider apart and spat on his cock. He eased the head in me and then shoved the rest of the way with one hard push. I shrank away from the sudden intrusion until the tree trunk blocked my retreat and then began to shove back against his piledriving cock. I reached for my aching dick and stroked it as he quickly worked himself toward a climax. He grunted a few times and then went rigid, and I felt his load fill me and dribble back out and down my thighs. A moment later, I sprayed a generous load against the tree trunk.

After washing ourselves off, we lay on the soft mat of leaves for a while and let the wind dry us. I had fallen in love with his smooth, even dick, and I gently stroked it and fondled his balls until he went soft.

"How'd you start doing this?" I asked, not really expecting him to answer. He surprised me.

"A fellow gobbled me off in a gas station men's room when I was about fifteen," he said. "I liked it, but I didn't get any more chances for a long time. Then a guy your Grandpa had working for him when I came to live here started sucking me off in the barn at milking time. I made sure I was there just about every afternoon. One day he said he had a surprise for me. He dropped his pants and got on his knees and showed me how to put it up in him." He looked at me and grinned. "How'd you get started?"

"You know the whole story," I said. "I've never done anything except with you."

"Aw, you're shitting me. You mean I got hold of a cherry?"

"Yeah, except I know now that I had been wanting to do it with somebody like you for a long time. But this guy—did you ever do anything to him? You know, like suck his dick or let him fuck you?"

"Hell no. I couldn't ever do any more than give a guy a hand job," he said firmly. "I've got a girlfriend and all. She won't let me do it with her yet, but I'm getting closer." He laughed, low and contented, and punched me in the ribs. "But until I do talk her into it, I sure do like for a guy to take care of it for me.

And, man, you do it better'n that other fellow ever did. I don't know which I like more, your hot mouth or tight ass."

"Well, I like your dick," I answered. "I think it's pretty. You can do it to me any time, as long as we don't get caught."

Buford laughed heartily. "Yeah, we will have to be quieter in bed, won't we?" He reached for my dick. "But we're not in bed now, and there's nobody to catch us." He rolled me onto my side and pressed his full body against mine. "You want to suck or get fucked?"

"It's up to you," I said, grabbing that beautiful stiff cock that I had come to crave. "It'll always be up to you."

THE WATCHER IN THE WOODS

Tony Anthony

Rod and I were doing it in the woods out on the edge of town. We could have been in our apartment but we'd been living together just long enough to want a bit of variety. So I was down on my knees, surrounded by trees and green brush, with Rod's big dick filling my mouth while he watched. He loves doing that, loves being a voyeur, and we'd got the apartment fitted out with big mirrors and enough video stuff to set up a porn studio.

So there I was with my hands on his bare butt and his dick feeling good and hard in my mouth.

"Someone's watching us," he said quietly.

Wondering whether it might be a cop I pulled away from Rod's dick.

"I think it's okay," Rod said. "He's a watcher."

"Is he going to join us?" I asked.

"I don't know. Just stands there watching."

Getting to my feet I kept one hand on Rod's dick and looked around. Sure enough, barely visible through the underbrush, there was a young guy in gray sweats looking at us. He could have been eighteen or twenty. His hand was inside the front of his sweats. He didn't move. Turning to face him I let my dick and balls come into full view. My erection is pretty big and I reckoned it'd bring him closer. If he joined us it could be great, especially for Rod's restless needs.

He didn't move towards us so I made a bigger gesture, circling the base of my dick with my fingers, and thrusting my hips. Staring at us he remained motionless.

Seeing the guy as something of a challenge I said to Rod, "Let's see if we can have him. At least get closer."

We moved slowly towards him, trying to appear totally safe to be with. If he thought we were going to mug him he'd probably disappear. For a while I guessed he was going to let us come to him. Then he began edging away, watching us nervously over his shoulder.

"Let's see if we can herd him into the dead-end canyon,"

Rod said.

The woods were on rough ground with lots of little ravines among the trees. Most of the fissures petered out but the one Rod had in mind was steep sided and ended in a vertical cliff that couldn't be easily climbed. The idea of cornering the guy and maybe fucking him began exciting me.

"Let's spread apart a bit," I said. "If he goes to your side, you go forward and head him towards me. Then I'll go forward and turn him again."

Moving slowly we got the guy edging towards the little canyon that he still couldn't see. It became a sort of game, with him watching us and responding to our moves. He was getting close to the mouth of the canyon and my heart was beginning to thud in anticipation. Then something must have spooked him because he headed straight across our front and disappeared among the trees.

"Fuck it," Rod said. "I thought we had him.'

"Me too," I said. "I was looking forward to getting his pants down."

A horse neighed in the direction the guy had taken. It probably indicated a mounted cop on woods patrol. Then the guy reappeared coming towards us and I guessed he'd seen the cop and preferred us. Anyway there he was and we resumed herding him.

In a short while he saw the cliff and knew he was trapped.

"Hang back a bit," I told Rod. "I'll go to him and calm him down."

With my fingers circling the base of my dick and pushing my balls forward I moved slowly towards the guy. Now that I could see him clearly his good looks came through. He was fair haired and his eyes matched the light gray of his sweats. Looking at my dick he pushed his hand down inside the front of his pants.

When I was closer to him his eyes looked scared, and he glanced from me to Rod, who was now much closer.

"Don't hurt me," he whispered.

I could have said we didn't intend to hurt him but I thought he was enjoying the fear so I let him sweat on what we wanted. When Rod and I were standing close to the guy he seemed to be paralysed. Reaching forward I put my hand on his crotch. He pulled his hand away and I could feel his dick and balls, lumpy inside his sweats. His long eyelashes fluttered and I put a finger to his cupid's bow lips and traced their curves.

Rod pushed his own pants down and showed his dick and balls. The guy still seemed very nervous.

"Now just take it easy," I said quietly, holding the waistband of his sweats and pushing them down. White briefs bulged over a big dick and heavy balls. I cupped them in my fingers and stroked the white cloth softly. His eyes were twitching nervously; so I said, "You've got a great pack there. It looks beautiful."

Lifting his top revealed washboard abs and a chest totally free of hair. His nipples were pink and tiny. Rod came closer and the guy turned to face him.

This brought the guy's butt into my view, and it looked perfect, rounded and very male. Gently I stroked the globes with my finger tips and felt under his crotch and found the cloth-covered bulge of his balls. My touch made him give a little jump.

Rod dropped to his knees and put his mouth to the guy's genital bulge. As he looked down I saw his eyes widen. The shape of his dick stiffened and straightened. He looked at me with his gray eyes troubled, as though wanting reassurance, so I nodded.

With the fingers and thumbs of both hands I pulled the back of his briefs away and looked down inside them. The swelling curves of his butt were perfect, smooth and white as marble.

Rod eased the front of the guy's briefs down and the dick they had held flipped out, nearly fully hard.

Pursing his lips, Rod kissed the long shaft from the thick base up to the head now emerging from its foreskin. The sight of all this was so sexy I had to hold my dick and give it slow and steady strokes. My balls were out of my pants, so I grasped them and let their sensitive areas send little shocks into me.

When Rod eased the guy's foreskin down I watched the red head emerging, gleaming wetly, pumped hard with internal pressure. Knowing Rod so well, I could guess how strongly tempted he was to open his mouth and fit it over the swollen, flared tip; but both of us are so shit scared of infections I wasn't surprised when I saw the red disappearing into a condom.

Still fisting my dick slowly, I watched Rod begin to suck on the guy's dick, and cradle his balls in one hand. Spasms in the guy's major muscles were making him thrust his hips forward.

Putting my hand on the bulge of the guy's butt I carefully felt into the lightly haired cleft. My fingers felt good in there and I found his pucker. It was tightly closed.

The guy glanced at me and then back at the kneeling figure of Rod expertly swallowing a now-massive dick.

While Rod was occupying his attention I felt around his pucker, circling it with a finger and testing its resistance. After a while I could feel it relaxing a little. An urgent need to fuck the guy filled my heart and mind. I rolled a condom down my thick dick and lubed it. With my finger slicked I pushed a bit harder, trying to work it into him.

He glanced at me quickly as though he was going to raise an objection but he couldn't keep his attention away from Rod's licking and sucking. I knew just how good Rod was at blowing and I could understand how the guy felt.

His pucker eventually parted enough for the tip of my finger to get in. Working slowly I got the full length of my digit sliding smoothly into his depths. Fucking him with my finger seemed to suit the guy because a second finger went in with little resistance. He was bending forward now and I slid his top up revealing his back and broad shoulders. His sides tapered down nicely to his butt and I wanted to have him even more.

Parting my fingers inside him, I tried to stretch his sphincter enough to take my thick dick. His nervousness suggested he might be a beginner; I wasn't sure a new boy could accept me in comfort. Lubing my fingers some more, I worked them inside him; his sphincter still felt tight.

My dick was so hard now it was aching to get into him, but I forced myself to wait. There's no point in hurting a guy unless he likes it.

Rod was having no trouble under the guy, slurping and working away like a fanatic. He had his hand on his own dick and I watched its familiar head appearing and disappearing through his circling finger and thumb. Rod is a natural for sex. He's totally involved in it and I love him for that.

The ache in my dick reminded me of my own needs and I wondered whether the guy's ring could take me now. His entrance was feeling more relaxed, not cramping down on my fingers.

Leaving them still in him I brought the head of my dick forward into his cleft. It looked really good, big and thick and ready to go into him. With fingers and condom well slicked in lube I put the head next to my fingers and pushed. The blunt head didn't make much progress before it stopped, blocked by his pucker still engaging my fingers.

Keeping the forward pressure on by pushing with my hips, I drew my hand back hoping to get the head in before his ring closed up tight. The idea worked at least partly, with the big head halfway into the sphincter when it tightened.

"Jeeze, that's big," the guy said, in a strained tone.

"You're doing just great," I said. "Try to relax and it'll go in."

"I don't know," he said.

"You can do it," I said. "And you'll love it when it's in."

I gripped his hips firmly and pushed with my hips. Having a big dick can be great but it can also get in the way.

The head felt as though it was slowly entering, parting his ring and easing into him.

He threw his head up, arched his back, and gasped, "Fucking hell."

"Take it easy, baby," I said, sliding my hands down his back, soothing some of the tension out of his muscles. "You're doing great. It's nearly there."

In fact, there was a long way to go, but I felt the flare of my dick slip past his ring before it tightened. I stopped pushing and gave his sphincter time to get used to the stretch. Getting the rest of my dick in ought to be easy.

Rod was having fun judging by the sounds coming from him, enjoying the big dick in his mouth.

I was so keen to get my length fully into the guy my whole body was trembling. The temptation to simply ram it all the way home was getting very hard to resist. Trying a steady push I felt my shaft slide a short way through his constricting ring.

Things were going my way at last. My dick was so sensitive I could feel every fraction of movement in the rectum. It was like paradise.

From somewhere below I felt Rod's hand suddenly grab my balls. I nearly jumped out of my pants. "You bastard!"

"I knew you'd like it," he said, chuckling.

Holding our new friend by the hips I began long, slow, steady thrusting all the way into his deepest recess. At last I was fucking him and it felt very satisfying. He seemed to be settling to it as well. The build-up of tension in my groin started and I widened my standing stance while continuing to do the fuck.

"It's so fucking colossal," the guy whispered.

"You're doing well," I said. "Good man."

An electric thrill from my dick shot up my spine and arched my back. Talking at that moment was out and I gasped and gasped again.

Rod emerged from under and stood at my shoulder watching me. His dick was standing big, an engorged stick of bone-hard flesh. His knob gleamed, purple as a plum. He was staring at my dick so I leaned back and let him see the thick erection passing in and out of the guy's butt.

Pumping steadily I let the tension build inside my groin and felt it spreading like an electric buzz.

Rod kneeled on the ground and I realized he was looking up at my dick, seeing it from below as it plunged. It must have been quite a sight because he was down there a long time. When he stood up he had his dick in his hand and he was pounding it hard.

"You've no idea how sexy it looks," he said. "Your dick looks huge and his hole is incredibly tight around it."

The idea of it excited me and my thrusting quickened. I felt I was akin to a bull, doing the big male job. My dick was easing along like a well-oiled piston, and I increased the pace a little. A tremor went through the hips I was holding and I guessed the guy was feeling some good things too.

Rod's hand swept over the curve of my butt and the burning ecstasy it created stopped me completely. When the feeling died down I resumed the long steady strokes. It was like starting from fresh and I could feel the tension growing again.

"Fucking hell," the guy said, quietly. "It's ... it's ... it's."

I know what you mean, I thought. *I feel that way myself.*

Rod groped under the guy and his hand came away holding

the limp condom. Then he groped again and his arm began moving as he jerked the guy off.

"Not now," the guy said.

So Rod straightened up and again watched my dick pumping at the guy's cleft. Looking down I had to admit it was a fine sight, parting the guy's cleft, a thick rod doing its job. My breathing was becoming heavier, forward strokes faster.

Rod closed his hand over his own dick and started pumping. He's got a fair piece of meat and I was struck suddenly by the scene being so totally male, men doing the fuck thing, big dicks and swinging balls, grunting a little now, eyes staring, excitement rising.

Inside the guy's rectum my dick felt as hard as steel, a blunt probe seeking blindly but actively, striving for the magic that would happen. A brush of electric shock drew my balls up tight to the base of my dick making it one solid unit of male fuck-thing. My back arched in a sudden spasm and my eyes closed as I fought the ecstasy.

Rod bowed, his upper body hiding for a while the busy working of his hand. Then he straightened up again and I knew his immediate agony had passed. His dick stood out like a thick flagpole, the head so purple and pumped up it seemed ready to burst. Clear liquid glistened at its eye like a tear of joy. He panted for breath.

Another spasm arched my back and held me there longer this time. When I resumed thrusting with my pelvis I could hear myself grunting, at every stroke, "Uh, uh, uh."

"I can't stand it," the guy gasped. "It hurts too much. Give me more. Give me that big fucking dick up my shitter. Why don't you fuck me? Fuck me with that big fucking thing of yours. I want it. Bang me hard."

My whole body seemed to be gripped in continuous electric shocks. My eyes were screwed up so tight I could barely see and I knew my face was twisted into a fierce grimace, mouth open, teeth bared. The dick sticking out of my groin had seemed big before this but now it felt as thick as a beer can, dominating everything in my life. My heart was racing and I strained for breath, panting like a runner in the homestretch.

"Yes, yes," Rod was gasping. "Now! Do it now!"

"I can't," I gasped. "I can't come! Help me."

My dick was racing so fast it felt like one continuous and ecstatic movement. I could hardly see. My mind was reeling. Feeling unsteady on my feet I expected to fall.

"For fuck's sake," Rod said. "Do it now."

"I can't," I sobbed. "I can't do it. Help me come."

Rod's hand brushed against my butt and I realised that he knew how to do it. He knew what to do and he would help me come and I knew it would work and I would come. His fingers were in my cleft and I could feel the cheeks of my butt clenching on them and releasing them rapidly. One finger found my pucker and pressed against it. But it didn't go in. It pressed again harder, then much harder. Suddenly my pucker opened a little and the tip of his finger was in and creating such incredible rapture I couldn't believe it and the ecstasy was rushing and rushing and my mind was racing and then, in a convulsive surge, my dick shoved a massive charge of semen along its length and another and another. The rapture was so painful I thought I was going crazy and my body twisted and jerked uncontrollably. It seemed to be lasting forever.

Then things were slowing down, easing and relaxing; but looking at the bare back of the guy I was fucking I saw a line of white semen looping down on it.

Rod was coming, big time, his hand racing along the shaft of his rigid dick, spurting spunk onto the guy, line after line of it, until he too was slowing and a last gob of cum rolled over his fingers and stuck to them.

When I drew my dick out of the guy, he straightened up and I saw that the whole length of his dick was glistening, wet with semen. He looked at his hand. It was wet too.

It took us some time to get ourselves together but we did it eventually. We spoke to the guy and he told us his name. Rod asked if he would like to come around to our place sometime and he said yes. Then he asked, when? So we said, why not now? We can clean up together and you can stay for a while.

So we went back to our place together and made it the start of a great friendship—one that looks like holding good for a long time to come.

OFFSHORE DRILLER

Corbin Chezner

At the tender age of 13, quite by accident, Cliff Wyler discovered the merits of jacking off to allay what ailed him. Later on, sex with other males taught him the therapy could be even more effective, particularly if he hardly knew the men but found them physically appealing. God knew, he needed the prescription now. He understood his own motivation quite well; as for the stranger piloting the helicopter, he hadn't a clue. To Cliff, sex with a stranger was merely a way to relieve stress, a method of ridding his mind of tension, if only briefly. Some harmless play would provide a buffer—for a few moments, at least to the turmoil he expected to encounter once he arrived at the offshore rig.

All the way from Houston, the two men had exchanged idle chat and telling glances. Although neither had broached sexual matters, Cliff thought he sensed an intense sexual tension between them. Or was it his imagination? The cauldron he was about to enter had his judgment off kilter—he knew that."How far have we gone?" he finally asked the pilot.

A beefy redhead who'd introduced himself as Dave Williams, the pilot glanced at Cliff and smiled."About 25 miles already. Won't be long now."

Won't be long? Cliff, dark-haired and handsome, began to doubt he'd get to see Williams' cock after all. Soon, the offshore rig would loom into view. Perhaps he'd misread the pilot's body language. Perhaps his "gaydar" was as out of whack as the offshore rig itself.

Then, just as the oil company executive was about to give up hope, without warning, Williams suddenly slammed on the chopper's glide slope antenna and the automatic direction finder. Before either of them could say something that might kill the spell, he unzipped his pants and, after a brief struggle, managed to pull his big, throbbing cock into view.

As his eyes riveted to the pilot's beautiful dick, Cliff heard himself gasp; on its own volition, Cliff's tongue licked his lips hungrily.

A growl erupted from Williams' throat as he glanced over at the passenger. With a wink he beckoned Cliff to him by flexing his rock-hard cock. Thrusting his hips upward from the cockpit seat, he commanded, "Suck it, dude!"

No one, particularly a good-looking redhead, had to ask Cliff twice. Reflexively, Cliff crouched down between the pilot's thighs; his hungry mouth, as if guided by sonar, immediately located Williams' tasty tool and took to it, like a newborn to tit. Smirking, the pilot steepled his fingers behind Cliff's head and guided the passenger to the base of his throbbing cock. "You like my big pole?"

Cliff's answer was to bear down on Williams' shaft. By now, he was determined to taste the redhead's cum—before they reached the rig. Because the pair had been fucking mentally ever since they'd lifted off the 50th-story helipad at Zandex Oil Company headquarters in downtown Houston, the actual act took only moments. Soon, the pilot tightened his grip on Cliff's head, and he blasted his load down the passenger's throat. "Ahhh man!"

Cliff had been pumping his own meat, and as he fought to swallow the sweet-tasting cum, he shot his own load against the floorboard of the cockpit.

Williams regained control of the 'copter, and the pair continued the trip to the offshore oil rig in silence, as if nothing out of the ordinary had occurred.

As the chopper's blades whirred overhead, Cliff began to re-examine his feelings regarding his assignment. Sexually, of course, he was excited about spending a whole month on a rig with forty hunky, horny oil field workers. What gay guy wouldn't be? Yet a pesky voice of reason reminded him this was no a pleasure trip. Far from it. As much as he wanted to believe otherwise, he knew damn well most of the men on the offshore rig—all of them, perhaps—would consider him the enemy. Nevertheless, he had a job to do. If he valued his position as operations analyst for Zandex Oil, he had to find who—or what—was causing problems on the giant oil rig.

Finally, the oil platform appeared. "Here she is," Williams bellowed over the whirring of the chopper blades.

Cliff looked out the cockpit window at the mammoth yellow platform looming out of the choppy blue-gray Gulf waters.

"Looks like a giant groping for butt," he said, smirking.

"Never thought of it!" Williams laughed and slapped his beefy thigh. He adjusted the throttle and leaned the bird toward the platform. "You got a point, though. Hey, it's none of my business, dude, but this is one hell of a time for you to be comin' way out here!' He eyed his passenger curiously.

"When you got a job to do, weather ain't a factor." Cliff raked dark hair away from his forehead and peered back down at the deck of the 40-ton oil platform. He learned long ago his job required discretion. Besides, most people didn't give a shit about the details. Not really.

"Chilton send you out?" the pilot asked.

"A good guess."

"Earl Chilton's one bad-assed dude, they say."

"Depends," Cliff said, shrugging. "You take care of him, he takes care of you. "

Williams cocked an eyebrow but kept his thoughts to himself. Cliff considered elaborating on his mission to the oil rig but decided against it. He had to be careful whom he confided in. Cliff continued scanning the rig as the'copter approached the helipad. Zandex Oil Company had named the platform El Roy, and it was as big as a battleship. From their vantage point inside the whirlybird, the men working on the drilling rig looked as small as toy soldiers At the pits, a couple of deck hands worked feverishly adjusting mud viscosity while their two buddies waded through the recycled mud checking for rock shavings; on the opposite end of the platform, just outside a welding shed, three men fumbled with a strand of pipe destined for the doghouse; halfway up the 40-foot tall Christmas tree, a couple of derrickmen stood on the safety platform playing with their crotches and pointing toward the sky; on the floor just outside the derrick three roughnecks were disassembling drill joints.

The day was warm and bright, and many of the men had removed their shirts. Cliff s heart raced, and he felt his dick stir. He still couldn't believe he'd be spending two shifts—a whole month!—on this drilling rig in the Gulf of Mexico. What an assignment!

"Radio says the storm could be a bad one," the redheaded pilot said, jerking back on the throttle.

"Hell, I hear El Roy could damn near survive a nuclear blast," Cliff answered with a shrug.

"Damn near." Williams looked over at the smaller man, a glint in his green eyes. He scratched his balls with his left hand and adjusted some controls on the instrument panel with his other hand as the 'copter settled against the pad. "Still, you might end up stayin' out here a few days longer than you expect." Cliff knew damn well a hurricane was churning its way across the Gulf, but he'd put off his boss as long as be could. Third-quarter reports had indicated something was awry at the drilling rig, and Earl Chilton, the CEO of Zandex, demanded some answers.

"Good luck." Dave leaned over Cliff and slid open the helicopter door.

"Thanks. I'll need it." Cliff grabbed his leather travel bag and jumped out; he waved as the copter went back into the air. As Cliff stood on the helipad and peered at the vastness of the Gulf, he suddenly felt eerily vulnerable. No land was in sight; nothing but choppy, blue-gray water as far as he could see. He closed his eyes and took in a deep breath of the salty air. There was no turning back now. His windbreaker flapped angrily as brisk, hot winds slammed waves against the platform's huge pilings; he crossed his fingers and hoped for the best. As he opened his eyes again and turned to look for a ladder or stairway down to the main deck.of El Roy, a crew member suddenly bounded into view.

Despite his recent encounter with the chopper pilot, Cliff's big cock stirred as he surveyed the young blond swaggering toward him. He was young—21 or 22, Cliff guessed—and he wore faded, oil-stained Levis and a black sweatshirt with the sleeves cut out. A Walkie-Talkie was clipped to his belt loop. Extending his hand, he smiled and introduced himself."Kevin Johnson, roustabout." His teeth were strong and perfect, like his body. In contrast to his bronzed skin, his teeth looked very white.

Cliff introduced himself, and the good-looking crewman motioned him toward a ladder that led to the main deck. Cliff and the roustabout climbed down the ladder and started across the deck toward the three-story building that housed the sleeping quarters, cafeteria, and offices.

"Wind's startin' to pick up," Kevin said, glancing toward the older man. The roustabout lifted his hard hat and raked strands of thick, sun-streaked blond hair away from his forehead. He put the hard hat back on, cocking it toward the back of his head. "Damn storm has us all a little on edge."

"I can imagine."

"I hear you'll be with us for a while," Kevin commented, with a sidelong glance toward Cliff.

"A couple of shifts."

"A month?" Kevin Johnson looked surprised. "That could be rough—you being way from home that long, I mean."

"Guess I'll just have to make the best of it," Cliff said with a shrug. "Just like the rest of you." Peering over at the young blond, he winked.

Kevin pointed toward the metal building that loomed over the deck. "Derek's in his office now."

"Hey, Kevin," a man called out as the pair passed by the mud pits, "tell Derek the rock shavings are comin' up short." The roustabout and Cliff stopped near the three men who stood by the pits. Two of them, roughnecks apparently, were shirtless and caked with mud. In contrast, the man who had called out to them was clean. Tall and lean, he looked to be in his mid-30s, and he was wearing tight Levis and a yellow pullover. The men were on their haunches, examining a circular filter trap set on a platform above the pits. Kevin crouched down beside the man who'd summoned them. Cliff looked on, mesmerized by the blond's butt: twin moons beneath thin, faded jeans.

Absently scratching his own crotch, the spokesman looked darkly at the roustabout. 'We've had nothin' but mud for over an hour now. Make sure the driller understands we've got a problem."

"How serious is it?"

Grasping the roustabout's shoulder, he warned, "If we don't slow down, we're in trouble. Big trouble."

Cliff closed his eyes and the aroma of sweaty men, salty air, and dank mud besieged his nostrils. Suddenly, his dick pulsed as he imagined the men wrestling naked in the pits. What a show the hunks could put on!

When he opened his eyes, Kevin was looking up at him.

Grinning as if he'd just read Cliff's thoughts, the roustabout groped his own crotch and winked as he stood and waved the older man toward the driller's office.

"What does it mean—no rock shavings?" Cliff asked as the two men continued toward the office of the man running the rig.

"I ain't no expert," the roustabout admitted with a shrug, "but it looks like we're goin' too fast. The driller wants to get to 4,000 feet by tomorrow night!" Meeting Cliff's gaze, his blue eyes darkened. "We've still got a thousand to go."

"That much? Why the rush?"

"I don't know a hell of a lot about it, but earlier I heard Dan Smathers tell Derek that if we're not past the limestone strata when the storm passes over, the well could cave in."

"Smathers? Who's he?"

"The dude at the pits who told us about the rock shavings. He's our geologist."

"Sounds like the rig is between a rock and a hard place."

"That's one way of putting it."

. . .

"So, you're the man Earl Chilton sent to spy on me."

Peterson's sharp words sliced to Cliffs core as the driller directed him to a straight-backed metal chair in front of his desk. "What will you need?" Peterson asked abruptly. Obviously, the man did not mince words. His intense brown eyes bore into Cliff's.

"The logs, of course."

He nodded. "I thought as much. Anything else?" he asked, leaning forward.

"I'll have to look around some."

"A man's got a blank check from headquarters, I suppose he can do all the lookin' he wants."

Cliff decided to stuff his inclination to protest. Peterson's resentment, however unfair, was understandable, he supposed. Absently stroking his dark moustache, Peterson weighed his next words carefully. "There is one more thing..."

"Shoot."

"It don't take a rocket scientist to realize why Earl Chilton sent you out here."

Cliff nodded. "I suppose not."

Peterson met his gaze again. "I don't like it, but Zandex is spending big bucks out here, and, if I was in Earl's position, I'd probably do the same. Hell, I know how stockholders scream in a CEO's ears." Pulling his muscular frame from the chair, he began pacing the floor behind his desk. "But there's a line that can't be crossed here."

"What's your point?"

He stopped pacing and peered intently at Cliff again. "Most likely, you're aware of my reputation. I can't argue it's deserved. I do push my men hard. When they're out here on the rig, I expect 110 percent, and not just some of the time. So when it comes time to relax—to play—they play hard. That's an arena I don't interfere in. If it comes down to that, Earl can find somebody else to run this goddamn rig."

"Hold it, Peterson," Cliff shot back. "Nobody said nothin' like that. You think I don't know how hard it is on these men working way out here for two weeks at a stretch? What these men do on their own time is of no concern to me ... unless what they do affects the company's bottom line."

Peterson seemed to relax a bit. "We understand each other then...."

As Cliff studied the driller, Cliff noted that the man's facial features were pleasant but describing him as handsome would be an exaggeration. On a body like Peterson's, though, too handsome a face would be a distraction. Derek Peterson's appeal stemmed from the size and shape of his build. That and his dynamism. The driller's intensity filled the room.

"You got anything, Kevin?" the driller suddenly asked the roustabout. Because the driller had absorbed his attention, Cliff had damn near forgot the younger man was still in the room, standing behind him.

The roustabout looked up, apparently startled himself by the sudden shift of conversation. He cleared his throat. "Dan says the rock shavings are coming up short."

"Damn!" Peterson pounded on the desk and stared grimly at it for a few moments. He raked his hand through his short brown hair and fingered his moustache. Finally, he looked back at the roustabout. "Get your butt back out on the floor. Tell Dan we're gonna keep drilling. But if it gets any worse, I want to know."

The roustabout started to protest, but Peterson interrupted. "I don't want any lip, dude," he ordered, glaring at the roustabout. "You hear me?" Checking his watch, he added, "I'd best get back to the grindstone. Show Cliff here his quarters."

The sleeping quarters reminded Cliff of army barracks. Beds were on each side of a long hallway that bisected the floor. Portable cubicles, about five feet tall, provided a semblance of privacy between beds.

Halfway down the hallway, Kevin pointed out a cubicle on the right. "This is where you'll sleep. You can leave your gear here."

Cliff's heart sank as he viewed the sleeping quarters. A plain wooden stead with no headboard supported the single bed. Ugly gray metal shelving next to the bed functioned as a chest of drawers. A door with a key sticking out of it covered the bottom fourth of the shelving unit.

Kevin pointed toward the shelving. "You got anything you don't want messed with, use the lock box," he suggested. "The key's there."

Cliff tossed his leather travel bag on the floor next to the bed. His only valuables were his watch and wallet, so he didn't bother with the lock box at the moment. "The head's down here," Kevin said, motioning Cliff to follow.

"Must have been designed by a military contractor," Cliff said sarcastically as he eyed the bathroom. Toilets and showers alike were out in the open—no partitions.

"You get used to it," the blond retorted.

Cliff looked on with interest as the blond hunk again fondled his protruding crotch. As in the helicopter, he began to doubt his ability to read a sexual come-on. Was this a signal? Was this blond really interested in him?

The blond gazed at Cliff with impassive blue eyes. "Is what the driller said true?"

"What do you mean?"

"He said you're here to spy. Is that true?"

"What do you think?"

He considered the question for a moment. "Beats me," he finally said with a shrug. Then, his gaze met Cliff's again and with a smile he added, "Hell, it don't make a hell of a lot of difference to me, to tell the truth. Only damn thing I care about right now is getting off. I woke up this morning horny as hell." Eyeing Cliff again, he beamed. "How about you? Care to join in?" Although blood was already surging into Cliff s big cock, he was nevertheless nonplussed by the blond's words. Was this some kind of set-up? A test? His heart pounded as he peered over his shoulder toward the hallway. Incredulous, Kevin Johnson arched his head toward the ceiling and roared with laughter. "Didn't you hear? Out here, man, nobody gives a shit."

"You mean Derek condones....?"

"Hey man, out here, a man has to take care of himself when he's horny." Readjusting himself into a wide-egged stance, his blue-eyed gaze bore into Cliff's as he began to unbutton his Levis. "He'd go nuts otherwise."

Cliff remained cautious, recoiling a half step.

"Hell, all the guys do it," Johnson urged. "One time or another."

Thrusting his hips forward, the blond ripped open the remaining buttons on his Levis, and his cock flipped into view.

The older man's gaze riveted to the blond's fat, engorged cock, which was between seven and eight inches long, with a full foreskin. Smooth as velvet, it beckoned. Cliff s mouth watered, but still he was resistant.

"I ... ah ... I don't know," Cliff stammered, glancing over his shoulder again; he leaned on one foot and then the other as desire pulsed through his loins. All the while, he was thinking that today the elements were with him. One dick down, and if his luck held, forty to go. The roustabout was so young, so uninhibited ... so damn sexy!

"C'mon, man, don't be such a puss," the roustabout urged, thrusting out his hips even farther. The action set his big dick to bobbing like a dashboard figurine."You like my big meat? he asked suddenly, grinning wickedly. Hadn't Cliff heard that earlier today? Ah, words that were music to his ears. Johnson's cock was already rock-hard; the long, thick shaft pulsated with his heartbeat, demanding attention. Suddenly, his foreskin retracted, and his pink cockhead thrust into view. Glistening blond pubic hairs peeked from his open crotch."Suck my dick," he demanded.

Cliff nervously looked over his shoulder again.

"Nobody's gonna find us, man," Johnson snorted, yanking on Cliff's shoulders. "Everybody's busy on the deck. But even if they did, nobody would give a shit. I'm tellin'you, man, it's different out here."

Capitulating at last, Cliff's knees buckled, and a moment later he was eyeballing the blond's pee slit. The blond's big cock flexed, and his young voice urged, "Suck it, dude."

Drawn irresistibly to the tool, Cliff's eager mouth engulfed the fat, hot cock.

"Ah, man," the blond clucked huskily. "Suck it. Suck it good, dude."Arching his head toward the ceiling, he thrust his hips forward, offering Cliff all his cock. He began fucking Cliff's face, slowly at first, then faster and harder until, finally, he squeezed the dark-haired man's shoulder and gasped,"Oh, man. Take all my dick."

As the blond continued to hammer Cliff's face, the production analyst ripped open his own jeans and began jacking himself off. With his other hand, he cupped the blond's gyrating buttocks as they worked their magic into his grateful face.

Finally, Cliff tasted the roustabout's salty pre-cum and an instant later the blond squeezed Cliff's shoulder blades again, harder this time. Arching his head toward the ceiling again, Kevin Johnson suddenly slammed a stream of thick, hot cream against the back of Cliff's throat."Ahh, man!" he hissed.

An instant later, Cliff's thick cock was spurting its load on the floor. Then, the roustabout backed out of Cliff's mouth and shook the remaining cum off the end of his dick, splattering it against the floor. "I feel for you, dude," he finally said.

"How so?" Cliff asked, looking up at him.

'The driller—he don't like nobody snoopin' around."

. . .

"Blowout! All men on deck!" The foghorn was blaring as Cliff awoke from a deep sleep. Someone switched on the lights and his eyes sprang open. "Blowout! Blowout!"

The foghorn blared again and a cacophony of curses erupted in the room. Grumbling men pulled themselves from bed and reached groggily for their clothes. Cliff looked at his watch: 3:30 a.m.! "Blowout! All men on deck! Blowout ...!"

Cliff looked toward the voice, and he saw that it was Kevin Johnson yelling. The youthful roustabout was wearing only Levis, and most of the men heading for the deck didn't bother slipping on shirts either.

Cliff pulled on his pants and followed the others to the deck. Chaos appeared to reign, but it was easy to see, at least. The deck was well lighted, and a full moon loomed overhead, adding to the brightness. Muddy strands of pipe were strewn haphazardly across the deck. Both shifts—around 40 men—huddled at the bottom of the derrick around the doghouse, where drill pipe was fed deep into the earth.

Kevin Johnson stood to the side watching.

'What happened?' Cliff asked, sidling up to the blond.

"A gas pocket. Belched the damn pipe right out of the ground."

"Anybody hurt?"

The roustabout pointed toward the mud pits. The victim lay on a wooden platform next to the rock filter. He appeared to be conscious, and Derek Peterson and Dan Smathers, the geologist, were giving him aid. Kevin told Cliff the victim's name was Bill Cravens. As the men looked on, Smathers tucked a blanket around Cravens while the driller finished bandaging the roughneck's head.

Smathers and the driller worked well together, Cliff decided, and they made a good looking pair to boot.

"He should be all right," Kevin said. "The 'copter's comin' to fly him to the hospital."

"Pipe hit him?"

Kevin shook his head. "The blast knocked him against the derrick. Gashed his head in."

"Might be worth getting slammed in the head to be doctored by those two," Cliff whispered, leaning closer to the roustabout.

"If you hadn't been in such a damn hurry," a voice suddenly roared, "this wouldn't have happened!"

Kevin and Cliff looked toward the voice. Peterson and Smathers were staring each other down, their fists drawn, their faces red and pinched tight with anger."Look, motherfucker," Peterson shouted back, grabbing the geologist by the collar,

"I'm fuckin' in charge here! You don't like what I do, you can get your motherfuckin' butt off this rig!"

Smathers knocked Peterson's hand away. "You don't give a fuck about these men! All you care about is makin' yourself look good to those damn Zandex big shots!"

Peterson took a swing at Smathers then, hitting the geologist square in the jaw. The force of the punch knocked Smathers against an aluminum drain pipe that ran from the doghouse down to the pits. Smathers crumpled and landed against the deck.

The driller rushed over and got down on his haunches to examine Smathers' head. He looked up then toward a clump of men standing near the doghouse. "Fletcher. You and Cox take him down to the commissary, will you? He'll be all right."

The men worked feverishly to get the pipe back in the ground. Derek Peterson, gesturing like a maestro, directed much of the emergency operation from the lower platform halfway up the derrick.

Cliff went into action, helping in any way he could. He lifted pipe; he lugged pails of water; he fetched huge crescent wrenches and other tools he'd never heard of. He even brought towels up from the laundry room so the men could wipe the grime out of their eyes.

A couple of hours later, Derek Peterson wearily climbed up in the derrick one last time. Like most of the others by then, he was shirtless. "Looks like we've got it under control," he bellowed, looking down at his men. His muscles rippled in the moonlight, and he smiled for the first time that evening. "The bar is open, and the drinks are on the house!" He waved the men toward the living quarters.

A skeleton crew of five stayed behind to keep the drilling unit going; the rest headed for the three-story tin building. Peterson climbed down from the derrick and caught up with Cliff halfway across the deck. Cliff was still leery of Peterson, but the driller appeared friendly now. With a smile, he put his arm around Cliff's shoulder. "Let's go get drunk!"

The bar was on the top level, next to the cafeteria. By the time Peterson and Cliff stepped into the room, some 20 men were sitting at round tables nursing longnecks. The pair stopped at the bar, and the driller looked over at Cliff."What'll you have?"

A mirror stretched along the length of the barback. Cliff peered into the mirror at the five tables of men."Looks like the longneck is the drink of the evening."

The bartender was darkly handsome, a Spanish-looking dude with a big, droopy black moustache and shining brown eyes. A white T-shirt and black Levis showcased his well-packed physique.

Derek turned toward the bartender and held up two fingers. The bartender slammed two bottles down on the bar and the driller introduced him as Ramon. Peterson told Cliff that Ramon also cooked for the night crew.

Ramon worked quietly, his face inscrutable; Cliff had no hint as to what he might be thinking. He delivered drinks like he was on skates, gliding between the beer cooler and the barback, along the length of bar, and out to the tables. Suddenly, Cliff had a hankering to rip Ramon's shirt off. Not that he didn't have enough to look at. He turned back toward Derek, who like most of the men, was still shirtless. Every time the driller took a drink, muscles rippled. His chest was big and hard, rugged, with good definition. Just the right amount of dark chest hair narrowed to a thin line that plunged to his navel. After several more beers, Derek loosened up even more.

"Hell, man," he laughed, slapping Cliff on the back again, I just might have to hire you on as a roustabout. You did a damn fine job tonight."

Cliff smiled. "Thanks. I tried."

"Still, I can't forget why you're here." The warmth drained from Derek's eyes as suddenly as it appeared."He's wrong, you know."

'Who? Earl?"

"He thinks we're doin' something wrong out here. He thinks it's my fault we're not makin' any wells."

"I don't think Earl's questioning...."

"The hell he ain't. Look, I understand the bastard, okay? I know what makes the man tick."

Laughing suddenly, the driller tossed down half his beer. Then he slammed the bottle back against the bar and wiped his mouth on his bare arm.

"What's so funny?" Cliff asked.

Peterson looked back at Cliff, mirth lingering in his brown eyes. "Your eyes——they look like they're about to pop out of your head, dude."

Averting Peterson's gaze, Cliff's eyes inadvertently fell on Ramon. Leaning against the barback, Ramon winked and fingered his crotch. Suddenly, Cliff's heart raced in fear; he'd been exposed.

Peterson laughed again. Placing his hand back on Cliff's shoulder, he said, "Hell, out here, that shit don't matter, man."

Pushing away from the bar, the driller stood wide-legged, staring into the long mirror above the barback. He plucked a comb from his back pocket and ran it through his brown hair. Then, clasping his hands above his head, he flexed his biceps, which bounced like testicles freed from a tight jockstrap."Hell, with a body like mine, a man can't be modest." Looking over at Cliff, he winked and smiled.

Returning his smile, Cliff nodded in agreement The noise level inside the bar had picked up considerably. Suddenly someone yelled, "Let's get some action goin'."

Anybody ready for some wagerin'?'

"How about jack in the ring?" a second voice called out.

"I'm game," the first voice said. "How about you guys?"

Voices from around the floor grunted in agreement.

Cliff looked quizzically at the driller. "What's jack in the ring?"

Leaning closer, Peterson whispered,"Enjoy yourself. I've got to take care of something."

Jack in the ring turned out to be a jack-off contest. Even men who had wives and families back home took part, seemingly without guilt. Somehow being out here in the middle of the Gulf of Mexico gave the men permission to do things they'd never consider otherwise. The men drank for what seemed like hours, and, eventually, Cliff lost track of reality; the last thing he remembered was a group of men wrestling naked in the mud pits.

Despite his drunkenness, Cliff experienced a fitful sleep, his dreams full of revelry and swirling, surrealistic sexual fantasies. Or were they just fantasies? Off and on throughout the night, he felt his butt plugged by a big, hot cock while someone's hungry mouth ate his dick and balls.

"Looks like he's comin' around, finally," a voice commented.

Cliff's mind, still swirling from the group binge, slowly returned to reality. As his eyes fluttered open, his ass felt exceptionally warm, and he realized a cock was indeed inside it.

"You like wakin' up to a big cock inside you?" a husky voice inquired. Hands grasped his shoulders and slowly the cock began pumping his ass.

Lifting his head off the pillow, he looked around and realized, with a start, that Derek Peterson was fucking him. "You really tied one on last night, dude," Peterson said, laughing wickedly.

Just then, Cliff realized someone had gone down on his dick and balls; the hungry mouth slurped down the shaft of his throbbing cock and then began to explore his big balls. The mouth stopped for a moment and said, "Welcome to El Roy."

Peering toward the voice, Cliff realized while Peterson was fucking him, he was being sucked off by Dan Smathers, the company geologist. It was damn near more than Cliff could take. "Ah, man," he muttered as the men worked him over, "this is one hell of a way to wake up."

Just then, Derek Peterson stopped fucking in mid-stroke, his dick still plugged into the hot ass of the company executive from Houston. Leaning toward Cliff, he placed his head next to the dark-haired man's ear and throttled it with his tongue. Squirming with pleasure, Cliff could only moan. Then, his hot breath still next to Cliff's ear, Peterson began pumping Cliff's butt again. He whispered huskily, "You like my big cock in your butt?"

In ecstasy now, Cliff writhed against the bed.

Peterson stopped in mid-stride again and demanded once more, "I asked you a question, dude. You like my big dick in your butt?"

The best Cliff could manage at this point was a mere whimper: "I like it."

Slapping Cliff on the butt, Peterson exhorted, "*Like* it? You mean you don't *love* my cock?"

Whimpering again, Cliff managed, "Yes, I do. I do love it. I'll do anything to keep your cock in me."

Fucking Cliff full force now, Peterson said breathlessly, "Anything?"

"Anything."

Patched through the company's satellite up-link the next day, Peterson finally got hold of Earl Chilton at Houston headquarters. "How'd it go?" Chilton asked, flipping on the speaker phone so he could light a cigar.

Smirking, Peterson toyed absently with the mobile telephone chord. "With a cock like mine, you have doubts, Earl?"

Chilton laughed. "You arrogant bastard!"

"I can remember a time when it worked on you."

"So, I can assume Cliff is on our team, then?"

Peterson reached down to fondle his big cock, still half hard from the previous night's activity. "He's our boy now."

ROOMMATES

Mario Solano

It's two a.m. and Shawn sits on the moonlit deck thinking about his new girl. His hard-on protrudes from his plaid boxer shorts. He's finishing his sixth beer and puffing on his last butt. His hands caress the outside of his smooth, tan, thighs. His surfer streaked hair falls casually to his green eyes, brushing his long lashes. He licks his dry, round lips, then lets saliva roll over his tongue. He pays no attention to his roommate, Rick, stumbling in. Rick's large muscular frame is never quiet, especially when returning from a night out on the town. He undresses in his room, weaving, while checking himself out in the mirror. Not bad for thirty-five. His gray-blue eyes are bloodshot. His mouth is dry and he feels chalky saliva on his teeth and tongue. He stands tall, to his full seven inches. He holds his stomach in, expands his chest, then runs his hands over his pecs and fingers his hard nipples. His huge hands rotate over his stomach, between his legs, where they massage his big round balls, causing his knees to bend as his ten inch cock points toward the mirror. From the street, he had seen Shawn's cigarette burning. Without hesitation he walks out to the deck.

"Hey, man," Shawn says. "What's up?"

Rick reaches down and rubs the boy's flat stomach, then sits next to him. "Hi, Buddy," he slurs, as he continues to rub the kid's stomach as his head leans toward his. Their heads touch.

Shawn is woozy. As he turns toward Rick's, their lips get dangerously close, for two straight guys. Rick fingers the elastic of Shawn's shorts. creeping an inch inside the band. The boy does not resist or assist, but, for the first time, he notices Rick's nakedness and his throbbing hard-on. He doesn't know what to do, so he does nothing. It's strange but not unpleasant. He wishes his dick were that big so he could fuck his girl with it. She would love that. His six inches seems to satisfy her, but, at this moment, he's aware of what four more inches could do.

Rick's fingers are now in his pubic hair; his fingers fondle the top of Shawn's cock. The big hand slips down into the crevice where thigh meets balls. Shawn's prick jerks.

In an instant, his cock is out of the top of his shorts, and he feels a warm mouth engulf it before he sees Rick's head going down on him. His body becomes rigid, causing his pelvis to move upward, which shoves his meat to Rick's tonsils. There's a gagging sound, then his whole cock, up to his golf-ball size nuts, is imbedded in Rick's mouth. Shawn feels Rick's tongue lashing his cock and balls. His breath leaves him as Rick kneels between his legs, yanks his shorts down to his ankles, and blows him.

As Shawn is about to shoot, Rick stands. His gigantic cock drips with pre-cum. It's in Shawn's face. He's never been this close to a cock before and he thinks it odd that it's not repulsive. Is it the beer? The hour? His horniness? He doesn't know and he doesn't care. His cock and balls are aching. Rick has been good to him, letting him move-in and helping him out until he found a job. If this is what he wants, he can do it for him. He wipes the jizz from Rick's pee-hole and puts the head in his mouth. Rick rubs the back of his boy's head and moans. Slowly, Shawn takes an inch of the shaft, then two. Rick gyrates his hips, demanding him to take it all. Shawn gags. The cock flops out momentarily, and Rick holds Shawn by his shoulder-length hair and maneuvers the kid's mouth over and around his cock. The boy opens his mouth and allows Rick's prick to roll in and out slowly while his tongue licks the shaft. His hands massages the man's big, musky balls.

Rick takes Shawn by the armpits and raises him to his feet. Rick is a head taller and fifty pounds heavier, Shawn's chin is on his shoulder. He reaches down and around, takes the boy's asscheeks in his massive hands, pulls him close. Their cocks rub together. He turns the kid around, holds him by his waist, and rubs his fat prick against the virgin ass. He bends Shawn over the chaise, works-up whatever saliva he can and lubricates the boy's asshole with his tongue while a finger penetrates the sweet, young, asshole.

Shawn's hands are spread-out on the arms of the chaise. His knees feel weak. He's never been rimmed before. When Rick spreads his cheeks, his ass moves backward toward the pleasure.

Rick stands-up and places his cockhead on the sloppy-wet

hole. As it starts to enter, Shawn's body gets stiff. Rick coos, "It's okay, baby, just relax."

Shawn hears the words allright, but he's so lightheaded, his body crumbles. It's no longer his body. Rick holds Shawn's torso and penetrates. The boy feels intense pain at first, followed immediately by pleasure, and a long, loud moan escapes his lips. Rick places his hand over the boy's mouth and fucks him. He fucks him for a long time before Shawn feels his cock explode. Five, six, seven gobs of cum land on the chaise and the wall. Then they fly backwards over his undulating prick onto his own belly.

Rick holds onto his hips and keeps plugging Shawn's ass. Shawn is nearly unconscious now; he wants it to stop. Everything is reeling, but he's speechless. His head reels from the pounding. He's about to scream. Rick pushes his head down into the cushion, which muffles the sound. He thrusts his prick up into the boy's belly and holds it there as his cum fills the boy's aching hole.

Shawn is pinned between the massive man's body and the chaise. They remain like that for a long time, sweating and breathing hard. Shawn is grateful that it's over, and he swears he's never going to do this again. Rick's cock is three-fourths out before Shawn feels some relief.

Then, with his knees, Rick pushes against Shawn's thighs, causing his legs to spread apart and his cum-filled hole to open wider. As Rick jams his half-hard prick back into the boy's hole, Shawn cries out, "No, no...."

A FARM BOY'S WHIRLWIND ROMANCE

Mario Solano

I'm a professional organic baker, and the Good Gay Lord gifted me with looks, charm, and a ten-inch-long cock that is as fat as a beer can. I'm half Sicilian and half German, two strong persuasions. My astrological sign is Taurus the bull. My home town is Manhattan, New York City. Obviously, I'm not shy. I've got an olive complexion, mink brown hair, which changes length with the seasons. Now, in Indian summer, it's a buzz cut. My eyes are hazel. I'm six feet tall and two hundred pounds. I'm not buff but I do some exercise and I eat well, so my body is lean with no extra fat.

Today I'm standing outside the bakery where I work and I'm holding two large, firm zucchinis. I'm gathering ingredients to make zucchini/pumpkin cake. I do what's called "Nineties Baking—no sugar, salt, oil or fat. I use apple sauce in place of oil and rice syrup for sweet flavor.

I hear his voice first: "Did you grow those?"

Then I look upon him. He's a teenage beauty: Five-ten, one hundred and fifty pounds, blond hair, big, bright blue eyes, freckles, and a warm, innocent-looking smile. He's looking at my zucchini.

"No," I answer, then ask, "Are you interested in home grown?"

"Yes." His eyes gleam when he proudly says the words, "I'm a farmer. I encourage young things to grow." I'd like to encourage him to grow.

"What do you grow?" I ask in earnest, as I check him out from his luscious, rose-colored lips to his well-worn brown leather work boots. He denim overalls are torn at the knee, with one strap missing. The bib hangs down exposing a T-shirt that says "Zig Zag." Farmer Boy recites an impressive abundance of vegetables and herbs. I touch the silk screened Zig Zag man on his chest and ask, "Do you grow this too?" He looks at my hand and smiles mischievously. I caress his pec, put pressure on his nipple and say, "I'd love to see how your garden grows." My eyes purposely wander from his eyes to his bulging crotch.

That's how it starts between Farmer Boy and me.

An hour later, he's giving me a personal tour of his garden. Farmer Boy is on his knees digging into the soil showing me the healthy roots of his prize pumpkin. I'm crouching down, so close behind him I can smell the sweat on the back of his sun-burned neck. My nose grazes the blond hair on the back of his head. I close my eyes and taste him. My lips touch his ear lobe. He turns his head back toward me and our lips brush, gently.

I'm apprehensive about what will happen next. Was he surprised at my boldness? Will he be angry? How is he going to react? I'm sure this is the first time he's been kissed by a man. He doesn't react at all. He just looks at me. His hair falls in casual bangs over his forehead and down over his eyes. His innocence makes him appear goofy looking—like an adorable sheepdog. With my fingers, I brush his bangs aside. He doesn't budge. I put my lips on his again. He doesn't resist. I kiss his top lip, lower lip, each corner of his mouth. I'm still behind him. His head is turned backward and up toward me. I lick his lips with my tongue and coax them open. They're soft, warm and supple. His tongue timidly licks mine. He smells like the field—earthy and fresh. He tastes like the sun—warm and comfortable.

My right hand moves down the inside of his overalls to his crotch. He wears no underwear. His cock is long and thin with an inch of foreskin. His balls are big, round and solid. My hand feels his moisture. As I wrap my hand around his cock, it throbs. I move the skin up and down. His body becomes limp and he falls back into my arms. We whip off our clothes like a whirlwind.

He lies on his back in the pumpkin field as naked as the day he was born. I kneel between his spread legs and observe my prize. He's very pale except for where the sun has made his skin various shades of pink, beige and tan. There's a scar on his chest that winds itself, like a snake, from the nape of his neck, in an "S" shape, down toward his navel. It's nasty. I imagine he usually wears a straw hat so his face is a beautiful beige. The back of his neck and his arms are darker than the rest of his youthful body which features love handles around his middle. His golden hairs are interspersed with sweat leaving moist ringlets on the side of his face and his forehead. His eyes are only half open and yet his blue irises peek out from his lowered lids like sapphires. His lips are chapped and dry. They look like crevices in a scorched desert anxiously awaiting a springtime rain. He licks them with a moist, rose colored tongue. I envision a halo over his head. He looks like an angelic cherub, and I'm about to devour him.

I lie on top of him and we kiss. His arms wrap around me. His beefy hands wander, grasp and grab at my back, neck and buttocks. He squeezes, pinches and explores all of me. His callused fingertips dig into my skin and probe my hole. I lick his mouth, ears and eye lashes. I raise his arms over his head and lick his musty armpits.

"Oh," involuntarily escapes from his lips in a whisper, followed by a sigh. His breath becomes labored and his legs spread farther apart. The hot sun helps our bodies to sizzle. I feel its rays on my bare ass as my cock presses against his cock and our bodies slither and slide against each other. I suck on his nipple. His hands grip my head like a vise and he guides me to his other nipple. My hands surround his pec and form a suckable breast. My teeth clamp on his nipple and I chew. The tip of my tongue enters into the deep scar and licks its way down along its path to his belly button.

"Ohhh...," he moans, as he raises his pelvis up and grinds it into mine.

My tongue licks the sweat from his belly as I attack his large, round, juicy belly button with fervor. He's putty. His arms stretch out like Jesus on the cross. His hands grasp hands full of grass, weeds and earth. His head passionately moves from side to side. He moans and groans.

I continue to lick and lash at his pelvis with my tongue. I chew on his pubic hair, nibble on the space where thigh meets groin, lick the peach fuzz on his pink balls.

I hold both balls in my hands, which causes his prick to stand at attention. The skin is halfway over the bulbous head of his dick. Like a spotlight, the sun shines on his cock. His balls glisten like two priceless Faberge eggs. I look up at his face. His eyes plead with me. I know what he wants but I want him to ask for it.

"Say it," I say softly. He looks at me confused, but still pleading.

"Suck it," he says in a whisper.

I lick the shaft, roll my tongue around the skin, then nibble on his balls.

"Say it," I repeat, in a loud whisper.

"Suck my cock," he gasps as he grabs hold of my head with force and guides my lips toward his throbbing prick. He lines up my mouth with the head of his cock, which is now completely out of its covering and dripping pre-cum. He tightens his huge hands around my head. My mouth opens to protest. He shoves his big boy-cock in my mouth and forces it down my throat. He holds my head in his grip and pounds my tonsils. His thighs open and close like a nutcracker on speed. It doesn't take long. I feel his jism hit the back of my throat and slide down like honey. I need to breathe. I try to lift my head off of his monster prick, but Farmer Boy holds tight. This is his first blowjob and he wants to make it last....

SEX ON THE RUN

Thom Nickels

I'd been searching for Mad Dog all over town. I even put signs up on random telephone poles:"LOST: One cute skinny white boy with tattoos & piercings. Sometimes has bleached blond hair; light brown goatee. May carry a knapsack filled with angry poetry and violent prose exhortations. Pale skin; sometimes wears vests and funny hats. Answers to Mad Dog but may answer to Lord Byron–at least he thinks he's Byron."

I placed an asterisk next to Byron and then in small print on the bottom of the poster I inscribed:"Has a nice hairless, very boyish body–but a small dick. Italian (!) And a beginner-poet."

I hung the flyers all over town. There was a phone number to call--my own. Of course I didn't expect a response. Hell, I'd already given up on Mad Dog. Hadn't he always told me that he was a player? Hadn't he always had three girlfriends at once? One early call I got about my posters was from a girl. She sounded hurt and on drugs."I know who he is," she said. "I should have smashed him in the mash pit at South Station. (South Station was a club that Mad Dog frequented). He's a motherfucker; he's a father fucker–he fucks everyone and he fucked me. If you find him, try and find out where he is and then give me a call. My name's Cindy." Then she left me her New Jersey number. "Yeah, Mad Dog's a player," I thought after she called. "Hell hath no fury ... He burned her...." Indeed, Mad Dog always delighted in telling me how he had dumped one for another, for no good reason other than he felt like it. "I have no feelings," he used to tell me. "My father is Satan. I have no loyalties. I would betray my own friends." But I didn't believe him; little did I know. He told me these things the first day I met him. He was walking behind me on Philadelphia's Pine Street. I turned around because I felt an intense presence. That's when I saw him: his striking long hair flat against his head like a '60s folk singer's. He was in a trenchcoat but I could still see that he had a nice body. There was no way I could not say hello. His whole demeanor was 'soft' and receptive.

He introduced himself as Mad Dog and said that he was a poet. That's all I needed to hear. I'd just finished watching Leonardo DiCaprio in "Total Eclipse" and my head was full of sixteen year-old poet Arthur Rimbaud. In a way it seemed as if Arthur Rimbaud had come to me, albeit in a new form. Mad Dog even looked like Leonardo—sea shallow green eyes, thick sensual lips, translucent skin, soft but firm voice. Sometimes the sexiest men—the sexiest boys—are petite rather than muscular.

"I was about to brew some Columbian," I lied. "Would you like to join me upstairs—I happen to live in this building."

He said, "Yes, right away."

I was amazed at the quickness of it all. As he followed me upstairs, it occurred to me that maybe I'd made a mistake; that perhaps I was going down the path of trouble. What if he'd been canvassing the streets just to find someone to rob? That feeling disappeared the minute he took off his trenchcoat in my apartment.

There was a relaxed quietness about him and yet at the same time he seemed distant and preoccupied, as if something was bothering him. I took this for poetic angst. Besides, with his trenchcoat off, I was enjoying him totally. He chose to sit on the small sofa adjacent to the big sofa where I normally sit when I have guests (I like facing people at an angle), and so I had an excellent view of his body.

As the coffee brewed, I asked if I could see some of his poetry. He opened his knapsack and took out a wad of papers. He started reading the titles: *Throat Cut Love; New Wave Vengeance: Cafe Blood; Punch and Judy Accidents; Head First Into The Mash Pit; Sickle Cell Orgasm.* He began reading from *Sickle Cell Orgasm*, which was not about an orgasm at all but about his wanting to lash out and kill everyone before he did himself in.

I was shocked. "Everyone?" I said, wondering if there were any notable exceptions—like me, for instance, whom he had just met. I didn't press for an answer. On one level he seemed like a twentysomething Ghandi; on another level there was this thing eating away at him. Perhaps this 'thing' was a lot of repressed violence, his desire to destroy everything he touched. Not an exterminating angel but an exterminating devil.

"Wow," I told him, after hearing how he wanted to rip a knife into the entrails of some girl who had betrayed him and then wash the streets with her blood before slitting his own wrists in a bathtub. "Wow," I said again, "I would hardly call you the poet of discretion. No one would guess judging from your calm demeanor." I was looking at his legs. I had already made a friendly gesture which included brushing my hand against his left kneecap which was very close to mine. I did my usual routine "sex testing" by mentioning queer writers to see if he was well-read or even a likely candidate for one of my rub downs. He passed with flying colors. William Burroughs was his favorite writer and he was well aware that on numerous occasions Jack Kerouac received some blowjobs from Allen Ginsberg.

I asked him to read another poem as I made plans to place my right hand on his kneecap and then let it slide up his leg. The plan was thwarted when he changed positions: he was now slouching away from me, a maneuver that had more to do with his own comfort than avoidance. I realized that I was going to have to mouth my proposition instead of moving in with my hands.

I offered him a foot massage for seven dollars. Why seven dollars I don't really know; it just felt right. Plus, I felt he needed the money. All poets need money.

He said yes to the massage. That's when I told him that this would be an erotic foot massage, much more than just a touchy-feely thing that went nowhere. He still said okay. So off came his black combat boots and white socks. He had nice feet. Very nice, in fact. I started on his left foot: I kneaded, rubbed and sucked his supple skin. He closed his eyes. I grabbed the other foot so as to have both his feet on my lap. He smelled like clean gym equipment and freshly peeled potatoes. Wow. I really liked this kid. I held his left foot in the air and then swayed it out to the side in order to get a better view of his crotch. There was no indication of a hard-on. Then, after concentrating some more on his feet, I let my right hand move up his leg till it glided near his penis.

Poet penis—a special one to be sure.

"No, not that," he said. "No dick. I don't let any man touch my dick. Only my girlfriends can touch it."

I could not believe what I was hearing. Only his girlfriends? Was he a poet or was this some Mormon missionary from Salt Lake? Arthur Rimbaud would never say such a thing. Nor would Leonardo, for that matter! I felt he should be ashamed.

I wanted to lecture him but bit my tongue.

"Nothing I can do or say to convince you?"

He shook his head.

"Not ever?"

The way he kept shaking his head 'no', I knew it was a done deal. He had been "brainwashed" by the culture: same sex sex was too hot to handle. I did not want to push my luck so I made do with worshipping his feet and then, after I came, I handed him seven dollars and my business card. It was better than nothing. "Call me again and come over," I said. He said he would. I thought I'd ask him later whether he had ever let a guy suck his dick but, in the meantime, I decided to just play it cool. What else can you do with a guy who looks like Leonardo and who says that his father is Satan? And, if his father is Satan, why in hell is he saying 'no' to getting his cock sucked. Was this a new kind of Christian Coalition Satan?

Well, how Mad Dog eventually let me suck his cock is an interesting story I shall get to soon enough. But I can tell you that the change did not come easily—and it took an entire year! During that time I had to make do with his feet, which were wonderful specimens and which pleased me to no end. The most exciting foot sessions were those in which he read his poetry aloud with his feet propped up on the edge of my love seat. Kneeling on the floor in front of his feet as he recited his work propelled me to great orgasms—he'd read even as I came and his perfect nonchalance even went to heighten the experience.

For the longest time after he allowed me to suck his cock, I had taken to diving down between his cheeks and letting my tongue run up inside him like a driving snake. He'd often contract his ass checks like a tight clamp so that my tongue could not enter as freely, yet as I licked and nibbled he'd eventually loosen up and further in I'd go. When this happened I knew I had at least a minute to taste his delectable interior, for soon he'd relapse into the clamp stage, the ass being one area where he was the most uncomfortable. The reason for this is that when he was very young, maybe nine or ten, he had an uncle who raped him for a period of time. The memory of that rape was so severe that he could hardly bring himself to talk about it: if he tried his face would redden and the words came out only after great effort. I could see that just remembering the incident was ripping the wounds wide open inside him.

My focus on his ass–the position I asked that he assume so that I could orgasm in splendor–was the death knell, though it took months before the damage was noticed. I first noticed a change when Mad Dog refused to answer my pages. He was usually good at returning these, even if to say that he could not meet up and would be indisposed for a while. He had proven himself to be an excellent communicator, but suddenly my pages went unanswered for days, and the frustration of being ignored only increased my pages until I was buzzing him ten or twelve times a day, if only to prove a point. His replies, when he did get back, were always the same: "I was in New Jersey and couldn't get back to you." "I was with my girlfriend." "My pager was off." "I was knocked out stoned." All of these ecuses sounded legitimate even if they were a stretch of sorts. The thing is, I'd forget all the slights and frustrations once he called and said he was on his way over. That in itself became the healing balm: his coming to see me with the gift of his melon ass and cock that I loved to milk.

When Mad Dog talked he talked only of his own life: who he was living with, what he was writing, what clubs he was hanging out at, or what jobs he had. Very early on I learned that he was not interested in hearing what was happening to me. His interest in that department barely spanned twenty seconds. I'd talk about myself and he'd start to drift. He was the heart and soul of self-absorption. Usually we'd "talk" for ten or fifteen minutes, sometimes less. Then Mad Dog would lean over and unlace his boots, a signal that he wanted to get going. Sometimes he'd even take his shirt off and sit there bare-chested, cracking his bones and turning sideways to stretch his muscles. He was nearly always in a rush. There were appointments with friends or girls in coffee houses, meetings on street corners or in bars. "We should get started," he'd say, "because I have to...."

Later, after Mad Dog let me suck his cock, he never hurried

love-making. Once he was in bed he never looked at the clock; he also never suggested that I hurry up and he certainly never cut things off before both of us had had our orgasms.

Our foot session went like this: he would lie on my bed with his boots and socks off with his legs draped over the edge of the bed. I'd be on my back on the floor with my face positioned directly under his feet. The second time we were together–and this was way before he let me touch his cock–I asked him if he ever let a guy suck him. He said yes but told me that he charged fifty dollars. "I didn't like it. I don't like it when a guy sucks my dick, but I needed the money."

"So you'd do it now for fifty bucks? Is that it?" I asked.

"Well, probably ... but not necessarily," he said.

I was in no mood to spend that kind of money so I let the matter drop.

During the early sessions I'd ask him to roll up his trouser legs to about his knees so that I could massage his lower legs and get in a few tongue licks as well. His skin tasted good, this son of Satan, and his legs were hairy, just the way I like them. Sometimes he wore a five-pointed star and talked about a number of Black Magic Masters. He told me was telepathic, which was not a lie as it turned out since in the coming months there would be many instances when I'd suddenly sit back during the course of my day and get an this intense image of his face in my mind's eye, only to find him calling me five minutes later. This happened too frequently to be called a coincidence.

"I always know when people are thinking about me," he said.

"You know that little fucker?" The voice was harsh and boozy sounding. I pictured a strung out guy in some sleazy flat, perhaps one of Mad Dog's former roommates. He had had many roommates: girls, guys, married couples. Without fail, each of these relationships had come to a bad end. Fights or arguments erupted and in some instances Mad Dog was thrown out on his ears. Those times he'd wind up calling me. "Can I come over? Can I spend the night at your place?" I always said yes. By that time I was sucking his cock and doing his feet and laying on top of him in heavy grinding fashion. I was even kissing him behind the ears. It had taken a year for him to get used to me and to let me do what I wanted to do.

. . .

I'd known Mad Dog for almost two years before he betrayed me. That's not a bad record. Girls never lasted that long with him. He just stopped calling. We never had an argument; there was never a hint of disagreement or displeasure. We never raised our voices at one another. I'd simply outlived my usefulness, and Mad Dog, the ultimate player, had to move on. Like the host of violent fantasies tucked away in Mad Dog's subconscious, the one physical act that may have eaten away at him over time was the position I had him assume after he had had his orgasm. That position was essential to my getting off: I'd request that he'd prop himself against the side of my bed in a kneeling pose with his legs spread wide enough so that I could kneel between his legs and jerk off onto his petite boy's ass—that shapely melon that never failed to take me over the edge whenever I'd feel or sniff it at close range. It was the most beautiful of asses: firm and small with two dimple-like indentations along the sides.

The cock sucking explosion occurred when he came over to my place one afternoon for our usual foot routine. He was sitting on the small sofa after updating me on his activities. Suddenly he got quiet. The air seemed heavy and I felt a strong sexual vibe. Then I saw his eyes glance down at my crotch. It was extraordinary. The quick glance, coming from anybody else would not have meant much, but with Mad Dog, who was always careful where he let his gaze rest, it was significant. Telepathy kicked-in big time: He never glanced at my crotch before and the two second focus told me that he wanted me to suck his cock.

I did not ask him if I could touch and suck his cock until I had each of his pant legs rolled up around his kneecaps.

"If I give you ten or fifteen, can I blow you or work you up with a lubricant?"

I heard the word I'd waited so long to hear:"Yes."

Afterward, I felt only joy and anticipation. Despite this, I was not one to leap on the experience, but bided my time by stroking his legs and running my tongue over his calves. I had waited too long not to savor this graduation to the next level. With my left hand, I stroked his upper thighs as my right hand proceeded further up into the once forbidden region. His cock, I noticed, was not particularly large; it was also not hard when I first touched it but that remedied itself in several seconds. Soon it was gallantly stiff as I pressed down on it. I was at last going to suck off little Arthur Rimbaud/Leonardo.

While undoing his belt and slipping off his jeans I feared that he'd change his mind and tell me to stop. My heart raced as I unzipped and unsnapped. Yet he lifted his ass off the bed so that I could slip his jeans down around his ankles and then slide them off his body entirely. His red boxer shorts hid his erection but I had only to insert a hand into the crotch slit before I found his cock standing straight up. I brought his cock through the slit and looked at it for several seconds.

Then I lowered my mouth in a seagull-like swoop till I had the small mushroom head between my lips. At this point, what would normally be considered a below average cock became the most desirable cock in the world. I lowered my mouth to the base then brought it up again; I repeated this four or five times to see if his body moved on the bed but Mad Dog remained motionless. I took his boxer shorts off and let them drop to the floor. That's when I was able to see his body for the first time. My heart raced: the beauty of it was its smallness, its perfect form and symmetry, its tiny waist, its boyish chest and pale skin.

"Can you do me a favor, Mad Dog, and move up on the bed so that you are laying square in the middle?"

Mad Dog did as he was told. Once he was on the bed I got up myself and knelt between his legs. He had his head slightly off the edge of the bed and his eyes were wide open. I thought this odd. He was not blinking but seemed to be staring at the ceiling. I don't know why but I expected him to have his eyes closed. For a minute or two I just looked at him. I could not believe my luck. He was just lying there on his back waiting for me to do almost anything—lay on top of him, suck his cock, turn him over and work his butt. Anything seemed possible at that point. My eyes were drawn to his stomach and to the downward slope of skin created by the elevation of his rib cage. I noticed that his navel formed a perfect oval. His cock was almost soft until I lowered my body on his. I knew I could get it erect by sucking but I wanted to test Mad Dog's response by grinding on top of him.

"Leonardo," I wanted to whisper, but didn't.

He was hard in less than a minute as I wiggled and pressed my body into his. I happened to notice that his eyes were still open and that they were still focused on the ceiling. As I looked at him I felt that part of Mad Dog was not there. His eyes were empty. I thought I could also feel a rage boiling somewhere inside him. That's what his eyes seemed to be saying. They had a vacant fixed quality but there was also rage somewhere in the mix. I hoped it wasn't because I was doing what I was doing.

"Are you okay?" I said.

He didn't answer. I had to repeat the question again.

"Yes," he said.

I continued to wiggle and press my body into his. I inhaled deeply: his smell got me more excited. I planted a kiss on his collarbone, then positioned his cock between my legs. I started to move in a fucking rhythm. Mad Dog continued to lay there with his arms at his side. He kept his body still. Part of me liked the corpse-like quiet, as it made me feel every bit the conqueror. Another part of me wished that at least he would wrap his arms around me and feel my ass.

Sucking Mad Dog brought me the greatest pleasure if only because it took him a while to orgasm. Not too long, mind you, but enough time so that I felt that I had adequately tasted him before he finally shot. Later, of course, I would learn that his orgasms were similar in that he would grab the base of his cock with his right hand, a sign that he was ready. It meant that I had better remove my mouth. I'd usually tell him just to moan or give me another kind of sign when he felt close. I said this because I did not particularly like having his cock whisked away from me just at the crucial time. I wanted to feel it erupt between my fingers and I wanted to get as close as I could to the sudsy aftermath. Mad Dog, ceding to my wishes, learned to grunt when he was close and on some occasions he let out a sigh. The flow from these orgasms varied. Some were copious and spilled out onto my blue bed quilt like great quantities of whole milk; others were not so large, yet still substantial.

He loved two blowjob positions: the first was with his body positioned across my bed so that his feet touched the floor, his head resting on a pillow that he would prop up against the wall the bed itself rested against. Here I could kneel between his legs and let my tongue race over his balls, occasionally taking nose-dives into his butt. Sometimes I'd lift his butt up from the hips so I could get a better tongue-plunge, but these times were rare. I always felt waves of uptightness coming from Mad Dog whenever too much focus was put on this area. It was as if the rape of yesteryear came creeping into the room and contaminated everything in its tracks.

"Please don't be afraid, darling," I wanted to whisper. Of course I never really said that as it would make me sound like a queen. Or like Marlene Dietrich.

Sometimes when I would look at him sprawled out on my bed I'd get the feeling that he wanted me to overpower him and that somewhere in his twisted psychology he had a desire to be forced into submission. I felt that a part of his psyche was still feeding off the rape experience. The imprint of that had an S&M cast; he would never admit to it or talk about it but just watching him sometimes I'd feel something in him reaching out to me from 'underneath,' an unspoken forbidden thing that caused me to at least think of doing something I would never normally do.

Mad Dog always refused to climb on top of me and feed me his cock in the doggie position I loved so well. I know the reason for this: the pro-active pose was too involved; it showed a positive participation whereas Mad Dog saw himself as a completely passive partner who was only doing it for money. To climb on me and assume a "mounting" pose aped the role he took with girls. I know he felt it would have put him into a different category. Still, I'd ask him from time to time if he wanted to climb up this way and he always told me that he didn't like it.

Out of respect for "The Son of Satan," I would remove the crucifixes and icons from my wall whenever Mad Dog came over. I don't know why I went to such lengths. One time I hid the crucifixes under the seat cushion of my favorite chair. When Mad Dog came over he instinctively went for this chair but when he started to sit down he looked at it as if something was wrong and then grabbed his ass as if something had pained him. I later told a friend, "I think I have a devil on my hands."

He feels crucifixes even when they are hidden under seat cushions!"

Sometimes when I was blowing Mad Dog I wanted him to move his body in fast thrusting motions. He habit was to lay as still as a corpse. I'd prompt him with my free arm and yank his body back and forth as I sucked him. Then I'd stop the motion to see if he'd continue on his own but this never happened. I wanted him to show some passion and enthsusiam, to fuck my mouth with jack-rabbit energy but this he never did. My forcing the motion was the only thing that did the trick.

There were moments of genuine affection between us. After sex I'd rub his back; tell him how beautiful his body was; offer to make him a sandwich; tickle him—anything to get a reaction. Although I could get him to smile and sometimes break his pattern of doing and saying everything in monotone, he would always remain fixed in a fairly depressed state.

He often said that people were after him. That this or that person wanted to kill him. So-and-so wanted to break his legs. Sometimes he'd show up at my place with bruises on his body. These marks were from the mash pit at South Station but sometimes they were from actual fights. He'd jump into the mash pit when he was clubbing and get pushed around by other kids; sometimes he'd get stomped. His body was so small and fragile it's a wonder he didn't break bones. Usually I couldn't see these so-called "hurt spots," but he'd insist that they were there, or that he could feel them. Generally, he was always having accidents. He'd slip off his skateboard or run into a car while riding his skateboard.

One time when he lived in a neighborhood far from mine and didn't have any money to come to my place on the bus or subway, I told him to just ride over on his skateboard. The bonus, of course, was the ten or fifteen dollars I'd pay him after our sex session as extra transportation money. But when he arrived all he could talk about was how a car had plowed into him and knocked him on the street. He said he was hit in the ribs and that the pain was really intense—but, it seemed, not intense enough to be taken to a hospital.

"Look, you shouldn't take chances with your ribs. That's dangerous," I told him. Of course, I knew I'd have to be careful making love. Mad Dog was unusually sensitive. If I sucked too hard, he'd wince and say that I was hurting him. If I buried my head into his balls or sniffed his ass too passionately, he'd say my beard was hurting him. My beard? I can barely grow a beard, and my skin is almost translucent, like Pope Pius XII's. If I wrapped both arms under his back while grinding on top of him, he'd say that his ribs were hurting. So I had to be careful for the longest time.

One time Mad Dog was living with a friend in an apartment house downtown. He was living rent free, as usual, and spent his days there alone although he never knew when his friend would come home. The friend had two part-time jobs and was involved in some shady city deals, so there was a lot of traffic going in and out of that apartment. Mad Dog called me from this place one afternoon and said he wished he could come see me but that he had to stay put because the apartment security guard had banished him from the building and didn't know he was living there. It seemed his roommate had let a number of people live with him and the guard was told to keep an eye open. I told Mad Dog I'd visit him. Since I had lived in this apartment house when I first moved downtown, I knew it well. Mad Dog was on the fifth floor whereas I had once lived on the sixth floor, so I felt quite at home revisiting the place.

The apartment, as I expected, was a mess. Dirty dishes were piled sky high in the sink. Trash and papers of all sorts were scattered in the living room. Dirty clothes were heaped in large bundles. A soiled bed sheet doubled as a curtain and covered the apartment's two small windows. The large double mattress on the floor had more soiled sheets twisting every which way.

Mad Dog secured the lock and then wrote a handmade sign and posted it outside the door in case his roommate came home. It read: "I'm having a business meeting. Please knock--be patient." Both of us were afraid that the roommate would walk in unannounced and see me blowing him. I certainly didn't want that to happen. To be safe, we had to hurry. Mad Dog put on a porn video and turned the sound down low. It was the one and only time we had sex watching a porn video. It was straight porn, with lots of big-busted girls getting fucked.

Then Mad Dog stripped and lay on his back on the mattress. I took off my clothes and climbed on top of him. I began to obsess on his beautiful body, thanking God for the opportunity to screw this beautiful Son of Satan.

Mad Dog, as usual, did nothing except lay there with a glistening hard-on. When I sucked him, I noticed that he was harder than usual, which I attributed to the grunts of the porn queens who were getting fucked in the ass and loving it.

The tension of not knowing when the roommate would enter made the sex very exciting. When Mad Dog came, it was one of his bigger explosions. His semen was everywhere. On the pillows. On my forehead. On his chest. The room reeked of a young man's sweat, chalk, and musky ass.

After he came, I asked Mad Dog to turn over so that I could look at his wonderful ass. He did as he was told. I spread his legs so that I had an easy thoroughfare. Mad Dog's ass was to be "savored," not consumed in a hurry, like eating chop suey. I put my nose to the crack and inhaled the musky aroma. I felt his cheeks contract (memory of the rape) as I inserted my tongue half an inch inside. He had a pure, foresty taste; a truly delectable boy rump. I was beside myself, what with the new surroundings and Mad Dog's rump propped up like pork loin. I pushed my tongue way in and rotated it round and round; I was hoping to get a sound out of him and make him like the porn queens but no such luck. He lay there like a patient etherized upon a table.

But I didn't care. I could no longer hold back: I exploded all over the side of the mattress. I really wanted to explode on Mad Dog's ass, or better yet, slightly inside the crack. That would be heaven. In my intoxication—and to my embarrassment, I must say—I felt some of the "uplift" the rapist must have felt. I loved having sex with this guy, no question about it. He was worth every dime of the ten or fifteen dollars I was about to give him. He was worth almost every risk.

When I left the apartment building, my nose and mouth were filled with the taste of his body. I purposely did not wash up before I left so I could savor the after-aroma. We beat the roommate; we had sex on the run. Mad Dog called me one week later.

"Hey, this is Mad Dog. Can I come over?"

I never once said no. Often I thought about swallowing him but for some reason I could never actually do that. I would toy with the idea while sucking him and then when he was about to come I'd always remove my mouth. But a couple times I told him not to say anything when he came and to just let me guess. Those were the times when he squirted cum over my lips or on the roof of my mouth.

I knew I was falling for him when I'd repeat his name over and over while I was blowing him.

"Mad Dog, Mad Dog, Mad Dog!"

I felt that a part of him must have been falling for me because of the regularity of our contacts. He was calling at least once a week; sometimes twice. The weeks turned into months, the months into a year and a half. There might be random weeks when I did not see him but he'd always get around to calling. And when he said he was on his way over he never stood me up, which is a lot more than I can say for the gay boys I've met on chat lines.

I should have sensed that the end was near when he told me that he'd met a woman who was paying him to have sex. Turns out, she was dominatrix. I couldn't believe it: A woman, especially such a woman, paying for sex? Wasn't that a gay thing? I felt only jealousy but I knew I couldn't let Mad Dog know. After he told me this he came around for a while but eventually he stopped returning my beeps and then his beeper was tuned off. He called me once—it was a fluke since I hadn't paged him—but told me that he'd dialed the wrong number. "But I'll call you when I get into the city anyway," he said. I believed him.

"What did he do to you?" I asked a caller who said he had seen my poster. The voice on the other end of the phone was excited. "He blew up my VW van. I gave him a job at the South Station. He was a sweeper; he cleaned up the place, you know. Sometimes he stored empty bottles in the recycle bin. He helped set up. My wife liked him—at first. She felt sorry for him. You know, misunderstood poet, struggling artist. Then she caught him giving away liquor. We fired him and he came back and blew up my van. I'll take his legs off the next time I run into him. Little fucker."

I took down the guy's number and said I'd get back to him if and when I ran into Mad Dog. Poor Mad Dog. The whole city was after him. He was hated all right, but girls could not forget him. One taste of his body meant that you were addicted forever.

Then I bumped into him when I happened to be with two gay acquaintances. When he saw me I saw a look of panic cross his face. I was shocked to discover that he knew both the people I was with. They greeted one another like old friends, saying, "Where have you been?" and all of that.

Later I discovered that they never had sex with Mad Dog and that they were actually friends of friends and didn't know him all that well. In any event, Mad Dog told me once again that he'd call me when he came into the city.

That was two months ago and I've heard nothing from him since. The adjustment has been hard: I still think of his boy's body, his wonderful chest and his otherworldly behind. I can't believe he's gone. He didn't have to leave. I would have given him a raise; I would have altered the pork loin rump prop that made him think of the rape. I would have done almost anything. He didn't give me a chance; he just blew the joint without looking back.

But as I tell the others who keep calling me from the posters, "What else can you expect from the Son of Satan?"

The Divinest Boy: This delicious faux photo of Leonardo DiCaprio from the Internet served as the inspiration for the ollowing story, in the same way that watching Leonardo in "Total Eclipse" did it for the author of the preceding story.

THE DIVINEST BOY

John Patrick

"Bosie, where have you been?" complained Oscar.
"Don't be so pathetic," sneered Bosie.
"I've found you the divinest boy!"
-An exchange in the film "Wilde"

"Oh, c'mon," Alberto said. "Why did we bother to come out here anyway? A little change would be good for us."

We were on vacation, traveling from Miami to Tampa and we had stopped at the only gay bar listed as being in Naples. For some odd reason, Alberto thought that finding a partner for us to share would be easier in a little town. God knows, if the size of the town had anything to do with it, it would have been much easier in Miami. No, this was about Alberto watching me have sex with a stranger, and I had managed to avoid it for a year. If this was about me having sex, I wanted it to be on my terms, not Alberto's. Now here we were at another crossroads. We arrived to find the bar closed. Not closed permanently, just CLOSED MONDAYS, as the sign on the door read.

"Is it Monday?" Alberto said, standing there with his hands on his hips. "Is it fucking Monday?"

"It is," I assured him, "Monday. Yesterday was Sunday, remember?"

"This is just fucking great." He kicked the door with an unsatisfying thump. "Now what?" Alberto folded his arms.

"I'd say we find a liquor store, then find a motel."

"Shit," Alberto said, kicking the door one final time.

We found a liquor store and a nice motel with a huge pool. We were the only ones there for a long time, enjoying dips in the pool between tumblers full of rum and Coke.

At one point, Alberto went to get ice and he came back not only with a bucket overflowing but with a youth in tow. Alberto explained they had struck up a conversation at the ice machine. It was obvious to me why Alberto done so: the boy, who was skinny, barely legal and even younger than me, wore a Speedo that left little to the imagination. He wasn't the cutest guy perhaps, but he seemed pleasant enough. He said his name was Chris and he was a college freshman, on his way to his grandparents' place after a few days of spring break in Fort Lauderdale. To me, he looked as if he were still in high school and not of legal drinking age in Florida, but Alberto immediately poured him a drink.

I proceeded to get drunk, of course, which is everyone's excuse for the fuck they might regret or want to pretend to forget.

Chris was quite a swimmer and I leaned back and enjoyed the sight of him diving in and getting out of the water, and swimming lap after lap.

At one point I realized Alberto was looking at me looking at Chris. "What?" I barked.

He gave a little smirk. "You're so ... into this. Your eyes are bugging out of your pretty head."

"Give me a break," I said.

"Oh, I intend to, darling."

I was shaky, in need of a little assistance when I stood up, finally, after sitting so long and having way too much to drink. I let Chris help me, and Alberto went before us, opening the door to our room. Chris hesitated at first, but Alberto practically dragged him in and closed the door behind us.

I fell on the bed and Chris just stood there until Alberto threw him a towel. "You want to take a shower?" he asked.

"I'd really better be goin'," Chris said, fumbling with the towel. "Really."

My head had begun to clear a bit, and I knew that if I was going to do anything, I had to make my move. Alberto wanted it and now I wanted it too—and we had my ideal stranger right here in the room with us.

I rolled over and fell off the bed. On my knees, I scrambled over to Chris. "Will you let me kiss that nice dick goodnight?"

Chris backed up, and his ass hit the doorknob. "What?"

"C'mon, don't be shy. Anybody who wears a bikini like that is proud of what they have."

Chris pushed me away, but gently. I fell right back on him, tugging at his Speedo. Chris relaxed. I pushed down his Speedo to reveal a truly beautiful erection. I don't know how else to describe it. Neatly circumcised, his cock curved upward at a graceful angle and had a certain symmetry about it. The sight of it made my mouth water and my ass ache. I thought about all the dreams I'd had of this other person who was fucking me in the dark while Alberto watched. But I wanted a cock that was different than Alberto's, and this was it. A blond boy instead of my dark, hairy Latin lover. Yes, now I could see the tool for the job and I wanted it—desperately. All right, I'd had enough. I'd tortured myself long enough. And I was drunk enough. I reached a hand to the shaft pointing toward me and gripped it gently in my fingers. It felt rigid but velvety, and I tugged him closer to me.

Chris, stunned, was staring down at me now, this total stranger wanting his penis, wanting it madly. His gaze flickered from my face to his cock sheathed in my hand. Then he turned to look at Alberto. Alberto got up. "Three's a crowd," he said, and went into the bathroom.

Chris took my hand off his cock and pushed me slowly but firmly back onto the bed. He climbed on top of me, his cock pressing hard against my butthole, and said, "Okay, you want me? I only do it one way."

"What do you mean?"

"I mean, I can only do it like this," he responded, rolling me onto my back, "as if you were a bitch."

"Okay," I said, smiling.

He started by stripping off my swimsuit. Then he lifted my knees and spread my thighs. "Oh, god, you got a nice pussy here." He ran his hands up my thighs but did not touch my cock. He spit on his fingers, then slid them down into my asshole. I thrust my hips up a little at him, wanting to feel him in me. He ran his finger around in a circle and I moaned.

"You want my cock, don't you?"

I groaned, "Yes. Oh, god, yes!"

He got up on his knees but kept fingering me. "Look at me, man. Look at my nice cock."

I smiled. God, it was a nice cock. Such a *nice* cock! Not large, but perfect. It was easy to worship this cock. It was redder now, flaming in fact, and I wanted to touch it, to lick it, to wet it, get it ready for shoving inside me. I lifted up and he brought it to my lips. I kissed it, then took the head in my mouth.

His finger made deeper circles. "God, you're tight, so tight.

Are you sure you can take it?"

"Yes."

"All of it?"

"Oh, yes. I'm used to big ones."

"All seven and a half inches of it?"

"God, yes," I said. "It's at least all of that, Chris."

He pulled his fingers out and got off the bed for a moment. He saw the condoms Alberto had left on the nightstand and he put one on his erection. He returned to kneeling between my legs. If anything, his cock looked bigger now that he'd slid the rubber into place. He pressed the head against my asshole and rubbed it back and forth there, smearing the lube around. Then he sank in about a half an inch. "Okay?"

"What?"

"It's what I say to every pussy I fuck. I don't go any farther 'til I hear it from you that you want me to. That you are absolutely sure you want to go through with this."

"Oh, for chrissakes, yes," I said, and I put a hand on his chest and stroked the fine hairs there.

"Really?"

"Oh, god...."

"You want me to fuck it until I'm satisfied?"

"Yes! Yes!" I tried to pull him down onto me. He held off for a second, but I wrapped my legs around him and pulled another inch onto me. He let his weight drop then and, as I fell back onto the mattress, he sank into me. True to his word, he began to grind. It was a tight fit, but I didn't mind. I sucked in my breath as he doubled his speed, slicking in and out fast, slapping our bodies together on the springy bed.

"Oh, yeah, you like that don't you?"

"Oh, yeah," I gasped. The angle and the rhythm and the speed and the duration all worked together and I began to come. I tried to hold back, but it was no use. The orgasm had been building since the moment I laid eyes on Chris, and letting it all out just seemed like the natural thing to do. And somewhere in the midst of all the noise I was making, the kid came too.

I blanked out for a while. Then, blissed out, lying there in a wet, happy heap, I managaed to forget who we were, where we were, why we were here. It wasn't until the kid pulled away and began peeling the condom off that I stirred. Then Chris said, "I wonder where Alberto got to?" Now I came back to reality. I realized I hadn't noticed Alberto wasn't there, watching the drama he had so carefully orchestrated. I looked toward the bathroom door; it was open a crack. Yes, I figured, he had been watching after all, seeing the fuck reflected in the mirror over the desk. "Come on out, Alberto."

Sheepishly, Alberto came back into the room. We eyed each other, wary now. I found myself staring into those dark, once more questioning eyes, a little apprehensive perhaps. The haughty smirk was gone; his lips pressed together in a thin, tight line. He stood facing me, his slender fingers played nervously at the bulge in his swimsuit.

"I've been waiting for you to fuck it," I said curtly. "What have you been doing?"

"Well, you were having so much fun, I didn't want to interrupt."

"We're done now, so stick it in."

Alberto looked at Chris, who was leaning next to me, nervously playing with the spent condom. His eyes were on Alberto as my lover slowly tugged the suit down and kicked it off his feet.

"Oh, god," Chris gushed when he saw Alberto's cock. I saw a new respect creep into his eyes. Although Alberto is not a handsome man, he does have a firm, muscular body and the biggest cock I have ever seen. It measures eleven inches and is very thick. Chris was astonished by it. His lips parted, but no sound came out. I waited, tense and keyed up, scarcely dating to breathe. Alberto's giant cock swayed seductively as he made his way forward, finally to kneel between my parted legs and he stopped there, stopped there to look at me, then at Chris. I couldn't help smiling as I looked down at Chris's hand. This self-proclaimed hetero stud was about to touch my lover's cock! Grinning, I reached down to fondle Chris's sopping cock, savoring the feel of it.

Chris was beginning to respond despite himself. His eyes had become curiously vacant as I slowly rubbed his cock while he stroked Alberto's. He let out a long, shivering breath as, using both hands now, he was mauling the cock.

"You like that, don't you?" I demanded with sudden

vehemence.

"Ooooohh ... yessssss!" Chris hissed through clenched teeth. "Ohmygod... yessss. I've never seen anything like it." His voice trailed off, low and throaty.

I let him go with a vicious twist of my hand, and his renewed erection swayed seductively. His shoulders heaved as he leaned forward with bowed head, panting. With a single thrust, Alberto shoved the cock at Chris's face and the head bounced off his cheek.

"Go on, it's okay," I said, holding the back of Chris's head steady. "Nobody here but the three of us. Go ahead, kiss it."

"No," he complained. "I just wanted to...."

Alberto took over, holding Chris's head as he peeled the foreskin back and exposed the enormous cockhead. He steadied the cock with one hand while he guided Chris's mouth to it. Chris tried to pull away. "You want to see what it would be like, I know," Alberto said.

"No, no," Chris protested.

But Alberto was intent on humiliating this stud. "Come on, open wide. As wide as you can..."

My eyes were soon glued to the sight of Chris's mouth wrapped around the cockhead. He nodded as Alberto slowly slid inch after inch into Chris's by-now-accommodating mouth.

The face-fuck that followed was a sight to behold. Chris gagged several times but stuck in there, even taking Alberto's hairy balls in his hand and playing with them while Alberto slid the cock in and out. The saliva was flying all over by the time Alberto decided enough was enough. "Now I'm going to fuck my boy while you watch me. You're gonna like this..."

"Oh, yesssss, I want to see that!" Chris said. But his hand stayed on the cock. He was surprisingly reluctant to give up the prize.

I was ready for it now. All my inhibitions had melted away. I had never imagined I would enjoy it this much, sharing Alberto. I got into position. Chris's hand did not leave the cock; in fact, he helped Alberto stretch a condom over it. Normally he didn't use one when he fucked me but I knew there was a reason he was using one now, a reason that would soon become evident. Chris followed the upward curve of the cock as it entered my ass.

"Oh ... baby, you've got such a perfect little ass," Alberto breathed. "I love fuckin' it...."

"Oh, yes, he does. It's a beauty. And so tight," Chris affirmed.

I stiffened, lying tense and expectant as I always did when Alberto began the fuck. I knew how much it hurt when it was first thrust into me. Then a single exquisite thrill shot through me. Alberto was half-way in and Chris's lips were on my hurting behind. I felt the cool slither of the tongue licking me, lapping up the creamy smooth curves of my ass that clenched in pure delight as Alberto drove the cock home. I couldn't help squirming excitedly, rubbing my cock as the two men were electrifying me, one with his kisses, the other with repeated stabs of blinding pleasure. The velvety wet feel stopped momentarily, and suddenly Chris was in me again. I spread my legs to provide even greater access to Chris's skillful fucking. I felt suddenly, gloriously, free. My legs spread even wider in happy exultation.

Now Alberto's tongue was on me and I sighed as Chris burrowed into me. My head was thrown back, my jaws clenched against the maddening thrusts of pure pleasure. They were driving me wild, and they both knew it. It would not be long before my own raging lust would be out of all control once again.

Alberto scrambled off the bed and ran his flattened tongue into Chris's exposed asshole. Chris arched up and tight little whimpers escaped from his pressed lips. In a heated rush, Alberto entered Chris's tender butt, and Chris groaned. He opened his eyes and looked down on me with hard, cold, desperate eyes. I smiled. Then he reached for Alberto in a vain attempt to restrain him. Alberto was not about to stop humiliating this boy once more. He showed no mercy, and Chris was pushed down on top of me by the sheer force of Alberto's full entry. As Alberto tore into Chris, Chris kissed me full on the mouth. And I accepted the kiss, letting my mouth fall open. Soon our tongues were dancing in an exuberant *pas de deux.*

"Oh god, yeah," Alberto breathed, kissing Chris's back, hungry for him, moving with a mounting intensity, a terrible urgency. Chris pulled up as the cock slid all the way in. Then

I was being kissed again, hard, and this time I returned the kiss with even more vehemence, thrusting my tongue into Chris's mouth, reaching out to clasp the hot, writhing body to my own.

Totally enthralled by the searing sight of raw lust, of Chris and me squirming on the sheets, our bodies writhing in a passionate embrace as Alberto fucked. It was as if Alberto was fucking both of us at once.

"Ohh," Alberto breathed, a long deep sigh that turned into a low plaintive moan as he continued to jam his cock in, getting a tight grunt from Chris.

"Oooooh ... yes ... yes ... yes," I mumbled, tossing my head from side to side each time my big-dicked lover jammed the stiffened cock deeper into Chris and came.

Alberto pulled out and Chris stepped up his pistoning of my asshole.

Alberto dropped down beside us. "You love it, don't you, you slut?" he spat at me all the while Chris was fucking me. I could do no more than whimper.

"Say it ... say it ... say 'Fuck me, Chris,'" Alberto screamed at me, twisting his hand, stroking my cock.

"EEEEh ... eeeeh, ooooh, yes ... fuck meeeee!" I whispered urgently, pleadingly. And Chris, driven crazy with passion, obliged happily, thrusting into me in a frenzied blur of motion till I was twisting and raising my hips off the mattress, arching up with every fiber, straining as I was suspended in the air for an impossibly long moment. My hips bucked furiously as Chris tore into me, a wild stud, his own excitement raging out of control. We raced together to a mutual orgasm that had both of us thrashing about uncontrollably and reanimated Alberto's semi-hard penis which now rose up in proud salute of our performance and began gushing cum.

Gasping, I let my head fall back on the pillows and closed my eyes. Chris pulled out of me and went to the bathroom. Then I felt my lover's lips as they paid their obsequious devotion. Satisfied at last, Alberto smiled and said,"That was a divine boy. Divine! Two divine boys...." He wrapped me in his arms and held me tight. I hated to admit it to Alberto but it had been worth the trip after all.

BOYS LIKE HIM

Barry Alexander

Cody's heart pounded as he drove down Sixth Street. He was going to do it. He was actually going to do it. A delicious shiver of excitement ran down his spine. His cock stirred inside his jeans, but his mouth was dry and sweat dampened his arm pits. He was overwhelmed by his own sense of wickedness. He swallowed hard when he saw all the cars parked outside the Adult Emporium. Cedar Rapids wasn't that far from rural Hazleton. Oh God, what if there was someone he knew inside?

But most of his friends would be at work or out in the fields cultivating while the weather held. Which is what his folks thought he was doing while they spent the day at his uncle's farm. Reassured, Cody flipped on his turn signal and glanced in his mirror. There was a pickup right behind him. A lot of his dad's friends drove pickups. What if they told on him? His dad would kill him if he found out. Panicked, he turned off the signal and kept driving. The truck pulled up beside him. Nervously, he glanced at the driver. It was no one he knew.

Cody circled the block, determined to stop this time. If someone saw him, they saw him. Ever since he'd heard of this place, he'd waited for his chance to see it. He'd worry about an excuse later.

He parked beside a van so his car wouldn't be visible from the street. Gravel scrunched under his boots as he crossed the parking lot. A car door slammed and he jumped, tugging his baseball cap down as a rusty Chevy rattled past.

Cody came to an abrupt halt outside the door. He hadn't expected the sign—WARNING! YOU MUST BE 21 TO ENTER. What if they ID'd him? He would die of embarrassment. He hesitated. Then he took a deep breath and pushed the door open. Fuck it! He hadn't come all this way to turn back now. He was an adult, damn it! He had a right to be here.

The Emporium was brighter than he had expected, more open. He took a deep breath, expecting the scent of wickedness and brimstone, but all he smelled was Pine Sol. Cody moved inside, tripping over the doorway. The men perusing the shelves didn't even glance up. Cody was too embarrassed to really look at them, but they were different than what he had expected, quiet, well-dressed, not at all like the dirty old men in raincoats he'd envisioned.

Two walls were lined with boxes of videos, the bright light reflecting off their plastic cases. In the middle of one of the walls was a curtained doorway, framed in marquee lights. Up by the cash register was a whole corner full of oddly shaped packages and boxes. Condoms and stuff, Cody supposed.

As if he had done this a hundred times, Cody walked boldly across the room to the videos. He didn't want a video; he'd never be able to play it on the family VCR, but all the other men were looking at the videos. He joined the silent line—studying the videos, keeping his distance, not looking at anyone. Naked women with humongous breasts sprawled across the boxes, legs spread wantonly. Cody felt a little dizzy. He glanced quickly down the aisle, but all he saw was a giant wall of pussy, pink and pulsating.

Maybe this store didn't even have gay stuff. Maybe they kept it segregated, hidden behind that curtain, so that everyone would know you were queer. He picked a video off the shelf and turned it over. There was a man. Cody couldn't see much of him, his crotch was covered by the long, wavy hair of the blonde going down on him. He slid the video back and picked up a couple more. He could see the back and shoulders of a naked man as he humped a woman. Cody's breath quickened. He could see the dimples in the man's butt, the dark hair shadowing his cleft, and the base of the man's cock, fat and veiny as it plunged inside the angry red cunt.

There must have been hundreds of videos. Blondes, Hispanics, Oriental, African-American—every kind of woman a man could want—if he wanted a woman. But Cody didn't.

Just when he was beginning to think there was nothing in the store for him, he found a single shelf of gay videos. No one seemed to be watching, so he pulled one out. He couldn't believe it: men sucking men, men fucking men, naked men posing with big, thick hard-ons. Oh God, yes! This was what he'd hoped for. Eagerly he grabbed the next box. The men were even better looking, smooth-chested golden men, bulging with muscle, smiling proudly as they displayed rock-hard erections. Cody felt like he'd died and gone to heaven.

Cody had known guys did stuff like this—guys in California, guys in the big cities—not regular guys like him. Somehow it had never seemed real. But to actually see it! To see the faces of real men touching each other, loving each other. And they seemed so comfortable with it, like it was the most natural thing in the world. Cody guessed maybe it was—for guys like him.

As Cody reached for another box, a man rounded the corner and started down his aisle. Cody jerked his fingers back as if they had been burned. Quickly he grabbed a box depicting two women going at it. Cody pretended to be interested. He started moving down the row again, pulling out boxes at random.

As he moved along, he spotted the magazine rack towards the front of the store. A guy was checking out the rack, so he kept looking at the videos, waiting for him to leave.

When he reached the lighted doorway, Cody glanced inside, startled to see a man slouched against the wall, studying him. He was an ordinary-looking guy, tall and lean with the unmistakable bulge of a long cock riding his thigh. For a moment, they made eye contact. The man jerked his head towards the darkness behind him. "Wanna see a movie?" he asked softly.

Cody shook his head and hurried past; he was relieved when the man stayed in the shadowy alcove. Cody wasn't ready for anything that daring yet.

When he saw the merchandise beside the register, Cody couldn't believe his eyes. Cocks! Dozens and dozens of cocks! Cocks with balls. Cocks without balls. Vibrating. Pulsating. Toy-sized. Horse-sized. Ribbed. Knobbed. Veined. Flesh-toned latex. Hot pink jellied. Metallic gold. Cocks of every color and persuasion. Awesome!

And that was just the beginning: handcuffs, cockrings, flavored oils, chocolate sauce, feathers, whips, inflatable dolls—male and female, edible underwear, nipple clamps, glow-in-the-dark condoms, dog collars, plastic vaginas, chain-link jock straps. Things that looked like his mother's cookie press. Strings of giant plastic beads. Pink plastic mushrooms with pointy caps. Cody asked himself, *What the hell were you supposed to do with this stuff? Did they give instructions?* No one was watching so he flipped a package over, but the back provided no clues. Puzzled he hung it back up, then he saw the stocking tag—anal plug. Blood rushed to his face. He pictured a naked guy bending over, spreading his white cheeks, and shoving one of those plugs up his butt. Did men really do that? Were men walking around wearing these things all day under their business suits? But they were huge. God, some of them looked like they would stretch a horse.

Cody had no idea this kind of stuff even existed. Who would have the nerve to buy it? Did respectable people have this stuff hidden in their closets, tucked away in the sock drawer? Did the banker keep butt plugs in his bureau? Did the dentist have a dong in his desk? Maybe he wasn't the only one who had a secret life.

No one was looking at the magazines, so Cody wandered over. His heart pounded in anticipation. But the magazines were as bad as the videos—all devoted to the glories of straight sex: *Big and Busy, Naughty Nurses, First Time Foxes*. Disappointed, he tried the other side.

There they were! A whole shelf full of gay magazines—gorgeous guys smiling right at him. Hi! they seemed to say, We've been waiting for you. What took you so long? Cody felt a little dizzy. Hands trembling, he picked up a magazine. It was sealed in plastic so all he could see was the covers, but it was enough. His cock was pushing so hard against his jeans, he was sure everyone would see it. He could feel the dampness soaking his shorts and smell his own ball sweat. He wanted to study every issue, but he was afraid he would have an orgasm from just *looking*.

He wanted every single copy, but the magazines were expensive, and he only had twenty bucks. Which ones should he pick? While he was trying to make up his mind, another guy started looking at the magazines on the other side. Quickly, Cody grabbed the two closest magazines and hurried to the register. He was afraid the clerk would make some kind of comment, but the guy didn't even blink. "That'll be $14.74." Cody handed over the twenty. If he dug the change out of his seat cushions, he'd have enough for another magazine, but he didn't think he'd have the nerve to come back inside. He grabbed the black plastic bag and hurried outside before someone could stop him.

He'd done it! He'd actually done it! Cody felt a delicious thrill of decadence as he climbed back in the car. His insides were still shaking. His breathing didn't slow down until he was out of the city.

He couldn't wait to get back home. He was dying to look at the magazines. As he drove down the interstate, his eyes were irresistibly drawn to the discrete black sack lying beside him. He rested his fingers on the slick surface, imagining the gorgeous guys inside, just waiting for him. He checked his mirrors. Traffic was light; it couldn't hurt just to look at the covers.

Setting the car on cruise, he slipped the magazines out of the bag. The covers alone were enough to blow his mind. A man with smoldering eyes and dark rumpled hair lounged against a leopard skin couch, his gray long johns unbuttoned to reveal one nipple and the start of his bush. Indulge. Boy, did they have that name right. Cody could think of lots of ways he'd like to indulge himself with that gorgeous body.

The next magazine was even better: two really cute guys about his own age, bare-chested, one incredibly smooth, one a bit hairy. One guy pressed up close to the other, his arm around his shoulder, one finger just grazing the flat pink aureole around his nipple. *In Touch:* "Hold Me Closer," the cover demanded. Cody brushed his finger over the shrink-wrapped nipple. He could almost feel the little point rising to push against his fingertip.

Even the advertisements on the back covers were hot—a young guy talking on the phone, the cord coiled around his naked torso, one hand dipping into his low-riders. "Wanna Play With Me?" Oh boy, did Cody want to play with that guy. On the other, a bronzed young stud smiled at him, hands on hips, daisy dukes popped open: 1-888-BAD-BOYS was written right across his crotch.

Cody ached to release his cock. For a moment, he considered doing just that. Then he imagined trying to explain why his dick was hanging out to some hulking highway patrolman if he got pulled over. Strangely, that thought made his dick even harder, but Cody settled for giving the hard bulge a couple of consolation strokes. He'd just have to wait. Miles of farmland rolled past, exactly like the landscape around Hazleton, acres and acres of corn and soybeans and pasture. Cody didn't know how he was going to stand the hour's drive home with temptation right under his fingertips. He tried to concentrate on the scenery.

Funny, he thought, he'd never noticed how much silos looked like giant cocks—the smooth, round caps with the vertical slit, the long, thick pipe running up the side just like a fat cum tube.

The hell with the scenery, there was so little traffic, what would it hurt if he just glanced at the pictures? Fingers trembling with excitement, Cody ripped the plastic and slid out the first magazine. Driving with one hand, he flipped it open.

Holy shit! Cody thought. The first image was a real shock! A gigantic cock, corrugated with thick veins, jutted from the heavy bush of a man wearing some kind of crotchless leather pants. Black leather straps, studded with silver spikes, crossed his massive chest. Cody had never seen anything so decadent. The figure was almost repulsive, obscenely muscled, legs spread arrogantly, fist clamped boldly around his bloated cock. Cody couldn't look away. He felt a little queasy. The picture was harsh and brutal and incredibly exciting.

Arousal battled conscience. Before there was a clear victor, Cody heard the warning strips rattle under his tires. Quickly, he swerved the car back into the lane. He caught his breath when he saw how close he'd been to driving into a deep ditch. He could just hear the gossip at his funeral:"Did you hear how the Miller boy died? Ask Margie, I can't even say it, it's so disgusting. Well, no decent boy would do it. I heard he was looking at those kind of pictures. No, it was much worse than that—there weren't any girls—if you know what I mean. His family must be devastated!'

Cody flipped the magazine shut, but in spite of the voices, the images burned inside his head all the way home. He'd read enough that he knew liking men wasn't something he had any control over and right here in his hands he had proof that there were lots of other guys like him. He had no need to feel guilty, but he felt a secret pleasure, an intoxicating sense of wickedness at doing something that would shock all the staid, respectable people in town. And maybe they weren't so respectable! Somebody bought all that stuff in the Adult Emporium.

Even though he knew his folks should still be over at his uncle's helping out, Cody slipped the sack under his shirt before he got out of the car. He thought about going to his bedroom and locking the door, but it would be easier to explain hanging out in the barn than locking his door.

He climbed up to the hay mow, startling the sparrows that nested in the rafters. He grinned to himself; no one to shock up here. The loft was half-filled with green bales. Spears of sunlight, sparkling with dust motes, poked through the gaps in the weathered boards. The loading door was wide open, pouring golden light over the stacked bales. Cody arranged the bales to form a hard recliner.

Cody flipped through the magazines, dazzled by the words and images. Hard Cock. Dripping Prick. Tight Ass. Bold words. Provocative words. Words he had never dared say aloud blazoned across the slick pages. Photos of gorgeous models. Short stories. Advertisements for gay videos, gay sex toys, gay phone lines. Reviews of gay books. Classified ads from young guys looking for Mr. Right. Letters from horny young guys who boldly talked about doing the things Cody had only dreamed of and a few he had never imagined. It was amazing: a whole world devoted to guys like him. Cody felt like he had finally found the place he belonged.

He didn't know what to look at first. Every word, every picture sent blood surging through his cock. He couldn't decide who was hotter. Richard with his richly furred body posing on the spiral staircase surrounded by lush tropical plants. Blond beefcake Darien with the boy-next-door-smile and dragons tattooed on his smooth, golden skin. Cute Devon drowsing naked, his slender body arched over a rough boulder, hard cock shadowing his navel, legs and arms spread, totally open and exposed. Cody felt like he was at a candy store. Everything looked so good and so completely edible.

But as he looked through the pages, he kept returning to one set of images. The two cover guys together. It really got to him seeing two men with their arms around each other, touching each other, proud and unashamed.

Cody touched himself and felt his cock arch under his hand,

begging to be free. He unbuttoned his jeans, letting the zipper slide down on its own from the pressure of the urgent mass behind it. The warm pungent scent of trapped sweat and musk and piss mingled with the dry sweet scent of hay. Cody squeezed the thick shaft, delighting in its size and rubbery hardness. He'd drooled so much precum that he could see his raspberry pink glans clearly through the damp white briefs.

Cody raised his hips to slide his jeans down. He should have thought to bring a blanket, he realized, as the broken hay stems stabbed through his briefs. He wanted to take everything off, but if his dad came home early it would be much easier to just pull his jeans back up.

It took a minute to find the best position. Propping the magazine against his left knee gave him free use of his right hand. He unbent his cock and threaded it through the opening. It snapped erect, smacking against his hard stomach. Cody dug out his balls, spreading the loose pink bag over his briefs. He cupped the fuzzy globes in his hand and turned to his favorite guys.

He loved the first picture: Two beautiful men with jeans down around their thighs. One man was smooth-chested with a head of dark curly hair that Cody would have loved to run through his fingers. The man appeared to be shy, with a vulnerable expression. The other man appeared older, with an experienced, all-knowing look. He possessed a sprinkling of soft brown hair over his chest Both with sexy, deep brown eyes. The older guy stood behind the other, his arm resting on the other guy's stomach, his long, veiny cock just touching a rounded, blushing asscheek. Cody wanted to be both men. He wanted to run his hands over those rounded cheeks, to kiss the hollow above them, and trail his tongue up the curve of his spine. He wanted to feel the hot cock pressing against him, to feel the warm hand against his stomach.

Cody knew exactly how the younger guy felt in the next picture, sitting on the edge of a white fur-covered bed and staring longingly at the hard, slender cock still sheathed and waiting for his hot mouth. He'd never sucked a cock, but his mouth watered just thinking about sliding down that slippery prick.

There were several bedroom shots: on the bed, standing in

front of the window, looking at each other, looking at the camera as if they couldn't wait for the photographer to leave. What would they do when the cameras were off? Was it all just a job to them? Cody didn't think so. He thought he caught a look between them, a moment when they looked directly into the cameras as if they wished they'd disappear.

Cody was sure they would go someplace where they could be alone together, someplace where they could act on their desires, someplace with soft music, flickering candles, and total privacy. He could see them kissing each other, touching the secret places of each other's body with long, lingering caresses. If they fucked, who would offer up his ass to the other? Did it even matter? Which would feel better—the tight embrace of a hot ass around his penis or the surging fullness of a rigid cock driven deep inside his hungry guts? Cody couldn't wait to find out.

Cody wondered how it would feel to press his cock against those white cheeks. The picture was so sharp, he could see every hair. Holding the magazine in one hand, he laid his cock across the glossy page. He could almost feel the heat rising from that firm ass. He slid his cock across the page a couple of times, imagining that it was slipping up that dark channel. Would the fine hairs prickle or would they be smooth and silky? A clear stream of juice oozed out of his cock and slimed the picture. It looked so good glistening on those cheeks, Cody couldn't resist licking it off. The taste of his own juices was like a jolt of electricity right to his nuts. If he tasted this good, how would it be to taste another man?

The best, the absolute best was the two of them lying in each other's arms, their bodies relaxed and sprawled across the white fur spread. Their eyes were closed as if they had exhausted themselves with every possible pleasure, but their cocks were still hard, arching towards each other even in sleep. In a moment, they would awake and begin again.

If he were there, he would ease onto the bed quietly. He would lick up the inside of a hairy thigh, lap the smooth pink balls and suck them gently into his mouth. They would waken slowly, smile and encourage him to explore their beautiful bodies. He would lick nipples, nuzzle into the dark tufts under their arms, taste sweat and ball musk, explore all the secret hollows and crevices.

They would caress his body, holding him between them, their hands cupping his ass and stroking his cock. They would pass him back and forth between them, aiming his hungry mouth at hard shafts and tender balls as they made out above him. Holding and kissing each other, and finally pulling him up to join them, the three of them open-mouthed, two dueling tongues filling his mouth.

By some unspoken agreement, they knew exactly what he wanted -- everything. Sandwiched between two warm, beautiful bodies, Cody knew his dreams were finally going to come true. A dancing cock inches from his mouth. A long, hard cock plowing the furrow between the smooth white boulders of his ass. His cock imprisoned deep inside a hot mouth.

He wanted that cock so much he knew he would have no trouble swallowing it whole, just like the guys in the stories. The warm meat slid easily down his throat, and he remembered to swirl his tongue over the head and caress the man's scrotum, just like the man was doing to him.

The guy behind him sucked his ear lobe as he slid his cock along the sweat slick crevice. Do you want me to fuck you? he whispered in Cody's ear. Cody groaned in response. Say it! You've got to say it or I won't do it. "I can't." Yes, you can. It's easy. Just do it. Cody let the cock slip out of his mouth. "Fuck me! Oh God, please fuck me!"

All right! Cody! "Wait, you have to have protection." The guy touched Cody's ear and pulled a condom out of thin air. "Where did you get that?" It's your fantasy. Where do you think?

The huge cock slid as easily into his ass as the one packing his throat. Cody had never felt anything so wonderful. Then blond beefcake Darion and hunky Ricardo walked into the bedroom and put their bursting cocks into his hands. And Devon climbed over their tangled, sweating bodies to suck his nipples.

Wrapped in warm bodies, mouth and ass and fists filled with hard cocks, hands and lips and tongues on every inch of his body, Cody couldn't hold back.

Cody rolled the magazine around his bursting cock, rubbing it up and down over the golden flesh. His nuts tightened, sending fiery tingles up his shaft. He groaned and trembled as he shot all over the models, drizzling their picture=perfect bodies with thick splats of cum. He carefully licked every drop away, hoping he hadn't ruined the picture.

Cody spent a lot of time in the barn the next week, reading every story, looking at every picture, every ad. By the end of the week the pages were glued with cum and some of the pictures had been rubbed clear away. The pages were permeated with his own scent. Every time Cody picked up the magazine, he got hard just breathing in that pungent reminder of his own sex.

Cody had gotten off on the pictures, but it was the stories that really got to him. The models were gorgeous, but they were like movie stars, people you dreamed of, fantasized about, but could never touch or even hope to meet. The stories made the guys seem real, like people he could actually know and care about. They made him believe it was possible to be gay and happy, to find one special guy and build a life together.

Somewhere out there were thousands, no hundreds of thousands of guys just like him. Cody couldn't wait to meet the first one.

SEX WEEKEND

R.J. Masters

"I wasn't sure I could get away," Brian told me, as he entered the cabin. "I'm sorry I had to bring little Matthew with me."

"Oh, that's okay. It just makes our fishing weekend all the more innocent, bringing your kid brother along," I replied, resting my hand on his shoulder. "We'll just have to wait until he falls asleep tonight."

The truth was, I could hardly wait for bedtime—to get Brian alone. My balls were churning and my cock was lengthening into the leg of my tight jeans, making me very uncomfortable. It had been a while since we had gotten away together and despite the on-again-off-again nature of our relationship, I was faithful to Brian.

I watched Brian as he bent over and unrolled his sleeping bag onto the bunk, yearning to reach out and grab those firm, round buttcheeks and ram my hardness into the crevice between those inviting mounds.

"I want you so bad," I whispered. "It's been too long."

"I know. I can't wait to wrap my lips around your hot cock. But we've got to be careful that Matt doesn't see or hear anything. "

"We will, I promise," I reassured. "He won't see or hear a thing. But he went out to the truck for a minute, so come here. Let me have a quick kiss."

I wrapped my arms around his waist and crushed our bodies together. He pressed his lips to mine and let his tongue slither into my mouth. His swelling cockmeat pushed against the front of his jeans struggling to escape from its prison of denim. His breathing was ragged and his chest was heaving with the intense desire—need we both felt.

I unzipped my jeans and hauled out my aching boner, jamming it into his hand. His fingers circled the fiery flesh and gave it a couple of yanks.

"Oh man, I'm so horny," he groaned into my ear.

The sound of footsteps on the porch forced us apart. I

quickly stuffed my cock back inside my jeans and pulled up the zipper, as Matt entered the cabin.

"Aren't you ready for bed yet?" Brian asked.

"You know, we've got to get to bed early, if we want to catch anything tomorrow," I added.

"Yeah, just about," he replied, disappearing into the bathroom. "I thought I'd crash early so you guys could have some time alone," he added knowingly.

Brian and I looked at each other, then toward the bathroom door.

"What did you mean by that, 'Giving us some time alone?'" Brian called.

"Do you think I'm still just a kid, that I haven't caught onto what's going on between the two of you?"

"What makes you think anything is going on?" Brian demanded.

"I don't know. Maybe the way you look at each other, just like my friends Steve and Josh. To tell you the truth, I've even gotten in on the action a few times. So I know all about it. Now, if you don't mind, I'm going to take a shower and go to bed."

He grinned mischievously and disappeared back into the bathroom. Brian looked a little shocked, but finished making his bed, the bed we would share for at least part of the night.

"Think that was a hint?" I asked, looking toward Brian. He and Matt looked so much alike. They both wore their blond hair long and they both had the most intense blue eyes I had ever seen.

I could easily imagine what it would be like to enjoy both of their hard, sexy bodies—to be fucked by Brian while I savored Matt's young tasty cockmeat. Just the possibility made my cock ooze gobs of precum into my shorts.

But Brian didn't respond, just seemed to be lost in his own thoughts. I moved toward him, wrapping my arms around his waist. I didn't see any sense in playing games when everything was out in the open. Brian tensed, but he didn't push me away. I brushed my lips softly against his, then let my hand seek out his throbbing boner.

He moaned softly and humped against my hand. I couldn't wait any longer. I had to have him, wanted desperately to rip his clothes off and bury my cock in his hot tight manhole.

"You know, I'm glad we don't have to sneak around this weekend. It'll be a lot more fun, being able to relax. If only the rest of my family were *so* understanding," he whispered.

"You're just lucky to have someone like me who'll take it when he can get it."

He smiled and his hand groped my oversized basket through the stiff fabric of my jeans. "You're *so* hot, Greg. So *fuckin'* hot!"

"So are you, man."

He didn't resist, though he seemed a little nervous as I unbuttoned his flannel shirt. I licked my lips as I eyed his tanned, muscular pecs and large pink nipples. I pinched the rosy buds between my thumbs and forefingers causing them to harden immediately. He groaned as I pulled and twisted more roughly, sending waves of pleasure-pain through his sexy body.

"Geez, that hurts. Feels like you're gonna rip them right off."

"Yeah, but it feels good, doesn't it?"

He nodded, so I continued to tug and tweak them until they were bright red and rockhard. I ran my hand across his rippled abdomen, then followed the trail of dark hair to the waistband of his jeans. I fumbled with the buttons on his fly, finally gaining entrance and shoving them to the floor. He stepped out of them and I tossed them into the corner in a crumpled heap. His impressive cockmeat was tenting his white jockey shorts. I wanted to yank them roughly from his body—leaving him naked and vulnerable, while I remained fully clothed, but I did not. I wanted to savor each moment.

I dropped to my knees in front of him, licking my lips and teasing him even more. Then I wrapped my arms around his waist and shoved my nose into his groin, inhaling his masculine aroma. I cupped those sexy buttcheeks, massaging them through the cotton fabric, dragging them apart so I could run my fingers along his crack. Like a heat-seeking missile, I immediately located the entrance that led to the center of his being and pushed against the tight ass-ring, forcing my fabric-covered finger ever so slightly inside him. He moaned and began to hump my face, his hardened cylinder sliding alongside my nose.

"Suck it, please," he pleaded.

I wanted to oblige as my own cock was now leaking its juices through my undershorts and into the stiff denim of my jeans. An obvious dark wet spot was forming where the head of my cock was resting. I wanted him desperately, to strip him, to take his cock into my mouth and to fuck his tight ass. I had been fantasizing about this night for weeks, but now that he was here all I wanted to do was tease him—bring him to the brink of orgasm, then retreat. I wanted him to want it, to beg me for it, to know how badly I needed him. It had been too long.

I reached down and squeezed my meat, stroking my length, wishing it was his hand fondling me. I ached for his touch—yearned to taste him—to feel him fulfilling my every desire. Instead I let my teeth scrape across the pulsating mass of cockmeat, still sheltered by the white cotton. He moaned and thrust himself into my face harder than before. His huge thigh muscles tensed, his body nearly as needy as my own.

"Suck it, Greg. C'mon, don't be a tease," he groaned, his voice now hoarse with excitement.

I slipped my thumbs under the wide elastic band and inched his shorts down, first exposing the thick purple cockhead of his monster meat, then his curly blond bush, and finally his big, heavy ballsac. My pulse raced as I stared at the swollen tip, oozing its pre-cum. The skin was stretched taut along the engorged, throbbing shaft. It was so glorious I wanted to shove him to the floor in front of the roaring fire and impale myself upon his impressive sword but, instead, my fingers lightly caressed the fiery flesh, then pushed through the curly bush before cradling his lemon-sized jewels in my palm and rolled them gently.

I looked up into his eyes and could see the frustration—the desperate hunger growing. Without saying a word, he reached for his jacket and retrieved a handful of foil pouches and a tube of KY jelly. He lay the lube on the coffee table and handed me a rubber. "Safety first," he whispered.

I stood up, quickly shedding my clothing. I pressed my lips to his, driving his tongue into my mouth, while I crushed our hard bodies together, enjoying the familiar sensation of his stiff prick alongside my own. I could wait no longer. I dragged him to the floor, positioning him on all fours on an old patchwork quilt. He remained motionless as I slid a condom over my cock and greased his hole. In moments I was pushing against him, stretching the tight muscle ring until it gave way and admitted my thick cock into him. Deeper and deeper I plunged as he moaned and humped backward, grinding his ass into my groin so that my curly bush was mashed against his creamy mounds.

"Fuck me hard! Harder! Harder," he pleaded.

I couldn't help noticing Matt standing in the doorway as I rammed into Brian's hot ass. Matt dropped his towel and leaned back against the wall, his hardening cock in his hand. He was really getting off on watching us, and I was getting off on watching him watching us fuck. I wondered if Brian knew he was there, but doubted that he did. Brian almost always kept his eyes shut when we fucked. His clenched fist slid along the slippery stock as he coaxed himself closer and closer to explosion.

I gestured to Matt, inviting him into the room. He hesitated for a moment, then approached Brian. Brian looked up, seeming startled to see his brother standing naked before him. Matt aimed it toward his brother's mouth. I waited, anxious to see whether Brian would comply—would allow two cocks to slam into his body simultaneously.

Brian hesitated, staring at Matt for a moment.

"Come on, suck it," Matt pleaded. "I really need to get my rocks off."

I couldn't really see what was happening from my angle, but I could tell that Brian had relented. Matt wrapped his fingers in Brian's hair and thrust forward, so that Brian's nose was buried in Matt's golden bush. I pulled back, my thick cock retreating from his violated manhole, then slammed forward, again reinvading his ravaged flesh. I jabbed at the tiny fuckhole, harder and faster as my hot wad churned. My balls contracted against my body as I neared an explosive release.

I reached around his slender waist, pushing his hand aside, and let my fingers curl around his engorged stock, positioning my thumb on the pulsating vein just below the rim of his mushroom-shaped head. I squeezed hard, while I made one final lunge into his slick manhole. My load coursed through me and erupted into the tip of the latex sheath, causing it to swell in his belly.

"Oh, that was so fuckin' hot," I moaned, releasing my hold on his stiff cock.

When I looked up, I could see that Matt was coming. His muscles had tensed and his face was contorted as though he were in pain. His eyes were squeezed shut as his body began trembling uncontrollably. He kept his hold on Brian's hair until the every last moment when he released Brian and his huge load had exploded onto the quilt. Then he collapsed back into a chair. "Wow, that was hot," he sighed. "That was so hot, watching you fucking his ass, while I was fucking his mouth."

Meanwhile Brian rolled over, my softening cock sliding from his stretched manhole. He looked up at me, frustration and anger showing in his eyes. "Why'd you do that?" he demanded.

"I didn't want you to come yet," I answered honestly, as I slipped off my condom and wiped up with a damp washcloth.

Without saying another word, he reached out and grabbed me by the hair, forcing my face down into his groin. He seemed not to care that Matt was watching us. He was too horny and anxious to get his rocks off.

I pursed my lips and planted a kiss on the tender cockhead, letting my tongue push into the cloaked pee-slit, then began to lap at the smooth hardness of his length. He was so hot I could feel the heat through the rubber covering. He thrust his hips upward, attempting to ram it into my mouth, but I resisted--wanting to tease and torment my lover a little more before I allowed him release.

I gently slapped his horny cock, so that it bounced against his belly, then cupped those big hairy balls. He moaned as I rolled them and massaged them, carefully pushing them upward in the loose ballsac.

"Suck it Greg, please," he begged.

But I ignored him, continuing my torture. While I worked his balls, I let my left hand creep upward to lightly caress the bulging vein on his throbbing shaft.

Finally I lowered my lips and allowed his painful erection to slide into my warm, wet mouth. I swirled my tongue around the rim of his pulsating cockhead, then let it inch into my throat—swallowing the squirming cock.

His breathing was rough and ragged as I let his length slide into my gullet. I buried my nose in the coarse hairs of his bush, taking all of his solid cylinder and contracting my throat muscles around it. He thrust harder and faster until his balls began to shrink into his groin. I knew he was nearing climax and I was not yet ready to let him come. I wanted him to fuck me—to slam his hard, horny cock into my vulnerable flesh—to torture my body with his rough assault of my tight fuckhole.

I quickly pulled away, abandoning his horny cock and staring down at him. His muscular arm shoved me to the floor next to him and he expertly pinned my back to the floor, as he had done many times when we wrestled in high school.

"You think you're funny?" he demanded, anger flashing in his blue eyes. "We'll see how funny you think this is," he growled, moving between my thighs and driving his ungreased length into my hole in one quick lunge.

I yelped as the pleasure-pain swept through me, but he did not relent. He banged, harder and faster, with all the force of the sexual tension that had built up within him, and did not let up until the waves of ecstasy overtook him. He tensed and his entire body shuddered as the snake within me began to wiggle and twitch. When he was through coming, he collapsed on top of me, his menacing cock sliding from my raped manpussy. He mashed his lips against mine, kissing me passionately. I melted beneath him, wishing this moment would never end and that my valiant lover never had to leave my embrace.

"Oh man, I've never been fucked," Matt claimed in on our special moment. "Would you do me next time, Brian."

"Why not? You might as well learn from your big brother instead of from some stranger," he agreed. "But we ought to wait a while. Have a beer or two, then go another round? What do you say? Hell, you might even learn a thing or two from Greg, if you pay close attention."

Matt said nothing, but he seemed to agree, eagerly retrieving a six-pack from the fridge. I sat back and looked at the two of them, thinking how lucky I was. Our weekend had gotten hotter than I ever thought possible. Instead of one sexy blond bottom, I now had two to fuck.

WITHOUT YOU

R.J. Masters

"...Our kiss was long and filled with passion, as though we both had been waiting forever for this day...."

I stood on the steps of Peter's apartment for a few minutes before ringing the bell. *What if he were with someone, or just didn't want to be bothered?* I asked myself. We had been best friends, confidantes before he moved upstate to take this new job. But three months had gone by since then. We hadn't even talked on the telephone, I guess because we both knew it just wouldn't be the same.

But then everything in my life had seemed to be closing in on me. I had driven three hours to get here, needing desperately to speak to Peter. He always knew what to say to make me feel better. He never condemned or criticized—just listened. I knew I couldn't just turn around and head home without seeing him. I pushed the buzzer and waited. There was the sound of footsteps inside the tiny apartment, then the door opened and we stood face to face.

I felt awkward for a moment, then he smiled and wrapped his arms around me, pulling me inside.

"Marc, it's so good to see you. I missed you."

He still held me tight, his solid embrace making me feel warm and safe.

"I missed you, too," I confessed.

He closed the door and took a step back. "Why didn't you call? What's wrong?"

His dark eyes were warm and filled with concern.

"Cari and I broke up. This time it's for good."

"Well, it's about time."

I was shocked by his honest reaction. He had never said anything against her, despite the several times Cari had broken up with me, the many times I had cried on his shoulder. He had always been supportive and understanding.

"Things usually turn out the way they are supposed to. You said yourself you weren't happy, weren't satisfied. And you deserve a lot better than what you were getting from her."

"I don't know. There's always been something missing. Maybe it's because I just didn't love her enough."

"Maybe love didn't have anything to do with it," he replied, taking two beers from the fridge. "Maybe Carl just wasn't what you were looking for."

"Then how am I going to find out what I'm looking for?"

I sat down on the sofa feeling hopeless.

"You'll figure it out. Sometimes what you're so desperately searching for is right in front of you, has been all the time."

I heard his words, but they didn't sink in at that time. I still didn't make the connection between my loneliness, the terrible void in my life, and Peter's move.

He draped his arm around me and pulled me close. I rested my head on his shoulder like a little boy who was afraid and was seeking the safety of his father's arms.

I recalled the many times Peter and I had spent the weekend at my family's cabin at the lake. We guzzled beer and talked, just like we were doing now. I couldn't count the number of times we had fallen asleep in each other's arms.

"Things haven't been the same without you."

I was a little embarrassed that the words had come tumbling out like that. I knew he took this job because it was the offer of a lifetime—a chance to become state director of public safety. I didn't mean to make him feel guilty. I was relieved that he was no longer out on the streets, putting his life in danger every day. But I did miss his nightly visits, when he got off work at midnight and stopped by to chat. Lots of times I was waiting for him, wanting to tell him about something that had happened during my day.

"I know," was his only reply. He went to the fridge and got us a couple more beers. We talked about his job and how I was doing in school; then there was silence. I guessed he was feeling as good as I was, all snuggled up together on the couch. It wasn't long before we had both dozed off.

When I woke, the sun was just coming up. He was lying on his back, one foot draped over the back of the sofa and the other resting on the floor. I was sprawled on my belly between his tree-trunk thighs, my face resting only inches from his cock. His dripping cockhead had poked from the leghole of his shorts and was oozing pre-cum onto his bare skin.

I stared at his cock, wondering how it would feel to hold it in my hand. I looked up to be certain he was still asleep, then let my fingertips lightly stroke the hard, hot flesh. I inched my face closer to the deep red cockhead, brushing my lips across the very tip and smearing his sticky pre-cum. I licked my lips, tasting the salty liquid, then kissed his cock once again.

I pulled away when he stirred, not wanting to be caught in the act. When he snored and I knew he was still sleeping soundly, I again let my lips touch the spongy head. I let my lips caress the smooth skin, from the rim to the sticky, wet pee-slit. It felt so good that I drew it into my mouth, letting it rest on my tongue for a moment.

I sucked on the pulsating monster, letting my tongue swirl over and around it. I wrapped my fingers around the throbbing shaft and could feel each beat of his heart as the blood pumped through the bulging vein.

He moaned and squirmed in his sleep, while I continued to pleasure his monster cock. I loved the feel of the thick head and pulsating shaft sliding over my tongue. I devoured his throbbing meat like I was starved for cock. His hips thrust upward, pushing the spongy head even deeper into my throat. I gasped for air, then recovered. I picked up the pace, letting my head bob up and down as my lips caressed his cock from the gaping slit to the crumpled fabric circling the oversized base.

When his hand rested on the back of my head, my first instinct was to pull away. My heart thumped in my chest as I awaited his reaction. I let his cock slide from my mouth and looked up into his eyes. But the heat of embarrassment flooded my cheeks and I couldn't face him.

I didn't resist as his hand guided me gently back to the glistening cockhead. I knew I wanted to finish what I had started, to feel his hot cream exploding into the back of my throat. But I didn't know what he thought of me now.

Still I went to work in earnest, slurping hungrily on his slick cock. His throbbing boner pistoned in and out of my mouth until I could feel his cream shooting through the thick stem. I readied myself for the oversized load that was about to drown me, but still I was not really prepared.

I locked my lips around the twitching cockmeat, trying to

capture every drop of his tasty prize. But despite my best effort, some of his white cream trickled from the corner of my mouth.

I released his cock from between my lips, being certain I had licked it clean. Then I nuzzled my nose against the thick stem. I closed my eyes and lay there for a little while, thinking that I had never enjoyed anything so much. I had never imagined it would feel so good to have a hard cock plunging into my mouth. But it was, somehow, so incredibly satisfying.

"That was good," he said, his voice hoarse with excitement. He put his hands under my arms and pulled me close. He pressed his lips against mine and his tongue dove into my mouth, sending erotic shock waves through my body. My cock was already hard and pushing against the front of my jeans. I reached down and tugged at the annoying bulge, trying to make myself more comfortable. My cock ached for his touch, but I couldn't say the words. So I sat there, wishing he would reach out to me.

Without saying anything, he proceeded to unbutton my fly and let his hand slip inside my briefs. I moaned and humped upward as he made contact with my fiery flesh for the first time. His expert touch made my asshole twitch in anticipation.

"Oh man, that feels so good."

"That's nothing. You just lay back and relax. I'll give you a treat."

He stood up and yanked my jeans and briefs from my body, leaving me naked and vulnerable. He dropped to his knees on the floor. His lips inched slowly toward my throbbing cock. His hot breath caused goose bumps to spread down each thigh. Then his tongue flicked against my sensitive cockhead, sending jolts of pleasure ripping through my bloated ballsac.

"Suck it, please," I pleaded, unashamed of my body's desperate need.

But he ignored my impassioned pleas, giving his undivided attention to my crinkled ballsac. He sucked and lapped each tender jewel before drawing it into the warm wetness of his mouth. My body was on fire as he pleasured me in ways I never thought possible. No one had ever worked my balls the way he was doing, and that was only the beginning of the new sensations he was inflicting on my already-aroused body.

His tongue flicked against my tight, virgin manhole, then burrowed into the heat of my insides. The tiny snake wiggled and squirmed inside me, massaging my inner walls and teasing the previously untouched nerve-endings. I moaned and thrashed, my cock oozing a puddle of pre-cum onto my belly. I knew I couldn't hold off much longer.

Then his lips were wrapped around my aching cock, caressing the head and drawing it into his mouth. He let it slide deep into his throat until his nose was buried in my curly bush. Then he swallowed, contracting the powerful muscles around the throbbing intruder.

I couldn't wait any longer. My long pent-up load blasted into his throat. He swallowed quickly, consuming every drop. The second and third bursts were smaller, but he held on, devouring them as well.

He released my cock from his mouth and looked up at me. I could see that his hunger was still not satisfied.

"I want to fuck you," he whispered.

I could only nod my consent and watch as he smeared saliva on his oversized cockhead. I was so afraid, my heart began to pound wildly in my chest. I had never even finger-fucked myself when I jerked off. Now he was going to plow his cock into me. I took a deep breath, hoping it would calm my nerves.

He pushed gently, letting the massive intruder slowly stretch the reluctant muscle-ring. The initial wave of pleasure-pain shot through me, forcing the air from my lungs.

"It's going to be all right," he reassured. "Take another deep breath."

When I inhaled, he pushed harder and a couple more inches of his lengthy shaft invaded my body. He paused for a moment to allow me to become accustomed to the incredible fullness, then pushed again. I couldn't believe my tiny manhole was handling his oversized monster, but I had soon taken it all into my belly.

He began to fuck me, with long slow strokes, deliberately teasing and tormenting my tiny prostate. The thick intruder rubbed against it, each time it thrust forward and retreated. Again and again he pulled back and reinvaded my body. I couldn't believe it felt so good. My cock was once again hard and throbbing and oozing pre-cum.

His breathing was loud and ragged as he neared his second explosion. He pounded me harder and faster, so that his heavy ballsac slapped against my asscheeks. Each time he slammed forward, my cock bounced against my belly nearing an eruption of its own.

"You're so hot," he growled. "I've wanted you for *so* fuckin' long."

I blushed, though his words were reassuring. Then I felt it. His cock jerked and twitched in the limited space of my body and his hot cream exploded into my gut. That was all it took to send another load of my sticky goo shooting from my slit. My chest was spattered with white specks, while a stream of the hot cream dangled from my throbbing cockhead.

He collapsed on top of me, smearing my cream between us. His lips once again found mine. Our kiss was long and filled with passion, as though we had both been waiting forever for this day.

When I could finally speak, I asked him, "How come we never did this before?"

"Because you weren't ready. You had to discover your feelings for me on your own. I didn't want to push you into anything."

"But how did you know I'd come?"

"I could see it in your eyes, could feel it in the way you would snuggle against me, clinging to me in the night."

"I'm glad you waited."

"So am I. But then, I knew it would be worth it," he said, wrapping his arm around me and pulling my lips to his.

I kissed him back with a hunger, an urgency that almost matched his. I knew I was where I belonged and I never wanted to leave.

We fell asleep with his cock still buried deep inside me. I had finally figured out what was missing in my life and was sure I would never be dissatisfied again.

GOING WITH THE FLOW

David MacMillan

There was no way around it: I'd just been fucked! Mike's hard dick was still buried in my ass—his chest against my back, his pubes tight against my butt-cheeks, and his lips at my ear. My pole was half-hard and its head was trying to reach my belly button again through a puddle of my own spunk on the floor under me. Yeah, I was butt-fucked all right. Like one of those dick-crazy homos my father was always going on and on and on about.

"You going to let me up?" I asked, breaking into the silence between us carefully because I didn't know what this was going to do to our friendship.

"I like the way your ass feels on my meat, Gary."

"That's my butt you're talking about," I mumbled, feeling really unsure of myself.

He chuckled. "And my dick filling it up."

"So, take it out and let me get up."

"What's your hurry? They know each other now."

He was right—his dick and my butt did know each other. Intimately. Because, somehow, I'd screwed up royally and let myself get butt-fucked. I resigned myself to having him lie on top of me with his pole buried in me and tried to remember how I got into this mess. Mike and I were roommates at a small college in the center of Georgia this past year and we'd already taken an apartment together for next year.

We became best buddies from the get-go. We got along like brothers—maybe better, because we managed to avoid the petty squabbling. He came from the coast and I was from a hole in the wall in the south-central part of the state, but it was like we'd known each other all of our lives.

I arrived at his home for a week of soaking up sun and hanging out with him. College didn't start for another month. I had just turned nineteen and was still a virgin figuring to change that status during my week at Mike's with one of the honeys who wanted sun and fun, away from my parents' watchful eyes.

After he showed me the town and we cruised the beach until dark, we picked up a bag of fast food and headed back to his house. His mother was in Washington for the week getting certified in something for the Navy base where she worked.

We had his house to ourselves. It sounded like it had a lot more possibilities than I'd ever had at my house with my mom's nose always stuck in my business and my father preaching hellfire twice on Sundays, and once on Wednesdays, at church.

"Want a beer?"

I shrugged. I didn't particularly like the taste but I'd go along with the flow.

He grinned. "We've got dibs on the liquor whenever you want something harder." I smiled at that. I'd come to like a drink or two the past year and he knew it.

We headed for his room after pigging out and downing a beer apiece. He carried a bottle of rum and glasses; I brought a two-liter bottle of soda and a bag of chips.

Setting his things down on the dresser, he pulled off his shirt and began toeing off his loafers. "We're in for the rest of the night?" I asked, setting my things down and turning to watch him undress. He had pecs and abs I wished I had. I was just skinny.

"Yeah." He grinned. "Never drink and drive. Besides, I thought you might like to check out my stuff."

"Huh?" I glanced quickly at his crotch. He couldn't mean...? No, no....

He reached under his mattress and pulled out a couple of magazines that had women on the cover with less clothes than I'd ever seen. He handed them to me and wiggled his jeans over his ass. I allowed myself a smile as I watched him bend over to push them off his legs. Mike had a nice, round butt. It had real character.

Standing up in his briefs, he went to the dresser and poured drinks for us. Turning back toward me, his hand shoved an old Oktoberfest mug off the dresser and onto the floor. It didn't break and he grinned raunchily as he handed me mine. "Down the hatch, Gary."

I took it and turned to the centerfold, where a girl was spreading her legs and showing herself off. I blinked. Her sex didn't look a thing like I'd somehow expected it to look. I'd expected some character like I figured Mike had in his shorts. Like I had. Not like ours exactly—but something.

"Come on, get stripped for action because I'm going to take you all the way to the mat just to show you who's boss around here."

"Yeah?" I growled in challenge. He might be bigger than me and have better definition, but he'd never been able to get me to my knees in all our months of wrestling in the dorm—much less all the way down.

I took a swallow of my drink as I toed my docksiders off. And felt the stuff burn all the way down to my stomach. "You trying to get me drunk?" I gasped.

He laughed. "I don't need you drunk to take you. Drink up and enjoy the glow you get."

I took another swallow and pulled off my shirt.

"How'd you like to lick that?" he asked holding up the magazine's centerfold as I pulled my zipper down.

"Shit." I pushed my jeans to my knees and pulled them off my legs.

"Maybe you'd like to lick something else, instead?" He cupped his groin and grinned at me.

I stared at him in surprise but didn't say anything. We'd never carried on like this back in the dorm. I decided it was the magazines and put it out of my head.

He flipped to another page and pointed to a girl bending over showing lots of butt. "How about porking those chops?" He groped himself through his underwear and I saw he was growing an erection.

I gulped the rest of the glass of liquor and wondered what kind of week I'd got myself into. This was definitely a new side of my college buddy I was seeing and I was uncomfortable with it. It put me far too close to all that curiosity I'd been hiding from since I learned what the thing between my legs could do for me. A curiosity I knew got me close to being queer. I checked his dick out quickly. It'd already snaked across his groin and looked awfully thick beneath his underwear. I was having a hard time keeping mine down.

He dropped the magazine on his bed and, grinning, grabbed my arm. "Now, I'm going to show you just what you've been missing." His leg shot between mine and I just barely stepped away before he could trip me.

We wrestled, gripping each other's arms and trying to take each other down. It took a while but I was beginning to figure Mike would win our match eventually. I resolutely told myself I sure wasn't about to go down without making him work for it and struggled to stay with him. Neither of us called a truce as we both sweated buckets in the hot, damp air of his room.

My hand slipped on his biceps as he flexed it; he was suddenly pulling me toward him and stepping aside so he'd be behind me when I got there. One arm went around my chest as he sent a leg between mine to trip me. His other arm circled my waist. He followed me down. My hands shot out to break the fall.

He lay on top of me, his chest pinning me, and I realized Mike had a full hard-on in his underwear and it was wedged between my asscheeks, spreading them wide. I felt blood rush to my face as I accepted just how compromised I was.

I forced that knowledge away and waited for him to get tired of holding me down. I told myself he wouldn't think about things like his meat in my crack, because buddies didn't think about butt-fucking their buddies. I saw pencils and a handful of rubbers beside me where they'd fallen out of the stein when Mike knocked it over.

I was just starting to imagine lying out on the beach in the morning when I felt his hips move against my ass. The movement quickly became a steady one. His dickshaft trawled my asscrack through our underwear.

"Mike, you'd better get some glasses tomorrow, old buddy," I mumbled even as my face burned hot all over again. My dick started to swell. "You've got me mixed up with a girl." It was a lame joke, but I hoped it was enough.

"This feels good, Gary." His voice was huskier than I'd ever heard it.

I raised my head and tried to look over my shoulder at what he was doing. His nose rammed my cheek and I couldn't see anything except his eyes squeezed shut.

"Let me up," I growled.

He continued to hump my crack.

My dick found the waistband of my briefs and the head of

it was free. I was surprised at what he was doing. And at my reaction to it. "Mike, get off me," I demanded.

I could feel his hot breath on my neck. His chest pressed against my back. As he pulled his arm from under me, his hand moved slowly across my stiff dick, helping my shaft past the waist of my underwear. My face burnt with embarrassment that my buddy knew I had a hard-on. A moment later I felt the back of his hand on my butt, and his pole lifted part of the way out of my crack.

I learned just how wide his dickhead was as it tried to dig me a new hole right under my tailbone. I was scared at how things were going. This was too damned close to what I'd been fantasizing about all these years.

But this was reality. "What're you doing?" I demanded. He'd got me down, but that didn't mean he could play with my butt. It sure didn't mean I should like it. And I sure as hell didn't want him knowing I was liking it.

His thick pole came back down hard between my crack and his hips wiggled on my butt a little. The back of his hand moved half-way down our knees and I felt his briefs bunch there across the back of my thighs. His hand came back up my leg quickly, grabbed the elastic of my briefs, and pulled them over my buttcheeks.

I was suddenly one ever-more exposed boy. I got harder. "Jesus, Mike!" I growled. "Let me get up."

He didn't say anything. His dick moved hot and throbbing through the valley of my ass, oozing pre-cum on my bare butt. I felt his elbow brush my flank as he picked something from the floor and brought it to his face. I heard something tear and his hand went between his groin and my cheek. It felt like he was stroking his meat. His movements were making about as much sense as me having a hard dick while a guy dry-humped me.

I was in shock! Here was my best buddy trawling my asscrack! Jesus help me, it was naked dick on bare ass! I was just as shocked that my own meat had decided it liked being caught between the throw-rug and my hard abs with him doing it. I couldn't believe it felt good. The whole thing was too queer.

I tried to decide if I should put up a fight or just lie there and let him get off on my backside so I could get up and decide what I was going to do about this shit. I sure didn't want to remind him I was hard too—he might get worse ideas than he already had. My pole decided it for me; it blew a load there on the rug and stayed hard. I told myself we'd both blame booze for this and pretend it never happened.

He raised his hips and it was his dickhead trawling my crack again; only it reversed direction and was now heading toward my balls instead of drilling a new hole under my tail bone. His finger touched my pucker and I jerked. It started working into my hole while the rest of the fingers of that hand guided his dickhead to my asshole. I finally understood Mike wasn't planning on just dry-humping my butt.

Hard-on or not, I'd better do something or I was a fucked duck. "Bastard," I growled and pulled my knees up under me. "We're going to stop this shit right now." My wildest fantasies were close to becoming real—but Mike would have me pegged as queer. I had to stop that from happening.

My hands were on the floor in preparation of pushing me up, my ass hiked in the air, my knees pulling up under me, and my head and shoulders were rising. My pole dug into my belly button. One of his hands moved to circle my meat. His other hand left my hole and grabbed my hip.

All I had to do was roll from under him and I was free. But his fist beginning to work my finest feature caught me. I froze for a moment, trying to understand why he'd started jacking me. Boys didn't do that shit to other boys unless they were queer.

His dick rammed into my ass, pushing deep into me before I even thought about closing things down at my rear entrance.

"Mike!" I cried and collapsed with him following me down. My tight abs hit the throw-rug and he pushed the rest of his dick into my virgin ass, his knees pressing my thighs apart. Pain flooded through me. "It hurts, Mike," I groaned.

"I'll hold still till you get used to me being there," he mumbled against my ear and let my shriveling meat go.

"Get your dick out of my ass!"

"Sshh. Just relax, Gary. I've got a rubber on."

"I'm no queer for you to butt-fuck."

He started to move inside my ass and all I could do was

ineffectively pound my fists on his back and sides.

My prick decided to come back to life—like some queer who got off on getting butt-fucked. His dick thatch scratched the insides of my asscheeks. His pole was still lodged inside me. He ground his hips slowly against my ass. His meat was full-sized hard all over again. And mine was too. He wasn't going to let me up. He was going to butt-fuck me again.

"Mike," I moaned, tears welling in my eyes. I had a hard dick up my ass, a hard-on myself, and was about to have my ass pummeled the second time in a few minutes. It was enough to bring tears to any man's eyes.

"Your ass feels *so* good, Gary."

"Cut it out, Mike."

He pulled several inches of his pole out of my ass and pushed it back in experimentally. It went in easily and I was surprised the movement of it through my chute felt good. "Grind your butt around on me while I'm feeding you my meat."

"I don't want to be butt-fucked," I groaned helplessly and liked how the throw-rug under me made my seven inches feel when he pushed into me. I accepted I liked how his dick in my ass felt too. I worried just how queer this was making me.

He ignored me and his pole proceeded to establish a slow, steady rhythm in my chute. "Come on, Gary, grind that ass for us," he mumbled at my ear.

His balls slapped my the back of my thighs each time his thick slab of meat pushed into me. His chest still pressed against my back and his arms held me close. His lips were on the nape of my neck.

I guessed there wasn't a whole hell of a lot I could do to give myself my cherry back. And there wasn't going to be any way I'd ever convince Mike I wasn't queer after this. It probably didn't matter how queer having my ass fucked made me because I liked it. I wiggled my butt against his pubes tentatively.

The additional movement added immeasurably to what his dick was doing for me. It felt as good as my hard pole dribbling on the rug under me.

My meat was alive. He moved in me slowly as I ground my ass under him; and my seven inches were getting as good a jerk-off as they'd ever got from my fist. Better, because of all the good feelings coming out of my hole.

"It feels good," he mumbled against my neck.

I gave up trying to understand how I'd got into this jam and how I was going to deal with it when I didn't have his hard meat in my chute. I went with the flow.

"Grind your ass against me harder," he commanded and nibbled at my ear.

I ground harder and felt my balls churn. I was close. I wanted to come. Even if I did have his dick fucking me while I was shooting.

His movement inside me stayed slow and steady. But it massaged my lovegland and that was sending new sensations through my body and my chute knew how to handle hard meat in it now. My ass and dick had somehow become connected since he shoved his pole into me the first time. Now, they were also connected to my balls. I groaned and shot a load.

Mike continued to plough my ass and I stayed hard under him. I ground my butt against him and laid my cheek on my hand. I was into the good times rolling out of my ass and dick.

Instinctively, my butt rose to meet his pole and ground itself on that slab of meat each time it pushed into me. My porker rubbed the rug and my hard abs. My balls started to strangle my seven inches again. I moaned and wiggled my ass with abandon.

"You like my dick in your butt, don't you, Gary?" he whispered at my ear. His hand went to my hard meat."You want me fucking you in the ass, don't you?"

"I ... yeah." I decided then and there that I might as own up to it; Mike sure knew I liked it well enough. His fingers had found my prick hard as a rock and were now a fist around it. They felt better than the rug.

"You want me to come in your ass too, don't you?"

I nodded and ground my butt against him."Let's get you up on your knees." His hand pulled my hips off the rug and I pulled my knees up under me at his direction. His meat stayed deep in my canal. I sighed. Fantasy had finally become reality for me; and it was as good as I'd ever dreamed it would be.

"You're going to come with me fucking you, aren't you, Gary?"

I was close again and the pending orgasm just added to the sensations flooding over me. "Yeah."

One hand held my hip loosely, the other returned to pump my hard-on in time with his movements behind me.

I moaned and wiggled my ass on his porker. And simply stopped caring what liking this made me.

An eternity later, Mike's tempo changed. He humped me with fast, short strokes for a minute before his hips lunged forward, pushing everything he had into my hole. His meat widened deep in my ass. My asscheeks were spread wide as his pubes pressed hard against them, his thatch scratching my asslips. He held himself there, and I felt warmth blink into existence somewhere near my stomach.

I blew another load as he filled my hole with more of his jizz. He pulled his dick out of me and pushed himself to his feet. "You want a drink?"

I lay on my stomach and gazed at him over my shoulder, wiped out from our sex—my ass feeling empty but a good kind of numb too. My eyes went to his dick. I'd never seen it out of his briefs, though I'd sure been feeling it up my ass.

It'd felt like it was a mile long and a mile wide, filling me all the way up. Looking at it now, still more hard than not, I was willing to bet I couldn't get my fingers all the way around it. The thing definitely had character. The kind that demanded immediate and continuous attention. It'd felt good in my ass when he ploughed me with it and I was sure I'd never get enough of it.

I pulled myself back to reality with difficulty. Mike now knew I was queer. I was going to have to find a new roommate. It'd be all over school. The folks would find out. I was going to be one fucked duck unless I could find a way to undo what had happened.

"How could you?" I mumbled, trying to sound as uptight as I figured I was supposed to. Only, I was a lot more confused than I was uptight. His cock had felt good in my butt and I had got off with it there—four times! It had taken possession of my ass and I accepted it had dibs on it. I figured all he had to do was get hard and I'd be dropping my shorts and bending over. That confused the hell out of me.

He poured us drinks and squatted at my hip to hand me

mine. I guessed it didn't matter he was going to see my dick—he'd already fucked my ass and jacked me off while he was doing it. I turned over, sat up to take the glass, and gazed admiringly at his softening dick.

I admitted to myself it had taken on a lot of meaning in my life the last half hour. It had my undivided attention; I just couldn't think of anything to go with it—except my ass. I wanted it there again. "How big is that thing?"

He grinned. "I guess it's about eight inches, hard."

I believed it. "Maybe nine...." I said.

"Whatever, I'm glad you liked it, Gary. You know, I kinda figured you would, the way you were always checking me out at the dorm this past year. But nothing I tried got you going..."

I raised my eyes to his. "And now you raped me," I mumbled, still looking for a way to explain away what had happened—and suspicious at how much I wanted to reach out and hold his soft meat. At how much I wanted it hard and back inside me. At how right he was about me.

He chuckled. "Ha! Look, nobody raped you, man. I just gave you what you wanted. Hell, it was what we both wanted. You sure got off on it."

I started at him. "You're saying I'm queer," I groaned and shuddered because even more of me wanted his meat in me again. Even if that did make me queer.

He shook his head. "Look, I'm just statin' the obvious. Your ass likes dick." He smiled. "I hope it continues to be mine you want in there."

I stared at him and silently prayed he meant what he was saying. If he wanted my ass even half as much as I wanted his dick, I was safe—no one was going to know. I shivered and reached out to touch his meat. He smiled and spread his legs wider. My fingers went around it and it started to grow. I couldn't take my eyes off its wide head getting wider.

"You ever have a blowjob?"

I stared back at him in shock. My prick decided it liked what he seemed to be suggesting and got as hard as his was. He reached out and pulled my bunched underwear down my legs. He grinned as he pulled them over my feet. I was as naked as he was and wasn't scared anymore. I smiled back at him.

"Drink up, Gary. Now we know you like the basics, we've

got all week for us to decide what else we like and don't like".

I tried to sort out what Mike was saying and got nowhere. "Are you saying you suck dick?" I asked, immediately accepting a blowjob from him would definitely keep Mike quiet about how fuckin' queer I really was.

"Now and then. If the guy's got a nice hot rod and I like him okay. It keeps things even while I fuck him."

"Do you get fucked?" I asked even more cautiously.

"No...." He glanced down at my hard slab of meat. "Maybe I'd better say I haven't yet."

"What's that supposed to mean?"

"It means I like you a lot, Gary. You aren't just another beach bum with an itch up his ass letting me give it a quick scratch. It means if we continue with me fucking you this next year, sooner or later I'll probably decide to try out what you already like."

He pushed himself to his feet and downed his drink. Setting the glass on the dresser, he reached down to me. "I want a taste of you."

He grasped my wrist and pulled me to my feet, my seven inches jutting out between us. "That looks good, Gary," he mumbled and knelt before me. I watched him take my hard dick in his hand and pull it to his face. "Tomorrow we find out how big you are."

I didn't tell him I'd already measured it.

His other hand went to my nearest asscheek and pulled me closer, pulling me into his mouth.

It felt good having my favorite body part in his mouth. His tongue a chute guiding it in. His throat muscles clamping down on it. His hand on my ass where it belonged.

I took a slug of my drink and relaxed in the feelings coming out of my pole. I finished off the glass and decided I could get into what Gary was doing with my meat. My balls were already tightening and he was kneading my cheeks with his free hand. Yeah, I could go with the flow.

I grinned as I realized I wasn't a virgin any more. My ass knew how to handle his hard cock. I grunted as my nuts churned. I was about to shoot a load down Mike's throat. And my fuck-tube was about to be tamed by a hot mouth. Maybe it was queer but it felt right. And it wasn't hurting either one of us.

Yeah, he could suck me off because it meant I was going to have his dick in my ass again—where it belonged. We were going to have us a hot night tonight—and a hot week. One the beach honeys couldn't come close to imagining.

I suspected I was going to know his dick as well as I did my own by the end of the week. I figured I could get into that—just as long as we kept it here and at college. It sure wasn't going to happen at my house, though. Mom'd probably be listening at the door.

I shot my load down his throat and gasped. I thought I was going to sink into the floor I was so weak. I shuddered and pulled my suddenly super-sensitive meat away from his tongue. He took a deep breath. And grinned as he stood up and took a step toward the bed. His dick was hard and grabbed all of my attention. "Come on, Gary. I'm ready for some more of your ass."

I pulled myself out of the euphoria of my orgasm immediately and, grinning back at him, started for the bed. I wanted him too—all eight inches or so of him.

"Lie on your back and put your feet on my shoulders," he told me as we faced each other in the center of his bed. "You'll like it this way." He grinned as I lay back and looked at him expectantly. "You get to watch me fucking you and work your meat at the same time."

I raised my legs and he crawled between them, taking my ankles and lifting them onto his shoulders. I started at the thick red head of his meat pointing angrily at me from between my balls and dwarfing my own hard-on. "God, just *how* thick is that thing?" He grinned as he leaned into me and I felt that head find my hole. "We'll measure that in the morning, too. You want to jerk off while I fuck you?"

"Yeah," I gasped as his dick slipped easily through my stretched assmuscle and dove for home.

"Ohhhh," I moaned as I grinned up at him and grabbed my hard meat as he crushed his thatch against mine. He was in all the way. "Oh, that feels good, Mike," I mumbled and watched him pull his hard-on almost completely out of my ass before plunging it back into me. "Oh, yeah," I moaned. By now I had decided could definitely go with the flow....

DOWN 'N' DIRTY

David MacMillan

I glanced over at Ian and grinned as we both stepped onto the sidewalk in front of the restaurant. He plopped his butt on the hood of the car and looked back at me.

"Jose is the sweetest guy," I told him and felt warm and toasty all over as I thought of the manager of the restaurant we were about to enter. I sat down beside him and took his hand in mine.

"Knowing you, I imagine he's got a big dick, too."

"Fuck you," I growled good-naturedly. "Hey, he's only the third guy to plug my butt—you and Manny were the only ones to hold that honor until a week ago."

He looked away. "Sorry, Geoff. I didn't mean anything by it. It's just that I'm going to miss our getting together."

I realized Ian was hanging back. It was almost like he didn't want to meet the man I'd decided to give myself to. Even after he'd pestered me the past two days to introduce them. Ever since he found I wasn't willing to drop my pants and bend over for him anymore.

"We'll still get together, buddy."

"Yeah. But we won't be fucking like we were doing."

Ian was a strange duck. His next door neighbor porked him every night. He considered his butt belonging exclusively to Manny; only, he liked to fuck me every chance he got. Ian was in love with his neighbor but he wasn't completely ready to give up his image of what makes a man a man.

I hadn't been around much the last week to give him the relief his dick thought it needed, though. I'd been with the Mexican inside the restaurant every chance we had to be together. And I didn't have any delusions about wanting to be a top—not with Jose and his dick to love me like I knew I wanted to be loved.

Ian was right, though. Jose did have a big dick. It fit my ass perfectly—filling it up so much I couldn't think of anything except blowing loads while it was inside me. And I couldn't imagine anyone else ploughing my butt now that my own personal young Mexican had claimed it.

"He's a lot more than just a big dick, Ian. I think I'm in love with him."

"Jesus!"

"You've got Manny."

"Yeah...." He looked down at his hands. "And you deserve more than being just being my fuckbuddy, Geoff. You deserve somebody really special."

"Hey!" I threw my arm around his shoulder. "You just got lucky first. And I'm not complaining about what we had, it's just that I now have a chance for the whole enchilada. Like you've got. I want to take that chance."

"Just make sure you're protected, Geoff."

I pushed off the hood as I growled: "Nobody gets through my backdoor without a cover. Not you, not Jose, not anybody."

Jose stood at the register as we stepped into the restaurant. Shiny black hair cut short, wide chest, tight abs, slim hips. Liquid brown eyes and pearly white teeth. A permanent bulge in the front of his jeans I had come to know well. Twenty he was, and I knew that only because he'd showed me his papers. He looked up and saw us—and smiled from ear to ear. "Geoff!"

"I brought a friend over to meet you," I told him. "Jose, this is Ian Norton. Ian, this is Jose Corrida."

"A social meeting?" The smile disappeared as he looked from one to the other of us.

"Ian's been my best buddy forever."

Jose's lips twitched. "And he maybe wants to make sure I'm good enough for you?" Ian blanched, then turned crimson. Corrida studied me for a couple of moments and nodded. "It's a good idea. I'll show him what I'm made of, Geoff."

Jose led us into the supply room/office of the restaurant and pushed the door closed behind us. "It is only three o'clock, mis amigos." He looked from me to Ian and back. "We've got half an hour now—even an hour—when it's dead and mis muchachos don't need me." He raised a brow questioningly.

I understood immediately. Jose had loved on me enough the past week that his body language came across loud and clear. I didn't know how I felt about this guy I already saw as my lover showing his stuff to anybody, Ian included. But I also understood it was a matter of pride for him. Jose had something to prove. My claim to him had to take second place to that.

I frowned and glanced over at Ian. "If you think he's nice in his clothes, you ought to see him with them off."

"Geoff!" Ian's pale English complection again turned crimson before our eyes.

"You would both like to do something, yes?" Jose's hand touched my thigh and I nodded, accepting that was what he saw as being necessary.

"I think Ian would like to check your equipment out."

"You would want me to show him it is in working order?"

His pride thing was tantamount. I could understand that. But I had some pride myself. "This one time only," I told him.

He nodded and grinned broadly. "Then, we must get down and dirty, *mis amigos*."

Ian stared at me for a long moment and I couldn't read what he was thinking. He turned slowly toward Jose. His eyes didn't get above Corrida's chest but quickly found their way to his crotch. The restaurant manager pushed off his sneakers and opened his jeans, exposing a triangle of flat, tight, brown skin beneath his shirt.

Ian sighed and reached out to pull the lapels of the jeans apart.

Jose wasn't wearing underwear today any more than he had any other day the past week, and his penga quickly sprang out for my best buddy's inspection.

"My god," Ian groaned and licked his lips.

"You'll help me out with this, Ian?" the restaurant manager asked as his fingers wrapped around his cock and pointed at it my buddy. His cock became the *penga grande* and I grinned at how my buddy's eyes bulged as he stared at it.

Ian nodded and leaned forward to lick the nearly exposed cockhead before him. His lips pulled the skin down over Jose's helmet. His teeth nibbled at the hem of that skin. Corrida shuddered and moaned his approval.

"Come, Geoff," Jose whispered. "I want a taste of yours?"

Ian sat on a box that elevated him just enough so that his face was even with Corrida's groin. He wasn't paying any attention to our conversation—he was nursing a cock that was as big as Manny's and twice as nice—and making every attempt to take it all.

"You want to?" I asked in surprise. Me getting blown hadn't been on the menu since the firsttime we got together. Ian was the only guy who regularly tooted my horn. I slurped on Jose'sjust enough to lube it for the main event of our sex together.

"*Si. Tu eres mi amor.* Sit on the box above Ian so I can reach you."

I happily shucked shorts and briefs and climbed onto the box, grinning back at Jose as he put ahand on each of my knees and leaned into me. My cock rode my stomach. My balls fell across my asspucker. My legs splayed as I gingerly moved my butt to the edge of the box to give himbetter access. His tongue touched my ballsac, his lips outlining my nuts. They nibbled up tomy root and out along my shaft. I lay back against the boxes stacked behind me and gave my dickto the very best of young Mexico to possess as he had already come to possess my ass.

His lips reached the head of my skinned dick and spread over it until they were anchored behindthe flange. His tongue pushed into the slit before he brought his teeth gently down around my shaft just behind the flange. As his knowledgeable lips slid toward my pubes, he directed one set of fingers to pull on my ballsack.

I leaned back and gave myself up to what he obviously knew how to do well.

His other set of fingers moved to begin exploring my abdomen, pushing my T-shirt up on mychest.

I lay back and listened to the slurping noises coming from beneath me, my ass planted on the edgeof the box, and let myself slide toward orbit the slow and easy way.

The fingers that had tugged at my balls traced ever tighter little circles around my asshole and the ones from his other hand tweaked one nipple and then the other. I was close and getting ready tojump over the edge.

I didn't even realize Jose's lips had left me until he spoke.

"Reach above you, Geoff," his voice caressed me. "Hand me one of the packets you find there."

I reached above me automatically. My fingers found condom packets on top of the box aboveme. His fingers left my nipples and I felt a sense of loss. I smiled as I remembered his other fingers now plugged my butt. I tightened every muscle I had in my gut and ground against them.

As I handed the packet to Jose, I leaned forward and looked down between my spread legs to see Ian still slurping on Corrida's tool. It took a moment for Ian's fist moving on his hard, jutting cock to register. It took another moment for me to realize he'd pulled his shorts and underwear off and they were bunched at his ankles.

I grinned. My best buddy was naked and about to find out just how nice Jose really was.

Ian gave up the cock in his mouth and he looked up as Jose put both his hands on his shoulders and pulled away from him. That blank look that covered his face told me he wasn't even thinking about me. No, he wasn't even thinking about Manny. He wasn't thinking about anything but Jose's dick and what it could do for him—just like me when I was alone with Jose.

Jose smiled and raised the condom packet between them. "I'm going to show you all of me so you'll know I am good enough for your friend."

Ian sighed and a shudder ran through him. But he turned around to kneel over his box beneath me, hiking his butt up for the taking. I lay back, my legs spread. I stroked my meat slowly, then moaned in appreciation when Jose's fingers returned to my ass.

Ian's grunt as Jose entered him brought my favorite Mexican back to my horn. His lips caressed my cock helmet. My feet found his shoulders again. His tongue tortured my meat with ecstasy, his fingers came out of my butt and pulled gently on my balls, and his other fingers again tweaked one nipple then the other forever.

Ian's soft moans were a constant, as were the soft splats of Jose's thighs against his cheeks, a rhythm carrying me deeper into orbit. "Oh, shit!" my best buddy groaned below me. "I'm going to ... yeah!"

My balls rode my shaft and Jose pulled on just the skin of my sac. He deep-throated me in synchronization with his continued movement in Ian's ass. My hands moved to Corrida's head to push him away. "I'm almost there," I mumbled and Jose's lips moved to my shaft and started to jack me. Ian's voice was a continuous moan beneath us.

I was coming and grabbed Jose's hair, pulling his lips into my thatch. Rope after rope of cum splattered against his neck and onto his back.

He groaned again, pulling me back into reality, and I let go his hair. He smiled up at me as he let my shriveling cock go. "You like what Jose does for you, Geoff?"

I pulled myself out of the euphoria sweeping over me. I nodded and smiled at him—and ruffled his gleaming black mop of hair.

"You'll come to my place tonight after work?"

Our eyes locked on each other's, he kept his dick's tempo in Ian at a steady pace.

I nodded again, immediately looking forward to having what he was giving Ian and getting hard all over again.

"I want to give you all of my love." Both his hands roamed over my backside to claim me gently.

I nodded again and leaned forward to kiss him.

Below me, long, steady strokes possessed my buddy's ass. Ian ground against the invader that had taken his hole. His moaning got louder and I broke contact with Jose's eyes to watch his penga's thrusts into my friend's lovechute. I continued to watch for several moments and thought of my best buddy's nice mouthful of meat for the first time since I realized Jose Corrida was enough for me.

"Can I suck him off while you're fucking him?" I asked.

"You want to do that?"

"This one last time only, Jose," I said carefully as I tried to understand what I was really saying. "I want to say good-bye to what we used to have in a really nice way."

He nodded. "You must do it then, Geoff. He's your good friend."

As I hopped off the box, Jose's hands went to Ian's chest and pulled him back against him. My buddy's face was a picture of a saint's hitting rapture.

I knelt beside them as Jose tweaked Ian's nipples. My buddy moaned as my fingers touched his nearest hip and caressed their way toward his bush and the hard, drooling dick poking out from it. Jose continued to move slowly in his ass, ploughing his guts gently.

I sat on the box before Ian and smiled up at my buddy as he

reached behind him, behind both of them, to grab Jose's backside. I reached out and cupped his balls as I knelt beside him. He stared blankly down at me as I spread a rubber over the wide head of his cock. He moaned as I pulled all of him into my mouth.

"Suck him well, Geoff. This afternoon needs to be a special memory for long years to come."

I nodded around the cock sliding in and out of my mouth. Jose understood me completely.

Jose's forward movement pushed Ian's dick shaft past my lips, his head hard against my tonsils. His dick's retreat from my best buddy's ass pulled Ian from me, leaving just his covered cockhead. I laved it with my tongue each time before re-forming a chute on which Ian's meat slid back into my throat.

I pulled on his ballsac, my finger slipped between his thighs to feel Jose's cock slide across its tip into my buddy and pull almost out. I kept my lips tight on Ian's shaft as it moved through them.

"I'm close, *amigos*," Jose groaned. His thrusts into my buddy's ass quickly became short and hard, pushing Ian onto his toes each time Jose banged into him. Ian was singing a soft moan continuously and, no matter how much I tugged at his balls, they bunched around his dick, strangling it.

Ian's hands grabbed the back of my head and pulled me on to his dick. My face buried in his abs and his bush tickled my nose. His cockhead grew in the back of my throat, pushing at my tonsils as Jose banged his ass hard. He held me there, and then unloaded. I could feel his cum blasting into the rubber wedged in the back of my throat as he jerked and shuddered to his orgasm.

Jose heaved against my buddy one last time, shoving Ian up onto his toes. And held there. Blasting his cum into the rubber deep in Ian's guts.

It was I who was the first to break the sexual magic of the moment. I had to breathe. I pulled off of Ian only to return to kiss the head of his dick. I rose from the box and took his face in my hands. And kissed his lips.

Jose pulled out of him and Ian collapsed against me. Both of them were gasping as their bodies cooled down from the twin work-outs that had got them off. I watched Jose's cock soften and smiled as Jose remembered to pull the rubber off before it could slip off by itself.

Ian pushed off me stiffly. He looked from me to Jose as if he were trying to figure something. He turned and faced Corrida. And stepped up to him without a word. He kissed him, his arms going around his back and pulling him to himself. Jose's fingers caressed his buttcheeks in appreciation.

Ian pulled away and smiled at the man who'd fucked him. "I think we need to go." His smile widened and he nodded. "Just take care of Geoff here, Jose. He's a very special buddy."

Jose nodded back, his face serious. "I'll keep him well as long as he wants."

My buddy picked up his clothes and started pulling them on. He glanced up at me and shook his head, wrinkling his nose. "Damn, Geoff, I've got to get home before that big-ass Manny does. You're driving, remember?" I nodded. "Well, get the lead out. This really nice guy is going to be here tonight waiting for you—just like he will be every night."

I picked up my clothes. Jose patted my butt and I looked up to see him smiling at me. I smiled back and started pulling on clothes. "I'll meet you here at ten?" I asked. He nodded.

As I pulled up in front of Ian's house, my buddy turned to me and nodded. "You're a lucky man, you know. You've got just about the best guy in the world in love with you."

"Manny isn't so bad, either."

Ian chuckled. "You're right. All of me is his now—after this afternoon. Just like you'd better be Jose's, if you know what's good for you." He moved closer and reached out to pull my face against his. "For old times' sake," he mumbled as our lips touched.

He kissed me—and what we once had together—goodbye.

—Adapted especially for this collection from material that originally appeared in *In Touch*.

COCK-SURE

Peter Gilbert

"An excellent day! An excellent day! I can't recall ever having had a day like it. A really excellent day!" said Professor Evans.

Mike felt like screaming. Nobody he'd ever known talked so much as Professor Evans. It wasn't so much talking as lecturing and it had gone on non stop all day from the moment they landed at the site. "What is it?" he asked, peering into the box. The creature waved its antennae threateningly.

"A giant cockroach," said the Professor. "I wondered if we might be lucky enough to find one. This is the ideal place. Thousands of human corpses to feed on after the bomb. I suspect, too, that the radiation was a factor in making them grow to this size."

"Why are they called cockroaches?" Mike asked.

"Corruption of the original Spanish, that's what it is. It's interesting how words change over the centuries. Take that thing you brought to sleep in. What do you call that?"

"A slibag, of course."

"Precisely! Now, in the olden days that would be called a sleeping-bag. See? A bag to sleep in."

"So now you know," Kevin whispered, "though why the hell you lumbered yourself with it, I shall never know."

Mike wasn't going to enlighten him. On that hot afternoon he hated Kevin. Kevin would dance for Professor Evans if called upon to do so; he was sure of that. Kevin carried the specimen boxes so that the Professor (who accompanied everything he said with hand gestures) should not be too heavily laden. On the rare occasions when the man fell silent, Kevin was more than ready to start him off again with a question or a complimentary remark. Kevin, in short, was an ass-licking creep and just as despicable as the creatures that swarmed on the half-eaten bodies in the city ruins.

The only problem was that Kevin wasn't just attractive. Kevin was magnificent. He was tall, and he had very long legs. Even his arrogant smile made Mike tingle with excitement. There had been times when they were in the library together, sitting at opposite ends of the room. Some strange impulse would cause Mike to look up from his book and find Kevin staring at him. He'd smile. Kevin would smile back; and all the facts that Mike had gleaned from his reading were erased from his memory before he could commit them to paper or his computer. Kevin had extraordinarily fleshy lips. "He mutated that way through sucking up to Professor Evans," one student had said.

The invitation was the first time Kevin spoke to him. Mike was in his usual place in the library reading a book about Cambrian fossils The desk lamp threw a pool of pale yellow light on the page. Anomalocaris; a two-foot-long monster which, for years, had defied every scientific attempt to classify it. He stared down at the picture of its 'pineapple ring' mouth with its soft outer parts.

"I thought I'd find you in here."

Mike nearly jumped out of his chair.

"I've just been having a chat with Professor Evans," said Kevin.

"Oh yes?" If any other student had said it, Mike wouldn't have believed it. Professor Evans was an Olympian figure whom hardly any of the students knew. He lectured about twice a year and spent the rest of the time on research. Kevin was the exception to the rule. Everyone knew how he crept round the Professor. It was sometimes diverting to watch a lecturer reduced to a mumbling wreck when Kevin interrupted him or her with "Professor Evans says...." But it went further than that. There was even a rumor that Kevin had discovered the Professor's birthday and had been seen on his way to the house with a birthday cake.

"The Professor wonders if you'd be interested in going on one of his expeditions."

Mike wouldn't have dreamed of accepting had it not been for the fact that the number of job vacancies for biologists was limited and "Invited by Professor Evans to go on one of his expeditions while still a college student on a CV would certainly unlock any number of sealed doors.

"You're honored," said one of the Professor's post-graduate students when he heard.

"I guess I am but he's such a bore," said Mike.

The older man laughed. "I guess you could say that," he

said. "If you want a tip from me, take a slibag with you. That will lessen your chances of being bored."

It didn't work. By the time they reached the hut on the first evening, Mike was desperately tired. It was too hot to sleep in the slibag so he undressed completely and lay on it. The Professor took an inordinately long time to undress. Finally, stripped down to his undershorts and a singlet, he lay down. Not once did he stop talking. Kevin stripped off and lay naked on a blanket he spread on the floor. So as not to look at him, Mike turned his face to the wall and closed his eyes. Sleep proved impossible however. The Professor and Kevin talked and talked well into the night, almost exclusively about blood-sucking insects. Not the best soporific for a nervous eighteen year old on his first expedition.

There was only one way to get to sleep; the way Mike had used when he was a high schooler. How many insects had names prefaced by another word? Cock for instance. Well, there was the cockroach and the cockchafer....He couldn't think of any more. Okay... expand the field. Cockroach, cockchafer, cockatrice. That was cheating really. Cockatrices were mythical. Cockroach, cockchafer, cockatrice. There was that fishing fly his uncle had shown him: 'cockabundy'. Any more? Well, if you're going to include a mythical beast and flies made out of feathers why not go avian as well? Cockatoo, cockroach, cockchafer, cockatrice, cockabundy, cockatoo. Cockroach, cockchafer, cockatrice, cockabundy, cockatoo, cockroach....

"What I find so extraordinary is that they are adapted to feed on blood," Kevin said.

"Terrestrial ones are but of course we have no idea what's out there in space. Sooner or later some careless astronaut is going to come back with alien eggs on his boots and then we shall be in real trouble," the Professor replied. "It would be interesting in many respects. Life is just starting up in some places. We might get a few specimens of creatures we've only seen as fossils."

"Cockroach, cockchafer, cockatrice, cockabundy, cockatoo. Cockroach...." Mike mouthed the words and then realized that the Professor and Kevin had stopped talking at last. He looked at his watch and realized, with a shock, that he had actually slept for a few minutes. The old method was infallible. The other method, equally efficacious, required privacy—and pleasant thoughts. He turned round so as to get a better look at Kevin. Beams of moonlight shone through the numerous gaps in the walls. Mike wasn't at all happy about those gaps. Giant insects were all right in their place. Indeed, some of the mutations were interesting but their place was in collecting boxes - not in the base hut. The hairs on Kevin's legs shone silver. His chest rose and fell and he was making slight snoring noises. He was probably dreaming about the time when he would be a Professor, Mike thought. Kevin made no secret of his ambitions. Unfortunately, he had covered his most interesting aspects—the parts of him which Mike most wanted to see at that moment—with a rolled-up towel. It was extraordinary that a man so full of himself in conversation, not to mention a student of biology, should be so modest about his sex-organs.

If they were anything like the rest of him, they'd be worth admiring—even from a distance, thought Mike. He closed his eyes again the better to envisage them. Kevin's cock first. The 'Cockevin.' A nice word. Limp it would be about an inch thick and five inches long and have a pleasantly rubbery feel. It would be uncut of course. The parents of such a god-like creature wouldn't dream of mutilating anything so beautiful. Erect, he guessed it to be about nine inches—maybe even more and it certainly wouldn't feel like rubber in that state. It would be as hard as steel. If you held it and closed your eyes, you'd only know it was alive by the throbbing in the veins lacing the ivory-colored skin. And would it...? Well, yes, he thought so. The head would peep out of its covering foreskin like a priapulid worm emerging from its sheath. Not exactly priapulid. Priapulis meant 'little penis' and Kevin's certainly wouldn't be little.

What about hair? Kevin's chest and abdomen were not hairy. He wasn't one of those students who looked as if they were wearing coconut matting. Kevin's pubes would be very soft and silky. They'd feel delightful against his cheek as he licked up and down the shaft.

"Some chance!" he muttered to himself and his imagination moved downwards to explore Kevin's scrotum. It was like a large, over-ripe avocado pear, he decided. Pear—pair. But you'd never know there were two testes in there until you felt it, or—better still—licked it. And, of course the surface wouldn't be anything like the coarse skin of an avocado. It would feel soft and slightly furry like the skin of a ripe peach and wrinkled like a walnut shell and its taste would be a subtle combination of all three. The sweetness of a peach, the somewhat musty flavor of the avocado and that lingering nutty taste would grow stronger as his tongue explored the smooth skin behind that monster sac.

Kevin groaned in his sleep. Michael opened his eyes, shut them and then opened them again. Antennae; waving antennae! He lay still, paralyzed by shock. What he had thought to be a decorative border of a towel was a band of color round the animal's body. It obviously wasn't a full-grown specimen. It was little more than a foot long but what he had taken for a towel was an Anomalocaris. It figured. The only people who ever came to Death Vale were scientists. Scientists often went on space expeditions. An egg carelessly dropped there would mature easily enough. He looked over again to make sure. The creature's tail was on Kevin's knee. He couldn't see exactly where its head was but he soon found out.

"Oh yeah!" Kevin gasped.

"It is surmised that the creature used its feeding appendages to place the prey against the fleshy mouth-orifice. The food would then be sucked in. No fossils so far found have indicated the nature of its principal food...."

It was odd, Mike thought as rational thought returned. No scientific discoveries had yet been made in the semi-darkness of a derelict hut in a deserted valley. Some creatures fed on blood. Anomalocaris fed on a body fluid of a different kind and Kevin was happy to feed it.

Kevin flung his legs apart. "Oh yeah! That's great!" he groaned as if Anomalocaris could understand. "Oh yeah! Take it. Take it all! Mmmm."

Mike lay on his side and propped his head on his hand to get a better view. The creature had arched up like a huge caterpillar. He'd been right about Kevin's dimensions. Half his penis had been swallowed but about four inches of glistening flesh were still visible. Kevin's body flexed upwards and another inch disappeared.

"Ah! Ah! Ah!" Kevin panted. "Oh yeah! More! Ah! Ah! Ah! Comin' soon ... Oh yeah! Ah! Ah! Ah! Aaaah!"

The he lay still. Millimeter by millimeter the creature withdrew from his rampant shaft like a glove being peeled off backwards, making squelching sounds as it did so. The thought suddenly struck Mike that he was the only person alive who had seen a live anomalocaris and watched it feed. He'd almost certainly be invited to lecture on the subject—possibly even at the Smithsonian.

Professor Evans would come along of course and inevitably he'd bring Kevin with him as a specimen on whom Anomalocaris had fed.

Professor Evans already had enough specimens named after him. He might even allow the creature to be named after Mike. Anomalocaris Websterii. It sounded good. So did the creature itself at that moment. It was still sucking as it moved slowly up the shaft. He could hear it savoring the last drops.

"Distinguished guests, ladies and gentlemen. I am honored to be here as the first human being to have set eyes on a creature long thought to be extinct and to have watched it feed. I have persuaded my colleague, Kevin Lawlor, who provided Anomalocaris with its first feed to stand naked in front of you...."

No. That would be a disaster. He could hardly expect the cream of the world's scientists to pay attention to his lecture when they could drool over Kevin's superb reproductive organs. Kevin would have to sit in the audience. He might get him to stand up but that was all.

"The creature appears to move by ripple-like movements of the flippers which were once regarded as swimming fins..."

He hadn't actually seen it move but that had to be the method. He glanced in Kevin's direction again and then stared. Kevin's blanket appeared to be empty and there was no sign of the creature that had sucked him dry. A creature a foot long, dependent upon a series of overlapping flippers for locomotion couldn't have crawled off somebody so rapidly but it had and it had apparently taken Kevin with it.

And then he knew. Of course! He must have dozed off for a second or two and Kevin had gone outside to wash his cock. It had happened to Mike often enough at home. However careful you were with a tissue, spunk had a tendency to run down the shaft and get into your hair. Kevin was an idiot of course. He should have taken a swab at least so that Anomalocaris' saliva could have been properly analyzed. The Professor would be furious with him. That was a pleasant thought.

He jumped as something touched his right leg, just above the knee and then, paralyzed with fear, he lay still. He knew what it was. You didn't have to be a trained biologist to realize that one ejaculation wasn't sufficient to feed a creature that big. It wanted more. The touch was feather light, amazing for a thing of its size. A pair of flippers encompassed his knee, held it for a second and then moved upwards. He put down a hand to push it off but then stopped. It hadn't done Kevin any harm. He'd sounded as if he had enjoyed the experience. Why not let it have its fill?

Kevin would drop right out of the equation. It would be Mike Webster, alone at the Smithsonian. The only man who had both observed Anomalocaris and let it feed on him—just like that time when Professor Evans had let a leech feed on his arm in the lecture theater, an occasion marred by the professor asking Kevin to operate the video camera and complimenting him on his skill in getting good close-up shots. It would be so good to hear Kevin well and truly put down one day, Mike thought.

The flippers moved upwards. "A very good specimen. I thought it would be."

That was the professor's voice! So near and so clear that he might have been less than a yard away. He couldn't be of course. The professor was sleeping at the other end of the hut. Mike closed his eyes and then opened them again. There was absolutely no difference. The interior of the hut was pitch dark. One of the feeding appendages grasped his cock.

"Not like that, you fool! It's flesh and blood, not bloody plastic. How many times have I done it to you?"

"Dunno. About eighty maybe."

"And you haven't learned a thing. Take it gently. Put your hand under his balls."

The lobster-like tail of Anomalocaris curled between his thighs. Mike knew what it was but it was much more pleasant to imagine Kevin's fingers down there. The feeding appendage slackened a little and then gently retracted his foreskin. He pictured the creature rearing up. It was almost as if the nerves in his thigh had become super sensitive. He felt the flippers on his skin, seeming to caress the hairs as it slid upwards.

At home, in bed, that feeling would have turned him on fast. Unfortunately, the greatest scientific experience of the 22nd Century threatened to be a complete wash-out. There was no way he could get his cock to respond to a foot-long fossil. There was only one answer. As he had done so often in the night-time hours, he'd have to rely on imagination again. That wasn't Anomalocaris. It was Kevin Lawlor, Professor Evans' star student. Kevin's fingers were on his cock. Ah! That was better. Kevin's fingers were tickling his balls. Mike's cock reacted more quickly than usual.

"There! He's coming to." That was the Professor's voice again. He'd never been able to imagine a third party before. It helped.

"Coming too," Mike murmured happily remembering the slurping noises from Kevin's blanket.

"Go down on it then. Lick it first. Make it nice and slippery."

Kevin's long tongue felt great. Mike arched upwards. He couldn't help it. The tip of Kevin's tongue caressed his cock-head. Kevin's fingers retracted his foreskin and his lips encompassed the tip of Mike's cock. It was almost as though he was kissing it.

Mike thrust his groin upwards. Kevin's fleshy lips slid down the shaft. His mouth was warm and wet. His lips tightened. For a brief instant, Mike's mind returned to reality but all thoughts of Anomalocaris soon vanished. Kevin's mouth was much more satisfying than the sucking mouth parts of a living fossil and Kevin's fingers felt better on his perineum than the caudal parts of any creature, however well adapted to its needs.

The professor spoke again, this time from seemingly farther away. "You've got a nice ass, young Kevin."

Those seven words were all Mike needed. He ignored the warning messages from his cortex to the effect that he'd imagined them. He knew that Professor Evans was the last person in the world to confirm his own evaluation in such terms but, nonetheless, he gave himself away to the most enjoyable fantasy of his life.

It wasn't just a "nice" ass. Heavens, no. It was a perfect ass! In any ways, Kevin's butt symbolized the man. It was a jutting, arrogant butt. In fact "butt" and "bottom" were the wrong words. "Apex" was a better word. When Kevin stood on the little step-ladder in the library and reached for a book, it was almost as if that tightly muscled sphere were sneering down at you.

"Look at me; admire me but that's all you're going to do. I'm the guardian of Kevin's asshole and nobody, absolutely nobody is going to get past me."

Mike would show him! That little step ladder would be ideal. The library would have to be conveniently empty. He'd put both hands in that thick embossed belt Kevin always wore and pull him down. He'd undo the belt and wrench Kevin's jeans down to his ankles. Then he'd bend him over the stepladder. Kevin would whimper a bit, especially when Mike tore those powder-blue undershorts off.

"What? ... What?" he'd say and Mike would reply, "I'm going to show you what it's like to be fucked. That's what I am going to do."

His hands would be on Kevin's hips. His cock would ream its way between Kevin's tight buttocks until it found the entrance. It would feel warm and wet and amazingly smooth. A pause for breath. Ignore Kevin's pleadings. No lubrication. Forget the tonguing he'd contemplated often enough in the past. Kevin was going to feel every millimeter. The first thrust. An agonized howl. Another. Kevin shouting so loudly that his voice echoed round the library. It would be a bit easier then. Gradually, Kevin's muscles would relax as he accepted the inevitable. The inevitable. A good name for eight inches of tissue as stiff as steel gliding like the piston of a steam engine into Professor Evan's star student.

Professor Evans. None of those neatly written little pencil notes this time. "You haven't really come to grips with this assignment. Suggest you have a word with Kevin Lawlor, who is very good on vertebrate anatomy."

In many ways, it would be a pity the professor couldn't be there to watch. Mike would show him what "coming to grips" really meant. Kevin would wriggle so violently that it would take all Mike's strength on his hips to stop him falling off the step-ladder. As for "vertebrate anatomy," by stretching his thumbs inwards, Mike would be able to feel Kevin's spine under the snow-white, smooth skin of his back. It would be Kevin who couldn't come to grips. The feel of Mike's cock in his anus would be so delightful that those tight sentinel muscles would slacken, allowing even more to slide into him. He'd feel so good; warm and moist. A long thrust; then another; Kevin made a strange gurgling noise. Mike's balls ached. He gasped out something—and came. His glutes tightened as the first stream shot out. Again for the second and yet again.

He sank back onto the slibag. Slibag? He opened his eyes and stared. He had to be still dreaming. Kevin Lawlor, Professor Evans' star pupil was kneeling next to him. Like snail tracks, trails of semen glinted in the moonlight on his chin. Professor Evans was sitting, cross-legged like a guru on Kevin's blanket and grinning.

"How did I do?" Kevin asked, wiping his mouth with the back of his hand.

"Reasonably well. You'll get better at it," said the Professor. "He's the ideal partner for you. I knew I was right."

Mike had to speak. He didn't want to but he knew, somehow, that speaking would shatter the illusion.

"I was dreaming," he said.

And both the professor and Kevin laughed.

"Indeed you were not," said the professor.

"What about Anomalocaris? Where did it go?"

"Anomalocaris? That became extinct about five hundred million years ago," said the professor.

"So...?"

"Welcome to the club," said the professor.

"Club?"

"Professor Evans' potential post graduate students," said Kevin. "This is how he selects them."

"And you?" said Mike.

"Kevin will be good," said the Professor. "He'll be even better when his attitude has been altered."

"And how will you achieve that?" asked Kevin.

"Very simply. In the old days I'd have done it myself but Mike will probably be even better."

"Better at what?" asked Kevin angrily.

"Fucking your ass on a regular basis. There's nothing like it for showing a young man like you his real place in life. When you've taken all that Mike can offer, you'll still be cocksure but in a different sense."

Mike sat up and put a hand on Kevin's shoulder. Doing that dispelled all his doubts. That smooth, rather cold and shivering skin was real enough. "I'd be happy to oblige," he said and mentally added "cock-sure" to his word list.

TRUCKSTOP BOY

Frank Brooks

Tommy sneaked into the truckstop by the back door, which was reserved for truckers only, and headed for the restroom. He had to take a crap, but he knew that if he tried to enter through the front door of the diner, he'd be kicked out on his ass, dressed as he was in nothing but a pair of ragged, threadbare shorts that revealed glimpses of his baby-smooth ass. It didn't matter that his ma was a waitress here. No shirt, no shoes, no service was the policy, and his ma enforced it as vigorously as the management. It didn't matter, though—he couldn't get into the restaurant even if dressed in a tuxedo. His ma would throw a fit if she caught him trying to come in, since she'd strictly forbade him *ever* to show his face at the truck-stop, which, she said, was too rough and dangerous—not a proper place for a boy. Strange, since before she started working here as a waitress, she and pa—before the divorce—used to bring him along here whenever they ate out. But now that she worked here, it was off-limits for Tommy.

Fuck it! Tommy thought as he tiptoed down the dimly lit hallway past the dormitory where truckers could rent a bunk. Rough place or not, he was old enough to take care of himself. And besides, he had to take a crap, and he had to take one now, and he didn't have time to wander across the flat, barren desert landscape in search of a rock big enough to squat behind so he'd be out of sight of the highway. The truckstop sat in the middle of nowhere, two miles from the nearest trees, which were the cottonwoods down by the stream where Tommy had spent most of the day fishing, not to mention stroking his throbbing hard-on, which never seemed to go down these days. He pushed open the restroom door and smiled with relief to see that one of the two toilet stalls was vacant. Latching the stall door behind him, he dropped his ragged shorts and sat down stark-naked on the toilet and instantly relieved himself, sighing out loud at the pleasure of it. Damn, a good shit was almost as good as coming!

The guy in the stall next to him loudly cleared his throat,

then shoved the toe of his boot into Tommy's stall and started tapping his foot. Tommy watched the tapping toe of the black boot, fascinated in an absentminded sort of way. He thought the guy must be listening to music through headphones. Then some movement higher up caught his eye, and he realized that there was a fist-sized hole in the partition between the two stalls, and that the guy was peeking at him through the hole! Goddamn! Tommy was about to sneer, impulsively, "What're you looking at?" when the guy pulled his face away. Brazenly, Tommy leaned forward to give the guy a taste of his own medicine. He put his eye to the hole and stared for several seconds before he realized what he was seeing.

Damn, the guy was sitting there with a boner—a really big one, a huge one, in fact, standing straight up between his hairy thighs and throbbing away! Tommy gulped at the sight of it and moistened his dry lips with his tongue.

"Like it?" The man stood up and rammed his massive boner straight through the hole, and if Tommy hadn't jerked back, he'd have got torpedoed in the eye.

Tommy gawked at the donkey-dong throbbing in his stall. He'd never seen a cock that big. He had a big one himself—over seven inches long—but it was nothing like this. He was not only stunned by the size of it, but he was dumbfounded by the fact that it was sticking through the hole into his stall. What a sight! It made his own cock stick straight up in the air and throb away as well. Leaning closer, he studied the huge cock, nearly touching it with his nose. It smelled sweaty, and had fat veins bulging all over it. It's maroonish head was shiny and moist, and only half covered with foreskin. Some clear juice oozed from the half-open pisshole. Tommy's heart was thudding away and he found himself stroking his own cock, sliding the foreskin up and down, turned on by the close-up view of this big, throbbing man-schlong.

"Lick it," the man growled, trying to push his cock farther through the hole. He was hanging from the partition now, rubbing against it, fucking the hole as if it were a cunt.

Tommy felt dizzy and a little dazed, and he was trembling all over. He kept sniffing the big man-cock, and studying it so close from balls to tip that his eyelashes almost brushed it.

"Lick it!" the man repeated.

Slowly, Tommy eased the tip of his pink tongue from between his hot, tingling lips. The tip of his nose touched the man's cock, which jerked in response, and the man gasped. Tommy's face felt flushed and burning-hot, and, panting like a dog, he tasted the man's cock with the tip of his tongue.

"Ohh ... yeahhh!" the man groaned. "Great! Keep at it, baby!"

After a few tentative licks at the throbbing fucker, Tommy started lapping with long strokes of his dripping tongue. He reached up and peeled back the man's foreskin completely so he could lick the head and the sensitive area of the shaft just below it. The head tasted especially salty, and Tommy slurped at it, getting more and more turned on. Clear juice bubbled from the slit and he let the salty-sweet fluid run down his tongue.

"Oh baby, you're a licker! Now suck it!"

Tommy gripped the shaft of the man's cock, hardly able to close his grubby, tanned fingers around it. He could feel the man's dick arteries pulsing wildly, making the whole cock throb. Tommy squeezed, enjoying the bull's-horn hardness of the huge prong. More juice leaked out.

"Oh Christ! Suck it!"

Tommy opened his mouth as wide as he could and engulfed the apple-sized knob. His lips, stretched like rubberbands, slid down the shaft. He could swallow four, maybe five inches, and no more. His spit flowed copiously as he munched on the big slab of man-meat, more turned on than he'd ever been in his life.

The man was panting, grinding his cock in Tommy's mouth. "Oh baby, you're good! Use your tongue too. You know where. Oh yeah, that's it! That's good! Oh baby, suck it!"

Delirious, Tommy churned his tongue at the underside of the pulsing slab of fuck-meat as he slowly bobbed his sandy-blond head and sucked. His spit ran down the man's veiny shaft. His thick forelock had fallen over his eyes and was tickling his nose. He had his own young fucker gripped in his brown fist and was pumping it like never before. Pleasure seemed to shoot from the man's cock and into Tommy's mouth and through his entire body. He tingled all over. Not just his cock and balls, but his mouth and tongue, nipples, toes, and asshole all throbbed with a delicious, maddening pleasure.

"Baby, I'm gonna come! Oh God!" The man shuddered against the partition, rattling it. His cock flexed powerfully, contracting and bucking. A jet of sizzling man-cum shot down Tommy's throat and made him gag. A second jet spurted down his gullet, then a third. "Drink it, baby! Suck it down!"

Dazed, dizzy, delirious, grunting and gagging, Tommy gulped the man's cum to keep from choking. The huge fucker swelled again and again in his mouth, then contracted, shooting round after round of thick, hot, man-spunk down Tommy's throat. Tommy's gagging eased and he found himself sucking hungrily, trying to get the big fucker to shoot more. He'd never been so excited in his life. A maddening jolt of electric sensation surged through his cock, through his balls and asshole, and his own jism shot straight up, pelting his chin and heaving chest, creaming the rippling muscles of his tanned belly. His grubby toes worked madly, clawing the floor as he came. The air reeked of freshly shot boy-spunk.

"Oh Christ!" the man said, easing his softening cock out of Tommy's mouth. "I ain't come that good in years. What a mouth you got, boy!" His shiny, dripping, slightly drooping, but still huge cock disappeared through the hole.

Tommy slumped back on the toilet seat, his heart slamming as he tried to catch his breath. He had cum all over himself. Splats of his cum were all over the floor. His cock was still in his hand and he was squeezing it and pumping it slowly, still milking pleasure out of it. He slumped there dazed as the man next door zipped up and left.

. . .

Tommy lay naked and hot on his bed, listening to the coyotes yap in the distance, probably down by the creek where he spent his days fishing. It was three in the morning and he'd hardly slept. The light of the full moon glared in through the window of his bedroom in the house trailer. The air hadn't cooled off tonight and no breeze came in through the window. He got up and crept down the long hall of the trailer, past his mother's closed bedroom door, and went outside, walking around naked in the moonlight, his hard prick wagging from side to side.

He was crazy with horniness even though he'd jacked off three times since going to bed. He couldn't get that trucker's big, juicy cock out of his mind. It was the first cock he'd ever had in his mouth and he couldn't get over how much it had turned him on to suck it. Nor could he stop thinking about how the man's hot, thick spunk had shot down his throat, and how he'd gulped it, and how much that had excited him, and how now he was craving more of it. His mouth watered at the thought of sucking more hard man-cock and of drinking more hot man-cum. He could still see that big man-cock, bulging with veins, sticking through the hole at him, throbbing and dripping. No sight had ever excited him more, and he'd been jacking off again and again, unable to sleep thinking about it.

He walked away from the trailer, over the moonlit landscape, which could have been the moon itself, barren as it was, peppered only with small rocks and small tufts of sagebrush. Between him and the cottonwood-flanked creek where he fished stretched five miles of this barrenness, with only the signs of civilization in that expanse being the highway, the truckstop, and a handful of scattered houses and house trailers. He could run around stark-naked all night—something he did now and then—without anybody catching him. The warm air licked his moist crotch and fat brown nuts like a tongue, and a phantom mouth seemed to nibble at his cock, which wagged from side to side like a stiff tail.

Damn, he was horny, and he'd already shot seven loads since waking up this morning—rather, since *yesterday* morning, since it was after midnight. In addition to the hot scenes sizzling in his mind, it turned him on to wander around outside without a stitch on, and the farther away he got from the safety of the house trailer, the more his nudity excited him. He imagined getting caught like this, getting his ass whipped, then getting thrown naked into the back of the sheriff's squad car. The danger of his wicked state added to his excitement.

In the distance he could see the moving lights of cars and trucks on the highway, and the cluster of lights at the truckstop. His large bare feet carried him toward the truckstop, his body drawn forward by his ramrod-stiff cock. He envisioned himself sneaking into the truckstop stark-naked, slipping into the restroom, and sucking off a horny big man-cock. If he was lucky, maybe somebody would even suck his own cock. The thought of it made him dizzy and he staggered forward.

The truckstop never slept. All night long, trucks were arriving and leaving. It was the only truckstop within eighty miles or so, so it seemed that almost every truck that passed by made a stop. The diner served food all night, the jukebox blasting. When he finally got there, Tommy paused outside the lighted vast back parking lot where at least thirty trucks were parked, their engines idling and perfuming the desert air with their diesel fumes.

The truck drivers came and went across the lot, moving between their rigs and the back door of the truckstop. A few stood outside talking. Tommy's bold spirits faltered. No way he was going to make it across that parking lot without being seen. He sat on the rocky ground in the dark, working his stiff boy-meat and watching. What a dope he'd been, thinking he could sneak into the truckstop naked, even in the middle of the night, without being caught.

As warm juice oozed out of his cock, he wiped it off with a finger and licked the finger clean. His prick-juice had a salty-sweet flavor. It turned him on to eat it, just as it turned him on to taste his own cum after he shot. He watched the movements of the men, wondering if they all had huge cocks like the man he'd sucked off this afternoon. They probably did. He'd sure like to suck one of them now!

After he'd watched awhile, he noticed that some truckers made frequent trips back and forth between their rigs and the truckstop. Also, some truckers left their own rigs and joined other truckers in their rigs. There was the sound of a female voice and giggles as a trucker came out the back door with his arm around a woman's shoulders and he took her into his rig. Not long after that, another trucker came out of the truckstop with another woman and took her into his rig and Tommy knew intuitively that these men were going to screw those women. He was tempted to climb up onto a rig and peek in the windows. Man, that would be hot!

Damn he was horny now! There was fucking going on around here, and damn it, he wanted in on the action! At the very least he wanted to watch it!

As he sat there sweating and stroking his cock, two men

came out of the truckstop and came his way. They moved behind the truck closest to him, speaking with low voices, and stopped not more than fifty feet way. Tommy, crouched down, pricked up his ears and heard the jingling sound of metal, then a sigh and a groan. His heart pounding, on his hands and knees, he crept closer. He could see fairly well in the moonlight, but the men were in the shadow of the semi's trailer. Soon he was so close to them he could hear their breathing and their whispers: "Suck it! Yeah, suck it!"

Tommy, beating his throbbing young meat, strained to see. As his eyes adjusted, he could make out one man standing, the other man kneeling. The kneeling man's head bobbed as he sucked with juicy, slurping sounds.

"Ohh yeahhh!" the man getting sucked sighed. "Great!"

The man doing the sucking had his dick out and was jerking himself off. Tommy could hear the squishy, rhythmic sounds of the man's foreskin slipping repeatedly over the moist head, and he sniffed the air for the scent of hot dick. In his excitement, he moaned out loud.

"Christ, we got an audience!" the standing man said, and suddenly both men were looking straight at him as he crouched not ten feet away, the moonlight revealing him in his nakedness. In seconds they'd caught him and dragged him into the shadow of the truck. A large hairy paw was clapped over his mouth.

"Can you believe this!" one of them said. "Where the fuck did this come from?"

"I don't know, but he looks like he wants some action," the one with the hairy paw said. "Is that what you want, boy?"

Tommy, trembling helplessly, nodded his head.

The hairy paw eased off of his mouth. "That's what I thought. OK, now don't make any loud noises. We don't want another audience." The man pulled Tommy to a kneeling position in front of him and rubbed the sizzling head of his dick across Tommy's cheeks. "Is this what you want, boy—some hard man-dick?"

Tommy was panting so hard he thought he was going to faint. Before he could say anything, the man stuffed his mouth with hard, hot, salty dick. Drooling, he began to suck like a starving calf.

"Oh fuck!" sighed the man getting sucked. "What a mouth!"

"It's what he wants," the other man said. "Jesus, what a cocksucker!"

As Tommy bobbed his head, his sandy hair bouncing in his eyes, the tip of his nose tickled by the man's pubic hair, he massaged the trucker's sweaty ball-sack, which was bristling with hairs and swollen with nuts as big as hard-boiled eggs. He tickled and caressed and squeezed the big nuts, enjoying the heft of them in his hand. They were filled with sperm, he thought, hot, thick sperm that was going to shoot down his throat. He sucked hard and fast, wanting that creamy load of man-spunk.

The other man crouched behind Tommy and started playing with Tommy's ass, squeezing and petting the velvet-smooth cheeks, kissing and nibbling and sucking the hot boy-flesh. He spread the cheeks and licked Tommy's crack, then slipped his tongue up Tommy's ass and Tommy would have shot off instantly if he'd been jerking his cock instead of letting it throb and drip untouched in hot night air. Still, each flick of the man's tongue inside him was like an electric prod that almost blew his fuse.

The standing man gripped Tommy's head and worked his cock in and out of Tommy's rapidly sucking mouth, sliding it deeper into Tommy's throat with each stroke until all eight inches of throbbing cock were buried in Tommy's face. The other man kneeled up behind Tommy and rubbed his sizzling, spit-lubricated cock up and down Tommy's asscrack. The knob felt like a hot potato against Tommy's throbbing pucker and Tommy wiggled his ass reflexively.

"Hey baby," the man behind Tommy whispered, breathing hotly on Tommy's neck and causing him to flash with goosebumps. "You want it, fuckboy? Huh, you want it?"

Tommy didn't know exactly what was happening. Delirious with excitement, he could hardly think. He felt a searing sensation in his asshole and a feeling of sudden pressure. He gasped, but his gasp was stifled by the cock in his throat. Then he felt a hot, slippery cylinder sliding inside him, the hot tip of it jabbing the pit of his asshole. It was as if a huge, greased rattlesnake were slipping in and out of him. The searing sensation melted into a feeling of intense pleasure, as if his asshole were about to have an orgasm. He grabbed his cock and started pumping it. Jesus Christ, he was being fucked up the ass! And the feeling was sensational! He'd never in his life felt anything so intensely pleasurable.

"Damn it, man, you're screwing the little bugger, ain't you," said the man fucking Tommy's mouth.

"Damn right!" panted Tommy's fucker. "Never felt anything this hot or tight! Damn it, I'm gonna come already!" Digging his fingernails into Tommy's hips, the grunting trucker went into a wild, thrusting, screwing rut. "Fuck yeahhh!"

"Fuck yeahhh!" the other trucker echoed, hugging Tommy's head as he buried his swelling cock in Tommy's face again and again. "Suck it off, baby, suck it off!"

Tommy thought his entire body was going to come, as if all of him had become a huge cock that was going to go into spasms. The cock in his mouth shot pleasure down his throat. The cock in his ass shot pleasure up his butthole. His jerking hand squeezed such intense pleasure through his own cock that he'd have howled if he'd been able. The two men grunted in unison as they shot their hot spunk down his throat and up and ass. His senses filled with the taste and scent of fresh hot man-cum and his eyes rolled with the delirium he felt. A jolt of electricity shot through his asshole and cock, through his nipples and toes, and the jism erupted from his cock, splashing on denim and boot leather, on pebbles and sand. As he squirmed with his spasms, he nearly blacked out.

When he'd recovered enough to know again where he was, he found himself lying on the ground moaning softly as the two truckers stood over him, zipping up their jeans. Without a word, the men left, each going to his own rig, and soon their trucks were rolling out of the lot and onto the highway. The moon had disappeared behind clouds and Tommy, once he got his strength back, stumbled home naked in the dark.

. . .

Over the next week, Tommy couldn't keep away from the truckstop. He'd lost all interest in fishing. Who wanted to walk five miles to the creek when the truckstop was only three miles away! Who wanted to sprawl beside the creek, jacking off by yourself, when you could jack off at the truckstop while sucking a cock, or where you could get sucked off yourself! Who wanted to jack off by yourself with a skinny finger up your ass when you could jack off with a hot, thick, throbbing man-cock up your ass! The truckstop restroom was a wild place, as wild as the desert itself, and Tommy wished he'd discovered its wildness years ago.

He started going there early in the morning and only leaving when he had to be home for supper with his ma. Truckers came in and out of the restroom all day long. Not all of them were interested in getting sucked off, but most of them were, and some of them were even interested in sucking some boy-cock, or in fucking some tight boy-ass through the gloryhole. Tommy wished he'd found out a long time ago about the pleasures of getting screwed up the butt. He'd never imagined that it could feel so fucking good. He couldn't get enough of it. He thought he could live with a hard, fat man-cock up his ass 24 hours a day. That would be fucking heaven!

For a week Tommy was enjoying life as he never had before—until one day he got home from the truckstop to find his ma in a bad mood. She had to be on the rag, or something, he thought—until he heard what she was ticked off about.

"What were you doing down at the truckstop this afternoon?" she started bitching. "I saw you leaving by the back door. Don't go telling me you ain't been there."

Tommy felt himself redden. "I wasn't doin' nothin', just passing by coming back from fishing. I had to go to the bathroom, if you want to know."

"Ain't I told you ten million times I don't want you down there? It's a dangerous place for a boy. Them truckers are always getting into fights. I don't want you caught up in the middle of a brawl and getting your dumb head knocked off. I can't afford doctor bills for shit like that."

"I can take care of myself."

"Yeah, sure you can! I'm telling you for the last time, I don't want you down there—ever! And that's that! You hear!"

"Well, you're down there everyday. You ain't been beat up yet."

"You think I enjoy being down there, working my ass off all day to support the likes of you. If your worthless pa hadn't left us, I wouldn't have to be down there slaving everyday."

"You were working down there before pa left," Tommy said. "He didn't want you working down there. Remember? You told him you made more on tips than he did at his job."

"That's enough of your back-talk!" His ma made like she was going to slap in across the face. "I don't want to see you down there again, and that's that! End of talk!"

Later, when Tommy tried to bring up the topic of the truckstop again, his ma ignored him and started harping about how worthless he was and that he ought to go out and find himself a job instead of spending all his time fishing and bumming. Tommy laughed out loud. Where in the fuck was he supposed to find a job around this fucking place? he asked her. The only place within 50 miles where he could possibly get a job was the truckstop, and she wouldn't let him go near the place. Well, that shut her up.

Tommy stayed away from the truckstop for a few days, but he thought he was going to lose his mind. All he could think about was that gloryhole and those big, juicy man-dicks sticking through it. He went fishing, but he spent more time beating off than watching his bobber. Finally, he decided to sneak back to the truckstop at night, while his ma was asleep.

Before he left for the truckstop after midnight, he paused a long moment at his ma's bedroom door, his ear pressed to it, listening hard for any sign that she was still awake and might hear him sneaking out. He heard nothing and, as soon as he was safely outside, he ran. Tonight he wasn't naked but was wearing jeans. He still wore no shirt and no shoes because of the heat, but at least he could walk across the parking lot tonight without causing a commotion. He didn't need shirt and shoes to sneak in the back door and into the restroom.

He ran all the way there and had worked up a good sweat by the time he reached the parking lot. He stood out of range of the parking lot lights, catching his breath, rubbing his stiff cock through his tight jeans. He was salivating. He could already taste those big hard man-cocks. He imagined himself sucking off a hundred of them before dawn.

He was starting across the lot when he heard raised voices and saw a trucker come out the back door with his arm around a woman's waist. The woman was carrying on and giggling like a teenager on her first date. The trucker guided her to his rig, which was at the far end of the lot and nearly out of the lights, and Tommy knew without any doubt that they were going to screw! He'd never before seen a man and woman fuck except in pictures, but tonight he was going to. He was feeling fucking bold. Sneaking through the darkness behind the lot, he made his way to the rig and cautiously climbed up it to peer in through the open window.

He'd been right. They had their clothes off already and were going at it, grunting and moaning. The hairy trucker was seated facing forward. The woman was on his lap, her arms around his neck, her cunt impaled on his upright cock as she bounced up and down. Through the open window Tommy could hear their panting and whispering. He could even hear the squishing of the woman's juicy cunt around the man's cock as she rode up and down. He couldn't make out all the details that well in the dark, but he could make out the woman's tits flapping up and down and the man licking and biting them as he fucked her.

"Fucking whore!" the man growled. "Baby, you're hot! I think I might just pay you tonight for two rounds."

"You got the dough, I got the pussy," the woman said. "Fuck me, you horny bastard!"

Tommy, rubbing his dick through his jeans as he watched, was on the verge of creaming in his jeans—he *had been*, anyway, until he'd heard the woman's voice. There was no mistaking it, he knew that voice—it was the voice of his ma! His ma was riding that trucker's cock, and she was doing it for money. His ma was a fucking truckstop whore! He couldn't believe it. Dazed, he eased down off the rig and staggered away in the dark, hardly knowing where he was going. It was only when something hot and wet splashed on his bare feet that he snapped to his senses and jumped backward a yard.

"Woe there!" said a voice in the dark. "Who're you?" The voice belonged to a trucker who was taking a piss behind his rig.

"You peed on my feet," Tommy said.

"I didn't see you coming," said the man. "You almost ran into me. What're you doing out here in the dark?"

"Just walking," Tommy said.

"Kinda late to be out here just walking," said the man. "You wouldn't be out here looking for something else maybe?"

"Something else like what?"

"Maybe something like this." The man pulled Tommy's hand onto his naked, piss-dripping cock, which swelled instantly when Tommy touched it. "Feel it, boy. Is this what you're after?"

Tommy didn't answer. Trembling and weak-kneed, he allowed the man to push him down. He knew what the man wanted. Without being told to, he took the man's throbbing cock into his mouth. It was huge, the hugest cock he'd ever sucked. It was so big he choked on it, but he didn't mind the choking. All he wanted to do was suck it, even if he choked to death on it. He wanted to suck that cock right out of the man's body and swallow it whole. Damn it felt good to have a cock in his mouth again!

"You're good," the man whispered. "Real good! I heard about a young cocksucker hanging around this place lately. Are you the one? Yeah, you must be the one. Damn you're hot! And I can tell you're cute as blazes even here in the dark."

Yeah, I'm the one, Tommy thought. I'm the young cocksucker—that's what I am. He drove his tongue under the man's foreskin, then twirled it around and around the huge, sizzling cockhead. The man started gasping. Tommy was darting his tongue-tip into the man's open pisshole when a flood of hot jism burst suddenly from it. The big cock pulsed, fucking cum, cum, and more cum into Tommy's mouth, filling Tommy's mouth and throat until they overflowed. Tommy gulped to keep from drowning—sucked and gulped and sucked some more—until finally the man pushed him away, begging for mercy.

"Phew, I ain't never had a blowjob like that! You're good, boy. You're the best. Come on up in my rig. I got lots more juice for a hungry young cocksucker like you."

. . .

Tommy was sprawled bare-naked on the seat of the humming semi as Matt, his jeans open and lowered and with Tommy's bare feet in his lap and wrapped around his nearly ten-inch cock, steered the big rig down the highway. Tommy worked the man's foreskin up and own with his toes, which were slick with Matt's pre-cum. From time to time he wiggled his toes under Matt's huge, heavy, hairy balls as he grinned up at the horny trucker and licked his lips.

"You're gonna have me squirting jizz all over your toes if you keep that up," Matt said, rocking his hips. "You're gonna end up getting us in a wreck, boy."

"You want me to stop it?"

"Fuck no! Keep them sexy bare feet of yours wrapped around my dick. Keep working that foreskin. Baby, you are a catch, you are!" Matt lowered the window visor as the sun rose above the horizon ahead and flooded the truck's cab with orange light. "Damn right, you are one fucking catch!"

Tommy grinned ear to ear. He liked being appreciated for once in his life. And he liked even more being wicked and dirty like this. He also liked Matt. The husky trucker had fed him three hot loads since they'd run into each other hours ago in the dark, not to mention shooting a load up his ass.

"I'm getting hungry," Tommy said, rubbing his skinny tanned belly. He tensed his abdominal muscles to make them stand out.

"You can chow down on this again, if you want, cocksucker. I got another hot load ready for you." Matt waved his big, drooling dick at Tommy, who squirmed forward across the seat on his belly until he had his face over Matt's lap and Matt's dick buried in it. He growled as he went to work.

Matt rocked his hips. "Go for it, boy! You sure love dick."

Tommy humped the truck seat as he sucked, and Matt reached over and worked a finger up Tommy's asshole.

"Baby, I can't wait to get my dick up this tight little hole of yours again. I ain't never fucked a hole this hot, and I fucked a lot of holes. Shit, I've fucked a thousand pussies, and a thousand assholes, both male and female, but I ain't never screwed a hotter, tighter, sexier hole than this one. You were born for fucking, boy, you know that?"

Tommy rotated his ass as Matt finger-fucked him. He felt like getting up and sitting on Matt's lap, fucking himself on Matt's cock as Matt drove, but Matt had told him that that wouldn't be wise. They might crash, and besides that, what if some state trooper spotted him driving down the highway with a naked boy bouncing on his lap?

"Christ baby, you got me coming already!" Rocking his hips, humping upward, Matt shot spurts of man-cum straight down Tommy's throat. Simultaneously, he churned his finger wildly in Tommy's asshole and Tommy, grinding against the truck seat as he gulped cum, saw stars and squirted hot spunk under his stomach. Tommy sucked and squirmed until both of them had pumped themselves dry.

"What a mess!" Matt said as Tommy sat up. Then, with a wicked grin, he wiped up Tommy's fresh jizz with his free hand, lifted his dripping fingers to his mouth, and licked them clean. "You can squirt this stuff on my cornflakes for breakfast, boy. It's tastier than cow's milk. Mmm, and it's still warm! He wiped up some more boy-jizz and ate it.

A half hour later Matt pulled into a truckstop twice the size of the one near Tommy's home. He gave Tommy a shirt and shoes of his own to wear so Tommy could get into the restaurant. The clothes were ten sizes to big for Tommy, but that didn't matter. Inside, Matt bought him whatever he wanted to eat, and Tommy ate like a pig. After their meal, they both visited the large restroom with its dozen stalls. Matt pissed and left, but Tommy stayed behind and entered a stall, and over the next half hour he had his dessert: three big horny man-dicks. He could have spent the whole morning there, sucking off one trucker cock after another, but Matt showed up and knocked on his stall door and told him that they had to get moving.

Before they left the truckstop, Tommy made a phone call. The answering machine at the other end came on, which meant that either his ma was still asleep, or that she hadn't come home yet from whoring all night at the truckstop. Even though it was something he was trying not to think about, it was a fact he couldn't deny: His ma was a whore, selling herself to men at the truckstop—and she wasn't doing it because she needed the money. The waitressing job alone brought in enough tips. She was doing it because she liked to screw, because she loved to fuck different men. There was no denying what he'd seen last night. She really loved her job, and she had probably been doing it before the divorce. In fact, Tommy realized now, her whoring was probably what caused the divorce in the first place.

"This is me," Tommy said to the answering machine. "I'm on the road, hitching around, looking for a job. Don't know when I'll be back." He paused, thinking maybe he should say something to let her know that he knew all about her whoring, but he decided to keep his mouth shut. "See you later then," he said, and hung up.

"So, how many big dicks did you blow in that john?" Matt asked when they were back on the road.

"Ten," Tommy said, exaggerating to see Matt's reaction.

"I believe it," Matt said. "Fucking boy-whore! You are a catch, you know that?" He reached over and pulled Tommy next to him and put his arm around him, then he kissed him. "Yeah, I got me a fucking little boy-whore all of my own. Every man should be so lucky."

As the big rig rolled down the highway, Tommy fell asleep with his head on Matt's shoulder.

At dusk they pulled off the highway into another rest area. Lots of trucks were parked here, and Tommy looked forward to jumping out and sucking several fresh cocks in the john. But Matt had other ideas. He pulled Tommy into the sleeping cubicle behind the front seat and stripped him naked. He also stripped himself naked. He was a big man with large hairy muscles. His cock, standing straight out and hard as a crowbar, looked a foot long! He greased it with lube, pushed Tommy onto his stomach on the sleeping cot, and mounted him from behind. His cock was soon buried in Tommy's asshole and Tommy moaned, feeling it throbbing in his assguts. Matt began thrusting, slowly, methodically.

"You're my boy," he growled in Tommy's ear as he licked and nibbled on the back of Tommy's neck. He bit Tommy's shoulders and ears. "Yeah, you're my little fuckboy."

Tommy felt alternating hot flashes and chills as he sank into the padded cot and felt the hairy trucker cover him totally and fuck him so deep that he expected the huge cock to pop out of his mouth. He squirmed and moaned as the man fucked him faster, driving in deeper and deeper. Each screwing penetration deep into him sent pleasure swirling and pulsing through his own cock. Whatever Matt was feeling in his cock, Tommy was feeling as intensely in his own cock. He whimpered and moaned and squirmed, wiggling his ass, wanting Matt to go on fucking him all night long. But the big trucker had a shorter fuse than an all-night one. With a final barrage of thrusts, he started to grunt and gasp and shudder, and then his lava-like man-cum was erupting deep in Tommy's guts. As the spurts of man-spunk splashed inside him, Tommy's own jism shot in hot bursts under his heaving stomach and into his navel, and Tommy nearly jumped out of his skin.

BODY CHECK

Thomas Wagner

Even before that stunning U.S. Olympic victory turned American college students on to hockey, I was out there on the ice practicing my slap shots. In the late '70s, I headed to a Canadian university to pursue the sport I loved best. I had to push myself hard to impress my Canadian-born teammates, most of whom had been swinging a stick since they were just out of diapers. Still, they seemed to accept me because of my intense determination and sincere passion for the game. I never bothered to mention that the main reason I spent so much time on the ice and in the locker room was to check out all those sweaty, well-toned Northerners.

I body-checked one guy in particular over and over: our husky left wing, Jean Paul. His eyes were as blue and hard as the ice, and he thought nothing of displaying every inch of his hairless, well-hung frame in the showers and around the locker room. Though I was afraid to come on to him, I spent many a night whacking off imagining his strong, steely jaws clamped around my rod while his full lips sucked me off.

The night our university won the championship, I got into a fight and received a bloody gash over my left eye. In spite of the pain, I managed to swoop down on the opposing team's goalie and score the winning goal. At that wonderful moment, pandemonium broke loose in the seats. The fans went crazy, and so did my teammates.

To my astonishment, they lifted me on their shoulders while they waved their sticks in the air. Since I'd always been wary about revealing my horny proclivities to them, I got a little jittery in response to all those well-built shoulders nestled under my ass. Soon my other stick was standing at attention along with the ones held by my teammates as we glided across the ice to soak up the glory.

Back in the locker room, we all stripped down and ran for the hot spray of the communal shower. Only Jean Paul lingered outside the cubicle, his body language strangely reserved. As I soaped myself up hastily, trying to hide my pronounced erection, I stole quick glimpses at the white towel hugging his trim hips. The knot in my skull began to throb as I clearly discerned the outline of his thick, curved cock lying flat against his leg like he'd stuffed a hockey stick between his thighs. Was it my imagination, or did it seem to stir a little bit every time I glanced in his direction?

His own stare remained as cool as the breeze in the rink as he finally shed the towel and stepped in beside me. By then, most of the other guys had taken off to go celebrate our big win with their waiting girlfriends. He and I lingered a while, not speaking to each other, until at last we were the only two under the hot spray. I could barely make out his outline through the rising curtain of steam.

The pulse in my cock began to beat as wildly as my heart. Despite the hot water drumming on my shaft, it reared up hungrily between my legs. Suddenly I noticed him staring at my crotch. When I lifted my chin and flashed him a quick, horny smile, he quickly looked away again.

That was when I got the distinct feeling that he wanted to celebrate with me in a much more personal way.

Taking a chance that I was right, I stepped closer and pretended to adjust the shower nozzle. In the process, I dragged my rigid cockhead against the back of his thigh. To my disappointment, Jean Paul tensed up and jumped back against the tiled wall.

"Oh, sorry," I said, getting ready to pretend I hadn't meant anything close to what I actually had! When Jean Paul looked up into my face, though, he didn't look a bit angry. Instead, I thought I noticed a distinct horny expression melting his stern features. But I figured that was just more wishful thinking on my part.

"It is all right," he said in that slight accent I found so appealing. His voice was so low and husky I could barely hear it above the drone of the water. Then he turned so that his own stiff cock jutted up between us, fully exposed through the tendrils of steam. It was bigger and thicker than I'd ever seen it before. Even the heat from the shower hadn't wilted it a bit. Apparently hockey wasn't the only game for which he had stamina to spare. "I am not offended. I am just...."

"Shy?" I finished for him with a hopeful grin.

"No...." Though his cheeks were already flushed from the heat, they grew even redder as he struggled to form the words. "I am...how would you say it?... new at this. Yes, very, very new."

My eyes widened, and my jaw dropped open. I just couldn't believe a guy with a boner like that had never stuck it where it counted. My hand trembled as I reached up and turned off the water. "Well, Jean Paul, if you're really interested, there are a few...uh...moves I could teach you."

The blush on his face and his cock deepened as he nodded furiously. At that point, I couldn't wait to score. I approached him and slid one hand around his big, low-hanging balls and cupped his stiff cock in the other. I could feel the big veins lining his shaft throb softly, like he was holding back enough cum to flood the hockey rink. Jean Paul leaned his trembling body against mine as my fingers roved through his matted, honey-colored pubic hair and crept toward his asshole. When I poked my fingertip inside him, he gasped and shuddered with pleasure.

I could hear his breathing grow heavy as he bent to give my earlobe a nip. He licked his way down my neck, and I reacted by pulling his sizzling body close to mine and digging my fingers into his taut butt-muscles. Our jutting boners wrestled with one another like warring swords. Hot water continued to flow down my aching body, but the scalding sensation I felt was coming from inside.

His hungry mouth sucked in my right nipple as his left hand tweaked and pulled at my right one. He was a fast learner, I thought as he lowered himself to his knees and began to rub his lips sideways over my shaft. For some reason, he seemed to avoid my bulging cockhead, almost like he was afraid of it. I figured he was insecure about tasting another man's cum for the first time; luckily, that was one pleasure I was most looking forward to introducing him to!

Taking hold of his head, I slid my fingers through my longish hair, nudging his lips toward my now painful erection. As he opened his mouth and tentatively took my torpedo-shaped dome and shaft inside, I thrust my hips into his face. Droplets of silvery water shimmered on him, making his bare body shine in the dim light.

"That feels fantastic," I murmured, as his mouth slid down past my cockhead and along my shaft. Getting into the game now, he started playing with my bloated balls and tantalizing my crown with his full lips. Meanwhile, his agile fingers eased their way through my sparse pubic hair. Pretty soon he was actually sucking me, though like most beginners his strokes were too hard and too fast.

He even grazed me with his back teeth a few times. If I hadn't been so turned on, my cock would have started aching from discomfort right about then.

"Whoa, whoa, buddy, take it slower," I murmured, holding his head and adjusting the force and depth of his mouth's fervent plunges. "Lightly at first, then build up from there ... oh, yeah."

Again I felt his eager teeth grate the tender skin of my shank, but this time he was moving more deliberately, teasing me instead of wolfing me down. He also figured out how to use the tip of his nose to nudge my base, his lips expelling hot breath into my sweaty, saliva-drenched bush. Eventually he got bolder still, and his right hand slipped between my tense asscheeks. His fingers toyed with my slick crack, his moans echoing through the empty shower stall as Jean Paul felt up my wet crevice.

Turned on beyond belief, I began driving faster into his mouth. I felt a little guilty when I heard him gag, but the mild discomfort didn't seem to bother him any. Just like on the ice, he was an agile performer, and my cock-shaft felt the rippling sensations as he widened his throat by relaxing his muscles. I smashed my groin into his upturned mouth, while he slurped down the pre-cum that was now flowing from my tip. My stiff meat beat against the pulp in the back of his gullet, coaxing small animal groans from his hard-working throat.

Just as I felt my load start to descend into my cockhead, Jean Paul twisted his cherry finger deep inside my burning bowels. I had no idea where he'd picked up that particular move, but my lower body sure as hell liked it! Losing control, I grunted and spewed a blazing load into his wet mouth.

I was again amazed at what a quick study he was when I felt his throat contract and swallow. Instead of backing away, or slowing his jaws, he just started sucking me harder. I couldn't believe I had any sauce left, let alone a whole waterslide of the stuff. But his incessant sucking produced even more warm jizz from the deepest reaches of my nuts. Grinning against my bush, Jean Paul swallowed load after load as I deluged his throat in spurts and then in more continuous streams. He guzzled and slurped my juices until I'd totally emptied my ballsac.

I slowly pulled out of his mouth and squirted my last drops of cum across his face. Then I stared down, awestruck at the state of his purple, incredibly swollen dick. The dick bobbed back and forth between his splayed thighs as he crouched in front of me, resembling a cobra enchanted by some horny snake charmer. His bloated nutsac gleamed with steam, sweat, and pre-cum.

I wiped my dick all over his face. Then I heard him groan as I pulled him to his feet and gripped his boner. His hips made small, spasmodic pushes as his groin rose to meet my manhandling. I could feel the hot blood whirring through his bloated limb, making him grow every time I jacked his shaft.

Soon he was fucking my hand like the wild beast he was, bucking and twisting and thrusting against me. His tight ass bobbed up and down, his fat balls smacked up against his flesh. When I finally saw the pre-cum trickle down the left side of his inflated rod, I hunkered down and shoved that delicious slab of Canadian bacon into my mouth. Jean Paul held on to the back of my head in order to balance himself as I bore down on him with pure suction. His grip became stronger as he came closer to coming. In two minutes flat he had blasted my own face with a steamy cargo of froth.

Tasting him had inflated my cock once again. It was like I hadn't even come a few minutes ago. While he was still recovering, I pushed him against the faded tiles beneath the showerhead. A look of fear passed over his face as I hoisted my cock up to his buns.

"Don't worry, Jean Paul, you're about to be the happiest guy on earth," I commented as I grabbed a bar of soap and lubed his asshole. "I'll take this nice and slow."

I spread his cheeks to give myself easy access. After I had finished the lube job, I entered him slowly with my cockhead and waited for him to adjust. When I managed to get about half of my dome inside, his cherry ass-muscles clenched my flange and quivered fearfully. Hoping to relax him, I reached around and slipped my fingers over his balls, kneading him slowly. Jean Paul let out an anxious breath and steadied his shoulders and hips with a visible effort.

"How is it?" I grumbled into his ear. My own balls were throbbing so hard now I could barely contain my load. But I held back for his sake.

"Yeah, much better now," Jean Paul whispered through clenched teeth. He was probably fibbing, but I didn't worry about it. He'd be loving it soon enough, I knew.

"Hang on, then." I gave his nuts another yank and then plowed all the way to his prostate. Jean Paul threw his head so far back it came to rest on my shoulder. A look of pure ecstasy crossed his chiseled features as I started pumping in and out of him with slow, shallow strokes that quickly became deeper and harder.

"I'm gonna lose it, Jean Paul," I finally croaked. I lifted my hand to his cock and started jacking him off, while he babbled something in French. In seconds, his cock went off like Old Faithful. He blew a geyser of white cream all over the ugly tiles in front of him. The sight of his shooting hose got me even hotter, and my hand dropped to his hips as I rammed into him again and again. He was fully open for me now, and I merrily fucked his ass while his rectum sucked down my spunk like he'd done it many times before.

Then I, too, let loose in his ass. Torrents of cum sprayed inside each of his virgin crevices. He slammed his virgin ass right back at me as the last droplets of cum shot from his swollen cockhead. I kept fucking him until I'd spewed every last bit of my own jizz, then gave his stretched-out goal a few more thrusts for good measure.

"*Oui, oui,*" he was rasping, juice running out of him and disappearing down the drain. He rocked back and forth on his bare feet until only a dribble dripped down his softening tip.

I then turned him around just as he sagged to his knees in exhaustion.

Laughing now, he bent forward and dutifully licked off my cock and balls one last time.

Then he looked up at me with a victorious, cum-stained

smile, like we'd just won the championship all over again.

Then Jean Paul spun me around with those powerful arms of his and started licking my ass to prepare for a rebound shot he had in mind. Hockey season was over, but that was the beginning of a winning season of a different kind!

BONES

H.A. Bender

"Are you the dinosaur guy?"

"What?" I turned around. In the 12 years since I'd graduated college and embarked on a career of paleontology, I couldn't remember anyone before referring to me as "the dinosaur guy." But I had no doubt the speaker meant me.

"Yeeees," I answered cautiously.

"Is your talk...are you going to...will you be talking about how to know if it's the right career for you...how to get into it...?" The young man with the buzz cut and the painfully erect posture was looking at me with such eager eyes. My own eyes took in his military stance, his muscular body, his youthful face, his pink cheeks, and those bright, luminous eyes.

"No, I'm here to speak on dinosaurs, not careers ... but I'd be happy to speak to you privately, later on. I'll be on campus till tomorrow. I have a room in Brandon Hall for tonight. If you'd like to come talk to me, I'd be pleased to try to answer your questions."

As I looked him over, I momentarily thought that I'd be pleased to do a lot more than that. Then I tried to put that thought out of my mind. Paleontologists who go around seducing boys at the schools they give speeches at soon get reputations that have nothing to do with their professional knowledge. I couldn't afford to.... I shook my head as if to clear it of lascivious thoughts and tried to concentrate on the earnest young man in front of me. But my eyes kept wandering and my thoughts with them. I flickered across his basket, trying to estimate the size of the young guy's equipment. I returned to his buzz-cut and pictured my fingers running through the stubbled hair. I looked at the smooth cheeks and wondered if the boy was even eighteen.

"I'll come see you this evening, Sir!" the boy breathed rapturously.

"Okay, but you can drop the 'Sir'," I urged him.

"Thank you, Sir," he said enthusiastically.

As I gave my lecture, my eyes roamed the auditorium. Most

of the cadets' eyes were on me with reasonable interest; a few eyes wandered or simply glazed over. But the young fellow who'd spoken to me in the hallway earlier was listening and watching so intently that it felt as if the sheer force of his concentration might swallow me up at any time. He was totally devouring me—my words, the sight of me, my very essence, it felt.

I registered no surprise when the knock came at my door, later on, after dinner. Opening, I saw the same young man. "Come in, Cadet," I offered, throwing the door wide.

"Thank you, Sir!"

"I told you, you can drop the 'Sir'! I'm not part of the school. I'm just a guest lecturer."

"Thank you, Sir...er, uh...what do you want me to call you, Sir?"

"I've been called 'Buddy' ever since I was a little kid. That would work."

"Buddy, Sir? Really, Sir? I mean...uh...Buddy?"

"That's better," I said, smiling at the kid and waving him in. Shutting the door behind him, I offered him the chair at the desk, perching on the edge of the desk myself. "Now, when did you develop an interest in paleontology?"

For the next ten minutes, he spilled out his story, and along with the tales of his digging expeditions as a seven-year-old came stories of how the other boys made fun of his paleontological interests and what it was like to be "different" in that way.

"Did all the kids tease you terribly?" I asked, leaning earnestly toward the apple-cheeked young guy with the close-cropped light brown hair and the fervently burning eyes. "How did it feel to be different from the other guys?"

He gave such a start, and looked into my eyes with such a hunted look, that I suddenly realized I had asked a loaded question—he was "different" in more ways that just his career interests. "I meant your interest in paleontology," I said softly, "but if there's anything else you want to talk about, I'm a good listener."

He stared deeply into my eyes with fear growing ever larger in his eyes. "You ... you can tell just from looking?" he finally asked.

I chuckled. "You know the expression: Takes one to know one."

"You, Sir...er...uh...Buddy?"

I dropped a hand onto his shoulder. I was only trying to be fatherly—or perhaps big brotherly. But the shudder that racked his frame at the feel of my hand was generated by a far wilder emotion, and it elicited an echoing response in me. Hesitantly the cadet—I still didn't know his name!—put his hand on my arm. I felt his warmth, his unsureness, his need.

"Have you ever done...anything...with another guy?" I asked.

"Yes...sorta. I fooled around with a couple of friends back home. We jacked each other, and one time Tommy and I sucked each other off. I'm not a total virgin!' he said proudly.

"Do these doors lock? And what's your name?

His name, it turned out, was Dwight, and his body was a work of art. With the door locked, he had stripped eagerly, while I pulled down the covers, and now we were lying next to each other on the bed. I traced a line down his hard, young, proud chest, innocent of any hair, with its two rose-tan nipples jutting insistently out like reaching fingers.

"So you've had a little experience?" I echoed as my fingers trailed their way down to his flat abs and into the tangle of coarse pubes that surrounded his swelling tree trunk of a dick. "Jack-off and sucking?" My fingers traced their way up the flat underside of his still-stretching shaft. "But you'd like to do more?" My fingers reached the spreading ooze of viscous fluid that was seeping from his willing piss-hole.

"Yes, Sir...I mean...Buddy. I want to do more of those things, and I want to do more things. I've never been fucked...or fucked another guy." His voice grew shaky as my hand wrapped around his shaft and began to tug at his uncut dick. The foreskin closed over his cockhead, then unfurled as I sharply pulled the skin down again.

"Which do you want to try more?" I asked, hefting his balls with my other hand and squeezing the cargo-laded spheres just hard enough.

"I don't know." His voice sounded very weak and shaky as I insistently tugged at his loose skin, which was much less loose now that his cock had swollen to its full potential. "I guess I want to try it all."

Letting go of his balls, I moistened my fuckfinger with his syrupy pre-cum and then squirmed it within the crevice between his taut buttcheeks. Those muscles were as firm and well-worked as any of his others, but he couldn't stop me from working my way to the puckered gate of his ass-chute. Soon my finger was squirming up into the humid interior of his anal canal.

A wild shiver racked his body as he felt my finger enter his rectum and begin to probe. At first I sought out his butt-nut and, finding it, gave the young cadet a massage he wouldn't soon forget. His dick began waving wildly as my finger skated across the walnut gland. He spouted a goodly spurt of lube. His body stiffened. I was afraid he was about to come—eons before I wanted him to—so I left off the prostate massage and just drove my finger in and out of his butt. Pretty soon I added another finger. And then another.

Now Dwight had three fingers earnestly dicking his hole. He began to hunch against them, his hungry ass swallowing my fingers each time he thumped his pumping ass back down against the bed. I crammed his ass as full of my fingers as I could, reaching as high as I could, spreading my fingers so they spread his walls. I wanted to fill him with my dick. I just wanted to open him up as much as I could, first.

When I decided he was ready, though, I prepared to fill him with something much more exciting than fingers."Okay, kid, pull your knees up!' I barked, patting his ass-cheeks and guiding his legs into the air.

Now his cute little pink ass-pucker was facing me, pulsating with expectant need. Quickly I faced off and prepared to indoctrinate him.

Applying a rubber to my throbbing organ, I got off the bed and stood alongside his head, telling him,"Lick this thing wet so I can shove it in you easier. Tongue the tip and get it good and lubed ... Go on...."

He hesitated, but soon he was earnestly encompassing my cockhead with his lips and sucking avidly on my corona. Carried away with excitement, he forgot that his mission was merely to lube my dick and instead began giving me a thorough sucking. His pouty lips travelled down and down and down till over half my thick prick was encased in his mouth. Then he began a seesaw suck-job that carried him down and up, down and up, tightening his grip a little more with every downward thrust. Soon he was doing a credible job of carrying me nearer to coming.

I let him go on as long as I could. I didn't want to come off in his mouth, or get so hot that I would spew my stuff within seconds of plunging into his ass-cavity. But it felt so good...and clearly my young novice was having a good time too!"So you're interested in studying bones," I said. "You're doing a good job with this one!" I chuckled at my little joke, but Dwight was far too engrossed in what he was doing to laugh along with me. His earnest expression never wavered, and he never broke suction to smile. He just went on chowing down on my rigid organ.

Encouraging him to take a little more in, I began taking a more active role in the cocksucking. Instead of just letting him swallow what he could, I began to face-fuck him. Rocking back and forth, I surged down his throat and gave him a little more dickmeat than he'd been prepared for. My young friend started to gag, so I backed up quickly. But he gamely kept sucking, and soon he had that much and more. I could feel his inexperienced lips growing surer of themselves, his sucking mouth learning just how hard it needed to apply the suction, and how much was too much. He experimented with his tongue and soon was flicking it across the flat underside of my dick as he sucked.

And then I knew that I had to stop him or risk blowing my wad sooner than I wanted to. So I regretfully pulled out of his mouth, saying, "I think you've got me lubed plenty," and I resumed my position at his butt-cheeks. Taking careful aim, I placed my glans at the puckered entranceway and gave a careful shove. His never-before-breached ass-lips parted hesitantly to accommodate my eager stiffy. I pushed a little harder, and more of my pointy corona made its way into his aperture. Another shove, and another, and the whole apple knob was lodged within his grip.

At that point my young friend was grimacing, but he never uttered a whimper. "Am I hurting you more than you can take?"

"No, Sir! Uh...Buddy. No, Buddy. No, it hurts good. Give me more?"

I gladly complied, threading more of my seething prick into his hungry ass. Then still more. And finally half my shaft was lodged in the grip of his channel. Dwight began making little hunching motions, trying to swallow up even more of my pulsating meat. If he wanted more, I had what he wanted. And I was very happy to give it to him ... hard and fast, now that I was sure he could take it.

Plunging as far as I could, I plowed my way into the blind end of his tunnel, thrusting sharply as I drove deep. Dwight was fully involved now. He was hunching his ass up and down as hard and fast as he could. Each time he thumped back down, his grabby rectum swallowed every inch of my palpitating cock.

Reaching up, I grabbed one of his pulsating, purple nipples. Pinching it, I turned up the sensory assault I was subjecting my young initiate to. It was the last straw as far as his dick was concerned. As I pinched the tough nubbin and felt the hardness of it, Dwight's hunching motions became erratic and his face flushed a deeper crimson than it was already. "I'm-I'm-I'm gonna-gonna come!" he managed to wheeze, straining under the rigors of his huge need.

"Do it, kid. Do it!" I huffed, more than a little breathless in the face of my own encroaching orgasm.

Dwight's face contorted in a grotesque grimace of need. Then he gave one powerful upward lunge, held the position, straining harder, and finally spewed his milky jism explosively, expelling his anal virginity along with his cum. I followed right behind, feeling my balls rise and clench as they prepared to jettison a heavy load. A second later and my dick was throbbing wildly in the young cadet's rectum as I spurted out my load.

The young guy was temporarily sated and temporarily exhausted. Looking at his watch, he realized he had to get going, too. "And I wanted to have the experience of...you know...fucking you," he lamented.

"Well, did you learn something about bones?" I teased.

"I still want to be a paleontologist...but I think this kind of bone is even more fascinating," he answered, squeezing my rapidly shrinking rod. Then he disappeared quickly, before he got in trouble.

I love addressing these youths; they're so eager to learn ... oh so many, many things!

A RAW FUCKING

John Patrick

Judd climaxed onto his hairy chest just as Matt slammed his cock rudely into his now spasming ass. Judd let out a long, low guttural cry as he felt one jolt, then another, then another. Then Judd shuddered as Matt came inside his ass. Juss relished feeling so filled, so full. "Ahhhh," he breathed, relaxing at last. Matt cried little whimpers until the spasms died away, then kissed Judd full on the mouth, the first time he had kissed him tonight.

Lying next to Judd on the bed, Matt resumed a feast at the boy's ear with his tongue. "You come like a real slut," he whsipered.

"So do you," Judd shot back.

Laughing, Matt turned Judd on his side, then slipped his cock into Judd's sloshy, wet asshole and he began a rude banging against him. Even only semi-hard, Matt's prick was enormous; it always seemed to be splitting Judd apart. Matt thrust into Judd slowly, almost affectionately, for several minutes. Then Matt changed positions, devouring Judd's body. From behind him, on top of him, side by side again, and then in poses that Judd wouldn't have believed he could manage. Matt was strong, turning the youth's body every which way, planting his cock with an incessant drive inside him. He slapped Judd's thighs and his ass until he could see in the mirror on the wall that they were red, becoming raw. But it wasn't painful as much as it was exhilarating for Judd. The raw fuck was lifting him away from everything but the present moment, and for that he was grateful. Things had not been going well between them but they could always, for a time, return to what had drawn them together in the first place: sex.

Judd's body heat was rising again, his cock pulsing once more. Matt's fingers massaged Judd's cute little six-inch cock until he could feel another orgasm mounting and ready.

Matt was behind Judd, his firm thighs thrust in an artfully consistent rhythm as he jabbed his cock into Judd's aching hole over and over.

"Ah, oh God!" Judd gasped. Again and again, he cried out with every jolt. "Augh, ah! ah! ah! Oh no!" The orgasm smashed through him, this time not sweet and not tender like the first one but matching the savage thrusts of Matt's cock behind him.

"Hmmmm," Matt grunted. He too was ready. Judd felt the shooting jolts as he milked Matt's delicious cock.

When Matt was finished, he collapsed against Judd. His hands had been squeezing his ass as if he had been kneading dough. And he didn't let go until every fragment of sensation, every pulse of his orgasm was finished and every drop of cum was inside Judd.

When Judd could breathe and move and think again, he looked at Matt, who smiled in an impish way, then stretched out beside him. Judd now remembered the quick taste of Matt's exquisite cock when they got back to the apartment. Judd had wanted to suck it for a while, but Matt wanted Judd's ass. Judd grew quiet under the touch of Matt's long, strong fingers."Fuck me," Judd begged. "Please, stick it in me!"

Matt grinned. He liked the sound of the boy's voice. The eagerness was there, coiled tensely inside his throat. But with the eagerness was submission, total submission to his will."So you want it, do you?" he asked quietly.

Judd nodded, obedient as always.

After undressing him, Matt gently pulled the asslips apart and stared in wonder. It was just as good as a cunt, maybe better, he told Judd. He licked at Judd's open, exposed asshole and his cock grew with desire. Hearing this now helped relieve the tensions Judd felt. Matt had left him, returned, left him again, always to go to his women, one of the many women Matt needed to feel like a man. To have his ass now judged"as good as" a cunt made the tensions all worthwhile.

Judd put his hand on the top of Matt's head as Matt licked away at his asshole. Judd shoved Matt's head forward and Matt shoved his tongue inside. It wasn't long before Matt had Judd in bed and he was sliding his cock into him.

Now, after the fuck, they lay silent and motionless. Judd did not look at him. Then, suddenly, Judd bent over him, laid his head in Matt's crotch. His nostrils quivered as he breathed in the strong, pungent odor of his maleness, mixed with the smells of their sex. His lips inched upward on his thigh; then he began licking the cock.

Matt lay motionless, his eyes scrutinizing Judd. Hardened, choking with willingness, the ruddy organ lifted high. Judd tasted it with the moist tip of his tongue. Stretching the foreskin to unsheathe the totality of bright pink glans, Judd brought his face forward and closed his lips around the huge head of the organ. His long blond hair would have fallen to cover the action like a curtain, but, Judd caught it with one hand and held it back from his forehead so that Matt could watch every movement of his mouth. Matt's strong fingers closed around Judd's arms, and he held him away from him. Still, Judd could remember vividly the feel of each hot, insistent thrust of his rigid prick deep in his ass. And he wanted it again.

Matt smiled, struck by the changes that three months of on-and-off raw fucking had wrought in the boy. He was, he thought, like a whip, growing better fitted to its task and to the hand of the whipper as the softening leather lost its stiffness and resistance. Matt's interest in men and women was that of a fine craftsman who, with consummate skill and patience, shapes raw material to the pattern of his fancy, then goes on to seek new talent. He had found Judd insufferably naive and unaware, and he had made a slut of him. He had uncovered Judd's capacity for suffering, and his pain and tears had made him radiant. He had made Judd alert to his senses, to the needs of a dominant top. But, now that Judd had given him so much, Matt thought, Judd no longer had anything to give him. He held Judd back from sucking his cock again, ever again. Today, he had decided yesterday, would be his last day with him. His last raw fuck of the boy. It was time he moved on.

Judd, sensing things had soured once again, looked at him uncertainly for a moment, then complied. He stood and went to the bathroom. Judd never argued with Matt. It would do no good.

Suddenly alone, Matt found himself becoming excited again. Judd's submissiveness, coupled with his knowledge that the raw fuck he was about to administer to Judd in the bathroom, in the shower, would be their last together, stoked his passions.

He followed his young charge to the bathroom. Judd was sitting on the toilet. "Open your mouth," he commanded, superfluously, for Judd had already anticipated his wishes. Then, seizing Judd by the hair, he thrust his throbbing cock between Judd's lips. Judd's fingers clutched at Matt's firm buttocks, pulling them to him. Judd's tongue and teeth played hungrily against Matt's huge, swollen shaft. Judd was so talented, Matt was soon close to the edge, and he pulled back. "No," he said. The last act, the final experience, should, he thought, be a total one—a total one for Judd as well as for him. It should be one Judd could remember him by, one that would burn forever in his brain as the last raw fuck he got from Matt.

Releasing his grip on Judd, Matt allowed the lad to get in the shower. As the water streamed over Judd's lovely young, hairless body, Matt stroked his cock. He told Judd to turn, present his ass to him. Judd loved the sudden rape, the grinding shock of Matt's prick being driven violently into him, Matt showing no mercy. Matt had taught him to thrill to it, and he did, like nothing ever before in his life.

Matt barged into the shower stall and tore into Judd with a savage fury. Judd's body buckled under the force of his assault. Then Matt began plummeting against Judd with hard, rhythmic strokes. With each thrust, Judd's body trembled. His fingers clawed at the tiles. "Matt, am I just the way you want me to be?" Matt said nothing. "I want it to be exactly the way you like it, so you'll stay. You like it this way, don't you?"

Matt's hands closed around Judd's waist, feeling the life pulsing through him.

"Oh god, I love it. I love you, Matt." Judd was hysterical; he seemed hardly to know what he was saying, except that it was wanton and that it excited him and that it would also excite Matt.

Then he fell silent as the long, slow, warm waves of orgasm inundated him. Matt's cock, sucked of its juices, slipped slowly out of Judd's ass. The job had been done. And it had been done well.

For all of a minute, neither of them said anything. Then Matt took Judd in his arms and kissed him full on the mouth once again. Then he pulled away and started to leave the bathroom, leave the apartment, leave the city.

But then Matt stopped, turned and gazed at Judd again. Judd. Beautiful Judd, smiling at him as he soaped his body. No, there was no way Matt could leave now. He couldn't. He didn't know why, but now after the raw fucking they had just enjoyed, and after all the raw fuckings over the past months, now he wanted it to work. No, he just couldn't let go. Despite everything, Matt could not let go of Judd.

Not yet.

A PUNK'S EDUCATION

Frank Gardner

When I was a teenager I did something really dumb and had to do some hard time. I thought it would be the end of me, that I'd be dead in a week, but then I saw my cellmate: a big Italian named Silvano.

That first night after chow, Silvano lay on his bunk waching me undress. He took one look at my ass and said, bluntly, "You've got a nice ass, kid, and I'm going to fuck it. You can take it up the ass either way, easy or hard. It's your choice. Now drop your pants, and bend over."

It looked like I was going to get a different kind of education. I knew I had a nice creamy, round ass, and that guys with creamy, round asses got fucked in prison. I didn't tell him, but I even liked to fuck it myself. I'd often stick my finger up my asshole while admiring my butt in the mirror. Maybe, I thought, Silvano's cock would feel even better!

And I'd read about the martial arts where you don't resist, but keep control by pushing the other guy in the direction he's already going. So I moved up close to Silvano and fondled his crotch. "I'll bet you've got a big one," I told him.

"Big enough to make you do some groaning," Silvano replied. But he was surprised. Most kids probably fought back, yelling, "No! Please don't! It hurts!" as Silvano grunted, "Take it, punk!" and rammed his big hot cock up into another tight virgin ass.

I continued to feel him up and Silvano's crotch bulged. I made my eyes wide and my voice husky."Gee! It feels big! Can I see it?"

"Uhh!" he grunted.

I unzipped his fly, reached in and ran my hand up and down his swollen cock, then cupped his balls."Awesome!" I fondled his balls. "Big ones!"

"Take my cock out," Silvano demanded, thrusting his hips forward.

I caressed his cock and balls with one hand, while I ran the other up over his muscular ass."You've got a nice ass," I said.

Silvano jerked my hand away. "Never mind my ass. It's your ass I'm interested in."

I didn't push my luck. I unbuckled his belt and pulled his pants down. His cock sprang up and I ran my fingers over it. "I'll bet you've fucked a lot of guys with this."

"Yeah, and they learned to love it," Silvano replied, "just like you will."

Yeah, I thought, I'll learn to love it if you give it to me just the way I want it. I pulled my pants down, revealing my own hard cock. "You sure all of them loved it?" I asked.

"Well...."

I reached over and twisted Silvano's foreskin, skinning it back. "I'll bet you've fucked a few guys that weren't much fun."

Silvano grunted, "Yeah. There were a few cold fish who didn't appreciate my cock up their asses."

"But it's beautiful!" I said, stroking his cock seductively. "Big and hard and hot!" He thrust his cock forward eagerly to get more of my warm caressing hands. I stripped back Silvano's foreskin and flicked my thumb over the tip. "I'll bet you like to get a little cooperation."

"Uhh!" Silvano gasped. "Yeah, I do."

"Me too," I pulled Silvano's hand over onto my cock while I kept pumping his stiff meat. I pressed his hand against my cock and moved it up and down. "Get me hot and I'll give you a really good time."

He smiled. "You will, huh?"

"Like you've never had before. Do you want me to squirm my ass for you when you stick this in me?" I asked, squeezing his cock.

"Yeah!" Silvano grinned. He was finally pumping my cock. "You'll really work your ass-pussy?"

"You'll love the way I work it. Play with my balls."

I spread my legs and worked my balls against his hand. "Oh yeah! That's making me hot."

Silvano grinned. He was getting what he wanted. He ran his hands up over my ass and fondled my buttocks. I wriggled my ass back against his hot hands. "Wanna' hear me squeal when you fuck me?"

"Yeah."

"Feel me up! Run your hands all over me. I can squeal real

good when I'm hot for a guy's cock." I kissed and nibbled on his tits. "Feel my ass!" He reached back and pulled my cheeks apart. "Oh yeah! Tickle my hole!" I grabbed his throbbing cock. "I'm ready for it now! Got any grease?"

"Yeah."

"Grease me up good," I spread my legs and bent over the bunk, resting my head and shoulders on it. I cocked my ass up.

"You've got a nice ass, kid." Silvano said as he worked the grease up into my ass. "This is going to be better than pussy. Nice and tight! Spread your legs wider and pull your buttcheeks apart."

I spread my legs, pulled my cheeks apart and lifted my hips. Fortunately, I also relaxed my hole, because he suddenly rammed his cock all the way up my ass.

"E-e-e-e-y-o-w!" I squealed. Then I squirmed my ass back over his cock to help him get it in deeper."O-h-h-h yeah! Give it to me!"

My squirming ass made Silvano hotter than hell and I got what I wanted. He was ramming his big hot piston in deep, and streams of hot energy surged through my guts.

I pulled Silvano's hand around onto my prick."Jerk it for me!" Now I was really squirming, and Silvano used my cock to make my ass squirm just the way he liked it.

When I shot into his pumping hand, I yelled again, and my ass muscles spasmed around his prick. He grunted, "U-h-h...Uh!" and I could feel his cum shooting up into my rectum. He kept ramming his cock in deep and grinding his balls against my gyrating ass until he finished shooting.

Silvano grinned and slapped my ass. "You are one hot pussy-boy!" he said. He must have thought so, because I got his big hot cock up my ass several times a week.

After a while, Silvano seemed to lose interest in my ass. I began to feeling lonely, deserted. I checked around and found out about an affair he was having with Jim, a new and attractive young inmate. They ever working on the same clean-up detail and they'd get it on in the john before they had to return to their cells.

Jim was barely eighteen, and a very willing and skilled cocksucker. He had built up a string of jocks down in the yard who liked having his warm wet mouth on their cocks. His talented mouth drove them wild. They had never had their cocks sucked like this before.

Finally some of them wanted more. They wanted to get into Jim's cute, plump ass. But Jim had a stock answer for them, "I'm saving it for my wedding night."

Jim was too popular to be abused. So the jocks settled for his cupid-bow lips, passionate tongue, and deep throat action on their throbbing cocks, while his fluttering hands played with their balls.

It was when Silvano discovered Jim's hot mouth that he lost interest in my ass.

I asked him, "What's the matter, Silvano? You haven't been giving it to me the last couple of weeks."

"I figured you didn't really like bending over and sticking your ass out for me, so I eased off," Silvano replied. He didn't mention Jim.

"Found somebody better, huh?"

"Well...."

"Yeah, you like Jim better, don't you?" I looked right at him. "What does Jim have that I don't have?"

"Hot hands and a warm wet mouth," Silvano replied. "He's soft, almost like a girl. The way he uses his mouth makes me hotter than hell!"

I thought of a prison joke about how a young kid is thrown into a cell with a big jocker. The jocker yells at the kid,"Look, kid, you better do this, or I'm gonna...."

"But I don't know *how!*" the kid protests.

"Okay, dammit, I'll show you one more time!" the jocker says.

Silvano had liked the way Jim sucked him. So maybe I could get him to show me just how Jim did it.

"You know, Silvano," I said casually, "I could suck your cock just like Jim, if you'd show me how he does it."

Silvano chuckled. "I doubt it, but you're welcome to try."

I sat on the bottom bunk, unbuckled Silvano's belt and pulled down his pants. I put my mouth on his cock and deliberately gave him a flubby blowjob with poor suction and no decent lip, tongue or hand action. He groaned in frustration."Don't you know how to suck cock?"

"No," I replied. "Will you show me?"

Well, he sure as hell showed me! And he was very, very good. I sucked him again, doing a little better. He had to show me again and again.

"You're gettin' better," Silvano would say, as he shot another load of creamy cum down my throat.

He continued giving me cocksucker lessons. While we lay in a sixty-nine position he'd say, "Do it like this," and I would imitate the way he was sucking me. But I added something. Where he had come up through the prison system he had probably taken plenty of cocks up the ass as a young punk. So while I sucked him, I worked my fingers back around his asshole.

And when he began working his ass back against my probing fingers, I knew he had learned to enjoy having a cock up his ass! So I asked him, "Silvano, could you teach me how to fuck a guy?"

"Y-e-a-h, I guess so." I could tell from the look on his face how much he still wanted it.

Silvano had a tight muscled asshole. I'd shove my cock up into him and he'd blush with pleasure as he told me about how he had been made into a prison punk. All the ways the jocks had shoved their cocks into his mouth and up his ass! As I followed his directions and we fucked that way again, a look of bliss would come over his face and we had some really great sex!

Eventually Silvano was released to a halfway house and I was left with just my right hand. After Silvano moved out, I had a quiet talk with Jim and invited him to move into my cell.

Our first night together, Jim said, "I know why you wanted me to move in with you." He worked his tongue over his lips. "It's this, isn't it?"

"What?"

"My mouth. You want my mouth, don't you."

"I wouldn't mind."

Jim had me sit on the lower bunk and spread my legs. He kneeled down, unbuckled my belt and unzipped my fly, then reached in and fondled my cock and balls. He slowly freed my hot swollen organ. "You've got a really big one!" he said, as he kissed the tip and fluttered his fingers delicately over my balls and painfully rigid cock.

Jim worked my dungarees down under my balls and lowered his lips over my swollen cock. His hungry mouth worked all over me! Lip nibbling, tongue lapping, quick little kisses, and a final deep sucking as I gasped and pumped into his mouth.

I came, "Uh!" Again, "U-h-h!" And again, "O-h-h-h!" as Jim's spasming throat muscles vacuumed my cock. "Ah-h-h!" Such sweet smooth suction! "Um-m-m"

After I came, I told Jim, "I can see now why Silvano liked you so much."

Jim grinned.

I put my hand on his thigh. "You're saving your ass for your wedding-night with Silvano, right?"

Jim's face softened and his eyes took on a dreamy look, "Yes. He said he would wait for me."

I caressed his swollen crotch. "You want to make it really good for him when you get out?"

"Yeah, sure."

"I can show you what he likes."

"You can?"

"Yeah, I can." I said. "Do you want me to show you what he really likes?"

"Well ... okay, I guess." He was hesitant, but he was also horny.

"Okay, let's get down to business." We stripped down and I showed Jim in great detail just what Silvano really liked. "Get up on the bunk on your knees and spread your legs."

He obeyed. "Yeah, that's it. Now stick your ass out."

Jim stuck his ass out. God, it was fuckin' beautiful! I fondled his asscheeks, and pulled them apart. "Okay, when I stick my cock in, you squirm your ass."

"I don't know...."

"It'll be fine. You'll see."

My cock was still wet with all of Jim's cocksucking spit, and I spread his cheeks as I stuck my cock in. "Yeah, that's it!" My cock just slid in, easy as could be. I had a hunch this boy had been around a bit. "Yeah, that's what he likes! Wriggle your ass back over my cock."

He obeyed. God, he was good.

"Oh, that feels s-o-o-o good!" I reached around and grasped his hot little cock. "He likes to play with your cock while he's fuckin' you. And he likes to hear you squeal, like this, 'E-e-e-e-y-o-w!' when he rams all the way in."

I rammed in, and Jim squealed, "E-e-e-e-y-o-w!"

"Oh, yeah, that makes him hotter than hell," I said. "Me too!"

I let Jim control it now, slamming back and forth on my cock, taking it to the hilt. I watched it disappear, re-appear—nothing had felt so good, ever. Jim came, his cum shooting onto the bunk. I continued to jack him as he squealed and I shot my load.

Breathing hard, I held him tight, silently thanking Silvano—for everything.

ONE MORE TIME

Jack Ricardo

Tommy grinned. "One more time?" His eyes were bright.

I grinned back. "You ain't got a chance."

"You're on," he challenged. He tossed the rope on the hay piled midway between us. We were in the barn.

Ever since we were nothing but snot-nosed kids, Tommy and I wrestled, seeing who can top who, who can tie who up. We graduated high school last summer. We'd both be leaving for college in less than a week. This was our last chance for a childhood fling.

"One more time," I said and pulled my t-shirt over my head. Tommy did the same. We pulled off our jeans and tossed them aside like always, and kept our briefs on. We were both bare-chested and build pretty much alike, although Tommy was dark-haired and I was light. And he had a mess of hair that crawled from his chest into his shorts. Chest-wise, I was pretty much hairless. Muscles? We both had them. We were a good match.

We were grinning like a couple of dorks when we circled each other round the haystack, each seeking an opening. I whipped a hand out, Tommy snapped back. Then he sprang out. I expected he'd try for a bear hug, instead he aimed for my legs with his shoulders and knocked me over. I landed flat on my back. He was atop me as quick as a spark and sat on my chest, then slid down, his butt on my crotch, his hands circling my wrists. I bucked like mad to topple him, flailing my legs, exerting pressure on my arms, trying to break the grips on my hands. Tommy was laughing and grunting at the same time, trying to stay on top, no matter that I was slamming his butt with my crotch to try and send him flying. When he went to reach for the rope, I had my chance. I back-circled my free hand around his waist and slapped him off me. Before he could gain another hold, I was on him from behind. I slammed down on his belly with mine, and grabbed his ankles. For a bare instant my crotch brushed his face, his mouth. He gripped my thighs and was shoving me lower and lower, pushing my body down until my chest was scraping over his crotch. The friction was building and I unexpectedly felt the same thing inside his underwear that I knew was in my own. A growing hard-on. This was a first for both of us and we both hesitated, both being aware that something had changed. I hopped up, somewhat confused and somewhat fascinated. Tommy hopped up, confident, buoyant.

Neither of us were grinning. We were serious, we were wondering, we were sweating and circling each other again. The noticeable silhouette in Tommy's shorts was like a bow, with its arrow. No, it was like a flagpole. Both. The shadowy profile of his hard cock was both mesmerizing and mysterious. Mesmerizing because I had never seen another hard cock but my own. Yes, it was inside his shorts, but it might as well not have been. The narrow dickhead was silhouetted distinctly, the veins of the shaft were prominent. And the whole was mysterious, yes. Because I didn't know why I was gawking at his cock so carelessly. I inhaled and sensed the same outline pulsing inside my shorts. Tommy was eyeing it, eyeing me. I stared at him with curiosity. He stared with, well, with lust. It was unmistakable. He swiped his tongue over his lips and gulped.

He lifted his chin high. Our eyes met. There was fire in his. Fear might have been in mine, not a frightening experience, a wondrous one. Before I could have a chance to define it, he was on me in a flash and grabbed me Greco-Roman style, his strong arms clamped around my bare back, my muscled arms surrounding his, our chests glued as one, both breathing as one. His lips were almost touching mine. I could taste his breath. We paused for perhaps one second, our cocks throbbed against each other through white cotton. I was stumped, I didn't know what to do. I was brazenly aroused! But this was Tommy, a guy, my best friend. Tommy must have been just as confused. He eased his hold. I thought he'd release me but he quickly re-clamped his arms round me. I didn't struggle. He lifted then jostled me backwards and let go.

I flopped on my back in the hay, the wind knocked out of me. My whole body ached, but not from the pressure of the landing, but from, from...well, I'm not sure. I coughed and turned onto my stomach, gasping for air. When I craned my neck around to face Tommy, he had the rope dangling from one fist. I coughed again, spit out some hay. I lifted a hand for a time-out, turned over, then rested my hands behind to hold myself up, and unselfconsciously spread my legs.

Tommy knelt beside me. I didn't know what he was gong to do. I was more than confused, I was dumbfounded. Without a word, he turned me onto my side, not gently, not roughly, casually. I didn't protest. And he tied my hands behind me. I let him, without a struggle. Again, I don't know why. Ours has always been an even challenge, utilizing equal strength. But now I was allowing him to take charge. I can't explain why, but it seemed appropriate. When my hands were bound tightly, Tommy stood up. He hadn't overextended himself yet his chest heaving, sweat was dribbling over his brow. His hands were dangling at his side, that stiff outline of his cock was still fronting his briefs and a noticeable dark slime appeared at the tip of the head.

My own breathing was stilted when I huffed and said, "Okay, Tommy, you win...this time." I pulled my legs under me to get up.

"What do I win?" Tommy said. The smile was back. It wasn't a grin this time though, it was careful, playful, anxious.

"I don't know," I said and meant it. I propelled myself to my knees. Tommy lifted a foot and set it on my shoulder. The weight of his muscled leg kept me on my knees. I was baffled. The match was over. Wasn't it? No. Tommy stood there, one foot on the ground, the other on my shoulder. I could see all too clearly his hard cock jutting from the front of his shorts. It was but inches from my face. I could also see each hair on his legs, hairs that grew densely and webbed up into his shorts where the dark flesh of his bare balls were blatantly visible. I could smell his sweat, and mine. The cock inside my own shorts gave out an involuntary leap, and that surprised me. Tommy saw it.

"What do I win?" he again said, not demanding, but playing, seriously playing. He swallowed loudly.

"What do you want?" I said, knowing, not knowing. But, yes, knowing.

Tommy didn't reply right away. But then he said quietly, "You." He kept his socked foot on my shoulder, then slid his leg down my back. The pouch of his balls settled near my neck and was hot, steamy and not entirely unpleasant. I could definitely smell his aroma now. The aroma of his balls. I peered up at him. I was frightened but not terrified. Something new was happening here. I'm not sure I liked it, but I'm not sure I didn't like it either.

Tommy lifted his other foot up and over my other shoulder. He was straddling my neck from the front. I was gently smothered. My face was mashed against the front of his underwear, his cock was twitching inside and tapping my forehead, his balls covered my entire mouth and nose. I was flabbergasted, aghast, annoyed, overwhelmed. I couldn't lean over, I'd break my back. But this had gone about as far as I wanted. I wrenched my face from side to side and mumbled, "Lemme...lemme..." I couldn't get the words out, his balls, his cock were rubbing harshly over my face. Tommy groaned, I groaned. His was pleasure, mine was exasperation, perhaps mixed with an unexplored thrill that kept me from protesting too much.

I fell sideways into the hay and lay there, my arms tied behind me. "Game's over, Tommy," I said, glaring at him, questioning him. "Please."

"Do you really want it to be?" he said. He stepped over me, one leg on either side of my hips, looking very much the giant from the childhood beanstalk. I dug my heels into the ground and pushed myself until my back was leaning against the hay and the wooden walls of the barn

"Yes," I said quietly, "No." Tommy was fondling the front of his shorts, his cock, his balls.

"You know what's happening here," he said. I think it was a question, a hope. I didn't say a word. I did know, I didn't know. I was frowning. His tone suddenly changed and hinted of a certain fear. He said, "I'm gay."

If Tommy had told me he was an alien from another world, I couldn't have been more shocked. "I don't believe you. Tommy, we're just fooling around together. We always did. So, we both got aroused this time. It doesn't mean anything, it doesn't mean that you're gay."

"It does. I'm gay, Mickey."

I sensed a plea somewhere in his proud proclamation.

"And I've always known it," he continued, "but I just never had the balls to do anything about it."

His words struck me as funny. I stared up between his legs. "Oh, no, Tommy, you have the balls." I couldn't help but laugh.

He coughed out a deep sigh of relief and hefted his nuts in the palm of one hand. "Yeah," he smiled. "I've got balls." He added, "And I've got you." He wrapped his other hand around the strong hard cock in his shorts. "All tied up, and all mine."

A fear tingled down my spine, but it was fear mixed with curiosity and, yes, excitement. I tried to smile and found it wasn't much of an effort. "What are you gonna do?" But I didn't give him the opportunity to answer before I asked, "You wanna blow me?"

"Yeah, I do," he said. "You're tied up, you won't stop me." He said this mischievously, playfully, still a kid. One more time. Yeah, a kid, with a stiff dick.

"What if I don't want to stop you," I said. Did I say that, I wondered. Yes, I did. I didn't want to stop him. My cock was pulsing, my balls were tingling.

Tommy was still standing over my waist when he lowered himself to his haunches. His butt brushed over my crotch. I lifted my hips and settled the stiff dick in my shorts directly in line with the crack of Tommy's cotton covered ass, and heaved up. His cock, his balls were crushed onto my chest. He sighed. So did I.

"I'm not gay, Tommy," I said.

"I know," he said.

It didn't matter. Not for the moment, not for today. I was his for today, for the last day of our childhood together.

He slid off me and slipped his fingers into the band of my briefs. He pulled them off. My hard cock flopped up and landed on my wiry and sparse cockhairs. My balls scratched into the hay. My arms behind me began to ache, the rope seemed to burn into the flesh. I stretched them to a more comfortable position. Tommy stood up and pushed down his shorts. He threw them on mine. His cock was jutting parallel with the floor, and it different from mine. Just as hard, yes. And pulsing just as vigorously. And probably hear the same length. But the head at the tip was narrow, almost an arrow.

Mine was round as a doorknob. Both were leaking slimy fluid. Coursing chills circled in my balls. I sat spread-eagled, my roped hands near the base of my spine, my back to the wall.

Tommy knelt between my legs. He set his hands on either side of my waist and bowed down to my chest, gliding his mouth over the muscles of my chest then flicking his tongue over one of my nipples. The sensation was as erotic a moment as I'd ever felt in my life. I'd had sex one time before with, with a girl, and it was I who flicked my tongue over her nipple. But now Tommy, a guy, was doing the same to mine. And it was remarkably invigorating, amazingly sensual, and I closed my eyes purred. I squirmed my bare ass into the hay.

Tommy licked over the ripples of my chest to my other nipple where he tapped it with his tongue, bit it gently with his teeth, and sent my senses soaring. I squirmed more, and the muscles in my arms automatically tried to break the bonds behind me. Certainly not to stop, Tommy. But to encourage him. I wanted to place both hands on his head and follow the path he was trailing with his tongue. He poked his tongue into my naval, and I sighed so loudly Tommy lifted his eyes to mine. I tried to smile. Dribble slid down my lips.

Tommy was drooling as well before he began scraping his chin over my cockhairs. My cock was nestled beneath his chin. I humped my ass up. Tommy trapped my cock with his chin. He chewed on my cockhairs than began gnawing at the base of the shaft of my cock. Gnawing slowly, wetly, lovingly, round and round the circumference of my cock, covering every inch, every pore, until my thickly rounded dickhead was sliding over the top of his lips before he lapped his tongue oven the underside of the head, slurped up the ooze leaking from the slit, then covered both lips over the entire head, warming it, wetting it, engulfing it, suckling it. I mooed like a more-than-contented cow. Tommy sucked down the rock hard shaft, sucked up. Tommy was sucking my cock.

"Tommy, Tommy, Tommy," I kept groaning, squirming, and all the time, flashes of pleasure surging throughout my entire body. Tommy kept sucking, slowly, easily. He seemed hypnotized by my cock, by the solid shaft of flesh that was sweeping in and out of his mouth, that was trapped between two wonderful lips that were getting as much pleasure as they were giving. It was a magnificent sight, to see someone, to see my best friend, delight in blowing me. My God, My Best Friend, Blowing Me!

He brought a hand over and covered my balls with his fingers. I cringed in sheer ecstasy. A thousand spiders with a thousand legs were crawling over the baggy flesh of my balls, tickling at the nuts inside. And Tommy kept sucking, and I kept soaring. He was holding my balls, he was sucking my cock, faster now, and a finger was tickling between my legs and under my balls, scraping over my asshole. I groaned louder. Tommy sucked frenetically now. He squeezed my balls tightly, his finger became persistent, poking open the wrinkles of my asshole and moving inside. Pinpricks of astonishing sensation raged through my body. Tommy downed my cock fully and stayed there. My eyes slammed shut. My cock was swelling to unexperienced delights inside his throat, he crushed my balls, his entire finger was inside my asshole and I yelped, and I yelled, and I grunted, and Tommy's throat muscles surrounded and pulsed against my cock and it was growing, expanding, shooting. Tommy sputtered but kept his mouth clamped over my cock. I shouted to high heaven and rammed my cock deeper into his gut until I was all juiced out and faded into the hay, both body and soul.

When I opened my eyes, Tommy was kneeling up at my feet, he was holding onto his balls, he was stroking his eyes, his eyes were wide and bright. He hunches his hips forward. The head of his arrowed cock grew wider, larger, redder. He grunted loudly and spurt after spurt of cum began shooting from his cock, landing on my feet, my balls, my chest, until his body shook, his cock spat out one more drop, and he collapsed his ass on the heels of his feet.

We both suddenly started laughing, almost hysterically.

I went off to college at the end of the week. So did Tommy. We write and talk to each other constantly. He has a lover. I'm engaged to be married.

ALL THE MAN I NEED

John Patrick

Lance's agent in Hollywood had booked him for a three-night dance gig at in Miami Beach over the Memorial Day Weekend. The first night, after his set, Lance was approached by an older man who said he had seen all of Lance's videos and wanted him to come back to his hotel. Lance demurred, saying he had a long flight from L.A. and was tired. But the man persisted, begging the porn star, saying all he wanted to do was give him a blowjob. Finally Lance relented when the man said his hotel was within walking distance. As they left the club, the man introduced himself as Moses, which made Lance chuckle and make a lame joke about his benefactor leading the way to the Promised Land.

At the motel, Lance stepped from the shower and toweled himself off, Moses tore off his shirt, and was quickly out of his slacks, shoes, socks, and underwear. He began pissing into the bowl, talking a mile a minute about how much he had enjoyed Lance's latest video about a football team gone sex-mad. Lance thought Moses was the one who was mad, running on nerves; it was so fucking weird it was funny. Finishing his toweling off, Lance stroked his cock but when it didn't harden immediately as it usually did, he decided that the moment of spontaneity had passed; he should have just let Moses blow him the moment they entered the room. Now sex was an obstacle that stood between him and his most fervent desire-to sleep. He made his way to the queen-size bed and crawled under the cool sheets. Moses came out of the bathroom and stood naked before the full-length mirror. He was proud of his body; he had retained the mesomorphic physique of the athlete he had once been. His white hair was snowy white and he had a lot of it. He had a naturally dark complexion, and so he religiously maintained a bronze tan.

And he had an eight-inch cock that was always ready for action, even at his advanced age. Seeing him naked, Lance thought, under ordinary circumstances, he might be able to handle him, but not now. Lance grunted and rolled over and then hugged the pillow. He closed his eyes.

"God," Moses gushed, stepping over to the bed and pulling the sheet back. "I've got the most gorgeous creature in the world in my bed and he has to pull a routine like this. I'm really disappointed with you."

The sight of Lance's magnificent ass, so white against the well-tanned rest of him, Moses thought of Lance's big, uncut cock hidden from view, the handsomeness of Lance's angelic face-the sum of it all caused Moses' cock to straighten up like a rocket. Lance rolled over and Moses saw that he was at last showing a bit of life.

"Oh my god," Moses gasped when he saw the cock, semi-hard, the massive head peeking out of the foreskin. But Lance was the one who took action. He grabbed Moses hefty shaft with both hands, like Louis"Satchmo" Armstrong picking up his trumpet at the beginning of a set. Soon his tongue was working it over. The thought of Lance in that video"Playing the Field", screwing an entire football team, or so it appeared, caused Moses to come in less than twenty seconds."My God," he said, "you sucked me dry. And I thought it was going to be a lost cause."

"You were really loaded," Lance chuckled.

"And you like that?" Moses asked.

"Yeah, I love it," Lance said, smacking his lips and continuing to stroke Moses' long, thin member.

Moses simply didn't figure Lance for this. No wonder he was such a major star. He sure seemed to like giving head. More to the point, he really seemed to have warmed to Moses. Lance lifted up and pulled Moses down to kiss him deeply, causing him to taste himself, which was, oddly enough, a first for Moses and a crazy kind of turn-on.

Lance wanted the kiss and more. Soon Moses was on the bed, between Lance's thighs, preparing to enter Lance missionary style.

Moses surprised himself; he had no trouble getting hard again. He put some lube up Lance's butt and then shoved the head of his prick into the porn star. His slow strokes gave way to faster ones. He went faster, harder, and deeper while Lance's low moans gave way to shrill cries of pleasure. Lance's nails dug deep into his back and Moses became lost in the experience of fucking someone so famous, and Lance too was lost in his own fantasy, pain mixing with pleasure. Moses found himself vanishing into an abyss of ecstasy until he came for the second time. Then Moses started to pull out but Lance wouldn't hear of it. Moses was to keep his cock in, was to continue fucking until the star had his money shot. Moses had to keep fucking harder and harder until Lance finally came, a pitiful amount, but cum nonetheless. Moses suddenly realized that fucking Lance had became work, a tremendous effort.

When it was over, Moses could hardly get any air and had to sit up on the edge of the bed panting. It dawned on him that Lance should pay him for such a Herculean effort!

"Hey, man, are you all right?" Lance said with a certain amount of professional concern.

"...Will be. Just give me a minute."

Moses got out of bed and went into the bathroom. He plopped two Alka-Seltzer tablets into a glass and watched it fizz, then he drank it down.

When Moses returned to the bedroom, Lance had turned out the lights. Moses got into bed. "For a minute there I thought I was having a heart attack. But I'm okay now," he said, still breathing heavily. He was utterly exhausted. He turned to Lance, who had rolled over onto his stomach and was already fast asleep, and kissed Lance's bare shoulder.

. . .

On the second night in Miami Beach, Lance had no pre-arranged "date" so instead of letting the other dancers roam the crowd and collect the tips, he decided to join in the fun. When he finished his first number, still wearing his jockstrap, he bounded from the stage and started making his way through the crowd. He did not linger the way the other dancers did, just took his dollars for a quick feel. Some men were bold and could not resist the huge bulge. Lance would adroitly squeeze their hand and push it away. They had seen the cock, it was allowed in Miami, and that was enough. If they wanted more, they could have a private show later. He had three more sets to do and by the last he would have picked out a likely prospect.

A fat man was very aggressive and wrapped his bear arms around Lance. Lance tried to pull away but the man, sitting on a stool at the bar, held him fast. It was then that Lance noticed the most handsome young man he had ever laid eyes on. The object of his desire was sitting next to the fat man who wouldn't let go. The object turned, opening his thighs to Lance. Lance reached out to the object and shoved his elbow into the fat man's gut. In a moment, he was between the object's thighs and the object's arms were around him.

"Well, hello," the object said.

"Hi." Lance looked into the azure blue eyes and couldn't help himself. He kissed the man on the mouth. The man returned his affection.

When their lips finally parted, the man said,"What are you doing later?"

"Nothin'," Lance teased, and danced away.

In the bathroom that passed as a dressing room, Lance asked Jeff, one of the regular dancers, who the man at end of the bar was.

"Cute isn't he?"

"Yeah."

"He's here a lot. His name is Hart. He's Senator Taylor's son, just slumming."

"Does he take anybody home?"

"No. He's just a looker."

"He's a looker all right."

"I mean, if you looked like that would you have to hire somebody?"

The Senator's son soon became the most unusual "date" Lance ever had. Lance went back on stage to dance his final set and when it was over, went directly over to Hart, who was still sitting at the end of the bar."I want to make love to you," the Senator's son whispered in Lance's ear as he held him. He introduced himself. He said he was in town attending a conference.

"Will you give me a ride back to my place?" Lance asked, running his hand up Hart's thigh.

"No, I'll give you a ride to *my* place."

When they arrived at the hotel, Lance went to the bathroom

and when he emerged, Hart had lit a vanilla candle. Except for the narrow flicker of light from the candle, the room was dark. A shadow danced erratically across the hotel room wall.

Lance was taken aback by the romanticism of it all. Soon Hart's lips were pressed against Lance's ear."Tell me what you want. Tell me." He kissed his cheek, his forehead, his eyes. "Please."

But Lance could not tell him what he really wanted—what he was really looking for—because he had not fully articulated it even to himself. But he knew he'd know it when he found it.

Even the slender light from the candle was far too bright. And Lance knew if he revealed too much, there'd be no place left for him to hide. Hart dropped to his knees and began sucking the limp cock. He worked it up to near-hardness and then stood.

Hart took Lance's hand and led him to the bed. They hardly knew each other and it made Lance vulnerable and apprehensive but he knew that in this case he couldn't say no. With a single kiss Hart had drawn Lance out of his hesitations.

"You!" Hart muttered, his voice deep. "You! You! You!"

He was all over Lance. His desire poured from him and cascaded into the stud. He covered him in kisses, nips, sucks. His lips, fast and desperate on the stud's body, sent currents of hard pleasure through Lance, who closed his eyes and felt his tongue slash across his nipples. He was pulling him, dragging him deep into a place he had never been.

His mouth found Lance's navel. Then he flicked the opening of Lance's ass, then plunged his tongue into the hole. Again and again, he fucked his ass with his tongue. A trail of hot saliva criss-crossed his skin. And further and further Lance slid into the abyss.

His predatory fingers lunged and Lance's monstrous sex became slippery with spit. He was hard, harder than he could ever remember being. Hart sucked the cock while he fucked the ass with his fingers. Lance, a willing prey, succumbed. As if there could have been any other choice but to spread his legs and arch up to meet his new lover.

"I can make you come. Just tell me how you like it," he whispered.

"Oh, god," Lance groaned.

Hart's breath was hot. And soon Lance was aroused to an unbearable, dangerous place—a place he thought he'd never come to. A constant throbbing radiated from between his legs.

As Hart entered him it was absolute pleasure, but he couldn't say it, no matter how hard the ache, how insistent the pressure. He could not admit to Hart that he was the first, that it was finally happening. But Hart had been here before. He knew Lance was home at last.

His fingers lingered on Hart's ass while he was battering him, pushing the cock even farther into his ass. Hart had been fucking Lance for over an hour. Or had it been two? Three?

Lance opened his eyes the tiniest bit. The room was darker. The candle flame leapt on the last of the wick. Hart began his orgasm. It was monumental. He shook and held Lance tightly to him, kissing him full on the mouth.

As they lay in each other's arms, Hart's semi-flaccid cock still inside Lance, Hart panted, "God, I can't stop. . ."

Lance moaned, then watched in anticipation as Hart lifted himself up and parted Lance's legs again. Hart looked down as he held the root of his cock and slid it back into the ass. Lance groaned now. He had never ached like this before, but his body was still shimmering with desire.

Once he was fully in him, Hart caressed his face with one gentle finger and then took him in his arms and kissed him. Lance kissed him back as the sex pounded through him.

Although his gig in Miami was over, he stayed on to be with Hart and dance for him alone.

Hart had turned the radio on and the music snaked into the bathroom like a thin spiral of smoke. Lance's reflection stared from the mirror. He had never felt so sexy. Alone, in the bathroom, he danced to please himself. He luxuriated in the swing of his cock as he moved. His hand slowly followed the thin line of hair that went from the navel to the pubic patch. He imagined Hart passing by, seeing him, desiring him like he now desired himself.

As if Hart could hear his thoughts from the other room, he came to the doorway of the bathroom. He simply stood there and watched as Lance danced. Lance felt lost in the music, lost in his incredible sensuality. It seemed as if Hart had a way of looking through Lance that sent a vivid sexual impulse careening through his body. Hart smiled and followed him with his eyes and a throbbing began in his cock.

Lance had always hungered for a man like Hart. One look and he was his. When Hart fucked him, he fucked him as if he were a pillow, ramming him, blasting into him, doing whatever he pleased. Hart could get as rough as he wanted, knowing Lance would never break. That was the attraction. Hart was already with someone who was fragile, someone he treated like a little doll: his wife. When Lance heard that news he was scared yet it was the fine line that he loved. He craved, for once, walking the edge between out of control and controlled. And Hart was an exquisite lover.

Hart turned from the doorway and Lance knew exactly where he was headed. He heard him changing the station, finding *that* song, Whitney Houston's "All the Man I Need." It was the song that was playing as they left the club.

Lance entered the bedroom and began teasing, tempting. He danced to please them both. He wanted Hart to watch, to become so aroused that he could barely breathe. Hart made no effort to come to Lance but he felt him soar across the room and grab him, shake him, devour him. His eyes took in every move he made. Soon he began masturbating.

Lance brought his cock up to semi-hardness. From opposite corners, they made love. Lance swirled his hips. Hart didn't move from the bed yet he was at Lance's side, all the same. With a pleased nod of the head he caressed Lance. He danced, danced, danced, working up a sweat. Hart came. The scent of sex spun around them as Lance moved closer and closer to the bed. His nipples stood like hard cranberries and his fingers grazed the tips, pinched them, plucked them. Hart lifted up and Lance let him slip his aching nipple into his mouth and he simply sucked.

Not allowing Hart's now-outstretched arms to capture him, Lance danced in a steamy circle around the bed. He felt exhilarated. The more he moved, the deeper he descended into another dimension. They were separate yet intertwined, all at once. Soon, he was on the bed and soaked.

Pulsating, churning—Hart wanted more. He rammed Lance as best he could. Lance was trembling.

"Oh yes!" And Hart plunged.
"Oh yes!" And Hart thrusted.
"Oh yes!" And he fucked him again and again.

Their lovemaking became poetry and art. Hart's fiery words aroused Lance intensely while he was being fucked. But it was not one-sided. At last Hart let Lance fuck him as well.

But when they were finished, Hart stood at the window, deep in thought. Something was off. Something desperately guarded. "I have to tell you, we need to keep things safe. No involvement beyond right here in bed. Agreed?"

"No involvement," Lance replied. "Yeah, exactly what I want, really. "

"Believe me, it's best."

Lance went to him. Hart wrapped his arms around Lance, pulled back slightly and peered at him. "I have to go home tomorrow."

"So do I."

"Will you be back this way soon?"

Lance looked away. He didn't want to think about it. "What's the use?"

Hart understood, but chose not to acknowledge it. He only wanted to have his cake and eat it too.

Hart cupped Lance's face in his hands. His voice was soft and soothing, but the azure blue eyes now held a sliver of dishonesty. Although Lance knew Hart was the son of a senator, he never let on he knew. Hart merely told him his family was in banking and he was attending the conference without his wife because that was his one chance to indulge his "other side."

Lance did not press his lover for more; indeed it was as if Lance did not want to know more. But the hopelessness of the situation was evident now. Still, Lance would not let it spoil their last night of sex.

Lance knew now that Hart wasn't looking for love. Hart only wanted to feel a transitory touch, enjoy homosexual intimacy for a moment in time, with the sexiest boy he could find, that his inherited money could buy. He was not looking for anything more, surely not looking for a relationship.

Lance was the one who had walked that tightrope—and fallen. For three days, Lance was caught up in his own moment in time, his own love story, a kaleidoscope of all that a great love—with a wealthy, handsome young man—could be.

For days after Hart, Lance could imagine making love with no one else. After Hart, for Lance there was nothing but the feel of the older man's touch, the scent of him, and his dirty, lewd whispers as he fucked.

—This tale was adapted from material originally appearing in *Lover Boys*.

PAYING FOR IT

Joe Sexton

I realize that seventeen is a little late for a "First Time," but I grew up the only son of strict Baptist schoolteachers in Broaddus, a small East Texas town, and had little opportunity until I went off to college. Once there, I hardly knew how to begin—I was shy, and much too naive and ignorant to know what I wanted or how to get it. Ripe for seduction, I surrendered without much of a struggle. But even afterwards I didn't become instantly promiscuous. There was something special about that first time, but I was confused and full of guilt, wondering if this was love. Later, memories of the affair overwhelmed me, and I spent many futile years trying to recapture a feeling that probably never existed, and to find a partner like that first one, whose attractions became magnified in my mind over time, impossible standards by which I measured all men.

I turned seventeen as I began my freshman year at the state college in Nacogdoches. This town of about 35,000 seemed a metropolis to me compared to Broaddus, a "broad place in the road" some fifty miles away, where I had just graduated as valedictorian in a senior class of twelve. In 1949 Nacogdoches *was* a metropolis in some ways, a center of culture and learning for all of the eastern part of Texas. There Danilova danced, Rubenstein played, and Metropolitan Opera stars on their way to Dallas or Houston made one-night stops for concerts. I attended everything available to me on my student activities card, eager to fill what I perceived as a yawning gap in my cultural experience; I had read widely, but had *lived* hardly at all.

To supplement my $100 a month allowance from home, I worked part time as a waiter in Nance's Cafe, near the campus, a popular gathering spot not only for students, but faculty and local residents. Instead of living in the men's dormitory as I would have liked, I rented a cheaper room nearby in the home of a retired couple, former teaching colleagues of my parents.

The first time I saw John, he came into Nance's Cafe with a group of other sophomores late one night looking for freshmen to haze. They rounded up a few of us and took us back to the men's dorm for haircuts. I was delighted. I wanted everything college had to offer, including participation in this barbaric rite. John seemed a little older than the others, and more serious. He took charge of me, and seemed to derive a malicious pleasure in reducing my abundant reddish curls to a single forelock, roughly maneuvering a pair of rusty clippers. The other freshmen were given similar haircuts, we were warned not to appear on campus without wearing our freshman beanies, and released.

Months later, near the end of the semester, I was taking my usual short-cut across campus through the men's dorm, enjoying occasional glimpses of naked flesh through doors left ajar, when a voice stopped me.

"Hey freshman, come here." I walked hesitantly into the nearest room and there was John, his entire body on a level with my eyes, as he lay indolently on the upper bunk, clad only in shorts. He was propped on his elbow, staring at me.

"Close the door," he ordered. I closed it. He surveyed me silently for a few moments, fondling his crotch with one hand.

"What's your name?" he asked, continuing to look me up and down. I told him. I didn't dare ask his. My mouth was dry, I was afraid, and excited, and hopeful. I wanted to run.

"Well, Red," he said, ignoring my real name, "how about a blowjob?"

"What's that?" I wondered. I had never heard or read the term before, although I could guess from the sound of it, and the circumstances, what it must involve.

"Come on, don't give me that shit--you must have done it lots of times." I shook my head and he stared at me in disbelief, then slowly began to smile. "Damn, I think I got me a cherry. Okay, I'll show you." He jumped down from the bunk, pulled on a pair of corduroy pants and a plaid flannel shirt, and motioned for me to follow him. Quickly and rather furtively we walked down the hall to a small utility room; he pushed me in, turned on the light, and locked the door behind us.

"This is safer," he said, "in case my roommate comes back."

He leaned spread eagled against the shelves and pointed to the floor in front of him. "On your knees," he ordered. I knelt. It was so like one of my fantasies I felt I was dreaming. But I was quickly awakened by the sheer physicalness of what came next.

"Now take it out and suck it," he said. Surprised by the brutal directness of his order and the lack of any romantic words or foreplay, which instinctively I felt should be a part of such a scene, I began to stroke the bulge in his pants with one hand and his tight buttocks with the other, resting my head against his thigh. But he would have none of it: he grabbed my shoulder and shook me roughly. "Cut that out and get on it. Do I have to do everything?" Impatiently he unzipped his fly and extracted his penis, already hard and bucking, thrusting toward my mouth. As cocks go, and I've seen many since then, it was extraordinarily large, well formed and circumcised. I remember the odor of tobacco on his hands as he guided it into my mouth.

As this was my first time, I frequently gagged and attempted to resist the relentless pumping, which he accompanied by a running commentary in a sensuous, curiously caressing voice: "Slow down, Red, that's not a sausage you're eating—just the head at first ... that's it—a little more suction—slide on down an inch or two—that's the way--now almost all the way back—keep it up, nice and steady, you're getting the hang of it—you really love that, don't you, Red? Take it all the way now. Slower, an inch at a time, all the way down to the base ... They, that's good sucking. You're doing fine, Red. Don't gag ... faster now. I'm getting close. I want you to swallow every drop--ready? You're getting it! Ahhhhh!" As he filled my mouth and throat, his voice became gravelly and ended in a gasp.

When it was over, I didn't swallow; I ran—out of the utility room, out of the dormitory and into the woods, where behind a big pine tree I spit and retched and spit again, trying to expel onto the carpet of dry brown pine needles all the feelings of humiliation and guilt and uncleanness which this act of near-rape had caused me. Unlike most rape victims, however, I had been a rather willing victim, and it was this, I think, that aroused the most guilt. I was still young and idealistic enough to have visions of romantic love, where sex was an integral part of that love, and not a violent brutal act quite separate from all affection.

I rushed back to my room and washed my mouth with soap, hydrogen peroxide, and Listerine. But nothing helped. I still felt unclean, violated, sinful. Then, still under the influence of my Baptist upbringing, I prayed. But the prayer didn't seem to get through, I couldn't concentrate, I already felt cast out by God. Later I took a bath, the memory of John returned, and I masturbated to that vision of dark beauty.

During the next week my distress and confusion waned and life returned to normal. I did not mention my experience to anyone, not even to Roger, my closest friend at that time. It began to seem like just another fantasy; but I was puzzled and disturbed that the violence and brutality of the act was what now attracted me most.

The men's dorm was out of bounds for me from then on. Although I thought of John often, I dreaded meeting him again. However, the college was too small for me to avoid him forever, and one day early in the spring semester, I saw him in the campus cafeteria, sitting at a corner table across the room.

Hurriedly downing the remains of my lunch, I made for the door. But he saw me, and followed me outside. "Hey, Red, got that English?" he called, even before he caught up with me. I looked at him blankly—I was taking Freshman English that semester, but he certainly wasn't in my class. "Got that paper ready for English class? I need some help with mine."

Then he looked around—no one was near, but he lowered his voice. "Come to my room. In five minutes." He started off, then turned back. "And you better be there if you know what's good for you!"

Loping off along the path to the dorm, he looked back once and scowled. I felt so shaky I had to sit down, full of turmoil again and not certain what to do. I thought of going back to my room and ignoring him, of dropping out of school, of killing him, of killing myself, but of course in five minutes I was knocking on his door.

This time we stayed in his room. He must have known his roommate wouldn't be returning soon. But he locked the door anyway and leaned back against the radiator, half sitting on it. We stared at each other. Not quite as rattled as I had been before, I took time to study him more carefully: medium height, dark hair and eyes, smooth olive skin, a persistent five o'clock shadow, thick sensual sullen lips, and heavy brows drawn together in what seemed a permanent frown. His eyes were magnetic, deep set and heavy lidded, with a compelling, unswerving gaze. He wore black Wellington boots, corduroys again, and another plaid flannel shirt. This, as it turned out, was a kind of uniform—I never saw him in anything else. He always looked clean and neat and smelled faintly of shaving lotion and tobacco.

Finally he spoke. "Well, I haven't got all day. If you want it, take it."

Needing no further inducement, I took it, and again he began his commentary, a little more desultory this time, and less instructive.

"You're getting pretty good at that, Red. You must have been practicing. I bet you've been wanting it ever since last time, huh? Well, I'm going to let you have it at least once a week. How about that? Hey, not so fast, slow down, nice and easy, that's it. You ever seen such a big one? You really like that, don't you?"

He lit a cigarette and watched me for a few minutes. Then abruptly he withdrew his cock and held it, still throbbing, a few inches from my face.

"Tell me how much you love it," he demanded. But I could not bring myself to put into words what I was ashamed of even thinking. Impatiently he waggled it before my eyes. "Well, *do* you love it?"

I nodded.

"Say it," he ordered. "I love it," I whispered. He seemed satisfied then and began to stuff his still engorged member back into his pants. "I'm going to have to put it away, Red. I gotta save it for my girlfriend, or someone who can pay for it, and believe me there's plenty'd give their right arm for this cock." He disengaged it again from his pants and waved it closer to my mouth. I stared, hypnotized. "Tell you what: give me five dollars and I'll let you have it again. It's worth more, but what the hell, I like you, Red."

"I only have two on me," I managed to croak.

"Okay, get it and I'll let you owe me for the rest."

We completed the transaction, and I resumed my sucking

with even more excitement and abandon than before, the financial arrangement having apparently added spice to the act for both of us. Afterward, much to his disgust, I spat into his sink, and left without another word. Home again, I repeated my cleansing, but without quite the frantic desperation I had felt after the last episode.

During the remainder of the semester, despite all my efforts to avoid seeing him, the pattern was repeated numerous times, with two differences: I had learned to swallow it, even like it, and I was becoming increasingly angry and resistant to his demands for money. Finally I refused altogether, pleading poverty, which was in fact true. My allowance from home and my part time job at Nance's Cafe paid for rent, food, and other essentials, but little more.

Surprisingly, he capitulated. "I know you're broke, Joe, so I won't make you pay me anymore." This was the first time he had called me by my real name and I was touched. It was such an unexpected contrast to his previous manner of cool contempt.

ut it was too late; I had already met someone who was initiating me into the local gay scene, such as it was, and I was enjoying a sexual relationship based on mutual and equal interests and satisfaction. This was near the end of the semester, and, confident in my new life, I simply ignored his latest invitation to join him in his room. The next day he came to visit me in my room. This was a most unwelcome surprise. I don't know how he located my address, unless he followed me. However, he seemed to have hidden sources of information—he knew everything about me, and I knew nothing about him, not even his real name.

Fortunately I had a private entrance, and I hoped that he had not been seen. There was no rule against my having guests, but I'd never had any, and I knew that Mrs. Dunn, preparing dinner in the kitchen next to my room, would be suspicious if she heard voices.

"Please be quiet," I said. "My landlady's just next door." He stared at me and flopped across the bed, caressing the bulge in his pants. "You want it," he whispered. "I know you do. Come and get it." I felt the familiar stirring of desire; I wanted to throw myself at his feet and bury my head in his crotch, and worship that firm strong masculine body and all it symbolized: power, force, violence, qualities all alien to me. I hated myself for being attracted to such things, and I hated him for making me feel that way.

The thought of Mrs. Dunn on the other side of the thin wall brought me back to sanity with a jolt, however, and I shook my head. I was terrified of having any hint of my sexual proclivities reaching the ears of my parents. Taking his cock from his pants and beckoning me with it, he began to stroke it softly as he urged me forward with a low almost gentle voice, staring at me with those dark hypnotic eyes.

"C'mon, Joe. It's free. You can have it anytime for nothing. Tell you the truth, I like it as much as you do." This was a surprising admission, and I realize now what it must have cost him to make it. But I was frantic to get him out of the house and felt a sudden surge of anger.

"Get out of here and leave me alone, you bastard!" I said, immediately aghast at my nerve in thus confronting him. He was off the bed in an instant and slammed me against the wall, his left hand at my throat and the other a fist poised for action.

"What did you say? What did you just call me, you fucking queer?" For the first time I was truly afraid. He seemed perfectly capable of murder.

"I'm sorry. I didn't mean to call you that," I hastened to assure him. "Please ... I'm just upset." He let go my throat and dropped his fist, but continued to glare inches from my face. I knew I had done the unforgivable, first in refusing him, and then in calling him a name no macho Texan could accept from anyone, least of all from one considered to be at the very bottom of the social scale, a queer.

"I'm going to beat the shit out of you, you little faggot," he promised. "I should have done it a long time ago. You've really been asking for it."

"Look, let's go outside. I don't want to mess this place up," I said, hoping to lure him out of my room. I had become much more frightened of an unpleasant scene before the Dunns, and the threat of exposure, than of getting beaten. Without waiting for an answer, I hastened out of the door and began walking up the hill toward the campus. John caught up with me and attempted to take my arm, but I pulled away and continued to walk at a fast clip away from the house. He seemed less sure of himself now and what his next move should be; he continued to walk beside me, crowding and jostling me occasionally on the path.

"I think the dean's going to be interested in what you've been up to this year," he said, finally ending the ominous silence. "They don't like cocksuckers around here, you know. This is Texas, it ain't goddam California. You're gonna wish you hadn't tangled with me, buddy!"

"That may be," I said, my courage somewhat restored, now that we were back on the main street. "But I'm just seventeen, still a minor, and you're over twenty-one," I hazarded a guess here, and it must have been to the mark, for he paled visibly. "It takes two to do what we did, and you could be charged with contributing to the delinquency of a minor."

He stopped, pulling me around to face him--I'm sure he would have hit me if there hadn't been people around. We were in front of Nance's Cafe by then. "Listen, punk. Don't you get smart with me. I'll whip your ass! Just remember, I know where you live. I'm going to be around next year and you'll be hearing from me." He gave my arm a vicious twist, turned on his heel and swaggered off in his brightly polished Wellington boots, giving me the finger as he walked, without even turning around.

After finals were over, I went home for the summer, then moved to Austin to attend the University of Texas. For a while I was greatly relieved to be rid of him, but gradually, as the years passed and I became more experienced, I began to suspect that I had let a potential treasure slip through my fingers. He had been gradually accepting what we had together when I ruined it with my sudden anger.

Later, when I returned to Nacogdoches, fresh out of a California graduate school, to teach art as a one-year sabbatical replacement, I made an effort to find some trace of him. In the library I pored over old college annuals, hoping to come across his picture and find his real name. But he appeared nowhere-- he was a loner, I suppose, not involved in campus politics or clubs or extracurricular activities. I had a slim hope that he would find me, that perhaps he had lingered all those years, just to get even or give me another chance. Several times I walked through the men's dorm, expecting to hear at any moment, "Hey, Red, you got that English?" But I couldn't even remember which room was his.

The following year I obtained a teaching position in San Francisco, a town I grew to love and which became my permanent home. My obsession gradually faded, and at last I stopped seeking John's likeness among the young leather studs cruising Polk and Castro Streets.

I think of him now only occasionally, but when I do, or when he comes to me in a dream, my desire rises and burns as fiercely as ever. Waking, I lie bemused, pondering the mystery and lingering sadness of roads not taken; then, with a sigh, I turn to the warm familiar body next to me, wrap my arms around him, and, content, fall into a deep and dreamless sleep.

—*This story has been adapted for this collection from material originally appearing in RFD magazine.*

CAUGHT IN THE ACT
(First of Three Parts)

Ronald James

"Jesus! Jesus! What the shit are you guys doin'?"

I'd just walked in on my brother Frank and his best friend, Ty, jacking off.

Frank: "Close the fucking door, man."

Then Ty: "Close the door, fuckhead!"

I stepped into the bedroom we shared closing the door behind me, never talking my eyes off the scene; Frank and Ty sitting on Frank's bed, their backs against the wall, jeans and jockeys pushed down to their knees. Their cocks were hard,

Frank's hands were almost protectively on his jeans as though to pull them up; Ty's hand was still stroking, slowly stroking his bone.

"Are you guys crazy? What are you doin'?"

"What's it look like?" said Ty, "Jackin' off."

"Cool it, Ty, he's just a kid."

"Fuck that, he's old enough to jack off, aren't you Jamie? Bet you do it all the time, don't you ...? What's the matter kid, no tongue and no balls?"

"I got balls," I said.

"Well what we're doin' see, is havin' a contest to see who can nut first, see? Wanna join in?"

"Come on, Ty... don't... I told you he's just a kid."

By now I'd crossed the room and was standing next to Frank's bed.

"What's the matter little boy, never seen a man's dick before?" He pulled it down between his legs and let it pop up slapping against his flat belly.

"Come on, kid, show me what you got."

"Leave him alone Ty ... I told you."

"Shut the fuck up, Frankie, or no dick for your supper."

"Come on, Ty! Please."

"I told you to shut the fuck up. C'mon, kid, show me your dick... if you're man enough... tell him to, Frankie boy."

"Show him," said Frank. He spoke softly, quietly, not looking directly at me. "Yeah, show me or Frankie boy goes to bed without his supper," and once again he pulled his dick down letting it slap up against his belly.

"Frank?" I said.

"Show him for fuck's sake. What's the big deal, I seen it plenty of times, you seen mine plenty of times."

Slowly, I unzipped my jeans and fished inside my shorts. I was hard and it was hard to get it out, then it was out.

"You got a nice one dude. What are you ashamed of?"

"I'm not ashamed!"

"Got fur yet?"

"Um, no, not really."

"Let's see, push 'em down."

I pushed my jeans and shorts down. As I did Ty wrapped his hand around my brothers still hard cock. Frank pushed back against the wall raising his hips, moaning softly.

"He likes when I do that. You ever squeeze his dick?"

"No."

"No?"

"No."

"Wanna see something?"

"What?"

"Head, Frankie."

"No!" Then more softly, "No."

Ty turned slightly, grabbing my brother by the throat.

"Do it now, right now... or never again... I mean it!"

"Ty, please."

"Fuck it, I'm outta here." Ty made to get up.

"Wait man... I mean, c'mon, Ty, don't leave."

"What do you mean? You mean shit! Suck my dick, dude. Ty now had his hand behind my brother's head slowly pulling him forward, forward and down.

Then it happened, my brother was down on this guy's dick. Frank grunted.

"You like it don't you?" said Ty.

Frank grunted again.

"Yeah, you like it, you love it, man, you love suckin' my fat one don't you?"

Again the grunt.

"Now you stay down on it while I talk to Jamie here. Did you know your brother ate bone?"

I didn't say anything.

"He ever suck yours?"

I shook my head no.

"Anybody ever suck it or jack it off for you?"

"No."

"No what?"

"No, nobody ever did it... I mean either one."

"Come here, get up here." He patted the bed.

I managed to get up on the bed, on my knees, my jeans and shorts still around my knees, still watching my brother.

"That's it, babe, that's it, suck the dick, dude, suck my fuckin' hot cock."

Ty was in the middle, my brother on his right, me on his left.

"He loves eatin' my dick, know how I know?" He didn't wait for me to answer. "'Cause his pecker stays hard while he does it... that's how I know."

"Up, off my dick, show little brother you got a hard-on just like him."

Frank let Ty's cock slip from his mouth and raised himself up onto his knees. His cock was sticking straight out from his bush, his hands dangled at his sides.

"See what I mean," said Ty, squeezing Frank's dick again. Then he reached for mine, squeezing a little, jacking a little.

"Both brothers turned on by my big one!"

"Okay, girl, more head." He tugged on Frank's bone and Frank went back down on him.

"Stick out your left hand Frankie and get some young stuff."

My brother reached blindly across Ty and closed his hand over my dick.

"Feel good, kid?" asked Ty. "I said, does it feel good?"

"Yeah."

"Your brother's a good cocksucker ... know what else?" He let his left hand slide down Frank's back to his ass, squeezing his asscheek, "Know what that means, Jamie?"

I shook my head no.

"Means he's so crazy about my dick he takes it anyway I want, anytime I want. I want to get jacked off, he jacks it off for me. If I want a blowjob he sucks it off for me. And if I feel like a fuck and there's no bitch pussy around he spreads his ass for me... don't you, baby? I said, don't you?' and he pinched Frank's ass really hard, so hard Frank winced as he grunted never letting his friend's dick slip from his mouth.

"Wanna see me fuck your brother up the ass?"

"No."

"No? Don't you want to see me stick my big one up that pussy ass?"

I didn't answer.

"Yeah, well, I guess you are kinda young, anyway I feel like somethin' else ... here, sit next to me."

I moved next to him.

"Closer."

I moved so close our thighs were touching.

He took hold of Frank's ear. "Come on, Frankie boy, you know what I wanna see, don't you? Come on, like the last time. Come on babe do it, just fuckin' do it!'

Frank's head came up and he hunched across Ty and suddenly my brother was sucking my cock.

'That's it, bitch, suck it down! Suck that young stuff! Yeah, babe, lookin' for that young squirt. Bet you been wantin' that young pecker a long time! Suck it! Suck it, faggot! Bring him off, bitch! Bring him off and swallow it!'

I started to come. "Fuck, oh, fuck I'm gonna come!" pulled Frank's head forward; I wanted more of my dick in his mouth....

And then it was over. "Okay, okay, I did it."

"Okay, bitch boy, now blow me."

I watched again as my brother ate his friend's dick.

'That's it, bitch boy, suck me! Eat dick honey! Eat me off, fuck face ... ! Oh, here it comes! Fuck, here it comes!'

Ty's body tensed then jerked. I knew each time he shot, each time he shot jism into my brother's mouth, then it was over.

"Okay, you can come now ... like I showed you before." Frank raised up on his knees wildly beating his dick.

'That's it, girl, beat it off. Jack-off like a good little bitch." As he spoke he reached for Frank's balls playing them between his fingers. Frank shot long ropes of white jiz across Ty's legs and jeans. Then, without a word being spoken, he fell forward onto his hands and licked up his cream. He licked it first from Ty's legs, then off his jeans. from

"I gotta go," Ty said, rising from bed and pulling up his jeans. As he tucked away his still-hard cock, he said, "I got a hot date tonight: real pussy, real bitch cunt."

And then he was gone.

Now my brother finally spoke, still not looking me in the eye: "Don't say anything to anyone, Jamie. Please, don't say anything to anybody, and I'll do it to you whenever you want. Please, Jamie ... please...."

(More to come)

WATCHER IN THE SKY

Barnabus Saul

I guess you're expecting some kinda history all about me an where I come from an who my parents were and all that sorta crap, but I don't feel like setting out my family tree or nothin'. Most of it just goes by and isn't worth notin', and the bits that are really worth notin' are the bits you can't share anyway because they're too close.

What I remember mainly was that it was the first day back at school and it was the last term and all and I knew I probably wasn't gonna make it because my grades had been shit all along and all through the holidays my Dad had been in these secret negotiations with the school authorities not to have them drop me just right away. We had one of those long 'Last chance or hit Cannery Row' kinda talks where he did all the talking and I did all the listening and said 'Yep' at the end of it. I mean what else is a guy gonna say? He knew and I knew that nothin' was gonna change, because nothin' ever does, no matter how much you want it.

There was four of us guys sharing and we spent the evening unpacking our stuff an stuff and then I musta gone to sleep because when I woke up they were gone and I thought 'Well, I bet I know where they've gone, but if they didn't bother to wake me I guess they're managin' okay without me.' And I was right, they'd ducked out after lights out for a midnight wank in the woods. It was a favorite to play 'dare': You hung around in the bushes till someone heard a car comin', then you had to run into the central reservation and beat off, and you couldn't come back till you'd shot some juice. You just had to stand there right in the headlights, buck naked pumpin' your whammer. It was easy for the first couple of shots, but when your jism stocks started to deplete and you couldn't whack off quickly enough some of the guys on the highway got a hell of a treat.

'Round about two o'clock this bundle of clothes comes hurtlin' through the open window, and another and another followed by Dave heavin' himself up over the ledge and tumblin' buck naked on the floor. Then Jimbo appeared and struggled in landin' on Dave and both of them got up and hung out the window pullin' Lawrie up by the arms. It's quite a reach up to our window, you gotta stand on a guy bendin' over and the hard bit is pullin' the last guy up. I lay and watched Dave and Jimbo's quivering butts as they strained out the window an I thought, 'Wow if a guy wanted to plug a guy...' so I started to massage my pecker. They got Lawrie in through the window, complainin' about the rough wood of the ledge scraping his belly and tool. They were all pretty high and laughin' a lot, they all had long floppy schlongs that were still engorged from being worked off too many times but they didn't have any wood left between them.

They said I oughta have gone with 'em, but I jus said well heck I was too tired anyhows and turned over and went back to sleep. But before I did I had made my decision to get out.

First I had to get my motorbike back. I'd lent it to Jeff long-term 'cos I didn't never use it. Good ole Jeff always had the key on a string round his neck . I asked around and good ole Jeff was playin' some dumb ball game as I mighta guessed so I high tailed it down to the sports area. I don't do sports, never really had the energy to get fussed whether the little ball went in a certain place or if it just stayed home and played with itself. A sport is so repetitive, a guy throws a ball at another guy, the second guy hits it and a third guy goes and picks it up. Fair enough, but then they go and do it again, and again, and they jus can't get enough of going round in this eternal circle. You ask them to do it in a factory they'd all be out on strike, but give 'em a bag of popcorn and they'll sit and watch this stuff over and over. You might guess I'm not that popular with the sports set. Jeff was in the showers which was kinda embarrassing to go in there as if you wanted to go lookin' at naked guys or somethin', but the guy who told me seemed to think it would be more embarrassin' to be shy about goin' in there with a bunch of naked guys so I thought what the heck and went in. It was hot and steamy and Good ole Jeff and about twenty other guys were horsin' around buck naked under the hot water. I shouted for Jeff and some of the guys looked at me like I was an intruder and I thought they might take it into their heads to grab me and have some fun with me. But they were jus jokin' around and Jeff came out drippin' wet and gasping with his hair all wet and plastered to his face. I noticed he didn't have the key round his neck. I noticed that even before I noticed he was pokin' a huge boner straight out in front of him like he was riding on a broomstick or something. I told him not to tell anyone but that I was thinking of clearing out and I needed the bike. He looked a bit sheepish and sorta stood there shuffling his balls with one hand without meetin' my gaze so I guessed somethin' was wrong. Maybe he'd got a flat or something. I could get that fixed.

"See it's like this," he started. Apparently there had been some kinda accident during the holidays. He'd taken my bike to his home and somehow, he wasn't too specific on the details, somehow it had gotten wrote off. He stood there pumping his dick as he told me this. I guess looking back this might have been some sort of nervous reaction, sort of comforting himself. But right at that time I took it the wrong way. I sorta lost it. I mean he had just destroyed my way outa all this.

"You wrecked my bike, my bike!" I screamed at him, like I had ever given a toss about the old thing, I mean it was hardly roadworthy. "And you can stand there wanking yourself while you tell me you wrecked my bike!"

I could tell he didn't know what to say at this, sports types don't usually have much in the verbal department, he looked really sheepish as I paced back and forth screechin' at him like I was teacher and he was a little boy 'cos I didn't know what else to do. Sure I wanted to hit him, but look at my weedy frame and look at this bulked up hunk with fur on his chest and thighs like tree trunks. Then one of his mates rescued us from this, grabbing his balls between his legs from behind and an arm round his neck and dragging him back to the rough and tumble.

"Look I'm really sorry," he called and I guess I believed he really was so I dropped it and went off to find a plan B.

Ed owed me money from last term so I headed off to the room he shared with Rick Paxton and knocked on their door. "Come in," they shouted and inside they were watching a video. They were side by side on Rick's bed, pants open and stroking their rigs. I coulda been anyone comin' in, they wouldn'ta cared. I thought that's really pathetic, I mean two guys side by side, sharin' an experience but each completely separate like that. I shut the door and squeezed myself onto the bed between them. But I didn't unzip 'cos I didn't really feel like it. I took over instead. I took Rick's prick in one hand and Ed's prick in my other hand and started to work them real gentle. "Ow ... wow!" gasped Ed, and then Rick said it 'cos Rick usually did what Ed did anyway.

"Get the shirts off," I ordered 'cos I reckon guys oughta be buck naked when they wank otherwise it's just devalued if you know what I mean, and, anyhow, I quite get off on the smell of teen armpits. I started using my thumbs on their rock solid prongs. I wasn't pumping them, just massaging the heads with my thumbs, squashing them hard and stroking the rough bit of my thumb on the very tip where the tiny little lips open up. Then I ran down in the cleft underneath, where the skin joins, and that made them both shudder with pleasure, and then round and round the hard ridge where guys are really sensitive. They were both starting to dribble a little lubrication by this time, like I said Rick usually does whatever Ed does, and my thumbs spread it all over to make their cockheads real shiny and glowing. Then I had an idea. I ordered them up on the bed, side by side, belly down and tugged off their jeans and boxers. I tugged them right off 'cos as I say I wanted 'em buck naked and I wanted their legs spread wide. I knelt on the bed behind them, I was astride Ed's right leg and Rick's left leg and I ran my hands over the tight packed row of four hard buns, slightly raised because of their legs being spread so wide. They were all smooth buns, but the backs of Ed's legs were matted with thick black hair while Rick's were boy smooth. You could see quite a bit of beard protruding from between Ed's buns. I slipped a hand deep between Ed's legs and under his belly.

I grabbed his tool and pulled it downwards so it appeared between his legs and pointed randily up at me. His nuts were big but tight in their sac and fairly hidden by his copious bush.

"You need a shave, Ed," I said tickling my fingertips softly through his undergrowth. Rick's balls were smaller and had hardly any hair. I reached under his belly and pulled his rig into view.

For the first time, I saw the pair of them catch each other's eye and exchange a glance of anticipation. "Hey you guys," I said bringing an open palm down firmly on each of the two outer buttocks, "let me see you kissing." They weren't keen on this at first and complained. "I don't do kissing, that ain't my style." But they were hardly in a position to argue. I took both sets of balls in my hands and gave them some gentle encouragement. They gave in pretty quickly and gave each other some half hearted pecks on the lips. "Come on, let me see those tongues. Put an arm round each other's shoulders. That's more like it. Now lemme see those tongues workin' together, you guys."

While they obeyed I gave them some further massage with my fingertips on their shiny, inflated knob heads so that their kissing was interrupted with little gasps whenever I caught a particularly tender sex nerve. And so I played on these two youths, like some exotic musical instrument.

See what I mean about sport, though? It's repetitive. Pretty soon I was looking for something to do more than just tickle these guys' prongs while they snogged. I leaned across and found a box of candles in the bedside table drawer that the guys kept for use after lights out. Some candles had rounded ends to fit in a candle holder, and other candles had sharp, square ends for standing alone. I picked a couple with sharp ends. Ed and Rick were still snogging happily. I put a hand under each of their groins to indicate I wanted their butts raised a little higher and their legs spread a little wider. I took Ed's buttocks firmly in my hands, thumbs addressing the crack and pulled him wide open. I heard him gasp as I blew cold air on his freshly exposed ring, then fired a wad of spit firmly onto his target. I rubbed the warm wetness over this very sensitive muscle and really enjoyed hearing him gasp with pleasure. Then I did the same to Rick, rubbing warm spit firmly into that smooth, tight little pucker with my thumb and hearing him make little high pitched gasps. That was when I reached out for the candles. I used the flat ends with the sharp edges and pressed them firmly against their little brown holes.

I used the flat ends with the sharp edges and pressed them firmly against their little brown holes. I pushed them determinedly so that the boys knew what was coming in, and

I gave them a few little twists now and then to ease them deeper into their passages. Those guys stopped snogging then, their minds were on other things and they kept on giving little whimpering noises every time I pushed those candles a little further home. I left them at about an inch and a half in, and boy I've never wished I had a camera more in my life than I did at that moment looking at Ed and Rich with candles sticking out of their butts.

I carried on massaging the guys over their dicks and balls and occasionally gave their candles a little flick which made them wimper and gasp.

It was while I was doing this I remembered why I'd come and all so I said to Good ole Ed, "Hey Ed, you remember that loan I gave ya last term. I need that cash back. Ya got it?"

I guess in his current state Ed didn't like to come out and say "No" right away so he dithered a bit and got himself gingerly off the bed, walking in a kinda funny way due to the candle rammed up his arse and fetched his wallet from the drawer. I watched him bend down to get it and saw the candle rise to point like a cannon, then fall back to pointing at the floor. "I got 15 bucks," he said. "Sorry that's all I got. I'm gonna be gettin' a cheque from Dad in a coupla weeks. I can give you most of it then." Fifteen bucks would just about get me a bus ticket. Shit. Just briefly I wanted to take that candle and shove it all the way home. I just sat there though, lookin' at his hairy dick pointing at me.

"Shit," I said, "you might as well get back on the bed." Which he did. I watched him get wrapped up again in Richie's arms. Good ole Richie. I left 'em to it.

That night I sneaked out of the dorm anyway. I waited till the other guys had wanked themselves to sleep so nobody saw me go.

I wandered around half of that night. I didn't have nowhere to go. Then I remembered this teacher called Jerry who had left at the end of last term who had always been kinda one of the guys. I kinda liked him he was cool. He lived somewhere round these parts and he had given us his number. Don't sit on a homework problem, or any other sort of problem, he said. So I had his number in my book. So I called good ole Jerry, and not only did he still live there but he was actually in. He sounded kind of funny but he said I could go round. It was late, I hadn't realized how late, and they were dressed for bed in robes over pajamas, but his wife Jane made me hot chocolate and a big sandwich and he made up the bed on the sofa. We talked for a little while then his wife went back to bed and he followed her a little while later I didn't have any pajamas so I stripped down to my vest and boxers and got under the quilt. I didn't want to shoot my load or nothin' but I started playing with myself to bring on that dreamy imaginative state that leads to good dreams and I didn't notice when the door to their bedroom opened 'cos Jerry was just suddenly in the room.

"I had to get this book," he said. I mean lame or what? And he grinned conspiratorially at me 'cos he'd obviously seen the quilt pumping up and down round about my groin area.

"Jacking off helps to relieve tensions," he said approvingly, dropping onto one knee beside my sofa."Here, why don't you let me help you with that." And before I could react I felt his hand slide under the quilt and up my leg. My dick and balls were out the leg of my boxers and he knew where to find them anyway so pretty soon he was giving me a real sweet relaxing rub.

He put a finger to his lips to indicate to keep quiet not to wake his wife and started kissing me on my cheeks and neck while his free hand felt down into my t shirt for my nipples. I didn't know how far he wanted to go with me but I hadn't felt this good in ages and it didn't really matter. He was nuzzling my ear, licking around there and rubbing my lobe between his teeth when he whispered urgently"You wanna do it for me?" I didn't know what he meant, I just said"Sure," figuring that whatever it was if it carried on being this good it had to be great.

He let go of my dick and said "Ssssh," again a few times. Then he stood up and opened his robe. His prick and balls were out of the fly of his pajamas. His balls were not too big and they were tugged up tight and almost hidden in hair. But his prick was arched upwards like some giant butcher's hook. You coulda hung a side of beef on that hook. The smell of it hit you like some giant exotic flower suddenly opening and shoving its scents in your face. It smelt sultry and musky and hot and up for it. He leaned forward and pressed it against my face. I didn't know what I was supposed to do so I licked at his balls as he stroked them sideways across my mouth. Then with a single agile movement he was over the top of me, supporting his hands and feet on the arms of the sofa and with his gown draped over us like we were inside a big tent. He shoved the end of his dick into my mouth and started raising and lowering himself, doing press ups, so that his big curved piston slid deeper and deeper into my throat.

It didn't take him long. When he fired I copped a load in my mouth which was so unexpected I turned my head and took the rest over my face and in my hair and in my ear.

He jumped off the sofa and tied his robe around him. I started to gargle, trying to spit his spunk out. He managed to silence the noise I was making and he kissed me on the cheek again and whispered"Thanks kid, we'll talk tomorrow ok" Then he got me a glass of water and chucked me the tissue box to clean up some of the jism off my face.

I still hadn't come, and I went back to stroking my own tool and wondering about tomorrow. My bone had gone and I was just rolling a big softie. I knew what would happen tomorrow. He wouldn't mention what happened, it would never have happened, and I'd get up and go on my way. I decided to do that early, and hoped the sun would wake me before they woke up and I could be gone.

There was this program I saw on television once, all about spy planes and espionage and stuff. People were saying how bad and evil like it all was that their privacy was being invaded, and I guess that's so. But I kinda thought that when I got out of school maybe that's what I'd like to do. I could operate surveillance camera or just go sit in some big hot air balloon in the sky looking down at all the people. And that way I could be the Watcher in the Sky, and every gay could know that whatever he was doin', in every snog and every wistful glance I'd always be up here, watching and rootin' alongside him and helping him along a little.

THE NAKED ALTAR BOY

K. I. Bard

Moving,
a scary-excitement,
anticipated,
dreaded.
Saying Good-bye
to the class
left to graduate
without me,
I've no idea
exactly what I'm leaving.
In Minnesota
there won't be
graduation
ending Grade Eight.
All I know
for sure
is the empty feeling
digging in my gut
making me feel
awkwardly off balance
when classmates
shake hands,
wish me well,
hand me
a parting token,
a holy card,
all conducted
under the supervising gaze
of Sister Felicita
who tops all,
sending me away
with a coloring book
of Christ's life.
I feel humbled
and shamed.

I'm too old
for coloring
and just on the edge
of seeing Christ
more man than God.
The pathos-scene
of Christ
on the cross
used to fill me
with sorrow
for mankind's sins.
That was when
my own sins
were small,
infrequent,
innocent.
Now I see
the cross-bound
body
that of a man
in rag underwear,
almost nude,
intriguing
in a way
that makes me
uneasy
at the path my eyes
follow
in searching that body
for clues
about my own.
If He was truly
made flesh
to teach us something
what did having

a body
show?
Sometimes,
alone in my room,
I strip
to underpants
that I tug
into a fashion
of His.
Then I stand,
feet together,
arms spread,
in an attempt
to feel Christ's
final Passion,
an act which somehow
becomes
merely my passion.
What I used to feel
has been replaced
by confusion,
excitement,
reality of self
pushing aside
the old drama
of God's human death.
I continue to tell myself
I believe,
doing so
even as my private rituals
see my innocence
transformed
into mockery,
a pious pose
usurped by
impure thought
bound resolutely
toward sin.
I cannot stop
this relentless process
of comparing
my body to His,
of questioning His Passion
against mine.
With a curious twist
I offer up
my body
and my sins
to Him,
telling myself
He will love me more
if I am abject
in human failure.
In this way
I justify
my acts
in compromise.
As a child,
His child,
I grasped
this fact.
There was no need
of forgiveness
if there was nothing
to forgive.
Being sinful
therefore
made me human.
The more human
I made myself
the more He
might love me.
It was a good excuse,
if nothing else,
for indulgences
I tried to expunge
with Indulgence Prayers.
If you are
old Catholic
you'll understand

the pun.

My farewell
had to have
a final act,
an honor, really,
to serve High Mass.
Late spring
in Illinois
is steamy,
even by
mid-morning
when I must robe
myself
to take my part
serving aongside the Priest.
Another boy,
selected to match me
in size,
and I
are head servers,
a distinction
usually reserved
for the oldest,
most reverent,
priestly boys.
Head servers
are supposed to hear
their vocation.
They are supposed
to heed
the Altar's call
and with folded hands
and bowed heads
subject themselves
to God's will,
making His plan
their own.
We are told
in ways subtle
and direct
what is expected.
I've heard it,
one way or another,
almost every day
for years.
So I've no excuse
for what I do,
which is to imagine
myself naked
under all those robes.
Repeating Latin prayers
while sweat beads
on my upper lip
I feel the heat
of my body
rising
in equatorial pulse
and power.
Despite those efforts
designed to tame me
I fail to escape
thoughts of
my body.
I am a naked altar boy,
hands folded in precision,
lips repeating
God's rote.
There's no way to know
by looking.
Only God can see
my secrets.
They belong
to Him and me.
In this way
I am more thoroughly
God's
child
than anyone
could imagine.

In sight
I am every inch
chaste, innocent.
But in my heart
I am His
naked altar boy,
the one He
will love and remember
above all others
because I cast aside
all veils
and give myself
body/soul - ALL.

A BOY'S BEST FRIEND

Antler

A boy spends more time looking at his boner
Than looking at his face in the mirror
Enjoys playing with his new-sprung-cock
More than any other part of his,
More than reading or listening to music,
More than smoking grass or watching TV,
just to get off by himself and consult
His miraculous oracle-he is familiar
With its every visage from limp to stiff,
From shrunk from swimming to super-bloated,
From many a jackoff holdoff brink, amazing!
What is more fun, more mystical, magical,
Meaningful than those secret chosen moments
Alone with your new-grown-puberty-dick—
Just you and it!
You know how they say
A dog is a man's best friend?
A boy's cock is a boy's best friend.
A whole night together—a boy delighting
In his beautiful, boundless, insatiable,
Inquisitive, playful, mischievous prick.

The sailor-stud featured in the photo on the preceding page can be found in the Euros book "Herve Bodilis," from Bruno Gmunder, and available from STARbooks Press.

"He was someone who turned military chasing
into military delivery...."
Mark Simpson in "Military Trade"

The Making of a Solider

A Collection of Erotic Stories
Edited by
JOHN PATRICK

STARbooks Press
Sarasota, Florida

Contents

INTRODUCTION:
A TASTE FOR BOYS IN UNIFORM
John Patrick

A PRIVATE'S PART
PFC Rick Jackson, USMC

A BIRTHDAY AT THE BATHS
William Cozad

ROCK-SOLID STUD
William Cozad

TERRY, THE NEW RECRUIT
Bill Nicholson

THE MAKING OF A SOLDIER
Peter Gilbert

SHIPMATES
Tim Scully

THE RECRUITING OFFICER
Peter Gilbert

THE CALL OF THE COCKPIT
Thomas Wagner

INQUISITION
David MacMillan

THE BEST COCKSUCKER
IN PHILADELPHIA
Thom Nickels

CAPTAIN, MY CAPTAIN
Tony Anthony

SERVICING SARGE
Aaron Mitchell

"...My cock stands up for the kind of guy who is usually a mechanic or a sailor. Unfortunately, after we climax, what else do we have in common?"
—Tom of Finland

. . .

"He may have a yen for raw recruits
or mountain goats...
offer him girls,
offer him boys."
—Lyrics by Noel Coward,
"The Passenger's Always Right"

Introduction:
A TASTE FOR BOYS IN UNFORM

John Patrick

"The history of soldier lovers spans the globe," *Military Trade* author/researcher Steve Zeeland says, and predates the word "homosexual" by several thousand years: "And if a taste for uniformed trade is politically unfashionable, it is not unpopular. ...No theory of sexuality can adequately account for personal quirks. But most military chasers can be said to have in common a passion for an organic, embodied, archetypal, 'authentic' masculinity; for immersion in numbers of servicemen; and for a 'pure' homosocial camaraderie or 'buddy love'—but one that allows for sex between men."

One of those Zeeland interviewed, John, gives a blunt example of what most military chasers want:"In most cases, you're guaranteed that if the guy's a soldier, he's gonna be a real man." A gay academic agreed: "Among the reasons that immediately come to mind are a certified masculinity; the association of masculinity with potency, with aggression, with being on top, with large genitalia, with buckets of semen."

And speaking of semen, John Butler recalls,"One of the most exciting single moments of sex I remember was one night in the hobby shop of the USS Lexington. This super-hung, sexy sailor I had been working on finally agreed to let me have him, and he lay on the deck while I worked on his huge cock the way I'd been wanting to for so long. Previously, he'd let me jack him off—and I didn't know how to really enjoy myself at that time in my life or I would have been riding that thick meat. Moments into it, he said, 'I'm gonna come, kid,' I raised up to say, 'Get it!' or something like that, and before I could get him back in my mouth he blasted a spurt way over his head and onto the bulkhead. As I said something clever like 'Wow!' he shot another spurt that hit his face. I was able to gather my wits quickly enough to get my mouth around him so he didn't waste any more."

And Talvin DeMachio, noted porn star and dancer who

served a four-year tour of duty in the U.S. Navy, finishing up in 1996, says: "Don't believe what you hear about the Marines! They're the biggest bottoms there are. They love getting fucked! I fooled around a lot, including with a lot of married men.

"I was in the Navy in San Diego. It was my first time away from home, and I was on the military base. And I took a taxicab to some gay clubs, and the one I went into was for ages 16 to 20. Anyone who was 21 or older couldn't get in. So I was dancing, and these cute guys came up and started dancing with me—they were, like, 24, and had sneaked in. There was this really hot, hot, hot guy. So we started talking and talking, and the next thing I knew, my heart was beating like a thousand miles an hour. He wanted me to go back to his house.

"So we got there, and he was sitting on the couch, and I was eating chips. And he put his hand on my leg, and immediately I got a woody. I was just eating chips and looking at TV, and I almost came in my pants. He kissed my neck, and I told him I'd never done it before and was nervous, and he told me to relax. We started kissing and making out. It was one of the biggest turn-ons to me when he sucked my dick. I fucked him and came in a few seconds because it was so incredible. Sex with a man was great! Once I went there I never even looked at another woman. We had sex all night long."

Another popular porn star stud, Rod Barry, was a Marine, and he says, "I think there's a lot of it in the Corps. A lot-lot-lot. And I realized that after I got out. Well, anybody who's gay, why not join the biggest gay club where there's the most men? I mean, shoot, it's all there. I think that's what it's all about. And it helps that obviously a lot of people think that the military's hot—a man in the military's hot—so they join the military to improve their image. I think that's what a lot of it's about. It was really funny—when I got out of the marine corps and I started dancing in San Diego, I saw a lot of the people whom I knew."

In his book, *Buddy Babylon*, Buddy Cole recalls taking a hike in the woods and coming across a small shack. "I had been tramping about these woods all my life, and never had I come across this particular abode. *Tres mysterieux.* I went up to the window and looked in. Bent over a woodstove was a strikingly handsome black man, about thirty years old, with no shirt on.

I could see what looked like dog tags around his neck. To this day, I think I've never seen a finer sight. As he turned from the stove our eyes met and I freaked out, tearing off into the woods. I heard the slamming of a door behind me and knew that he was in hot pursuit. I tripped over a branch and fell.

"'Who are you?' he barked in strangely accented French.

"'I'm Buddy Cole.'

"'What were you doing?' he said.

"'I'm lost. I didn't mean anything.' I began to cry. He immediately softened, picked me up in his arms, and carried me inside. My ploy worked. As he carried me I took the opportunity to read his dog tags. They said PRIVATE LINCOLN TOUSSAINT. A real ragin' Cajun. Inside, the cabin was very cozy. I felt faint with hunger as we passed by the sizzling pan of bacon. He laid me down on his unmade bed and then brought me a plate of bacon and eggs. I realized how famished I was and took it...."

Sad to say, although he spent the night, the closest Buddy got to sex was falling asleep with his face buried in Lincoln's armpit.

For others, such masculinity *was* attainable. In *Wilde's Last Stand*, Philip Hoare says The Guards regiments represented the apogee of aristocratic military narcissism:"It was the Brigade of Guards in which Osbert Sitwell felt most comfortable as a newly-enlisted officer, describing in almost fetishistic detai: the fitting of his tunic of scarlet Melton cloth, the all-important smoothness of shoulders and waist, and accoutrements requiring 'esoteric' perfection. Stationed in London, the regiments were open to the capital's temptations: Sitwell received his cultural education whilst barracked at St James's, running up huge bills with ticket agencies as he attended the ballet, theater and opera.

"For some Londoners, the Guards represented an attainable masculinity—their other ranks were notorious for their sexual availability, 'a bit of scarlet'. One relic of the Nineties, Charles Dalmon, told the writer Michael Davidson: 'My dear, my ambition is to be crushed to death between the thighs of a Guardsman!' London's sexual subculture had always existed, but in wartime, a hedonistic spirit of *carpe diem* combined with the throwing together of large numbers of young men to bring many into contact with worlds they would never otherwise have experienced. The capital had escaped the moralizing campaigns, leaving it with the reputation of 'the nation's pleasure ground'. The theater was the nexus of this culture of pleasure, and was also peculiarly open to outside influences; from the new syncopation from across the Atlantic to the avant-garde from Europe, their influence was often felt first in the world of the theater. Here Londoners first heard American slang such as 'kid' and 'okay', and saw dances like the Apache, the Tango and the Bunny Hug, unprecedented in their body contact. It was also a liberating arena for women. The stage was one of the few places where they could pursue and succeed in independent careers, and stars like Gaby Deslys, Phyllis Monkman, Beatrice Lillie and Teddie Gerrard led fast lives in modern revues; many, like Gerrard, also worked their way through a string of lovers, male and female.

"The theater's mixing of class and sexuality, and its susceptibility to the suspiciously new, combined to produce a threat to the moral status quo. The old social demarcations had gone. For Captain Leo Charlton of the Royal Flying Corps, 'it was so ridiculously easy, during the war, to hob-nob with women, and men too for that matter, whose names and faces were continually advertised in the dreary photographic pages of society weeklies'. Charlton, an aristocratic Catholic homosexual, was representative of a subculture within the armed forces. His London home boasted an indoor swimming pool where he would entertain 'young officers of the Flying Corps in whom he was interested' and 'one or two of the West Indian boys, his gymnastic pupils ... It cannot be claimed that the scenes which were enacted late at night were uniformly decorous. Much license was allowed, especially to those who had just come from, or were immediately returning to, the agony of life at the war.''

American historian George Chauncey's remarks about Wartime America hold equally true for Britain:"World War I was a watershed in the history of the urban moral reform movement and in the role of homosexuality in reform discourse. The War embodied reformers' darkest fears and their greatest hopes, for it threatened the very foundations of the nation's moral order—the family, smalltown stability, the racial and gender hierarchy—even as it offered the reformers an unprecedented opportunity to implement their vision.' Mass troop movements through major cities and ports created conditions in which any sort of sexual behavior was opportunistic: Chauncey describes the attempts of various welfare and moralist societies to control such behavior in Wartime New York.

"As the War progressed, the societies were astonished to detect an apparent increase in male perversion. Agents report seeing perverts approaching soldiers and sailors on the streets, in theaters, and in hotel lobbies, meeting them in bars, and taking them to assignation hotels. They saw suspicious-looking civilians inviting servicemen to join them in saloons and hotel bars ... Agents had noticed fairies fraternizing with sailors for years, but it was at the beginning of the war that they witnessed the spectacle of 'sex mad' sailors near the Brooklyn Navy Yard 'walking arm in arm and on one dark street ... a sailor and a man kissing each other ... an exhibition of mai[sic] perversion showing itself in the absence of girls.'

"At the moment of their triumph, the social-purity forces were confronted with mounting evidence that the War somehow unleashed the most appalling of urban vices.' The same sort of behavior was becoming all too obvious in England. During the War, ports such as Plymouth, Southampton and Portsmouth were venues for homosexual soliciting in the streets. So socially unacceptable did the morally outraged find this behavior that they could not accept that it was a British phenomenon. It had to be the product of German infamy: hence the scenes of dockyard entrapment that were directly alluded to and recycled in *Mr. Billing's Black Book*.

"Rather than expunge a tendency towards unBritish perversions, for one young officer at least," Hoare says, "the Billing affair served to rouse interest in the very subjects it sought to proscribe. Charles Carrington, later an eminent man of letters and biographer of Kipling, wrote about Oscar Wilde: 'Until his trial, he had been so innocent as not to know that sexual aberrations existed in Society and can describe my experience only as being a king corrupted by what I read in the newspapers. Some morbid streak in me was strangely stimulated by these new suggestions ...'

"Carrington's Wartime sexual experiences had been exclusively heterosexual, from a sexual initiation with a prostitute picked up near Leicester Square with whom he had had sex in a taxi going round the Houses of Parliament, to the brothels reserved for serving officers in Paris, complete with Louis XV furniture, ceiling mirrors, pornographic films and girls dressed in baby clothes. But such experiences turned Carrington against mercenary heterosexual sex. One night, after a particularly unsuccessful evening with two street walkers in Amiens, he and a fellow officer fell into bed together. In the morning, they regarded each other guiltily, and did not speak of the incident. Although Carrington found himself attracted to fresh-faced recruits, he had no further homosexual experience in the army until the end of 1918, when he was posted to Valdagno in Italy.

"There he became close friends with a wealthy, handsome young officer, Owen Butler, who modelled himself on Byron and had been expelled from Harrow for sexual misconduct. Butler, the only son of the first baronet Sir William Butler, was promiscuous and, although younger than Carrington, much more sophisticated. They would remain close friends until Butler's suicide in 1935. Together they founded the Valdagni Binge Club, devoted to strict military discipline by day and debauchery by night. They drank heavily with two like-minded young sergeants—in another instance of the cross-class experience which war and sex induced—calling each other by their Christian names and even exchanging clothes to make matters equal. Butler's behavior was particularly flagrant, and he wanted to invite 'Jimmy' James, the best-looking boy in the regiment, with whom he had already slept. Carrington vetoed this, feeling obliged to protect 'Jimmy's' honor, even though he himself was attracted to boys in the regiment, and had once surprised a handsome corporal by kissing him goodbye."

In Michael R. Gorman's biography of Jose Sarria, *The Empress Is A Man*, the way the entertainer screwed himself into the Army is delightfully articulated: "There was a major working with the enlistment officer in San Francisco whom Jose had met years earlier—at various gay parties. In the 1940s gay parties were relatively secretive affairs. Guest lists were carefully controlled, and those who attended agreed to an unspoken rule to guard the identities of the attendees in the outside world. Being identified as gay in the straight world more often than not led to loss of job, discharge from the service, shunning by parts of society, and often loss of family. There was a tight bond among gay men based on shared experience, but also on the vulnerability that each had to the others.

"The major had taken a liking to Jose from the first time he met him at one of the parties. Jose was no wallflower, and the combination of his youthful beauty and his playful gregariousness charmed the military man. Jose flirted with the major as he did with most men at such affairs, and the major finally asked Jose to spend the night with him. Jose was flattered and a little interested, but he preferred to play hard to get. Despite the man's repeated requests over a few years' time, Jose continued to refuse. That, of course, was before he decided to join the Army.

"...Jose went to meet him for lunch so that they could discuss his enlistment. The lunch was a fine one at the Saint Francis Hotel. When they were finished eating, the major paid the bill and led Jose up to the room he had rented. By the time they emerged some hours later, the major had promised to see that Jose would be in the Army soon." And, of course, he did.

A black man once wrote Boyd McDonald about his sexual adventures, including many while he was in the Army, and the letter eventually ended up in the book *Lewd*: "Around age sixteen, I got the chance to see my first white cock. I was working loading watermelons, and this white guy went to the bushes to pee. I saw this as my opportunity to see my first white cock—and look I did. I knew he had a big cock, and to see all that red meat hanging out provided me with jack-off material for years. His cock was larger soft than mine was on hard at that age. I made a promise that some day I would get me some white cock.

"At age twenty, I joined the Army and remained in the Army for twenty years. My first duty assignment was at Hunter Army Air Field in Savannah, Georgia, and it was there that I sucked my first cock—a white cock. My roommate became drunk and was running around the barracks naked for two hours before he passed out in the room. He had a tiny cock but I licked and sucked on it for thirty minutes and then turned him over and ate out his ass. From that day on I was hooked on white cock.

"At twenty-one, I sucked my second white cock in the Greyhound bus station in Orlando, Florida. He only had about three inches hard but it tasted good. Because of where we were I didn't get a chance to suck it like I wanted.

"I was sent to Vietnam. I would sit in the outdoor toilet and watch guys come up to piss outside the toilet and jerk off. It was a real treat to watch all those cocks of different sizes, shapes and colors!

"...I was stationed at Fort Hood in Texas where I received my first blowjob from a white college student I'd picked up in the Trailways bus station. We went to a motel and he was the first guy I ever fucked. He wanted me to suck him also but his cock was leaking. At that time I didn't know that guys' cocks leaked when they became excited. While still stationed at Fort Hood one night coming back to base on the bus, I convinced another soldier to suck my cock on the promise that I would get him some black pussy. I busted a nut all in his mouth but he spat my hot cum on the floor. Everyone gave us a strange look, but I had a happy look.

"...I was sent to Germany, and with all that available white cock I had a ball. I was gang-fucked by six white guys in Denmark and walked wide-legged for a week. When I was stationed in Stuttgart, Germany, I would visit the toilet and take out my nine-plus inches and jerk off while the Germans would watch and beat off as well. I never touched anyone or would let anyone touch me. After shooting a big load from watching all those white uncut cocks I would then leave and go back to my barracks.

"...When I was twenty-six, I visited Copenhagen. They love blacks there and your ass can get pretty sore! The biggest blackest cock I've ever seen was there. He had about a foot. I have a big mouth and couldn't even get the head in. All I could do was to lick it. During that period a young blond was giving me head. He pushed my legs around my ears and started eating out my ass. I became hotter than a pistol. The next thing I knew, a guy was holding each of my legs by my ears and the suckee was ball deep inside my ass and I was hollering. After he came, another guy got into the saddle. I was fucked by seven guys, one right after another. After they had all fucked me, one guy sucked me while one had his finger up my ass and a man was on each nipple sucking. That was the strangest nut I ever had.

"...Later I returned to the States and was stationed at Fort Lee, Virginia, and on weekends I'd travel to Washington, D.C. I'd spend the night at the baths, and I sucked over a dozen cocks one night. Incredibly, I sucked *five* loads out of a black guy from Baltimore. His comment to me was, 'You are very oral.' I guess that was his way of telling me nicely that I was a cocksucker.

"I found that the bigger the cock, the more of a pussy the guy is. I saw many guys with million-dollar cocks with their legs up in the air—me included. At least we have something for the person to hold on to while plowing."

And speaking of finding someone to "hold on to," in the interesting book *Take the Young Stranger by the Hand*, about same-sex relations and the YMCA over the years, John Donald Gustav-Wrathall states, in the 1930s, men knew that the 63rd Street YMCA in New York was "notorious," though they found sex easier to obtain at the Sloane House. Discovering the public cruising scene could be a first step toward learning about the existence of a gay subculture, and a first step toward internalizing a new homosexual identity. The *Scarlet Pansy's* main character, Fay Etrange, was portrayed as being initiated into Baltimore's gay subculture in the years before World War I at the YMCA. On the other hand, entry into the gay community through other means made one aware of the availability of public cruising as a form of sexual release. Furthermore, the sexual interaction of "queers" with "normal" men as "trade" became an important part of emerging sexual identities and patterns of male-male sexual interaction.

The YMCA cruising scene was intensified during World War I by the boom in YMCA army and navy work. Armed services work had the effect of bringing a huge influx of men into YMCA dormitories and gymnasiums. The effect of armed services work on the YMCA cruising scene was even more dramatic during World War II, and initiated what could be called the golden age of YMCA cruising. Paul Hardman recalled that "World War II opened the floodgates [of cruising at the

YMCA], though before then, the gates leaked a lot." William Billings recalled that "there was a lot of activity . . . particularly since World War II." As Alan Berube has demonstrated in *Coming Out Under Fire*, a study of homosexuality in the armed services during World War II, psychological screening had the effect of spreading popular awareness of homosexuality, while the concentration of men and women in coastal military cities gave individuals opportunities to explore their sexuality and connect with already existing gay communities.

In these volumes, we like to spotlight those among the famous, both past and present, who share our interest in military sex. One of the most notable was Ludwig, king of Bavaria.

In *The Mad King*, Greg King reveals that Ludwig had a thing for his officers and stableboys: "He faithfully recorded his every caress, kiss, and sexual thought, along with his heartfelt declarations that he would never again yield to temptation". On January 21, 1877, Ludwig wrote, "That what took place yesterday night was the last time forever; atoned for by the Royal Blood—the Holy Grail. Absolutely the last time under penalty of ceasing to be King." But, naturally, the King couldn't keep his hands off for very long.

"Often," King writes, "members of the king's household unwittingly found themselves the object of his affections. Ludwig's favor often fell on the handsome stableboys and young soldiers who were posted to do guard duty at one of his castles. The new favorite would find himself showered with expensive gifts or granted privileged appointments, taken on midnight sleigh rides and nocturnal visits to remote hunting lodges high in the Alps. Flattered by such royal attention, few of these ambitious young men resisted Ludwig's attentions, submitting themselves to his 'sensual kisses' and sexual passions. But the king's tastes were subject to quick change, and he became easily bored with these new friends. 'Many a Bavarian cavalry officer,' wrote an historian, "was thus subsequently amazed to see his horse washed by a newly assigned stable boy who was wearing a diamond ring he had gotten from the King.'"

Ludwig was 28 when he first met Baron von Varicourt, a handsome former officer in the Chevaux-Legers Regiment;

entranced with the baron's name and its associations with the Bourbons, the king asked him to provide a family genealogy. Varicourt complied, slyly writing the document in French; Ludwig was delighted and immediately appointed the baron as a personal aide-de-camp. Within a few weeks of their meeting and Varicourt's meteoric rise, the King wrote:"You know that you owe the appointment as aide-de-camp to my interest in the history of France in the past centuries...." Two days later, Ludwig sent along another letter with a photograph of himself.

"Ludwig was enraptured with Varicourt," King asserts, "believing that he had at last discovered his one true friend, destined by Providence.... Even in this blissful state, however, the king apparently feared that this new friendship would follow the path of other failed relationships.... Ludwig was infatuated with the handsome young officer, but Varicourt did not share his feelings. He was not averse to the royal friendship, but he continually tried to direct it along platonic lines. Despite Ludwig's protests of love until death, the inevitable break came soon enough, as it always did in his liaisons."

In her book about Arthur Rimbaud, Enid Starkie says that before the poet met Paul Verlaine he spent some nights in barracks of the Rue de Babylone, when he is said to have been assaulted by the soldiers. At that time he wandered about the city in the direst poverty, picking up a night's shelter wherever he could find it. He wrote a poem, *Coeur Supplicie*, which was the outcome of some very bitter and painful experience which left an indelible mark on him. "...It is probable that some startling experience shocked and terrified him, driving him home for refuge. ...This is the first poem that expresses profound feeling, a deep wound in his nature....

"...Up to now Rimbaud had remained, in spite of his intellectual maturity, a child in experience, who had been carefully sheltered from the ugly side of life. It is true that like all imaginative children he had thought much about love and passion, but only in a literary manner. It is quite obvious from the poems he had written before he had as yet had no sexual experience and singularly little sexual curiosity; even his imagination had remained innocent and child-like. The only person ever to have stirred his emotions was Izambard and his affection for his master was shy, unexpressed and probably not fully realized by himself. At sixteen, when he went to Paris, he still looked a bit like a girl, with his small stature, his fresh complexion and his reddish-gold wavy hair. It is probable that he then received his first initiation into sex and in so brutal and unexpected a manner that he was startled and outraged, and that his whole nature recoiled from it with fascinated disgust. But though this experience brought him shock and revulsion so great that he fled from Paris to heal his wound at home, there was more in it than mere recoil. It was not solely an unpleasant experience that had disgusted him and against which he could stiffen himself; it was one that did not leave him indifferent, nor his senses untouched. It was a sudden and blinding revelation of what sex really was, of what it could do to him, and it showed him how false had been all his imagined emotions."

In F. Valentine Hooven's perceptive biography of Tom of Finland, he quotes the artist as saying, "I was always attracted to the men of action. My father was not a real man in my eyes, though he was really very handsome—and very well hung—but he wore a white collar and worked indoors, using his mind rather than his body, so he didn't have the appeal of a soldier or a policeman.

"...At the peak of mobilization, sixty percent of Finland's male population was in the military. This is the maximum amount a nation can call up, because nonfighting individuals—those who are too young (fifteen percent), too old (fifteen percent), or disabled (ten percent)—total about forty percent. In other words, every able-bodied man Tom met for the next five years was wearing a uniform!

"Sometimes the attraction to the uniform is so powerful in me that I feel as if I am making love to the clothes, and the man inside them is just a convenience to hold them up and fill them out—sort of an animated display-rack."

Hooven says, "The primary purpose of the warrior is not a sexual one. Yet paradoxically, nothing emphasizes male sexual iconography more than war. This goes far beyond the obvious Freudian connection between a hard cock and a spear, a rifle, or—the ultimate erection—a nuclear missile."

Tom related, "Every night there was the blackout. Ah, if you never experienced one of the big cities with all the streets in total darkness, you really can't imagine what it was like! For some reason it aroused me sexually—maybe it was just because I was young—but I would go out, night after night, and cruise the pitch-black streets and look for sex. I was not the only one turned on. I got all the sex I wanted. There were a lot of other soldiers and sailors prowling in the dark."

Hooven says that Tom's blackout experiences were not unique: "For some reason, war and the threat of death are an aphrodisiac to many people, making them willing, even eager, to indulge in behavior that in peacetime would be considered promiscuous or worse, even by the participants themselves. Freud thought that perhaps the increase in sexual activity was generated from the life instinct, urging people to procreate before it was too late. Jung felt it might be caused by the disruption of familiar patterns and restraints; such chaos throws an individual back on more primitive urges. In Tom's case, his lustiness might have been due simply to his youth (and to the effect of pointing that huge steel phallic symbol into the air all day long)."

Whatever the cause, at last Tom found sex that was as exciting in reality as it was in his fantasies:"I had sex in some fantastic situations thanks to the blackout. Once, in the very heart of downtown Helsinki, at the crowded trolley stop in front of the Swedish Theater, it was so dark, all I could tell about the man standing next to me was that he was large and, like me, wearing a trenchcoat and boots. Then I brushed against him and discovered that he had his cock out and was playing with himself. Casually, I turned my back, took his cock in my hand, and beat him off, with at least a dozen people all around us waiting for the trolley."

Tom found himself bombarded with all the erotic enticements of uniforms. He was working, relaxing, eating, even shitting in the constant company of other young men, all wearing uniforms. When they weren't in uniform together, they were sleeping in their underwear, or naked while they showered and (being Finnish) took the sauna. The bodies of the other soldiers, whether dressed or undressed, constantly stimulated Tom's desire to draw them....

"Gradually," Hooven notes, "Tom's aimless wanderings in the

blackout coalesced into a pattern. First, he would walk along beneath the trees of the Esplanade, where some of the outdoor cafes were open for business even in the blackout, with barely visible patrons murmuring at the little tables in the dark. Then he would cross the cobblestones of the old Market Square and stroll along the waterfront, listening as waves lapped against the sides of unseen ships full of sailors. If nobody struck his fancy along the way, he would finally arrive at the park on the knoll at the southernmost tip of central Helsinki. There he would wait, surrounded by the pale buildings of the eighteenth-century Swedish Observatory (appropriately, its original purpose had been military). Someone would come along; someone always did. His presence would be revealed by a gleam of moonlight on the polished visor of a cap or the smell of leather and wool on the night breeze, just before Tom heard the guttural whisper, 'Come here!'

"Sometimes, on a really cloudy night, you wouldn't even know some guy was there until you touched him or he touched you. Sometimes nothing was said at all. You'd just hear breathing and the clink of a belt unbuckling....

"...Only in a dark park could he come into brief contact with men who were, or pretended to be, the masculine lovers of his fantasies. Or so Tom believed. The fleeting relationships with the men he met in the streets could not be expanded into anything more lasting. These partners preferred to be nameless and unattached. Anonymous promiscuity was a major part of the erotic appeal, not just to Tom but to most of his partners as well. If the man was basically heterosexual, which was frequently the case in street sex, after orgasm he wanted nothing to do with the person with whom he had just performed a forbidden act. Conversely, if he was just faking his masculine pose, he did not dare hang around too long or the hairpins would begin to drop and he would ruin his image. But the most frustrating encounters for a well-educated, culturally sophisticated gay man such as Tom were those in which his sex partner turned out to be exactly what he dreamed of: a real man's man who was uninhibitedly happy to have sex with another man."

Another great artist who had yen for military men was Paul Cadmus, who, at 94, recently had a show devoted to his work.

"'Men Without Women' is a provocative title for a rather sober survey," Richard Goldstein reported in the *Village Voice*. "A few bulbous buttocks are the only sign of what is called homoeroticism today. But in the front room, all decorum departs," Goldstein reports. "Here are some of Cadmus's most notorious works, including *The Fleet's In!*, the 1934 painting that made him all art star. In this knowing study of carousing sailors, there are not only buns and baskets on proud display but loose ladies admiring the briny trade and even a fey gentleman offering a cigarette to an eager gob. The navy was not amused. An outraged admiral had the painting removed before it could be shown in Washington, D.C. A sequel,*Sailors and Floozies* (1938), featuring an angelic seaman in slumber, grasping his crotch, fared no better in San Francisco; 'in the interest of national unity' it was taken off the wall.

"Fifty years before Robert Mapplethorpe became a catalyst of the culture wars, Cadmus was a symbol of the enduring American conflict between artists and puritans. It's a sad sign of the times that Mapplethorpe was largely lambasted while, back in the '30s, the press mostly sided with Cadmus and the artist ultimately prevailed. ...(His) fleshy appreciation of the male body may echo the Renaissance, but in the context of modern culture it signals a sensibility that is very gay. ...Cadmus was definitely taken with the working man. ...(And) a gay figure, sometimes Cadmus himself, appears in the recesses of many of his paintings, observing or sketching but never joining in the action. This outsider stance is also very gay—or was until the peephole became a pridefest."

"My work was never in the closet for people with eyes to see," says Cadmus, and in *Shore Leave* (1933), for example, a gay man is clearly propositioning a willing sailor, but what one notices first is the ripe women in the foreground and a recumbent swab with his bulging crotch in full view. Goldstein comments,. "...Looking at this pantheon of locker-room studs, seafood Sampsons, and young waifs lounging in the playground with baseball bats jammed between their legs, one sees a quality beyond the ideologically mandated worship of the working class. Call it longing."

"I was fascinated by the sailors, and I used to sit on a bench and watch them all the time," Cadmus recalls. In fact, Riverside

Park around 96th Street was a prime cruising ground in the '30s, largely because it was where the warships docked."The uniforms were so tight and form-fitting that they were an inspiration. I was young enough to be propositioned by the sailors, who would offer to take me back to the boat, but I never went. They were too unattractive, or maybe I was too timid. I don't know."

Timid too was Allen Ginsberg before meeting Jack Kerouac. In Ellis Amburn's revealing look at Jack Kerouac's"hidden life," *Subterranean Kerouac* (from St. Martin's Press), the author states that Kerouac had been described to Allen Ginsberg in heroic, irresistible terms: a football star, poet, novelist, and sailor. But at the time, Ginsberg was still a timid, virginal teenager, but intrigued by Lucien's depiction, he summoned the courage to call on Kerouac....

"...Ginsberg arrived at noon," Amburn reported, "Jack had just gotten up, and he came to the door fresh from a bath. Ginsberg recalled that Jack was 'very beautiful looking' in his white T-shirt, and Ginsberg's eyes fastened hungrily on his 'sturdy peasant build.' ...To Ginsberg, Jack was a desirable 'big jock who was sensitive and intelligent about poetry.'

"Kerouac's own account of the visit was markedly different. He disliked Ginsberg on sight and 'wanted to punch him in the mouth. He was a pushy little kike who had no business hanging around us older guys.' He dismissed Ginsberg as someone who wanted to have sex with everyone he met, in a huge tub of dirty water."

Later, Jack was introduced to William S. Burroughs, and, again, Jack was just stepping out of the shower, to the delight of Burroughs, who would later write of a character in *The Wild Boys*, "Johnny has just taken a shower. Flesh steaming he walks across the room."

"Perching primly on a hassock," Amburn says, "Burroughs quizzed Kerouac about life at sea on a merchant ship, but it was clear to Kerouac that Burroughs was interested in him as a piece of 'rough trade'. Nonetheless, he took an immediate liking to Burroughs and relished his macabre sense of humor".

Through Burroughs, Kerouac met Herbert E. Huncke, a small- time con man, thief, and gay hustler from Chicago, who Kerouac later recalled had a "radiant light shining out of his despairing eyes," when he approached him in Times Square one night. "I'm beat," Huncke said, a word Kerouac speculated he had picked up from "some Midwest carnival or junk cafeteria. It was a new language. Beat originally meant poor, down and out, deadbeat, on the bum, sad, sleeping in subways."

Ginsberg fell in love with Jack but was too timid to confess his passion, according to Amburn. Nevertheless, Jack sensed it and warned Ginsberg that "queerness" made him feel anxious. Ginsberg then reversed his strategy, dropped the sex issue, and attempted to snare Jack by spiritual means, contemplating a union of souls. But that didn't work either: Kerouac resented Ginsberg's self-appointed role as a "diabolic" despoiler of his spiritual life.

Eventually, Kerouac and Ginsberg did have sex together. Passing "the trucks" (the Village's notorious meat rack) the two would occasionally stop and masturbate. "We were horny," Ginsberg told his biographer Barry Miles, and they "jacked each other off. Kerouac allowed Allen to blow him. (And) Allen fell completely in love." Huncke concurred: "Allen and Jack slept together occasionally. Allen was in love with the whole bunch". According to Ginsberg, Kerouac at last began to be more reciprocal in their lovemaking, and thereafter their friendship deepened. "He was bending and stretching quite a bit to accommodate my emotions," Ginsberg recalled. "That's why I've always loved him, because I was able to completely unburden myself...and he was able to take it." According to Ginsberg, Kerouac became homoerotically aggressive on speed, hitting on men in public, saying, "C'mon, I'll fuck you." Kerouac blamed his burned-out condition on New York and on his former mentor, Burroughs. Having plundered each other for drugs and intellectual booty, neither showed concern any longer for the other's welfare, and their friendship deteriorated.

Amburn also reveals that the group participated in the historic Kinsey study in the late '40s. "Kinsey's variable straight-gay scale had perhaps never been more to the point, but the Beats made the same mistake as the greater society, separating individuals into artificial sexual categories....

"Jack's only relief from his heavy work of writing was occasional sex with Ginsberg.

"It was interesting because Jack felt there was nothing homosexual about being the blowee, only the blower," Ron Lowe, Kerouac's Florida friend, recalled. "Jack said, 'Gin used to blow me under the Brooklyn Bridge. I was young then and I came slow.' To hear a man that freely admitting, despite his distinction of being the beneficiary instead of the benefactor, didn't cut it with me. It was a distinction without a difference as far as I was concerned."

"Yet the distinction was important to Kerouac," Amburn said, "and he managed to convince himself that he could dip deeply and regularly into homoeroticism and still be a part of society's heterosexual tyranny. The price for living so dishonestly? Ever-increasing amounts of alcohol and drugs."

In his interview in *Freshmen* with Jamoo, porn star Sandy (of *Stag Party* from All Worlds, among others) Sloan said the particular type of guy he usually goes for is Latino, and, even better if he's in the military! Sandy has worked with a couple of Latinos on porn sets, as a bottom. He says he'd like to work with Mike Lamas. "He's not my ideal man, but I think he has a great body, and I like uncut dicks. Foreskin drives me crazy." His fantasy movie would be a Latino group scene. "I like to have threesomes with my lover," he says. That lover (in San Diego) hails from Puerto Rico and is "a Navy Boy."

The legendary porn filmmaker William Higgins drove down from Holland through Dresden in 1989 with a Russian friend, who was to act as his interpreter: "We drove through Terezin, which was built as a military fortress town by the Hapsburgs to staunch the Prussian hordes that were flooding in from the north. Today, it is still a garrison town. In the town center, we spotted a handsome young soldier hitchhiking his way south. I stopped the car and he got in. He had been in the car for less than half a minute when I said to my Russian companion, 'offer him 60 DM to have sex with me.'

"The Russian made the offer. The soldier didn't hesitate even one second, when he answered in Russian, "Sure, why not?"

"We drove on into Prague, found a room in a private apartment. The rest is kind of history.

"It turned out that was the kid's last day in the army and he was hitching home to Slovakia. He didn't have a job, and he and his buddy, who was even more handsome, wrote me in

Amsterdam and asked to move in with me. They lived with me for six months, and are both still living in Holland. I made plans to find a way to move to Czechoslovakia. My early history here will fill, I'm sure, many subsequent columns. For now, back to the topic at hand, 'hitchhiking.'

"Recently on a Friday afternoon at 15:00, I headed out with my driver Dan to do some 'research.' On Friday afternoons, Prague, along with every other big city in the Czech Republic, becomes a ghost town as families head to their little dachas (Czech: *chata*) in the countryside. You will never meet a Czech boy who has no carpentry skills. They spend virtually all of their weekends during their youth either building or repairing these little dachas. It's well known by Czech gays that every Friday after three o'clock thousands and thousands of Czech soldiers hit the roads hitchhiking home with their weekend passes. Soldiers have traditionally been easy 'pick-ups' in CZ for lots of reasons. Dan and I pushed off and immediately ran into an enormous Friday afternoon tail back, when we arrived at my favorite hitchhiking point (there are dozens of them around Prague), the clouds burst open with an enormous spring thunderstorm. So much for 45 minutes of driving. I said, 'Let's go to a service station and wait for ten minutes.'

"Sure enough, after ten minutes, the skies cleared and out popped the sun. Dan and I hightailed back to the pick-up point just in time to see literally hundreds of young hitchhikers emerging from shelter to try and catch rides. The bulk was soldiers, many students, and a few hippies with guitars. Thanks be to goodness that we haven't had any John Wayne Gacys yet to ruin an old Czech tradition. But the ways of the West are rapidly encroaching. I quickly ran out of film, and had to settle for handing out calling cards to all of the remaining soldiers who wanted to be photographed.

"In the Czech Republic, if you see someone interesting who is standing at a bus stop and offer him a ride, chance are about 80% that he will accept and hop in the car. By so doing there are no implied sexual connotations. Still, I have had some very worthwhile encounters with Czech hitchhikers. Military guys are particularly malleable since they are only paid about $12 or $13 a month." And, for us lovers of men in uniform, that sounds like heaven on earth!

A PRIVATE'S PART

PFC Rick Jackson, USMC

The United States Marine Corps has a lot going for it. The very name smacks of exploits in far-off lands and challenges that test a man's mettle. A Marine spends his life among men like himself—men who keep themselves in condition a Greek god would envy and never shrink from adventure. It goes without saying that many Marines are *very* close to their comrades and share more than duty assignments.

The one area where the Corps needs to rethink its program, though, is how it treats those of us who are still at the bottom of the food chain. Once a Marine makes Corporal, his life changes dramatically. He earns more money and no longer has to do every shit job that comes along. Those of us who are still privates, however, might as well be slaves. I don't object to working 36 hours a day, but I don't like being taken for granted.

That was what pissed me off about Lt. Miller. I'd liked him from my first day at Marine Corps Barracks, Yokosuka, Japan. Well, I have to admit I did more than like him, but I didn't expect him to suck my dick. All I wanted was to be treated like a human being instead of some mindless robot.

One of my jobs was to clean out the officer's head—do the deck, the crappers and basins, and even wash the spooge stains out of their shower. When the LT stroked in one day and popped into a shower stall, I was busy doing the crapper immediately opposite. Granted Marines are used to seeing each other naked, but he should have given me a break and shut the shower curtain.

How was I supposed to do my job with him slathering slick suds across his firm, hard body? I had to pretend not to watch, but I wondered whether he subconsciously wanted me to see what he had or he'd have shut the curtain. The way his hands massaged that lucky soap between his legs and up through the hard Corps-built mounds of man-muscle that guarded his virtue was so fine my dick didn't have a chance. I had to shut the stall door and beat a load down the drain while watching through the crack in the door as he twisted and turned that gorgeous body under the hot shower spray as though I weren't even there.

Afterwards, it was even worse. I'd no sooner blown my load and moved on to work in the next stall before he was out, standing naked as Temptation in the middle of the floor rambling on about something or other while he used his rough white towel on his flesh. Huge drops of water gleamed as they rolled off his massive shoulders and dripped from the dick I needed so much.

His huge hands flowed across his tanned pecs and down between his legs, dragging that coarse cotton where my tongue longed to go. He stroked and rubbed and twisted and talked until I was about to cream my cammies. Then he turned that heart-stopping ass of his to me and ambled towards the door. Only just as he stepped out into the passageway did he bother wrapping the towel around his ass. You can believe I nipped back into the stall for a second live fire exercise the minute the door slammed behind him.

I discovered the next day that I wasn't the only one jacking off. In a way, that was an even more insulting experience—at first. We also clean the officers' rooms: do their decks, empty the trash, wipe out the sinks, and so on. About 1000, I knocked on his door and waited. When I didn't hear anything, I used my key and stepped inside—to find him stretched out in his rack, naked, with his stiff dick towering towards the overhead.

It had been hard enough to ignore the day before, swinging thick and low between his thighs. Now it was impossible. Yet as I stood there in the doorway with my mouth agape, he didn't even glance in my direction, but kept his huge hand sliding up and down his glistening shank. I saw his legs twitch slightly as his knees parted to make him more comfortable, perhaps pretending some stiff dick was about to do him hard.

I don't know how long I stood there, gaping like a bootcamp having his first shower, before I let the door slam behind me with a cataclysmic CLANG! I was confused. Did he think so little of me that he would keep stroking off with me standing there? He could have at least reached down and pulled a sheet over him. On the other hand, maybe his slow strokes along that fine Marine shank were an invitation. If he'd been another private, I'd have been up his ass from the get go; but the guy was a Marine lieutenant.

His hard, sweat-speckled body gleamed in the light pouring through the windows. I saw his hips begin their roll, fucking more and more dick up into his massive paw. It was time for a command decision—one that could either get me what I wanted or have my ass thrown into the brig and out of the Corps on the double.

I took a step closer, hoping he would give me some clue; but he just reached up for another load of spit to slather over his enormous purple dickhead. His eyes were almost shut in private pleasure, but he knew I was there—watching, waiting, wanting.

Finally, I couldn't stand the strain another second. My hand pulled me to his rack and cupped his heavy, low-slung commissioned nuts as his thighs spread wider to let me in. LT's crotch was hot and sweaty and smelled of musk. He'd obviously just come back from PT and decided to stretch his most important muscle while he was at it. As I looked up across his powerful body, I could only think of a cheetah lying in the sun, waiting to jump the first poor gnu who wandered past.

His belly was flat and hard and as narrow as his tight hips, but powerful flanks rippled up across awesome pecs to broad shoulders that were even better. His strong jaw and brow, the green eyes now all but shut, and his cute little jarhead ears made my guts churn almost as much as the handful of sweaty balls I found myself juggling.

His body arched upwards, driving his crotch into my hand and putting pressure on his sack as he drove my fuckfinger down into his sweat-slicked butt-crack. Pretty clearly if the LT was going to burn my ass, he was going to let me have my fun first. I decided to give us both something to remember.

My face slipped to his crotch and inhaled those huge nuts, sucking and slurping and tugging at his 'nads as my pulse pounded in my ears. His legs spread wider yet, and his left foot reached over to pull me towards him. I managed to wriggle out of my T-shirt and UDTs and up onto the rack, but left my boots on rather than hold back another second.

The rangy, rough, spicy taste of man slashed across my

tongue like a wildfire, driving me to suck harder at his bumpy ballsack and the long hairs that dangled off it. His crotch rocked against my face like a childhood Christmas morning, begging for more, eager for everything I had to give.

Once my mouth was full of his nuts, my hands couldn't help themselves. They eased across his belly, following a thin ridge of blond fur up towards his chest. By the time they were on station, tweaking his furry tits and gliding in worshipful tribute across those powerful pecs, the LT was moaning like a raw recruit and we both knew rank wouldn't matter for the next hour or two.

His hand kept busy at his crank, sliding farther down towards the broad base of his ten-inch bone, pulling his skin tighter down his shank and stretching his plum-sized perfection more with every stroke. He wasn't in any hurry, though. That hand was teasing his tool, yanking out every possible sensation while he worked his way slowly towards the firing line.

My tongue needed down that dick in the worst way, but the LT's hand was first on station and didn't seem eager to surrender its position. For four or five more minutes, I chewed on his nuts and played touchy-feely with his tits; then the miracle happened. His feet lifted to snag on the underside of the rack above him.

As his ass followed upward, pushing that paw-powered prick forward against his belly, he took my mouth with him for a moment and then used his free hand to pry my face off his nuts. I didn't know where he dragged the rubber from and still don't care. He handed me one, though, and clenched his ass-crack in a mute invitation for me to drill my first commissioned shit-chute. I looked up between LT's solid infantry legs and discovered the green twinkle of his eyes peering out from between his dazed lids.

Now I was in charge—and I intended to make the most of it. Looking back, I saw he hadn't been ignoring me at all, but testing my initiative, begging for the hard fuck I wanted to give him. That latter realization didn't mean I'd completely forgiven his ass, though. As his crack pulsed open and shut, eager for all nine thick inches of my private's part, I hefted his heavy ballbag with my left hand while I slipped my right fuckfinger into my mouth for a generous load of spit.

My slick finger slid between the tight cheeks of his ass. Inside, muscle bound hard against muscle like coiled springs waiting to explode, but outside his skin was soft and supple as a virgin's hope. His left foot prodded me to hurry; but I let that fuckfinger keep on sliding, deep into the sweaty, hairy crack of his jarhead ass. He didn't know whether to bear down on my hand or use my finger to scratch away at the itch driving us both crazy. When I slipped across his asshole, his body nearly jumped up my arm to get a grip.

I pulled back and teased him some more, coasting around the tender rim of the pink pucker he'd hidden from his platoon. His ass accepted the challenge and tried to track me down, twisting this way and that to force his way against my finger while his own paw picked up speed and jacked away, jiggling his nuts against my hand. Finally I decided he'd suffered enough—and that I couldn't wait another second.

The rubber was tight around my dickhead and a steady stream of pre-cum oozing out of my piss-slit had turned the cloudy latex crystal clear. I thought about taking my time, teasing his shithole with my dick the way I had with my finger, but something told me he didn't want love. He wanted to be fucked—hard and deep and as long as I could keep my bone banging away.

The greedy look on his face told all. Far from ignoring me, getting me up his ass was a priority. I wasn't sure whether he was afraid to let his brother officers know what he liked, or if he just wanted me to do him as some reverse prestige symbol, rather the way the old planation masters had used their slaves. Whatever the case, I didn't do him to service the massa, I did him because I needed to.

He still hadn't said a word; but when I slammed my way through his shithole and up into the slick, hot guts that lay beyond, the bastard made more noise than Desert Storm. Maybe he'd underestimated how much first class privates I packed between my legs. Maybe he just hadn't been fucked open in a while. In any case, his body just didn't know what to do with all I had to give.

On the one hand, his ass clutched tight around my shank, desperate to keep me deep inside him and make the most of my meat until I'd launched my load where it would do us both all the good in the world. On the other hand, his ass hurt like hell when I split him open. I saw his eyes and jaw clench tight as one seizure after another rippled up from his tail to tear the leer from his lips. The lean muscle of his torso and limbs had nowhere to go, so it just knotted tight and held on through the storm.

I lay still, pulsing deep inside him for a time while his tender tail took measure of this grunt's gear. Soon enough the pain of entry had transformed itself into a satisfaction of absolute fulfillment and his feet wrapped around my ass to urge me on.

I moved my torso lower, partly to find more room to wrangle, partly to smell the sweaty heat of his body while I fucked him. I made him grunt with every vicious stroke up his ass. My swollen knob plowed a frantic furrow through his prostate and kept on going deep enough to teach his liver some manners. Every hard, butt-busting thrust through his ass told me I'd been right. The LT didn't want love. He didn't need any more respect. He needed to feel a man's meat buried deep up his ass, to be possessed by member of his warrior brotherhood while he lashed his log and dreamed of martial glory.

I could almost see his wheels turning as his fist pounded that meat between our ass-humping bodies. Whether Pork Chop Hill or Khe San or Iwo Jima, he had some great battle whirling away in mind and was dashing to freedom's defense as both our weapons loaded to fire.

I sank my lips to his furry chest and locked them around his hard, heaving tits. My teeth followed a moment later, anchoring us together as we bucked together like wild mustangs in heat. The LT was long lost in fantasy, moaning and grunting like a wounded bear as his hand picked up speed only to find my unit passing his on the straightaway. My hands locked hard around his shoulders, and then I turned The Monster loose up his ass.

One wave of blinding frenzy after another ripped upward from my rod and carried me off to a world of my own. I still saw the twisted grimaces of a tormented lust parading across the LT's boyish face, but I was too far gone to give him the attention he deserved. My balls were busting open with the consummation of every private's dream come true: reaming his LT up the ass and fucking him into a stupor.

I don't know how he held out as long as he did. I had to have been slamming away up his butt for at least fifteen minutes, and he'd had a major head start on me. I just know he jolted my ass back to reality when his body bucked and heaved and slammed upwards as his jack hand ripped the head off his dick and sent creamy commissioned spooge flying in all directions. The stuff slammed into the bulkhead beyond the rack and covered us both in his pearly ball ballast.

If his ass had been tight before, when he let loose his load, the jerk-off did everything but break my bone off at the joint. Only by slamming down on his legs and twisting his hole up to take better leverage was I able to keep fucking that incredible hole to my satisfaction. Unfortunately, the change of position meant the LT's dick was splashing spume straight into his hunky recruiting-poster face. I took one look at his tongue snaking out to lick a glob of his jarhead jism off his nose and lost every drop I had.

My balls clenched tight and convulsed in an instant, splashing a battalion-sized load of sperm up through my weapon and out into the LT's ragged ass. Only the rubber kept his gizzard safe from the shellshock it probably deserved. I know I kept at it, reaming and ramming and tearing my tool up that tight ass until I thought I'd pass the fuck out. By then, the LT had run out of ammo and was working his shithole like a velvet glove to jack my joint until my balls surrendered.

Once I was dry, I splash-landed onto his chest, ready to be nuzzled and kissed and congratulated, but the bastard wasn't interested. He eased his ass off my dick and reclaimed possession of his rubber. The LT was more interested in stirring my cum together with his and rubbing our cream across his belly than he was in rewarding my performance. Still, I'd gotten what I came for, so, knowing no one was about, I picked up my clothes and headed for the shower, naked from the ankles up.

I got as far as the door when the bastard finally deigned to recognize my existence: "Be back here at 2200."

I gave him a long look and then said, "Sir, with all due respect, suck my dick!"

He just gave me that studly grin of his, but as the door slammed into my ass on the way out, I heard him yell, "Right.

2200."

Fortunately, his supply of government-issue rubbers seemed as endless as our supply of jarhead juice. We went through a half dozen rubbers that night and have been busy burning rubber and cranking up the Federal Military Budget ever since.

A BIRTHDAY AT THE BATHS

William Cozad

It was my birthday and I while I pondered how to celebrate I stopped in at what had become my favorite diner to treat myself to a big mug of coffee and piece of their specialty: coconut cream pie. As I cleaned the plate, I had come to a decision. I didn't want to just go to a bar and get drunk. No, I would go to the baths. Hell, I could at least get a blowjob on my birthday.

I was about to split when into the diner strolled two cute young guys. They sat down beside me at the counter and ordered. Cokes and fries. Right away I got the hots for the tall, slender blond. The short guy was dark and muscular. Both of them were smooth-faced, boy-next-door types.

Usually I'm shy with strangers, but I couldn't keep my eyes off the blond. There was just something about him I liked. When he glanced my way, he smiled and I struck up a conversation. "You guys just get into town?" I asked.

The blond beamed now. He had bright, perfect teeth and such kissable lips. "Marines. Just got out of the Academy. Going to pick up our first ship," he said.

"Hey, that sounds exciting." But then I found myself tongue-tied. I figured it didn't matter much because I was wasting my time. No way I could get the blond away from his buddy and sneak him back to my hotel room for a little fun. No way.

They scarfed down their fries and slurped their sodas. I drank the dregs of my coffee. I knew it was stupid, but I just couldn't let the blond get away without trying for him. He chatted a little more and was very friendly; his buddy didn't say a thing. They were perfect together.

Suddenly an idea popped into my head.

"Yeah, well, I'm kinda new in town myself, and it's my fuckin' birthday."

"Oh, yeah?" the blond asked, green eyes sparkling.

"Yeah, and I wanna celebrate. How'd you guys like to have

a drink with me?"

"Shit, we'd love to, but we're only 18, man," the blond said.

I was thinking about taking them to my room at the hotel but nixed the idea. There were no visitors allowed after six P.M. Besides, it was risky, with two guys. They could start some trouble, maybe beat me up—or worse.

"Yeah, well, I know a place we can go, it's like a club."

"Yeah?" the blond was interested.

"Yeah. My treat."

The blond smiled and looked at his black-haired buddy, who shrugged.

"Okay, let's go, man," the blond said.

In a rare burst of generosity—and perhaps thinking of making a good investment—I sprang for their tab. Then I stopped and bought a bottle of good vodka at a corner grocery. From there I escorted them to the downtown baths. They gave me a funny look but didn't say anything. I paid the admission, and the clerk gave us a special large room upstairs, like he sensed what the hell the situation was—so I pushed a fiver at him and he smiled.

Most of the clientele at this early hour were older men, and damn few of 'em. Some of them eyeballed us, but we just kept walking.

I got soft drinks out of the machine in the lobby, then we headed for our room.

The seamen sipped the soda, and I filled the cans with generous portions of booze. I soon learned the blond was named Bobby, the black-haired guy was Wade. Bobby rambled on about the training at the Academy and how he was excited about going to sea. They had to report to their ship at the pier by midnight. Wade just stared at the walls.

"Well, guys, we'd better get undressed. It's a bathhouse, you know," I said. I stood up and started shedding my clothes.

Used to following orders, they too started to undress. It was a feast to the eyes. Both of 'em had nice, smooth bodies. The blond had an above-average-sized, clipped cock. The swarthy one had a big, uncut dick, with enormous balls. I got undressed too. We sat on the large bed wearing just our towels and sipped the spiked sodas. They toasted my birthday.

Horny and not wanting to waste time, what with the clock

ticking away, I decided to get things rolling. "Bet you guys are horny, all that time in Basic, no chicks and all. Bet you're needing it pretty bad by now." Both were silent, just staring at me. But then I noticed their dicks were going hard, making their towels stick up over their crotches. The brunet let out a laugh. "Fuck, man, you were right. The dude's a fag." The blond smiled back at his friend, then at me. Then he just dropped his towel open and spread his legs. "Shit, man, go for it." That was all the invitation I needed. I crawled between his splayed legs. I inhaled the ripe smell of his musky crotch.

As soon as I touched his dick, it became fully engorged. Hard it was around eight inches, but thick. Leafy blue veins showed beneath the skin of his shaft. His mushroom cockhead was rosy. His dick throbbed, and a strand of silver pre-cum clung to his pisshole. His pendulous balls heaved in their mossy, chicken-skin sack. Excited by his blond pubes, I did something that I'd always fantasized about. I just started to lick his pubic bush. His dick bobbed around, and I clasped it while I bathed his blond bush in spit until it glistened. He squirmed around on the bed. I stroked his shaft and lapped at his nuts. They were big and full of cum, but I managed to stuff both of them into my mouth and hum on them. I sloshed them around, then spit them out.

By now clear goo oozed out of his pisshole. Gripping his pulsing shaft, I dug my tongue into the slit, slurped up the sweet pre-cum and swabbed the rosy crown. It turned a purplish hue. I fastened my lips around his cockhead. I sucked on the knob while I tongued the sensitive ridge below it.

"Oh yeah. Suck it. Suck my dick," he moaned. Meanwhile his buddy was leaning in close to watch my every move. I jacked the shaft, then let go of it. I bobbed my head up and down on his gristly dick. I tugged on his spit-soaked nuts while I deep-throated every inch of his eight-inch cock. I drooled spit down onto his soppy blond bush. Somehow I managed to devour his cock and balls.

"Oh, shit, man, I'm fucking coming!" he screamed. His dick was hard as a rock and it just gushed, squirting down my throat and filling my mouth with sweet cream. I siphoned his balls until his dick softened and his jewels slipped out of my mouth. When I glanced over at the swarthy guy, Wade, he'd already dropped his towel. His dick was monster meat, over nine inches and beer can thick. He lewdly stroked it.

Like a trained seal tooting horns, I waddled over to it on my knees. It jutted out from his dense black bush like a tower. He had jumbo-egg-sized balls. I gripped his shaft by the base, which was even thicker. I licked his dickmeat up and down, coating it in spit. Out of the corner of my eye, I noticed the blond gulping vodka straight out of the bottle.

I continued with my cocksucking routine. Fascinated by the cowl of foreskin, I pinched it over the crown like a sausage, and jacked his dick while I lapped at his bullnuts. I sucked them separately, unable to stuff both of them into my mouth at the same time. I was caught off guard when the swarthy seaman grabbed me by the hair on my head and shoved his big dick between my lips. He nearly choked me to death with it. Tears stung my eyes. He pumped his massive prick down my throat, with his wet balls slapping against my chin. My towel had fallen off in the cocksucking fray and my own dick begged for attention. I wrapped my hand around my meat and fisted it in the same rhythm that the black-haired seaman fucked me in the mouth.

Suddenly Wade yanked his dick out of my mouth. He pointed at his buddy. Bobby was passed out on the bed and snoring. Clasping his dick, Wade slapped me in the face with it. He smeared the clear pre-cum all over my lips. I was about to gobble up his dick when I got a brainstorm. My asshole twitched. I hadn't been fucked in a while, but I wanted to get fucked by this big-dicked seaman. I plopped down on the lumpy bed on my belly and nearly bounced Bobby off it, but he didn't wake up. Reaching back, I spread an asscheek. I poked my middle finger in and out of my butthole. I glanced over my shoulder.

"Fuck me, Wade. Fuck me with your big dick." I didn't have to tell him twice.

He straddled my legs. "Fucking's my specialty," he said. He slapped his huge, hot, hard dick against my butt like he'd done against my face earlier.

I could feel the sticky goo on my buns. I was kind of scared by the size of his dick, but I wanted it real bad. I had to have it inside me.

"Spit in my crack," I said. He drooled warm spit into my ass ditch. That, along with his oozing pre-cum, made the penetration possible. He pulled back his foreskin and popped his bullet-shaped cockhead into my pucker.

"Oh God, it's so fuckin' big," I gasped.

He inched in some of the shaft and my hole relaxed. I would take it or I'd die trying. I backed up on his dick. "Fuck me, sailor. Fuck my tight ass."

He lay on top of me and then relentlessly ground his dick up my ass.

I humped back; I wanted it so bad: "Fuck harder! Deeper!"

I buried my face in the pillow. He jackhammered my asshole until I saw stars. My head was spinning. I was in orbit. It seemed like forever. He plowed my ass like there was no tomorrow. His dark, cum-filled nuts banged against my buttcheeks.

Soon he was breathing heavy, dripping sweat onto my body His dick was steely when it exploded and gushed wads of molten cum deep into my assguts. At the same time my own dick went off and gushed a puddle of cum onto the sheet underneath me. I didn't even touch my dick. It just happened. My hole spasmed around the big dick inside me, which softened and slid out.

Amazingly, Bobby was still passed out cold on the bed next to us. So Wade and I ventured down to the steam room, where I gave him a blowjob and jacked off all over his legs. Back in the upstairs room, Wade and I polished off the bottle of vodka, then woke Bobby up. We all got dressed and left the tubs.

It was sad to say good-bye to them at the bus. They were nice, horny sailors whose big, fat dicks made my birthday one I'll never forget.

THE ROCK-SOLID STUD

William Cozard

The summer after I graduated high school I enlisted in the Marines and was sent to camp. Boot camp was supposed to be tough physical training, and it was. Our DI worked our tails off and ran us ragged, but damned if I didn't like it!

I became tight with a recruit named Robinson. Unlike me, it seemed he did everything right. He could tear his piece apart and put it back together in a flash, not to mention tear up the bullseye on a target every time.

Robinson was tall, rock solid—and black. What attracted me to him, besides his being a gung-ho Marine recruit, was what I saw in the showers. Naked, Robinson showed a dick that was at least seven inches *soft*. His delicious-looking, uncut manhood swung over huge, pendulous balls. I blinked in utter disbelief!

However, in the beginning, I was too busy—not to mention too damn tired—to give it a lot of thought, but, over time, I guess you could say I became obsessed with Robinson. He was handsome in his own macho way, with a big nose, full lips and perfect teeth. And of course that dick. I knew was that I was attracted to Robinson, and I guess he liked me okay, too. At least he was real friendly to me, skylarking and teasing in what little free time we had. He never said anything but I could feel the vibes and caught him staring at me sometimes, like he was mulling me over. I figured some day something had to give. At least I hoped so.

I was working my butt off and sweating plenty to make it through boot camp. Some recruits were set back in their training, others were discharged as unsuitable for military service, but most of us made the grade. I was proud to wear the uniform, just like my dad before me.

After graduation from boot camp we all got time to go home on leave before reporting to our duty stations. I was assigned to a detachment just outside San Francisco, while Robinson was going to be stationed in North Carolina. When we took the bus to downtown San Diego I sat beside Robinson. I wanted to tell him I was going to miss him, but it seemed too wimpy. But maybe he was thinking the same thing because, all of a sudden, he said, "Party time!"

"Huh?"

"Yeah, man, let's you and me have a little farewell drink."

"Shit, man, a bar's not going to serve us, you know; we're both underage," I reminded him.

"Fuck 'em. You just leave that to me." Robinson took charge. He found an older Marine on the street who bought us a couple of six-packs of Bud and a bottle of whiskey at a store. Robinson paid the tab.

"So where we going to drink this?" I asked. 'We'll get busted in Balboa Park."

"Let's get a hotel room. Can you pop for a twenty? Gonna need the rest of my bankroll for that plane ticket."

"Sure."

Robinson checked us into a downtown hotel.

It all happened so fast. There I was in a hotel room alone with Robinson.

"Call your folks and tell them you'll be a day late," he said.

"Won't matter. I'm taking the bus. I already wrote them that I'd be home sometime this weekend, but nothing specific." Robinson got on the phone and changed his plane reservation, then called his folks collect to tell them when to pick him up. Suddenly it dawned on me that we'd be spending the night together, just Robinson and me. I was nervous as hell, but ready for whatever happened. Tell the truth, I wasn't much of a drinker. Oh, I'd drunk beer at parties, but never touched the hard stuff. Whereas Robinson considered himself an expert on booze.

"Beer's for wusses," he teased. He poured us glasses of whiskey. We gulped it and chased it down with beer. A couple of those and I was feeling no pain.

"I'm glad we're celebrating together," I confessed.

"Shit, we deserve it after all the crap we been through."

"You were the best fuckin' recruit in the platoon, man. Even the DI said so."

I must have been getting drunk to talk so sappy.

"I always wanted to be a Marine," Robinson said. "Yeah, my dad was a Marine."

We clicked our whiskey glasses and guzzled the suds, sitting at the small table by the window, looking out at the San Diego skyline.

"I'm gonna miss you, Robinson." Guess I was getting loaded.

"Yeah? So how much you gonna miss me? Just *how* much?"

"A whole lot, man," I responded. "A whole lot."

"How about my black dick?"

"What about it?" I didn't know if he was goofing or what.

"You gonna miss looking at it like you always do?"

"What...?"

"Shit, man, you know what I'm talkin' about. And I ain't stupid, you know. Look, I know damn well you didn't come to this hotel room with me to just get drunk...."

"I...."

"Well, did you?"

"Well...."

What I saw next blew my mind. Robinson leaned back in his chair, unzipped his fly and whipped out his cock. Then he just started stroking his dick. It was already semi-hard. Damned if I didn't get a boner from watching him. I was hoping he'd want to jack off together. But it turned out he had something even better in mind.

"You like black dick, don'tcha?"

"Man, what are you sayin'? You think I'm queer or something?"

"I ain't sayin' nothin'. I'm just sayin' that you like black dick. I'm just remarkin' about the obvious."

"Hell...."

"Oh, c'mon, buddy. Ain't no need to pretend no more. You been wantin' this big dick since you first saw it."

"You're crazy. Or drunk."

"Go ahead. Feel it."

My eyes bugged out. Robinson took my hand and placed it on his black manhood. It was hot and throbbing. I squeezed it. "I never did this before," I protested.

"Go ahead, take your dick out. Show me what you got." On an impulse, I unzipped my pants and freed my cock. It was hard and sniffed the air.

"Man, you got a helluva *big* dick for a white guy!"

"Well, I guess it gets the job done," I said shyly. "But, speaking of that, nothing gets the job done like yours. Jesus, I bet it's a foot long!" It was true. I bet it would have measured a foot if I'd had a ruler handy.

"Like it, do you?"

"Yeah."

So there we were, both in uniform, with our dicks out and stroking them, watching each other, 20 inches of dick between us.

"Let's get out of these uniforms," Robinson said, taking charge, as always.

We both stripped naked, wearing only our dog tags. He lay back on the bed and spread his legs invitingly. I might have been a little high, but it seemed the most natural thing in the world to do. I went over and lay down next to him. Robinson and I got on our sides facing each other and embraced. Our two hard, young Marine cocks dueled. Then he kissed me. My body was on fire. I'd never felt so horny in my life.

"Are you going to make me suck your dick, Robinson?" I asked hopefully.

"Uh-uh." Robinson rolled me over on my belly. I realized that he wanted to fuck me. Don't think that didn't sober me up fast. Looking over my shoulder, I took another gander at the foot-long dick he was stroking. Totally engorged, it was as big around as a beer can, I swear. The very thought of it crammed up my ass sent goosebumps up and down my spine. "I don't think I could ever take that big thing up my ass, man. It's like a fucking telephone pole."

"I'll go easy. You want it, I know you do."

Next thing I knew Robinson spread my lily white buttcheeks. I couldn't believe it. He just stuck his tongue in my crack and lapped at it.

"Oh, shit, that feels good," I squealed. "Eat out my Marine butt."

"Do more than that, white stuff. Gonna give your ass a taste of my big, black dick."

Looking back over my shoulder at the sight of Robinson slapping that black snake on my buns was serious business, knowing he was going to bury it up my ass. He greased his dick up with one of those little complementary tubes of lotion, then rubbed his cockhead in my spit-soaked crack. He nudged at my pucker and I felt my asshole opening up. He punched his prickhead inside.

"Holy shit!" I yelped.

He eased in an inch or so of veiny shaft, and my assring expanded around it. Felt painful, but I liked the way he was taking charge, making me take it. "Want it?" he asked. "Want that big black dick up your tight white ass?"

"Yeah," I whispered. I didn't believe I said that. But as I felt him cram my butthole with black dick, I knew I was getting just what I needed. Amazed that the pain had subsided, I craved that black dick reaming my fuckhole more than I'd ever wanted anything before in my life. "Fuck me, Robinson. Fuck me with that big, black dick."

"You got it, you pussy."

I bucked back and moved my ass around. Soon I felt his wiry pubes scratch my asscheeks. That meant he had the whole thing up my ass. I was delirious. "Ram my hole. I can take it. Everything you got, black Marine motherfucker. Give it to me."

It felt like a jackhammer up my ass. I loved his sweat, his smell and the sound of his heavy breathing. "Like my big, black dick? I thought so. Man, was I ever right about you. I didn't know where or when but I knew that I was gonna fuck you. I had wet dreams about your hot, white ass. You acted so innocent. I knew you was cherry."

"Yeah, make me take it. Drill my ass open. Tear it up. I love the way it feels. It's like I've been waiting all my life for this to happen." Robinson was a natural sex machine. His 12-inch cock was bloated and pounded my guts to mush. His dog tags jingled. Soon his cock was like a crowbar. "Fuck, yeah! I'm comin' in your tight ass!"

"Oh, I feel it! I can feel it! Fill it up!" I was sweating and panting as much as him as he grunted and shot his cum into me.

After what seemed forever, his enormous black dick deflated and plopped out of my now so wonderfully deflowered butthole. Suddenly I became aware of my own hard-on. All my sensation had been focused on my sensitive butthole when he screwed it, but I realized my cock was a real diamond cutter, in need of release.

I bucked the Marine stud off me and rolled over with my prick towering in the air. "Yeah, beat that dick," he said. "I like to watch a punk play with himself."

I just grinned at Robinson as I spewed my spunk onto my sweaty chest.

In the morning, Robinson straddled my body and docked our dicks. Pointing our cockheads together, he slid his velvety black foreskin over my rosy white crown and masturbated our 20 inches of meat. I held our turgid pricks together and jacked them until they erupted and coated our crotches with cum. Robinson showered, but I let the cum cake onto my skin—something to remember him by for as long as possible, I suppose.

Outside the hotel he shook my hand and I hugged him just before he got into the airport taxi. Lugging my duffel bag, I hiked to the nearby bus depot.

I still get off remembering the way Robinson's big black dick popped my tight Marine cherry.

JERRY, THE NEW RECRUIT

Bill Nicholson

It was Colonel Nasser who was responsible for my coming into contact with Jerry.

For those of you for whom this name means little or nothing, Colonel Nasser was a Middle-Eastern leader who took it into his head to precipitate, in 1956, what became known as the Suez Crisis, blocking the Suez Canal with scuttled ships, which caused our British government some concern.

His timing couldn't have been more disastrous for me. I had already served my enforced two years of National Service, every moment of it begrudged, as it had interfered with my college life. Now I was an equally reluctant Army Reservist, liable to be called-up at a moment's notice to help sort out any foreign foolishness. Sure enough, my call-up papers arrived just a month before I was due to start my first job. I was not pleased.

However, resigning myself to the old maxim, "What can't be cured must be endured," I stiffened my British upper lip and reported to the same dreaded camp in Yorkshire where I had begun my National Service. Here I was kitted-out in the same scratchy (and decidedly unbecoming) type of uniform that I remembered all too well. After a day or two spent in reconciling my digestive organs to the Army's idea of "Egon Ronay," and having various pricks (not the interesting kind, but those from hypodermic syringes, which were designed to immunize me against Nasser-type foreign bugs), I was sent to a God-forsaken transit camp in Wiltshire, quite near to the famous Stonehenge on Salisbury Plain. It was here that I first set eyes on Jerry.

His real name was not Jerry; it was Peter. He was not a reservist, but a fresh National Serviceman. He was in the Pay Corps, and allocated to my barrack room; I am reminded of the "fickle finger of Fate" motto of Charity Hope Valentine—but that's showing my age, which in 1956 was twenty-four.

Jerry, as a new National Service recruit, was just eighteen, and looked even younger. He was about my height, 5' 8 or so, with black hair and a knowing twinkle in his eye that set my testosterone on "Red Alert." Unlike my North-of-England self, he was a Londoner, with the Cockney accent with which Dick van Dyke was so gamely to wrestle eight years later in "Mary Poppins." He had acquired the "Jerry" nickname due to a [slight] resemblance to Jerry Lewis, combined with a zany persona. He brought to mind the "class comedian" type from schooldays, only far more attractive than most such. Unlike many, the "crew cut" suited him ideally.

During my two years of National Service, I had elected to become an office clerk. I thought that it might be useful to learn typing, and, probably as a result of my being quite a competent pianist, I had 'passed out' as the most efficient typist of my section. All the other lads, as far as I remember, remained "two-finger" exponents. My talent was quickly spotted by the officers of our transit camp, and I was given my own tiny office, where I spent the days pounding out correspondence of "Great Import" concerning the Suez Crisis.

It's strange, but I can't remember the first occasion on which Jerry, as I shall continue to call him, brought me a batch of letters from the orderly room to type. What I do know is that a regular pattern emerged. He would deposit the letters on my desk, and then, obviously in no hurry to leave, lean back against the wall with that seductive look and an enticing bulge in the left leg of his trousers. Quite soon this was accompanied by, "Fancy an 'ard?" [or "a boner" or "a beat" or "a stiffy," or one of his apparently inexhaustible vocabulary of synonyms for what dictionaries call an "erection"]. Eventually this ritual was inevitably concluded by my grasping, squeezing and kneading what was straining behind that rough fabric, and finally saying, with feigned boredom, "That's your ration for now. I've work to do."

We were at the camp for several weeks. Each evening, we would listen to the radio in the "N.A.A.F.I.", to hear how the Suez situation was progressing. In the meantime, I availed myself of what was, for me, one of the very few advantages of army life: the showers. In those days, showers were almost unknown in British homes. Some houses didn't even have a bathroom, until a spare bedroom was converted into one. In my part of Britain, some families were just converting from outdoor toilets, primitive though that sounds now.

So, making the most of the luxury, I showered almost daily, although the shower-hut was some three or four hundred yards away. I'd possessed myself of a large, soft, plastic toilet bag, which contained a bar of soap in a hard plastic box, a bottle of shampoo, a face-cloth, a large, round, synthetic sponge and a rubber sink-plug, this last because nowhere in the British Army was a single one to be found. In my Basic Training days I'd found, to my surprise, that one was expected to make a wad of toilet paper to "bung up" the sink outlet, in order to wash and shave in the mornings. On such economies, I gathered, was our Empire built! Well, my portable, flexible plug served to block up the outlet from the shower base in which I stood, so that my feet could enjoy the soaking they needed.

It was not to be taken for granted that the water from the showers would inevitably be hot, but it was, mercifully, more often so than not. Even when it wasn't, I still went ahead, though I cut the proceedings short and did not shampoo my hair.

There were two varieties of shower. The first was when there was company; that is, when one or more of one's fellow-unfortunates were already at their ablutions, or came in while one was on one's own. Either way, this was when "window-shopping" took on new meaning! So did "frustration." On two occasions I was lucky enough to be showering close to a lad from Newcastle-on-Tyne, to whom I ever afterwards mentally awarded the nick-name "Donkey-man." God—what a tool he had! The second variety was when one had the shower-hut to oneself. These were the occasions when the hot water, the soaping and the memories of those desirables who had already stood naked in the same spot caused a chronic onslaught of tumescence which could be relieved only by "wanking oneself senseless".

Sunday morning's shower was one I never missed. Being the day of rest, a lot of the lads stayed snoring in their "pits". I rose, though, and went for a mug of tea and a slice of fried bread with an egg, foregoing the jaw-paralysing porridge and grease-swimming bacon. Then I lay on my bed for a few minutes, after which I picked up my towel and toilet-bag.

That was the usual procedure. What made one Sunday

different from all the the others was a stirring from the bed four down from mine, and the voice that said, "Where yer goin', Nick?"

Nick was not my name, any more than Jerry was his. Mine was derived from an abbreviation of my surname.

"For a shower," I said.

"Hang on a minute! I'll come wiv yer."

He jumped out of bed in his underpants, pulled on his denims and boots, picked up his towel and soap and stood grinning [knowingly? expectantly?]. It crossed my mind, briefly, that it was a 'dare.' Who cared?

"C'mon, then," I said.

We walked to the shower-hut in the bright August sunshine. If we spoke, I don't remember.

We went in. As usual, on Sunday morning, it was empty. The showers were in a double row, back to back, with a space between. I led the way through, heading for the cubicles that I knew provided the most powerful sprays.

"These are good ones," I said, throwing my towel and bag on the wooden wall-seats. "I'll see if the stokers have done their duty."

I fiddled with the hot and cold taps, adjusting the temperature.

"Yes", I said, "it's good and hot."

"Right, then," Jerry said, sitting down and pulling off his unlaced boots. Then he stood and began to strip.

Taking off my own gear more slowly, for some reason I didn't look at him. He was naked while I was still throwing aside my shirt. He went to the cubicle next to the one I'd set off, and, leaning forward, began to adjust its taps. Then I did look. The August sun shone through the windows, its glare illuminating the whole of his rear view. My scrotum received what I can only describe as a contracting, mini-electric shock as that lithe, supple, yes, beautiful body imprinted itself on my retina. The legs, slim rather than thin, were covered in tiny black hairs, each one of which glistened in the light. The curve of the spine led my eye downward to the perfect twin globes of his buttocks. I shut my eyes and instead finished my own undressing. As I did so, Jerry turned round and, after a second or two, chuckled. I opened my eyes.

"What's funny?" I asked.

"You," he said. "You're so fuckin' 'airy."

This I could not deny, but being slightly rattled by the remark (did he find hairiness repulsive?) I replied,"We can't all be like new-born babes."

"Oh, yer?" he said, "'and 'ow many newborn babes like this 'ave you seen?"

With that he put both hands behind his head and rocked from side to side, causing his cock to slap against each thigh in turn. Again my retina clicked—the front view was even more devastating than the rear one had been. The slapping cock was uncut; somehow I knew it would be, though the office groping through thick trousers couldn't have told me so. It hung from a luxuriant pubic bush whose curling black hairs caught that brilliant sunshine just as enticingly as had his leg-fur from the back. Above that foliage was a thin line leading up his flat belly to the navel. Dear God, please help me!

"We came here to shower," I said, desperately, and went with all my toiletries into my cubicle. Jerry stepped into his and for a few minutes nothing was heard but splashing water and soaping. Jerry began to sing, tunelessly, the song "Maybe it's because I'm a Londoner." It really was excruciating.

I made it an excuse, though.

"Anything's better than that," I said. "Come here and I'll wash your back, if you'll shut up."

"I'll bet you say that to all the boys," he replied, but he came.

I soaped my sponge and set to work, my left hand on his shoulder. I didn't hurry; I covered that smooth expanse with slow, what I hoped were titillating strokes. I squeezed the sponge and watched the line of suds course down his back, some of it making its way into the cleft between those twin mounds. All this was having its inevitable effect on me, if not on him, and I felt the first stirrings of my equipment.

"Oh, that feels great," he said suddenly, and that did it.

With my soapy middle finger, I slowly went where the soapsuds had gone before—into that enticing cleft between the mounds. Slowly, slowly, so very slowly, until I reached a small ridge, at whose edges I paused.

Jerry turned his head to the right. "Naughty, naughty!" he said, but the tone was not one of anger.

I decided to press on, in more ways than one. I slowly massaged the spot I had found, then gently pushed the one finger just inside the muscle. His shoulder blades tensed, and I heard a sharp intake of breath.

"Now, 'ang on...." he said.

"No, you hang on," I replied. "Step backwards. Come nearer."

He obeyed, feeling with his heels for the raised base of my shower tray. A couple of "sploshes" and his feet were inside my cubicle. My middle finger left its target and slid forward along the area between his pucker and his ball-sac. I applied upward pressure to what I knew was the root of his penis. It started to swell, and my tool continued its own enlargement.

I removed my hand and turned off my shower spray. Time for more soap, with not too much water. I grabbed my cake of soap, bent down for a couple of handfuls of water from the tray and began to work up a slippery mess in both palms.

"Time for you to hang on," I said. "Grab the bar up there."

[This was the metal bar which would have held up a curtain in showers designed for modest female soldiers.]

Once again, Jerry did as he was told. ['Good boy!"]

I got to work on that beautiful, boyish body, reaching round with bare hands, first to tease his armpit hair with short tugs, then moving inwards until I found both pointed, erect nipples. These I tormented with my thumbnails, raking slowly over them a few times. There were moans, and his hands clenched and unclenched on the bar.

Now it was time to home in. My hands made the journey south, down his chest and abdomen [with a brief "whistle stop" at the navel], down his belly, into the forest and....

Bingo! My prize! A proud English oak, if ever there was one; strong and sturdy and pointing to the heavens, standing triumphantly clear of all the surrounding foliage. As my slippery hands explored its length, it squirmed and bucked.

"Nick! Oh, Nick! What if somebody comes?" came his anxious voice.

"I think that's highly unlikely," I replied.

Fondling his balls with my left hand, I worked his foreskin back and forth with my right.

"I haven't got one of those knob-cosies," I said.

"So I noticed." His right hand left the bar and reached round to grasp my tool, which was by now poking the small of his back. [My turn to shudder deliciously.]

"Roundhead pricks can be quite pretty, though." He gave a couple of squeezes, then let go his other hand and turned to face me. I glanced down; the sturdy oak still had ambitions to reach the ceiling, rising higher than his navel.

"You are a Guinness Book of Records new-born baby, aren't you? I'd no idea. I can give you six years, and by the look of it you can give me two and a half inches."

"You jealous old queen," he said, putting both arms round my neck and drawing me close, squeezing our hot, slippery cocks side by side between our bellies. He leaned his head on my right shoulder and I began to run my nails down his back, from neck to the rise of the mounds. I knew from my explorations of my own body that the end of the journey could result in a tingling that runs through the entire loins. The purrs from Jerry's throat soon proved to me that he had the same mechanism.

"Fuckin' lovely," he murmured, and twitched his cock a couple of times in appreciation.

I could feel his heartbeat strengthening, and my own too. The Gates of Paradise were preparing to open, I thought. I brought my right hand round, eased back, grasped his prick and persuaded it to take a new home, under my balls and between my thighs. My hand went round to continue gentle nail-scratching in the small of his back.

We began a mutual slow rocking back and forth, accompanied by the quiet "suck-slurp" sound of well-soaped flesh on flesh. Like fellow-mountaineers, we worked steadily and single-mindedly to attain the summit.

Soon it was so close that, in the excitement, it seemed that it wouldn't have mattered if all the rest of our barrack-room mates had suddenly made an appearance to witness our achievement.

Through the noise of the now frantic gasps and violent heart-hammerings came Jerry's anguished, "Nick! Nick! I'm... going ... to...."

My right middle finger found the sphincter whose opening it had lightly teased minutes earlier, and this time it plunged, raping, as far as it could go. My left hand squeezed and scratched the right arse-cheek frantically.

I thought, momentarily, that Jerry's now-violent stranglehold might cause me to black out. I can't attempt to describe the sounds that came from his throat as he reached the pinnacle. I do know that his final roar set echoes resounding round the roof of the hut; the decibel level must have been at least the equal of the last seconds of Ravel's "Bolero."

Nor can I believe that my own orgasm was silent, but it was certainly drowned by his.

Eventually, the earth stopped spinning.

My back was pressing against cold tiles; a shower was splashing in the next cubicle. A young man was standing just outside my own cubicle, in the bright August sunshine. He was stroking his belly, which was glistening with a mixture of soap and cum. His still-impressive, though now flaccid, penis was coated with the same mixture.

He looked at me.

"I need a shower," he said.

I turned on my own spray again, at the same time letting out the water from the tray. Spirals of jism made their way down the plug-hole.

We both showered and dried off like any pair of "buddy" regular soldiers. I sat, drying my feet in readiness for dressing. Jerry, having finished, made for his clothes, lying next to mine. I took hold of his hand as he reached for his denim trousers, and drew him in front of me. I looked up at his boyish, cheeky face. I thought there was a slight frown on it.

"For God's sake, don't feel ashamed," I said.

His groin was level with my face. There was the winking navel, the dark line of belly-hair, the luxuriant bush. I leaned forward, buried my nose in the pubes, now sweet-soap-smelling and moist-crinkling, and gently kissed the penis, not yet shrunken to its smallest size. The glans still projected slightly past the foreskin, and there was a late "dew-drop" shining at the slit. I licked it off, and looked up again. "Please."

Suddenly he beamed his wonderful, boyish smile at me. He stroked my chest hair for a second or two, then gave it a vicious tug, which made me wince.

"Yer great 'airy fool," he said.

On the way back to the barrack-room we met two other soldiers coming in the opposite direction. One was a lanky, carrot-haired lad, the other short, dark, and very attractive. Both carried rolled-up towels.

As we met, the latter asked, "Is the water hot, lads?"

Jerry winked at me. "It was hot enough for us wasn't it, mate?"

I had to agree.

When the Suez affair was over, we exchanged addresses. I wrote, but he never replied. Nevertheless, I have to say, Thanks, Colonel.

THE MAKING OF A SOLDIER

Peter Gilbert

Was it James's jug-ears or his conversation that first attracted John's attention? To this day he doesn't know and you don't tell a young man that he has elephantine ears. John wouldn't dream of doing so, even though James is now a twenty-five-year-old Army captain.

Whatever it was, it certainly wasn't the boy's figure. That was covered by a long raincoat. He came into the restaurant with an elderly couple and a younger woman. They took off their wet coats and sat down. John ordered his lunch and a beer. Of all the pubs in the area, the Schwarzer Ochse was probably the best, not that the catering there was anything wonderful. He looked at his watch. Michael was due to arrive in fifteen minutes. He took a sip of beer.

"You can take that back and bring another. It's flat!" he said to the hovering waiter.

"*Wie bitte?*"

"Oh God! This beer is flat. Bring me another," he said in fluent German.

In fact it wasn't too bad but it did no harm to keep them on their toes, he thought. The waiter shrugged his shoulders, picked up the glass and returned to the bar. He came back with a glass with so much froth that it formed a dome on the top of the beer.

"That's better," said John. He sipped it and wondered how long he would have to endure his present life. His research on the old Wartime secret weapons factory at Mettenheim had really only just begun. It would be some time before he could finish the book—and then who would read it? A few retired officers like himself. One or two historians. Was it worth it?

Life in retirement in Germany did have certain advantages. The first was Michael, due to arrive at the Schwarzer Ochse in fifteen minutes—if he was on time, which was unlikely. Michael was nineteen, tall and superbly fit. Fit for anything. The thought of spending a wet afternoon pushing into Michael's squirming ass; holding him tight and hearing him gasp as he got his weekly refill was enough to give any man an appetite. John beckoned to the waiter.

Hans served very well on Tuesday evenings after his diving class at the local swimming pool. A few minutes under the hot shower in John's apartment dispersed the smell of chlorine and allowed John to work the boy's enormous cock into a state of rigid anticipation.

Friday evenings were reserved for Peter. John had never before known a young man with so much hair on his body as Peter. "Peter the Gorilla" he called him. It was a pity that this particular gorilla had the power of speech. That, he reflected bitterly, was the trouble with all of them. They wanted to talk, to practice their English or hold long conversations in German about their girl friends, pop groups or favorite football teams. John didn't waste time talking to them. They had nothing of value to say anyway. Like the soldiers he had commanded, they were there to do a job—to "give their all." They did what they had to do, picked up their money and left.

He ordered his meal and another beer. That was the trouble with twentieth century young men, he thought. They just didn't know their place. They needed discipline, military discipline. Not the insipid regime that passed for discipline in the Army he'd just left but the nineteenth century version. A good flogging never did anybody any harm.

Feeling the strange tide of uncontrollable anger sweeping over him again, he turned his attention to the group at the next table.

"I wish I'd brought the magazine. We might have been able to find them if I had," said the boy. It took some seconds for the fact that he had spoken in English to sink in. He wasn't bad looking, John thought. Pity about those jug-ears and, of course, an English boy would chatter even more than the Germans.

"There'd be nothing to see after all this time," the elderly man replied.

"The article said the tunnels and bunkers are still open. It's the trees that make it so difficult."

"You'd only have got yourself dirty, darling," said the younger woman. "What do you want to eat?"

"Oh, anything. Anything that's handy. I wish I'd packed the magazine."

"Don't keep on and on about it, James. You'll spoil Mummy's holiday." That was the elder woman.

John hadn't noticed the waiter's approach. "Excuse me. Colonel Winslow?"

"Yes."

"The young Herr Stocker has telephoned, Herr Colonel. He has to work today and cannot join you. He says he will see you here next Saturday."

"Oh, thank you."

"Another beer, Herr Colonel?"

"Yes, I might as well."

That was typical of Michael, he thought. He must have known that he was due to work. Why the hell didn't he call last night? He would have saved John the trouble of driving out to the Schwarzer Ochse in the pouring rain and saved him the expense of a meal. They were all the same. No sense of responsibility whatsoever. The waiter brought his beer. He sipped it reflectively.

Like many other faculties, John's imagination had been honed to perfection by thirty-five years service in the army. A glance at a map was sufficient for him to visualize the countryside perfectly. He didn't just imagine the deployment of an enemy. He could even tell what their officers were thinking and what they had in mind.

Michael strung in one of those triangular frames they used in the good old days. Strung tightly so that every muscle was tense, especially the muscles in his butt. In contrast to the rest of him, burned brown by working in the open air all day, Michael's butt was milky white. It would show off the weals perfectly. "This will teach you to keep appointments in future."

"I really did want to see Mettenheim. If it wasn't for those trees, I could have found it." Mention of Mettenheim in that youthful voice jumped John out of his reverie. He must surely be wrong. Young people weren't interested in his research. They were only concerned with themselves and silly pop singers.

He hardly noticed as the waiter brought his meal. Instead of sending it back to the kitchen as usually did, he picked at it, listening intently.

"We found the cement factory all right and we found the

path. If only it wasn't for those trees," the boy continued. "I remember. It said the path led right into the works. There was a map too. There were no trees on the map."

"Because the bloody cartographer left them out, that's why," John barked. He hadn't meant to speak but he'd been boiling with anger about the article in *Battle Scenes* ever since the issue with his article appeared.

They all stopped eating and looked across at him with the incredulous expressions middle class English people adopt when spoken to by a stranger. He half expected the older woman to say something like "I do not see you, sir!" Instead, she just stared.

Suddenly remembering that the Schwarzer Ochse wasn't the officers' mess and that these were not junior officers who needed to be put in their place, he clambered to his feet.

"I beg your pardon. I couldn't help overhearing what you were talking about."

"Oh! You're British!" said the younger woman.

Resisting the temptation to say "Of course I'm British, you stupid woman!" he nodded. "Colonel John Winslow. I wrote the article the young man was referring to," he said.

"James. My son," she said proudly. "He's mad on the War. He's studying it in history, aren't you dear?"

James didn't answer her. He stood up. "You really are Colonel Winslow?" he asked.

"I'm not in the habit of telling lies,"

James put out a hand. He had a surprisingly firm handshake for a kid. He was well built too. With eyes trained by years of inspecting soldiers on a parade grounds, he took in his broad shoulders, smiling face, and long legs. If it hadn't been for that ghastly raincoat, John would have taken an interest some time previously.

"We tried to find the ruins," he said.

"So I heard. I put the pine forest in on the original map but the stupid cartographer said the trees masked too much detail. That's grown since the War of course."

"I only wish I'd managed to see it," said James.

"I could take you there after lunch but there really isn't a lot to see. This gentleman is right."

"Oh sorry. Mr. and Mrs Foster, my grandparents, and this is

my mum."

They all stood up and shook hands. James's mother suggested that he might like to join them. He beckoned the waiter who brought over the remains of his meal and his half empty glass.

All that remained of the underground V2 factory at Mettenheim, he explained, were some ruins and a couple of tunnels or bunkers. It was hardly surprising that James hadn't found it. Several readers had written in to complain that the pine forest made it impossible to find and the locals, understandably in view of the horrific treatment of the slave laborers there, refused to answer questions and never went near the place themselves.

"Can I go, Mum?" James asked.

"I don't know, darling. You haven't written your postcards yet."

"I haven't done anything to write about, have I?"

"Don't be cheeky dear," said his grandmother.

"Let me. I'll be quite safe."

Not for the first time in his life, John's military training came to the fore. Instinctively, he contradicted the boy."Neither you nor I can guarantee absolute safety," he said. "We can say that we shall take every possible precaution."

James's grandfather laughed. "Just like my old Major!" he chortled. "Always absolutely honest, you chaps, aren't you?"

"One has to be," said John. "There is an element of danger in everything. One tries to minimize it.."

"Of course, of course," said the old man. "Let the boy go, Marianne. He'll be a damn sight better off with the Colonel than sitting in a hotel room writing postcards."

"I don't see how," said James's mother. Neither for that matter did John and it took some moments to secure her agreement.

"I knew she'd agree in the end," said James when he was finally in the car and fastening his seat belt."It's really good of you."

The drive to Mettenheim was not long—which was just as well. John was furious again—this time with himself.

It would have been easy to tell them that his name was Mr. Smith and that he knew the ruins. He could have taken James out there and he might—one never knew—have stood a chance. James was a powerfully built lad but then, so was he, and he had unarmed combat training to his advantage. It wouldn't have been that difficult to get the lad into a suitable position, wrest his jeans down and feed on his cock until, having reached his boiling point, he stopped struggling and did what was expected of him, thrusting into John's spunk-hungry mouth, eventually shooting his warm cream and then lying exhausted while John licked the spillage out of his groin and pubic hair.

"Bloody idiot!" he said aloud. Coincidentally, a car overtook them going at far more than the speed limit for a country road.

"They do go a bit fast, don't they?" said James.

What about James himself? John wondered. Did he go fast? Was he like the German boys who shot within minutes, desperate to be done with it and on their way? He would never know. He glanced down at the boy's muscular thighs and then caught the reflection of James's face in the mirror. He really was a good-looking boy and those thighs must indicate a fully fleshed, muscular butt. Getting into that on the first meeting would be well nigh impossible but there were the cells in one of the Mettenheim tunnels. The steel gates were still intact though the locks had rusted. He could keep him in one of those until his resistance went. His very own boy, reserved for him alone. Not like Hans or Peter. He was pretty sure that those two were being screwed by somebody else. There would be a police hunt, of course. That was a difficulty. He'd probably have to keep James in the apartment at first until the excitement blew over. That wouldn't be such a bad thing. He'd keep him tied up. Whip him once or twice to show him who was master. If only he hadn't given his real name and rank.....

"I can't wait to tell my friends I've met you," said James suddenly.

"I can't imagine that many people of your age have even heard of me," said John.

"Oh, we have. There are six of us at school. We all want to go into the Army."

"You want to go into the Army?" John repeated, incredulously. All the other young men he knew were ardent pacifists.

"If I can get in. Mathematics is letting me down at the moment."

"Rubbish! Mathematics is an intellectual discipline. It never let anyone down. It's your approach that's wrong."

For a few moments, James was silent. Then he said, "You're a very honest man, aren't you?"

"As I said, I'm not in the habit of lying."

"No. I don't mean that. You told my mum that you couldn't vouch for my safety and now you've said something that none of the teachers at school have said. You're right. I suppose it is a question of attitude. I sort of know I'm going to fail every exam before I even start."

"That's where you go wrong. Do it the Army way. Prepare carefully. Consult the experts over everything you're not actually sure of and then go in to win!"

"Does the Army have a way of doing everything?"

For the first time in days, John actually laughed. "Not quite everything," he said. "Just most things. Anyway, here we are. We have to park here."

They got out of the car. It had stopped raining and the sun was attempting to break through the clouds. The trees shone with an almost luminescent green. John took his torch and his camera and, together, they crossed the field and entered the forest.

"Always mark your route," said John. "See those chalk marks on the trees? Watch them carefully and you won't get lost."

"But you know the way," said James.

"If one of us breaks a leg the other's going to have to come out to get help. Watch them. Count them. First duty of every officer. Look after the men."

"It's sort of eerie quiet isn't it? Like a graveyard," said James when they were well into the forest.

"In many ways it is. Thousands of prisoners died here. It's one of the reasons none of the locals will come anywhere near the place. It brings back memories they'd rather forget and they reckon it's haunted."

"So you could do anything here and nobody would know."

"If you're thinking of an illicit cigarette, forget it. Pine forests are the last place in the world for that."

"No, no. I don't smoke. But I could murder you, for instance."

"That would be singularly thoughtless. I grant that it would take them a long time to find my body but the nearest bus stop is over a mile away and the buses are about every three hours."

"Or you could murder me."

"Why should I want to do that?"

"Oh, I don't know. You might want to keep me quiet about something."

"Like what?" John was beginning to find the boy's conversation interesting.

"Well, we might find some treasure and you'd want to keep it all for yourself."

"Oh, is that all? Well, you can forget that idea. There's no treasure in Mettenheim."

"Of course I know you wouldn't because of what you said about looking after the men." James stopped short in his tracks, surveyed the scene that had suddenly opened in front of them and gave a long whistle.

"Impressive, eh?" said John.

Vast, unrecognizable concrete structures loomed all around them. There were gigantic arches from which huge lumps of concrete dangled, supported by rusting re-reinforcing rods. Blocks bigger than houses lay around as if an incredibly powerful giant had thrown them in a fit of rage. The whole place was extraordinarily quiet. No birds sang. Their footsteps on the rubble were the only sound.

James found the sheer enormity of everything as breathtaking as John had on his first visit. For some time they wandered around the ruins as John tried to explain the various departments of what had been one of the most important and secret sites of the German Reich. He took one or two photos of James clambering over the concrete. "Definitely not for your mother," he explained. "She'd have a fit. Watch out for that rusty iron. Some of it's sharp."

"Don't worry. Where are the bunkers?"

"Follow me." They left the factory site and re-entered the forest, coming soon to a square hole in the ground. "This was the main command bunker," said John. "The main entrance was in the factory itself. That's buried under several feet of rubble. This was the emergency exit."

James peered down into the dark void. "We can get down

there. There are steps in the side of the shaft," he said.

"Sure. There's nothing much to see down there though."

"Can we try?"

"Sure. Let me go first. Be careful, though. Some of the rungs are a bit loose."

With his torch stuck through his belt, he clambered down and James followed. At the bottom, they both looked up at the square of light far above them.

"Deep," said James.

"Thirty-two feet," said John. He switched on the torch and they moved off. James amazed him by the second. The boy knew so much and, furthermore, he was interested, unlike Michael, Hans and Peter who thought John's fascination for the the so-called "haunted ruins" weird. He showed James the empty rooms which had once been offices and pointed out the gun ports in projecting walls. "No invaders would have had a chance," he said. "Every tunnel has these. They'd run up against a hail of machine gun fire and no hand grenade in this world would break down three feet of concrete." His voice echoed back from the gray wall.

"And what were these rooms for?" asked James, swinging one of the rusty steel gates.

"A bit of a mystery at the moment. Prison cells or kennels for guard dogs but they're too big for either."

"What I can't understand," said James, "is why the place closed down so suddenly—just at the very time the Nazis needed a new weapon."

"That, my dear James, is what I am trying to find out."

John could hardly believe his own ears. Had he said that? "My dear James." He'd never called anyone "my dear" in his life. And if anyone else had been swinging the gate as James was swinging it, the creaking would have got on his nerves in seconds.

"1944. Germany is on its last legs. Six members of the Hitler Youth guard run away. The Chief Scientist is removed and the entire facility is shut down. It doesn't make any sense," said James.

"I agree. I've been through all the papers in the Reich Archives and they don't shed any light on it."

"You said something about two tunnels."

"The other one is flooded. I've tried to persuade the local fire brigade to pump it out, but they won't."

"Can we have a look at it?"

"Sure."

They made their way back to the entrance. "You'd better go first. I'll follow you," said John.

James clasped the first rung and heaved himself up. John waited till he was half way up before clambering up the steps himself. Army training resulted in him going faster than James. The top of his head touched James's behind. "Sorry," he said.

"Okay. Here we are."

"Without thinking, John put up a hand to help James over the top. The feel of the boy's tightly muscled backside sent a frisson running up his spine.

"You'll never change, will you?" said James when they were both above ground again.

For a moment John panicked. Had the boy realized?

"How do you mean?"

"Always the officer. Just like you said when we were walking here. Putting up a hand to help me. Nobody else I know would do that."

"Always look after the men," said John.

"But I'm only a boy. I won't be eighteen till the beginning of next year."

"A very good age to be. Now the other tunnel is over there. When the Americans bombed the place in 1945 the craters flooded, forming the lake, which is down that slope. You can't see it because of the trees. The water has seeped in as you'll see."

They reached the place and James bent over the square hole in the ground. "How deep is the water?" he asked.

"About four feet."

"I could wade through that."

"But there's no point. There can be nothing worth seeing."

"I'd like to have a go."

"At last a boy with some guts!' John thought. How different from the German boys! "You won't hurt me will you, Herr Colonel?" and "My friend told me that I might catch a disease from doing that." How pleasant to dissuade rather than persuade!

But James wouldn't be put off. "I'll be okay," he said, "and I can clean up afterwards in that lake you mentioned. Mum will never know."

In the Army, of course, that would be John's role. "You stay up here and keep watch, Sergeant. I'll strip off and go down and take a shufti." But he wasn't in the service any more and what could be more pleasant than watching a good-looking teen strip off his clothes?

Which James did, without the least show of embarrassment. Quite different to the "face the wall" fumblings of the German boys—and the boy had a superb body. At first John faced away and took an occasional surreptitious glance. Then, realizing that James didn't object, he turned round and feasted his eyes on the boy's broad shoulders and suntanned belly.

"Nude bathing in a flooded tunnel. A new experience," said James and slid his underpants down.

His cock swayed as he threw them onto the pile of other clothes. He might have jug ears, thought John, but his cock made up for them. It was at least four and a half inches long, quite thick, and it tapered to an elegant point. His pubic bush was thick and gleamed in the watery sunlight. He turned to look down into the tunnel again. His bottom was an almost perfect, white hemisphere.

"I'll pass the torch down to you," said John, getting to his feet with some difficulty.

"Okay. I'll keep calling out, okay?"

"Do that."

James swung his legs over the edge and, bit by bit, disappeared from view. First his legs. Surprisingly hairy for one so young, John thought. Then his midriff. What couldn't a man do with a cock like that? How big was it when it was erect? Pretty big certainly. And those balls! John only caught a glimpse of them but they'd certainly make more spunk than the dribbling emissions of his German boys....

"Ready for the torch." John jumped out of his reverie. It was just as well that James was out of sight. He'd certainly notice the bone-hard lump in John's immaculately pressed trousers.

The water came up to a point just above James's navel. "Throw it down. I'll catch it." he said.

John did so. "Is it cold?" he asked.

"Yes. Pretty dirty too. I hope that lake is clean."

"No worry about that. Go carefully now."

"I will." And the boy moved off.

"See anything?" John called.

"Load of broken wood. Looks like bits of desks. Going a bit farther. It's deeper here." James's voice grew fainter and fainter. The water sloshed around under the entrance.

"You okay?" John called after a few minutes had gone by.

"Sure. It's like the other one really. Lots of rooms off the sides. Just going into one now."

Silence fell. The water below stopped moving. A large piece of wood hammered repeatedly against the concrete.

"Okay?" John shouted. No answer. "James! Are you okay?" He bent over the hole and shouted in his old parade ground manner.

"Yes," came a faint voice. "On the way back now. I've found something."

Realizing that his heart was thumping and his mouth dry from anxiety, John sat on the edge and waited. His first view of James was not his head but of a book. James was carrying it above his head.

"Can you come down and grab this?" he asked. "I don't want to get it wet."

John climbed down the first six rungs and took it. It was remarkably heavy. He climbed back again and James followed him.

"God, you're a mess!" he shouted. The whole of James's body from his chest down was smeared with gray mud. A piece of string had got wound round his right leg.

"What is it?" James asked.

"The find of the century. Where was it?"

"There's an opening in the ceiling about half way down. It's an office. There's rusty bed in there. A desk too. The desk is completely rotted and this seems to have fallen out of it and there's a really badly corroded typewriter too but I couldn't manage to bring both."

"It's a diary," said John, flicking through the mildewed pages. Several stiffer pieces of paper had been inserted at the back. He opened the book fully to see what they were and shut it again.

"You'd better go and clean up," he said. "Go along that path and down the slope."

"Aren't you coming too? I mean, I might drown. Look after the men and all that."

"You won't drown in five feet of water. I'll be along in a minute. I want to have a look at this first."

"Okay. See you there."

John waited till he heard the splash of the boy entering the water and opened the book again.

Photographs. Horribly moldy photographs but what photographs! They were all big half plate enlargements. The boys were all Hitler Youth members. In two of the pictures they wore their forage hats but nothing else. Erect cocks pointed proudly and their owners smiled at the camera. In one, the photographer had caught the exact moment of the boy's ejaculation. His eyes were closed and his mouth open and a rainbow shaped arc of semen linked his penis with his right thigh.

John slipped them back and flicked through the pages. In the course of his research he'd seen several photographs of Ludwig von Rosenheim, Chief Scientist at the Mettenheim Revenge Weapon factory. He was a military-looking man and there was no hint in that smiling, confident face of the man's secret life.

One by one, he read and turned the pages. Some were almost indecipherable and would need a lot of skilled restoration before they could be read. ".. beautiful bottom." "balls in my mouth when...." "right inside him. Hope I didn't hurt him but..." Heinz tomorrow. Too young really but anxious to join in my scheme. Had a good look at him in the showers. Nice. Not a lot of hair yet but nice cock and....'

He shut the book and looked at his watch. With a shock he realized that he'd been engrossed in the past for over half an hour. Putting the book under his arm and the camera over his shoulder, he made his way along the path and down the slope to the lake. For a second or two he was panic-stricken. There was no sign of James.

"I thought you'd never come," said a voice behind him. He turned round. James was lying on the grassy slope idly chewing a piece of grass.

"I was reading this," said John.

"Learn anything?"

"An awful lot. Thanks to you, the mystery is explained."

"Tell me."

"I'm not actually sure that I should. It's a bit sordid."

"A juicy sex scandal?"

"No scandal at all but sex certainly. Have a look at these."

He passed the photographs down. James threw away the piece of grass. "Wow!" he said. "Who took these?"

"None other than Honorary Colonel, Herr Doctor Ludwig von Rosenheim, Chief Scientist. The six boys were his personal bodyguard."

"He chose well. They're all good lookers. This blond one especially. Big cock, too."

"You're not shocked?"

"When you go to a school like mine, nothing shocks you. What happened to him and them?"

"As far as I can make out, he gave them all copies of his notes and let them escape, hoping that they'd reach the Allies. He must have been sent to a concentration camp. Without him they couldn't continue and he probably told them that the secret of his Vengeance Weapon was in Allied hands."

"A brave man," said James.

"A very brave man. And he was genuinely concerned for their well-being. He got extra rations for them and special medicine. He got them special leave."

"And had it off with them?"

"Yes."

"Nothing wrong with that. They probably got the best of the bargain. Is the diary all about his work or does he mention the sex bits?"

"It's all about his sex life."

"Read me a bit."

"I'm not sure that I should."

"Go on. Just a page at random."

"Well, the more legible bits are at the beginning and the end."

"Give me a sample of both."

John opened the book.

"'May 8th,'" he read. "'Der Commandant ist einverstanden—The Commandant has agreed to my request. Six Hitler Jugend boys to be my personal bodyguard. I am to choose.'

"'June 9th. Kurt. Willing. Nice one.'

"'July 11th. Commandant agrees. My boys might have picked up sensitive aspects of research. They will be moved out of barracks and will live in command tunnel. I am to select the ones for duty every day. (and night!)'

"'August 3rd. Hans and Robert. Drank both. Delicious! Robert very worried about his mother. See Commandant tomorrow to arrange special leave for him.'

"'September 9th. Sven my Nordic beauty. Reticent at first but I told him what I had in mind. Agreed. Nice balls and even nicer cock.'"

"That must be this fair haired one," said James, picking up the photo.

"Probably. Then, 'October 11th. Rode Kurt for the first time. Wonderful experience. Difficult to get in him at first but he tried hard and succeeded.'

"'October 14th. More difficult to persuade Doctor than it is to persuade boys but he agreed that my boys should have extra rations. They can't protect my 'valuable person' if they are starving. Neither, for that matter, can they perform well in bed but I didn't tell him that.'

"'November 11th. Only Robert. The others are all on special leave. Rode him twice. Nice bottom. Soft and warm. Hope the others are all right. Air raids very bad.

"'December 25th. Christmas day. Gave boys their presents. Only one who gives presents but they deserve them. All very thankful. Drank them all, one after the other. Great fun. Hung Christmas baubles on their cocks afterwards and we sang carols.'

"'January 12th. Exhausted all day. Not surprising. Rode Hans and Kurt last night. Must see Doctor and get special medicine for Kurt's acne. Even some spots on his back but not (I am glad to say) on his bottom which is perfect.'

"'February 8th. Spent two hours with young Heinz, helping him with his Physics and Maths courses. He is so anxious to be a doctor and a credit to his parents. Poor kid is frightened of being sent to the front and dying. His brother was killed last week. Told him all about my scheme, which cheered him up. I am to help him with his studies every day and in return he will do what I want. Drank him after the lesson. Very tasty.'"

"Go on."

"Well, the next pages are illegible. There's just this bit at the end: 'No doubt now that Germany has lost the war. Have made six copies of all my research notes. Boys will break out in the spring. Hope at least one of them meets up with the Allies. God knows what will happen to me but it is the boys I worry about. They have all been so good to me.' It ends there."

"He sounds like a nice guy," said James as John closed the book.

"Some would say...." but John couldn't finish the sentence. James's cock had thickened and lengthened and projected and lay over his belly like a hook.

"Like you say, he looked after his men," said James. "He helped them in their careers." He stared at the photo again and his cock twitched upwards as he did so. "I wonder if Heinz ever made it to be a doctor," he said.

"There's no way of knowing."

"I hope he did. If someone were to help me get over my math problem and help me get into the armed forces, I wouldn't mind what I did in return."

"Even...?"

"That too. I mean, I'm not gay. At least I don't think I am. I don't suppose any of these boys were. Whoever it was would have to teach me what to do."

John put the book down onto the grass and very gently placed a hand on the boy's belly. James didn't move but looked at him quizzically.

"You?" he asked in an amazed tone. John didn't answer but slid his hand downwards, running his fingers through the bristly hair until he touched it. It seemed to spring to life, thickening as it did so. His fingers encircled it and then tightened on the rising flesh.

"That feels nice," said James. He dropped the photograph, lay back and parted his legs. His cock hardened. His pulse began to race. Gently, John pulled back the foreskin. James's cock-head popped out. It was so much nicer and healthier looking, he thought, than any of the German boys and a German boy by this time would be gasping "Do it faster, Herr Colonel. I mustn't be late."

"I come pretty quickly," said James. For a moment John

thought he was going to be like the rest of them until James added, "If you want to drink it, go ahead."

A teenager's hard cock, the property of the nicest young man John had ever met, slid into his mouth as if it actually wanted to be there. There was no need, with James, to wrench away a protective hand or to shove his legs apart. James grinned encouragingly and then lay back to enjoy it. He did, too. Did he ever! He supported himself on his forearms and brought up his knees so that his feet were flat on the ground. John slid a hand between his damp thighs, felt his balls and then pushed an exploratory finger further in. James wriggled delightedly as it found his tight entrance and then gave himself up to his mentor. John savored the salty sweetness of his cock and let his tongue play on the stiff shaft. He tickled the boy's asshole and James thrust his body upwards. He said nothing but his panting breaths were more expressive than any speech. Even "Oh ja, Herr Colonel! Ja! Ja!" lost it's charm when you knew that the moment the boy had shot, he'd remember a pressing appointment and ask for the money.

A thought struck him. It would be possible to pause and get undressed. That tight little orifice was definitely more responsive than those of Hans, Peter and Michael. It was from them he had learned that you could do anything with a boy with a hard on like James had at that moment."Oh nein, Herr Colonel! I not do that," soon turned into 'Ja, ja, Herr Colonel.' He stopped sucking for a moment. It wasn't just the cynicism of an old man that told him what would happen at the end of that afternoon. James would say something inane about not telling his mother and would run up the hotel steps like a frightened faun and that would be the last he'd see of the boy. Yes, he thought, that's what he'd do. What did the military manuals say? "Advance whenever an opening presents itself." Well, this opening was certainly showing signs of presenting itself. He'd just bring the boy to boiling point with his tongue and then.... At which point James gave a huge heave upwards and came. Not the viscous flow over his tongue and between his teeth that he was used to. It cascaded against the back of his throat. He gulped and another flood filled his mouth. He was shamefully aware of dribbling it down into the boy's pubic hair. He swallowed again and then licked round his mouth. It tasted warm and syrupy with a tingle of saltiness; the delightful taste of a delightful boy.

"Was I okay?" James panted.

"Superb. Absolutely superb!" said John, licking his lips.

"I guess I'd better get cleaned up again before I get dressed."

"It seems a shame but I suppose you had. I guess you want to get back pretty soon."

"I suppose I should. You know what my mum's like."

James got up and walked down to the water's edge. It had been a wonderful experience, thought John, but it would never be repeated. The next thing the boy said was sure to be a request to take him back to the hotel as soon as possible. There was bound to be something he had to back in time for. They were all the same.

"Colonel!" James was standing waist-deep in the water.

"John to my friends. What is it?"

"Did I see your camera?"

"You did."

"Why don't you take some pictures? Colonel von Rosenheim did."

"Are you sure? Nothing you've got to rush back for?"

"The family are going to an open air concert this evening but I can get out of that. Is there enough light?'

"Plenty."

The boy was unbelievable. Only in the services had John found youngsters who did exactly what they were told and none of them would have obeyed the orders he gave James that afternoon.

"Lie back with your legs apart. That's it. Hmmmm ... Can you get it up again for me? Oh, yes. It's such a nice one."

"I don't think I can come again," said James.

"No matter. Keep on doing that. That's great. Get it right up if you can. Let's see the head. Good man! That's beautiful! ... Now turn over and kneel down. Yes ... Open it up for me. I want to get right in there ... if I can."

Did James get the double meaning? Maybe. He giggled.

Finally, the camera was put away. John went back to retrieve James's clothes and they were on the way to the hotel with the precious volume on the back seat. John was well aware that, at any moment, James would start making excuses. He decided to bring the matter up first.

"So, you've got concert tickets for tonight?" he said.
"Yes, but I'm not going."
"Won't your mother insist?"
"Not if I've got a math lesson."
"Have you? Who with?"
"You, of course. She'll be thrilled to bits."
"It will be maths, James. If you're quite certain..."
"Quite certain."
"You're going to really work hard to pass math and then go into the Army. Have I got that right?'
"Absolutely and you're going to give me the shove I need."

It wasn't really a shove. It was more a long, slow thrust and it happened, as John had stipulated, after an hour and a half of math tutoring. But now, the books were on the little writing table and James lay on the bed. John's shoulders, more used to carrying weaponry, bore the boy's long legs. His cock was more accustomed to the use it was being put to, but had never been in a more responsive ass.

They'd talked a lot before that. John promised to arrange for the Education Officer at a military base near James's home to give the boy math tutoring.

"But when shall I see you again?" James asked.
"I shall have to be in England fairly often in connection with von Rosenheim's diary. That will have to be published, together with my own research. *Our* research, I should say."
"You're going to put my name on it as well?"
"Of course. We're a partnership; a couple."
"We soon will be. That stuff feels cold. What is it?"
"Jelly. It'll make it easier for you."

Whether it did or not, John didn't know. James cried out just as loudly as the German boys and tears formed in the corner of his eyes. But James didn't mutter swear words. He just bit his lip and lay there. Then, after some minutes, he wriggled slightly. "I think it's okay now," he said.

It was far more than okay, of course. James's own frantic squirming made John's efforts almost worthless and, unlike the German boys, he grinned as John's rubber-sheathed cock massaged his most sensitive places.

Amazingly, it was James who came first. John was surprised

that he came at all. None of the German boys did when they were fucked. Indeed, if he felt under them he was invariably disappointed to find a cock which might as well have been made of soft rubber. James's cock had popped, erect, out of his pants the moment he got undressed and stayed that way, pointing at the ceiling, the whole time while John carefully lubricated him and then entered.

For the second time that day, the boy's violent ejaculation took John by surprise. He gave a few more thrusts. James managed a slightly tearful grin as he came. The boy's soft tissues clenched against the rubber as if they were reluctant to let him go. He waited a long time before he withdrew.

"How was it?" he asked.

"It hurt at first but it was nice after that," James replied.

"Spoken like a true soldier. You'll be a credit to the Army," John replied.

SHIPMATES

Tim Scully

"You don't suffer from seasickness, do you, Tim?" Mr. Parsons looked at me over his half moon glasses.

"No. Why?"

"Just as well. I want you to spend a week or two on board H.M.S. Albion. 'Stingray' you know. Usual teething troubles."

Teething troubles with 'Stingray' had been going on for years. The damned thing had had time to grow wisdom teeth. The missile had been in production for some fifteen years and the computer system had been playing up all that time. The model on board the Albion was one of the latest, too. It was not an assignment to relish. For one thing, Danny and I had just moved into our new apartment and when you've got an ass or a cock like Danny's to look forward to at the end of a long working day, you don't feel very keen on spending time on a destroyer.

And there were my weekends with Dhasan and Neil and my occasional weekends with Barry. 'A week or two' might not seem very long to Mr. Parsons but to me it was going to seem like an eternity.

But there was nothing for it. I reported, according to instructions, at Portsmouth Dockyard and, after all the usual security checks, a rather handsome young sailor showed me to the gangplank that led up to H.M.S. Albion's deck. He helped me get my bag and the two bags of equipment up.

"Welcome on board, Mr. Scully," said the Lieutenant at the top.

"Thank you."

"Let me show you to your cabin."

I followed him down companionways and staircases. We ended up in a narrow corridor. "In here," he said, opening a door. "I think you'll be comfortable. The Captain would like a word or two with you when you've unpacked. I'll come and collect you in about an hour if that's okay."

"Perfectly okay."

I looked round the cabin. Two bunk beds, a wardrobe, a

desk and chair. Even the paint was the same color. Memories came flooding back.

...

"Do you fancy a cruise in the summer holidays?" asked Tommy, as he wiped spunk off my legs.

"Ha-ha! Canapes on the sun deck and dinner with the Captain?" I said.

"Not exactly. My dad's arranged for me to go on a trip on his ship and says I can bring a friend."

"I'd have to ask my folks," I replied. "When are you going to ask Matron for a new towel? That one's stiff with the stuff."

"I'll try to wash it in the wash basin," he said. "There. It's all off now."

We were both fifteen and boarders at Yarbridge School, albeit in different classes and, sadly, in different houses. That made our meetings a bit difficult. It all started with a chance meeting in the school library. Tommy was engrossed in a book. I sat next to him, working on an essay. Somebody made a noise behind us. We both turned round to see what had happened and something fell out of the book he was holding.

"Here, let me," I said and reached down to pick it up. So did he. We nearly fell off our chairs. It had fallen nearer to mine so I grabbed it. He went to snatch it out of my hand. It was a magazine. The title, "'Time for Bed," was somewhat misleading. True, the boy on the front cover was in (or rather on) bed but he showed no sign of going to sleep. He was grinning at the camera and holding his erect cock.

"Give it back!" said Tommy.

"No talking!" the librarian called.

"Let's have a look at it," I whispered.

"Why? .... Are you?" said Tommy.

"Let's read it together," I whispered. He tucked it back into the pages of "Revision Exercises in Biology" and we both bent our heads in study.

There wasn't a lot of reading matter but there were pictures. Pictures of boys wanking and sucking each other's cock.

"He's got a big one," Tommy muttered.

"A nice one too," I replied. "I'll bet he shoots a lot."

"Do you?"

"Quite a lot, yes."

"Me too."

"Where did you get this from?" I asked, but he wouldn't tell me.

He kept turning the pages. He came to the centre - spread. A boy of about our age lay on his stomach. Tommy went to the next page almost immediately.

"Hold on," I whispered. "Let's have a good look."

"But you can't see his cock," said Tommy.

I suppose my orientation. Or preference. Or call it what you will. It had already been established even at that young age. Reluctantly, Tommy turned the page back. I feasted my eyes on the boy's long back and perfectly rounded, dimpled butt. It was infinitely more aesthetically pleasing to me than the penises on other pages.

"Can't see any fun in looking at a shit hole," said Tommy.

"I've told you two once. If you talk again, you'll be out!" called the librarian.

"Let's go," said Tommy.

"Where?"

"We could go to my room. My study. My mate's playing squash."

"Risky," I said. You were supposed to get permission from a teacher to visit another house. Something to do with fire regulations.

"Nobody will notice. Old Rice will be asleep anyway."

Mr. Rice was his housemaster. A dear old man who wouldn't retire, preferring to mother his boys.

So we went back to Tommy's room and studied his magazine —and that led to us both getting erections and that led to us ending up with our trousers round our ankles, wanking each other furiously. All good, if not clean, fun. He made a hell of a mess.

His study-mate's addiction to squash was very convenient. After that, I spent an enjoyable hour every afternoon manipulating Tommy's surprisingly large penis and playing with his equally large balls.

"You ever sucked a cock?" he asked one afternoon.

"No," I replied. In fact I had. My roommate, Adam, couldn't

get to sleep until I'd sucked him dry.

"Want me to show you how it's done?" he asked. I made a token show of distaste which, fortunately, he ignored and he got his first mouthful of my adolescent juice. On the following afternoon I was similarly fed. Tommy tasted nice.

He told me about his family. His dad was a Commander in the Royal Navy and his greatest ambition was that Tommy should follow in his footsteps. He wasn't keen.

"You might like it," I said. "Rum and buggery from morning to night."

"Blow that! I'll bet it hurts," said Tommy. I said nothing. Adam had done it to me—not very expertly and it did. On the other hand, Tommy had a nice bum and I was beginning to have ambitions in that direction....

My parents said I could go. Indeed, they seemed keen on the idea. Thus, the following August, I met Tommy at the station and we took the train to the docks. Tommy's dad, resplendent in gold braid and medal ribbons was waiting for us and took us on board. Midshipman Williams, who was deputized to show us to our cabin was a rather pleasant-faced young man. I guessed him to be about eighteen. He was fair-haired and, though his torso was lean enough, the lower half of him was pleasantly convex. His trousers appeared to have been cut to show off a series of bulges. His backside bulged. You could make out the curve in the backs of his legs and his behind seemed to stretch the material almost to the point of tearing. Watching him negotiate a companionway (as they call a ladder in the Navy) was quite an experience.

The cabin was pretty sparse but compared to Yarbridge it was luxurious. Just two bunk beds, a wardrobe, a desk and a couple of chairs. The light from the solitary porthole shone down on a tiny wash basin on the cream-painted steel bulkhead which looked just about big enough for a person to clean his teeth.

"Does the door lock?" I asked.

"Commander McCormack would prefer that you didn't lock it," he said. "If there were to be a sudden emergency, we'd need to get you out fast."

I suppose I should have been happy to think that the Navy considered us worth saving but I wasn't. We'd discussed possible opportunities on the train journey. No squash playing roommate or aged housemaster was likely to gatecrash, but a Naval officer was as just as dangerous—if not worse.

"You won't be disturbed at all," said Midshipman Williams, apparently able to read thoughts. "The Captain has put this cabin out of bounds to everyone."

"What about my dad?" asked Tommy.

"I think the Commander's going to have his hands full on this voyage. You won't be seeing a great deal of him," said Midshipman Williams. Tommy smiled at me. One of the things we'd planned (for 'we' read 'I') was the penetration of Tommy's still virgin asshole. Not wishing to tell him the truth about my roommate and me, I spun a long and involved tissue of lies involving me at the age of thirteen and a non-existent kindly uncle.

"And it didn't hurt at all?" Tommy asked.

"No. It was a great feeling. My uncle had some special stuff. I've got a tube with me as a matter of fact. Bought it yesterday just in case. If the person on top does it carefully and goes in slowly, it's the best feeling in the world."

"Mmm. I don't mind wanking or sucking but I wouldn't fancy that."

I did. When we got undressed that evening, after a long and (to me) boring day of meeting officers and seeing over the ship I fancied it a lot. I sat on my bottom bunk and watched Tommy at the wash basin. It was the first time I'd seen him completely undressed and he was nice! His legs, unfettered by trousers and undershorts, were superb. The last rays of the setting sun lit up the fine, fair hairs that were just beginning to grow on his shins and thighs. His butt was a perfect, cream-colored hemisphere. I'd only ever seen it compressed against his school bed. His position at the wash basin, with his legs slightly apart showed it off to its full advantage. My cock twitched upright pretty quickly.

He noticed it, of course. I made sure he did. I sat with my legs dangling over the edge of the bunk. He looked in the mirror, smiled, and turned round.

"You're keen tonight," he said.

"I always am," I replied. "You're not exactly uninterested yourself."

His tool hung, semi-erect but showing distinct signs of life.

"Where shall we do it?" he asked. "Shall I get up there with you?"

I thought carefully. The Yarbridge-sitting-on-a-bed position wasn't going to be a lot of use for what I had in mind.

"No, I'll come down," I said. I dropped onto the floor.

"Do it standing up," I suggested. That was easier said than done. The H.M.S. Grampian was under way and we were somewhere out in the English Channel. Tommy had to reach behind him and hold on to the bunk beds to stay upright. I held on to Tommy. To Tommy's cock to be exact. Tommy's cock had a quite distinctive feel. It was colder than most and had a wonderful silky texture, and the veins on his were not so prominent as mine. More important, it was the sort of cock that responded well to be played with—which is precisely what I did. We stood facing each other.

"I like your cock," he said, putting his fingers round mine.

"Yours is nice too. Did you bring that book?"

"It's in my bag. Oh, that feels good. Do it again."

I had got my fingers under his balls. His cock rose rapidly. I tickled them gently. I could feel his breath on my face.

"Going to suck it?" he whispered.

"Too right," I replied. "In a minute." I moved my hand forward. He parted his legs. My fingers found the hard surface behind his balls. I knew I had to go slowly. I tickled.

"That's nice," he said. He was breathing heavily. A bit farther forward....

"Watch out. You're near my asshole," he said but made no move to get away. I found it and tickled. I was expecting some sort of reaction. He said nothing. "Like it?" I asked.

"Yeah. It's okay," he said. I continued for some minutes. It felt really good; rubbery and pliant. Then, without the slightest warning, he came. I was amazed. Tommy's comings were usually noisy affairs, prefaced with warnings. He just jetted it out all over me.

"Sorry," he said. "I wasn't thinking."

Well, of course, it didn't matter. What did matter was that once Tommy had come, he lost all interest. I tried to persuade him to bring me off but he said he felt tired. He did get the book out of his bag and I jerked off that night to the centerfold boy.

The second night was a bit better. I persuaded him to suck me off before I started to work on him. I could tell by the way he hung onto the bunk supports with his legs wide open that he really did enjoy having his asshole tickled. Again, he came copiously but at least he gasped out a warning.

The third evening was almost a disaster. We'd both undressed. Tommy had been taking a shower and stood drying his hair while I sat in a chair and watched him. The violent movement of his arms made his cock swing from side to side.

"I was thinking...." he said.

So was I! "Oh yes?"

"If you're sure it doesn't hurt, I wouldn't mind trying it. Stand up for a minute." I did so. He threw the towel down onto the floor and put his fingers round my cock. Just watching him had made it hard.

"Are you sure it's not too big?" he asked.

"'Course it isn't. My uncle's was much bigger. The bigger they are, the better it feels."

Then everything seemed to happen at once. The door swung open, wide open, framing the shape of a man. I caught a glimpse of white lapel patches and brass buttons. Midshipman Williams!

I can't remember exactly what we did. I know I ended up by the wash basin. Tommy must have grabbed the towel because in a split second it was round his middle.

"Going to bed so early?" said Midshipman Williams. "It must be the sea air. Sorry to disturb you but we're doing speed trials tomorrow. The Commander says if you'd like to be on the bridge you're welcome."

"Oh... er... thanks," said Tommy. "What time?"

"I should get up there as early as you can," said the Midshipman. "It could be quite exciting. Anyway, good night."

"Good night." We spoke in chorus.

"Oh, one other thing," he said. "It would probably be best if you both stayed in the cabin tomorrow afternoon. We're all going to be up to our eyes in work. There's a hell of a lot to do after a speed trial."

"Christ! Do you think he saw us?" said Tommy, after he'd gone.

"No. He'd have said something."

"He must have noticed your prick." Tommy's face was quite pale.

"He'd have thought I needed a pee. It's not just hands that make cocks hard you know."

"That's all very well but if he tells my dad...."

"Of course he won't. Stop panicking. The great thing is that we've got the whole of tomorrow afternoon to do it."

It certainly wasn't just hands that made my cock go hard. Just the thought of penetrating Tommy's virgin asshole brought it up again. It was even twitching slightly during the speed trial. The sea crashed over the bows and the ship left a broad, creamy wake as it sliced through the waves. Tommy seemed genuinely interested. They let him hold the wheel for a few minutes and, as he stood there, gazing at the compass, with his feet slightly apart. I stared at his ass, imagining how grand it was going to feel.

We had lunch and went down to the cabin. Tommy quibbled a bit. I knew he would. I got the book out and that worked quite well. I watched it harden up under his jeans as I commented on the pictures, passing over the pages that featured the bottoms I'd admired so much.

"This one's got a lovely cock. Just imagine that sliding into you. God! I'll bet he'd feel good!"

Twenty minutes of that treatment did the trick. I could smell his excitement. I put my hand on it. He did the same to me. In minutes we were both undressed. I got the tube out of my bag. At four thirty, my friend was lying on the floor on his back. His legs were on my naked shoulders and my well greased finger was working overtime.

"Go easy," he gasped as I pressed. "That hurts a bit." I pressed again. He groaned. Suddenly, he surrendered. My finger sank into him. "Ow! Ah!" he yelped.

"Okay?" I asked. He nodded—and the door was flung open.

"I thought as much," said a familiar voice. Midshipman Williams! Tommy seemed to leap into the air, though how he managed it I don't know. I guess I did too. The tube slithered across the floor and then slithered back again as the ship rolled.

"Having it off were you?" he said. Neither of us said anything. We just stood there red-faced. My heart was pounding.

"Stand up facing the bulkhead," he ordered. We did so.

"To attention!" he barked. "Let's have some discipline, shall we?" We brought our feet together.

"That's better." There was a period of silence, broken by Tommy.

"Please don't tell my dad?" he whined.

"No. It was all my fault," I said.

"It was, was it? You like fucking ass, do you?" said the voice behind us. I didn't answer.

"How many times have you done it?" asked the disembodied voice.

"Never." We both spoke at once. "That was the first time," I added.

"Looks like I came in just in time," said Midshipman Williams. "A few minutes later and you'd have been up to your nuts in guts as we say. Turn round!"

Both our cocks had subsided—not surprising. He glared at us.

"You won't tell my dad, will you?" Tommy pleaded.

"I'll see. I'd prefer to deal with you myself. You. Scully isn't it?"

"Yes."

"Do you know the forward chain locker?"

I didn't. Neither did I know the medieval system by which the Royal Navy keeps time. He had to explain in landlubber's terms. At 7 that evening I was to go into a small locker at the front end of the ship and wait for him, making sure that nobody saw me go in there.

I was frightened to death. The chain locker sounded ominous. I had visions of being imprisoned in fetters for the rest of the voyage. But there was nothing for it. At five to seven I crept along like the rat I felt, keeping close to the superstructure until I found the grey painted door marked CHAIN LOCKER: There was nobody around, I opened it, slipped in, found the light switch and closed the door again. I was slightly reassured to find that nobody could possibly have used that chain. You'd need to be Tarzan to pick up a single link. I sat on it and waited.

The door opened and he appeared. "Anybody see you?" he

asked.

"No."

"Good. Get your clothes off."

"Why?" My voice trembled.

"Don't ask questions. Do as you're told." He sat on the chain.

With shaking hands, I took off my shoes and socks and then the rest. I put them on the floor beside me.

"That's better. Now come here."

I took a step towards him. "Closer," he said. I took another step. "Closer for Christ's sake. I can't get at you from that distance." I took two steps forward.

"That's better. I'm not going to eat you but, by God I'm going to drink you."

I couldn't believe it. He took my cock between his finger and thumb and popped it into his mouth.

"I... er... I...." I stammered. He said nothing. He couldn't and, very soon, I wasn't in a mood to protest further. He was good at it. My frustrated cock rose immediately. His hand massaged my balls. I closed my eyes. Midshipman Williams caressed my ass, pulling me even farther towards him. His breath wafted through my pubes.

"I'm coming!" I gasped. His mouth remained clamped on my cock. I spurted. He swallowed and let me go. He produced a handkerchief and wiped his lips.

"So you are too?" I said.

"Don't be impertinent. Now, let me see. The Commander has his conference in the second watch.... Tell Tommy to be here at two bells. Nine o'clock in the morning. As for you, you'll come back here at two in the afternoon and again at this time. Keep your appointments punctually and I'll keep my mouth shut. That is, I won't say anything. Bit difficult to keep it shut with a cock like yours in it. Same goes for Tommy. Know anything about Naval history?

"Nothing at all," I said, getting dressed.

"Well, in the old sailing ship days they used to keep a cow on board to provide milk for the crew. I've got two. You and Tommy. I shan't want for vitamins on this voyage."

"What did he say?" Tommy asked when I returned to the cabin.

"Oh, he just told me off. He wants to see you at nine o'clock in the morning. Same place."

"Is he going to tell my dad?"

"I don't think so."

I was quite amused at ten o'clock the next morning. Tommy looked a bit pale.

"Everything okay?" I asked.

"Oh. Yeah. Fine. He's not a bad guy."

At two o'clock it was my turn again. Then Tommy. Then me again. Naturally enough, Tommy clicked pretty quickly."He's sucking you as well, isn't he?' he asked. I nodded.

Midshipman Williams was no fool either. Once he realized that each of us knew about the other, we went together. As a matter of fact I enjoyed watching Tommy wriggling around and I loved the way his ass went taut at the moment he shot his load in Midshipman William's spunk-hungry mouth.

The ship cruised up the west coast of England, passing Ireland. When we were not in the chain locker we got wonderful views and quite a few photos of the Scottish islands. Then it was time for the return voyage.

"You still got that lubricant or did you throw it away?" asked the Midshipman one afternoon as we got dressed.

"It's in my bag," I said.

"Good. We're due in Portsmouth on Thursday. No. Don't get dressed yet."

"Why?" asked Tommy.

"Don't ask questions." He stood up and came towards us. He patted Tommy's backside. "Mmmm," he said, and then he did the same to me.

"Both ripe for it," he said. "I'll do you first, Tim. Tommy afterwards. Stay in your cabin on Thursday morning."

Neither of us slept much on Wednesday night. Not because we were thrilled at the prospect of going home. I think we were both a bit scared. Tommy certainly was. He kept asking me if it hurt. I couldn't see Tommy as the great naval hero his father was anxious to make him.

Midshipman Williams arrived at exactly nine o'clock. He produced a huge key from his pocket and locked the door behind him.

"Still in bed?" he said. Tommy said something about not

having had much sleep.

"So much the better," said the Midshipman. "I'll need that bottom bunk, Tommy. I don't want to roll off the top bunk with my cock in your friend's ass."

Tommy got out of bed. I did likewise and crawled into the warm lower bunk. I watched as the Midshipman undressed. I wasn't wrong about all those bulges. His ass was massive and so was his cock. It sprang out of his underpants like a jack-in-the-box. I think he'd been circumcised. I can't be sure. Certainly his cock head was totally visible but with an erection like he had, that wasn't surprising. He'd had erections before in the chain locker but they'd always been covered up. Seeing it stiff and swinging from side to side was quite an experience and mine followed suit.

I gave him the cream. He wanted me flat on my stomach; the first time I'd been had in that position. Thinking about it, it was the only way he could have done it in such a confined space. I tried, and I think succeeded, in giving the impression that the only thing that had been in there before was a thermometer. On the other hand, thinking about my own goal and looking at Tommy as that massive member screwed down into me really got me going. I tried not to cry out, even though it hurt like hell. I even managed a happy grin as the last few inches reamed in and he started to fuck in earnest.

After that, there was no need to pretend. He was as good at fucking as he was at sucking. I think we came together or at least at about the same time. I wasn't that keen on having my ear bitten but, to tell the truth, I was sorry to relinquish his cock.

Tommy met his nemesis about an hour later. Talk about keeping animals on board. Anyone passing the cabin door that morning would have been forgiven for thinking that a pig was being slaughtered in there.

He screamed. He struggled. But he was no match for a young man who had come through the Royal Navy's arduous training program so recently. I sat in the chair, watching and fondling my cock lovingly, mentally promising it that it would be next to penetrate Tommy's neat little ass.

After a time, he quieted down. All that you could hear was their stentorian breathing (and mine!) and the creaking of the bunk supports.

"Oh god, you're good."

"You're beautiful!" gasped Midshipman Williams. "Oh my god! Aaaah!" and his powerful buttocks stopped clenching.

The thought of his semen flooding into Tommy made me feel even more excited. Tommy continued to wriggle for a few seconds and then he too stopped moving and they both lay motionless.

I enjoyed watching eight inches of greasy cock sliding out and Tommy's ass reverting to its usual rotundity. I also got the impression that Tommy was reluctant to release it.

When we went back to school in September, Tommy didn't seem to want to know me. He spent a great deal of time telling his class mates about the girls he'd met during the holiday and of one in particular who was mad with lust for him. I minded at first but then I found other fish to fry. We left school at the same time and I never saw him again.

. . .

I felt really miserable as I struggled up the gang plank on to H.M.S. Albion with my bags. It was going to be a horrible job. I was missing Danny already and we hadn't even left port. Somehow the presence of double bunks made me feel even more lonely. This time I had no Tommy with me—not even Midshipman Williams. I dedicated my first wank on board to their memory.

The Captain and the officers were friendly and helpful. Able Seaman Russell was taken away from his usual duties to help me. He wasn't a lot of help but it was nice to have him around. He was just eighteen; a fresh-faced youth with a happy smile, long legs and a very attractive butt indeed. Interestingly, we hadn't been together for more than a few minutes before he started to ask searching questions. By the end of the first day it had been established that neither of us was married or had a girlfriend.

"You don't get the opportunity in the Navy like people with shore jobs," he explained.

"I see," I replied as I peered into the fifth junction box that day. Privately I wondered how the many thousands of married personnel had managed it.

"Course, I've got loads of good mates," he said.

"Oh so have I." I screwed the lid back on. Nothing wrong with that one.

"I was at school with my best mate," he said, which made me think of Tommy again and wonder where he was and what he was doing. "Where did you go to school Mr. Scully?"

I told him.

His eyes lit up. "That's a boarding school, isn't it?"

"Yes."

"Cor. I've read about them. Are all the teachers homos?"

"Definitely not!" We agreed as we walked to the next junction box that it was possible that some boarding school teachers might be that way inclined. I think he was slightly disappointed to hear that I had not been pursued and bedded by an elderly gentleman in cap and gown.

'If only you knew,' I thought as I cleaned the caked salt off the next box before opening it. A sort of mental litany went through my head; a name for every stroke of the wire brush. Adam Wheelwright, Adam Trenchard, Tommy McCormack....

"Did you ever get punished?" he asked.

"Lots of times." My patience cracked. "And so will you be if you don't help!" I snapped. "Why am I getting this stuff all over me while you do sod all except ask questions?"

We worked for the rest of that day, finally finding what might have been the cause of some of their problems. By nightfall we were well out to sea and I slept like a log.

On the next day he returned to the subject. "I suppose it's only natural really," he said. "I mean, keeping a load of boys together. It's bound to happen. It happens in the Navy too."

"On this ship?" I asked as I tested yet another circuit.

"One or two are. One or two of the cooks and a steward."

"And you?" I asked, deliberately not looking at his face.

"Christ no. I've never done anything like that. It's too risky. Sex between sailors can get you thrown out of the Navy. There were two stewards on my last ship. The officer caught them at it." He giggled nervously. "One of them had his cock right up the other one's ass," he said. "One of them tried to get me to do it. Said I had a lovely little ass. That sort of thing."

There was a long pause. Should I? I had just as much to lose, if not more but he was attractive. The steward had been right. Bell-bottom trousers are appropriately named. They show off a young man's butt to perfection. They are also loose enough in the front to show an erection and Able Seaman Russell was performing a very good imitation of a stallion in heat. I'd never seen anything like it. It looked as if he were trying to conceal a hammer in his pants. He blushed slightly when he saw me gazing at it. I grinned.

"I see. This ship's the same class as H.M.S. Grampian, isn't it?"

"That's right."

"Then I think we ought to make our way to the forward chain locker,"

"Why? There aren't any computer connections in there."

"Well, it's a bit more private, if you know what I mean," I said.

For a moment he stared at me. Then he grinned."Oh, I see," he said. "Could do I suppose."

He helped me carry my tool boxes and we made our way along the deck to the chain locker. We went in and I switched on the light. It was exactly the same in every respect as that on board H.M.S. Grampian. The Royal Navy is obsessed with absolute uniformity. There was the massive chain, coiled up exactly as H.M.S. Albion's chain had been.

"You won't say anything, will you?" he asked, as I closed the door behind us.

"Don't be daft. I've got as much to lose as you have."

He flinched as I felt it through his trousers. "Hang on a minute," he whispered. I took my hand away. He undid something and his trousers fell round his ankles. He pushed down his pants.

"That's better," he said. It was. His cock was truly magnificent and I liked the glossy brown of his pubic bush. It shone under the lamps. I put a hand under his balls. I wondered what his reaction was going to be. I needn't have. He grinned. I moved his foreskin back, revealing a very appetizing purple, plum-like head.

"Be careful. I'm pretty close already," he said. That was apparent. A long, sticky stream hung down, broke and landed on the steel floor at his feet.

I was desperate to take it into my mouth, but something, some instinct, told me to take things slowly. Thus I contented myself with hand-work. That was a shame.

After only a few minutes he was so far gone that I could have done anything.

But there was always tomorrow and the next day; and the next.

"You like this, don't you?" I murmured in his ear.

"Mmm."

"Shall we come in here tomorrow?" I asked.

"Could do. Oh! That feels good. Do you do anything else?"

"I do a lot of things. We'll come in earlier tomorrow."

"Sounds... good.... ah! Watch out. I'm....."

His ass cheeks clenched together. I just had time to reach down and grab a piece of paper from the top drawer of the tool chest. He put a hand on my shoulder to support himself as thick, creamy gobbets spurted out of him and splashed onto the paper. Navy life must be very frustrating indeed, I thought as it turned into papier mache in my hand.

"Christ! That was great!" he said as I wiped the last stream. "I've never been wanked by anyone else. Sure beats doing it yourself."

"Tomorrow will be even better," I said. "Now we'd better get back to work or someone will wonder what's going on."

That evening, at dinner in the wardroom, I had a lot on my mind. Principally an eighteen-year-old with a delightful cock and a very pretty behind. I also had to think up a good story to cover the disappearance of a top secret wiring diagram. 'It blew out of my hand' was all I could think of.

"...a signal from your firm," the engineering officer was saying.

"Oh yes."

"They want you back. There's a chap called Lyons coming to take over."

"Oh yes, Adrian. When?"

"We're putting in tomorrow morning to pick up some officers who've been on a course. He'll be waiting for us."

I was glad to get off the ship but annoyed that I shouldn't be able to achieve my ambition with Able Seaman Russell. I managed to find him that evening, sitting with a pint of beer with his mates in the Ratings' Mess. I gave him my card. "If you're ever in the area, call me," I whispered.

"What about your home number?" he said, turning the card over.

"No. Use the firm's number. I'm not often at home." The last thing I wanted was Danny to know about him.

He stood at the top of the gangplank the following morning and waved.

I'd left the firm's bags on board for Adrian so was able to wave back.

A knot of officers stood on the quay side. One of them stared, looked down at his feet and then stared again. He came over.

"Excuse me," he said. "Were you on H. M. S. Grampian years ago?"

"Good Lord!" I said. "Midshipman Williams!"

"Lieutenant Williams now. I'm joining today." We shook hands. I explained what I had been doing.

"You've lost contact with Tommy?" he said.

"Yes. Haven't seen or heard from him since we left school. A pity. I liked him, as you did, as I recall."

He smiled. "Very much," he said. "I'll tell him I've met you."

"Why? Do you still see him?"

"Very often. Of course, he never put you in the picture did he?"

"What picture?"

"We first met when his dad was a Lieutenant Commander at the Royal Naval College. He was only about thirteen but I fancied him even then. We kept in touch by letter. Then Commander McCormack and I ended up on the same ship. The Commander wanted him to spend some time on board. Tommy wrote that he'd found someone at school who was keen so I suggested to his dad that he might feel a bit lonely on board and should bring a friend. It worked out rather well, don't you think?"

Up to that moment I'd considered myself the planning genius. This guy was streets ahead of me. I laughed.

"So what brings you on board one of Her Majesty's ships this time?" he asked. I explained.

"I guess you've been pretty busy," he said. "Did you manage to sort out the problem? How far did you get?"

"Part of the way. I didn't get a chance to taste, I mean, *test* it."

THE RECRUITING OFFICER

Peter Gilbert

"What you don't seem to realize," said Major Mitchell, "is that it's not as easy as that."

He was in an irritable mood that morning. One or two little barbed remarks about the new training schedule had been made at the Colonel's daily briefing. Nothing serious, just hints that the old man was not entirely happy.

When the phone rang he thought it might be a call from the Colonel or his aide to apologize. It wasn't. It was Alan. There were times when he wished he'd never met the man. In the middle of every month he determined to tell him that the 'arrangement' would have to stop. Then came the end of the month. A weekend away from the base in a comfortable hotel; a comfortable bed and an extremely compliant, good looking young man lying next to him grinning while his hand worked on a superbly stiff cock or lubricated a welcoming ass. Those weekends were the only thing worth living for. There had been a time when he'd enjoyed army life. Now he saw it as a succession of niggling details.

"Good God, man. You've got over a thousand eighteen-and nineteen-year-olds at that place," said Alan. "Don't tell me that you can't find one that'll take a cock up his ass for a weekend pass and a bit of pocket money. If I could get in there I'll bet I could find a dozen in as many minutes."

He probably could. Peter tried, again, to explain. There was no way that he, as an officer, could proposition them. He was supposed to be the distant figure of authority. Finding companions for Alan and his friends was becoming more and more difficult. He was keen to oblige. In return for his services he got a boy who was nothing to do with the Army and was happy to believe him to be a travelling salesman, a teacher or, as in one never-to-be forgotten weekend, an extremely helpful psychiatrist.

"Well, do your best," said Alan. "I've got a nice one lined up for you."

"Oh yes?"

"Eighteen. Blond and *very* well built. He's a farm worker—and hung like a prize bull."

"Mmm. Sounds interesting," said Peter. His cock stirred under his uniform trousers but he wished Alan wouldn't be quite so outspoken on the phone. One never knew if the lads in the exchange were listening in.

"So get off your backside and find me a soldier," said Alan. Peter put down the receiver and sighed.

"Just find a soldier," he murmured. "Easier said than done."

It worked well enough at first. He hadn't, he reflected ruefully afterwards, properly assessed the risk. So much for 'officer quality'. 'Assessing the risks' was drummed into potential officers time and time again at the Military Academy.

Peter had sent a lad called Harrison. A tall, good looking, strong young man who was, he knew, in desperate financial straits. Harrison didn't have a girl friend. He was a very lonely loner; ideal for what Alan had in mind.

So he turned out to be. Alan sent the video tape he and his friends had made. Young Harrison joined in everything with a will. He was wanked and sucked. His spunk spattered everywhere, including the camera lens. He was whacked and fucked. The shot of one of Alan's friends screwing his virgin ass was a real turn-on.

Sadly, he turned out to have a big mouth and whined on his return about having been abused. Luckily, Peter was in the clear. As far as he was concerned, Harrison had been sent to Alan to paint chalets at a nearby holiday camp as part of the old man's policy of keeping well in with the locals. How was Peter to know that the owner was that way inclined? If, in fact, he was. The Colonel agreed that young men were prone to imagine things at times, and Harrison was a strange, lonely young man.

Harrison was posted away immediately after his basic training was completed and none of the others caused problems as Peter's secret collection of video tapes testified but it taught him to be more careful in selecting suitable 'volunteers.'

He got up and picked up his hat and cane.

"Going for a stroll, Bates," he said passing through the clerk's office on the way to the door.

"Sir!" said Bates. "Were you expecting any calls, sir?"

"One's quite enough. If Mr. Pennels rings again, tell him I'm out looking for a volunteer."

"Would that be for the holiday camp work, sir?"

"It would. Bloody nuisance."

"The Colonel's very keen on the project, sir. I wouldn't mind lending a hand down there for a weekend pass, sir."

"I don't need you to tell me which projects interest the Colonel, Bates," Peter snapped. "Anyway, you're of more use here." He just caught the tail end of a comment as he closed the door behind him. "..... him? Miserable old sod!"

He couldn't resist a smile as he stood on the steps and surveyed the parade ground. He wondered what Alan's reaction would be if he sent thirty-two year old, fat, balding Bates.

The smile soon vanished. A drill sergeant was putting a platoon through its paces. Second Lieutenant Rooksby-Mills' platoon, and, as always, the silly little idiot was making a fool of himself.

"Now do come on, chaps. You can do better than that. Try it again, sergeant."

"Sir!" the sergeant shouted. He saluted and turned to face the men again. "You heard what the officer said. Now then.... wait for it... wait for it.... Atten....shun!"

The days when rich fathers bought their sons commissions in the British Army have long since gone. They now do the next best thing and send their sons to the expensive private school that produced Marcus Rooksby-Mills and several hundred other, equally useless officers some of whom are sufficiently senior to ensure the continuance of the tradition. It is said that the atmosphere of the officer selection board changes instantly once the candidate mentions the name of the school. Frowns turn to smiles. Barked questions about sporting achievements turn to 'Did you know so-and-so?' and 'Good Lord! I saw that match. Was that you? Damned fine game!'

Rooksby-Mills was just nineteen years old; no older than the men he professed to command. He'd been a thorn in Peter's side ever since he arrived at the camp in the Porsche that his father had given him. His cheerful, schoolboy manner and his loud, affected laugh were a constant irritation.

Peter stood there watching. With the skill that comes from

years of experience, the sergeant transformed a motley group of individuals into a corporate entity. Boots crashed onto the tarmac simultaneously. In less than half an hour, they were marching in perfect unison. It was an impressive performance and would have taken an even shorter time without Rooksby-Mills's constant interruptions.

Finally, they marched off. Rooksby-Mills approached, stood at the foot of the steps and threw a perfect salute. Saluting was of enormous importance to Rooksby-Mills. He always took the long way round when walking to the Officers' Mess, just to receive and return as many salutes as possible. Secretly hoping that some of the men in the platoon would notice, Peter touched his hat with the tip of his cane as sloppily as possible.

"Out to enjoy the sunshine, old chap?" said Rooksby-Mills, bounding up the steps.

Peter glared. "To 'sir' I will answer. I will even, if it is used at the right time, answer to my name but I am not and I never will be 'old chap'," he snarled.

"Sorry, sir. I've just been putting the platoon through their paces."

"The sergeant has been putting your platoon through their paces. From what I could see, your presence was entirely unnecessary. You are supposed to concentrate on their welfare and leave the training to the people who know how to do it."

"Oh, I know. I like to be around though. The chaps appreciate it."

"I'm sure they don't. Where are they going now?"

"I've given them a half hour break before gym."

"They don't need it. Where are those two going?" He pointed with his cane to two soldiers who had broken away from the rest.

"God knows, old....sir."

"*You* are supposed to know, not God."

"I'll go and chase them up," said Rooksby-Mills.

"No you won't. You stay and keep an eye on the rest of them. I'll see to them."

Rooksby-Mills pouted and Peter set off. He had to walk briskly to keep up with the two figures ahead of him. They were obviously going somewhere. They certainly weren't out for a stroll. They stopped at the end of the road by the sign that read 'OFF LIMITS.' Peter nipped behind a building and watched. They turned round and, seeing nobody, ducked under the barbed wire.

The area in question contained several old huts that had been used when the base was first opened. Derelict now, they were used for street fighting practice. The sensible thing to do, as Peter knew well, would have been for him to detail an N.C.O. to arrest them. He would have to discipline them and couldn't be both judge and witness.

Curiosity got the better of him. He watched as they approached one of the huts. One of them wrenched the door open. They were both tall, good-looking lads. The one at the door grinned. He wouldn't be grinning tomorrow morning, thought Peter. They both went into the hut. He waited and then set off again. Climbing under the wire was undignified, even though he lifted it with his cane. Stealthily, he approached the hut. For years, inexperienced soldiers had sent bullets flying in all directions. The walls were pock marked and all the windows had been smashed. Bending double, he approached and then stood between two windows.

Almost certainly marijuana, if not something harder, he thought grimly. A few days in the cells and then an ignominious discharge. They deserved it.

"Your hands are cold," said a voice from inside the hut.

"Soon warm up," said the other. "You're hot for it though."

"Always am ... Oh, Christ! That feels good."

As rigid as any sergeant major on the parade ground, Peter stood, unable to believe his ears. There was a moment of silence and then a slight scuffling noise.

"Lick round it a bit first," said the speaker. "That's it. Mmm! Now my balls. Jesus, that feels good!"

For some time, neither said a word. A sound reminiscent of a child drinking through a straw drifted through the window.

"Oh yeah! Yeah! Any minute now," said a breathless voice. "Ah! Ah! Aaaah!"

Another silence, longer this time, followed by the unmistakable sound of webbing belts being clicked together.

"Good one," one of them said.

"Always ready to oblige," his companion replied. "How many more weeks before we get a weekend pass?"

"Three."

"I'm not sure I can wait that long."

"Nor me. We dare not do it in camp, though. Anyway, it'll be better in a decent bed. Christ! Just the thought of fucking your lovely little ass turns me on."

"Me too. What's the time?"

"Eleven-thirty."

"Great. The gym session's well under way. What are we going to say this time?"

"We've been to see the M.O.?"

"We've used that one twice before. Tell you what... we could say that Major Mitchell sent for us."

"Too risky."

"No it isn't. Rooksby-Mills won't check up. The major hates his guts. Did you see the way he returned Rooksby-Mills' salute?"

"Yeah. Okay then. We were on the way to the gym and Major Mitchell stopped us."

"What for?"

"Oh, I dunno. He wanted to know if we were happy here."

"That's a laugh. He's the most miserable bastard here. It could work though. Come on. Let's go."

Peter bent double and dashed under the windows to the back of the hut. He heard the door creak on it hinges and then slam shut. He took off his cap and peered cautiously round the building. They were both good-looking lads. The backs of their necks had been shaved smooth but enough hair projected under their berets for him to see that one was blond and the other dark. The blond one clambered under the barbed wire. His companion put one hand on a post and vaulted over it. Peter smiled. Alan liked them long-legged.

They would have to walk to the gym by the prescribed route. By cutting through the officers' mess, he would encounter them long before they got there. Waiting until they were out of sight, he set off.

It was probably just as well that he never heard the comments of the various people who saw him.

"Never seen old Mitchell walk so fast. I wonder where the fire is," said the driver of a small van to his mate. They were in the process of 'transferring' a quantity of bacon and butter from the catering store to the grateful manager of a local hotel.

"You don't reckon he's got wind of us and is going to check the stores?" said his mate, anxiously.

"Him? No way. He's pissed out of his mind most of the time. My mate knows his batman. He reckons old Mitchell's home consumption liquor bill is bigger than the Colonel's."

"Maybe he does a lot of entertaining."

"Don't make me laugh. Who'd want to spend any time with 'im?"

And, equally, they would have been surprised (to put it mildly) to have overheard the conversation between this most hated officer and two soldiers he encountered as they were on their way to the gym.

"And where are you two going?" he enquired after returning their salute much more smartly than his acknowledgment of Rooksby-Mills'.

"Gymnasium, sir," said the blond one.

"A bit late, aren't you?"

They exchanged anxious glances. "Not that it matters. I'm glad to come across you," Peter added. "You know where my office is?"

"In the admin block, sir."

"That's right. Get over there right away. Tell Corporal Bates I sent you. I want a word with you both."

Again they exchanged glances. Frightened glances.

He stopped at the mess for a quick coffee and to think things over. Then he sauntered back to the office to find two very nervous privates standing rigidly to attention by his door.

He slung his hat onto the hook, placed his cane on the desk and sat down.

"Looking forward to your first weekend pass, I imagine," he said with a smile.

"Very much, sir," said the dark-haired boy.

"Going home?"

"David, I mean Simmonds, is coming home with me, sir."

"That's nice. How would you like a pass this weekend?"

They stared at him, puzzled. He explained. Mr. Pennels, owner of the holiday camp at the end of the lane wanted a couple of lads to help get the place ready for the summer rush. The Colonel was keen to help.

"I don't know this man very well," said Peter. "I've met him but I have no idea what he's like or even what he wants you to do."

"We'd do anything he wanted, sir," said the blond one enthusiastically. Peter smiled.

"Splendid! I'll tell Corporal Bates to make out your passes. You'd better give me your names and numbers - first names too. The civilian world sets store by such things."

Privates David Simmonds and Ross Masters left the admin block unable to believe their luck. "Bloody amazing," said Masters. "It's like a dream come true, and he really did ask if we were happy!"

"He's not nearly such a miserable bastard as people think," said Simmonds.

Marcus Rooksby-Mills would not have agreed. He called in during the afternoon.

"Excuse me for asking, sir," he said, "but what's this about Simmonds and Masters going away for the weekend?"

"Perfectly true. They're going to help down at the holiday camp."

"Don't you think we should have discussed it first," said Rooksby-Mills with his usual pouting expression. In many ways, Peter thought, it made him look more attractive. Out of that incongruous uniform he'd be a nice-looking boy...

"No, I don't. I am the officer in charge of training. I do not discuss my decisions with second lieutenants."

"But they're not really suitable," Rooksby-Mills continued. "There are heaps of chaps who'd be better."

Peter glared at him across the desk. "Are you criticizing my actions?" he said.

"No, no. It's just that those two are loners. They don't mix much with the other chaps. No corporate spirit, if you know what I mean. They find any excuse to miss gym and they don't play games. They're the sort of chaps we'd have given a rough time at school. Actually, they're the two you spotted sloping off this morning."

"I am well aware of that. I caught them and reprimanded them. That incident is closed."

"Went for a quick smoke I imagine," said Rooksby-Mills.

"I repeat. The incident is closed. Now if you've nothing else to do, I have."

"Where exactly is this holiday camp?"

"At the end of Sea Lane."

"Oh, I know where you mean."

"It's reassuring to hear that you know something that you haven't learned from military manuals. That will be all."

Peter waited until he was well out of the building before picking up the telephone to call Alan.

. . .

A few days later, the same hand picked up another telephone. Not a 'telephone, desk model, black' but a sleek avocado-green instrument.

"Your nephew has arrived, Mr. Rooksby-Mills," the receptionist said.

"Good, send him up." Peter put down the phone and tucked his copy of *Stallions at Stud* under the pillow. The idea of using Rooksby-mills' name had occurred to him during the drive to the hotel. As for a profession... something slightly unusual but not so much as to provoke questions. He decided to be the manager of an aluminium foundry. Most youngsters didn't even ask but it was as well to be prepared.

Alan's description of Robert Lang proved to be true in every respect. Peter had never seen a cock like Robert's. It was fully ten inches long, thick and easily roused. His balls were the size of apricots. He was delightfully hairy in all the right places and, to Peter's delight, Robert actually enjoyed being fucked. Boring into the boy's soft but powerful butt, feeling Robert squirm under him and hearing him groan more than compensated for a miserable month of military existence. There was one moment when he wondered about Masters and Simmonds. He was licking Robert's balls, but by the time the boy's gigantic and already-dripping cock was in his mouth he'd forgotten them too.

On Monday morning, feeling twenty years younger as he always did after his weekends away, Peter drove into the camp. He even managed a watery smile to the sentry on the gate. He went to his room, changed and then walked over to the office. It was there that depression took over.

"Good morning, sir. Good weekend?" Bates asked.

"I am not in need of a weather report and my weekends are my business," he growled. Submissively, Bates bent his bald head over the file he was reading.

The 'In' tray was overflowing as usual. Peter read the top set of papers, initialled them and then pushed the tray aside. His hat was still swinging on its peg when he put it on again.

"Going out, Bates," he said as he went through the clerks' office.

There was no good reason for calling on Alan. During the course of a year dozens of senior officers, politicians and other famous men visited the base. All had thrilling, sometimes hilariously amusing stories to tell but none of them were as fascinating to Peter as Alan Pennels'. He knew that associating with Alan was dangerous. But ever since that evening many years ago when they had stood next to each other at the bar of the White Lion waiting to be served, Alan was like a python to Peter's rabbit: a lethal trap from which he couldn't escape.

A tall, fair-haired young man had stood up behind them and made his way to the door. "If you fancied blonds, that would be quite a dish." The words were directed to Alan's companion but he had made no attempt to keep his voice down. Peter looked over to them and smiled. Alan paid for his drink so he felt obliged to sit with him at least for a few minutes. Alan's companion, Geoff, said very little. Alan made up for it. His conversation was peppered with cliches. In anyone else Peter would have found it irritating, but Alan's overworked vocabulary was so often used to put Peter's secret thoughts into words.

"Nice eyes," he said on that first evening, turning round to look at a young man playing pool. At least, that's what Peter thought he said.

"I didn't notice," Peter replied following Alan's gaze.

"None so blind as those who don't want to see. I wouldn't mind a slice of that, if you know what I mean."

His companion nodded. Peter nearly choked over his drink.

"His mate's not bad either," said Alan. "A bit slack possibly, but I wouldn't mind putting my cue against his balls. Know what I mean?"

At no time that evening did Peter give the slightest

inclination of his own preferences. Alan just kept on, following every double-meaning remark with "Know what I mean?"

He'd been glad to spend the following day at Alan's holiday camp; largely because it was pleasant to be with someone who was so contented with his lot. Alan had inherited the land from a relative and, having no interest in farming, had set about building the camp. There were six family bungalows, twenty four chalets and an area of hard-standing for trailers. A restaurant and toilet facilities had been built and the sports hall was in the process of construction.

"It has its benefits," Alan explained. "It pays for itself financially and I like to do a bit of butt-hunting in the summer months. Amazing how many of the lads who come down here for a bit of the other with the other sex will take it, if you know what I mean."

Alan showed him a video to prove the point. True enough, one of the lads who had been sucked by Geoff and fucked by Alan said "We'd better get back to the girls, Alan. They'll be wondering where we are," as he pulled on his flowery Bermuda shorts.

The little favors started. A weekly bottle of Scotch at the special armed forces' price soon became two bottles. Alan wanted a large party of soldiers together with a bulldozer to clear some land. The Colonel had to be brought in on that one.

"Sounds a splendid idea to me," the old man had said, beaming over his half-moon glasses. "Tell this Pennels chap that we'd be glad to help him. Good for the young soldiers too. Keep 'em out of mischief."

It wasn't long after that before young Harrison was sent to 'paint chalets' to be followed at monthly intervals by others equally amenable but more discreet. It was all horribly risky, Peter thought as the car swept in under the gaudily painted arch with its slogan 'WELCOME TO WIBCHESTER'.

Alan was in his office. "Nice weekend?" he enquired.

"Very pleasant. How about you?"

"A bit of all right. Geoff's got the video to make a copy for you."

"They performed well, did they?"

"Well, needed a bit of persuasion at first. They wanted to do it to one another. We let them at first. Nice bit of footage that is. That David's got a nice cock on him. Ross appreciated it too. First time apparently. After that we had 'em. Both very tasty and accommodating boys if you know what I mean but that other one. Wow!"

"Which other one?"

"The one who came down on Sunday evening. Nicely spoken boy."

"Not from the camp?"

"Yes."

"I don't know of a third."

"He knows you," said Alan. "Said you were the most miserable, bad tempered sod he'd ever met."

"Did he indeed? What was his name?"

"Peter somebody. I never asked for his surname. He turned up at about seven. Geoff had just left with Ross and David. He wanted to know if they'd been satisfactory."

"And you said?"

"I said very. He wanted to know if they'd done everything I wanted. I said 'Yes' and asked him in. Well, of course, the place was a bit of a mess. It always is after a session, if you know what I mean. Towels on the sofa; oil tube on the floor and all that... Well, one thing led to another. I could see he was worked up, if you know what I mean. Ha! I soon had it out. First time since he was at school, he said. Used to have it off regularly there. One of those posh boarding schools, it was. Ha! He even got fucked by the chemistry teacher. Imagine that!"

"Did you get him on video?" Peter asked. A nasty suspicion was forming in his mind.

"No. Nobody to operate the camera. Got him on audio, though. Used the cassette recorder in the bedroom."

"Let's hear it," said Peter.

"Not a lot to hear and I'm not sure you should. He wasn't very complimentary about you, if you know what I mean."

"I couldn't care less. I'm not in for a popularity competition. Let's hear it."

Ten minutes later, Peter's mouth had dropped open and he sat, looking like a marooned codfish. There was no doubt about that voice.

"He's made my life a misery ever since I was posted here. I hate the bastard."

"Well forget him for now. Nice pair of trousers. You never got them in Wibchester."

"In London, actually. Be a bit careful undoing them, old chap." If anything was needed to clinch the speaker's identity it was those last two words. Rooksby-mills!

"Sure. There! By God, that's a nice one. Just how I like 'em."

Rooksby-Mills giggled. "That's what Mr. Arnold used to say."

"And who was Mr. Arnold?"

"Chemistry teacher at school."

"You had sex with the chemistry teacher?"

"Quite a few of us did. Good way of getting good grades and free private tuition. It was fun too. You know ... Saturday afternoon tea parties at his house..."

"With lots of cream too, I bet,"

"Quite a lot, yes. Ah! Ah!"

"And I bet Mr. Arnold liked your buns as much as you liked the ones he gave you."

Rooksby-Mills giggled again. "I think so. Mmm!"

"I'm not surprised. So will I. There. Let's have you up on the bed."

"Is that thing working?"

"Yes but don't let it worry you."

"You won't play the tape to anybody else?"

"They wouldn't know who you are anyway. Don't worry about it. Come on now."

Bed-springs creaked. Rooksby-mills groaned. Slurping noises came from the loudspeaker. The springs protested even louder.

"Oh! Ah! Oh! No, don't stop."

Alan obviously had no intention of stopping. The gasps and grunts became louder and louder. Finally, Rooksby-mills gave what sounded like a long, drawn-out sigh. Then there was silence.

"The next bit was about two o'clock in the morning," said Alan, turning the cassette over.

A strange squelching noise, followed by "Ah! Ah! Oh yes! Fuck me"

"Just as well I had another bottle of oil," Alan commented, lighting a cigarette. "Lovely ass the boy's got. Much nicer than Ross or David. A real classic if you know what I mean. Knows what to do with it too. Cigarette?'

Peter shook his head. It was odd, he thought. He had never paid attention to Rooksby-Mills' physical attributes. He'd stopped soldiers on hundreds of occasions for minor breaches of service discipline, just to admire a hot, young bottom. There had even been times when he'd insisted on a few press ups and feasted his eyes on a khaki-clad butt rising and falling, tensing and relaxing as he counted. The only thing he'd ever noticed about Rooksby-Mills was the immaculate polish of his shoes and shoulder-strap.

"I think I will have a cigarette, after all," he said. Alan's gasps and grunts merged with Rooksby-Mills' groans and sighs. Peter lit the cigarette and leaned back to enjoy the rest of the performance. At last, Rooksby-Mills was doing something he was good at and learning that it was good for junior officers to have someone to look up to—at least metaphorically speaking. It was pretty obvious from the muffled sound of his groans that all he could see was a pillow.

He yelled out. "That's when I touched his button," said Alan, exhaling a twisted wreath of cigarette smoke. "That's when he really started to go."

Peter said nothing. The bed-springs groaned. So did Rooksby-mills. Alan gasped like a long distance runner. Rooksby-mills muttered something. Alan gave a long, contented sigh and then there was silence.

"Are you sure you don't know him?" Alan asked, switching off the recorder.

"I don't get to hear their voices. He could be any one of several hundred," said Peter.

"Goes to prove my point," said Alan. "If you'd only get out and find 'em, we'd have enough to open this place as the best boy-brothel in the country. I hope that one will come down again. He said he would but for some weird reason he doesn't want any of the others to be here at the same time. Stupid really. Ross and David wouldn't mind. It's better when there are two, especially when Geoff's here. Two boys being fucked simultaneously is a symphony in sound. That's why I have the recorder in the bedroom. Got time to listen to Ross and David?"

"Not really. I ought to be getting back. Some other time," said Peter. He stood up and stubbed out his cigarette.

There wouldn't be another time. Of that he was quite sure.

He drove into the camp and astonished the sentry by smiling at him.

Rooksby-mills was on the parade ground again.

"May I have a word with you, Lieutenant?" Peter asked.

"Sir! Carry on, sergeant." The sergeant saluted. Rooksby-mills bounded over. He really was astonishingly good looking, Peter thought.

"Sir?" Rooksby-mills saluted. Peter returned the salute as smartly as possible.

"What are you doing this evening?" he asked.

Rooksby-mills' face fell.

"I thought you might like to come over to my place after dinner for a drink and a chat," said Peter.

Rooksby-Mills frowned. "I could do," he said, "I've got nothing planned actually, sir. Did you want to see me about anything in particular?"

Peter glanced downwards. He could just make out its outline under Rooksby-mills' immaculately tailored trousers.

"One or two things actually," he replied. Alan hadn't said anything about the boy's balls. They should, he thought, be pretty big and as for that ass.... "Nothing military, er, old chap," he added.

. . .

"What we *could* do, old chap...." said Marcus. He lifted his beautiful, naked butt off the bed to enable Peter to take the towel from under him.

"Mm? What could we do?" He folded the towel so that the damp patch was underneath, placed it on the chair and sat down again. Chairs, wicker ... Officers' were most uncomfortable if one was unclothed.

"I was thinking," Marcus continued. "Masters and Simmonds don't like Army life and they don't really fit in. You could get them quietly discharged on sexual grounds. You could get them jobs down at the holiday camp with this Pennells chap. Then, whenever we felt like it, we could toddle off down there for a spot of lolly-licking or bottom-boring."

"Are they Mr. Arnold's expressions too?" Peter asked, laughing.

"They are actually, yes. What do you think?" He turned over onto his back. His cock was already beginning to show signs of life again. It was one of the nicest Peter had ever had his hands or lips on.

"There's only one sort of discharge I'm interested in at the moment," he replied. The feel of Marcus's plump buttocks pressing up against his groin as the boy wriggled, trying to get as much into him as possible had made him almost faint.

"They're both rather pretty, don't you think?" Marcus asked. His cock twitched as he spoke.

"I hadn't really noticed."

"I've seen 'em in a gym a few times...." It twitched again.

"Then you're luckier than the gym instructor! He hasn't. There's a memo on my desk from him at the moment."

"A couple of fine, upstanding lads," said Marcus in a voice that was not his own. "That's what Mr. Arnold used to say when he came round the dorms. He used to feel the bedclothes. 'You're a fine, upstanding lad,' he'd say and then you were away. Special tuition; a word in the ear of some visiting general and hey presto, you're in the Army. Brilliant chap, he was. I miss him—or, rather, I did until tonight."

Peter reached over and felt it. It was hardening fast. Marcus grinned. "Lolly-licking or bottom-boring?" he asked.

"Perhaps a bit of both. And tomorrow we'll discuss this little plan of yours. It seems to have definite possibilities. So does this...."

THE CALL OF THE COCKPIT

Thomas Wagner

From the moment I joined the Navy, I'd been burning to meet as many hunky sailors as that particular branch of the military had to offer. As soon as I got my orders to ship out, I headed for the aircraft carrier with a lump in my pants and a smile on my face. Once I got there, I began to check out my fellow shipmates. Each was in tip-top shape, and I would have been overjoyed to hump any one of them. But then I spotted Strom Sexton.

Strom personified any horny guy's image of a rugged sailor. His close-cropped blond hair, sparkling grey eyes, and quirky smile made me horny for him beyond belief. It was all I could do not to beat off whenever he strode by in full dress blues, gleaming saber and all. Needless to say, I was more interested in the saber that swung inside his pants!

Once we got out to sea it was especially hard to keep my eyes—and my hot fantasies—off him. All through meals, or when I was lying in my bunk at night, I tried to devise some foolproof kind of gaydar. I was desperate to know if there was any chance he'd let me suck him off.

At first, I just tried to make eye contact. Then I made sure to brush up against him in the narrow passageway below deck, searching his face for any interest as I apologized and struggled by. Unfortunately, there was no sign of any until one day when we were both on night duty. I waited until no one was in a certain out-of-the-way passage, knowing he passed by there on his regular patrol just after midnight.

Pretending that I couldn't see him, I stepped out in front just as he rounded a corner. Our crotches brushed together, and a hot spark seemed to leap between us. Strom caught me up in a powerful grasp and pushed me against the bulkhead, his rugged face hovering only inches from mine, the stark planes of his cheekbones and sturdy jaw awash in silvery shadows.

My jizz was about to explode right in my pants when Strom recognized me and set me back on my feet. He looked around and then lowered his full lips to my tingling ear.

"Meet me in the cockpit of Fighter Jet 59 at 0400 hours," he said quietly. Then he gave me a half-innocent, half-wicked wink and just kept right on walking.

I gave him a formal salute. I didn't see him for the rest of my shift and went through the motions of my typical after-hours grind, checking the equipment, swabbing the decks, and fantasizing about his thick dick in my mouth. I was salivating at the prospect.

By four a.m., I was so hot waiting for Strom that the front of my pants were soaked from sweat and pre-cum, though I didn't actually dare to whip open my fly and beat off. I wanted everything ripe and ready for him when he gave me the signal. The minutes ticked by like years stuck in the brig.

At last, it was 3:45, and I crept up to the deck with a controlled stealth that surprised even me. Silently, I walked down every out-of-the-way corridor within a hundred square feet of where he'd told me to meet him, taking the time to make sure we wouldn't get caught.

In the end, it took me fifteen minutes for a five-minute walk to the dark, quiet plane. But I was on time. Strom was already there, sitting in the co-pilot's seat, waving me to come inside the cramped cockpit and join him. There wasn't a sound except for the waves crashing against the hull of the ship. I got in and sat in the pilot's seat, waiting for him to speak first.

By the time we were settled, Strom looked me right in the face and made a shocking admission. As we sat face to face, he murmured, "Look, Jason, I've never done this before. I've wanted to be with a guy for as long as I can remember—hell, I guess that's why I signed up to live with a bunch of smelly sailors in this tin can of a ship—but I was afraid I'd get caught. Promise me you won't tell anyone about this, okay?"

"'Course I won't," I said, scarcely able to believe my ears. This strapping hunk was really a cherry waiting to be picked—and by me! "I'll go real slow. You have nothing to worry about."

It took every fiber of my strength for me not to leap across the plane and ravish him, but somehow I got myself under control and went down on my knees. First, I undid his tight shirt in order to massage his thick pecs and get him to relax more. My fingers coiled tighter into his sparse chest hair, wrenching it by the roots. With slow precision, I rubbed his body up and down and twisted his stiff nipples until they looked red and bloated. Next I reached for his crotch. His regulation zipper came undone in my hands at once, and I peeled his pants down around his flushed thighs. The polished gold buckle glinted in the moonlight as I pulled his belt through the loops.

Strom grunted, and I nearly fainted when I saw the size of his stones, with a giant boner to go with it. His balls seemed bigger than any one else's I could remember. They looked like two purplish mini-cannonballs about to explode. And here I was, the first guy to get a load of them, so to speak! I just couldn't believe my good fortune!

The sweat dripped off his groin, and I began to lick those fat suckers like Strom never dreamed possible. Then I slid my hands around his buns and lifted him up into my face. I could barely get a hold on those rigid glutes, which were streamlined like steel bands after months of rigorous workouts, military gauntlets, and 50-mile marches. His muscles were so taut that my fingers could hardly grip him as he squirmed in delight.

His nuts tasted of chastity and raw, hot lust all at the same time. I pulled at his blond pubic hairs with my teeth, inhaling the strong scent of his pre-cum, which had just started to trickle from the rigid cock poised above my face. Before we got too carried away, I pulled a condom from my pocket and rolled it down his throbbing cock.

I kept one thing in my head—the thought that mine would be the first dick inside of him. I realized my prep-work had to be enough to make him want it bad, since we couldn't dally around like this for too long. The longer we were out on deck, the more chance we had of being caught.

Strom threw his gorgeous head back with a grunt of ecstasy as my tongue rolled one of those big balls into my mouth. I sucked on it and chewed it slowly as it swelled even more. Soon I'd hauled in both of them, sucking and licking them in the warm recesses of my horny mouth.

At the same time, I lowered my fingers to his humid asscrack, swirling them around in his dripping sweat. I made use of the natural lube and played with the outside of his butt-hole long enough to slip my forefinger inside, just a bit. I then gave each of his tender folds special attention, causing Strom to aggressively push his dick right into my face.

Then, at last, my quivering lips latched on to his rubberized fuck-missile. Strom groaned as he traveled down the length of my throat, moving my way down his broad base. His rod palpitated in my mouth as my throat-muscles scoured every millimeter of hot, straining skin through tight latex. He rocked back and forth in his seat, humping back in response to my roughness.

Strom responded with a series of raw animal grunts. "Oh, yeah, suck me," he snarled. "I can't wait any more, man. Get me off."

He didn't have to beg. I already had him halfway down my throat. Then he gripped my shoulders with all his might with one hand and with the other pushed himself so deeply into me that I imagined he could spear my body straight through and emerge backward from my asshole.

I sucked on him harder until I felt all of him inside me. He began to plow my mouth even harder, and I was able to corkscrew my finger deeper inside his tight but voracious asshole.

Strom hammered his body against my thick finger, then up into my mouth, and back again. His body gripped mine from inside as sweat slithered down both our faces. His heavy, bloated balls rubbed my chin, leaving rug-burn on my close-shaved cheeks. Finally, with a wheeze that turned into a strangled scream, he let loose a torrent of jizz into the condom. I squeezed my tongue tight around the bloating rubber sheath while Strom kept pounding my mouth until he'd fired off a second hot load. He seemed to come over and over again, his first man-fuck driving him utterly wild.

After he finally softened and relaxed, he pulled out of me, still breathing hard. He took off the condom, tied it up, and shoved it in his pocket so no one would find it. His eyes drifted to my crotch then, and I immediately got down to business and unzipped. Strom anxiously turned around, kneeling with his bare ass sticking right up in the air while I slicked a second rubber over my meat. He gulped as I got into position, and his knuckles grew white where he was gripping the pilot's seat.

I put on a condom, then reached around and used the

remnants of his own cum as lube. Luckily, there was plenty of it, so I smeared wad after wad across his tight pink butt-hole. He lifted his ass toward me once again, and I hunched down on my knees and slowly entered him. I fed him a few inches and then stopped, giving him a moment to adjust, which he seemed to do quickly.

Strom's virgin ass-muscles gripped my missile hard, as I'd known they would. I then wrapped my hand around his belly, gripped his re-hardened dick, and started to jerk him off. As he got aroused again, his ass loosened up for me, and I lunged in as far as I could go. He was so tight that I heard him swallow a moan as I began to pummel his juicy ass. He was looking over his shoulder, watching me pound his chute, his face twisted with want.

I grunted with each thrust, my dick ramming him as forcefully as a heat-seeking missile plummeting toward its target. His body stiffened as I ripped my way to his prostate. His ass was virtually bubbling over with sweat, fortunately adding lube and flexibility. Urgently I lifted myself part way out and then plowed in again even harder, repeating the process over and over, keeping his butt in a constant state of fucking. The cheeks and hole flared crimson with heat and desire. For one wild minute I was afraid it might be glowing in the dark. At that point, though, I couldn't have stopped if I'd wanted to. I groaned as I thrust and twisted inside his hot colon.

My balls clapped against his hard, round ass, seeming to applaud our lewd little show. This only improved my performance, and I kept fucking him until I felt my load descend. Then I fired a torrent of jizz into the condom. I could feel it balloon deep inside of him, increasing his own pleasure. Just then, Strom let go of a load of his own, spraying his own belly with cream. He jerked his hips forward, and the jizz shot all over the control panel. Before long he had re-painted the interior of the cockpit with his cherry-flavored cum.

Unfortunately, just then we heard a noise. I had to pull out fast, my dick still half-hard with the unblasted part of my load, and we both dropped silently to the floor. Luckily, it was just a plane flying overhead, but at that point we hurriedly cleaned up and made a dash for our respective posts. However, we agreed to dock together at the next seaport.

INQUISITION

David MacMillan

We were face-to-face, both naked and tied to a separate sawhorse across the bonfire from each other. Our blond hair was cropped short to CSC specifications, our bodies were still teen-aged slim, but rippled with muscles built up from months of work at St. Ignatius Loyola Camp for the Christian Soldiers Corps. Now, our bodies glistened with sweat from the bonfire that lighted our inquisition for our fellow Corpsmen to watch as twilight became night on the Montana flatlands.

I'd made the mistake earlier in the afternoon of confessing to Preacher Man that Jimmy got off while relieving me. Jimmy had been hard and drooling a lot lately when I fucked him; but my identical twin shooting a load under me scared me enough I finally confessed it. It didn't take Preacher Man long to bring in Brother Ralph and let Corps discipline take over. It'd taken even less time for the two men to tie me up, gag me, put me in the barn, and send a search party to look for Jimmy. In less than a half hour, my brother was in the barn with me, as bound up as I was, and waiting the full, public inquisition the Preacher had ordered.

Brother Ralph was behind Jimmy, a Corps underleader behind me, and a fully-clothed Preacher Man stood between the two of us, holding an open Holy Bible in one hand and a riding crop in the other as night completely claimed our Montana camp.

Brother Ralph's shirt was pulled behind his head as he repeatedly rammed his cock into Jimmy's ass. The completely naked Corps underleader was buried deep in me, grinding his pubes against the tender sides of the cleft between my globes with his every downstroke. The faces of both men were masks covering the pleasure they felt at their coming orgasms. The Preacher watched our cocks—mine and Jimmy's—intently for signs of tumescence as the Corpsmaster and the underleader fucked us.

Corpsmen sat nude in a circle around us and the bonfire, witness to our spiritual reclamation. Senior Corpsmen sat in the first row of spectators and several of Brother Ralph's underleaders patrolled the sidelines watching for signs of prurient interest from our witnesses. Ten other sawhorses awaited sinners who got aroused at our reclamation.

"Sodomy is a sin against God!" the Preacher shouted into the growing darkness, making himself heard. "Hear me now, Soldiers—sodomy is abomination. Abomination is possession by Satan; it's taking pleasure in relieving others—it's submitting to the animal in us and denying our duty to be God-like."

He stopped and smiled when his sharp eyes caught Jimmy's cock beginning to thicken between his legs. Preacher raised the crop over his head and brought it down hard on my twin's shoulders. The report of leather slamming into skin and Jimmy's scream touched each Corpsman, and there was a ripple of movement through the assembly as each witness flinched.

Brother Ralph's pummeling of my brother's ass was becoming short and fast. Sweat beaded across the Corpsmaster's face. Beneath him, Jimmy's ass grabbed instinctively at his cock. Jimmy's fuck-meat drooled and grew as his love gland continued to be savagely massaged. I saw he was losing his concentration on keeping pleasure at bay with Brother Ralph closing in on an orgasm inside him. That was my twin all right—he'd come to really love having his butt plugged since we joined the Corps six months ago, right out of high school.

The pain of the crop hitting his shoulder shattered his concentration. His cock jumped immediately into full erection before the Preacher and all the assembled Corpsmen. Brother Ralph grabbed Jimmy's hips and pulled himself deep into his ass as his balls churned and pushed jizz into his dick.

"I expel you, Satan, in the name of the one God," the Preacher yelled and rushed around the sawhorse as the Corpsmaster pulled out of Jimmy, his cock still pulsing. The Preacher stopped before my twin's up-turned ass, pushed Brother Ralph away, and raised his crop.

The assembled Corpsmen listened in silence as the crop whistled through the night toward Jimmy's ass. "Out, I say! Leave him in the hands of the Father who loves him!" the Preacher yelled and Jimmy screamed as the crop slammed against his cheeks. Moments later the crop was whistling through the air again to crash against his backside.

I watched helplessly as his balls churned, his cock riding his tight belly. Jimmy lost the last vestige of control and his first rope of spunk erupted as the Preacher's crop found his ass again. I watched drops of blood erupt from the repeated thrashing and flash in the light from the bonfire as the crop fell on Jimmy's ass over and over again. His cock lost its size and his chest collapsed against the sawhorse; he stared dazedly at me as the Corps underleader's hands gripped my hips and his strokes in my ass became short and fast.

I concentrated everything I had on not getting hard. It was difficult because I had one of the few men I'd ever fantasized about in my ass and getting ready to shoot his load in me; but I held on, forcing myself to think of anything but the cock in my ass and the man it was attached to. I latched onto the whipping Jimmy had got, replaying it in my mind and hoping it and its pain would keep Satan away from me.

The Preacher moved to stand between us again and looked at the Corps around us. "It is right we help our comrades out, men," he called out to them. "We're animals and we have animal needs. Relieving each other is our Christian duty." His gaze fell to Jimmy and, then, to me as the man behind me wedged his cock as deep in me as it would go and unloaded himself.

"But...." The word hung for long moments in the air over us all. "Even as we give ourselves to our duty and help relieve our comrade's need, we must be vigilant. We must guard against Satan slipping into us during that most intimate moment. We must guard against the pleasure of succumbing to animal lust. Helping one another out is Christian. Enjoying it is sodomy. It's Satanic. It's abomination."

He glanced at Jimmy beside him as he raised his head and looked again at the assembled Corpsmen. "You!" He pointed to a non-commissioned Corpsmen in the first row. "Come up here and relieve yourself with your comrade."

The man pushed himself off the ground and started toward us, pulling on his meat as he moved. Randy Homell! He was the biggest buck rabbit in camp, ready to fuck anything anytime. He'd lucked out in getting Jimmy, even if my twin's ass was bloodied and already abused and he was half-unconscious from his beating. I noticed Randy was doing a damned good job of keeping a grin off his face as he approached downwind from Jimmy.

"Relieve yourself, soldier-boy. Your comrade gives himself to you," the Preacher told him. That was all the invitation Randy needed; he walked right up to my brother's ass, pulled it up to groin-level, and sank his putt.

The Corps underleader pushed off me, patting my butt affectionately with one hand while wiping sweat from his face with his other arm. The Preacher glared at me like he was unhappy his crop hadn't tasted my ass yet. He pointed to a Corpsman in the third row and called: "Come up here, man. Relieve yourself in your comrade." I watched the man approach. He was new to the Corps and I'd never seen him naked before. Only, now, I was happy the Corps underleader had stretched me some and left me lubricated with his slime. This boy was huge as he got his cock hard about the time he reached the bonfire and started toward me.

One of the non-commissioned officers yelped and grabbed a Corpsman from the circle. Two more men joined him and they pulled the poor boy up to a vacant sawhorse and tied him to it. The man's eyes were round as he stared at me, then Jimmy, and finally the Preacher with his crop and Holy Bible.

The Preacher hurried around the bonfire to him, his face a knowing smile. "Satan hardens you to defile these boys' purification," he purred, loud enough for everybody to hear, his craggy face a loving, knowing smile. I saw the Corpsman was still hard despite his fear. So did the Preacher.

As Big-cock situated himself behind me and placed his meat at my already spunk-coated asslips, the Preacher circled behind the new man and raised his crop.

Big-cock began to ease into me as the kid screamed as the crop crashed against his ass.

I groaned softly. This boy knew how to fuck a man. He wanted his partner to feel him in his ass and enjoy it. Jimmy would be raving about him for days. But he was pushing inch after inch of thick, hard meat into my ass—in front of the entire Corps and with the Preacher ready to use his crop at the first sign of carnal interest.

I was in trouble and knew it. My cock twitched between my

legs and sweat beaded on my forehead as I concentrated on the flailing the boy down from us was getting. Anything—just so I didn't get hard with Big-cock deep in my ass.

Only, it wasn't working. My meat welcomed the man inside me the only way it knew how. It oozed ball-juice and grew as those inches massaged my love gland. I forgot the men circled around me. I forgot the beating my brother had just taken and the one the new man was now getting. I forgot the months of control I'd perfected. My cock was already eight inches of throbbing, hard man-meat when Big-cock's pubes pressed against my cheeks the first time. All I wanted was him fucking me forever.

Big-cock's hands splayed out over my back as he continued to press against my butt. "You're tight," he mumbled and his hips withdrew most of him, leaving me feeling empty.

"Fuck me!" I hissed under my breath.

His hand went around my hip and found I was hard and drooling. "You're getting off on this," he whispered and didn't miss a stroke. "I like that—a tight ass that knows what it wants. Yeah."

I backed into him, surrendering to the pleasure shooting out of my ass and covering all parts of me simultaneously. "I'm going to want more than just this once," I told him, forcing myself to think enough that I could see more good times.

"Not like tonight, though, baby." He ground his meat as he pushed himself back into my ass, touching it all and claiming it as his own. "I don't turn on too much to spectators."

The Preacher was through expelling Satan from the newly tied Corpsman and turned him over to another senior Corpsman to pummel. I knew I had to somehow establish control of my cock before he could reach me. I knew it, but my cock and balls rejected the knowledge. Instead, my nuts climbed up on either side of my cock, trying to strangle it. I was close. My pole rode my tight abdomen. I wanted to shoot my load with Big-cock in my ass.

His tempo speeded up inside me, his massage of my love-gland became rough, short jabs punching at it. I moaned and knew I was finding heaven here on earth. Its name: Big-cock. Randy Homell was already through in Jimmy, pulling out of him and stepping back to leave my twin's ass to leak his spunk. Through the haze of my pleasure, I saw him leer at my brother's ass. The asshole had finally scored one of us after six months of trying.

I didn't see the Preacher's approach. The first warning I had he'd found me out was when I heard the crop's whistle as it came down against my shoulder.

I screamed as pain spread out over me, pushing the pleasure Big-cock was giving me before it. I jumped, the after-effects of the pain quivering through me and spasming my ass all along Big-cock's meat buried in me.

It was enough. He unloaded deep inside me, giving me one last moment of the heaven he'd brought me to with his fuck.

"Get out of him!" the Preacher growled, his hand and Holy Bible pushing Big-cock from me. "This is abomination!" he screamed to the assembly, his crop pulling my hard meat from my belly and showing it to any who could see it. He pulled the crop away and my cock splattered against my belly, still hard and demanding more relief.

I was somewhere between heaven and realization of where I was when I heard the whistle of the riding crop diving through the air toward me. I braced myself just before it could hit my ass globes.

Pleasure and pain stood together, holding me in the limbo between the two of them as I bucked. My cock was hard, my balls tight, my sweat ran into my eyes, my ass leaked jizz. The next time the crop splayed across my ass, I shot my load. My balls emptied themselves and I cried out.

"There are others," the Preacher told me and the rest of the Corps. "I want their names!" he demanded as the crop landed across my asscheeks. "Help your brothers. Help me rid them of Satan." The crop landed again.

I lost count of how many times he hit me. My throat was sore from screaming my pain. My cock shriveled. Parts of my brain were turning off.

Others? Who?

"Randy Homell!" I screamed with what was left of my throat as the crop landed against my ass again. And blacked out, my head hanging over the sawhorse pressing into my chest.

I passed in and out of consciousness. Hoarse screaming from the ring of spectators pulled me back into awareness and, mercifully, the Preacher had decided he'd bested Satan in me. Another scream and I turned my head in its direction. Two of Brother Ralph's burliest non-coms had Randy Homell firmly by the arms and were leading him into the circle lighted by the bonfire. I saw the fear in his face as one of the non-coms tied him to a nearby sawhorse. I also saw most of the sawhorses now held men tied to them. More of Brother Ralph's boys were slipping into the lighted circle, carrying their own crops. The Preacher had a full-fledged inquisition going now.

I passed out again, but a groan pulled me back to the circle. I watched a Corpsman sink his meat into Randy's ass. Across the flames from me, Jimmy's chest rode the sawhorse as yet another Corpsman relieved himself in him. His cock wasn't getting hard this time, though; and I knew the Preacher had expelled Satan from him.

It took me several more moments of consciousness to realize I had another groin grinding itself against my ass. Slowly, I raised my head enough to look over my shoulder and saw a man piledriving into me—and I wasn't even feeling it.

I smiled. Satan was out of me too. I'd been right to confess to the Preacher after all.

It was only then I remembered Big-cock and what he'd been doing for me. No matter what Preacher said, that'd felt too much like heaven to be the work of Satan. I guessed it was sort of like how Jimmy felt when I was working his ass.

I sank back toward unconsciousness, telling myself I was just going to have to be very careful when I was getting it on with either of them because I didn't want to be an intimate member of another inquisition any time soon.

THE BEST COCKSUCKER IN PHILADELPHIA

Thom Nickels

"I believe in human beings, relationships, and boys' asses."
—*Somerset Owl*

Excerpted from Billy Goodwin's Sex Diary, 1982:
Today, Ken from Scranton telephoned an apology. It was a stilted delivery, motivated more, I think, by the possibility that he'd lost a good cocksucker and would have to search the city for a new candidate by standing on street corners. It can take a long time to find a reliable cocksucker. Not just any cocksucker, mind you, but a good one.

I don't know why he got cocky on me and wrote me that nasty letter accusing me of sucking every cock in town. Perhaps he was feeling some guilt at letting another guy suck his cock. Or perhaps there's something wrong with him. I just know that his letter was pretty insulting and that I was ready to cross him off my list. I wasn't even going to respond to his wacky letter but in fact had made my peace with never seeing him again when his call came through. "I'm sorry," he said, "I don't know what got into me. I just started to hate myself and hate you. Now I know that was wrong. I like you and I want to see you again and I want you to suck my cock."

I know that Ken felt a genuine reluctance to contact the Philly transsexual who was his first blowjob contact, an irresponsible girl who'd never commit to a time or date and who very often left him stranded near her tiny apartment. I, at least, was as reliable as most Amtrak trains, and could be counted on for spontaneous visits as well as planned sessions.

Besides which, I suck better than any girl.

. . .

I called the gypsy seer, Miss Mitchell, on Pine Street and she wants to see me tomorrow at three. She says I'm to bring one pound of coffee and 2 pounds of sugar for a prayer ritual she'll perform for Jason. Am I nuts? She says I will get a phone call from Jason very soon. And when that happens, he'll lower his pants. "Don't worry," she says, "everything is going to work out! He will let you suck him!"

My other favorite seer, Lucy Jackie, has scarlet fever—how gothic—so I can't get a reading until she's better.

February 24

Miss Mitchell leaves for Italy and England in three weeks, but she says, "I will see you again." She assures me that Jason will call or write and that he does not love the current man he is dating. She also advises me to go back to school. I don't know where this idea came from, unless she thinks I have too much time my hands and that school will take my mind off Jason. She promised me that when Jason calls he will have a big boner and will want to see me as soon as possible. She said, "He likes to see your head go up and down like that. Bobbing. Dancing. You do it like nobody else, right? Well, be patient, okay?"

. . .

It is so odd to have Jason's parents follow me through the foyer of a restaurant, especially when his mother calls my name and hands me an empty cloth wallet. The wallet has many plastic containers for photographs but it is empty on all counts. I can't figure out what to do with it, or what purpose it is supposed to serve as I flip through it. People in the restaurant are all staring at me, and this is disconcerting, to say the least.

Then everything changes and I'm dressed in a tux and seated at a table eating with some people. In the fog that surrounds me I can't determine whether they are my family or friends, though I do know that Jason's family is sitting across the room. As soon as I notice them Jason's mother looks up and utters an "Umph," a disagreeable snort to be sure. Then I notice Jason stealing a glance at me—"stealing" I say because he was made to sit behind some rather large people so he wouldn't be able to see me. His look tells me that he wants a blowjob. Since I can't control events, everything shifts, and I'm suddenly in this white wedding dress and climbing stairs to where Jason is. In a flash, his parents appear and I move discreetly downstairs as Jason's mother covers his crotch with a frying pan.

I don't understand dreams.

After that, the dream ends and I'm awake in my room. This is where I want to be, of course, even though I don't like the way my waking life is going. Today being the 26th, I wrote and read for many hours and then as evening approached I felt an urge to go out. I had a big boner and I was thinking of Jason and all the other boys in the city. I had to go out because nobody was calling me, except my ex-lover Mark, and I needed fresh air for my sanity.

I decided to hit the bars, and went to Woody's bar for wine. The place was packed but I managed to find a nook by the cash register. The bartender was somebody I tricked with years ago, a guy I can't relate to on any level at all, so I felt pretty awkward standing there since his wasn't the gaze I wanted to meet. I found a seat at the bar, and soon an attractive fellow came and sat beside me.

A half hour went by during which we checked each other out. But just as things were getting hot and both of us were close to saying something, a friend of his came over and sat between us and ruined everything.

Feeling the effects of the wine, I didn't want to go back to my lonely room, so I walked around the city—avoiding all the peep shows like a good boy should—until I spotted a sexy blond youth in a leather jacket fumbling with pocket change inside a telephone booth. I was attracted yet repelled by his drunkenness, for he could hardly stand up. Yet I was also excited by the prospect of finding someone who might be easy to snag. Especially a sexy young drunk.

The blond kept banging his head on the telephone when he stooped down to pick up the money that he kept dropping. Though something told me not to, I asked him to come home with me. My boner was doing the talking.

While walking together, he told me he was bisexual and could definetly get into getting sucked. With a pleasant smile, he added, "You can see that I have a good head on my shoulder, even though I'm a little drunk."

The guard at my building noticed his condition and gave me

the evil eye, making me feel like a cheap whore. It was unnerving standing in the lobby waiting for an elevator—where are the damn things when you want them?—the blond wavering back and forth and the guard trying not to stare. Finally, I got the blond into an elevator without an accident of any sort, although on my floor he began to stumble against the walls and talk in a loud voice. I was starting to wonder if he could get a hard-on.

In my room, he fell back against my bookcase, knocking over a few treasured knick-knacks. I almost asked him to leave but he saved himself by apologizing nicely. When he undressed I noticed that he had a very nice cock. It was one of those angled-to-the-side cocks. I went down on him under the covers and sucked for what seemed like hours, but he does not orgasm. He stayed hard while asleep.

The next morning, when he was in the shower, I noticed that a ten dollar bill was missing from my wallet. I asked him,"Did you take it?"

He swore that he didn't, that he was not a thief."Want to check my pockets?' he asked.

I should have said yes, but instead told him,"No, anyone who swears he didn't do something on his little son's life, must be telling the truth."

Oh yes, I did eventually suck him off in the morning. It was an uneventful blowjob if only because he came so quickly. Ten strokes with my mouth and there was cream everywhere. And he was a dead fish after that.

March 7

Who should call again but Ken from Scranton, livening up a meditative Sunday night.

"Guess where I am?" he says, the sound of passing traffic in the background. "The Greyhound bus station at 16th and Market!"

It takes him twenty minutes to walk to my place, and as soon as he's in the door he lowers his trousers and flops down on my one overstuffed chair, dick erect and throbbing.

That was all I needed. In no time I was on my knees. He was insatiable, though he only orgasmed once. Then I took him to Equus where we had a beer. On our way back, we passed Little

Jason. Jason was walking real fast, both his hands in his coat pockets, his elbows stuck out in such a way that he resembles a little bird. Naturally, I did a double-take. Two cocks in one fell swoop—it's too much."There's the person I'm in love with," I told Ken from Scranton. "And I can't believe I just walked past him without saying a word!!'

Since I'm sure that Jason went into Equus, I tell Ken that we must go back and search him out. He agrees, but there's no sign of Jason in the bar, either upstairs or downstairs, so I check the deli next door and then go back to the bar.

Back in Equus, I spot him at the bar, walk up behind him and touch him on the shoulder. "I just tried to call you!" he says, turning around, his cheeks flushed. He has a worried look on his face like his life has been rotten since the last time we met. I sit down beside him and he buys me a drink as I talk about Lucy Jackie's astrological reading, and listen to tales of his mother reading the novel, *Consenting Adult*. Jason tells me that there's been some progress on the home front, though his love life for the past month has been hell.

I tell him about Ken from Scranton, calling him"a straight guy I blow from time to time." Of course, I make it sound casual, which it is, because I don't want him to confuse a simple blowjob with French kisses, hugs, and anal intercourse. I figure: the truth is better than a lie though in Jason's case anything is awkward. I really want to go back to my room and be alone with Jason. Jason has the biggest cock in Philadelphia! I must have sucked it about a hundred times and each time the experience only gets better. The last time was over a month and a half ago; since that time I have fantasized about this moment. I knew there would come a time when I'd bump into him.

So we go back to my room where Ken is sleeping.

My mood? All white lotus leaves as I introduced the boys to one another. "I'm glad you found your buddy," Scranton Ken finally says, sitting up in bed and squinting through the darkness. Jason is looking at Ken's manly, hairy chest and I see lust in his eyes. It's obvious Jason wants a threesome although what he doesn't know is that Ken just likes to get his cock sucked. Two top guys meeting one another is only hot on the surface. Then there comes the big problem of what to do.

Through it all, I'm hoping that Jason is making some kind of resolution to win me back. "If you two would like to use the bed, I can get up and go somewhere for a while," Scranton Ken says. I'm on pins and needles, hoping Jason says yes when he does a radical U-turn and blurts out, "No, I didn't come here for that, no." Of course he didn't come here for that. He came here for a threesome. The bloody opportunist. It was Ken he was after. Not me. How I wanted to pull down his trousers and suck him off then but he held me off at the pass. "Let's just kiss," he tells me, just hoping to make Ken hot and bothered. But Ken could care less. Ken thinks I want to be married to Jason and in some way he is happy for me. The thought of kissing another guy would make Ken run in the opposite direction.

"Good night," Jason tells me, guarding his mammoth hard-on with his right hand.

"Maybe for you," I say.

Miss Mitchell says she needs a hundred bucks to complete the marble crosses she's making. These crosses are to be used to melt the wax walls and get rid of the curse she says my family has been dealing with for centuries. She says she needs the money for the crosses before she leaves for Canada, which is in a few days.

I wreck my head worrying about where to get the money, deciding that I can ask my great aunt for twenty bucks and then chip in twenty myself. Forty dollars would take half the curse away, and then I could do forty later. Then I'd be home free: Jason would telephone and say, "Suck my cock!"

I regret having met Miss Mitchell and wish that I had just stuck to Lucy Jackie, since she never mentioned curses or wax walls or even wanted extra money for "holy work." Half of me does think that Miss Mitchell is a fake, though the other half knows what she can do. When she says Jason will call, he calls; when she says he will visit, he visits. And so on. Not only that, there is something about her that gives me courage. After visiting her, I feel revitalized and have a renewed sense of hope. That counts for something.

I agreed to meet Miss Mitchell on a Friday, which is a pay day for me—something I'm sure did not escape her expert eye. But the preceding night, a Thursday, I was feeling the pain of giving up twenty bucks as well as feeling guilty for conning my great aunt into giving me twenty bucks for food. I also knew I had forty more dollars to pay if I wanted the curse lifted, and I did not look forward to shelling out more money the following week. All that to suck the big dick of a pretty boy is a bit much.

In the midst of figuring out my finances, I was also trying to figure out what Miss Mitchell meant when she said she was making marble crosses. Did that mean she took a saw and cut through the marble herself, then sculpted each piece over a fire till she'd etched out the form of a cross? This seemed unlikely. Perhaps, I told myself, she meant the making of little crosses, thimble-sized figurines fashioned into cross shapes, that might then be sold in novelty stores. The second was more likely, as part of me could see her scraping and cutting with a kitchen knife on crude chunks of marble purchased from "the churches."

But even the second scenario was problematic. What did getting marble from the churches mean? In all my days as a Catholic, I had never heard of anyone getting marble from churches, be they architects with open access to materials of every sort, or parish priests with a penchant for chipping away at marble interiors. Marble, after all, is inlaid securely in church interiors, whether in the form of sculpted altar stones or as steps around communion rails. Excess marble, in the manner of altar lace waiting to be chopped up into segments and sold to the devout, wasn't a commercial option in the house of God.

So how did I come to believe Miss Mitchell? Because she was a gypsy, I let myself believe that she must have known some obscure gypsy churches in old neighborhoods, where access to marble was something like the mainstream Catholic's access to Lourdes water or Fatima paraphernalia. I also wanted to believe Miss Mitchell had connections with priests who recognized her talent and who gave her what she wanted—crosses, holy oils, saintly images, bags of sweet rolls, donuts. This sort of relationship between priest and believer was something the typical suburban Catholic might be at a loss to explain.

I convinced myself that even if Miss Mitchell was lying, and needed the money to pay her phone bill or feed her children, that my giving her money would work good energy. That energy would help transform anything negative I was generating, since her appreciation for my efforts would be translated into feelings of friendship and warmth, in turn having some good effect on her powers of concentration and focus when it came to Jason and myself. After all, she knew how I longed to be back in Jason's arms and suck his big dick again. She knew the power of big dicks: this knowledge was written all over her face. Once when I visited her I met her boyfriend and I spotted huge pecker tracks in his trousers. Miss Mitchell had the face and lips of a cocksucker: thick lips that seemed to extend out and a nose shaped like the angular protrusion of some cocks.

I called Lucy Jackie for some feedback, since she was always telling me to call her whenever I had a question. When I finally got something other than her machine—her messages were always sassy, as if she were in bed copulating with a client—she told me that she was with a client (drinking scotch, skirt pulled up around her legs?) and that she'd get back to me later. Since it was not her style to pinpoint a time—she often talked about the infinite stretches of psychic time, or "the grey horizon where one day can mean five years"—I was left guessing, and so spent the better part of Thursday afternoon waiting in my room for the phone to ring.

When I hadn't heard from her by sundown, almost five hours later, I gave her another call and discovered, to my amazement, that her machine was on. This time her message had a snappier ring—something about rushing to South Street for a Greek salad, the message accompanied by a giggle (a man tickling her pussy?). Disappointed as I was, I wanted to believe she was hungry from an afternoon of Readings and had rushed out for nourishment.

"I'll try in a couple hours," I told myself, satisfied with my take on the situation, not yet realizing that Lucy Jackie suffered from the disease affecting most psychics and astrologers: a flakiness that makes more promises than it can keep. And the reason for this? Why, she too, is a cocksucker-compulsive, I might add. That's why she encouraged me to bring Jason to her house. She was hoping for a bit of the hose, since I'd told her how big it was and how much I needed it.

Am I being overly sensitive concerning this? Perhaps, but

this didn't help me explain Lucy Jackie's cold, almost abrasive tone when I called her later that night and asked for help. Gone was her initial sweetness, the attitude she demonstrated when she kept pouring me scotch. In fact, she spoke so fast I imagined a speeding train running through her house; I only knew that she wanted me off the phone so that she could resume her life, minus my interruption, despite the fact that she said she'd get back to me, which I now chalked up as something she never even remembered saying. And I knew what she wanted to get back to: seducing another client, some pale young man slouching on one of her fluffy sofas.

"Will Jason let me do it sometime this week?" I managed to get out. "We haven't had sex in almost two months. I don't know how much longer I can stand it!"

She did mention that Mercury was retrograde, meaning a time of confusion and missed communications, when projects or jobs or relationships started at this time almost always fail. A time when cocks go down or don't cum. A time when guys withhold their cocks and say no or maybe or just leave you hanging. A bad time for cocksuckers. Mercury retrograde was a sort of penalty phase, like having to walk barefoot over a garden of thorns.

That Thursday night was pivotal for me in that I learned to use my own psychic resources, calling into myself the spirits or whatever deity may be hanging around. Some big-dicked archangel perhaps. I asked that the situation with Miss Mitchell be rectified overnight so I could find some peace. While "tuning into" these spirits I definitely lost it, lying curled up on my rug crying the blues and in utter confusion concerning Miss Mitchell, eventually falling asleep as memories of past tricks moaning and ejaculating on the same rug filled me with erotic torment.

I wanted Jason's big dick and I wanted it now.

On Friday, I called Miss Mitchell, just as she requested. My spirits soared when I heard a recording say that the phone was temporarily out of order. That meant that the big-dicked archangel had listened; it also meant that I was off the hook. If I choose not to go to Miss Mitchell's and give her the money, I had a valid excuse. No additional curses would be leveled against me. Still, I could not sandbag the bargain and decided to make a personal visit and give her forty bucks for the good counseling she'd given me.

The visit proved worthwhile. Her two children clustered around me and said, "Billy, when are you going to bring more presents?"

Afterwards, Miss Mitchell told me that Jason's mother is on the verge of accepting her son completely. "Don't be surprised if you receive some contact with her," she said.

March 14

I'm trapped in this awful love for Jason. He came over early one morning. Apparently he'd been out all night but couldn't start his car when it was time to drive home. So he headed for my place, the doorman ringing me up, saying a Jason Armstrong was in the lobby. When I opened my door, Jason had tears in his eyes, and the first thing he did was embrace me.

A little later, when we sat on the edge of the bed, everything happened in a telepathic way: before I knew it I was unzipping his zipper once he stretched back on the bed. Tears were still streaming down his face as I withdrew the treasure and held it in my hands. I positioned my head on his abdomen and placed my lips at the base of his pecker. I licked the shaft and kissed the holy dome, running my tongue up and down the shaft many times before taking the whole thing in my mouth. I know how excited Jason can become so I held back because I wanted to see the slow seepage of pre-cum trickle down the shaft. This I scooped up with my tongue and when the well was dry all I had to do was manipulate the head a little and another long stream flowed down. I did this for a long time, tears welling up in my eyes. Jason, too, came between sobs. Big hearty orgasms that covered my face. "Miss Mitchell's magic," I thought, inhaling the chalky aroma of his life-enhancing cum.

The very next night I saw him in Equus with a stranger. We noticed each other, nodded, but that was all. That's when I felt like a ball was crashing smack into my stomach. That's when I felt like he'd stabbed me through the heart with his big dick.

Jason takes the love I have to give and says 'Fuck you.' Afterwards, I'm left with a feeling of emptiness but still with the illusion that everything will be okay. How do I deal with it?

I burn a candle for him like a crazy gypsy lady every Sunday morning in the church next door. What I'm doing is praying for a miracle. I want the big-dicked archangel to come to my rescue again. But the process is wearing thin; I'm stripped to the bone. My tears last night as I sat on the toilet were so bad my eyes were bloodshot the following day. The walls being so thin here, I know that my Polish neighbor, who also has a big dick, heard me rant and rave, and was probably thinking something like how hard gay love is, while his own straight life explodes with joy and sex, considering how he's always fucking his girlfriend at all hours, she moaning constantly like a stuck motor. To be sure, I don't think there's ever a time when those two do not fuck. Still, I know how she must be feeling: I once caught a glimpse of his long cock snug against his pants leg when he wore a pair of tight trousers. It was as big as Jason's, maybe bigger, and as fat as a beer can. She must be addicted to the feeling of having him inside her. She must be a person obsessed. Like Lucy Jackie. Like myself. We all love big dicks.

He's as straight as the Polish pope because I once slipped him a note, asking him to visit me for coffee. He never came over but he must have told her about the note because whenever she sees me she gives me a cross-eyed look and a disapproving frown, as if I'm trying to steal him from her. She must be a jealous bitch and a whore.

I know she screams and moans just to get my goat.

If I shut Jason out—tell him I don't want to see him when he calls—I suffer the torture of not knowing if things will ever get better. No matter what I do, I can't get rid of the pain of losing him. I can forget him if I don't see him but when I see him my system breaks down. I am so sorry I met him on that warm May night. If I could undo everything concerning him, I'd edit it all out, everything that has led absolutely nowhere. Everything is wasted on this Big Dick. So, as I write, I have absolutely given up—there will be no more prayers, no more lying awake at night meditating on him: I commit his soul and his dick and my love for him to the gods. I am, I suppose, not meant to be happy or to have a big dick to call my own. It is a very sad day.

. . .

A drag queen first told me about it. We were walking together on Walnut Street when he pointed his finger in my face and said, "*The New England Journal of Medicine* says there's a deadly disease you can get through sex. It causes cancer, and eventually kills you."

I thought he was speaking out of his anus, since he had a habit of speaking out of his anus. Then he went into detail about how people afflicted with the plague lose weight and turn into walking skeletons, or how they get big sores all over their bodies.

Since he was very competitive in the tricking department—we had locked horns many times in peep shows, trying to hit on the same guy—I was sure he was trying to scare me into not cruising and giving up the peep show circuit altogether, making it easier for him to score when I was not around. But his report sounded so fantastic I barely knew what to say. Though I half dismissed his warning as drag queen poppycock, I was worried because he had an ashen look on his face when he talked about it. And his eyes had a frightened quality that I didn't like at all.

"How do you catch it—specifically?" I asked.

"Through sperm. Cum. Eating sperm, drinking a man's cum, sipping a boy's milk. By blowing people and by getting fucked," he said, smiling wickedly. I've never seen him look so happy.

"In other words, what the whole world does, what every gay man in America does, what every gay man in Philly does," I said. "That covers an awful lot of territory, wouldn't you say? Then again, how do you know this isn't a campaign by scientists or doctors to keep gay people from meeting people and having sex?"

"It's not that at all. The sperm goes to your brain and rots it. It makes a cancer."

"Of course, this is before the aliens come down and sip it out with a straw," I replied, thinking of all the men and boys I'd sucked. The hundreds, thousands really, from Boston to Denver to New York to rag tag Philly—boys in alleyways, boys in the baths, boys in peepshows, boys in parks, automobiles, movie theaters, men's rooms. Too many boys to count, from five-minute quickies to 12-hour marathon sessions. How many gallons of sperm would that be if it could all be collected and put into gallon jugs? Ten, twenty, thirty? Was my brain already flooded with the fluids, corroded, packed with maggots and getting ready to turn to pulp?

I put the drag queen's prediction out of my mind when I read nothing about the plague in the papers. I chalked it up as a rumor, to his having heard a medical rumor or an out-of-control *National Enquirer* story. Though an RN, the drag queen was actually a psychopath, at least according to my ex-roommate Mark, who urged me to stop associating with him unless I wanted "something terrible to happen to me." I knew that whatever the case, oral sex was okay and that if there was a disease he was fucking up the facts.

The second person to confirm the plague's reality was an old friend from Boston. Somerset Owl was an overweight poet, literary genius, Harvard alum, and a lover of young U.S. Marines.

I met Owl for the first time when I was eighteen and in love with somebody he knew, a beanpole of a gentleman who loved to fuck me but who wanted no part of a long-term relationship. At that time, I was too young to understand the dynamics of casual romance (or the "fuck buddy" syndrome), and so made many dramatic scenes, some of which included running into the arms of the all-understanding Owl, who more often than not told me things that I did not want to hear, namely that Jack the Beanpole was hopeless, that he needed variety in his love life and that the last thing he wanted to do was settle down with one person.

During one counseling session, I let Owl suck my cock when he let me spend the night in his place. Since he lived close to Jack, running to Owl's place whenever I was upset with Jack was easy. Owl had a rustic-looking apartment on top of the most popular gay bar in Boston, Sporter's on Cambridge Street. The apartment was a haven for cockroaches; they covered his bed, kitchen cabinets, bureau drawers and closets. Owl cultivated them for the most part although he did have a preying mantis on hand to eat the overflow. But his preying mantis never ate enough of the roaches to reduce the population significantly, so hundreds of bugs were always running rampant.

Owl's blowjob failed because I could not focus on anything but Jack. I was also distracted because roaches were crawling up my leg and belly as he sucked me. Some were even trying to crawl up my cock. It was all I could do to keep from shaking them off or scratching where they had been. As a result, I could not settle into getting sucked at all, so Owl and I both wound up cuddling while doing battle with the roaches as well as the ones dropping off the ceiling into his loft bed.

The next morning, Owl made breakfast and we ate by a window overlooking Boston's Cambridge Street. Then he took out a stack of tarot cards. It was my first tarot card reading, and I was impressed by his ability, even if he told me to forget Jack. "Jack," he told me then, "is a beanstalk to nowhere, big dick or no big dick."

But I'm getting way off course. When Owl read my cards in Philly many years later, the plague came up. Of course, that's all Owl thought about then, as I noted in my July 12th entry: "...All Somerset Owl talks about is the Gay Plague. He's afraid to meet anyone for sex because of it. As a result, he seems very frustrated and unhappy..." In the actual Reading, Owl told me I would tailor my sex life to fit the "current health situation," meaning of course, what the drag queen talked about months before when he mentioned sperm rotting the brain. Which wasn't true at all. Regardless of both warnings, I was still continuing to meet people, and had even recently discovered the delights of a nearby arcade, where teenagers and young men congregated by the dozens to play pinball and video games.

My method in those days was to scan the arcade for a suitable boy, then stand by him as if fascinated by his playing skill, or as if I were impatient to play the game myself. Usually, I'd exchange a few words with the boy in order to measure his friendliness potential: if he was taciturn and uptight or seemed suspicious of strangers, I'd move on, but if I got a small indication of friendliness and openness, I stayed put until I felt the time was right to hand him the note I'd written in my apartment and had folded inside an envelope.

"—Hey, you seem like a cool dude, cool enough to appreciate the fact that I have a great porno collection and a VCR. Look, I invite you to give me a call if you want to come up to my place and watch a film. The truth is, I'd also like to blow you—no strings attached, no reciprocation. I'm a friendly guy and you'll feel comfortable in my place. So, please call me at 226-0808. but give me time to get there before you call."

I had put the note inside a sealed envelope because that bought time in case the friendly prospect turned out to be a crazy homophobe. By the time a homophobe unsealed the envelope and read the note, I'd be across the street and inside my apartment lobby, time enough to beat any mad dash on his part to track me down. The one existing danger, of course, was that an enraged prospect would follow me into the lobby and show the note to the doorman, thereby creating fuel for the doormen's round table of gossip. This was worth the risk, however, since many guys who hung out in arcades were rather sexy in a strange way and always up for the adventure I had in mind.

I met many guys this way. Before my card reading at Owl's, I landed a Native American boy, about 18 or 19, five-eleven. He was very nice and wore a pair of sexy shorts that were easy to unzip and slide down around his ankles. His dick was long and slender and stayed hard even after I sucked him off two times. When he came he not only shot all over himself, he hit my bookcase and one of the paintings on the wall. I gave him my telephone number and urged him to call me whenever he was in town, but I never heard from him again.

At this stage of the game, I was still trying to track down psychic Lucy Jackie. But I wasn't having much luck because she was always with a client; if not that, then her answering machine was always on. She was putting me on hold indefinitely, and I was feeling frustrated because I now wanted to ask her about the Gay Plague, and whether or not I was infected, and who among my friends had it, and so many other things. I had to find out what was going on.

In the meantime, Jason came into my life again.

July 15

I slip out of my apartment and see Jason walking up 13th Street. I assume he's going to the train terminal, so I call his name and he stops and turns around. We walk to the corner of 13th and Market; as we stop at the intersection he tells me he got my letter. I tell him I'm glad he got it on a Saturday morning when he could read it in relative peace. Then I ask him when he got into the city.

"Four this afternoon," he says.

"Four o'clock!" I repeat, wondering who he spent the time with. He senses my distress and hesitancy in walking him any further and makes a not-so-subtle plea that I stay. Along the way, the only two people we pass are two gay men holding hands and laughing—a rare sight in provincial Philly. At the terminal, I sense his mood: he can see that I suspect that he has a new lover. There's a sheepish look on his face, and he can barely look me in the eye.

We sit down on one of the terminal benches. "Do you have a new lover?" he asks.

"Do you think getting a new lover is as easy as shopping in K-mart? Look, there have been lots of attractive people and good sex, and sometimes nice affection, but no magic!"

"Same with me," he says.

He tells me about a man he's seeing, a Ukrainian archeologist at the University of Pennsylvania, who speaks with an accent. Obviously, it's the archeologist whom he spent the afternoon with, and I want to know details: "Is he fat or thin, ugly or handsome, rich or poor?"

"Chubby," Jason says, "chubby and blond." At least the archeologist didn't walk him to the train station—that would smack of true affection. I make a mistake and tell Jason that I'm always bummed out on Sundays. "Sunday used to be our day, you know," and he says, "Well, I'll make it up to you next Sunday."

I think, but do not ask him: "Does that mean I can suck your dick?"

Dream: Another man and I are begging Jason to let one of us suck his cock. Jason lets me do the honors (I suppose because it's been so long since I've sucked him), but when I go down on him his cock resembles the sword of a swordfish and is as dry as a stick and about as sensual.

Dream No. 2: After the swordfish episode, I'm in the bathroom combing my hair when out pops a tiny white bird or dove. It can barely fly and is about as big as a butterfly.

One week later. Sunday. Jason comes over. I take him out to dinner and tell him what my big dream in life is: to live with him in another city. His face lights up at this ('seems to,' because I can never be sure about anything when it comes to him). "Well, I guess if it's karmic—at least it'll be out of Philadelphia; this city's the pits," he says.

After dinner, I ask him if he wants to go back to the apartment with me (my code line for "Want a blowjob?") and he says no, that he has to get back to his house in Lansdale before his parents return from New York. I sense this may be a lie. The fact is, he's probably unsure about starting up sex with me again, unsure about where it will lead. Or perhaps he planned on visiting the archeologist. Or better yet, maybe the archeologist has already sucked him dry and he has no energy left.

I go home and jerk off and think evil thoughts about the archeologist. I also begin to wish I knew a psychic or a gypsy who could put a spell on all the men Jason comes into contact with. Everyone I meet talks about "letting go" and accepting destiny. Nobody yet has offered me any alternative but to accept what is. The fifty dollars I gave Miss Mitchell towards the crosses perhaps produced 50% good luck; that's why Jason is so ready to have dinner with me but not go the full route and get his cock sucked. Lucy Jackie has no powers except in doing astrological charts, even though she claims her Will is so strong she can make a person break their leg if she thinks on it hard enough.

Is that arrogance, or what? That's why she says she has to be careful not to think "the wrong thing," because she can do some heavy damage. But that's why I need to speak to her because I need to get her to make Jason want me to suck his cock.

But what if heavy damage is what I want? Where do I go?

Somerset Owl does not believe in God or Love. "I believe in human beings, relationships, and boys' asses," he told me when I went to see him again for a second reading. Owl told me that I will emotionally withdraw from a relationship because of sexual restlessness. The end result of this, he said, will be added dedication to my work. This in turn will make me prosperous. "The World" card turned up which means liberation, cosmic consciousness. He sees a long-term affair for me in the future (within the next three or four months) providing I don't withdraw because of fear.

Before I let Owl read my cards, I paid a storefront gypsy to read my palm. The truth is, I am becoming addicted to gypsies and to a certain extent I am worried about that. I was walking around town when I saw this woman's shop and I stopped dead in my tracks; it was too difficult to stay away. She told me that people stand between Jason and me, that they want to keep us apart, but that we will be together someday. She said nothing about letting go, which made me breathe easy. Still, I felt there was something canned about her delivery, though I was still excited by her take on the situation. When I saw Owl later that day, I couldn't resist asking him for another reading; I guess I am a glutton for punishment, especially considering that Owl's first reading left me feeling depressed. But I felt that if he could only confirm the gypsy's reading I would start feeling really good and stop worrying so much about Jason.

Unfortunately, Owl's reading threw out the whole works when he predicted a withdrawal from a relationship. All of this has made me fairly crazy, and now I don't know what to do or whom to believe. Owl is naturally negative and takes a dim view of anything like "living happily ever after": he even tempers his most positive views with so many "tough reality pies" that they don't seem positive at all. I want to believe the gypsy more than Owl, so that's why I returned to her the following day for a more elaborate read-out, plus to tell her of Owl's reading and get feedback on that. I have so many questions. How can two sets of tarot cards say different things, or two psychics for that matter?

The gypsy wanted twenty bucks for a full card reading, plus money for candles she said she'd burn for "spiritual work" I had to have done to change "bad luck" regarding Jason.

"Bad luck? I thought you said things were going to work out? I thought you said we were going to be together?" I told her.

She said that "things change" and that the negativity around Jason is so high that things might not work out if I don't let her burn some candles.

"How much do the candles cost?" I asked, flush red in the face and about to burst from more frustration.

"Forty dollars," she said. In the background I heard her little gypsy children talking, making me wonder whether they were playing "tarot cards" on little tea tables or practicing reading each other's palms. Then it hit me that maybe this gypsy was a relative of Miss Mitchell's and heard that I was an easy mark, and that's why she was now talking about candles and curses and money.

I declined the offer, deciding that I'd work to abolish the negativity myself. After all, anybody can burn candles; it doesn't take a gypsy to do that. Hadn't I gone into St. John's Church nearly every week for the last several months, burning candles before a statue of Our Lady of Fatima? Of course, it was the spiritual side of my love for Jason I was thinking about when I lit candles, not my desire to touch and caress him.

One of Miss Mitchell's predictions, after she told me to buy the houseplant, was that something extraordinary would happen on May 16. May 16 that year was a Sunday, a day on which I usually did my laundry in the Adelphia laundry room. As it happened, it was the day that I met Peter, a sexy Italian who'd been living in the same building for a number of years and whom I must have passed a hundred times in the lobby. Peter had dark hair and a 1910-style curly mustache that swirled around in a big spiral. Soft-spoken, unassuming, quietly masculine, Peter appeared—or was"sent" to me—just as I was tying up loose ends with Jason. My meeting him at that time had all the elements of what some call"perfect timing."

Seeing Peter a lot was an easy thing to do, considering that he lived only four floors above me. Within a short time, he was inviting me to dinner, cooking all the meals himself despite the fact that he had limited cooking skills—burnt pork chops were his specialty, as were fish sticks, crab cakes, sardine sandwiches or tuna and noodle dishes.

Peter introduced me to the pleasures of rum 'n' Coke, a drink I rarely cared about since I was mainly a wine person. He was generous with his food, his time, and even his money, lending or giving me cash whenever I came up short. This was happening a lot since the law firm laid me off and I found myself, once again, in the unemployment line. Sex between us was also abundant, even if it was mostly one-sided: I had now become the pursued, the beloved, the one who reclined on a sofa and munched an apple as I was being worked over. I was Peter's Jason in a sense, though I felt a genuine affection for him and did not torture him in quite the same way that I allowed Jason to torture me.

Two short dreams of Jason: I dreamt he came to me on a motorcycle. He was very muscular and swaggered when he walked. We stood face to face and engaged in telepathic communication. Then suddenly the dream switched to a large lake around a wooded area. I stood on a dock when somebody offered to sell me a canoe for fifteen bucks. I took the canoe and prepared to row out to Jason's house, which was across the lake at a considerable distance, reminding me in a way of Joseph Conrad's *The Heart of Darkness*. But as I gazed into the black where I knew his house to be, I got a feeling of entrapment and isolation, as if Jason were in prison or lost in a vast wilderness.

On the 29th, I visited Owl, who told me that I should concentrate on fiction and not journalism. During my visit, he lashed out at organized religion and spoke of "jerking God off or fucking God in the ass." I forget what brought this on. Perhaps I told him that I believed in a Supreme Being or a Cosmic Source. Anyway, the 29th was also the night that Peter spent the night with me, an experience that inspired me to write: "...I suppose it would be nice to fall in love with Peter. He is a good man, dependable, unique even. We've had some nice times together, and he gives me space when I want it. But I can't fall in love. My thoughts are still with Jason."

The last couple of days spent in mild distress. Long days cruising arcades, rushing back to the apartment waiting for phone calls. The monotonous cycle continues. Manpower, the temporary employment agency, has no jobs, and I'm too exhausted to put on a tie in this hot weather and walk the streets. An idea for a new novel haunts me but I tell myself that I can't write unless I know I have a steady job. Peter keeps me fed...last night we cooked a steak in my apartment.

Afterwards, I roamed the city looking for sex. No scores, except that earlier today a handsome guy came onto me in a peep show and suggested that we watch a film together. He was kind and eager with a nice cock, and he had me jack off into his mouth. I loved holding his head while he blew me.

Just as I finished the above paragraph, a sexy blond teenager I gave my telephone number to earlier tonight telephoned me.

He was breathing heavy and blowing wind into the receiver when I asked who it was. When he told me his name and what he looked like, I suggested he come up for a blowjob. He said he'd be up in ten minutes, but the Nordic lay never showed.

Later in the evening, feeling anxious and horny, I roamed the streets of the hot and humid city. Before long, on 12th Street, I spotted a blond male slumped inside a concrete tree bed. Going over to him, I noticed he was pretty well out of it. My attempts at waking him brought no response until I began to rub my foot against his legs while sitting casually next to him and pretending he was a friend who'd passed out. Finally, when he bolted awake, I recognized him: he was a sailor I had met some three months before in a bar. I brought him home, undressed him, and proceeded to massage his long lean body.

Despite his drunkenness, he was able to maintain a hard-on whenever I blew him, which was on and off until the sun came up. What I liked about the sailor was his expressiveness: whenever I'd lick his balls he'd let out a loud moan and then kick one of his legs against the wall, waking my Polish neighbor who then took it upon himself to fuck his girlfriend.

It took the sailor a long time to shoot his load, a fact I didn't mind since sucking him was such a sweet treat: a steady albeit slow stream of pre-cum, as delectable to the palate as the juice from a honey-dew, kept oozing out of his cockhead. I love men and boys whose libidos are sky-high; it's even better when they let you have them whenever you want. And this sailor was up every time I reached for him.

When the sun came up I only half-cared that I'd lost Jason and that Ken from Scranton was seeing me on a less regular basis. Besides, the sailor told me that the fleet—the U.S.S.. Forestall—was in the Navy Yard and that he and his friends would be in Philly for at least three months.

"Don't worry," he said, "I'll keep your number and even pass it to my friends, so don't be surprised if somebody calls you late at night and wants to come over. You suck soooo good."

CAPTAIN, MY CAPTAIN

Tony Anthony

When I was a boy I idolized my dad, as most boys do. He was a big man physically, about six foot I guess, and rugged rather than handsome. He was a sailor, a tugboat captain, and that made him seem extra special in my young mind. Unlike many tugboat captains he was seldom home. His boat was an ocean-going salvage tug and that meant he was away from home for long periods. A big salvage job anywhere in the world could claim him for months, and when it was over he might tie up or anchor in the nearest port and wait for another possible job.

My mother died when I was very young and I lived with an aunt. She rented two rooms to her brother; one for me and one for him. She hated males and gave me a lot of hell. Once when my Dad was home I told him I was unhappy and wanted to live with him. He said I couldn't live on the boat, and asked me to settle down and be a good boy.

I only once saw Dad naked. It happened when I was very young and I wandered into the bathroom when he was drying himself off. He looked terrific, a muscular and hairy giant with a big dick that hung down low and ended in a heavy round head.

My own dick was not cut and I remember taking a long time to work out what had happened to Dad. It was hard to believe that his skin had been intentionally cut off and, for a while, I thought maybe he'd lost it at sea somehow. Maybe it was something they did to sailors or captains to make them special.

He had a strong sense of duty and his behavior around me was always perfectly correct. In my daydreams he was always available and we'd do all sorts of male things together, the way I imagined other boys did with their fathers. The door to his room was usually locked when he was at sea, but one day I found it open and was sorting through his underwear drawer when my aunt walked in.

"What are you doing?" she demanded.

"Nothing," I said, always afraid of her.

"Get out," she said.

The door was always locked after that, and male things acquired a sort of magic that stayed in my mind like a memory of a perfect day.

Another memory that stayed with me was my father coming into my room late one night and sitting on the edge of my bed. Waking from a deep sleep I asked him what was wrong.

"A big salvage job has come up," he said. "I'm sorry son, I have to go. Maybe next time I'll stay longer, huh?"

He leaned over and kissed me on the forehead. It was something I often remembered, as he never did it again.

A lot of time passed and when my eighteenth birthday was coming up he wrote and asked what I wanted as a gift. Living with my aunt had become more and more unpleasant so, not expecting to get it, I wrote that the one thing I really wanted was an apartment of my own.

His next letter, to my surprise, said he knew a guy in town and would see what he could do. And a month after my birthday I had my own apartment!

It was in a tough part of town and was no showplace, but to me it was like heaven. I wrote the old man, thanking him sincerely, and saying I had a bedroom for him on his next visit home.

My increasing gayness had become very hard to deny to myself, and I revelled in the freedom to stack shelves with my gay books and stick posters of male physiques on the walls.

When my Dad wrote that he was coming home I, at first, decided to leave the gay stuff in full view and let him react in whatever manner he chose. It would be a good way for him to find out about me, I told myself; straight out and up front, as it should be.

The night before he was due I told myself it might be better to let him know gradually. After all, he was a big hairy sailor and he might not like the idea that his son was a fag. Cursing myself as a coward I took the incriminating stuff into my room and hid it away.

Next day I had to go downtown for job interviews so I left a note on the door reading, Dad -- Keys in bookshop on corner. Ask for Bob. I'm back tonight.

Approaching home that night I knew that changes were in

the air, and I wondered what they would bring. Dad looked fine, tan from real sun, big and happy. We shook hands and his grip was hard. There were beers in the fridge and I cooked stuff to eat and we watched Superbowl games I'd taped for him.

It was an evening of males together and I loved it. For the first time he seemed willing to see me as a man and he opened up, telling me about tug work and the difficulties in keeping a crew out of trouble while they waited for another race to a salvage job. First tug to arrive could get the big dollars.

Both of us soaked up some beers and I went to bed feeling extra good that my dad was with me in my own apartment. In the morning I woke with a big hard on and an urgent need to pee. Holding my dick I lurched to the bathroom and found the door open and sounds of my dad humming while he shaved. I'd never shared a bathroom with him in the past and I wondered how to handle it now.

"Dad," I said through the half-open door. "I've got to pee."

"Well, come in if you want to," he said. "I'm easy."

My dick was still hard, angling up through my shorts. Confused and embarrassed, I held it in one hand and went in. Dad was totally naked, looking in the mirror and shaving. Going straight to the can I leaned forward and pushed my dick down until I could pee into the water.

"I got used to being naked in my cabin on the tug," Dad said. "Got to liking the feeling too. You don't mind?"

"No, no. Suits me fine," I said, fighting my erection.

"You've got a good length there," Dad said, looking at me. "Maybe you take after me."

He half turned and I saw his dick curving down heavily out of a dark bush of hair. The big round head was there, just as I remembered it.

"Your mother wanted you circumcised," he said. "But I wouldn't let her get it done."

"Thanks," I said. His frankness and open display of his genitals was so unlike him in the past I didn't know what it all meant. There was a pause while the only sound came from my pee hitting the water.

"When you've finished," Dad said. "Sit down a minute. There's something I want you to know."

It sounded ominous and I wondered what sort of bad news was coming. Eventually I was able to sit on the lid of the can and say, "I've finished."

There was a long silence while he continued shaving.

"I don't like to keep things from you," he said. "Now that you're eighteen."

I waited, and murmured, "Uh huh."

"I'm gay," he said. "Used to be bisexual I guess, but now I'm exclsuively gay."

I was speechless.

"Maybe it was being at sea," he said, smiling. "You know what they say about sailors."

I managed a short little laugh.

"So what do you say?" he asked. "Tell me you're disgusted and I'll be very disappointed."

"I ... I'm gay too," I said. "I've been wondering about telling you."

"I had that feeling about you," he said. "Something told me you were gay."

Thinking of all those years when I'd wanted some sort of real contact with him I said, "Why didn't you say something before this?"

"You weren't eighteen before this."

"I wanted you. I needed you."

"And I wanted you," he said. "It nearly broke my fuckin' heart but I wasn't going to do anything while you were so young."

"I wish you had done something," I said.

"It wouldn't have been right," he said.

He was standing in front of me now, his big dick hanging in my face. It was rugged, like him, and his balls behind it were bulbous and hairy. My own dick was semi-erect, adding to the all-male atmosphere of naked and near-naked bodies, with sexuality on hold. I wanted to kiss his dick and take it into my mouth, swallow this basic part of my father and keep it deep inside myself. Instead I did nothing while thoughts and impulses battled inside my head.

"Tell you what," Dad said. "Wash yourself and we'll have breakfast, huh? You may need time to get used to this."

We had breakfast wearing nothing but towels around the

waist. Sitting opposite him and drinking coffee all I could think of was his sexuality and its beauty. In my mind I could see his crotch and his massive dick and hairy balls. All I wanted was to touch him everywhere, kiss every part of him and absorb him so he became a permanent part of me. Then when he went back to sea I would still have something of him.

Instead of doing it I just sat there sipping coffee and talking small talk.

Suddenly he said, "My god, you're a handsome boy. I'm proud of you."

My face burned, I could feel the heat in it, and I wanted to say the same to him.

He looked into my eyes and, in his deep voice said quietly, "I need you now, son. What d'you say we make up for some lost time?"

Standing up I led the way to my bedroom. Wondering what I ought to do I felt embarrassed and confused. Who does what when you're going to have sex with your dad? Maybe it would be best to simply relax and let things happen.

Dropping my towel I sat on the edge of my bed. Dad stood in front of me and dropped his towel. His groin was filling my gaze and I just stared at it, taking in its bulky maleness. He put his hands on my head and stroked my hair. There was a long pause.

Putting my fingers on the inside of his thigh I gently stroked the dark hair. His balls moved, lifting themselves a little in their skin bag. His dick, already long, began lengthening and stiffening. It seemed to be reaching out, trying to touch me.

At long last I was on the verge of getting what I had yearned for during the past many years. Still I hesitated, uncertain of whether I was ready to dive into this situation.

Then I pushed my face forward and buried it in his wiry pubic hair. It felt good, perfectly male, and it smelled faintly of good masculine things.

His dick erected itself quickly, reaching forward and angling up stiffly. Kissing my way along its shaft I reached the big round head, darkening now and developing a sudden flare and thick ridge. It looked flawless, dominant and godlike.

"Dad," I said quietly. "You look perfect."

"Nobody's perfect, son," he said. "But you look pretty good

too."

He sat next to me and put his arm around my shoulders. With his free hand he touched my dick and a current of electricity buzzed into me. Parting my legs I let him cup my balls in his hand, and another shock went through me.

His hand fondling my dick and balls made a picture that summed up a lot of what I wanted, so I put my hand on his dick and cradled his balls, completing my ideal picture of father and son.

When we were lying back on the bed I produced a condom and showed it to him, not speaking. He nodded and it was the sort of sensible thing you'd hope for from your dad. His dick was thick and rugged now, a rigid pole ready for its proper function. Carefully I rolled the condom down all the way to his balls.

He did the same for me and we lay together for a while. I kissed his lips and fingered the nipples on his hairy chest, but all the time I had my mind on his dick ... wanting it.

Kissing my way down his body my lips came to the round head of his dick. Opening my mouth I let him enter me and the reality of the situation came to me at the same time. I was with my wonderful father, naked with him, his wonderful dick was in me, a part of him was now a part of me. It was bliss.

His hand was on my back, sliding down to my butt, and tracing lightly over the bulges. A finger entered the cleft briefly and brushed against the hair around my pucker.

Hoping he didn't want to fuck me, I felt like telling him I was a virgin down there. Instead of talking I fingered his balls and then felt for his pucker. He parted his legs a little to aid me and I found the spot. He gave a little gasp. Did he want me to fuck him? It seemed too much to hope for.

Tightening my mouth around his thick dick I moved along his shaft, loving the sensuous feeling in my lips and on my tongue.

"Yes," he said, quietly, one hand stroking my head and neck. "That's great, son."

Speeding up my movements I felt his stomach muscles tensing and his balls tightening up against his shaft. He parted his legs, flattening his thighs, and I stroked them with a hand before feeling again for his pucker. It pursed itself firmly, not letting anything enter.

"Yes, yes," he said. "Oh God that's good."

The muscles in his gut formed hard ridges and I got an idea of his physical strength. He was obviously a strong man and I hoped he would never want to hit me. His hips started moving convulsively, making thrusts that pushed his dick farther into my mouth. I wished I could take the whole of his shaft deep into my throat but it was too bulky.

Deep in his cleft his pucker opened a little, enough to admit the tip of my finger. I worked it in little twitches, stimulating the sensitive areas of his ring. It was a trick I had discovered for myself long ago.

"Fuckin' hell," he gasped, and began writhing on the bed, twisting his upper body from side to side. His breathing became noisy, drawing eager intakes of air, sounding expectant, sensing that something big was going to happen.

My own groin felt as though it was blocked by a lump of lead and I realized how excited I had become. Lifting my mouth off Dad's dick I looked at him.

"Yes," he said, understanding quickly. "Let me do you."

I lay back and he brushed his lips along my chest and gut and I felt my rubbered erection enter his mouth. The head of my dick slid against soft wet tissues and the sensuous thrills drilled urgently into me. With his head at my groin his butt was within reach and I played fingers over the bulges. Things were happening quickly. I wanted all of him. Wanted to fuck him and hold him and suck his dick and kiss his butt and smell his armpits and nip his nipples and be above him and under him all at the same time. He was my father for chrissakes and I wanted to crush him in my arms until he became a part of me that could never separate from me again! I wanted him to crush me too, in a bear hug that would never let go.

My back was arching, forcing my head down and my chest up, shock after shock was zipping through my dick and up into my brain. I could hear my breathing, sucking air in urgent takes. My eyes closed and I knew my face was screwed up in a grimace that bared my teeth. The ecstatic delights flashing through my body were like pains, ice cold agonies that changed into burning heat glowing red behind my closed eyes.

"Fucking hell!" I sobbed. "Oh my god."

I felt desperate to see my father's dick again. Putting my hands on his head I lifted him away and pushed him down beside me on the bed. Scrambling up onto my knees I straddled his thighs and grabbed the condom off his massive dick, freeing it so I could see every detail of it and watch everything it did. And I tore the condom off my own dick and let it stand rigid, straining, red head nearly bursting with the pressing need to climax. Both dicks were wet and slippery, my hands racing along their lengths, racing forward and back as fast as I could drive them.

Dad was shouting something I couldn't make out, something that was expressing his passion and ecstasy. I was raising my butt off his thighs and letting it fall on them again, adding to the sensuous excitement that was burning in my body.

"Fuck, fuck, fuck," I heard myself saying.

"Yes, yes," Dad was saying, forcing the words as he gasped, his head rolling from side to side.

"Oh fucking hell," I wheezed, wanting to thrust my dick into his butt or mouth or something but wanting to see it too while it strained to deliver, big and rigid; like Dad's dick, big too, thick and rugged and hard in my frantically sliding hand, its round head bulging and purple.

Moving my butt to one side I got the cleft over his thigh and felt his hairy warmth stimulate my pucker. The electric shock was unbelievable, sending ecstasies flashing through my body and up into my mind.

I wanted to come, I burned to come, and the big man under me needed the same. The pressure built to incredible heights and hung there, poised, waiting for the final touch that would send it bursting over the top. My hands raced, searing the nerves, forcing them without mercy and at last ... at long last ... something opened inside me and the first jolt of semen loaded itself into the base of my dick and shot out in a stream of white followed by another and another.

The sight of my spunk seemed to trigger my Dad's orgasm. His big body bucked under me, thrusting his dick convulsively, semen jetting out of the purple tip of his dick, thick splurges landing wetly on his belly and chest.

My semen traced white lines looping over and under his emissions, merging with them, while the two of us gasped and grunted in our frenzied exertions.

And so it went until everything slowed down and lessened and eventually ceased.

Our breathing returned to normal and we blinked our eyes and looked at each other and relaxed.

"Fucking hell," I sighed, and flopped down next to Dad. "That was something."

"I know what you mean," he said. "It sure was something."

"It's been so terrific I can hardly believe it," I said. "I mean everything ... you and me together ... at last."

"It's been great," he said.

"I don't want you to go to sea again," I said. "You can stay here."

"I'm sorry," he said. "But I'll have to go sometime. I'll be back though."

"You better be back," I said. "Now we're together."

"I'll be back, son," he said, looking into my eyes. "Nothing'll stop me now."

SERVICING SARGE

Aaron Mitchell

A sense of humor doesn't get you very far in this man's Army. I learned that shortly after joining. I learned a lot of stuff, in fact. But the bit about humor ... that was one of my hardest lessons.

Joking around has always been my way of dealing with tension, handling unpleasant situations, generally coping. So when Sarge assigned me latrine detail, and I nearly gagged at the thought, I naturally said, "Sounds like a pretty shitty job."

Christ, I was just trying to break the tension. Sarge didn't see it that way, though. "Did you say something, Private?" he asked.

His tone of voice left me no doubt what my answer should be. "No, sir. Just joking, Sir."

"Drop and give me 50!" the sergeant barked. "This ain't David Letterman!"

As I was cleaning the latrine—and it really was a shitty job!—my mind wandered. And as my mind wandered, my dick rose. At first, I didn't know what thoughts had put starch in my stiffer. Then I realized I had been thinking about the way Rosenman's butt had looked when he was getting out of his skivvies. *Christ! Maybe I really am gay!* I thought to myself.

For the last half year in particular, ever since Todd and I messed around after my eighteenth birthday celebration, I had been filled with thoughts that made me wonder about my sexuality. I mean, messing around with a buddy to give each other a little relief, that's one thing. But actually getting turned on by asses, by dicks, by six-pack abs toned by weight-lifting ... hell, that kind of reaction can get a guy the kind of reputation I didn't think I wanted.

Although I couldn't deny the way my stiffer had throbbed to full erection the night before at the sight of Rosenman standing there, his pale, firm ass-globes jutting out toward me as if they were just begging me to stuff my pork between those cheeks and plunge in. I had sprung a major boner and dived under the covers without even taking a piss first, just to get my embarrassing woody out of sight.

And then, when I'd surreptitiously beaten my meat beneath the covers, it was images of Rosenman's buns that kept flooding my mind even while I tried to think about more acceptable turn-ons. As I jacked on my joint as silently as I could, I tried to keep my breathing in check, tried not to give away what I was doing, and tried my damnedest not to let the pictures of butts and hard dicks race through my mind.

But it was a losing battle. I couldn't keep my breathing calm, couldn't keep my hand from racing wildly as my balls got closer to spewing their creamy load, and above all couldn't keep from picturing hunks of man-mounds just waiting for me to slip my raging dick between them.

I'd spurted a hefty load of jizz between the sheets ... and that had been just the night before ... yet here I was, my mind wandering as I cleaned the latrine, and my dick throbbing to hefty inflation all over again. It was throbbing and pulsating as demandingly, as raucously as if I hadn't whipped out a frothy load just the night before.

I finally gave up trying to fight it and figured, I'm in the latrine—I might as well take a minute off to dump another load of jizz. Ain't gonna take me long, the way this sucker is throbbing.

So I opened my fly and hauled out my throbber. Spitting into my hand, I wrapped my fist around my meat and began whaling away at it. As I did, those same images glared at me in my mind's eye:

Rosenman, bending over to get into his footlocker, his tight butt firm and tempting, his browneye puckered and winking at me from between those twin manmounds of glory.

Simpson, who had the biggest dick I'd ever seen, and uncircumcised too, idly fisting his half-hard hose as he sat at the edge of the bed reading a letter from his sweetie at home, the pre-cum oozing in viscous droplets off the end of his swelling rod.

Irens, whose massive dick appeared perenially half-hard, probably because of its size, and who always appeared ready to prong anyone unsuspecting who bent over in front of him.

Yeah, there was a lot of grist for the fantasy mill around the barracks, but they were all the wrong kind of fantasies. I wanted to be thinking of chicks, and here my mind was filled with what I thought of as "faggot fantasies." What did that make me?

What it made me right then was hot. My throbbing meat seemed to sizzle as I stroked back and forth along the length of my vein-ringed shaft. I gripped my rod tighter and began rhythmically clenching and unclenching my hand as it stroked along the length of my humongous erection. I couldn't remember my hard-on ever being harder, or the size of it ever being larger, than it felt that day.

As I thought of prodding my stiffer up Rosenman's unsuspecting bung, another thought—an even more unacceptable one—popped into my head: Simpson's huge meat invading my tight bunghole. Christ, if wanting to pork Rosenman didn't make me a confirmed homosexual, this new image certainly must! But the more I tried to put the thought out of my head, the firmer it took hold.

My balls felt swollen, heavy, bursting, like they had boulders in them, or a full gallon of cream, or both. And now my anus started to pucker and throb. I dropped my drawers completely and, licking the middle finger of my left hand, took aim at my quivering bung.

"Private! Atten-hut!"

It was Sarge!

My middle finger had just pierced my rosy rim, probing for all those nerves I had read about. I pulled my stinky finger out of my back door and dropped my dick with the other hand. Yet there was no way I could deny what I'd been doing.

At least Sarge had no way of knowing what mental pictures had accompanied my self-pleasure ... I hoped. I kept imagining that somehow he knew, though ... that somehow he could guess what thoughts had been blazoned on my brain as my hand kept stroking my meat and my finger went questing for those buried nerves.

"What were you doing, Private?" Sarge asked.

"Taking a break from latrine duty, Sir."

"Did I give you permission?"

"No, Sir."

"Does this kind of work turn you on?" he sneered.

"No, Sir."

"What does turn you on?" he asked, looking at my dick, which seemed to have grown harder than ever.

I didn't answer. Sarge studied me a minute. Then he opened his fly and hauled out his wanger.

"Does this turn you on, Private?" he asked.

I still didn't answer. Sarge pulled a rubber out of his pocket. Snapping it into place, he advanced toward me, then said, "Drop to your knees." When I had done so, he barked, "Service this." He jerked his thumb toward his swollen weapon ... as if I needed to be shown what "this" referred to! I was a little less sure what he wanted me to do to it ... but it was obvious from the rubber that he was looking for more than a hand-job, and he'd ordered me to my knees. It was pretty easy to conclude he was after a blow-job.

Opening my mouth, I hesitantly approached Sarge's manmeat. If I took it into my mouth, I really was a cocksucker. Then Sarge punched his hips forward, and his meat jabbed into my mouth. Without conscious thought, I closed my lips and entrapped the meat, compressing my lips around the spongy pole.

My immediate reaction was how different a dick feels between your lips than it does when you just hold it in your hand. Instinct took over, and I began to suck. I drew Sarge's warm, living flesh as deep into my mouth as I could get it and trusted to instinct to tell me what to do from there. His rod felt so fine as it skewered its way into my mouth.

As my suckling lips fastened tighter around Sarge's beefy slab, he chuckled—not so sneeringly now—and said,"I thought ya'd like that."

I did like it! It horrified me, but there was no getting away from it. My new definition of "pure good times" was slurping on Sarge's swollen gristle. Growing more daring, I took yet more of the monster meat—and it was big, by anyone's account—deeper into my mouth, swallowing greedily.

Sarge began ratcheting his hips back and forth, dickfeeding me deeper and filling my gullet with his swollen pillar. As I sucked ever lower on that bloated shaft I had already fallen in love with, my nose approached his coarse curlies, ringing the base of his hard-on.

They exuded a raunchy odor, rancid with the day's

accumulated sweat. Yet, to add to the day's surprises, I wasn't grossed out by the stink, I was turned on even more. The fetid stench rose up my nostrils to my brain, inflaming me, setting both my brain and my balls on fire.

Easing off his dickshaft till just the tip remained in my mouth's grip, I slathered my tongue round and round his dickhead. My tongue probed for his recessed piss-hole, dipping into it to taunt him time and again. Inspired, I reached for Sarge's balls and began rhythmically squeezing them the way I sometimes liked to do to myself.

"Careful, boy. Don't mess up the family jewels," Sarge warned, his gruff voice mellower than it had sounded earlier. I dared glance up and saw his eyes were half-lidded, pure pleasure painted across his features.

Smiling to myself, I basked in the glow of accomplishment. Though new at this, I was obviously turning into one righteous cocksucker, if I could mellow out old Sarge like this and make him smile like that. Not bad for a barely-legal virgin from a small town in Indiana.

I tightened my liplock and ratcheted up the suction a few notches. Speeding the motion of my lips, I sucked Sarge faster as I sucked him harder. His dick speeded in and out of my mouth. My mouth hastened up and down his dickpole. There was nothing fancy or delicate about my sucking. There was certainly nothing experienced or well-practiced about it. But it was earnest and eager. It was insistent. It was more than merely willing. And Sarge was obviously having one hellaciously good time.

To keep things interesting, I varied my action. Now I sucked on just the head, so my tongue could run circles around his dickhead and probe his piss-hole. Now I took as much as I could into my mouth and tried to swallow him clear down to my belly. And now I took a middling amount in and tried to suck with a bit more finesse, varying the suction and trying other tricks.

A few minutes more and I glanced up again ... just in time to see Sarge's smile broaden as he had a new thought."Stand up, boy!" he barked.

I hesitated. I didn't want to release my liplock on his delicious meat ... and even with that yucky rubber, it was nothing but delicious, the way it filled my mouth and fulfilled my dreams.

"Now, Private!" His voice had the old steel and fire back in it. You didn't disobey that voice. I stood, letting go his dick, feeling terribly empty as the column of flesh-wrapped steel slid out of my mouth.

"Spread 'em! Bend over! Grab your ankles!" Sarge barked. "Bend your knees a little." Then I heard a spitting sound, and a nanosecond later something wet made contact with my rosy bung. Sarge's thumb followed his spit, rubbing it well into my rim, slipping into my puckerhole's grip and tantalizing nerves I hadn't known I had. Suddenly the void in my mouth, which had just lost its hold on that wonderful slab of meat, was nothing compared to the emptiness I felt in my asshole, which yearned to be filled with that same meat.

"You ready?" Sarge snickered, not waiting for an answer. He stood behind me, thumped his club of meat against my hole, and pushed forward. His weapon breached my defenses, but bolts of searing pain shot through me. My asshole caught fire. But up inside, where a phalanx of nerves I never knew I had resides far up in my gut, Sarge scratched an old familiar itch.

The more he pushed his rod in and out of me, the more he scratched that itch. And it was a funny thing, but the more he scratched it, the more it itched. But it itched so good! Even as it itched more, it began to feel satisfied at the same time.

I felt truly stuffed. His bloated meat spread my anal walls and filled every inch, every centimeter, every available area in my gut. It felt as if he was plunging so deep that his dickhead would pop up from my gullet at any moment. Then Sarge relaxed whatever minimal restraint he had been exercising, and he battered my bruised asshole with a vengeance.

"Gonna really let you have it, boy," he huffed as he energetically slammed in and out of me. "You can take it." Wham! he slammed into me again as he said it. Slap! went his balls as they swung against my asscheeks.

Suddenly, without my touching myself, my dick discharged like a fucking cannon. It was the most powerful, most explosive climax I had ever felt, and I hadn't had a hand anywhere near my dick.

A moment later, I felt Sarge's powerful weapon swell within

me, and then he exploded, sending a barrage of jism-shrapnel into the rubber.

When he pulled out, all I could say was, "Wow!"

"Your first time, wasn't it?" Sarge asked, laying a hand on my shoulder in an almost kindly way.

"Yes, Sir," I replied, almost forgetting protocol in the grip of sublime satisfaction.

"There's a lot of pleasure to be had in the Army," Sarge said.

"I never knew," I said simply.

Sarge understood. "Yeah, a lot of young men find themselves in the Army," he said.

I carefully wiped my weeping dick with some handy toilet paper as Sarge added, "The slogan is true, you know."

"How's that?" I asked.

"You know how it is here: we help you to 'Be all that you can be'."

"...I would come to find out that my fraternity brothers were very special boys, and very frisky, like me."

The Frisky Boys

A Memoir by
Kevin Bantan

STARbooks Press
Sarasota, Florida

> *"...our bellies together nestling,*
> *loins touched together,*
> *pressing and knowledgeable*
> *each other's hardness,*
> *and mine stuck out of my underwear....*
> *slowly began a love-match*
> *that continues in my imagination to this day...."*
> *—Allen Ginsberg, "Many Loves"*
> *about one-time lover Neal Cassady*

One

I guess that I could have called this memoir *A Son of the Circus*, but it wouldn't be original, or so I have been told. Besides, it would only begin to tell the story of a young life lived, if not to the fullest, at least to the sexiest. Maybe that's hyperbole. I'll let you decide. Anyway, this is my story, and you'll just have to take my word for it—although sometimes even I find it hard to do.

I really was born into the circus. Nothing grand, mind you, like Ringling or anything. The Raton Falls Circus mostly played the smaller cities of the east coast and near midwest, that the bigger companies wouldn't bother with. Names like Florence and Winston-Salem, Roanoke and Hagerstown. York, Wilkes-Barre, Binghamton, Syracuse. Names for places which all looked alike, because I never saw more than the identical dirt and scrubby grass of the fairgrounds where we performed. Well, 'we' was stretching it.

Mom told me that the elephants (there were only two) trumpeted for joy the night she delivered me. I thought that was kind of neat. Still do. I guess I'm not as jaded as I'd sometimes like to think, but that's not for lack of having tried, as you'll see.

My parents were acrobats with the circus. They almost got fired when mom got pregnant, because old man Wattley couldn't see how mom could continue to perform on the trapeze, while carrying around a coconut, as he called it. But she did. She hardly showed, actually. As a result, I was born healthy, if way small.

My earliest memories are of my folks dazzling me on those bars high above the ring, clad in lustrous, tight pink or sky blue costumes. I wore a matching unitard, even though I had no official function in the circus, except to look adorable for the paying customers. And with my golden blond curls and sparkling sapphire eyes I guess I did, because the audience seemed to find me irresistible. I loved wearing my second skin and did so most of the time. Unlike dad, I didn't wear a belt for support. There wasn't much to hold, of course. But I did wear a cup made of molded hard rubber over my boy parts, which dad had made for me, so that I would look like him down there. It made me proud to show off myself like that. And, in retrospect, it was pretty lewd-looking on a little boy. But in a circus you could get away with that and more.

My best friends, Benjy and Cubby, thought my boy bump was way cool. Benjy was my age. Cubby was older, maybe by a couple of years. They wore their own sexy outfits. Kiddie erotica in clothes is what it was. Benjy was the son of the ringmaster. He wore a tight-fitting, shiny, light blue shirt with vertical rows of black metal buttons and epaulets. His matching pants were equally form-fitting, as were his knee-high black boots. I loved seeing Benjy in his performing costume, and the feeling was mutual. As it was with Cubby. He rollerskated with a chimp named Bobo. Like ours, his costume was body-flattering, a pink bodysuit with powder blue tights to provide contrast. His skates were pink, as were Bobo's. Before going out into the ring, both Benjy and Cubby would rub my cupped crotch for luck. Everything seemed to involve luck or superstition among circus people. And that, you will learn shortly, was how my boyhood odyssey began.

During the day, when we were in our "civvies," I still usually dressed in my body stocking and slippers, as I said. With a sweater, if it were nippy. And athletic shoes, when I was doing chores, because the supple footwear offered no protection for my feet. Benjy wore jeans, T-shirts and brown boots, like his black ones. Cubby wore T-shirts and shorts, too, with sneakers. But he, too, liked to wear his tights all the time. Not until years later I would recognize the fact that the three of us were indulging ourselves in youthful fetishes; Benjy for his boots, and Cubby and I for our tight, shiny spandex.

We were great friends, although Cubby started to spend a lot more time with Bobo at a certain point. And it wasn't all innocent. He would tell us about how he and Bobo played with each other's wee-wees. Benjy and I thought that was so cool. Maybe because we did the same at bath time. Cubby also said that Bobo's wee-wee was bigger than his, but we never got to see it the way he did, at least not on purpose.

In fact they became lovers, as much as two disparate, yet anatomically alike animals could be, I guess. Well, not that different, given that chimpanzees are our closest genetic relatives. It got to the point that they were always together.

They would walk around holding hands, when they weren't skating together. Or Cubby would carry Bobo, and the latter would kiss him on the mouth a lot. The adults thought that they looked precious together. Honestly, they did, but Benjy and I knew better. It would be during those seemingly innocent embraces, with Bobo's leg's wrapped around Cubby's torso, his hands around his neck, that we were able to glimpse the chimp's erection pressing between them.

And I admit that I was often jealous of Bobo, because I came to realize that Cubby was beautiful. His dirty blond hair was cut short, but the color juxtaposed with his tanned face produced almost a halo-like effect, which was intensified because his eyebrows, lashes and eyes were dark brown. But he had eyes only for his skating partner. In fact, it was so gradual that Benjy and I almost didn't notice how the two of them were melding together, at first. But by the time Bobo was wearing the same costume as Cubby for performances, we realized our friend was really in love. Of course everyone thought that was great, the two of them dressed alike, because it made the act look more professional with them outfitted alike. The audiences loved it, especially the kisses Bobo gave Cubby at the end of their routine. How shocked these people would have been to see them together later, Bobo on his back, being kissed and caressed intimately by Cubby before the latter went down on his troglodyte lover.

Cubby never told us whether Bobo fucked him, but I was certain that he did and would find out that I was right. I guess at the time I wanted it to be so, even in the midst of my lingering jealousy, because, as weird as this will sound, they really looked handsome together. Benjy thought so, too. And it was Benjy who made their relationship tolerable, and then acceptable, to me. Benjy made a lot of things possible.

As long as I can remember, Benjy and I always bathed together. When we were little kids, one of our mothers would wash us in a big, round galvanized tub. Then when we got older, we washed each other on our own. No one seemed to think it odd that two boys continued to take baths together, even as the calendar pushed our ages toward double digits. We didn't, perhaps because we had always done it. Or it might have been what I came to look back on as the almost otherworldly world of the circus.

It was Benjy who began to play with me down there. Really play with me. I don't remember how old we were, but we were still steeped in what should have been our innocent boyhood years. He told me that his daddy did that to his wee wee at bed time, and that it felt good. It sure did. I loved bath time and the little erections we made on each other. They felt and looked so cool, like little fingers waving up at each other. That was how our sex lives began.

Although there were always chores, I enjoyed my life. My parents loved me. Benjy loved me. The other circus people did, too, except for Mr. Wattley. He hated children and animals, but in spite of that he had several dogs in the acts. Along with us three pretty boys. Whatever his feelings to the contrary, dogs and boys were good for business, and that was what Wattley was all about. In my more cynical moments now, I picture Wattley jerking himself off with twenty dollar bills wrapped around his hard shaft.

While Cubby had his chimp to experiment with, Benjy and I got further inspiration for our nascent physical relationship from watching the dogs mate. Naturally, we had to do it, too. Benjy was the first boy inside me, at age nine. It didn't hurt or anything, but it did make me want to go to the bathroom. At first we couldn't figure out why the dogs got so wound up about doing that, but we kept at it. Circus people are nothing if not troupers. However, it wasn't long before we both agreed that it felt kind of neat for him to put his wee-wee in me. Then it felt better. Then we loved to fuck every chance we got. Young guys, who shouldn't have known better, but did. Boys, who still looked that way, with our smooth, juvenile bodies. I forgot my jealousy for Cubby. Because I had Benjy to kiss and fuck with. And to love. For too short a time, as it turned out.

I'll never forget that fateful tour. It was our first one west of the Mississippi River. It was a matter of survival, my parents explained. There were too many circuses like ours vying for the same dusty fairgrounds and crowds. So, Wattley decided to take us west. We worked our way out to California, wherever that was. And it was there that my life changed forever. I even remember that I was wearing my soft blue unitard with pink slippers, when it happened. Mom and dad were practicing, as they did every day. I was watching, mesmerized, as always. I could never get enough of seeing their slim, shiny bodies flying through the air with breathtaking grace.

And then it happened. They fell. They did, from time to time, because they weren't perfect. Only this time a trapeze rope broke as mom grabbed dad's ankles. They plummeted. It was over in a second or less, as it always was. Except that instead of bouncing harmlessly on the net, that gave way, too, and their bodies bounced off the hard ground. They didn't move, and that sickening sight of the dull, dead fish bounce reverberated in my young brain. I knew, standing there frozen in place. My mom and dad were dead.

I remember Benjy's mom pressing my head to her big breasts as I cried my eyes out. Those cushioned female things smelled of sweat and sour milk, as if she leaked the stuff and the air curdled it. Whiskey from her breath mingled with them to make me nauseated.

Naturally, I was devastated, although everyone was really nice to me. Except Wattley, who had been with us all the way of the trip, which was unusual. Benjy and Cubby were the great friends I'd come to love. I slept with Benjy at night, and I can't tell you what his soft body and sweet breath meant to me. It was the first time I kissed another boy, although we didn't have sex. Neither of us felt like feeling good, given the tragedy. But the touching and holding and kissing were my lifeline. I still had Benjy. In a fool's paradise.

Because things began to happen so fast that my head didn't even have time to spin. Everybody else seemed to be taken by surprise, too, at first. Out of nowhere, two new acrobats materialized. Wattley called it Sarah something, although they were both guys. And cute ones, I would note later. As I would the word serendipity, and hate it. And before I knew it, I was being banished from the circus I loved, from the people I loved, from the place where I had always felt safe and nurtured. Worst, from the boy I loved.

Wattley told everyone that I was bad luck, a jinx, to have around, considering what happened to my parents. I was an unwanted reminder of that tragedy. He played to their stupid superstitions, and it worked. The only thing to do was to give me over to the authorities, he said.

So I was. To some childrens' services agency in a county named after one of Santa Claus's relatives. Santa something, anyway. The farewell was almost more than I could stand. I shed more tears than the off-season thunderstorms back in Florida. It was devastating to leave Benjy and Cubby. But especially the ringmaster's son, of course. My best friend. My lover. "Friends and wee-wees always," he whispered in my ear with his tear-choked voice. "I love you, Jason. So much."

But Jason Packer felt only loss through filmy layers of shock. No love. Just loss. And knew that he would never feel love again.

Two

The foster home I was placed in was better than most, I suppose, but how would a twelve-year-old know? These people, the Comptons, were nice and treated me well. But they weren't my parents, you know? They seemed to be professional foster parents. Of what seemed like thirty kids, although it was only eight, Sandy was the only one, who was theirs. Ugly, prissy Sandy. I steered clear of her, especially when she wanted to play dolls.

The bright spot in the otherwise bleak, loud household was Yuki (short for Yukio). We shared a bed and a blossoming friendship. He was thirteen, and we liked each other almost immediately. He was real cute, like Benjy and Cubby, and he had exotic eyes, which reminded me of Cubby's, only Yuki's were more almond-shaped.

He was about as happy living with the Comptons as I was, which was not much. He had been an orphan for most of his life, and he was amazingly cynical, which I would come to be grateful for. We quickly formed a bond against the other nine people in the household. I took Yuki's cues, because he was older, and he had been in the household for nearly a year. We weren't rebellious or anything, but we were able to minimize our contact with the rest of the brats and our foster parents by disappearing after our chores were done.

As often as not it was to the room, which we shared with two of the other boys. They were younger and part of the unwelcome cacaphonic atmosphere of that house that never seemed to rest, until the sandman had worked overtime to settle everyone down. Then, happily, the rugrats in the other bed would be dead to the world for the rest of the night.

Yuki and I didn't fall asleep right away. Part of it was wanting to enjoy the novel quiet of the house, which was so unrelentingly pulsing with raw human sounds all day. The other reason was that we enjoyed being together, our bodies touching, our subtle boy smells, like newly mown grass, increasingly irresistible to each other. For me, it also helped that Yuki became the beautiful boy he, in fact, was, the longer we were together. When I realized this and allowed my mind to accept the attraction he held for me, Benjy's stranglehold on my libido began to lose its grip, to be replaced by Yuki's.

He responded to my first tentative touches as if he had been waiting for me to unlock his own emotions with the key of my hands. His mouth welcomed mine, and we spent hours in the dark kissing and holding each other's erection in those early days of love, finally falling asleep with our heads pressed together, our hard dicks lying against each other in excited contentment.

It was rare for us to be able to get away by ourselves during my early days in the foster home but, thanks to Yuki, we found which of Mrs. Compton's buttons we could push to allow us to take off for an afternoon with the two sad-looking, barely serviceable bikes came closest to fitting us. We would pack lunches—tuna salad sandwiches, carrot and celery sticks, Cheez-Its, Fig Newtons—and ride to a park that we deemed a safe distance from our foster home. Yuki had seen it once on a ride to the Dairy Queen in what he would call now a photo op; the chance for the publicity-hungry Comptons to show off their unselfish, charitable natures by displaying the pitiable waifs in their care for any and all strangers to see. Hypocrites.

We would wheel our bikes through the tamed part of the park to a wooded area, where we would stow them in a thicket and walk in peace through the unintrusive presence of trees and bushes. Birds calling above us seemed to serenade Yuki and me with an avian symphony meant only for us. At least I wanted to believe it. I was falling in love with my room- and bedmate, despite the emotional tug of Benjy still strong on my heart's vulnerable core. We would eat our lunches sitting on tree stumps or a fallen log, talking easily in the way that had become the norm for us. Like lovers secure in each other's acceptance.

It was one such day, when our smiles seemed unable to leave our faces, except to masticate. Meatloaf sandwiches this time. Leftovers from Sandra the Queen's birthday dinner. She would be furious. Good.

After lunch, we walked deeper into the woods. Although neither of us commented, just shy smiles exchanged. It was the first time we had ever held hands outside of bed. That was how we always lay until the snotnoses in the other bed fell asleep. Sure, we kissed and groped like the preteen pubescents that we were, but holding hands in public was new. And it felt so good. We came upon a small outcropping above an algae-ridden, marshy pond, which probably had given birth to the dinosaurs millions of years ago. We sat on the rocky ledge, unafraid that anyone would disturb us.

Sitting there, I did something that my parents used to do, thousands of years ago when they were alive and held my hands. I raised Yuki's hand to my face and kissed it, then put it against my cheek. He looked at me with his straight black hair falling so sexily over his forehead, his black eyes reflecting light from an unknown source. They seemed so overcome by the simple heartfelt gesture. Then his face blossomed into a priceless smile. "I love you, Jase," he said.

"I love you, Yuki."

We kissed and fondled each other in unbridled excitement. We fumbled for the zippers, urgently grasping and pulling them down. Reaching, hands disappearing inside the material, feeling each other up, making each other hard. Lips sliding in desperate, exquisite pleasure over each other. Our little cocks sticking out of our shorts for each other, showing him what he'd made of them. Slobbering over each other's face as we jerked the other fast. Wet, boy stuff to make wet boy stuff. Except that we spasmed in each other's hand as our bodies froze but ejected nothing. So young. So horny. So in love.

After the fact we stripped and lay on the warmed rock above the dinosaur soup. Alone together. It felt so good. Naked, our young, skinny bodies exposed to the beloved.

The afternoons we spent at that outcropping were our favorite times. We could express our love for each other without having to worry about making noises thath would wake up the two brats barely feet away in that cramped room. In fact, we would almost shout in happiness as we orgasmed for the other. And then, lying sated, Yuki would always want me to talk again about my life in the circus. He never seemed to tire of hearing about it.

"Some day I want to see you in your pink bodystocking and blue slippers. I bet I'll come on you without touching myself, you'll look so hot."

"I don't now?"

"You do, but I can't come yet."

"Oh." As if what he said made sense. Being in love didn't, either, I realized later.

Yuki and I were often giddy for no apparent reason. Mrs. Compton would feel our foreheads, certain that we had fevers burning our brains into masses of hysterical cells.

Of course the telling of my previous life, especially the intimate part with Benjy, helped our own sex life. Yuki loved to put his dick in me, and I loved having it there. We discovered making it facing each other by accident, although why we hadn't thought of it before, I don't know. It was so cool to lie on my back with Yuki inside me, looking at me as he fucked me. His beautiful face lit up in happiness for having his dick in my body, making it feel good in there.

We discovered sucking, too, through the miracle of saliva. Being randy and all when we were pulling on each other, we often made our dicks sore from our youthful enthusiasm. Then we figured out that we hurt each other less if we wet our hands first. And how much more sensitive it felt to do it that way. Then the proverbial light bulb. Where did spit come from? Having Yuki jolt in helplessness on my lips felt great. Having his hot mouth on me made me shiver in exquisite boy satisfaction.

There was no doubt in either of our minds that we were going to be together for the rest of our lives. Except for his stinky farts, there was nothing about my wonderful lover that I didn't like. I even tried to like his farts, but you had to be there. Odious! If only I'd known the word then. If only I'd known a lot of things.

But that's the problem with young kids. Despite how happy we were, or maybe because of it, we couldn't see much past the other's hard cock. But why should we? As we were growing up in a household, which now seemed surreal, because we slept with the reality of our lives every night, we were also growing together as boys. Our experiences accumulated like layers of glue, bonding us relentlessly together. Yuki and Jase: two bodies, one mind.

So the import of Mr. Compton's being laid off from the box factory didn't make the immediate impression that it should have. But it did that evening, when Sandy said at dinner,

"Well, I suppose you should be getting on with getting rid of this riff-raff, so that I can still get that prom dress I'm simply dying for." It was then that Yuki and I looked at each other; what she'd said was suddenly sinking home. I was too shocked to want to slug her, for once. And although her parents shushed her, the hard truth was bearing down on him and me. We were wards of the State, and that meant that we wouldn't be together forever. The same naked fear my face showed him, Yuki returned. We were panicked and excused ourselves from the table. Fortunately, we didn't have to clear and wash that night.

"What are we going to do," Yuki asked, his voice breaking from the tears threatening to unleash a flood of emotion at me.

"I don't know." I was in shock. I couldn't muster an emotion, if I tried.

"We have to stay together, Jase."

"I know."

"Jase, we have to."

"I know, Yuki. But how?" Shock can be a wonderful thing. Coming out of it then was not.

"I don't know."

We were walking around the streets of the neighborhood, desperation growing like the shadows of evening as the sun deserted the world again.

"We'll have to run away."

"How?"

"I don't know, but we can't stay here. They'll separate us, Jase. We're not related. There's no way that another foster family is going to take young boys together." He was right. Yuki had been in the system too long not to know its evil ways. Running away was our only choice.

Strangely, once that was settled, we were hot for each other again that night. We sucked cock like it was our last best chance at sex. If it had been, we'd have earned a lifetime supply of it. I went to sleep happy, wondering what it would be like to have him come in my mouth.

The Plan was deceptively simple. It had to be. We were two ignorant young kids, and we were the ones who thought it up. We were also stupid enough to think that it was foolproof. Boy, give guys testosterone and watch the world go to hell. I wasn't thinking that then, of course. I was too preoccupied with trying to fantasize about Yuki ejaculating heavy cream from his cock. Well, that's how a former foster brother of his had described it to him, anyway. And what I was able to conjure fascinated me. Yuki, shooting like a hose from that eye of a slit of his. The slit he liked me to put my tongue into now to tickle him and make him hard and throbbing. Man, we were so sophisticated. Oh, The Plan.

The Plan was to hoard as much food under our bed as we could in one or two weeks, because the children's services people wouldn't be able to have us placed anywhere by then. We'd take along blankets from the bed for sleeping. We'd commandeer the bikes and make our escape just after everyone went to sleep. That would give us a good eight hours head start before anyone missed us. Maybe longer, because we were going to leave on a night when we didn't have chores the next morning. Were we smart or what? It was frightening how good we were. We decided to head east, which was a no-brainer. Heading west, we'd drown in the Pacific.

The sex we had in the meantime was great. It just kept getting better and better. Yuki and me against the world. And we would win, if our orgasms were any clue. If only young boys had any. Clues, that is.

Actually, The Plan worked to perfection. We figured that we had food for weeks, tied up in plastic garbage bags slung over our shoulders. We'd put air in the tires of the bikes that afternoon. And as soon as snot and nose fell asleep, we listened for the steps of the adults on the stairs. Then we gave them fifteen minutes and we were out of there.

I'll never forget that first night on the road. We were out of town in no time. The road leading east that we chose was lightly traveled. We couldn't see the city anymore. No lights, no nothing. It didn't help that we didn't know where in the state we had been living. Or what lay to the east. But that night Yuki held me from behind as we stood in the dark and looked up at more stars than we ever imagined existed. It was awesome. Then he went inside me, and I felt as if I were one of the stars and the rest of the galaxy swirled in my head. It was so special to be fucked on that blanket, under the stars, our bodies dim outlines to each other, our passion making those outlines glimmer like the sky. My feet rested on his chest; my toes played lazily with his nipples, which he liked. He stroked my thighs as he pistoned in me, great, hard boy-fucker that he was. He took my penis in his hand and made me rigid, not missing a stroke in me. He jerked me as wildly as he fucked me, forgetting the marvelous bodily invention of spit. I didn't care. This was what life was. Being with Yuki. Making it with him. Everything else was possible because of that.

I don't know how many days we were away. We'd forgotten to take a watch, naturally. The sun and heat were merciless. Fortunately, we were deeply tanned from being naked at our park hideaway. Yes, even this blond-haired, blue-eyed caucasian boy. Whose hair and eyes never failed to get Yuki's gonads going, deep tan or not. So the sun wasn't a problem, but the heat was. We nursed our milk jugs of water, hot now from the scorching atmosphere. We figured that we were in a desert, and it turned out that we were right. But we pressed on, despite what that implied.

We would have kept going, but nature intervened. Suddenly, one late afternoon, the sun disappeared. We turned and saw clouds, weirdly brown, like none I'd ever seen. A storm was coming. We looked desperately for a place to shelter ourselves. We saw some buttes in the distance and decided to make a run for them. We kissed and were off. But as the storm clouds got close to us, a wind came up and swirled the dirt, and everything else not anchored down, all around us. Visibility dropped to nothing. We were choking and blinded and lost track of each other, except for our scratchy, panicked voices.

Then I was knocked off my bike. I couldn't breathe, a river of dust was clogging my nostrils. I tried to cover my head and call for Yuki at the same time. He didn't answer, if I had managed any sound at all. Then I managed nothing. And I never saw my Yuki again.

Three

In my mother's stories, angels always had blond curls and blue eyes, like mine. But this angel was ugly. So I must be alive, I decided. I wanted to ask this repulsive guy if Yuki were safe, but my lips felt like sandpaper, as did my throat. I was barely able to make a sound.

"Take it easy, boy. Slow down. Here, drink this." Water. I wanted to empty the ocean, but he let me have only a sip. Frustrated, I closed my eyes. But after a while, the guy let me have some more water. And some more. Gradually, until my lips and throat felt like cotton. An improvement, trust me. Finally, "Yuki."

"Be quiet, son," he said.

"Yuki." I couldn't help it. "Yuki." He was my life.

"Was that his name?" Was?

I guess my brain shut down, because the last thing I remember was trying to cry at the realization of my loss, but none came, no matter how much I tried. I guess I was parched. And exhausted. So I conked out.

When I came to, I was given more water. My mouth almost felt moist. "Almost died out there, too, boy." Too? Yuki did? Then I felt a hand over the rough blanket covering me. It was rubbing me down there. Then kneading me. And to my surprise, I felt that part of me working. My nerves went crazy against the rasping fabric as my responding dick moved upward to point at my head. There was no hand on it now. Evidently the guy was watching me in motion. Watching my boyness harden, unable to resist even a strange hand. Was that all I was, I remember thinking. A cock that responded to anybody's touch. I closed my eyes harder. I didn't want to think about it, because getting hard always meant Yuki. Until now.

Then the hand was under the cover, stroking the erection tenting the heavy blanket, in spite of its size. The fingers moving up and down me were as rough as the blanket, but I was helpless not to respond. Then I felt air rush onto my naked body, as if the cover was being taken off me. But it wasn't. It was a head under there now, its mouth taking my little stiffness into it. Incredibly, I felt skin on me inside, too. How could that be? God, it felt so good that I relaxed and let that warm slickness take me higher. Whether it was my depleted state or the insistence of that strange orifice on me, I was being driven to moaning helplessness, as I twitched in velvet agony in him. Make me! Make me! I pleaded silently. Do it, man! Fuck!

My body arched, sending me as far into his mouth as I could, as I jerked in blessed relief. I flopped back onto the mattress, drained. God, what a blowjob that was! Nothing had ever been as good, although I banished that thought, so as not to demean Yuki. I opened my eyes and looked up at the smiling ugly face. "Never been gummed before, have ya, boy?" His mouth stretched into a grin, and I saw that he had no teeth. Damn. Gummed. Maybe I could love him, if I didn't have to kiss him, I thought, stupidly.

My days with the guy, whose name was Dan, were boring. He was a prospector, looking for gold in the buttes of the desert. Mojave, he informed me. I had heard of it, once I think, but I was there now. With an old guy, who struck me as a loon. He asked all sorts of questions about where I was from, but I was evasive in my answers, so he eventually stopped grilling me. He was not only ugly, he was smelly. His clothes were dirty and worn. His breath smelled mostly of whiskey, which might have been a blessing, considering how bad his body reeked. The food was awful, too. If it wasn't canned pork and beans, which made his farts worse than Yuki's worst, I regret to say, he would kill whatever crept or sidled up to him when he was working. I adamantly refused to eat the sidewinder he'd killed, until my stomach couldn't take the hunger pangs anymore. I suppose if I didn't know that it was snake meat, it would have been good. But it *was* snake. We had other things to eat, too, but everything was bad.

But nothing was as much as having to blow him. He smelled

putrid down there. But I sucked on him, because he forced my head down his shaft, and it was a cock, after all. Smelly to high heaven and not much longer than mine. But it did get hard, which I admit I loved feeling in my mouth. God, the things we do for sex, I thought. If I only knew. Then there was a further rude awakening. His come. I wasn't prepared to have him shooting his jizz into my mouth, because it had never happened to me before. And Yuki's explanation nowhere near described the reality of the experience. I choked on the gobs of semen, and when I tasted it, the stuff wasn't at all like cream. It was bitter and salty, like the guy it came from. Yuk.

He said that about once a month he went into the nearest town for provisions. He drove an old pickup, which was as ancient as he was. The town was a couple hundred miles away. The name didn't mean anything to me, but I still refused to go. He said that I couldn't be wanted for a crime, I was too young. Must have run away from home. He leered, the way he usually did before he pawed or sucked me, or made me do it to him. "And if you're thinkin' of runnin' away again, think twice, boy. Same thing'll happen to you like it did the first time. Only you won't be so lucky this time. Either the desert or me'll git you." Then he left.

So did I, in spite of myself. I decided that I'd rather die than stay and eat shit and have revolting sex with the old scuzz. Although the realization that there were snakes, in a place that looked as if it had no life, scared the shit out of me. Still, I went, I was that desperate to get away from the crazy asshole.

I took few things with me. Some of his water, and some oats he had. Honestly, at that point I just wanted to get far enough away from him to die. Yuki's death was still weighing pretty heavily on me, and I thought that joining him was probably the best way for this aborted adventure to end. But I didn't want to do it myself. I wanted the desert to kill me. Besides, I was too much of a coward to stick one of Dan's knives into me.

So I moved eastward, keeping on a line with the sun. At first I ran, but that tired me too quickly. At that point, I didn't want the old prospector to find my body. No telling what he would do with it. I wondered what he did with Yuki's body. *If* he even saw it. I had only his word for it. Maybe Yuki wasn't dead, after all. Then I thought of the bikes. Maybe the old fart saw the second bike and assumed that whoever was with me was dead, but he hadn't in fact, found his body. That gave me some hope. I wished that I'd risked looking for my lover, in spite of Dan's insistence that he was dead. The guy was crazy, I reminded myself. Why should I believe what he said? But where would Yuki be? Why hadn't he found his way to the prospector's shack. And the bikes. Where were they? Man, I could make much better time if I had one, such as it was.

As I walked on, a shiver went through me. If someone like Dan was out here in this godforsaken place, who else might I run into, before my body ran out of gas? Somebody worse? I didn't want to think about it. And I didn't for the rest of the day, I think. That is, until I saw the thing in the distance. It wasn't a butte, because it was moving, I was able to see. After watching the movement for several minutes, I could tell that it was a horse coming toward me. In the fading light, I couldn't make out who was riding it, but I was happy to see whoever it was, which surprised me.

As the horse drew nearer, I could see that it was a boy riding it. He looked naked, and I wondered if he were a mirage. Then I wondered if Dan had been real, but my nose twitched in response. Asshole, it was telling me. The closer he got, the nakeder he got. And he looked young. When he was practically on top of me, I was certain that I had gone crazy.

Four

I was so stunned by the boy's dark, muscular body and handsome face that I was rendered nearly speechless. Nearly.

"So there you are," he said, smiling. "I've been looking for you everywhere. One of the bikes?"

I nodded.

"Good. Come on, I'll give you a ride to my place. I take it you had the dubious fortune of running into that crazy old prospector."

"Yes," I managed, finally.

"I'm glad you got away. He was going to be my last stop in trying to find you."

He dismounted and helped me up onto the horse. Then he

got back on and galloped away from the direction I had come. Good. My arms held fast to his belly, which was as hard as a rock, with ridges of muscle I couldn't remember seeing on anyone before, let alone feeling. Although it was difficult to hear with the wind blowing hard from the streaking steed, he told me his name was Travis Ridgemounter. I told him mine. He said that Jason was a beautiful name. Yuki thought so, too. So had Benjy and Cubby. Why did I think about them all of a sudden?

We didn't say much else, but from time to time he put one of his hands on mine and squeezed. That gesture made me feel safe, for some reason. And he smelled good, too. It was a clean scent mixed with boy and horse sweat. A glorious smell, polished by the sun. I couldn't hazard how old he was, but he was older than me while still looking pretty young. I laid my head against his muscled back, happy to be alive and away from the scumbag. Even happier to have my body against one that even my eyes could see was magnificent. And my own body feel it.

This adventure hadn't gotten me to the point of being jaded yet, so I was impressed that Travis lived in a cave. A cave in the middle of the desert. It was so cool. And it was cool inside, too, after the blast furnace of the desert. The place was spartan, but he was anything but. It was while he was showing me around that I saw how beautiful his body was. It was like a tree stump. His torso went straight down. His calves were almost as thick as his thighs. And he wasn't quite naked. He wore a rough leather flap tied by a thong to cover himself. Oh, and a headband with a feather in the back.

After we ate (I resolved not to ask, he resolved not to tell me), he took me outside and down the slope from the cave to the desert floor. We walked a little distance before we came to two piles of rocks.

"What was his name, Jason?"

"Yukio. Yuki." I began to cry. Travis held me tightly to him and let me bawl. He rocked me, the way my mother had those eons ago, when I would have a nightmare or would hurt myself. In spite of the devastation I felt, his body comforted me. After a while, I stopped crying and wiped my eyes.

"I'm sorry, Jason," he said.

"Thanks. I loved him so much."

"It's obvious. I understand."

"You do?"

"The other grave. His name was Kurt."

We sat in front of the two graves, piled high with the rocks. I wondered where he found them in that wasteland. And the cave for that matter. As if reading my mind, he told me that he and Kurt had fallen in love on the reservation. He didn't tell me which one, nor which tribe he belonged to, except to say that he was from Arizona. Anyway, he and Kurt had been banished by their families, for all practical purposes, but the cave had been found for them, so that they would have a chance for survival together.

"Why didn't you just go to a city or something? Find work and live there?"

"Jason, life on the reservation was hell. The men in both families were drunks. They were unemployed. The thought of going out on our own scared the shit out of both of us. Especially into the white world. So we decided to show them that we could survive on our own, Indian-style. But we didn't."

"What happened?"

"Kurt got thrown by his horse, when it got spooked by a snake. He died instantly." He lowered his head. "We had it made. We not only survived, we thrived. We worked this desert six ways from Sunday. The best years of our lives."

"Man. How many?"

"I don't know. It doesn't matter. We were in love, and life was great. So much better than on the reservation. Then all of a sudden he was gone." Tears rolled down his cheeks into a steady stream. I put a hand on his shoulder. I wanted to ask how long Kurt had been dead, but I realized that it was a stupid question. Travis wouldn't know, and besides, he still missed him a lot. I looked at Yuki's grave and wondered how long I would mourn him. "I thought of killing myself, but the Great Spirit seemed to be telling me not to. I can't explain it. I just felt I had to go on. For what, I didn't have a clue. Maybe now I do." He fixed me with his soft black eyes, made more so by the tears. I thought that I knew what he meant, because my heart seemed to reach out to him, somehow. Then my smile. He returned it.

We got up and walked away from the tiny cemetery, where the loves of our lives rested side by side. I conjured the image of Travis and me resting side by side. Alive.

It was hard to believe that there was running water in the cave. Literally. At the back of it, there was a spring that pooled into natural basins before it continued on down farther into the earth. "There's a lot of water under this desert. Underground rivers. Like under Phoenix. Only the white man doesn't respect nature. That city has pumped so much water from them that the ground is sinking. And still they needed more. Any fool could tell you that you can't provide enough water for a million people in the desert, who shouldn't be there in the first place. I guess it shows that the white man is worse than a fool."

"Does that include me?"

"No, little one. Not you. You haven't been spoiled by the white man's way yet."

We bathed in the cold water, and finally my goose bumps went away. Travis scented the water, with sandalwood, he said. It smelled so clean. Like him. He had taken off his flap and removed his feather. I asked what the feather was for. He laughed and said to scare the shit out of the old geezer. I laughed, too, wishing I had seen him do it. After our bath, I felt refreshed and clean for the first time in I didn't know how long. I had tried to keep myself as decent as I could, but without proper facilities, it was impossible. Still, Travis hadn't seemed to be repelled, so maybe I didn't reek as much as I thought I did. And he'd said that the prospector's shack was the last place that he was going to look for me. Did that mean that I hadn't been there as long as it seemed? Possibly, because a day with him had been an eternity.

Travis's mat was surprisingly comfortable. He gathered me into his big arms and held me to his wonderfully scented body. He kissed my wet curls.

"No one's been with me here but Kurt."

"Is it ... is it ... is it all right?"

"Is it with you, Jason?" I responded by kissing him. His lips were so full, so earthy in color, so soft. So wonderful. Before long we were erect from the passion we'd kindled with our lips. He took hold of my bloated penis, and I grasped his. His cock was longer than Dan's and it was really fat, like his muscles.

"You're beautiful, Jason. Like the hunter's moon."

I didn't know what he meant, but I knew it was a compliment. That first night we fell asleep still holding each other in our hands.

The next morning was another matter. I woke up first. It gave me a chance to look at Travis in all his glory. God, his body was unbelievable. His reddish-brown skin was shiny and taut over those hard muscles. His areolas were darker, the nipples standing at attention. I longed to kiss them. I was hard just looking at the most perfect body I had ever seen. I'm sure that part of it was because he was so much bigger than Yuki. He was a man, no matter how young he looked. But his face was that of a boy's. And then I noticed something that didn't make sense. His hair wasn't long. Where in the desert could he get a haircut? I would find out that he had taken his knife and removed all of his hair, when Kurt died. Which meant that it hadn't been all that long ago, considering its length.

I was aroused from looking at his gorgeous physique, and my desire got the best of me. I snuggled up to his warm, soft skin and took his near nipple between my lips. My right hand slid down his torso to the modest nest of hair, and beyond to the thick maleness resting between his legs. I would have been shocked at the appearance of his cock, had I not been forced to service the stinking prospector. His had been the first uncircumcised penis I had ever seen. I thought that it was deformed, like his brain, but he told me that it was the way men were supposed to be. Then why did I not have that skin, I'd asked. Because I had been butchered was his explanation. But holding Travis and pulling back the flap I saw that we looked the same now.

He stroked my hair gently to tell me that he was awake. I couldn't get enough of the hard nub standing up from his chest. As I continued to suck, I masturbated him. The extra skin was like an extension of my hand. Then I felt his other one on mine. "Not yet, little one. Maybe tonight." Confused, I left his rock-hard penis to wither on his belly.

If I had wondered how Travis had gotten that splendid body, I didn't need to after that morning. Before the sun came into full heat, we ran across the country. At least that's the way it seemed. Well, he did. I got winded soon into the run. Travis laughed and kept going. When he returned, we did pushups and situps. I was pitiful; he was a machine. Then we had breakfast. He told me that their families supplied them with flour and oil and other basics, so that they didn't have to rely solely on the desert for nourishment. They never saw them, just the bags of supplies lying outside the cave. That was because he and Kurt were supposed to be officially dead. So they didn't know that Kurt was dead.

I got to help Travis feed Warrior, his horse. He seemed to like me well enough, considering that I was a stranger. After visiting the graves of our lovers, we rode Warrior for a while. Holding onto Travis was as good as having sex, I decided. So did my erection, which pressed against him. When we returned to the cave, we spent most of the day talking. Like Yuki, Travis was fascinated with my life in the circus and with how I came to be sitting across from him.

We napped during the heat of the afternoon. After eating, we bathed and then sat outside to look at the stars. At least that was what I thought.

"Look over there, Jason." Travis was excited by something he saw. I followed his pointing, eager to see it, too. But I saw nothing. "Keep looking." I did, and after what seemed like hours, although it wasn't, I saw a white streak in the sky."It's a shooting star." Neat. Then there were several more over the course of the next few minutes. Travis held my hand and squeezed. I returned the pressure, delighted for the contact with this beautiful boyish man. "It's a sign from the Great Spirit."

"Really? Who's that?"

"God."

"Honest?"

"I was praying for a sign to show me we're meant for each other, Jason."

"Really? And that's it?"

"Uh, huh. He approves."

"Wow, that's so neat, Travis!"

"You mean it?"

"You bet I do."

"Great!"

It was. We retired to the mat where we kissed and caressed

each other all over. His hands on me were feverish but gentle, as were his kisses. I returned his ardor in kind. We were just all over the mat on each other. Then he got me on my back and subdued me with his touch, his mouth. He went down on my cock, waving desperately for him. I couldn't stop sighing, his mouth on me felt so wonderful. Then he came off me to lick circles around my unguarded sex, the surrounding skin not yet having produced the confirmation of my pubescence. I was still bare, my erection achingly vulnerable to him. He murmured his appreciation of my unspoiled crotch and the soft boy perfume of my youth holding out there.

My scrotum was no match for his tongue. It was bigger than I was, even with my ripening balls growing inside the silky living pouch. I could feel the profound constriction of the organ in its defensive position. Yuki had only ever fondled it into submission. Travis's was full-scale oral assault. The delirium of sexual satisfaction that produced was followed by a new, equally intense sensation. The small, smooth area of skin behind my balls was set on fire by the lubricated raspiness of his tongue. Never had I been touched there, except for my own clumsy, incidental efforts at soaping it.

By the time he found the vulnerable spot between my cheeks, I was emitting feral sounds completely at home in the wasteland of the desert outside our love chamber. Another person was lying there being ravished, and he possessed a cock permanently engorged with desire. "Oh, Travis" became a mantra as he violated my young body, sending it into a dimension I couldn't comprehend. My naked rosebud puckered in response to his kisses and tentative penetration, the muscles desperately reversing their normal function in order to pull that probing tongue inside me.

The mantra changed to "Yes, yes, yes," as he left me so needy down there that I wanted to die on his cock, wanted it to split me open and kill me with its knifelike hardness and power.

When he entered me, I felt as if I were going to die, the pain was so searing. My belly and ass blazed with a pain that set off shooting stars in my head. But I wanted it, even as my tears fell freely down my cheeks. Hurt me, Travis. Make me yours.

The sharp ripples of hurt began to smooth out as the surface of water does after the pebble has done its temporary damage to it. I looked up at his beautiful face and smiled through my tears. He wiped away the lines of moisture on my cheeks. "We're one, little Jason."

We were, I realized, as the feeling of hurt diffused itself into a strange mixture of pleasure and pain. He began moving in me, and the nerves of my opening and the sheath of my bowel welcomed him as its new and permanent guest. I smiled as his awesome, toned body possessed me with its thick, rigid extension. I stated the obvious: "I love you, Travis," as if I finally knew what it was like to love another person in intense physical bonding. As the ache subsided into pleasure with each thrust, I did know, for the first time in my life, what it really meant to be joined to another boy. And this one was incomparable in beauty and desirability and in love with the young body I offered him for his gratification.

Sweaty and delirious with hormonal drunkenness, he rutted in me as I urged him on, desperate for his come, needing to be marked as his possession, because I knew in that act that I would always belong to him. He covered my face with kisses as necessity drove him into me again and again until he was helpless in the sheath of my love. We cried out, two young animals realizing the nirvana of oneness, one twitching, the other exploding in orgasm.

Then lying wet and exhausted and sated, to sleep the sleep of eternal communion.

My sleep was dreamless, as if the physical rigors of consummating our marriage had demanded so much that little was left in its wake. But I woke strangely refreshed the next morning, and my nether lips were alive with a need I had never felt before. I left Travis's strong arms to seek out that need. It pointed up at me in its male beauty, the head bared to me in its excitement. My mouth strained to cover it and take it into me. I took as much of the shaft as I could and fellated as much of his magnificence as I dared without asphyxiating myself. He groaned in waking pleasure as I sucked the organ I now belonged to. "Jason," he whispered. "Oh, god."

I straddled him, holding his throbbing sex to guide it into me, to scratch the itch of my lust. Slowly I sank onto the cock I now belonged to, the cock I was fated to pleasure. He opened his eyes and smiled at me the way only a lover smiles at his mate. His hands roved over me in silent communication as I moved on him. Travis. Travis, who loved me. My mate. Inside me. The beautiful mewlings he uttered drove me faster on him. He jerked me as he bucked into me, like a wild horse intent on throwing its rider. This human horse determined to possess me again. I sank completely onto the pole of his boyness and arched my back as my cock went wild in his hand, and my sphincter pulsed in the imaginary release of my semen. Travis melted into the whimpers of profound orgasm, and I felt him flood me again in wave after wave of cum against my bowel wall.

When the temblors of our union stopped, he was holding my sides firmly. He looked at me and smiled."Little Thunder," he said and grinned. My fate had been determined. I belong to Travis and would in the bliss of our love for the rest of my life.

Five

I grew accustomed to the rigorous morning training; in fact, I looked forward to it. Travis devised a small ceremony, where we exchanged thongs decorated with two brown and white hawk feathers. We girdled each other's genitals with the thongs, and thus adorned, they were the rings of our marriage. He fitted me with a headband like his and made a soft loincloth to cover me when we went riding on Warrior. He taught me to meditate, and we spent hours in the quiet of the cool cave, opening our minds to each other and communing in a way that shocked and pleased me. We were one in spirit and body. I grew to look like my mate, if only a smaller version. My crotch was crowned with blond hair that looked more golden against my dark skin, the tawny reddish undertone unexpectedly like Travis's. I had more blondness under my arms, and he loved to lick the downiness there, sending me into jolting happiness. Naked but for the feathers of our love hanging beside our manhoods, we lived and loved an idyllic life that I could never have imagined with the most powerful abilities for fantasy. But that was our life together.

The prickly pear cacti bloomed and grew and provided us

with nourishment and shiny bodies from their succulent viscousness. The blooms we picked and placed on the graves of the boys, who had made our present lives a reality. Yuki and Kurt held fast in our hearts and lived in our memories with a sweetness that ripens with the disappearance of hurt.

Travis taught me the self-sufficiency of living in desolation, aided by the foodstuffs that would mysteriously appear at unexpected intervals. Our identities were so intertwined with each other that I couldn't honestly say where I left off and he began. He told me that I was the most beautiful boy the dirt of the earth mother had ever fashioned for herself, and that probably no other babies were now being born on earth, as a result.

Our lovemaking was gentle and riotous by turns, Ridgemounter and Little Thunder true to their names. I loved sucking him to helplessness, as he lay under the spell of my mouth and tongue. And to have his burnished, dark cock fitted into me in joyous coupling. We arrived at an existence where every look and touch was insidiously sexual. Our auras melded and glowed in proximity to one another. We were one.

A self-contained existence admits no others, so the warning that Travis had given me early in our life together was forgotten in the happiness of our circumstances. And this was to be the spectacular fall from grace and expulsion from the torrid Eden I had come to claim as my birthright.

We had gone riding in the lengthening shadows and abating heat of a typical desert day. Our destination was the highest promontory in the area, even higher than our modest mountain. The table top of the hill provided us with a private outdoor playroom.

We meditated for several minutes, our arms raised to the Great Spirit. Then we would indulge in a ritual of cleansing and sex. As we did all the other times, we squatted near the edge of the mesa and dropped our loads on top of each other's, our bodily offering to the deity. Then we took turns lying with our lover standing between our spread legs.

We peed on each other, the warm, golden liquid covering our torsos. I loved feeling Travis' piss warm my face and fill my mouth and splash off my body and trickle down my sides and crotch. Then we coated ourselves with the fine dust of the tabletop altar. We resembled plaster statues as the moisture evaporated rapidly in the unforgiving dryness of the atmosphere.

Then I lay atop Travis and rubbed my powdery skin against his as our hands explored our temporary second skins. Our arousal rose to a frenzy as I humped him, our erections sliding on the silky dirt of our altered bodies.

We came almost at the same time, then lay holding each other as our semen mingled with the good earth of our open church. I had begun to come for my mate, to both of our delights. We were now equal in our male abilities and pleasure.

Afterward, we lay holding hands, letting the air desiccate our essences and the thermal fingers of the desert's hot breath scour our bodies of the ashes of our sacrament of love. It was almost miraculous that we were cleansed of the lubricant of our lovemaking by the time we descended from the altar of our bodily sacrifice to the Great Spirit.

So we returned to the cool womb of love, having stopped to pick up a gnarled piece of wood to place between the graves of Kurt and Yuki, as one would put flowers on a grave in a conventional cemetery.

Warrior had been uncharacteristically skittish as we neared home. We surveyed the landscape for a stray snake not yet slithered into its den for the coming cool evening, but saw none. We were at a loss as to its cause. After laying the offering in front of our departed beloveds, we stood in silence.

And in that silence I heard the sick whistle. My head jerked up to see Travis stagger back and fall onto his back, the shaft of a brightly-tailed arrow sticking out of his upper abdomen. I knelt beside him as he lightly caressed it in wonder. "My brother," he said, fingering the feathers at the end of the instrument of his death. "He found me. Kiss me, Little Thunder. Kiss my dying breath, my beloved, myself." I did, taking his dying breath into my lungs and making the death rattle in them that Travis was incapable of. I kept my lips pressed to still ones, refusing to believe that the phallus imbedded in him was evil, was his death. Then I collapsed on him and sobbed as the reality of my loss weighted me to him with all the gravity on the planet.

I sat, my arms hugging my legs, keeping a vigil through the

night, alternately wailing and moaning, focused on the handsome shaft of wood that had taken my life from me. My Travis, as beautiful in death as in life. But dead. By the hand of the brother, who he had told me hated him. More than anything, that had been the reason for their banishment from the reservation. The disownment had been for their protection, so outraged was his sibling over his brother's homosexuality. His exile to this place hadn't been enough.

My watery grief turned into a comforting shock, the vaguely familiar absence of feeling that my memory tugged on itself in vain to identify. I was a machine now. I painstakingly dug as deep a hole next to Kurt as I could. Then I dragged Travis's corpse to the excavation and gently eased it into its final resting place. I got in with him and pulled out the arrow. I sucked on the shaft, cleaning it of the congealed fluids of my beloved. I toyed with the idea of plunging the tip deep inside my own vulnerable belly to join Travis, but I hesitated. Why give the hated brother the satisfaction of having destroyed both of us? So instead I broke the arrow in half and hurled it away. I kissed Travis's lips gently. Goodbye, my love. Myself.

I covered him with the excavated dirt, still fortunately enveloped by the numbness of my loss. I don't know how many days I spent finding rocks to protect the flawless body, whose every inch I had known and worshipped. I sat in vigil for I don't know how long. At one point, I looked down to see a scorpion beside me, ready to menace me. My palm flattened its lethal-tipped spine, sending the needle of poison into the back of its skull. Its pincers quivered in shock that it had been wounded with its own instrument of death. Travis had told me that the denizens of the desert were immune from their own poisons. But not from their own swords. It seemed to look up at me, incredulous that I had buried its swaggering blade into itself. I resisted the urge to flatten its head, letting it suffer on its own impalement. Then I looked at the grave and swore a foolish youthful oath to avenge the beautiful creature who had been my life.

One day I realized that my mourning had run through its first stage. It was time for me to act. I got up and removed my thong and feather ring. I kissed it and placed it on top of the stones. I began to cry, and the tears were welcome. I looked at the sky watered by my tears and told the Great Spirit that I neither believed in it, nor needed its impotent power. I could no longer feel happiness, so I would become a boy without any emotions. I would become simply a body, and I would use it only for the main purpose for which it existed: sexual fulfillment.

After dressing in what was left of the ill-fitting clothes I had arrived in that place wearing, I said a last goodbye to Yuki and Travis. Then I mounted Warrior and rode south to where Travis said a highway ran through the desert. After a long time, I found it and dismounted. I put food and water on the ground for the horse. He nuzzled me, and I patted him for the friend he was. I walked to the other side of the road, confident that someone would find Warrior and take care of him. And that I would get a ride. To where I didn't know, except that along the way it would include a stop at an Indian reservation to accomplish the death of the most hated person on earth.

Six

I felt an electricity of sexuality course through me as I stood waiting for someone to stop to pick me up. My plans were in complete disarray, having no idea how I was going to make Travis's brother pay for his crime.

The first car that approached stopped. It was being driven by a middle-aged white man, who looked as if time had been his enemy. Still, it was a ride, and he was a male. He leered at me, when he saw my long blond curls and dead but glowing blue eyes. He told me to hop in. Warrior was still occupied with the food, and I wished him a silent goodbye.

As the man drove and made small talk, I slumped in my seat belt suggestively and kicked off the sneakers that were way too small for me now. He didn't miss the cue, soon covering my crotch with his hand. I slumped further, wanting him to use me. He unzipped me and put his hand inside my shorts, murmuring appreciatively at what he found there."Play with it, man. Do it like you own it." I wanted him to, just as I would want every other male I encountered to use my body for his pleasure. To own me for that time he was with me. A part of

Jason had died with Travis, the part able to love. The new, diminished Jason was capable only of sex. But his beautiful, muscled body was desirable, and that's what sex was all about. And this pot-bellied, balding guy knew it, if nothing else.

Eventually, he pulled over into a deserted rest stop and suggested that I get more comfortable in the back seat. When I was naked, his breath caught in his throat at the sight of me. "My god."

"Yes, I am." A statement of fact, said without emotion.

He didn't undress, just unzipped and pulled it out. His cock was respectably long, even soft, and he couldn't resist pointing out the obvious. I decided he was lonely and insecure and any number of other male failings. But I didn't expect him to pull the gun from his belt under his shirt. I started.

"Hey, don't be scared, beautiful. It's not loaded. I just like to play with it, while I'm getting in the mood, you know? I didn't have a clue. "It helps me get my own gun ready to fire." He laughed as if it were the funniest joke ever told. He put the barrel into my ass as he stroked his obstinate cock. He fucked me with it. The steel inside me felt good, although I only had his word that it was unloaded. But what did it matter if he intended to shoot it in me? Travis was dead, and so was I. Being fucked to death, I thought and laughed to myself. Funnier than his joke, even if the truth might turn out to be lethal. I encouraged the thrusting of the ersatz cock, wanting to make him stiff and replacing the gun with himself.

He did and handed the firearm to me. I put it into my mouth and fellated it. He licked his lips at the sight. As he pummeled me, I took it out and ran my tongue up and down its maleness, savoring the metallic taste as my cunt enjoyed the sausage he was shoving in and out of it. I kept fanning his fire with my oral antics, and he was sweating and puffing, desperate to shoot his load in me.

"What the fuck?!" he yelled, stunning me, and I pressed the trigger and the gun went off, shattering the window above me, raining pellets of glass onto me."Jesus! Do you know what you just did?!" Except scaring myself shitless? Not a clue. "You shot him!" Shot him? Who?

He scrambled off me and opened the back door on his side. I jumped up to see a body sprawled on the compacted dirt of the parking lot. I blinked, not believing what I saw. A guy wearing a headdress askew on his head. And tan chaps and moccasins. This couldn't be happening. I got out of the car as tentatively as I could manage. The sausage was already bending over the guy, muttering, "Jesus," over and over, as if he knew meditation.

Then I saw the feathers on an arrow peeking out from behind him. I smiled and closed my eyes to savor the fact. I had avenged Travis. The brother's nose was missing, where the bullet had shoved it into his brain. Blood pooled behind his head. One hell of an unloaded gun, I thought.

"Jesus, I gotta get out of here."

"You mean *we* have to get out of here, asshole," I said, brandishing the automatic handgun.

"Uh, right." His eyes were widening into saucers at the sight of the weapon in my hand.

"It was unloaded, huh?" I pointed it in the air and fired, scaring myself again, I admit. "Lucky for both of us it is," I said, carelessly pointing it in his direction.

"Look, it was a mistake. I promise."

"Liar. But you're right. We need to get out of here fast. Go."

We rode in silence, and his hands stayed gripped on the steering wheel. I told him I wouldn't hurt him, if he behaved. I also told him what a slimy fucking bastard he was to put a loaded gun with the safety off into my boy cunt. He was completely cowed, his sausage shrunken into a little wiener, as if all of its fat had been fried off.

We drove past the day and through the night until his gas began to run out. I told him that we might as well be stranded, because there was no way I was going to let him pull off the highway to fill the tank. It was then that he conveniently remembered the canisters of gas in his trunk. Kept there for driving through the Mojave, which we had left since I had serendipitously assassinated the evil brother. When he was finished filling the tank, there was enough gas remaining in a couple more red cans to take us into the next day and beyond. We stopped at a fast food restaurant somewhere in Arizona or New Mexico for badly needed food. We stocked up on fried dessert pies and coffee, which would carry our stomachs as long as the gas did. I wasn't crazy about the taste of mainstream food again, and my bowels were horrified. I shit out the window as we were driving along, making a mess of the asshole's car. He gave me his handkerchief to wipe myself, but I really wanted his tongue and lips to clean me. Unfortunately, I couldn't chance having him try to pull something. But it would have served him right to eat my shit.

When he had to get gas, the canisters now empty, I had him stop so that I could dress in the least repulsive-looking of his dumpy clothing. I kept the gun, warning him that if he went to the cops, it was still his weapon that had killed the guy. I could tell that he wouldn't by how nervous he acted. He drove off, and I walked to a ramp of an interstate going north. After he didn't return, and no cops came, I threw the thing into the brush. I wasn't sure where this road would take me, but I determined that my destination would be Florida. It was where I had spent most of my early years, when the circus wasn't on the road. I wanted to be on familiar turf. Although why I wasn't sure.

I had gleaned one piece of useful information from the asshole salesman. What date and year it was. So I knew that whoever Jason Packer was now, he was sixteen years old.

Seven

I decided that being naked from the waist up would improve my chances. As I waited, I was surprised that my thoughts returned to Travis and the days of our bliss. I stood, barechested, waiting for a ride with a persistent erection, the memory of his unbelievable sensuality bathing me in constant arousal. I didn't know it, but it was a great preparation for what was coming.

The car, which turned the corner onto the ramp, was a sporty model with its top down. The head sticking up drew my eyes to it. It was tanned and topped by very short dirty blond hair. The guy smiled, dimples showing on his cheeks, white teeth brilliant in barely tanned skin, as he passed me. He stopped just ahead of me. I walked to the passenger door.

"Hey, where you headed?"

"Wherever you are," I blurted. We both laughed, defensively.

Then he said, still giving me that great smile,"Okay by me.

Get in." I did, and we were off.

His name was Bart, short for Bartholomew. It wasn't a name I remembered hearing, but it was beautiful, like the guy who carried it. When I'd gotten in, I'd noticed that he was barechested, too. His muscular development reminded me of Travis's, and this surprised me. As we chatted, I took in more of him. He wore tight faded jeans and tall black cowboy boots. The boots were unadorned but had high heels and pointed toes. The new Jason wondered how much of that pointiness he could take up his ass.

"Seriously, where *are* you headed?"

"Eventually, Florida. I lived there when I was a kid. If I have one, it's home." But you don't, my internal voice reminded me. Yuki, and then Travis were your homes. People, not places.

"Well, I'm headed to Chicago. I go to the University of Chicago. I was visiting my folks in Austin. Although I prefer the north, I think I could get into the place. Well, some of the people, who live there, anyway."

"The boys are that cute?" That threw him, but he recovered and chuckled.

"I guess I didn't misread my gaydar with you, huh?" Nor maybe my hard-on sticking up, and still obvious now with my new, slouched posture.

"Not a chance. Life's too short for games. Except of the boy variety."

"I hear you, Jason. Got any you want to play right now?"

"Just to bury my face in your crotch. Make you want it more."

"Be my guest. I want you real bad now."

I felt the same way about him. I unhooked my belt and lowered myself into his crotch. He had a pretty bulge there, and I kissed it in homage. My lips went from teasingly chaste to wetting the well-worn material. I wanted to unbutton him and fish him out, to see what his maleness looked like, but I decided that just letting my mouth tease him was a better idea, especially in that little car, whatever the hell it was. No need to kill the golden goose in coitus. His free hand caressed my unruly curls, which cascaded down my back. Were it not for the headband, they would have been unmanageable. He stroked my bare skin with soft fingers. I felt strangely contented and connected with him in our unhurried foreplay. Even the air horns of passing trucks, signalling their approval of my crotch veneration, didn't deter me, although they did scare me with their sudden loudness. My nose buried itself into the creases on either side of his lump and inhaled a faint mixture of laundered denim and male scent. My hands brushed and kneaded his hard thighs. I couldn't wait to see his nude body. And I knew I would.

"Time to stop for lunch, Jason. You game?"

"Sure. I'm starved." I was, in spite of stuffing myself with those fast food pies. I kissed his excited trapped sex and sat up.

"You are one hell of a cock tease."

"Thanks. Years of experience."

"Since when? Nursery school?"

"I'll tell you over lunch, if you want to hear it."

"From a guy who looks thirteen or fourteen, sure. And although I don't want to know, how old are you?"

"Eighteen," I lied, easily. "My baby face is my curse."

"Some curse."

We drove off the interstate and stopped at a strip center, where Bart said the ribs were great. He always stopped here on his way back to Chicago. I wondered if they would discount his meal when they saw the high cowboy boots. Man, they were doing a number on me, and I knew exactly what I wanted to do with that number.

"You're not going to wear that shirt, are you?"

"It's all I have. I borrowed it. My bag was stolen back in New Mexico." Look, the only reason I was lying was for the sake of sex now. I meant Bart no harm. Okay, I really wanted to worship him and have him possess me the way Travis had, he was so beautiful.

"I have one you can wear. Shorts, too, now that I look at them." Yeah, they were ugly, too.

I changed right there in the parking lot. There wasn't any traffic, to speak of, to see my naked butt. I didn't know what people in the restaurant might be able to see, but, frankly, I didn't care. Bart was the one I wanted to see my body and personal stuff. He did and smiled, I noticed out of the corner of my eye. Travis had taught me a lot about keeping my wits about me, although he would have shaken his head over the firearm incident, fool that I had been. But I did shoot his fucking brother, after all. The way I figured it, he was as crazy as Travis said he was, and I'd bet that he was going to do the salesman and me, especially after seeing us in male fornication. So I got him first. I just wished that I felt better about having avenged my beloved.

Bart gave me a pair of athletic shoes to wear, too. They were too big, but they fit better than the T-shirt and shorts, which I swam in. Bart approved of that, saying I looked like a fashion boy. I had to take his word for it, having been away from the world for the best years of my life.

As I followed Bart into the restaurant, I put another item on my list of things to adore. His butt sat high and round and was molded to his jeans. He was wearing a black T-shirt now, and he looked so damn sexy that I was hard again. A good sign, if you've decided on sex as a way of life.

I couldn't get over how handsome he was, and, despite the cool boots, he looked like a clean-cut, grown-up kid. When I mentioned it later, he chuckled and said that he was terminally preppie, despite himself.

"Why do I have the feeling that you have a story, Jason?" I shrugged. "And that you're not eighteen."

"Bart, I'm sticking with the age thing, okay? I don't have ID to prove it, I admit. But why do you think I have a story?"

"Your hair is a mile long, and you have the deepest tan I've ever seen on a white boy. And it's even all over your body, too." He had me there. That's what living nude in the desert'll do. But if I told him the truth, he wouldn't believe me, and I told him so. However, when he saw me temporarily buffaloed by the flatware on the table, he said, "Jason, I'll believe whatever you tell me."

"I feel older than eighteen."

He smiled at my open, serious response. "Understood, man," and touched my knee under the table. I looked into his eyes and knew that I could trust him.

Actually, I got the hang of using a knife and fork again pretty easily, although the ribs and fries we mostly ate with our fingers. I tried not to be too enthusiastic in shoveling the food down, as Travis and I had. We had also fed each other. God, so in love. My eyes misted, remembering the young man, whose soul I had shared. I knew that it would happen, the tears. I expected it too many times, and I wouldn't be disappointed. I also wasn't surprised that the food seemed to be going right through me. As I said, that had been the emphatic reaction to my first "civilian" meal with the salesman, too.

As I was washing up after my gut churned into the commode, I was shocked to behold myself in the restroom mirror. I stared in wonder at this boy I didn't recognize. I touched the shiny, taut brown skin on my face, and it was real. As were the high cheekbones, which might as well have been islands suddenly erupting out of the sea, they were so unfamiliar. The intensity of the pure sapphire-hued corundum of my eyes made me blink first, they were so piercing. In spite of that, I spent the next several minutes trying to get acquainted with this stunning person I didn't recognize. I was shocked that I had changed so remarkably. Puberty had done much more than transform my dick into a cock and give me hard muscles. It had changed my face into an enhanced version of the irresistibly adorable kid I had once been. This was the face Travis had loved. The last one he saw before he died. This was Jason's face. And Jason's face was fucking gorgeous.

My golden hair, held fast by the leather headband, had been turned into platinum by the same solar rays that had done the opposite to my skin. Man. I turned sideways to see the white gold river, like a brook over rocks, like the water of a brook bumping over rocks. These tresses, the color and consistency of corn silk, I had often masturbated Travis to delirium with. That memory brought a rush of other wonderful images, which I stopped by closing my eyes and shaking my luxurious mane. Only my own newly met face remained when I opened them, but the moist, dark blue eyes I saw once more in the mirror held the glint of a promise, or more accurately a threat, that the past would eventually flow freely again, despite all my efforts at damming it up with denial. And that the truth that lay there, unwanted, would nevertheless assert itself and flow into the reality of my future.

Refusing to entertain the accusation of the honest sapphire orbs, I shook my head to make the bounty of my hair dance to distract those eyes. I smiled. People in the restaurant had kept staring at me, and now I knew why. The long locks looked completely out of place in a world of scissors.

A busboy came in to pee and gave me a sly smile."Awesome hair," he said, his lovely, rosy lips parted, as if their fullness prevented them from closing, or maybe they had been trained that way to allow his tongue fevered access to other boys' mouths, or to receive theirs, in kind. I realized that his lips reminded me of my own newly discovered bounty there. I lingered at the sink, partly because I was still taken by this new Jason I had met, and because the slim boy was pretty, and I found that beauty immediately arousing. I was rewarded for my indecision with the sight of him shaking off one last time in silhouette for my benefit. My mouth felt as if I'd held it open in front of the electric air drier on the wall next to me, it was suddenly so parched. The sight of such a long cock on that young, thin body was an eye-opener. I decided that it was time to get out of there before I acted on my desires. "See you," he said, but it was more of a question than a statement.

There was a hair salon in the shopping center, and that was where I left most of mine. The hairdresser asked how I wanted it styled, and I told her that I wanted it to look like Bart's. The only complication was that mine was curly, so she talked me into short on the sides with modest ringlets on top. I liked the look. And I'd only seen my long hair that once in the mirror, so I wouldn't miss it. Except when I thought of Travis. Except. Man.

"Will you marry me, when you're eighteen? I promise I'll wait, beautiful," the stylist said. Bart thought that was funny. He also thought that I looked dynamite. I thought I looked ten years old again.

For the rest of the afternoon, I told him some of my adventures over the past several years. I caught him looking at me at times during the narrative, but I think he believed me. And by the time we stopped at the motel for the night, his free hand had been resting on my left thigh for hours.

Eight

Bart was a surprisingly good kisser, which was something I

really didn't need to know. Travis could make me whimper with his kisses. But that was love. This was sex. Still, Bart was beautiful, and he seemed sincere. And his passion did arouse me. His kisses on my neck made me hot to shine his boots.

At first he was taken aback by my asking to do his boots, but he sat on the bed and watched as I licked up and down the long shafts and over the insteps and around the tops of the soles. He had insisted on wiping them with a towel first, which made sense. But he seemed to love seeing me worship him that way, because he kept remarking about how sexy it was seeing me do that, and fondling my new haircut. For my part, I was able to slip the toes of the boots inside me while I straddled them and licked the tops of the shafts. I was disappointed that they only kissed my sphincter, but I tried.

I had no idea where my craving for his black beauties came from, but I didn't question my needing to make love to them. By the time I finished and looked up at Bart, adoration in my eyes gleaming to match the laved polish, I saw that he had freed his cock from his jeans. He was pointing up hard. The stiff organ looked like a soldier ready for battle with its purplish, helmeted head. The sight of it made my saliva-drained tongue lick my lips.

"I want to fuck your pretty brown ass, Jason," he said, stroking my curls.

"I want your cock in me," I said, brushing the rigid shaft with my finger tips and feeling the moisture in my mouth return as awakening mini-geysers.

"Good. Make it real wet first." He put his hand behind my head and pulled it to his expectant cock. I liked that gesture of power and let him guide me onto him. The florid glans seemed to swell further in anticipation of my parted lips French-kissing it. A drop of precome oozed up as if unable to control its excitement at the prospect of my mouth on it. My tongue snagged it before surrounding it with fleshy warmth.

I fitted my mouth over the engorged cap, and it seemed intent on filling my cavity. My lips slid down the shaft to a mere sheen of silken brown hair, where I expected my nose to find a full bush of it. But I forgot about the sparsity of growth with his knob now lodged in my throat. I inhaled, and the suction made Bart moan. Then I eased him out of the constricted area and concentrated on slickening him for penetration. I was hard-pressed to make enough of the stuff after I'd left so much on his boots, but when you've lived in a desert for years, you learn to compensate.

I was proud of how shiny I'd made Bart's rod look with my spit, and he said it looked cool, too. There was a large mirror on the wall opposite the bed above the low chest of drawers. He decided that he wanted to take me on all fours across the foot of the bed, so that we could watch him fucking me. He still had on his jeans and boots, so I hadn't seen the rest of his great body bare yet. I was prepared to be patient, because the jeans looked so sexy. It was so neat to watch his cock disappear into me and feel it move up my colon. We grinned at each other in the mirror. I knew that I was going to get used to looking into them again very easily, given the fascination I was having with seeing myself being fucked, not to mention my newly reintroduced mug.

I smiled at the reflection of my erection angling away from my torso, then closed my eyes and arched my head and back, savoring Bart's cock in me and my waving in response. I loved feeling a man in me again. Even if it wasn't Travis, but I concentrated on feeling Bart's helmeted beauty instead. And being naked on all fours, emulating an animal while he was mostly clothed, gave my new determinedly submissive psyche a rush. I wanted to bay like a coyote, the way Travis and I had some nights in response to them, and each other, but I resisted the celebratory outburst. Besides, I was determined to leave my previous lives behind me, like the asphalt the car had barely skimmed and the telephone poles it had rushed us past.

However, youthful intentions are too easily countermanded by reality.

Bart's fucking was a celebration of male lust, and he drove himself into me one last time with, "Oh, god, beautiful," and surrendered his cum to me.

Then he lay, sweaty and satisfied, as I pulled off his boots, jeans and socks. I crawled back onto the bed and hovered over him, kissing and nipping his glistening, tanned body, as if I were one of the playful coyote pups Travis and I had too rarely spied at play from a distance. My erection remained waving proudly from my body, as a flag bearer of old marched confidently into battle.

"Man, Jason, you're a really frisky guy. You just don't quit."

I looked up from my ministrations to his body. "Well, I do like worshipping your body. And I haven't come yet, so I guess I'm still pretty wound up."

"Well, let's wind you down. Sit down on me and let me take care of you."

I straddled him and nestled my buns into his striated ab muscles, teasing his sensitized head with my cheeks. He smiled and took my hard-on into his right hand. A ring I hadn't noticed before glinted in the bedside lamplight as he masturbated me with the easy detachment of someone who had already experienced his own penis's pleasure but was still enchanted by another boy's erection. That was fine. Being handled slowly like that only prolonged my enjoyment. I sighed under his touch, content to be with this beautiful young man and have him play with me however he saw fit. My moans of mounting excitement gave way to soft mewls as he got more interested in the organ now that it was bloated under the assault of his silky fingers.

My body moved under his increasingly firm grip, watching him do me, making me helpless in his hand. Then I convulsed in orgasm. My come splattered his face and chin before falling exhausted on his chest. We grinned at each other, as if sharing a secret no other humans were privy to. Then I cleaned him while savoring the smell he had emitted in his now-evaporated perspiration.

Stretched out beside him on the bed in naked camaraderie, I remarked about his ring. After what seemed like a strange pause, he said, "Jason, there's someone in my life." Involuntarily, I stiffened, although why I didn't know. Consciously I had no expectations of Bart other than sex. Then why? "His name is Hank, and I want you to meet him. He'll find you irresistible, like I do. We've been together for almost two years and love to share." Share what, I didn't ask.

I distracted myself by admiring his ring, which had a black stone set in the center of a plain gold band. Dark passion, he said of the color. The cave flickered in my mind for less than a second. I don't know why, but I kissed the glinting stone. He liked that.

Then I turned over and Bart held me.

"You seem to be readjusting to civilization pretty quickly."

"Well, I did spend most of my life in it, after all, so eating utensils and bathtubs are not alien objects. Although I admit that toilet paper is still a challenge." He thought that was funny. Then I did, too, remembering being befuddled by what to do after my diarrhetic bout in the restaurant rest room.

"What did you do in the desert?"

"We had two pools. One we bathed in. The lower one we used as our toilet." I explained how we dammed and undammed our "bathtub" to "flush the lower pool."

"We weren't barbarians, Bart."

"That was obvious, when I met you. So what happened to Travis that you left?"

I knew that he could feel my muscles tense at the question. "He died," I said too hastily. "I'd rather not talk about it." But it was too late. The image of the beautifully feathered, deadly phallus in my beloved overwhelmed me. My tears burst forth in spite of myself, but they did stop the probing. Bart just held and nuzzled me. Then when I regained my equilibrium, he said, "You'll like Chicago."

"Really?"

"Yeah. Boys for days. And you'll be a star, Jason."

Before I could ask what that meant, he lifted my right leg a bit in order to fit the erection I'd felt pressed against my spine into me. I sighed as he slid in, grateful to be used by his cock. As Bart moved in me, I proclaimed silently again that that was what I wanted to be now: a vessel of pleasure for males. And I would get my wish.

Nine

The next morning Bart said that we were on the last leg of our trip. He still wore his boots, but they were mostly covered by khaki jeans with black side stripes. His T-shirt, like mine, was black, too. When I remarked about not wearing the cowboy boots out, he said that Chicago wasn't cowboy country. He could have said that Neptune was bombarding earth with radio waves, and I would have accepted the explanation. I, myself had on shorts and his sexy, albeit too-big athletic shoes. He said that my calves were too cute to cover. Except that he had that morning before we dressed.

He had me pull on those black boots, which I found so sexy. In fact, I experienced an insistent erection by the time the leather was hugging my legs. Then, standing in plain view of a wall mirror outside the bathroom, Bart fucked me from behind and masturbated me as I luxuriated in my reflection. Because I was shorter than Bart, the boot tops came over my kneecaps and made them look all the more erotic to me. I watched myself spew come all over carpet not deserving it, as Bart emptied himself into me.

Riding through the vastness of a country my imagination might never learn to grasp, I swore that I could still feel his sweet cum on my ass. It would spot the light-colored shorts I wore and leave the leather upholstery wet, but when we stopped to eat, the long T-shirt would cover it. Yet I almost wanted everyone to see the wetness on my butt, a silent testimony of what my gorgeous traveling companion had done to me. Yes, despite myself, I feared I was falling hopelessly in love with this boy.

I became captivated by the landscape as we drove on. Having become used to the shaded monochromes and scattered greens of the desert, even the new monotony of corn and wheat fields was a visual delight. Although not nearly in a league with Bart. I could look at him for all my waking hours, I'd become so taken with him.

After lunch that day he said, "I really am impressed with how well you're adjusting to the world again, Jason."

"So, do you believe my story?"

"Yeah. The hair was the real giveaway. Well, and your dark skin."

"It was real, that's for sure." Still too real. Travis. The tears came and my eyes blinked at the amber waves of grain we were passing. I willed them away and, when they dried, concentrated my gaze on the profile of Bart's beauty. After a while he must have felt my eyes on him. He turned and smiled. Then he unzipped me and pulled me out into the rushing air. As we sped north, he masturbated me, simply keeping me hard for his hand's enjoyment. More air horns blasted the air from horny truckers we passed.

"That reminds me," he said after one such salute. "I have this friend, Morgan, whom I think you'll find really sexy. He has eleven fat ones. He used to hang out at night at an oasis on the tollway north of the city. He was a skinny, pretty kid at the time, he said. He's a god now, by the way. But then his cock looked even bigger because of how thin he was. He used to let truckers blow him and then screw them while they were draped over the rear tires of their rigs, screaming and begging him not to tear them up with his big sausage. They remembered his tool all the way to Mobile." He chuckled. "He's a lot kinkier now."

"I can't imagine."

"You won't have to. And I guarantee you'll want to worship his beauty for the rest of your days."

"Sounds interesting."

"It will be. Trust me."

"I do." Fool that I was.

The skyline of Chicago shocked me. I'd never seen buildings so tall. My excitement was heightened by my shooting my load on the Dan Ryan Expressway, which almost caused a passing motorist to crash into the center abutment, when he saw my geysers shoot up and blow into my face. I was grinning like a kid with a surfeit of candy as I licked at my white-pimpled face. Welcome to Chicago.

Bart and Hank lived in a nice, quiet, tree-lined neighborhood north of the university. I was eager to meet Bart's lover, especially given that he hadn't said much about the man. That, of course only made me dying to see what kind of beauty this adonis had his way with in bed every night.

I wasn't disappointed, although I was surprised. Hank was a redhead with wiry, nearly orange-hued hair above facial features thath only the word "cute" adequately described. He was someone you had the immediate urge to cuddle in your arms, he was so puppy-dog adorable. He grinned widely as he approached me. He didn't waste any time pressing his red lips on mine and unzipping me. His hand was inside the shorts, handling me proprietorially. His kisses were hot and wet, his fingers making me hard in no time.

When he'd accomplished that, he told me to kneel and make him the same way. I didn't hesitate. I went to unzip him, but he told me to kiss him first. Then I was allowed to bare him. Which involved unbuttoning him I found out. I determined to ask them why these tight jeans didn't have zippers. I reached in and carefully freed him from his denim prison.

His cock was almost snowy white, like his lightly freckled face. There were no beauty marks down there, but the skin was almost translucent, which made his veins more prominent looking and the bluest I had ever seen. It was a good six inches at rest and on the lean side. I went all the way down on it and buried my nose in his musky orange pubic hair. I kept myself in that position for several seconds, during which time Bart unbuttoned the waist of Hank's jeans and pushed them past me. I heard the redhead sigh as Bart's beauty cleaved his ass cheeks. I felt Hank lengthen and grow hard in my mouth and throat withoutmy even fellating him. When I did move back up his shaft, it was rock hard.

As I sucked, my hands found his spread legs and stroked the leather of the motorcycle boots he was wearing. Man, these guys were into it, I decided. I also decided that I could get used to living in nothing but tall boots, specifically with these two guys.

After making him begin to pulse, I left his pale erection to attend to his low-hanging sac. Like Bart's it was smooth. And his tawny pubic hair was hardly visible, too. Kind of kinky, I decided. Little did I know, as I sucked and licked Hank's balls into retreat.

Then I returned to his hard-on, which was waving at me from the hard thrusts of Bart into him. I sucked him in earnest now and was rewarded for my labors when he cried out and gushed into my throat, causing me to choke on his pole. I left him to soften in my mouth as Bart brought himself off in the slick tunnel of his lover.

I slept with them that night, lying between them after getting blown and fucked by both of them. It was when I saw that Hank had a tattoo on his right biceps that matched Bart's I spoke up. They gave me a vague explanation about symbolism of the half inch solid black line that encircled each's arm. It was pretty much what Bart had told me, when I'd pointed it out that first evening in the motel. They looked sexy, but I wondered why guys would do that.

I found out sooner, rather than later.

Ten

Morgan was another boy who took my breath away. It was much like seeing Travis's naked perfection that first day. Still lean, but by no means skinny, he was dressed in leather, although he wore nothing under his motorcycle jacket. Silver chains swaggered in loops from both that and his jeans. He looked nearly bald under his peaked cap, his hair was cut so close to the scalp. His skin was the creamy brown of chocolate frosting left to soften in a warm kitchen before spreading. He made my mouth water.

I thought it strange that he greeted the guys by running his fingers over their cheeks in greeting. His hands were otherwise sheathed in gloves. Bart and Hank seemed to accept this gesture from him gratefully and even kissed the leather palm of his hand.

Then he turned his attention to me and appraised me as if I were something that he was considering buying. At least that was the impression I got from his dark, shiny eyes. They were riveting, no-nonsense eyes. God, one more thing that made him beautiful. This man was so hot that he had me hard just looking at him. Which reminded me to look down to see if there were any hint as to what that eleven-inch sausage had become in adulthood. There wasn't one. It was advertised! His cock lay down his left leg, almost as a threat, it was so long. Unconsciously, I licked my lips at the sight of it. I wanted it. Then I wondered if I could take it.

Morgan told me to strip off my clothes after our introduction. That threw me, but I complied. When I was bared to him, he ran his leather palms over my smooth body, including my cock, which he made hard again just by brushing it with his slick palm. He smiled, his eyes boring into me, as he handled me. Then he shocked me by kissing me with his plump lips. His tongue went inside my mouth, and I surrendered to his strong, leather-covered arms.

When he had made me desperate for him, he stopped. He sat down on one of the living room chairs, and Hank brought him a beer. Morgan motioned with his finger for me to sit at his feet between his boots.

I did so without question, feeling a thrill in submitting like that. The way I had determined I wanted to be for other men. Their sex toy. As he chatted with my hosts, about my potential for becoming a slave, no less! he caressed my golden curls. I could hardly believe that he was actually talking about me like that, my face, my body, and yet he didn't say anything directly to me. Yet he made me erect with the things he said.

When he'd had a couple of beers, he took hold of my chin and twisted my head to look up at him. "Let's go, boy," he said. I was dressed within a minute.

If Bart and Hank's place was the plushest apartment I'd ever seen, Morgan's took my breath away. He lived in a high rise building on what he called the Gold Coast. I saw why, when he pointed out Lake Michigan just beyond the picture window in his living room. I was naked again now, having disrobed when we got inside the door, and soon embarrassed, when he introduced me to his other housemates. One, his sister Michelle, was a strikingly pretty teenager. She carried the leather theme from Morgan with a black mini skirt and platform boots. Her straight black hair was styled simply but flatteringly around her head. Honestly, she was the prettiest girl I had ever seen.

Damien was a goodlooking guy in his early twenties. His skin was lighter than Morgan's and Michelle's. He wore only a pair of white nylon sweatpants and head wrap. His muscles on the slim frame reminded me of the tigers from the circus. The impression was reinforced by a series of horizontal scars on his cheeks, which looked almost like cat's whiskers. I would find out that a wealthy white lover had done it to him to make him resemble what he thought an African savage would look like. I would also see his penis head, which also bore lines radiating out from his slit. It was horrifying and yet intensely arousing to see how his glans had been altered. Not surprisingly, I guess, Damien was reserved in meeting me.

Then there was Buddy, a brown-haired white teenager, who had on a pair of expensive athletic shoes and a ball cap worn backward. Buddy was a doll. And he thought nothing of being bare in front of the others, it appeared. He was a flirt, too, which Morgan seemed to tolerate with no problem. Buddy, it turned out, was a cock hog, as the master put it. He loved sucking and did it to his heart's content, when the brothers came over, Morgan said. A few drinks and your cock sucked, too, I thought. I could see the boy's lips around even the fattest prick, his mouth was so conveniently wide. A boy who lived to taste pubic flesh and semen. Not a bad life, especially living in such a luxurious place.

After a late dinner that night, where we dined alone, Morgan took me to his bedroom suite. The bed was huge and covered with a black leather blanket. We had chatted for a long time over the meal about something called the Ebony Fraternity and my participating in the group as a slave. I assured him that I was willing to try, considering that what he told me made me hard again. The fact that he was so seductively handsome didn't hurt in the least, but the shiny skins he wore excited me even more.

He had me kneel and lick his boots. Because I'd already willingly done that to Bart, I had no reservations. Except that Morgan didn't clean his first. That was my job. Then, after gargled to clean my mouth, he made me worship his incredible cock. I choked several times, it was so big even soft, but he made me take his entire length into me. That was cool, though, because it was magnificent. Almost ebony in darkness, it was beautifully formed. I thought how I had an ideal of male endowments in me as I serviced him enthusiastically.

When he'd had enough oral worship, he told me that it was time to get fucked by a man. I gulped. That massive organ was going to tear me up. I thought briefly of all the truckers he'd sent on their ways with sore asses. Still, I wanted it.

He took me from behind, easing his head into me past my surprised sphincter, which screamed in insult. Then, before I could concentrate on the searing pain, I felt the organ push all the way up my colon, stretching it like a rubber band. I was impaled on every inch of his manhood and my gut was on fire. I blinked tears, but I refused to cry out in pain. How many other guys ever got to have a cock of this size stuffed inside them? I reasoned. As Morgan pummelled me, I clenched my hands on my knees and bit my lips. I refused to give in to the turmoil in my nether region. I wanted his magnificence right where it was, and I was willing to pay the price, even disembowelment, if that's what it took.

Soon, he was breathing raggedly and dripping sweat on my back, his fucking was so animated. The pain had mysteriously lessened the longer he used me, but I was reminded of what was in me every second it was there. He held me by the shoulders and pounded away inside me until he cursed and came. I felt the weird sensation of come blasting the top of my colon at short range. He actually had filled the entire descending part, I realized to my amazement. When he pulled out, I felt as if I were going to remain stretched permanently. And I decided that I wouldn't mind that a bit, if I didn't have to shit again.

"You have one tight pussy, slave."

"Thank you, sir. I mean, Master."

He chuckled and pinched my cheek. "Either, Jason." Then he went to a dresser and removed something from the top drawer. A chain with clips. He applied the clips to my nipples. They hurt, but they also engorged from the stinging sensation. He showed me what I looked like adorned, and the sight of the silver ornamentation pleased me. As did the dull pain now. Then he kissed me hard and long. I slept with him that night and relieved his need the next morning when I awoke.

Over the next week I met several of Morgan's fraternity brothers and serviced all of them wearing nothing but the chain hanging between my nipples. I was surprised and disconcerted that they were not at all as friendly, but rather they treated me as a piece of meat. They stroked my body and played with my penis and scrotum with detachment. However, I became glad for this, because it made me realize what the life of a slave would be like. It would be filled with worshipping these muscular studs but devoid of affection. I would merely be a body, whose purpose was to serve and give pleasure.

Something about that fact satisfied me. During my meditations after Travis's death, I had determined that the love I had experienced with him I couldn't possibly expect to find again. But I was still a sexual creature and needed the physical contact with other males, even if it was only to give pleasure or to be used for theirs. Love was out of the question. It had died with Travis. Considering how young I still was, perhaps I could be excused my emotional immaturity.

I passed the scrutiny of the men, who had "interviewed" me. This was after I had passed my physical and psychological evaluations. So the next week I was pierced. A rather ugly black man with a full beard came to the apartment to adorn me. Large silver rings were put into my ears first. Then my septum was breached, which hurt like hell and burned worse. My nipples got the same treatment, as did my cockhead and perineum. Despite the pain, I was pleased with how I looked, when my temporary master showed me the results. I knelt and kissed his feet, hoping that it was an appropriate response to my being altered so dramatically. It was.

I spent the rest of the day lying on a bed in my "slave quarters," a bedroom and bath off Morgan's suite. I tried to sleep off the pain, but I hurt too much. At one point, Michelle knocked and came in. She was wearing her mini skirt with a ruffled blouse, sheer hose and her boots.

"Do you mind if I come in, Jason?"

"No, not at all. If you don't mind listening to me moan."

"That's why I played hookey today. How do you feel?"

"Awful. But the rings do look cool. If they would only feel that way."

"They will. The pharmacy is sending up pain pills for you. Morgan's good that way, and he was impressed that you took it so maturely."

"Well, I am a slave."

"You'll be a great one."

"I hope."

The doorbell rang, and Michelle went off to see if it was the pain medication. God, she walked seductively, and I didn't even like girls. When she returned, I took one of the pills and lay back down. She sat on the bed.

"You really do look so sexy in your jewelry." With that she stretched out on the bed with me.

"Thanks, but I'm sure you realize that I'm not into girls."

"Of course, silly. I'm not either."

"Well, I would have guessed that. And as pretty as you are, you can have any boy you want."

"Sweet talker. But I'm not straight, either."

"Now I am confused."

"I'm a boy, Jason."

Michelle found the look of shock on my face amusing. He tittered as if he really were a girl. "When our parents died in the car wreck, Morgan was already a successful stockbroker. So I moved in here with him. But I made him promise that I could be the girl I wanted to be. I mean, how could he refuse, being Mister Leather Master and all? So he let me wear girls' clothes and makeup, and even enrolled me in an exclusive academy. They don't have a clue. I just pray that I don't need to shave before I graduate. But once I'm in Barnard, what are they going to do, right?"

"Amazing. And you really enjoy being a girl?"

"No, I enjoy being a boy dressed as a girl. I'm as queer as my brother and love it."

"Do you get it on with Buddy?"

"Are you kidding? Child, that adorable boy was made to have sex with. I love Buddy. He's Bart's cousin, you know. And I think he's going to be Morgan's personal slave, when he's old enough. I mean, he sees himself as Morgan's boy already, but my brother wants him to have a few more years to decide that that's what he wants. After all, he's only a kid. But he simply adores Morgan. And my brother has to be careful, because having a white boy as his boy is definitely frowned upon by the fraternity. Honestly, Jason, I think that Morgan would prefer to keep you to himself, but he is smitten with Buddy. He thinks you'll be a great slave. I can tell how proud he is of you already."

We spent most of the afternoon together. Michelle, well Michael, undressed to a pair of nylons and lacy garter. His body was boyishly beautiful. We kissed and played with each other, but we didn't come. And thanks to the pain pills, my erections didn't hurt. Besides, I loved spending the time with Michael. He was intelligent, in addition to being enticing. I also found myself admiring him, he was so confident of his sexuality and the persona he wanted to be.

He told me that Bart and Hank had sold me into slavery. Now it made sense why they lived in such a nice place. It was true that Bart had been visiting his parents, but he was also looking for cute boys for the Ebony Fraternity to domesticate, while he was down in Texas. Using his looks and high boots as the lure. I didn't resent what he'd done, because he and Hank were slaves, too, although they served their black masters part-time now. Morgan had been their patron, too, so he made sure that the fraternity provided for their well-being. And Michael said that slaves were now pierced instead of being tattooed and sometimes scarred, as they had been when Bart and Hank were inducted.

I decided that I preferred being pierced for the pleasure of the men I would serve. Now that I wasn't in pain, the heavy rings and balls were even sexier on me. Michael helped me move the jewelry, which I would do daily, so that I would heal with the holes remaining open.

Something else that made sense after talking with Michael, (he liked that I called him by his real name), was the Greek letter *epsilon* carved into Morgan's right pectoral. I was fascinated by its smooth surface and liked to lick it on the nights we lay together in bed. Morgan hadn't really said much about it, but Michael said that the letter represented the 'e' for ebony and members of the fraternity were permanently scarified to show their membership. I found the angular letter cut into Morgan highly arousing—as if I needed something else about him to make my hormones go wild.

Ten

Morgan said he liked my friskiness. It was something that Bart remarked about, too. I suppose that Travis and I had been a lot more like coyote pups at play than I had realized. But my Master enjoyed my enthusiasm, as short-lived as it was. And I loved worshipping his body and having his cock deep inside my boy place.

I received my first pair of engineer boots soon after my piercing, and I wore them with a pair of 501s (I finally found out what they were). I'd spent the better part of the day in the tub, emptying and refilling with hot water to fade the dye. Then I'd stood in the solarium letting them dry to shrink to the contours of my body.

Michelle, or Michael, as he preferred me to call him, was pleased to get to watch them dry on me. He had on a white blouse and plaid skirt, dark beige pantyhose and buckled patent leather shoes. "The nuns must have forgotten the old reflection thing," he said, looking down to see if he could spot his panties. "Nope, and they're plain white ones. But they are elegantly ruffled." Then he raised his skirt to show me and giggled. Honestly, I knew that I could easily fall in love with Michael, he was such a fun guy to be with, in addition to being more beautiful every time I saw him.

"Have you sprouted something unboylike all of a sudden," I asked, looking at his chest.

"Oh, the falsies. It's a training bra with socks stuffed in it. But the socks do have lace trim," he hastened to add. "Well, I *am* sixteen, and I should be showing something there, you know. After Christmas vacation I'm going to switch to rolled-up athletic socks. They'll just think I grew. Anyway, the other students, who had sisters who went to Annunciation, say that the girls practically bound themselves so they didn't show their cleavage, it was so strict in those days. The patent leather thing, right?" He looked down but saw nothing. Again. Which made him frown. "Stupid nuns." That made me laugh. He was rapidly becoming the neatest guy I'd ever met. After Travis. And Yuki. And.... "Now we're supposed to be proper young ladies, but we can have tits. Well, some of us. Just my luck." He giggled again. It was a melody learned from angels.

"I love you, Michael," I found myself blurting out.

"I love you, Jason." His beautiful dark eyes were serious as they held mine. He came up and kissed me with shiny red lips. Another one-time heresy allowed now by the nuns. "I really do. You're the most beautiful boy I've ever seen, and that includes Morgan and Buddy. In fact, Buddy was the first white boy I was ever attracted to. Well, Dexter Briley in grade school, but he was an almost white-skinned black boy." Then he threw me. "We're about the same age, aren't we?"

"Uh, well, I mean, Michael, I'm eighteen, okay?"

"Uh huh. The company line. I thought we were the same age." He kissed me again with those wonderful painted lips.

"Oh, sorry." It was Buddy. He had evidently just arrived for an evening with the master. He was wearing another pair of awesome athletic shoes in black with white accents."I didn't mean to interrupt you guys."

"Not at all, sweetheart. We were just sharing some personal feelings." He and the white boy hugged and kissed with even more feeling.

Then I had a strange thought. I wondered what would happen if Michael and Buddy fell in love. Would Morgan allow his brother to steal his future slave from him?

"And how have you been able to resist this blond-haired beauty?"

"By not being around him much. Besides, Master would beat the shit out of me, if I played with Jason. You know that, miss preppie girl."

"What Master doesn't know, Buddy." Then he lowered his panties and hose and took hold of Buddy's cock, which was still tumescent from their kissing. My hand surrounded his little semi-hard beauty, and Buddy played with mine.

The sun was streaming into the room, as we stroked each other. Buddy and I grinned at each other. I liked him. He was younger than Michael and I, but he possessed his own friskiness, which I enjoyed.

"You know, for sixteen years old, you don't have much in the way of mammaries, Michelle," he said, squashing the left sock-filled cup while still teasing Michael's glans."Boys dig them, you know."

"I wouldn't, and neither would you, you creepy faggot." We laughed. The three of us might as well have all been school girls in uniforms with falsies, we were so giddy. It felt so good to be with these guys. Guys my own age, although Buddy was younger by a year or two. But he was spirited, too, and I thought that Morgan was going to have a gem in him.

We were still keeping each other hard when Damien wandered in wearing lustrous red sweatpants and a matching wave cap. He smiled at what we were doing and rubbed his cock through the shiny fabric. It was so cool to watch him lengthen against it. Then he walked over to where we were standing and pulled it out for me to handle. The swollen cockhead, which had repelled me when I'd first seen it, now looked almost like a flower in bloom. And it shot its pollen for me after a few minutes.

Twelve

Morgan took me to a leather shop, which was located in the back of the fraternity's city location, to be fitted with my collars. I was dressed in my jeans and boots, the attire of a slave accompanying a master to the club. Most didn't, except on rare occasions, because any sex the members had in the city with white boys was done upstairs, Morgan said. But occasionally a member would bring the slave while he mingled with his brothers and had drinks. A new slave was usually introduced to whichever members were present at the club before he began his formal servitude. That was what would happen that night and the following to me.

The men in the shop were friendly to me, which I didn't expect. Morgan had told me that most fraternity members didn't dislike the slaves; they just considered us inferior. But at the same time, they respected us for our volunteering ourselves to their service. Even the out-and-out racists would treat me fairly, he assured me.

First my collar was fitted on me. It was a beautiful inlaid-onyx collar with rounded silver edges, about an inch wide. And a bitch to get around my neck, because it wasn't hinged. But somehow they managed to squeeze it onto me. It locked with an emphatic click. I would wear it for the next two years, at least. And even before I saw how great it looked, it felt really comfortable sitting in the middle of my neck. You see, the artisan, who had produced it and fitted me with it, had made an indentation for my Adam's apple in front, so that it rode on it when I swallowed. He was kind of effeminate and fussy, and it was so cute to see him pleased that he'd gotten the fit over the cartilage right. Morgan was amused, too, but I saw that he was also proud of me.

Being fitted with the genital harness was more time consuming. It wasn't that it was all that tricky to put on, but it was rigid, too, and the man had to be careful of my vasectomy scar on the seam of my scrotum. Well, it wasn't really a vasectomy. A surgeon, who was a member of the fraternity, had simply closed off my vas deferens with what he described as a kind of paper clip. He assured me that he could remove it with no injury to me, so that I could come again after my days of bondage were over. Slaves were altered so that we didn't have accidents if a brother was playing with us. The doctor also said that he would definitely see me later and winked.

So the stitches were out, but I was still tender. Mindful of this, the artisan was careful. The harness was the same as the collar, only narrower. The basic cock ring was intersected seamlessly by another which encircled the base of my shaft. A third curved length ran down from there over my seam and then up to the back of the bigger ring, where it locked. God, the harness looked beautiful! It couldn't be taken off, except with a special key. And it sure as hell couldn't accidentally fall off. It was a part of me as long as I was a slave.

I thanked the artist for harnessing me with his exquisite pieces of bondage by kissing the hands that made them. He was pleased by my obeisance. So was Morgan. He squeezed my neck on the way out of the shop.

When I was dressed again, we made our way out into club. I walked behind Morgan, being led by a leather leash attached to my penis ring, but he had me stand beside him to introduce me to his brothers. It was so cool to look down and see the strap coming out of the opened button of the fly. And to see the bulge the harness made, of necessity. Yes, I was going to really get into being a slave. And my psychological evaluations had confirmed it.

All of the men wore leather. Their ages ranged from twenties to sixties, it appeared. It seemed to me that the older men were the friendliest, and the younger ones were the most arrogant—and most likely to want to fuck me or have me blow them. But generally the men made me feel welcome. After all, I had volunteered to give up two years of my life to serve their every whim.

There was another new slave there that night. Morgan didn't know his name, but he had been introduced the night before. That night he was bared for the men. He knelt with his legs spread and his hands cuffed behind his back, on a pedestal about four feet tall. His penis was tethered to a bolt in the platform by a short chain attached to his head ring. That really turned me on, it was so arousing to see a boy helpless like that. Naturally, it was the first time I experienced an erection in my new harness, and I loved it. I also loved seeing the boy, who was adorned the way I was. Although he had an impassive expression on his face, he cracked a smile and winked, when he saw me wearing the common uniform. I grinned and winked back. I would come to find out that my brothers were very special boys, and very frisky, like me.

And I would be where he was the following night, and thinking about it made me all the harder.

Thirteen

The other fraternity building was west of the city. It was a resort, Morgan said. All kinds of leisuretime activities for the brothers. It was entered by an unmarked, dirt road and entrance to the grounds was gained by inserting a credit card into a slot and then punching in a code before the gate would open. I was shocked by how big the building was. And you would never guess that it was there, given how foliated the front of the property was.

When I arrived at the fraternity, I was greeted by Mister Jakes and ushered into a locker room to the left of the entrance. I undressed. He took my jeans and boots and checked to make sure that my name was in the clothes. I still did have a name, just not at the fraternity. Well, most of the time, but that was another matter. When he saw that my stuff was in order, he handed them to another slave to put away. The boy was brown-haired, blue-eyed and gorgeous, of course, as were all of the slaves. That was one reason that I was looking forward to serving there. The boy, whose name was Jonathan, showed me where my locker was. Like the others, it had no door, but there was no theft, so there was no need for them. And it was so cool to see all of the pairs of identical jeans and boots in them. We were all brothers, all equal, the sight said to me. Even if we were all lowly slaves.

Past the locker room was a bathroom and shower room. All of the slaves showered after being masturbated and shaved each morning. We would line up to be sexed by Mr. Jakes in order to lessen the possibility of hurting ourselves while on duty. I'll explain later. Then the boys were all shaved, which is what he did to me now. I didn't have much body hair to begin with, but he buzzed my head, leaving only a rime of a crew cut. I looked down to see my ringlets lying dead on the floor. Then the blond tufts from my armpits and crotch. The latter stubble was then removed with a safety razor to make me completely smooth. Then I showered. While I was soaping myself with leather-scented soap, it struck me why Bart and Hank had had such little hair on their bodies. They were shaved, whenever they were on duty. Now it made sense.

Our routine for cleaning ourselves was morning, after lunch and before retiring. The last shower was in case one of the members awoke at night and decided that he was horny and needed an ass or mouth to fuck. At least the boy's body would be fresh for him. We were kept scrupulously clean for the members.

After I was cleaned up, Mr. Jakes gave me a tour of the facilities and told me what my training would consist of beginning the following morning. I liked him almost immediately. And even though he was formal with us most of the time, he would pat our butts and kiss us to show us that we were his boys. Well, considering that we took most of our orders from him, and the fact that he denuded us to make us look like prepubescent boys, and masturbated us every day, we were.

I didn't get to meet my roommate before I dressed and was taken back into the city to be displayed for the members. That made me only more curious as to what the boy would look like. The reason was because the slaves were allowed to play with each other in the evening, after they were off duty. Morgan said that usually roommates had sex with each other, from what he understood. So I was hoping that I would have a bedmate whom I would want to do it with.

I have to say that I really enjoyed being bare and tethered on the pedestal, my body ogled and occasionally touched by handsome dark men in leather. When I was led in, another boy was already there, standing on a low version of the platform I would be on. Marvin, the member who had brought me back into the city, told me that the slave was being used as ornamentation, until I arrived. He, too, was very handsome and stood like a statue. His hands were bound behind him, and, also like the slave the previous night, his genitals were lifted and flaunted by the harness. Beyond that lewd display, I noticed that a black pole rose out of the pedestal between his legs. It wasn't until he was lifted off the little stage by two of the leather men that I realized that the pole was a sleek black phallus, and that he had been standing there impaled on it. The long, ersatz black cock had been buried in his ass, making him utterly helpless. Man, that was so sexy!

As a result, my own cock was waving at attention when I mounted the pedestal. Marvin and another man, whose name I never heard, had great fun joking about my organ's randiness. But their amusement wasn't at my expense, I realized. It was a shared male thing. We're guys, we get hard, sometimes in spite of ourselves. And it also didn't help my physical excitement that there was another aspect to my immobilization on that pedestal that I hadn't seen the night before. A short, but very thick butt plug was also there to hold my body in place. Very carefully they fitted me onto the monster. It filled me and made me sigh, it felt so good inside me. After a few more minutes, they were able to secure me to the ring, to my relief.

I was now kneeling with my legs spread wide apart, my ass held firm by the plug and resting on my calves, my cock tethered to the floor. The realization of my total dependency on the leather-clad beauties around me was heady. This was what my slavery was: complete reliance on men I didn't know for my well-being.

All in all, my stint on display went without a hitch, except for my penis responding to more than one fraternity brother's leather-clad beauty. But the pull of the chain on my vulnerable sex brought me back to the different reality of my own incapacitation.

The member, whose name I didn't know, drove me back to the fraternity. I blew him on the way, which I was glad to do. He had a short, fat cock, and I nursed on it for the twenty or so miles, finally making him come in the parking lot. He told me how good I'd made him feel. He was a nice person, and I was glad that I could give him so much pleasure.

A slave greeted my chauffeur and smiled at me, nodding. Then he led the man away. Another boy came out of the locker room, and we both laughed and hugged. It was the slave over whom I'd salivated on the pedestal. He introduced himself as

Todd. When I'd doffed my boots and jeans, he took my hand and led me farther into the building, where the slaves' sleeping wing was. We both had shit-eating grins on our faces, we were so happy at the prospect of each other's body sharing his bed.

Our area was simple painted cinder block. There were no doors on the bedrooms, but why bother? We were always nude, so there wasn't any need for privacy. And sex at night was expected, I gathered, so we wouldn't be doing something nobody else wasn't. The bed was the only piece of furniture. After all, we didn't need dressers. In spite of the spartan accommodations, there was a toilet in the room, which was thoughtful. It was one of numerous examples of kindnesses that the brothers did for their slaves without comment.

Once inside the room we were in each other's arms, our lips and bodies pressed together in urgent communication. Our genital adornments clinked and then sang as we ground the steel in our crotches against each other in unbridled excitement. I was still high from my recent presentation and being with the boy who had done it the night before me drove me on. We maneuvered to the bed and flopped onto it. Our mouths and tongues were everywhere, sampling the soft skin and supple muscles of our mutual desire. Predictably they ended up in each other's crotch. We couldn't resist the newly jeweled boy sexes we wore.

The taste of Todd's metal and jewel restraint set off explosions in my brain. The hardness; the smoothness; the reality of the onyx and stainless steel girdling us made me swell in his hungry mouth. And he returned the favor with body-wracking convulsions. We spasmed in each other's mouth again that night. It was the beginning of our falling in love with each other. It was also the real start of my intensive love affair with my harnesses and the fact of my slavery. See, that night the fact of my not being able to come was driven home to me. I equated that reality with my beautiful harness, and it gave me an indescribable mental high.

During my first official week of slavery, a young black boy came to the fraternity. He was beautiful and had a lithe body. I took him for a slave but was quickly corrected by Todd.

"Ricky is a boy."

"You can say that again!"

"Jason, he's not a slave. He's a boy. His master owns him, but he's taken the man's name, so he's his boy. He comes here so that Mr. Jakes can finish him for his master. Besides, he obviously isn't one of us, slave brain."

It was. In the first place, Ricky had creamy brown skin, so, by definition, he couldn't be a slave. In the second, he had pubic hair above his genital harness, which also made him superior to us.

And his master, Rasheem, was the only fraternity member I can honestly say that I came close to hating. I think that it was mutual. He would always find fault with me, to the point of calling me by my name. Which was the ultimate shame for a slave, because it singled us out and separated us from our fellow slaves. Worse, I always had to wait on him, no matter what damned hour of the day or night he decided to show up. He was able to get away with abusing me because, like Morgan, he was one of the richest guys in the fraternity. And as much as I hate to admit it, one day he broke whatever last mental barriers I might have still had to being completely submissive.

He made me bend over and put a dildo fashioned after his cock and balls in me right in front of a bunch of the members, and Ricky. I had to walk around with the fake balls sticking out of me. Later he attached a leash to my nose ring, for maximal humiliation, took out the dildo, then made me kneel and fellate it while he held it and the leash. I had to suck and lick my mucius and shit off it. After being made to rinse out my mouth thoroughly under Mr. Jakes' watchful eyes, he made me suck him off. It choked and hurt me, it was so big. He held me tight to him as he creamed my throat, causing me more discomfort from gagging on his flood of man come.

He completed my utter debasement by making me blow Ricky. Oral worship of a boy, along with being called by his name, was the ultimate degradation a slave could suffer. I made love to Ricky's cock as if it were my mother's tit giving me life-sustaining milk. It was while sucking and licking it that I fantasized about being his Boy. And then someone else's Boy, which came out of nowhere and totally confused me. But Ricky brought me back to reality by coming in my mouth, making me swallow all of it until he let me free.

...

Life at the fraternity was fulfilling, if demanding at times. There were always fraternity brothers there, but the weekends were the worst. That was the only time some of them could get out of the city for some relaxation. Most of my life was filled with menial exercises. But the daily activities I loved most, besides making it with my gorgeous roommate at night, were getting shaved and being hobbled. After showering each morning, Mr. Jakes would attach a short length of chain to the rings at the end of our cockheads and secure it to the ring in our perineums. This chastisement kept us from responding to the delightful sights of the muscular brown bodies we served. It was also why we were masturbated each morning. Thank Priapus.

Also, being neutered with the chain meant that we had to sit to pee. When we were done, we had to blot our slits to remove any remaining urine. As I said, we were kept meticulously clean for the brothers.

Despite the fact that I loved being submissive and obeying orders, I wasn't a saint. Even as docile as I was, I still mouthed off to Mr. Jakes in frustration sometimes. Once I even told him to fuck himself. Boy, that was a mistake. No, he said with fire in his eyes, I'm gonna fuck you, white trash. And he did, making me bend over in front of Todd and all the other slaves on the shift. With his index finger in my mouth, making me suck on it, he pounded my ass good. But then once he'd made an example of me, he held me, which melted my insides, it was such a neat thing for him to do, and the gesture wasn't lost on anyone. It was just one of the reasons we loved the slave master.

I do want to tell you about one event, almost a ceremony, which I will never forget as long as I live. It was an honor for a slave to be used for it, and Todd and I were on numerous occasions. It took place in a room about twenty feet square. It was called the Ritual Room by the young brothers, who played there. The walls were painted black and lacquered, and the floor was heavily padded under a thick white carpet. There were eight round pillars, also black, set about a foot out from the walls. There was one at each corner and the middle of the walls. Leather cuffs were put on our wrists and ankles, and we were secured to these columns by Mr. Jakes' lacing the cuffs together behind the pillars. The sight of twelve slaves lashed to those phallic symbols and suspended on them was indescribably beautiful. But it got better. Steel penile cages were fitted over us. They were snug and made our cocks curve upward to where a spike sat as a metallic extension of our further-harnessed sexes. Into the spikes black tapers were pressed and lighted. Helplessly tethered to the pillars, we were the illumination for the sex play of the young, buffed studs.

And it was only about ten twenty-and-young-thirty somethings, who participated. They all wore silver-studded black pouches over their scrotums, which were secured to the bases of their shafts by a studded strap. Man, they looked so hot naked in those adornments. And their oiled skins gleamed in the flames of us candleboys. If they had a boy, they would often bring him and make him sit against the walls next to us to watch them cavort.

What made it a ritual was that they began each session by kissing each other and then reciting a pledge of loyalty to each other in Swahili. Then it was an orgy. The men celebrated each other's body by kissing, licking and sucking seemingly every part of them. Morgan always participated, and I especially liked it when Rasheem licked his armpits. Of course that aroused me, which was hell to pay as my swelling cock pressed against the unforgiving steel cage. Still, it was captivating to watch the glistening bodies slide over each other and enter each other in lust. For some reason I especially liked seeing the men suck on each other's dark cock. And also seeing those beautiful boys' harnessed cocks in erection in response to seeing their masters cheat on them so sensually.

One gorgeous young stud, Steven, who liked for me to suck on the fingers of his one hand while he drank beer with the other (which I really enjoyed, by the way), would lie on the floor while another brother straddled him. Then he would grasp the man and pull himself up against him with his ebony beauty between the man's cheeks. Another participant would suck Steven to erection and then guide as much of the long cock as he could into the man. Then he would fuck Steven's exposed ass. And so on. Meanwhile, the man being fucked by

Steve would suck off another brother. Who would be fucked. And so on and so forth. Boy, talk about the cage hurting!

My favorite scene was when Morgan would take Rasheem from behind, while they were kneeling. Except that Morgan would kiss, fondle and masturbate him while doing it. Still, it seemed that my Master was doing it for me. At least that was what I wanted to believe.

At the end of the orgy, they all kissed each other one last time, and then they each caressed us on the head in thanks for illuminating their scene. Yes, even Rasheem, who did respect my slavery, while not liking me. I appreciated his pat as much as the others', although Morgan's meant the most to me, of course. And when we were taken down from the pillars, Mr. Jakes reattached our neutering chains. Then we went out into the hallway, where we were paid the highest physical compliment a brother could show to a slave. We lined up and, one by one, they would place their index fingers between our shafts and sacs. I don't know how that gesture came about, but it was awesome to have a brother do that to me, it was so rare and special.

Thirteen

My life for the next several years seemed to be assured. Todd and I were in love and among the most popular of the slaves. Jaytoh and Tohjay, we were called. (All of the slaves called each other by nicknames, our given names being pejorative, of course.) It was not only rightly assumed that we would re-up, there was talk of waiving the age limit for a slave, which was thirty, when the time came for us to leave the service. We were awfully young-looking for eighteen-year-olds, so I guess they figured that we had good genes. And believe me, we were both ready to spend our lives at the fraternity as slaves and lovers. But it was not to be.

Before the day came to officially sign up for another stint, I was called to Morgan's place. This did happen from time to time, so I thought nothing of it. Besides, I loved getting fucked by my Master and spending the night with him. I also got to see Michael, which was great. He had grown into one beautiful young lady.

So imagine my shock when I arrived and was told that I was not going to remain as a slave of the Ebony Fraternity. Instead, I was going to accompany Michael to college in New York. He'd been accepted at Barnard College and Columbia University. When I protested that I wanted to remain a slave, Morgan assured me that I would. He showed me the paper, which said that he owned me. Although I was formally owned by all of the fraternity members in common, Morgan held individual title to me. And as I clutched the paper and watched, Morgan sold me to Michael for one dollar. That was far less than Bart and Hank had been paid for bringing me into the fraternity, by the way. He also handed the key to my harnesses to his brother.

Were it not for Todd, I would have been thrilled. I had loved Michael almost from the day I met him, and I had fantasized that I was sucking his cock, when I would go down on one of the brothers. Still, I was in love with Todd and said so.

"You'll get over it, when you start to worship my hot body," Michael said. I would, but I never went back to the resort to say goodbye to Todd. And I also never knew if he was as crushed as I was.

We didn't fly to New York. That would have created an unwanted problem with regard to my genital harness, not to mention the other intimate piercings, at the metal detectors. There was no way that Michael would take any of them off my body, either. Instead, we drove to the city in the car Morgan had bought him the previous year.

I know that you must be asking what kind of a fool I was that I didn't realize that I was legally able to walk away from the situation. But to where? Besides, I had been a slave for two years. I had been completely obedient, well, pretty completely, to every man I encountered during those two years. I was conditioned to obey. And during that time, all of my physical needs were taken care of. I mean, remember, I was even masturbated once a day. So, what was I going to do? I was going to accompany my new Master to New York.

I had never been there, although Michael had visited several times. He was eager to get there and party, as he put it. That was why we left almost a month before school started. As he drove onto the skyway to head east for Gotham, I wondered what kind of adventure this would turn out to be. I could never have imagined what Bart's picking me up would lead to. Thinking about that made me miss Todd all the more.

God, we had great sex together. From cocksucking to fucking, although I never fucked him. And he did something sometimes that Travis used to do to me. I had told him about my life with the beautiful Indian and about my favorite thing.

I would just lie on our mat while Travis kissed me and caressed my body. My torso, arms and legs. God, it drove me crazy to be handled by him that way. My toes would curl, my back arch under his touch, he was so sensual the way his hands loved my body. Then when I couldn't take it anymore, he would masturbate me. Looking back, I could see how I was a submissive person to begin with. It wasn't just that. I let Travis take the lead in everything. As I had with Yuki. And the boy I loved from the circus, whose name I'd forgotten. And now my newest love had made love to me as erotically as Travis had. I told Michael again that I really missed Todd.

"Well, sweetheart, he was only a slave after all. Now you have a real ladyboy to love and serve. Besides, do you think for a minute that I wasn't going to do anything I could to get Morgan to give you to me, beautiful?"

"I appreciate that, Michael. I really do. I love you. But Todd and I spent two wonderful years together."

"As slaves, Jason." I winced, when he said that, and explained. "Sorry. But you have a name, which I love, by the way, and I'm going to use it. None of that slave crap like Morgan and his playmates, even if I do own you."

"But what I'm trying to say is that we were really, really in love with each other."

He was silent for a few seconds. "I'm sorry, Jason," he said, quietly.

But it was too little, too late.

Fifteen

Although I thought that Michael looked more like a boy now than he did when I'd met him, he was completely convincing to those we met. I never saw a double take or frown by anyone we encountered. His voice was only slightly deeper now, but he talked in a breathy way that disguised it. He rarely shaved, except his legs, and he kept his eyebrows narrow and beautifully shaped. His long lashes didn't hurt, either. Well, and he was more pretty than handsome to begin with, and he was achingly pretty.

I, on the other hand, got plenty of stares. Because he decided that I looked cute with them, I still had the nose ring and ultra-short hair. I also had all my other piercings filled, too, which I was glad for. I liked my bodily enhancements, and I didn't notice my nose ring unless someone tethered me there.

Michael had bought me a wardrobe of sorts, although wearing clothes still made me uncomfortable. He called the stuff punk, which is what he said I looked like. I hardly remembered the term, I was so young when kids started shaving their heads and wearing weird clothes. Now I was the one with the baggy T-shirt and shorts and heavy, treaded boots. All in black. Michael said I looked adorable. I doubted that's what most people thought, considering their expressions.

He had decided that we would stay in Indianapolis the first night. After Chicago the skyline seemed tame. But it was one of the two major cities in the midwest, besides Chicago, he said. Columbus was the other. We were staying at a hotel of a major chain, where there were doormen and bellhops. One of the latter carried our bags for us. He seemed fascinated by my nose ring, if my peripheral vision wasn't lying. See, I was checking out his uniform. It might be because of the costumes we wore in the circus, or perhaps the ritualized leather of my masters, but I was fascinated by his tight, ornate outfit. And by him, truthfully. He was blond, too, with crystal blue eyes.

"My, aren't you just an adorable, corn-fed Indiana boy," Michael said, barely disguising his male voice. What was he doing?

The gorgeous kid chuckled and said, "Yeah, and aren't you just about the most convincing *woman* I've ever met."

"You already know the answer's yes. How big do you want your tip to be?"

"Just make mine hard. And then some."

"It's a deal, pretty boy."

In the room he said, "I get off at ten."

"And afterward, too, gorgeous."

"Harlan."

"Michael. And this is Jason." We shook hands.

"I'll see you soon, guys."

"Not soon enough, Harlan. And keep your uniform on, hon."

"Why did you do that, Michael," I asked, when the door closed.

"Oh, come on, Jason. You've had nothing but black cock up your ass for years. Don't you want to see what a white one feels like for a change?"

"I know what it feels like, Michael. Todd was white."

"You're a total bottom, aren't you?" I nodded, aware that he was avoiding the subject of Todd. "Well, didn't he turn you on?"

"Yes, ma'am. I just thought that we were going to be lovers."

"We are, silly. But we can also share ourselves with others."

I needed a shower, which Michael understood. He knew of the regimen of the slaves. I was really disappointed that he wanted to go screwing with other guys, as attractive as the bellboy was. I cut myself shaving my pubes, which I had to do myself now, because Michael wanted me to remain smooth. That was fine. I liked being that way. But Mr. Jakes had always shaved my body, and, besides, I was nervous about getting it on with this Harlan person, although I didn't know why. Well, he was a stranger. Even the men at the fraternity I didn't know, someone else did.

And only once in my whole time there had I been hit. It was a guest, who slapped me hard on the face for something he thought I did or didn't do. Insolence, I think he said. Hardly. This had happened at the indoor pool. I loved serving there, because the brothers were out of their heavy leather clothing and boots. They were mostly young and built and wore only black leather briefs, thongs or G-strings, showing off bodies God could have created Himself. This guy was slim and buffed to mouthwatering, I remember. When he hit me, everyone froze in shock. One slave had the presence of mind to run for Mr. Jakes to tell him that Jaytoh had been struck, while the scene suddenly turned angry as the brothers recovered from their disbelief at what had happened. Mr. Jakes was of no mean height and build, himself. He was furious when he arrived. I was holding my cheek, and Todd was holding me from behind. Those brothers who weren't threatening to kill the perpetrator were asking me if I was all right. Mr. Jakes gave the member and guest ten seconds to clear out, or else. They didn't wait to find out what that would be. The member knew full well that his buddy had committed the cardinal sin. You never, ever, touched a slave in anger. Then I thought of all the times I had been touched sexually and smiled. The pats on the buns, the stroking, the groping. God, I missed that. Missed Todd.

Michael was wearing a filmy lavender babydoll with his black nylons and garter belt. I was still getting used to seeing people in "civilian" clothes after nothing but leather for two years, but Michael looked really sexy in his girl stuff. We kissed and played on the bed until Harlan showed up. My new Master wasted no time seducing him. The blond seemed both amused and turned on by Michael's crossdressing. After they made out for a few minutes, the bellboy knelt and pulled down the sheer panty. His mouth went onto Michael all the way, as if he had been deprived of cock for years. Watching him worship the rigid brown rod and stroke the shiny legs made me erect. Michael hadn't masturbated me that morning, to my chagrin, and I think that I was cranky, and horny, as a result. I would never underestimate the benefits of a daily sexing, even as perfunctorily as Mr. Jakes had performed it on me.

Michael finally had to stop Harlan before he shot his load in the boy's hungry mouth. He got the bellhop to his feet and helped him out of his uniform, swaying his narrow boy hips and round ass as he unbuttoned the charming tunic. Once Michael had disrobed him, I was fascinated with his nakedness. He had a solid body with fair hairs covering his torso and legs, reminiscent of the fur of an animal. Almost all of the people I'd seen nude in my life had been smooth. A few of the brothers had had sparse, kinky hair, so this abundance of straight ones was a novelty to me.

I approached him, and he finally tore his eyes away from sultry Michael. When he looked at me, his mouth opened. I guess that my collar and nose ring had been kind of quirky, but seeing the matching harness and the rest of my rings threw him.

"Jason is special," Michael said.

"Man, I'll say. More like exotic."
"That, too. With a tight boy place made for fucking."
"Yeah? I can't wait."

But he could, because he wanted to kiss me and play with my adornments. I was glad for the oral diversion, because I wanted to run my hands over the carpet of his body hair. He liked that, given that his cock responded to the fondling I was giving him. I felt him poke my abdomen, and I returned the excitement. I loved having my harness traced by a boy's fingers. Todd and I used to do that while we fellated each other. Why it felt so great, I don't know, but it did. And it sure did now. However, my own fingers found the silky hairs of Harlan's chest and belly luxurious.

Too soon his curiosity with my ornaments waned, and he wanted his stiff pole snugly inside my "tight boy place." I lay on the bed, raised and parted my legs. He pointed his erection between my cheeks and pushed into me in no time. I inhaled, when I felt his wiry pubic hairs scratching my sensitive skin, realizing that he was already in to the hilt. This was so unlike Travis, even Bart, and certainly not like the brothers, who, when they did my ass, did it slowly to make me know it was being done. But Harlan was young and needed the itch at the top of his shaft scratched, I guessed. Besides, he felt good in me, and he was handsome, and I did get to play with his hair while he pounded in me.

Which was what Michael was doing to him, much to the boy's dismayed surprise. "Hey, I don't get fucked," he said, when he felt Michael knocking. "You do now, honey. You want that precious ass, you get this precious cock." That made Harlan whine in discomfort but buck into me faster. God, he was like an animal in heat. So was Michael. He was twisting Harlan's tits, which looked so cool, and actually bit him on the shoulder. Man! And the boy seemed to love it, because he responded by fucking me even faster. He was drying out my protective mucius with the friction of his feverish rutting. It wasn't surprising that after a few minutes he froze and emptied himself into me.

Then he plopped out of me and bent over to take my needy cock into his mouth. His mouth seemed as deprived as his cock had acted. He went up and down on me like a madman.

Maybe it was Michael's internal massage that was driving him, but he made me cream him far sooner than I wanted to. When he straightened up and licked his mouth, Michael took hold of his reawakening cock and pumped it to hardness, never missing a thrust in the boy he now possessed completely. Harlan lolled his head on Michael's shoulder, and he bit him again. In response he moaned and shot one small drop of come onto my abdomen. Still holding him and nibbling, Michael groaned in coitus.

"See? That's what a blind date will get you," he said, after Harlan had left, and we were nestled under the covers.

"I'll take your word for it."

"Tell me you didn't enjoy that," he whispered in my ear. He was half draped on me, rubbing a silky stockinged leg over my sex.

"You know I did."

"Yes. And you'll have so much more enjoyment, love. And always remember, no matter what happens, I love you more than anything, Jason."

"Oh, Michael." I knew without a doubt that he meant it. His passionate kiss reinforced it. When he broke contact, I moved down under the covers to make him hard again. He was well on his way there from our brief lip lock, and I finished the job. Then he finished himself in me.

Sixteen

We did see downtown Columbus from Interstate 70. It's skyline wasn't much different from that of Indianapolis. We didn't stop, because we had several more hours to our destination for the day. Michael did say that there was a bar called BoyZenith, which was supposed to be the best one for gorgeous numbers between New York and Chicago. He'd seen a photo of the fabulous young owners and averred that he would die happy with both their cocks in him at once. I wondered if Michael had ever taken anyone's cock in him, but I didn't ask.

That made me think of Buddy. Man, what a beautiful kid he'd become in the two years of my slavery. And his cock had, too, not to mention how long it was now. Hard to believe that he was only sixteen. God, he was a boy stud. And more hopelessly in love with Morgan than ever. It seemed mutual, which made me happy. Especially considering my own lousy track record with the boys I'd loved. Suddenly separated from my first one. Yuki and Travis dead. Todd, alive, but lost to me. But at least I had Michael, and for beauty and intelligence, he was more than I could ever ask.

I got excited as we neared the West Virginia border, because the terrain began to get hilly. Then hillier, and soon we were in Pennsylvania. After so many years of living in flat places, I was delighted to see the cousins of mountains I'd looked forward to every year, when the circus moved northward. I didn't count the desolate peaks of the Mojave, because they were barren and more forbidding than welcoming. But these were covered with trees and seductively undulating.

Pittsburgh was full of hills, too. And tunnels and bridges. The downtown exploded into view coming through one of the former on our way to the downtown. Stopping there was out of our way, but we had a lot of time to kill, and Michael wanted to see places he'd heard about. We stayed at another fancy place, but none of the bellboys seemed interested. That was fine with me. Harlan had been a handful. But Michael was determined to sample the local cock here, too.

That evening he wore a sleeveless black blouse, tight jeans and knee-high, spiked-heel boots. He did look hot. I had always liked seeing him in drag before I went to the fraternity, and he turned me on with his outfits even more now. Silicone breast inserts had replaced the lace-edged socks of high school, but I found them curiously interesting, too. Perhaps because I knew that a handsome boy chest was lying under them.

The kid he'd insisted on picking up was named Dirt, or something. He had about a dozen piercings in his ears and a ball implanted under his lower lip. Michael decided that he was a rougher version of me. That was an understatement. Although he was really cute, his appearance seemed to do everything he could to counter the fact. He had a foul mouth to go along with his sullenness and overall mangy presentation. The cock he shoved into me did have another ball on the topside of his head, which was quite attractive, but he just didn't appeal to me. He was even more desperate to come than Harlan, if that were possible. And he cursed his cock the whole time he was rutting in me. And once he'd gotten off, he left, taking his half dozen tattoos and foul aura with him. Michael called it an adventure. I called it a night, after I shit the kid's come out of me.

I wasn't prepared for the Manhattan skyline being way more impressive than Chicago's. I remember thinking, out of the clear blue sky, which it was, that I really needed to be a lot more grown up in this intimidating city. I reminded myself that I had Michael to look after me, but I reminded myself right back that he was another eighteen year old. Certainly no Mr. Jakes. Whom I missed, too.

Morgan had rented an apartment for us not too far from Central Park. I would come to love the park's myriad natural sights and great human attractions. The apartment itself was as nicely furnished as Morgan's. It was done in browns, beiges and whites. "For us," Michael said and kissed me. I didn't know what he meant, but the decor was supposed to be a melding of our skin colors. Neat. And before we had a chance to christen the bed, he took me on the living room floor in his need to couple with me. I was hard from his kisses, as I always was, when I undressed. I lay down on the thick pile of the carpet, my feet telling me that it felt like the luxurious carpeting of the Ritual Room. My butt had never touched such plushness, except in fantasy. Michael shed his T-shirt, denim skirt and panties. He hooked his pantyhose under his balls, leaving his own erection to spring out into the air. He still wore his chunky black and white sneakers, which looked so sexy on him.

He leaned into me and kissed me at the same time his cock eased into my body. Home, I thought. I'm finally home. Coupled with this beautiful creature who cares for me. He continued to kiss my face, neck and lips and murmured words my ears welcomed and caressed. How beautiful I was, how sexy I was, how much he loved me, as he moved deliberately in me. I felt loved. More importantly, I felt safe lying on that carpet with Michael's cock buried in me, his warm, moist breath on my face. It was the first time I had since leaving the fraternity and its beautiful, naked slaves and shiny leather-clad men.

I cried out his name as I came without touching myself. Seconds later he called mine and God's together as I felt him spasm and squirt in me.

Seventeen

We spent the weeks before school getting acclimated to the island. It was as if we were on our honeymoon. A newlymarried young straight couple enjoying the sights of the big city. And I have no doubt that that's exactly what people thought we were. We held hands and kissed. Our different skin colors didn't seem to faze anyone. And we could get away with being amorous precisely because Michael looked like a woman.

We checked out bars we could get into with fake IDs he had somehow managed to have made. One of Morgan's contacts, I wondered. Probably not. For all of his cavorting with underage guys, he struck me as a pretty straight arrow. But everyone needed vices. His was young white boys. And one special one of them loved him. No, Michael had found a source but hadn't told me. Maybe he was thinking that it was better that I remain ignorant. That was fine. Besides, when we could get into them, I was fascinated by the boys and their fashions. So was Michael, to the point that he'd actually dress up as a guy in some really cool outfits when we'd go out. Still wearing his nail polish, of course. That seemed to be points for cool, as he put it. Then I got them, too, because I now wore black on my nails, at his insistence. He also made me let my hair grow out on top, because he adored my ringlets, he said. The sides were still shaved, so that I looked appropriately rebellious with my jewelry. And although I noticed that I was a minority with my jewelry and clothing, guys seemed to find me attractive. Well, I was. Even I knew that by looking in the mirror.

Michael made friends easily, whether as a girl or guy. He was determined to go through all four years of college as a female, and I admired him for his gambit. Hell, I did more than that. I worshipped him. He was my lover and my Master and whatever he said went. That he was so assertive made me feel that much more secure. The psychiatrist, who was a member of the fraternity and had administered the psychological tests had smilingly called me assertively passive. Not a term of the profession, he'd said, but the makings of one hell of a slave. Maybe he knew how right he was. And I was still a slave. But I was Michael's now. In bed and out.

For the first party we went to, Michael dressed me in tight leather jeans, leather vest and my latest pair of motorcycle boots. I'd gone through several pairs as my feet grew during my time with the fraternity. Morgan always bought me new ones, so that I could stay in uniform. And I was happy to know that Buddy was wearing a pair of my outgrown boots.

Although he sometimes mocked his brother for his own dress, Michael insisted that I looked *darling* in leather. As did he. He wore a leather bra, miniskirt and thigh-high boots, which really turned me on. No surprise. Leather was my scent. Michael was my man. We kissed before we left. I caressed his nylon-covered legs and fondled his breasts. We giggled and kissed some more. God, I had fallen so much farther in love with him that Todd was already a receding memory. And Michael thought that I was the adonis of his dreams.

The party was being given by someone we'd met at an after-hours club. That had been an experience. Just one of thousands Michael wanted us to have in the really big city, as if they might stop being available before we were able to have them. But I loved his enthusiasm for trying new things. I was also amazed at how accepting people seemed to be. I didn't get a second glance, unless I was being cruised, which was what Michael told me the stares from guys meant.

Anyway, this after-hours place was an experience. I actually looked pretty normal, considering how outrageous some of the other people there looked. Which made it all the more fun. One guy was wearing only hip waders and cutoffs cut off at his crotch. The only thing keeping his goods from hanging out completely was black net wrapped around them, I guess continuing the fishing theme. I was ready to take the lure and swallow his hook, so to speak.

There was also a humpy guy dressed as a cop, who was handcuffed and being blown by a boy dressed as a highway patrolman. What made the sight so sexy to me was that the cop's bubble butt was exposed to reveal that his nightstick had been put into his ass. *"Very* Tom of Finlandish," Michael said of the sight.

The "official" entertainment took place in a ring in a separate room. Two buffed, smooth teenagers, oiled and wearing only shiny white leather wrestling boots, were trying desperately to pin each other. It was a treat to watch their glistening, muscular bodies grapple on the mat. Especially whenever their cocks would appear, because they were both big-dicked. After a really well-fought, if slippery, match, I saw why each wanted to win so much. The victor got to fuck the vanquished.

The losing boy knelt before his conqueror and nuzzled his crotch, while he moved his hand slowly up and down the oiled male meat that would claim its final victory. I watched with riveted interest as his slow, manual worship caused the long organ to rise in the air. When he had the other boy hard, he lay down and reared back for the invasion. The other boy walked up to him and knelt, his hardness swaying deliciously for us. He braced himself on one hand and guided himself into the opening with the other, and then impaled the boy totally with his big, bloated cock. The fuckee let out a cry of pain and surprise at being taken so emphatically, and he grimaced as the daylights were fucked out of him. Some of the onlookers cheered as the winner celebrated his victory in the other boy's body. I watched the fucker's face intently for it to betray his orgasm, and I wasn't disappointed by the expression which registered there as he spewed his load into the boy writhing beneath him. "Cool," Michael said.

We returned to the larger room for another drink. Michael had introduced me to alcohol, and I liked the buzz it gave me. Rum and cola was my drink of choice. As I was waiting for Michael to get the round, I noticed three strikingly handsome boys standing together. Their shoulder-length hair was parted in the middle and swept behind their ears. They were all wearing high-necked, lavender satin blouses with waves of ruffles down the front and at the cuffs. Their black satin pants were pleated and wide-legged, and each wore black Cuban boots. Their nail polish and lipstick matched their shirt. What stunning creatures, I thought to myself.

"They're Fancy Boys," a voice beside me said. I turned to see a sandy-haired young man with gleaming dark eyes."The boys you're looking at, I take it."

"Yes, they're beautiful."

"So are you, if I may be so bold."

"Thanks."

"You're welcome. But they are, too. And they know it, and are snobs on top of it. They won't have anything to do with the hoi polloi, but at least they do let us look at them."

I was about to ask what hoi polloi were, when Michael rejoined us.

"Who's your friend?" Michael asked me, while giving the man the once over.

"He's Pierce Franklin," he said, offering his hand to my lover. Then he shook mine. Actually, his name was Pierce Franklin III, and he was quite wealthy, he managed to tell us. But he wasn't all that snobbish, as the Fancy Boys presumably were. And that was how we met this person, who would nearly destroy our lives.

Pierce lived not too from the park in a modern highrise. His digs were even more sumptuous than ours, which I didn't know was possible from my limited experience with decent living quarters. He greeted us warmly, having decided that we were financially able enough to be his friends. Not to mention the fact that he found Michael's crossdressing darling, and me to be wonderfully exotic. So I wasn't surprised that he heartily approved of our outfits.

As soon as we entered, Pierce got us beers. There were perhaps a dozen or so men and boys already there. He introduced us to several people, and I scanned the huge living room for cuties, while I sipped my beer. I saw two that made me stir. Luckily, our host decided that we should meet them. Rob had short, straight brown hair and intense dark emerald green eyes, which seemed to have their own light source. His lips looked as if they had been painted, they were naturally so shiny and red. His teeth were white and straight and seemed to conspire with the lips for maximal effect. He was dressed unpretentiously in a baggy white T-shirt and shorts and black lace-up boots with white socks turned down over the tops of them. Rob could have been a Fancy Boy, he was so stunning.

He was eighteen and belonged to an older man, Fritz, who reeked of money. I was smitten by Rob, and I wondered if his smile was telling me the same thing.

Damon had shelves for cheekbones and a square jaw which housed a dimple. His deep blue eyes were almost menacing-looking, they were so vibrant. And I had no doubt that those eyes were trying to draw me into them the longer I was in their presence, nor that I would go, given sufficient seduction. So I was relieved when we moved on.

After several beers, I needed to pee. For some reason, Michael seemed delighted that I did. Another guest pointed down a long hall and told me where the room was.

On the way, I was stopped by the scene beyond a partially open door. Two blonds, with what appeared to be almost identical tanned bodies were fucking and obviously not caring who saw their sweaty bodies joined by a cock. The boy on his back was holding the other's head as the other boy slid back and forth in him in short strokes.

"Oh, god, Scotty, your cock feels fucking great. Oh, man, I want this thing in me all night."

"Just all night?" They kissed. I smiled. They were really hot together.

At the door I thought I had been instructed to go to, I realized immediately out how wrong I was. It was another bedroom, and it was occupied. Neither person had heard the door open. A clothed young man lay on his side, his back to me. He was playing with the nude boy lying next to him. The boy's crotch was hairless, so I gauged him to be perhaps nine or ten. His left arm was draped over his forehead, a smile of pleasure on his lips as the other's hand slid up his body and then down his legs, stopping at the little organs to attend to them. Then I realized that the young man's penis was out and that the boy was playing with it.

"God, Josh, your hand feels so good. Do me with that soft hand."

"Yeah, I'm gonna make you spurt your boy juice, Sean." I should have left, but I was captivated by the arousing sight of each doing his bedmate. And the fact that I couldn't see Josh doing Sean only added to it. He whispered, "Close, love. So close." Seconds later he groaned and convulsed in pleasure, his seed whitening Josh's abdomen. Then he gathered it up in his hand and coated the boy's little sex with it. After a couple of minutes, Josh's face screwed up and his body jerked in dry orgasm, as he cried out. I closed the door silently.

My next stab at fending off wetting my pants rewarded me with the sight of the porcelain god. I had unzipped myself, in preparation to sitting down, as I usually did, when the door opened. I looked up to see Damon entering. He closed the door and smiled. "Pretty cock, Jason. And I love the ring."

"Uh, thanks. Why are you here?"

"Don't be bashful. Michael just wanted me to check on you."

"He did?" Why?

"Yeah, he thought I might help you pee."

"He did? He said that?"

"Uh, huh."

I couldn't for the life of me figure why Michael would let another guy handle me, but he was there, so I decided not to make a scene. That was harmless. His fingers felt warm and soft on my sensitive skin. In fact, it was really erotic to have another guy holding me while I peed. And when he shook me off, I began to get hard. He ran his finger over the ring, sending little vibrations of delight into my head and encouraging my ascent. I told him that this probably wasn't such a good idea, and he agreed, saying he had a better one. He held and kissed me, assuring me, every time he took his tongue out of my mouth, that Michael had okayed it.

For whatever reason, I chose to believe him. Well, he was gorgeous. After the kissy face, he ordered me to lick his face. God, my tongue went to heaven on the his facial structure. He had about a day-old growth of beard, which looked really sexy against the tan of his skin. And I enjoyed how they made the sensitive surface tingle. But not as much as tasting the outcroppings that were his cheekbones. Nor fucking the dimple and sucking on the granite that was his chin. Which led to my kneeling and taking his attractive maleness into my mouth and mouthing it to powerful hardness. Then I was aware of another presence. It was a guy I hadn't seen before. Curiously, he was wearing only a shiny white-striped red wrestling singlet under a shiny black bomber jacket. Big high tops of the same material encased his big feet. Long brown hairs covered his impressive legs.

Damon greeted him as Seth and told me to get him hard, too, after he removed the jacket. The male bulge stretching the slinky material made my mouth water. Big feet.... I kissed the lump and licked it for good measure before lifting up the leg of the singlet to free his fearsome endowment. Almost like a gun it raised itself and aimed its eye at me. I swallowed as much of it as I could, but he had plenty to spare.

Then Damon decided that he wanted me to suck both of them at once. They stood side by side with their arms around each other, two buddies having their cocks sucked together. It was really hot to look up and see them like that, sharing a boy's most intimate act. At the same time, my mouth was stretched almost beyond endurance to have both fat erections in me. But it was worth it, when Damon, then Seth creamed me. I gulped every last bit of them down. Then Seth masturbated me into the sink, while Damon felt up my leather ass cheeks, telling me how great they were, as he licked my collar. I got a better look at Sean's face and wondered what year in high school he was. After I noted how boyishly handsome it was.

After I came and Seth left after thanking me and giving me a clumsy kiss, Damon said he wanted to show me something. We went into a room, which was Pierce's study. Damon scanned the shelves, looking for something.

"What was the deal with Sean dressed like that?"

"Dressed the way you are you have to ask?" He shrugged. "Pierce likes to see guys wearing flattering stuff. Sean wrestles for a prep school, and his body should definitely be shown off, wouldn't you say?" I agreed. "And you should see Courtney in his lumberjack outfit. Flannel and pole boots really turn some guys on. Or little Max in his riding togs. I've seen men and boys beg to lick his boots right out there in the living room, he's so adorable." I thought of Bart. "He tricks with whomever he pleases. And he's wonderfully arrogant for a fourteen year old, it's such a turn on." Just the thought of little Max in his riding boots making me adore him while belittling me and making me serve him. No surprise there, being a slave.

At last he pulled down a leatherbound photo album. We sat on a velvet settee and he opened it. My eyes got wide at the first picture. It was of a nude white boy, standing with an index finger in his smiling mouth. The next one showed him bent over, showing the camera his little heinie. Damon pronounced him precious. The next boy was black and draped on the back of a white sofa, smiling widely. Then lying sideways with one leg crooked to show himself off. "Pierce is into younger boys. I'm not, but they are cute to look at."

"They are that," I said, feeling myself getting turned on all over again, by seeing these pretty bare boys. Then I thought of Josh, who did turn up later in several lewd poses in those pages. Along with one boy of indeterminate ancestry, who beguiled me for some reason. Perhaps it was the wet athletic T-shirt pressed against his body on one page. Or the ball cap he wore carelessly backwards on another. Whatever, he pressed a button and I responded. So did Damon, when he saw my renewed arousal. His hands and face went into my lap and engulfed me in their embrace. I gave him my own taste of boy.

Why Damon had shown me the album, I couldn't figure. Maybe to say, in effect, that Michael and I were trusted with this secret. Or maybe Michael had told Pierce my story, and he and Damon knew that I had been a slave long before I was legal.

Michael was acting weird when I returned to the party with my sexmate. Kind of lethargic, kind of dreamy. As were several other guests and our host. I couldn't imagine that the beer had done that to him. But that was my problem. I couldn't imagine.

Eighteen

As the weeks went on, I would often go to the park to boy watch and savor the fall air, after Michael left for classes. Our sex life was great, and I was happy to have stability in my life. But too quickly that changed.

It began with his asking me if I would run an envelope over to Fritz's apartment, which was in a building bordering the park. I had no idea what it could possibly be, but I didn't question Michael, because of my training. If he had told me to take him out and suck him in the middle of Grand Central Station, I would have, without hesitation. I was so thoroughly trained to obey, that I was helpless not to.

I was met at the door by adorable Rob, which surprised me. He seemed very happy to see me. As I was him. He was wearing a forest green T-shirt and matching tights, khaki shorts and woven brown clogs. He looked great in his outfit to the point of making my mouth water. The green of his outfit made his eyes seem that much brighter. And his lips redder still. God, he was gorgeous. I explained that I had the envelope for Fritz. He took it and invited me in. We went back into the apartment to what he referred to as the boy's suite, explaining that he and Fritz had been together for five years, and that he had only recently turned eighteen. I wondered if I had seen a much younger version of him lying seductively in the pages of the photo album.

His rooms were furnished tastefully, and they were unmistakably a boy's, albeit with a softness to them. Kind of like him. We sat and he slipped off his clogs. He had wide feet, like Michael. And his legs looked terrific sheathed in the opaque fabric. I wanted to caress them but knew what that might lead my hormones to do. He asked if I wanted to watch a video, and I said sure. I had nowhere else to be. I would just be reading or watching TV at home. Besides, being able to sneak glances at this beauty would be worth it. Mentally, I dressed him in lavender and black satin, those broad feet lifted by Cuban heels. It was when he was handling the video that I saw again that his nails were the same color as his legs and shirt.

"Have you ever heard of the Fancy Boys?"

"Uh huh. They're kept boys, like me. Really stuck up, though. I take it you saw them." I nodded. "They're stuck up, and they always go out dressed alike in precious outfits. Pretty, but pretty vapid, too."

"There is something to be said about pretty, though."

"Yeah, there is, and you and I both know it, Jason." He grinned, wickedly.

"But if they're kept, why would they be out in the middle of the night?"

"Because their daddies get off on them, if they can, and fall asleep, as old as some of these guys are. So they don't miss them. And at the after-hours places they can drink. Not to mention slum."

"Huh. What's the movie?"

"None you've heard of. This video isn't of the best quality, but I hope you like it." The smile returned. Even if I didn't.... I thought.

It looked like a black and white home movie. Rob was right about the quality, but it was good enough to see a teenager lying on a bed, rubbing his belly. His hands went to his nipples, and he tweaked and pulled them. Then one hand slid down to his crotch, and he played with himself leisurely. When he was hard, he was joined on the bed by another boy, who promptly took advantage of the nubile erection he found.

The hand went up under my big black T-shirt and rubbed my belly before I realized it was there, I was so focused on the two boys on the big screen. At first I didn't want to respond, but his touch was becoming more interesting than his younger self being fellated. I turned to gauge his intentions from his face. He was looking at me with lowered lids, seduction unmistakable in those eyes. That told me all I needed to know. I was out of my T-shirt and turned to meet those lusciously full lips. His fingers were now at my nipples, tugging on my rings. His mouth was hot on mine. I whimpered from the pleasure of having my tits under total control. I stroked his leggings, which felt as silky as I knew they would. He broke our oral contact to kiss my neck. "Oh, man, you're so beautiful, Jason," his warm, moist breath whispered into my ear. "And so exotic." Then his mouth engulfed the earring there and played with it. I shivered from the pleasure.

We managed to bare each other, and I went down on his glorious maleness. His scent, which had been trapped by the tights, intoxicated my nostrils, it was so delicate and youthful. I sucked and licked as deliberately as my desire would allow, managing to have him breathing more audibly within minutes. Then he eased me back onto the couch, pressed his bare crotch onto mine and humped me. Out of the corner of my eye, I saw the screen. On it, Rob was rubbing his partner in the same way.

We began to kiss again with a want that only fueled the want. I locked my boots around his legs to draw us even more tightly together. And then it was over. I heard the boys cry out in the video, as my cock let go. Fueled by my lubrication, Rob spent himself as I held his beautiful body.

We lay together for a good while before he lifted his head and kissed my nose. "Thanks, Jason, that was great. I'm sorry, though."

"About what? Oh."

I tried to think about how many times I'd cheated on Michael in recent days, and the answer didn't make me proud. I loved this guy so much, but I let myself go with people I didn't love. Well, I could love Rob, easily. But he was taken. It was on that walk back to our apartment that I wondered next if Michael were cheating on me. He was, but did I ever have his "tricks" wrong.

Nineteen

I had an epiphany in the park one day. It wasn't the one I needed, but it was one I did need, as it turned out. Although we were past Thanksgiving, which we had celebrated in the city, to Morgan's chagrin, the day was unseasonably warm. I was in a T-shirt. As much as I preferred warm weather, I did hope that there would be snow for Christmas. This was going to be the best one I'd ever had, because it would be with Michael. Things had been a little rough between us, but I chalked that up to Michael having a tough time adjusting to life in college. He was increasingly irritable, sometimes telling me to leave the apartment, saying he needed his space. Naturally, I obeyed. Sometimes I went to Rob's for much-needed sex with the beautiful kept boy. I felt guilty about it every time, but I went every chance I got. For his part, Michael seemed more relaxed, if not even more amorous when I would return.

I was such a familiar sight in that big park now that regular joggers and Rollerbladers would wave to me. Even nannies pushing those expensive prams with precious, rich babies in them. I guess that, despite my rings and collar, they knew that I was an okay guy.

I had stopped to sit and watch the human sights. A welcome one came toward me after a few minutes. A very cute boy I had not seen before was skateboarding my way like nobody's business. His straight brown hair was riffling in the wind under his ball cap. His unbuttoned flannel shirt flapped as if applauding the smooth, young skin it revealed. At the same time, the voluminous material of his white Pipes jeans revealed nothing of his boyness underneath.

He grinned at me, and his eyes flashed as he skated by. It wasn't just his sexiness that made me get up and begin to walk after him. There was something oddly familiar about him, but I couldn't figure out what it was. He shook his booty as the board rolled away from me. It was an unmistakable invitation. So I continued to follow those undulating buns.

He stopped and flipped the skateboard up with his foot, catching it and settling it in his right hand. He turned his head and smiled, as if he knew that I would be following him. He headed off the path across some lawn to a copse of bushes. I found him deep inside it. When I got close enough to see the perfect white teeth in his grin, he raised his hands, hooked his index fingers into my earrings, and pulled my head to his. His kiss was youthfully enthusiastic and had me pressing hard against the denim of the jeans in no time. He came off my lips and whispered, "Let's do each other in our jeans, sexy ring boy."

He unbuttoned me, and I unzipped him. My hand went inside the roomy jeans and found him ready and waiting. He forced his hand down my leg and stroked me. "Cool, huh?"

"Yeah." We kissed some more and moved our hips in response to being sexed. Yeah, it was cool to be kissing and doing each other in the middle of the park, even if we were well-hidden. "Wow, you got cock rings and one in your head, too. Awesome," he said, playing with it. Now he decided that he had to see it.

With difficulty he managed to move me upward and finally out. "Awesome." He molested my head now, paying attention to the ring. I liked that, because of the vibrations it sent into me. He also loved the fact that my harness looked like my collar. He was in lust with my cock, he said. I was quite happy with his and it showed. "Fuck, I'm gonna come, Jason." He pumped me hard, and I shot all over the front of his jeans as he let loose onto the inside. Then we kissed and closed ourselves up.

"Aren't you concerned about people seeing the wet spots on your jeans?"

"No, I have the come of a pretty boy on me." He looked down and chuckled. "I guess it wouldn't hurt to button the shirt down there. Hey, you want to walk around together for a while, stud puppy?"

"Sure. But how did you know my name?"

"The harness. When I saw the collar, I thought, 'I wonder if this is the famous Jason I've heard about.' Then when I was doing you, it dawned on me that the harness was the same, and you were he."

"So I'm famous, huh?"

"Uh huh. Rob thinks you're fabulous. Unfortunately, Daddy and I didn't get to meet you at Pierce's."

"This was better."

"It was. Oh, my name's Court. That's short for Courtney. Not my original name, but Daddy liked it, so that's what it is. I mean, the guy paid big bucks for me, so he deserved to do it, you know? Pierce said you're Michael's slave. Were you expensive?"

"No. Michael's brother bought me for a couple grand. But it was something I wanted to do."

"Really? Cool."

"It was. Do you love your daddy, Court?"

"Uh huh. He's a neat guy. And he's rich, too. And I will be for the rest of my life."

"I'm glad for you. Are you by any chance Courtney the lumberjack?"

"Oh, you heard. Yeah, I love to get their tongues hanging out. They want to lick my boots, Jason. Like Maximillian in his riding duds. We get it on, by the way, but we don't tell our daddies. But, honestly, as far as the flannel business? I think if I wore nylons they would have the same reaction. I mean, I am a pretty hot boy."

"An understatement. And for your information, Michael wears nylons all the time. He lives life as a girl."

"Really? Way cool."

"Yeah, it is."

I made a friend that afternoon, but after we parted I wondered if Courtney would tell Rob or Pierce about what we did. I didn't worry about it for long, because there were tears in my eyes as I made my way home.

Talking about being a slave brought back a vivid, painful memory. Michael had gotten a call from Morgan one night, soon after he came home from studying late. He seemed kind of spaced out, as he seemed to be more and more recently. The phone call got him all upset.

When he hung up, he told me that Todd was dead. He had killed himself. I remember our holding each other and crying our eyes out. I thought that he was sad for me, given that he'd never met Todd. But it was something else, and I found out when I got home that day.

Twenty

I found Michael unconscious. At first I thought he was sleeping, but I couldn't wake him, no matter what I did. Then I saw the powder. Oh, shit, how could I have been so dumb? I called emergency, and he was rushed to Columbia University Hospital. I was an absolute wreck. And it didn't help that we weren't related. Nor the way I looked, either. The emergency room personnel treated me pretty badly. Fortunately, they were able to do something to stabilize Michael. I called Chicago right away, not knowing what else to do.

Morgan cursed me up and down every telephone pole between New York and Chicago. He accused me of hooking Michael on drugs. I was in tears, pleading with him to believe me. I told him that I had had no idea that he was doing drugs and that I loved him more than anything, which was absolutely true. That only made Morgan heap more scorn on me. He said that he would be flying out right away, and he didn't want to see me anywhere near Michael, when he arrived at the hospital.

I was crushed. I went home, which is where we had our confrontation. Well, that word overstates the encounter. After telling me again what scum I was, Morgan ordered me to leave. I couldn't believe it. I protested again how much I loved Michael and that I didn't know that he was doing drugs, but he was having none of it. I was out on my ass.

I was able to make several calls before I left. Pierce's butler said that he was out of town, indefinitely. Rob told me that there was no way that his daddy would let me stay with them, although he did say that he was sorry to hear about Michael. I was in a panic, not knowing where I would go. Morgan did give me five hundred dollars before I left. I rented a hotel room that night, which was a hassle, looking as I did. It also ate into the money he had given me, which was all I had.

The next day I went to the park and sat with my belongings beside me on the bench. I looked like a homeless person, I thought, and then realized that I was. But I had no clue as to what I would do now. Travis had taught me to live by my wits, but that had been in the desert. Further, I had been trained to be completely reliant on others for my needs. Now I had no one. Worse, I didn't know anybody else, whom I could contact. Except that I did.

Then I looked up and saw Court skateboarding toward me. His face lit up, immediately. I broke down at the sight of him. He sat, put an arm around me and asked what was the matter. When I told him, he said that we were going to his place. His daddy would take me in, he assured me. I was so relieved, I cried harder.

Saul Bernoose was older than I had expected."Max's daddy's old, too. We're gonna get married after they die," Court said. "But I hope that's not for a lot of years, because I really do love Daddy, as I said." And I could have kissed the man, when he said that I could stay with them as long as I needed to. Over dinner he told me that someone like him would love to have me, but my appearance would turn off most potential benefactors. Even with my rings and collar removed, given the big holes that would remain. And I would have a deviated septum, he explained. It sank in that he was telling me that I was damaged goods. When had I not been, since my parents' deaths? Well, not with Yuki and Travis. And then at the fraternity. But, no, I was, and I knew that I couldn't live with Saul and Court. I would want to have sex with Court and feel guilty about it, because I knew that he would insist on it.

And, of course, he did. With Max, no less. Max was blond, too. His hair was fashioned into what he called a page boy. He was adorable and sexy, like Court. His brown eyes were shining, full of life, and lust, like his friend's. He, too, found me radical, fascinated as he was with my jewelry and by the fact that I was a slave. We spent many hot hours naked on the silk sheets in Court's room, kissing and sucking and celebrating each other's body with youthful enthusiasm. I delighted in their slim builds and soft skin. The first time Max wanted me to fuck him, but the idea was so alien that I couldn't. Instead, he and Court took turns inside my mouth and ass. It was great to be with young guys as randy as I was. At least for the moment. Afterward, I thought about Michael and felt the familiar pang of guilt.

A couple of days after moving into the Bernoose household, I received good and bad news. The hospital told me that Michael had been released. However, when I called his apartment, the computer said that the number had been disconnected. I realized that Morgan must have taken him back to Chicago. Although I was elated that he was alive, the devastating knowledge that he was lost to me forever began to sink in. I loved that beautiful young man so much.

Court and Saul were a great help. The latter understood what Pierce and his friends were up to with drugs, and that was why they weren't at the party Michael and I had attended. Looking back, I'd bet that the bathroom sex episode was to distract me from what Pierce was introducing Michael to.

"But couldn't I snort just once?"

"No, Courtney."

"Aw, Dad."

Domingo, their houseboy, was most solicitous, too. Not with sex, although I would have submitted to him. He wasn't interested. He also wasn't goodlooking, but he had a body of death. The reason we didn't have sex was because of Raphael, a drop-dead gorgeous guy of Italian descent. They'd been lovers for nearly two years, but Rafe wasn't sure that he wanted to live on Central Park and wait tables at a nearby hotel. It seemed too incongruous, he said. But it was obvious that they were in love, and that was what Saul was trying to foster. He didn't want Court to be fucking the hired help. Max couldn't be helped, he said. Nor I, for that matter. He said it with a wink, but I looked my sheepish slave self and told him how much Court loved him. "I know. That's why I tolerate his dalliances. Which aren't many, but he's a teenage boy. Besides, you are as irresistible as Max, Jason."

Mr. Bernoose had Domingo take me to a leather shop, which also had a piercing salon. The technician was a ruggedly handsome man with a trim full beard. Remembering the man in Chicago who'd altered me, I wondered if all piercers had beards. There was also a cute boy in the shop about my age. He wore a dog collar, leather jeans and lace-up boots. A rime of dark hair covered his scalp. Like me, he was pierced. His were half rings with balls on the ends. I took it that he was the other man's slave. I would love to have made it with the kid, imagining us two slaves in bed together, desperate to satisfy the other. Man.

The reason that we were there was so that I could be fitted with new silver jewelry. These were less dramatic-looking; only the ball ends of the short bars were visible. When the piercer got to my penis ring, he called the boy over. He unzipped him and pulled out his genitals to reveal his own ring implanted in his cockhead. We grinned at each other. Brothers. He also had one in his scrotum, whereas mine is in my perineum, as you know. The older man suggested leaving that one, so that Domingo could attach weights to it and make me walk around that way. Playing along, the houseboy said that he already did that, and winked at me. So I nodded.

I liked the look of the new jewelry. It was less ostentatious, but I still had my originals, which I knew I would want to wear still. They were, after all, the symbols of my slavery. Both Court and Saul approved of my new conservative punk look. That made me feel good.

Twenty-One

One night Domingo asked if I would like to go out with Raphael and him. I said sure, figuring that Court and Saul would have some privacy with me gone. He told me to wear my T-shirt, jeans and boots, so I did. I wore my motorcycle jacket, too, because it was getting cold now. I liked Rafe immediately, partly because he was effeminate. I had loved that about Michael, perhaps because of how different he was from the aggressively-masculine, leather-clad black masters I had served. "Well, girlfriend!" Rafe said, upon seeing me. "You look fabulous, Jason!" He had a friend for life, he was so affirming. And I was happy that he and Domingo had each other. It was so obvious they were in love that any fool could have seen it. I didn't wonder for long why this Italian adonis loved this plain-looking man from the Dominican Republic. Their hands always seemed to be touching each other, and they talked a mile a minute, discussing everything from football to hemlines.

"We don't mean to exclude you, Jason," Rafe said, putting his arm around my neck and kissing me on the cheek."But we just get carried away with each other."

"I understand. You guys are really cool."

"Thanks. And so are you, pal."

After we ate a late supper at a very good hamburger joint in the Village, they took me to a gay bar. I was amazed at the different types of people there. Others were dressed in leather, and Michael would have been the star among all of the guys dressed as women. Michael. Would I ever get over him? Or would he somehow convince Morgan that I had nothing to do with his addiction? That thought gave me hope. Because, after all, he was the one supposed to look out for me, not the other way around. If I held on to that possibility, I thought that I would enjoy the evening much more.

We found a narrow round table with three high stools and sat. A waiter, wearing a fawn-colored, fur-like G-string and matching footwear and antlers, took our order. It was getting on to Christmas, after all. And he did look awfully sexy in his scanty outfit. I noticed that all of the other waiters were similarly attired. Rafe and Domingo were pleased that I got a kick out of it.

The entertainment was a strip-tease show. No matter how they came on stage, the performers ended up with shiny, buffed bodies wearing only white fishnet pouches. All of them were goodlooking and desirable. But one appealed to me more than the others. He was white and about my height. Like me, he didn't look eighteen. He had brown hair and eyes. His nose flared at the bottom. His eyebrows weren't exactly thick, but they met in the middle, giving him a neat look. But his wide mouth just begged to be kissed. To top it off, his body was beautifully proportioned. He reminded me somewhat of Travis, with his thick forearms and calves, although this boy was slimmer. His ass cheeks made my tongue want to ski down their slopes, they were so nicely shaped. And then dying on those lips. He was dressed as a policeman, when he came out. The real treat, however, was when he got down to his G-string. He was built there, too. It was so much fun seeing him shake his pouch and his booty for us. Man, I was positively in lust. I wasn't the only one. He got a loud round of deserved applause.

Unbelievably, at the end of his performance he came off the stage and over to where we were sitting. He greeted and kissed my hosts. He was introduced as Ben. I couldn't believe that this glistening adonis was standing next to me, shaking my hand and drilling me with his eyes, while his smile made me weak-kneed. I was afraid that my collar and other adornments would turn him off, so I couldn't believe it, when he told me how cool I looked in them. Then, when he was talking to Domingo and Rafe, I couldn't help staring at the distended fishnet and licking my lips. What a great package of maleness he was.

Then Ben invited us back to his apartment, where we could have some drinks. Naturally my new friends accepted, for which I was glad. The prospect of spending more time with this fine specimen was one I welcomed. Ben said he would change and be right out.

"Well, what do you think of him?" Domingo asked.

"He's gorgeous. No, he's more than that. A work of art."

"Yeah, he is. Benjamin works with me," Rafe said.

"Really?"

"Yeah, and he likes you, Jason."

"He does? How do you know?"

"The way he kept sizing you up. And the fact that he invited you home."

"Looks like a successful matchmaking, dear," Domingo said, and they kissed.

I was in shock. Then I wondered why. I could hold my own against most guys, I knew. I guessed that it was my slave mentality that kept me from realizing how goodlooking I was. The guys kept ribbing me, as we waited. That was fine. The possibility that I might touch that muscular body and suck his cock had my hormones going wild.

Ben's apartment was a little uptown from the Village. I wasn't familiar with the particular area where he lived, but I knew approximately where I was on the island. I was also happy that it wasn't too far, because the air was colder and felt damp. He lived on the third floor of a five-story building. He got us beers and sat on the sofa with me, my friends having taken the less logical seating, considering that they were lovers. He lived with a roommate and his lover, he told me. Rafe and Domingo chuckled, but Ben told them to be nice. From their reactions, I wondered if the lover was a dog. It didn't matter. My date was anything but. And on the second beer, he kissed me. God, those lips. There was something else about him, but I couldn't for the life of me think what. He reminded me of somebody I knew, I decided.

When Rafe and Domingo announced that they were going to leave, Ben took my hand and asked if I would stay. The look he gave me was so earnest that my heart jumped. Domingo said that he would come back later that day to get me, which I appreciated.

Before retiring to the bedroom, we made out on the sofa. He unbuttoned me and took me out of my denim prison. I did the same. As he stroked me, he stopped kissing to ask, "God, Jason, are you bejeweled all over?" When I said yes, he said, "Come into the bedroom and show me." We undressed, and he played with my nipples, fingering and kissing them. He decided that they looked good enough to suck, which he did. He found my harness and collar a real turn on, he said. Evidently, because he was waving in the air. And what a salute it was. His cock was thick and a good seven or eight inches. His head seemed almost like an extension of the shaft, it was hardly bigger. I knelt and took the meaty erection into me, almost gagging to accommodate it. He eased me off him, and we settled on the double bed.

I kept him erect, alternating between his cock and low-hanging balls. He pulled me up to kiss me before easing my ass down onto him. I closed my eyes and savored the slow penetration of the fat organ into me. When I was impaled, I opened my eyes to see Ben grinning at me.

"You know, I think I'm going to fall hopelessly in love with you, Jason. Your blond ringlets remind me of my first love. His name was Jason, too."

"Really? I'm glad to hear that, because I feel the same way. And, somehow, you remind me of my first, too." I rode that beautiful erection as he masturbated my decorated cock with the same intensity. I felt connected to another boy as surely as I had known that I never would again, after Michael. And everyone before him. The pleasure of Ben's magnificent maleness buried deep inside me was indescribable. He touched something in me that sent my ass into a drunken spree on him. I was on the automatic pilot of heady physical desire. And his name was Ben. I froze as I shot in arcs onto him, baptizing him with my come.

"Oh god, Jason!" he yelled and began thrusting into me, pulsing and, finally, spewing his cum deep into me.

After his orgasm, we embraced for a while. Then I had to pee. At some point during sex, I had heard the roommate come home, but I didn't pay much attention, so happy was I to be with Ben. Now, on my way back from the bathroom, I heard a voice in the other bedroom. The door was ajar, and I stopped, for some reason. I think to see the dog, who was the lover. Only he wasn't. I mean, I couldn't see him, but my chin hit the floor, when I heard, "Oh, man that feels so good. I love you so much, Bobo."

I staggered back to the other bedroom, my brain reeling from the assault of realizations exploding there. He looked up and smiled that beautiful, boyish smile. Then his face went somber, seeing the tears in my eyes. "Benjy."

And then it began to snow....

The Contributors
(Other Than the Editor, John Patrick)

"Captain, My Captain" and "The Watcher in the Woods"
Tony Anthony
The author says he is a "handsome young stud (in his wet dreams)," who has been a draughtsman, storeman, truck driver, prospector, ship's steward, miner, hospital technician, technical writer, and physical security designer. He has boxed as an amateur, hunted big game, played rugby, cricket, squash, tennis and men's lacrosse, ran a half-marathon, and raced on bicycles and motorcycles. He has travelled in Africa, Australia, New Zealand and Europe. He says he has won the fabled Pulitzer Porn Prize no less than twice (again in his dreams), and enjoys writing fiction, especially for STARbooks.

"Boys Like Him"
Barry Alexander
The author is a frequent contributor to gay magazines and has had stories published in several anthologies.

"A Boy's Best Friend"
Antler
The poet lives in Milwaukee when not traveling to perform his poems or wildernessing. His epic poem *Factory* was published by City Lights. His collection of poems *Last Words* was published by Ballantine. Winner of the Whitman Award from the Walt Whitman Society of Camden, New Jersey, and the Witter Bynner prize from the Academy and Institute of Arts & Letters in New York, his poetry has appeared in many periodicals (including *Utne Reader*, *Whole Earth Review* and *American Poetry Review*) and anthologies (including *Gay Roots*, *Erotic by Nature*, and *Gay and Lesbian Poetry of Our Time*).

"Frisky Boys"
Kevin Bantan
The author now lives in Pennsylvania, where he is working on several new stories for STARbooks.

"Naked Altar Boy"
K.I. Bard

The author's first story for STARbooks appeared in *Juniors 2*. Future stories are in the works. He lives and thrives in Minnesota.

"Bones"
H.A. Bender

This is the author's first story for STARbooks. He is a major contributor to gay journals and has promised to give his stories featuring youths to us.

"Truckstop Boy"
Frank Brooks

The author is a regular contributor to gay magazines. In addition to writing, his interests include figure drawing from the live model and mountain hiking.

"A Fever in the Loins"
Leo Cardini

The celebrated author of the best-selling *Mineshaft Nights*, Leo's short stories and theatre-related articles have appeared in numerous magazines. An enthusiastic nudist, he reports that, "A hundred and fifty thousand people have seen me naked, but I only had sex with half of them."

"Offshore Driller"
Corbin Chezner

The author is an experienced writer of erotica who lives in Tulsa, Oklahoma. His credentials include a master of arts degree with mass communiocations. His first story for STARbooks appeared in *Sweet Temptations*.

"A Birthday at the Baths" and "Rock-Solid Stud"
William Cozad

A frequent contributor to gay magazines, the author resides in the San Francisco area. His startling memoirs were published by STARbooks Press in *Lover Boys* and *Boys of the Night*. His novella,"The Preacher's Boy," appeared in *Secret Passions*.

"Frankie and Johnnie Were Lovers"
and "A Punk's Education"
Frank Gardner
The author lives in Maine, where he is working on many more hot stories for STARbooks.

"Cock-Sure" and "The Making of A Soldier"
and "The Recruiting Officer"
Peter Gilbert
"Semi-retired" after a long career with the British Armed Forces, the author now lives in Germany but is contemplating a return to England. A frequent contributor to various periodicals, he also writes for television. He enjoys walking, photography and reading. His stories have swiftly become favorites of readers of STARbooks' anthologies.

"A Private's Part"
Rick Jackson
An all-time favorite writer of erotica, Rick recently saw another collection of his stories published by Prowler Press, London: *Shipmates*.

"Caught in the Act"
Ronald James
The author is a graduate student in Fine Arts at a university in St. Louis, Missouri. He is working on more stories in this vein for STARbooks.

"The Plowboy's Plaything"
Thomas C. Humphrey
The author, who resides in Florida, is working on his first novel, *All the Difference*, and has contributed stories to First Hand publications. A memoir appeared in the original *Juniors*.

"Dark Ride" and "Jack O'Lantern"
James Lincoln
The author is new to the erotica scene. He has a number of supernatural tales slated for publication by various magazines and anthologies. Originally from New York, he says he

currently resides in the deep south, "against my better judgment."

"Going With the Flow" and "Down 'N' Dirty"
and "Inquisition"
David MacMillan

The author was born in London, England, and entered the U.S. after the Korean conflict. He earned his masters degree from Columbia University and returned to England as a political analyst and organizer as well as a stringer for a number of publications before returning to the US permanently in 1977. His writing efforts are devoted to crime fiction, historical fiction, and dark fantasy. He is the well-trained pet of Karlotte, a 16-year-old calico dominatrix. She strokes him on average once a week—but only if he has followed his assignments faithfully and with at least some creativity. He has contributed to *The Mammoth Book of Historical Erotica* and *Skinflicks* magazine, and is editing books for Companion Press and Idol.

"Sex Weekend" and "Without You"
R. J. Masters

The author, who lives in Maine, is a frequent contributor to gay erotic magazines under various pseudonyms. His first novel, *Foreign Power*, an erotic tale of sexual awakening, a young man's introduction into the world of S/M, was published by Nocturnis Press.

"Night Mazes"
Edmund Miller

Miller is the author of the legendary poetry book *Fucking Animals* (recently reprinted by STARBooks) and frequent contributor of stories to magazines and anthologies, is the Chairman of the English Department at a large university in the New York area. His current major writing project is *Icons of Gay New York: A Celebration in Words and Pictures* a sonnet sequence with photographs celebrating the go-go boys of New York.

"Servicing Sarge"
Aaron Mitchell
The author is a frequent contributor to gay magazines.

"Terry, the New Recruit"
Bill Nicholson
Born in the North of England and educated there and in London. His interests are music, literature, and the cinema. He has composed music which has been performed locally and poetry which has been published.

"Sex on the Run" and "The Best Cocksucker in Philadelphia"
Thom Nickels
The famed Philadelphia-based columnist and writer's last work for STARbooks was "Once A Hustler," a bonus book-length work in the best-selling *Intimate Strangers*. Thom has prepared a major work for the forthcoming *Huge 2*, and contributed a lengthy essay on famed gossip columnist Billy Masters for John Patrick's *The Best of the Superstars 2000: The Year in Sex*.

"One More Time"
Jack Ricardo
The author, who lives in Florida, is a novelist and frequent contributor to various gay magazines. His latest novel is *Last Dance at Studio 54*.

"So Fresh, So Frisky"
Lance Rush
The author is a frequent contributor to many of the leading gay publications.

"Watcher in the Sky"
Barnabus Saul
The author, based in the U.K., says, "Barnabus Saul was one of the boy servers used by Elizabeth I's court magician, Joe Dee, to contact the angelic worlds." His stories have appeared in STARbooks' popular anthologies, *Smooth 'N' Sassy* and *Juniors*.

"Shipmates"
Tim Scully

A great friend of contributor Peter Gilbert, Tim is working on new material for STARbooks based on his life experiences. His previous work appeared in *Sweet Temptations*.

"Paying for It"
Joe Sexton

Joe's stories appear frequently in such magazines as *RFD*. This is his first story for STARbooks, and his second will appear in the forthcoming *Boys on the Prowl*.

"Roommates" and "A Farmboy's Whirlwind Romance"
Mario Solano

The author first contributed to STARbooks with a story in *Raw Recruits*. He now lives and works in Manhattan.

"Body Check" and "The Call of the Cockpit"
Thomas Wagner

The author is a frequent contributor to gay magazines.

ACKNOWLEDGEMENTS AND SOURCES

Our coverboys appear through the courtesy of the celebrated English photographer David Butt. Mr. Butt's photographs may be purchased through Suntown, Post Office Box 151, Danbury, Oxfordshire, OX16 8QN, United Kingdom. Ask for a full catalogue. E-mail at SUNTOWN1@aol.com. A collection of Mr. Butts photos, *English Country Lad*, is available from STARbooks Press. *Young and Hairy*, David's latest book, is enjoying huge success in the U.K.

The secondary cover illustration is from the best-selling video "Heartland," a hardcore production from the talented Kevin Clarke and Juniors Studios. The video is available from RAD Video at radvideo.com or 1-800-722-4336. The editor also features Kevin Clarke in *The Best of the Superstars 2000: The Year in Sex*.

Excerpt from John Patrick's "The Best of the Superstars 2000: The Year in Sex"

Kevin Clarke at Junior Studios has a knack for finding adorable young talent. Jason Miller, for instance, sent an e-mail to Clarke, who quickly replied:"Come in for an interview." The result was stellar sex in "The Pleasure Principle" and "Something Very Big..."

In an interview with Jamoo in *Freshmen* magazine, Jason explained the problems twinkies have performing in porn. Jason said he *sometimes* enjoyed having sex for the camera: "Sometimes it's fun, but sometimes it's not. It depends on who you're working with and what you're doing. I liked making 'Pleasure Principle' because Richie Fine topped me in that one". Miller, who has also appeared as Jeremy Lee in such videos as "Blade Studs" (All Worlds), says he loved meeting Johan Paulik when the Duroy superstar was in Hollywood:"I liked him a lot—we went to Universal City together. He has a really heavy, pronounced accent, but after a little bit you get used to it". Miller says his favorite thing is to give blowjobs:"Oral fixation, I guess. And I like to get fucked really hard. I like to start out really slow and then get pounded really hard". One would hope Johan did the trick!

Jason may have retired from video, but Clarke quickly replaced him. In "The Americam Way" he gives us three noteworthy discoveries: Christian Taylor, Ashton Ryan and Aaron Nichols. Like the boys in the videos of George Duroy, these guys seem to be really enjoying what they are doing. Critic Keith Bryan calls Christian Taylor"sex on legs. He's wild, passionate, and completely into what he's doing". The video really gets going when Taylor meets up with Ashton Ryan and Chuck Murphy. "Taylor, who has a light dusting of golden hair on chest, literally shivers and shakes when Ryan sucks his dick (or hell, for that matter, when he simply touches him). Murphy rapidly becomes the third-wheel and decides to make a fast getaway and vanishes from the scene entirely (sadly, we never get to see Murphy's dick, nor a cumshot from the lad). But back to our dynamic duo ... Taylor and Ryan exchange gonzo blowjobs (who knew that they were so proficient in deep-throating techniques?) and Taylor tops Ryan. ...Taylor fucks Ryan as if his life depended on it; saying that Taylor fucks energetically would be the understatement of the year. Ryan claws at Taylor and thrashes his head back and forth, mumbling incoherent words while in a state of complete ecstasy.

"After Ryan shoots his load (while Taylor is still pounding his ass, we might add), the two trade positions. Ryan oils up Taylor's back and begins an erotic massage before topping him. Again, Taylor is fantastic here, as he bounces wildly on top of Ryan's very sizable whang. Taylor shoots while mounted on Ryan. Later, Taylor is kicking around a soccer ball with Aaron Nichols, yet another great-looking twink. ...Cutie-pie Nichols mounts Taylor and fucks him for all he's worth; Taylor shoots while being fucked. Taylor sucks Nichols off until he shoots his load on Taylor's smiling, cherubic face."

Taylor commented, "All I can say for that amazing boy named Aaron Nichols is that he can sure keep quiet when he gets excited.... I think I also beat my record for getting off more then five times in a day!' Taylor and Ryan, of course, also appear to great effect in "Heartland."

In a later development, when asked about Chance, the adorable blond boy in "An American in Prague," Clarke says that he tried to lure Chance out more times than you can imagine. He has a standing invitation to work with me anytime. He is a good friend I have known him since before 'An American In Prague.'

"In fact, I was quite helpful in getting he and Bel-Ami together. And I spent a weekend in a hotel room in Vegas with him at the MGM Grand two years ago at the Consumer Electornics Show. Jason Miller and Cody Matthews were in the room next to us. I would love to say something happenned but the truth is nothing did. But I can tell you this he is one of the sexiest men on the planet and also one of the nicest guys I have ever met. I tried my best to get him into both 'The American Way' and 'Heartland,' and when I shoot next he will be the first call I will make. He will probably say no and I will cry for a week." We've heard of one-hit wonders in the music business, but this is ridiculous! Of course, after you've been with Johan Paulik and Ion Davidov, there's really no way to go but down!

John Patrick's "The Best of the Superstars 2000: The Year in Sex" is now available. Only $11.95 for 576 sizzling pages of gossip, reviews, and profiles. E-mail us at starxxx@gte.net or write STARbooks Press, P.O. Box 2737, Sarasota FL 34230. Add $2.95 for first class postage.

ABOUT THE EDITOR

The editor and his favorite frisky boy, porn star/escort Tony Cummings.

John Patrick is a prolific, prize-winning author of fiction and non-fiction. One of his short stories, "The Well," was honored by PEN American Center as one of the best of 1987. His novels and anthologies, as well as his non-fiction works, including *Legends* and *The Best of the Superstars* series, continue to gain him new fans every day. One of his most famous short stories appears in the Badboy collection *Southern Comfort* and another appears in the collection *The Mammoth Book of Gay Short Stories*.

A divorced father of two, the author is a longtime member of the American Booksellers Association, the Publishing Triangle, the Florida Publishers' Association, American Civil Liberties Union, and the Adult Video Association. He resides in Florida.